Orname

11

1819 – 2020

Chris Fogg is a creative producer, writer, director and dramaturg, who has written and directed for the theatre for many years, as well as collaborating artistically with choreographers and contemporary dance companies.

Ornaments of Grace is a chronicle of twelve novels. *The Principal Thing* is the eleventh in the sequence.

He has previously written more than thirty works for the stage as well as four collections of poems, stories and essays. These are: *Special Relationships, Northern Songs, Painting by Numbers* and *Dawn Chorus* (with woodcut illustrations by Chris Waters), all published by Mudlark Press.

Several of Chris's poems have appeared in International Psychoanalysis (IP), a US online journal, as well as in *Climate of Opinion*, a selection of verse in response to the work of Sigmund Freud edited by Irene Willis, and *What They Bring: The Poetry of Migration & Immigration*, co-edited by Irene Willis and Jim Haba, each published by IP, in 2017 and 2020.

Ornaments of Grace

(or *Unhistoric Acts*)

11

Moth

Vol. 1: The Principal Thing

by

Chris Fogg

flaxbooks

First published 2021
© Chris Fogg 2021

Chris Fogg has asserted his rights under Copyright Designs & Patents Act 1988 to be identified as the author of this book

ISBN Number: 9798599307839

Cover and design by: Kama Glover

Cover Image: Bradshaw's Defence of Manchester AD 1642, one of the Manchester Murals by Ford Madox Brown, reprinted by kind permission of Manchester Libraries, Information & Archives

The text for *Film #4: Learning to Walk by Night* on p388 is based on the poem On Learning to Navigate the Flat by Night by Lucy Cash and is used here with the author's kind permission.

This book is sold subject to the condition that it shall not, by way of trade or otherwise be lent, resold, hired out, or otherwise circulated without the publisher's prior consent in any form of binding or cover other than that in which it is published and without a similar condition, including this condition, being imposed upon the subsequent purchaser.

Printed by Amazon

Although some of the people featured in this book are real, and several of the events depicted actually happened, *Ornaments of Grace* remains a work of fiction. Some dates and names may have been changed.

Ornaments of Grace (*or Unhistoric Acts*) is a sequence of twelve novels set in Manchester between 1761 and 2021. Collectively they tell the story of a city in four elements.

The Principal Thing is the eleventh book in the sequence.

The full list of titles is:

1. Pomona (Water)

2. Tulip (Earth)
    Vol 1: Enclave
    Vol 2: Nymphs & Shepherds
    Vol 3: The Spindle Tree
    Vol 4: Return

3. Laurel (Air)
    Vol 1: Kettle
    Vol 2: Victor
    Vol 3: Victrix
      part 1: A Grain of Mustard Seed
      part 2: The Waxing of a Great Tree
      part 3: All the Fowls of the Air

4. Moth (Fire)
    Vol 1: The Principal Thing
    Vol 2: A Crown of Glory

Each book can be read independently or as part of the sequence.

"It's always too soon to go home. And it's always too soon to calculate effect... Cause-and-effect assumes that history marches forward, but history is not an army. It is a crab scuttling sideways, a drip of soft water wearing away stone, an earthquake breaking centuries of tension."

Rebecca Solnit: Hope in the Dark
(*Untold Histories, Wild Possibilities*)

Contents

"The peppered moth story is easy to understand, because it involves things that we are familiar with: vision and predation and birds and moths and pollution and camouflage and lunch and death. That is why the anti-evolution lobby attacks the peppered moth story. They are frightened that too many people will be able to understand. If the rise and fall of the peppered moth is one of the most visually impacting and easily understood examples of Darwinian theory in action, it should be taught. After all, it provides the proof of evolution."

Mike Majerus: Professor of Evolution, Cambridge University

Prologue: Ova   15

Chapter 1: Cutting the Ribbon   17
      2013 – 1959 – 2009 – 1999 – 2012 – 2013
      2002 – 2013 – 2012 – 2013 – 1898 – 2013

Chapter 2: Tracing the Source   51
      2020 – 2013 – 2020 – 2005 – 1996 – 1852
      1822 – 1852 – 1862 – 2010 – 2005 – 1996
      1833 – 1996 – 2020 – 2005 – 2020

Chapter 3: Walking the Tightrope   168
      2018 – 2019 – 2017 – 1947 – 2017 – 2013
      2017 – 2019

Chapter 4: Ex Machina   222
      2014

Chapter 5: Imitation Games   264
      2019 – 2013 – 1952 – 2019 – 1954 – 1951
      1952 – 2020 – 1819 – 2020 – 1955 – 1956
      1957 – 1958 – 1930 – 1958 – 1963 – 1964
      1959 – 1964 – 2020

Chapter 6: Amrit Sanskar 470
2013 – 2007 – 2013 – 2007 – 2013 – 2007
2013 – 2009 – 2007 – 2005 – 1955 – 2005
1966 – 2005 – 2013 – 2007 – 1976 – 2007
2011 – 2007 – 2013 – 2007 – 2013 – 2011
2010 – 2011 – 2012 – 1993 – 1992 – 2013
1999 – 2013 – 2012 – 1995 – 2012 – 2005
1947 – 2005 – 1947 – 2005 – 2013 – 2020
2013

Chapter 7: The Glittering Prizes 635
2013 – 1949 – 1954 – 1959 – 1965 - 1975
1987 – 1992 – 2007 – 2013

Epilogue: Larvae 746

The Life Cycle of the Manchester Moth	13
Photograph of Beetham Tower	16
Glossary of Sikh terms	748
Dramatis Personae	751
Acknowledgements	770
Biography	773

For Amanda & Tim

dedicated to the memory of my parents and grandparents

Ornaments of Grace

"Wisdom is the principal thing. Therefore get wisdom and within all thy getting get understanding. Exalt her and she shall promote thee. She shall bring thee to honour when thou dost embrace her. She shall give to thine head an ornament of grace. A crown of glory shall she deliver to thee."

Proverbs: 4, verses 7 – 9

written around the domed ceiling of the Great Hall Reading Room
Central Reference Library, St Peter's Square, Manchester

"Fecisti patriam diversis de gentibus unam…"
"From differing peoples you have made one homeland…"

Rutilius Claudius Namatianus:
De Redito Suo, verse 63

"To be hopeful in bad times is not just foolishly romantic. It is based on the fact that human history is a history not only of cruelty, but also of compassion, sacrifice, courage, kindness. What we choose to emphasise in this complex history will determine our lives. If we see only the worst, it destroys our capacity to do something. If we remember those times and places—and there are so many—where people have behaved magnificently, this gives us the energy to act, and at least the possibility of sending this spinning top of a world in a different direction. And if we do act, in however small a way, we don't have to wait for some grand utopian future. The future is an infinite succession of presents, and to live now as we think human beings should live, in defiance of all that is bad around us, is itself a marvellous victory."

Howard Zinn: A Power Governments Cannot Suppress

Moth (i)

"Using olfactory navigation the moth detects currents of scents in the air and, by small increments, discovers how to move upstream..."

Barbara Kingsolver: Prodigal Summer

"I've always preferred moths to butterflies... They mind their own business and just try to blend in with their surroundings and live their lives..."

Kayla Krantz: The OCD Games

"Judge the moth by the beauty of the candle..."

Rumi

Fire (i)

"The future of the world belongs to the youth of the world, and it is from the youth not from the old that the fire of life will warm and enlighten the world..."

Thomas Mann (co-founder of UK Labour Party): New Unionism

"Success isn't a result of spontaneous combustion. You must set yourself on fire..."

Arnold H. Glasow: Wall Street Journal

"Every person's work shall be made manifest, for the day shall declare it. It shall be revealed by fire, and the fire shall try every work of what sort it is..."

1 Corinthians 3: 13

A Brief Introduction to the Life Cycle of the Manchester Moth

The peppered moth, or *biston betularia*, is a temperate, mostly night-flying species, widely distributed across the world. Evolutionary polymorphism has produced variant phenotypes, more commonly called *morphs*. In Britain there are three such morphs of the peppered moth: the white morph – *typica*; the black – *carbonaria*, and the intermediate – *medionigra*.

The evolution of the peppered moth over the last two hundred years has been studied in detail. At the start of this period, the vast majority of peppered moths had light-coloured wing patterns which effectively camouflaged them against the light-coloured trees and lichens upon which they rested. However, due to widespread pollution during the Industrial Revolution in England, many of the lichens died out, and the trees which peppered moths rested on became blackened by soot, causing most of the light-coloured moths, or *typica*, to die off due to predation. At the same time, the dark-coloured, or melanic, moths, *carbonaria*, flourished because they could hide on the darkened trees. This led to the black peppered moth being given the name of the *Manchester Moth*.

The improved environmental measures introduced into cities, including Manchester, have resulted in a rise in the number of *medionigra* variants, with a gradual return of the *typica*. Examples of all three are now quite common, with inter-breeding occurring successfully between each.

The peppered moth is *univoltine*. That is to say, it has just one generation per year, one chance to make sure the species survives.

The lepidopteran life cycle consists of four stages: *ova*, the eggs; *larvae*, the caterpillars; *pupae*, the cocoons, which over-winter in the soil, and *imagines*, the adult moths.

Prologue

Ova

The male imagine flies every night in search of a female, whereas the female flies only on the first night she emerges from her cocoon, when she releases pheromones to attract the male. These pheromones are carried by the wind, so the male flies along what is called the 'concentration gradient', the diffusion of all molecular particles with temperatures above absolute zero, in order to find their source. This is a treacherous journey, for the male must fly the gauntlet of many predators, particularly bats and birds. Once he reaches his target, the male will guard the female from all other interested rivals, until she lays her eggs.

The female will lay as many as two thousand pale-green ovoid eggs, each approximately one millimetre in length, into crevices in the bark of trees, with her ovipositor, a tube-like organ especially evolved for the purpose.

The male usually stays with the female to ensure paternity. But not always. Sometimes they perish. Sometimes they simply fly away. A mating pair, or a lone female, will spend the day hiding from danger, protecting the eggs till they are ready to hatch. Once they do, they are on their own…

Beetham Tower
301 Deansgate, Manchester

1

CUTTING THE RIBBON

2013 – 1959 – 2009 – 1999 – 2012 – 2013 – 2002 – 2013
2012 – 2013 – 1898 – 2013

2013

Chloe Chang, final-year Media student at Manchester's Metropolitan University, rushes into the TV Studio in the Grosvenor Building of its All Saints Campus on Oxford Road, dropping papers and swearing as she does so. She looks up to the Control Booth at the far end of the studio mumbling apologies. Clive Archer, Chloe's tutor, taps his wrist, even though he isn't wearing a watch. She is exactly on time.

"Time's money in this business," he mouths.

"But we're not in business," replies Chloe, before she has chance to check herself. "Not yet anyway. When I last looked, this was still a university, not a cheap outsourcing site for one of the larger corporations."

"But in order for you to learn, for us to teach students like you, Chloe, we try to simulate, as best we can, the realities of day-to-day conditions in a working newsroom…"

"Actually," continues Chloe, ignoring what Clive has just said, "that mightn't be a bad idea. You're always saying that you're facing cuts – making actual programmes might be a neat way of earning a bit of extra cash. Of course, you'd have to pay us students as your news team, rather than *us* having to pay – well not *you*, Clive, obviously, but you get what I mean? And the money we earn might help us to pay off that pesky student loan a bit quicker, mightn't it?"

The other students, sprawling at the back of the studio, wake up to what might be a welcome change of routine. Chloe has a reputation. She's like a dog with a bone. Once she gets started, it takes a lot to stop her.

"I'm never going to pay off my student loan," moans Petros. "I mean – what are they going to do if I don't? Throw me in jail? The prisons are overcrowded as it is."

"They take it straight from your pay packet," Clive chips in.

"But we don't get a pay packet, do we?" insists Petros.

"Not if you don't get a job," says Clive, "and you're not likely to if you never hand in your assignments."

Petros smiles. How little you know, he thinks.

"That's playing to the system, though, innit?" It's Khavita's turn now to join in. Khav.

Lorrie, sitting quietly in the corner, bag perched neatly on her knees, above her 1950s retro bobby-socks, bleached blonde hair, who normally never says boo to a goose, removes the piece of gum from her mouth, and pipes, "Don't be such a twat, Khav."

"Ooh! Listen to Miss America over there. Khavita to you. Or 'B' Girl. I mean, I'm going to be a freelance guerrilla film maker, you get me?" She flicks her wrist and winks as the rest of the class jeer. Undeterred she carries on. "*Khalsa Kaur*," she proclaims, raising her fist. "*Warrior Princess*." And she begins a nifty hip-hop routine across the studio floor, finishing with a neat pose – arms folded across her chest, her turbaned head nodded down for further emphasis. "They pay me a fee, I ain't gonna declare it."

"No – you're just going to donate it to one of your worthy causes, I suppose?" asks Clive, though in truth he is beginning to enjoy the banter's back and forth.

"Like 'Underpaid University Lecturers', you mean?" laughs Petros.

"Underpaid, Undervalued, Under duress," chimes in Chloe.

"Ah, Chloe," says Clive, standing up, clapping his hands. "I'd almost forgotten you were here. Are we ready at last?"

"I've been ready all my life, Clive."

She calls up to Tanya, the Studio Technician, sitting next to Clive in the Control Booth. "You got my file, Tan?"

"Uploading as we speak."

"Thanks, Tan. OK then. Camera, lights…"

"Wait, wait, wait…" Lorrie again. "Can I snap the clapper board?"

Petros tosses one across, the crap, hand-made one they'd come across in a cardboard box their first day there.

"Action!" everybody shouts, as Lorrie claps the board shut.

Final Presentation # 1: Chloe

The Media Studies degree course at Manchester Metropolitan University – MMU – is a mixture of lectures, seminars and tutorials, combining written with practical assignments. Each student must give a Final Presentation on a topic of their own choosing. They do this in front of the Head of Department – Dr Clive Archer – and a small tutorial group, who support and critique it, in this case: Chloe Chang, Petros Dimitriou, Khavita Kaur (Khav), and Lorelei Zlatan (Lorrie). Today's presentation is Chloe's.

CHLOE:

First of all, I'd like to thank you for the opportunity of bringing this hot news story to your attention.

The rest of the students good naturedly jeer.

CHLOE:

OK, I know '*Queen Opens New Building*' doesn't sound like hot news, but the way I'm going to tell it, I think it will be. I want to bring a new angle to an old story, a human face to an anonymous corporation.

KHAV:

You need to know your history, girlfriend. The Co-op was set up as a profit sharing co-operative just ten miles from where you're standing to support the rights of poor working class people.

CHLOE:

That would be before their CEO Niall Booker collected his four million quid salary for a year which saw his bank make more than a six hundred million pound loss and shutting down one in five branches nationwide resulting in more than a quarter of its staff being made redundant, I suppose, while mis-selling PPIs to thousands of its customers, would it? Or maybe it was to pay off his predecessor Paul Flowers' cocaine debts – that's the *Reverend* Paul Flowers I'm talking about, the still yet-to-be-defrocked Methodist minister with a penchant for paying rent boys to eat nachos directly from his bare nipples. I don't think that quite fits in with what we usually associate with profit-sharing. Nor with how Niall Booker sees it either, it would seem. According to Wikipedia... (*She holds out her i-pad with the relevant source pulled up on it*)... he was promoted through the ranks, you'll be pleased to hear, while he was with HSBC, becoming Chief Executive of their India HQ, going on to head their Dubai operations before finally making a killing in the US sub-prime markets, where he was able to retire with a handsome profit – pity about all those poor buggers who lost their homes, eh? So earlier this year he comes out of retirement to sort out the little matter of the Co-op's one-and-a-half-billion-pound hole in their balance sheet. Easy peasy – a capital injection from some hedge funds to pay off that embarrassing inconvenience and it's back to the markets we go, boys. Abracadabra – now you see it, now you don't. The Co-op Group may have lost overall majority control of itself, but it still assures us it will continue to safeguard its historic ethical reputation by the introduction of a 'Special Code of Conduct' monitored by 'a Values Committee'. Phew, I was beginning to get quite anxious, but now we can all sleep easily in our beds again, especially those of us who, like me, just happen to have closed our Co-op account, along with 25,000 others. So congratulations, Mr Booker, it's clear you've earned your four million quid Christmas bonus this year.

CLIVE:
And your point is, Chloe? This is all old news.

CHLOE:
My point is this, Clive.

She taps a key on her i-pad and onto the screen behind her is projected an image of the Queen, smiling and receiving bouquets.

Petros stands to attention, finger of his left hand resting on his upper lip beneath his nose, right arm outstretched in a Nazi salute, singing the national anthem.

CHLOE: (*continues, smiling*):
The Queen, who wore a turquoise and indigo outfit by the designer Karl Ludwig together with his trademark patent bag – people are always interested in what she wears...

PETROS:
... like who?

CHLOE:
Like my gran –

KHAV:
– and mine...

LORRIE:
 – mine too…

CHLOE:
 So Golden Rule Number One, Clive: start with the frock… Her Majesty was followed closely by the colourful Duke of Edinburgh, 92, who looked fit and well despite a recent health scare, and who, after the ceremony was concluded, shouted cheerfully to the crowds waiting below, "Right, you lot, back to work!"

CLIVE:
 I have some sympathy with that remark.

KHAV:
 Well you're just a closet royalist, Clive, innit?

LORRIE:
 So are most of the country.

CHLOE:
 Thank you, Lol. Actually, that's what really interests me. Everywhere you looked the streets were lined with cheering crowds waving flags, and I'm not just talking about primary school kids who have no choice but to be there, but everyone else, all ages, all races, some of them who had travelled from miles away, camping out overnight to make sure they got a good view…

PETROS:
 How do you know that? How do you know they're not just homeless?

CHLOE:
 Cos I spoke to them, dickhead. It's called being a reporter. One guy I spoke to, he must have been about *your* age, Clive…

KHAV:
> Old then?

CHLOE:
> … and he told me he followed the Royal Family all over the country. He reckoned this was the 25th time he'd seen the Queen, and the 6th he'd actually spoken to her. She always knew exactly what to say, he said. "That's what marks her out as special. The common touch." When I asked him if he intended to follow her on to her next public engagement, he replied, "Most definitely."

PETROS:
> I'd call that certifiable.

KHAV:
> I'd call it stalking.

CHLOE:
> No. The atmosphere was happy, relaxed. Like a party.

PETROS:
> More like propoganda. It's just a way of keeping the masses in their place...

CHLOE:
> I don't think it's quite as simple as that.

PETROS:
> ...which I'm all in favour of, by the way.

CHLOE:
> And which I don't believe for one second. But it's complicated, this question of allegiance and loyalty.

KHAV: (*chipping in*):
> Home and belonging.

CHLOE:
Devotion and duty. It's all so ambiguous.

PETROS:
Tell me about it.

CHLOE:
At one point people started singing.

PETROS:
Not *'For She's a Jolly Good Fellow'*, please not that?

CHLOE:
'Angels'.

LORRIE:
Robbie Williams?

KHAV:
Look at Miss America there. That's perked her up, innit?

LORRIE: (*singing*)
'And through it all she offers me protection
A lot of love and affection…'

CLIVE:
A true son of Manchester.

KHAV: (*gesturing towards Lorrie*):
Don't you mean 'daughter'?

CHLOE:
And that's my point.

CLIVE:
Finally.

CHLOE:
Bread and circuses.

LORRIE:

Don't talk to me about circuses.

CHLOE: (*continuing*):

The banks threaten to bring down governments. Their greed and incompetence go virtually unpunished. One bank in particular lays off thousands, siphons millions to fund sex and drugs but not much rock and roll, and then erects a monument to its own glory with this so-called greenest building in the world, creating a future out of the ashes of its once ethical roots, with its biodiesel cogeneration plant powered by solar panels and rapeseed oil, with its double-skin façade, adiabatic cooling – whatever the fuck that is – rainwater harvesting, grey-water recycling, zero-carbon emission – naturally – completely paperless. Apparently the building would have had to be four storeys higher otherwise to accommodate all the paperwork they would traditionally generate. My grandmother, back in Shenzhen, used to squat beneath the skyscrapers that were being thrown up every five minutes when she was a girl, picking through waste paper. That was her job.

PETROS:

It's one way of ensuring full employment.

CHLOE:

And today crowds cheer and sing as the Queen cuts the ribbon. "I now declare One Angel Square open. May God bless her and all who sail in her…" You know, some people are already calling it 'The Cruise Liner'? Though some wags prefer 'The Egg Slice', as it leans over what was once called 'Hell on Earth' by none other than Friedrich Engels no less, whose family's factories were helping to create this hell, still euphemistically known as Angel Meadow, with its tanneries, gas works, lime kilns, brick fields, dyeing houses, tobacco plants, all belching black smoke into the air and pumping raw sewage into the black sludge of the River Irk, alongside which were huddled the largest proportion of cellars, courtyards, undrained lanes, filthy rows of badly built, unventilated back-to-back houses of any city anywhere in Europe, alongside the open burying grounds where more than thirty thousand bodies a year were tipped. Look.

She projects a series of old photographs of 19th century Manchester slums over the continuing soundtrack of Robbie Williams.

CHLOE:

This place really did use to be a meadow. Tinkers' Hollow, they called it, then Vauxhall Gardens, after its fashionable counterpart in London, and all the rich landowners used to promenade up and down it and ride in their carriages and listen to music and drink tea and chocolate, a bit like Shambles Square today.

Robbie Williams continues to sing while the images of Manchester's slums are replaced by a contemporary slide show of 21st century laughing young professionals standing drinking outside many of the city's new bars and restaurants.

PETROS:

So are you becoming a spokesperson for NOMA now, Chloe, as well as the Royal family?

LORRIE:

NOMA?

CLIVE:

Lorrie, please do me the small favour of at least pretending you have been paying attention to my lectures this term. Enlighten her, someone.

KHAV:

It's a sort of acronym, innit? "NOrth MAnchester".

LORRIE:

I thought it was a restaurant in Copenhagen.

CHLOE:

So it is, Lol, and apparently a very fine one, but it's also the 'Gateway to the Northern Powerhouse'. Let me read to you from their website.

She taps once more on her i-pad, which then shows what she has brought up there onto the screen behind her.

'If Manchester was the world's first modern city then NOMA is the place where it all began. The place where entrepreneur Richard Arkwright built the world's first steam-powered Cotton Mill and cemented Manchester's future as an industrial powerhouse, and where The Co-op grew on the founding principles of democracy, education and co-operation. In embracing the area's past, NOMA is inspiring its future, creating a new twenty-acre neighbourhood where you can live, work, create and innovate. Driven by the powerful partnership of The Co-op and Hermes Investment Management…'

PETROS: (*triumphantly raising a fist*):

Hermes – Mercury – Messenger of the Gods.

CHLOE:

Meaning?

PETROS:

International venture capitalism – way to go.

CHLOE:
So you're happy about off-shore pension funds buying up real estate here in Manchester?

PETROS:
Aren't you? US, Middle East, Russian, Chinese – let them all come, I say.

CHLOE:
Thank you. But I'm already here. Ever heard of Thucydides' Trap?

PETROS:
No. But I expect I'm about to.

CHLOE:
In his text on *The History of the Peloponnesian War*...

PETROS:
Touché...

CHLOE:
... Thucydides writes, 'The rise of Athens and the fear it instilled in Sparta made war inevitable.'

PETROS:
For Athens read China...

CHLOE:
And for Sparta read America...

CLIVE:
Where's all this leading, Chloe?

KHAV:
Right here, innit? Manchester. Collateral damage. Caught in the middle.

PETROS:
The centre ground suits me just fine.

CHLOE: (*continues reading from the NOMA website*):
> 'NOMA combines the enterprising vision of the industrialists and the spirit of community, opportunity and fairness blah-blah-blah... And at the heart of the project is One Angel Square...'

Voilà.

Chloe steps forward, takes a bow, then moves aside. Petros sarcastically applauds.

KHAV: (*throwing the clapper board at him, which hits him on the back of the head*):
Cut.

CLIVE:
Thank you, Chloe. Hardly what you might call an even-handed, balanced piece of journalism, though, was it? When last I checked, this module was called '*The Role of the Impartial News Reporter.*'

KHAV:
That's so last century, Clive. We're not all broadsheet-reading, BBC-watching, fair-minded liberals, you know? Ever heard of the internet? Youtube? We're all reporters now, a-bloggin' and a-postin'. I thought that was cool, Chloe.

CHLOE:
Thanks. But I've got to dash now. Is it OK, Clive, if I leave a few minutes early? I'll email my presentation to you, but the reason why I was arriving at the last minute is why I've got to go now. Sorry.

She picks up her things and hurries out, calling out a final 'Thanks' to Tanya, who responds with a cheery 'No probs.'.

CLIVE:
Can anyone tell me what's going on?

KHAV:
It's her gran.

CLIVE:
Is she ill? Why didn't she say?

KHAV:
It's a Chinese thing, innit? Close-knit.

PETROS:
I know all about that. Keep your friends close but your enemies closer.

KHAV:
And your family closer still.

*

Outside Chloe takes a deep breath. Then she quickens her pace and hurries down Oxford Road. She pauses briefly by *On The Eighth Day*, debating with herself whether to buy a take-away for her lunch, before eventually deciding against it. She is trying not to spend unnecessarily. She crosses the bridge where the murky, rubbish-filled River Medlock briefly emerges from its culvert, gasping for some much-needed polluted air. Leaning against the bridge's MDF-clad, graffiti-splattered iron grille, a woman of indeterminate age, wrapped in stained sleeping bag, much of whose stuffing has leaked out, holds up an empty Starbuck's plastic coffee cup.

"Any spare change?" she croaks.

Chloe looks down. The woman might be younger than *she* is, but looks much older. She roots in her pocket and finds a pound coin, which she takes out and looks at, as it lies there in the centre of the palm of her hand. The woman looks at it too, waiting, saying nothing. Slowly Chloe closes her fingers around it, mentally calculating. The young woman turns away, holding out the cup towards other passers-by, who all avert their gaze, ignoring her. Chloe pauses. After a few moments she uncurls her fingers once more.

"Here," she says, dropping the coin into the cup. "That's all I can spare today."

The woman looks up. For a brief second their eyes meet. Chloe catches a glimpse of a tattoo on the woman's shoulder, but she can't make out what it is. She walks on.

"Thank you," the woman calls after her, barely audible above the traffic's roar.

Chloe hurries past the waste ground where once the BBC Studios had stood before they moved out to Salford's *Media City*, opposite the former *Regal Cinema*, which once showed foreign-language films before turning into a porno-cinema, and which is now home to *The Dance House*, hosting classes ranging from ballet through to contemporary, where Khav sometimes teaches street and hip-hop for girls. Oxford Road was full of cinemas once upon a time. As well as the *Regal*, there was the *Gaumont*, the *Picture House*, the *Tatler*, the *Jacey*, and, tucked beneath the arches of the railway station, the *Classic*. All gone now, either burned down or demolished. Except for the *Cornerhouse* – although there are rumours that its days too are numbered. Even the three thousand-seater Art Deco *Odeon* is boarded up now.

Chloe turns sharply right alongside it, into Back George Street and the labyrinth of narrow alleyways leading into Chinatown. Her presentation went so badly. Not at all how she had intended it. Why had she let the others wind her up like that, so that what she had ended up talking about was a complete tangent, a sideshow to what she had planned? Urban regeneration is a complex matter, and she isn't at all sure how she feels about it. Maybe Petros has a point? People have to live *somewhere*. But the glittering palaces he dreams about are way beyond the reach of ordinary common people. She smiles. Just as that thought was occurring to her, Jarvis Cocker's knowing, northern twang cuts through the air from one of the crane drivers' CD players, slicing between the perpetual, pounding rhythm of the demolition and building work, which roars in her ears constantly.

"I said, 'Pretend you've got no money'
She just laughed and said, 'You're so funny'
I said, 'Yeah? Well I can't see anyone else smiling in here…'
Are you sure?"

Chloe *is* sure. Not about what is happening. But that she wants to be a part of it. One way or another. They all of them do. Petros, Khav, even Lorrie…

"I wanna live like common people
I wanna do whatever common people do…"

The truth is, in spite of everything, she had enjoyed seeing the Queen. She's looking forward to telling her grandmother, her *Wai Zu Mu*, all about it, and she thinks the building, the 'Egg Slice', is OK, however much the critics disparage it. Secretly she thinks she might even apply for a job with NOMA when she graduates later this year. They're always recruiting graduates, especially those from an ethnic minority, and she smiles to herself, just as she reaches the side entrance to where she lives. The rank smell of where someone last night must have pissed on the step on their way home from a late drinking session pulls her up sharply back to the present. She turns the key in the metal door and steps inside. "*Lao lao*," she calls. "I'm home."

She finds her grandmother in the back room, curtains still drawn, sitting in a chair, a rug across her thin knees, fast asleep. Chloe puts her bag down as quietly as she can and kneels at her side, waiting for her to wake. After a few moments she opens her eyes.

"Ah, *Sunnu*, there you are. I've been expecting you."

"Yes, *Lao lao*. Would you like some tea?"

"Later perhaps. First I have something to show you. Here." On her lap lies an envelope with a Chinese stamp and postmark. "It's from your father. Pass me my glasses, will you?"

Chloe does so, knowing already what the letter will say, and her heart sinks.

"He wants us to join him, to go back home."

"But this is my home, *Lao lao*."

"Your real home, *Sunnu*, the home of your ancestors."

Chloe switches on the small lamp on the table by her grandmother's chair and listens while she reads her the letter in growing excitement. It's in Mandarin, which, though her grandmother hardly uses it these days, preferring Cantonese, Chloe still roughly understands. It's full of a complicated legal wrangle. Following the repeal of the Property Act some five years before, it is now possible back in China to return houses that had previously been confiscated under Mao back to their original owners, but this has been slow to be enacted, with many village councils still holding sway, always finding new ways to obstruct these transfers. Chloe's father had returned to their home village in Guangdong Province, close to Shenzen, as soon as the new law had come into place and he's been battling with the authorities ever since, while at the same time investing in the building projects that are mushrooming everywhere there. Another issue has been the rampant corruption arising from land transactions. Under the 1982 Constitution the Chinese Government still preserves its right to reclaim properties from individuals if a case can be made that doing so would be for the greater public good – like being then able to tear it down to make room for a new six-lane highway – but just two years ago additional regulations had been brought in, providing greater transparency and a fairer compensation scheme. Chloe's father has, it seems, finally taken possession of the keys to the family home, with an accompanying letter promising an undreamt-of sum should it ever need to be taken back. As she reaches the end of the letter, Chloe's grandmother is both singing and crying.

"I can see how important this is to you, *Lao lao*, and you must go back to rejoin my father. I am very grateful to you for looking after me since my mother died and my father returned to China. But I am also English. I was born here. I want to stay."

"Yes, yes. Finish degree first – so proud is your father of this, the first person in our family to go to university, and a girl too – then go back, get high pay job with Chinese State Television."

"And would I be able to speak my mind there, say what I really think, even with all these new laws?"

"You say far too much already, *Sunnu*. Always have. You should learn when to stay silent."

"While this new property law undoubtedly increases protection for home owners…" begins Chloe carefully.

"Yes, yes. Did you not hear what your father said in his letter?"

"… doesn't this also erode China's socialist principles?"

"What do *you* know of socialist principles?"

Chloe smiles. "Is this another of your Great Leaps Forward?"

"This is no laughing matter, young lady. Your Aunts and your Uncles, they die in that Great Leap Forward…"

"I know."

"This is why we come here. But we always mean to go back one day. If we can."

"I know, *Lao lao*. But I don't feel ready yet." Privately she knows she never will, while the Scylla and Charybdis of Duty and Devotion rear their heads once more.

Her grandmother takes hold of Chloe's hand. "Finish your studies. Your father will want to come back see you graduate. Then let us talk about all of this again."

Chloe nods her head.

"Now – haven't you essay to write? Off to Library with you."

Half an hour later Chloe sits in the hushed Reading Room of Manchester's Central Reference Library, looking up at the newly redecorated domed ceiling. She reads the inscription that winds its way around the entire perimeter.

Wisdom is the principal thing. Therefore get wisdom and within all thy getting get understanding...

Chloe rubs the back of her neck, straining from trying to read its ornate script. She looks around at the other students sitting nearby, bent over their books or tablets, and wonders: is wisdom the same as knowledge? Not really. She understands this now as she opens her laptop and prepares to email the full text of the presentation she never actually gave earlier that morning to her tutor, Clive.

Her grandmother had been shocked when Chloe first mentioned his name. She tutted and shook her head. "How can you respect a teacher who does not insist you call him Professor or Doctor, or at the very least, Sir?"

Chloe smiles at the memory.

She decides to look through some of the footage she has collected once more before finally pressing 'Send'.

Reg, a retired soldier from the British Legion tells her how proud he is to be carrying the standard, the flag of his local branch. Lian, a pupil from Chetham's Music School, a Chinese clarinet player, who has been chosen to play a short solo as the Queen arrives in the Square, is more interested in looking at Chloe's camera. Asif, a seven-year-old Muslim boy from Blackley Primary School, whose art work decorates the foyer of the new building and which the Queen appears to enjoy looking at, admits to a slight disappointment. "I thought she'd be wearing a crown," he says, "like the one in my drawing." Chloe remembers how *Lao lao* would tell her of when Puyi, China's Last Emperor, was still on the throne, in her own *Zu Fu's* time, her grandfather, how every public building, and even some private homes, had pictures of him in all of his regal robes and splendour. Then, when he was forced into exile, she said that her *Zu Fu* would tell her of the shock they all felt when they saw this on the cinema, the travelling news films that from time to time would be shown in the village square. He was wearing a western suit. No wonder he was overthrown, they all said.

Chloe sighs. These old stories her grandmother has told her about the old family home back in Shenzen continue to interrupt her. She doesn't like to be disloyal, but it all sounds quite primitive, to be honest. No electricity or running water. A two-mile walk across flooded fields to collect drinking water each day. Pigs wandering underneath the one-roomed hut raised up on stilts to try and keep the rats from coming in as well. The rank smell of rotting fish from the lead and arsenic constantly being smelted over charcoal fires all across the valley. Not that dissimilar to the slums of Angel Meadows she's been reading about. But would the money her father might receive from the flattening of his village to make way for a spanking new skyscraper of steel and glass, like the 'sliced egg' she'd seen being opened last week, really compensate him for the loss of his heritage? All things must pass, as *Lao lao* always says, what once was old is new again, but some things are best forgotten. Or are they, wonders Chloe? Once again, she finds she isn't sure. Duty and devotion. Loyalty and allegiance. The ambiguities cloud her thoughts.

She needs a coffee. She walks down to the café in the Library's newly refurbished Media Centre, where she sits with a caramel latte at a touch screen in the Local History section. She scrolls down till she finds the archive film clip she is looking for and smiles. Another Royal Visit…

She collects these in the same way her grandmother saves string…

*

1959 – 2009 – 1999

On 21st May 1959 the Queen Mother opened the new Heinz Baked Beans factory at Kitt Green in Orrell, just outside Wigan, now the largest food processing plant in Europe. Fifty years later the current Queen, again accompanied by Prince Philip, commemorated its anniversary by opening a new packaging hall there. There are photos of the two of them watching the endless stream of the more-than-three million cans of baked beans the factory processes each day pour before their eyes on dozens of conveyor belts, reminding Chloe of a Spaghetti Junction of motorway flyovers. She wonders if the Queen likes baked beans, if she has ever tasted them even.

She is reminded of a story Petros told them one time at uni. Ten years before, his older sister, Callista, who lived in London for a while, briefly went out with Princess Anne's son, Peter Phillips. He invited her to stay over at Windsor Castle one weekend. Before she went to bed, he showed her where their private kitchen was, and told her to help herself to anything she fancied if she got hungry. The next morning she woke up early and, feeling decidedly peckish, not to mention curious, she took herself downstairs to the private kitchen. No one else was about, and so she had a good scout round, opening various cupboards and drawers. Pulling open one door she was faced with several shelves of Tupperware containers, all of them neatly labelled. On one of them was written: 'Anne's beans – keep off!' Giggling, Callista closed the door and went back upstairs.

Chloe doesn't know whether this is true or apocryphal, but she enjoys the way Petros tells it. For all their butting of heads in the studio and their seemingly always opposing views, Chloe likes Petros. And she can tell that he likes her too. They enjoy goading each other, seeing just how far they can push before one of them backs down. The one to lose their temper first loses. She chuckles once more at the thought of Callista's discovery of Princess Anne's secret stash of baked beans hidden in a Tupperware jar, and finds herself singing the words of Pulp's *Common People* to herself again.

"*She came from Greece and had a thirst for knowledge
She studied Sculpture at St Martin's College…*"

Now, Chloe reads, the Heinz Factory at Kitt Green, just twenty-one miles away from where she now sits, is listed by the Discovery Channel as one of the three largest industrial plants in the world, alongside the Volkswagen Car Factory in Wolfsburg and the NASA Kennedy Space Center in Florida.

The common touch.

Chloe scrolls further down and finds another example. This one's from less than a year ago. When the Queen visited the city as part of her whistle-stop UK tour to celebrate her Diamond Jubilee, like launching a new album. *Queen's Greatest Hits…*

*

2012

Daily Mail

24th March 2012

QUEEN GATECRASHES WEDDING

Frances and John Canning had the surprise of their lives yesterday while marrying at Manchester's Town Hall in Albert Square.

Just after Frances, a hairdresser, and John, a builder, had tied the knot and were preparing to leave for their reception, an unexpected guest turned up.

It was none other than Her Majesty Queen Elizabeth II, who, together with her husband Prince Philip, the Duke of Edinburgh, was in town to open the new Media City at nearby Salford Quays, just one of a number of engagements she was carrying out as part of her Diamond Jubilee celebrations...

*

2013

No – hilarious though it is – Chloe decides to set this aside for the moment. She'll come back to it later. Right now she needs something more personal, something more closely connected to her own direct experience...

*

2002

Ten years earlier.

A more significant example of Her Majesty's brushes with the common people.

Rising with a bullet, it's the opening of the Manchester Commonwealth Games...

This particular appearance in the pantheon of the Queen's Greatest Hits is especially close to Chloe's heart, for she was there. She took part in it.

The primary school she attends – St Philip's on nearby Loxford Street – is invited to be one of twenty-nine local schools to participate in the Opening Ceremony. Chloe is chosen to be one of the pupils.

For six months she rehearses once a week at Z-Arts, a mile and a quarter away in Hulme. Each week she walks in a crocodile escorted by her teachers. It takes them twenty-five minutes to get there. The route takes her past the Bridgewater Hall, where eleven years later she will graduate. It takes her past MMU, where she will study for her degree, then across the recently constructed Hulme Arch Bridge, awe-struck beneath its parabolic span, its six trapezoid steel boxes, which her teachers make her count and calculate every time she crosses it, past the *Munchies Pizza & Kebab House*, which all the children long to stop at on their walk back to school after rehearsal but which they never do, until they finally reach Z-Arts itself, the converted Congregational Church of Zion, on the edge of the newly laid out Hulme Park, with its BMX and skateboard zones, where the rehearsals take place.

The rehearsals are led by members of Weapons of Sound, a junk percussion orchestra. Chloe and the hundreds of other children taking part are encouraged to bring with them anything they can find that they might like to bang and make a noise with – buckets, bicycle wheels, paint cans, hub caps, shopping trolleys, knives, forks. Chloe brings a biscuit tin. The noise they make together is deafening and wonderful. Out of discord and cacophony come harmony and concord.

But no amount of rehearsal can prepare her for the night of the Opening Ceremony itself, which passes in a surreal blur of dreams and pyrotechnics…

A ceremony for the 21st century – with style, and edge, and wit. Pomp without pomposity. That's what's been promised. But even aged just eleven, Chloe can see that, for large parts of it, this is not the case. After the Weapons of Sound, the hiphop, Bhangra and capoeira dancers, which really get the party started, there's a march past by the Band of the British Grenadiers, which is out of touch and embarrassing, followed by the Royal Northern College of Music's Brass Band playing Walton's *Crown Imperial* for the arrival of the Queen herself. OK – Walton was born in Oldham, and this is his centenary year, but who knew? Who cared? She hopes there might be some compensation to be had with *One Nation Under a Groove*, a song she really likes, but why import West Coast rappers Bishop & Tyga to perform it? Don't we have our own rappers here in Manchester? Surely we do? And what's the appearance by S-Club 7 meant to be about? Or the Parade of ageing Coronation Street stars in a cavalcade of Morris Minors? Thank heavens for three other moments that are transcendently unforgettable...

First, there is the Lantern Procession of the world's major faiths that are all to be found jostling together cheek by jowl in the heart of Manchester. Lanterns in the shape of churches, chapels, mosques; synagogues, temples and gurdwaras, are carried on high into the stadium in a magical ballet of strength and fluidity. They separate and they conjoin, wheeling around each other in space, choreographed satellites in a shared orbit, coming together at last to embrace a mosaic of other differently coloured lanterns, which unite to form the recumbent figure of a perfectly proportioned Vitruvian Man. Not so much a man, but quintessentially human. Fluid, genderless, all-encompassing...

Next, there is the arrival into the stadium of the Jubilee Baton, a technological wonder, containing electronic sensors, which detect each carrier's heart rate through a series of LEDs, transforming into a shaft of continuous blue pulsating light, which synchronises with each new carrier. A living relay of slender aluminium, expressing the uniqueness of each individual within the shared rhythm of humanity. It is carried through five hundred cities, towns and villages right across the country, by five thousand individuals, each runner conveying it five hundred yards, before handing it over to the next in line.

Its arrival into the stadium is spectacular. An electronically-controlled hot air balloon, with a map of the solar system painted onto the envelope, hovers in the night sky above the fifty thousand open-mouthed spectators staring up at it from below. Beneath the balloon, instead of a basket, is a harness, from which a trapeze artist, Lindsay Butcher, who Chloe later meets and gets to speak to, hangs suspended. She performs a heart-stopping, slow-motion display hundreds of feet up in the air, before descending breathlessly into the arena, where, waiting in the centre to receive it, is none other than David Beckham, whose mission it is to run the anchor leg of the relay towards where the Queen, in a lime green coat and matching hat, waits to receive it...

And last, there is the moment when Beckham is joined for the final fifty yards of the Jubilee Baton's journey by six-year-old Kirsty Howard, born with a rare inoperable condition, one of just two people in the world known to possess a back-to-front heart, who Beckham first met the previous year when Kirsty was a mascot at Old Trafford for England's World Cup qualifier against Greece, in which Beckham scored the injury-time free kick to secure the nation's place in the finals, since when Kirsty has continued to raise millions of pounds for the Manchester Children's Hospice. She receives a louder cheer even than David Beckham.

The Queen accepts the baton from Kirsty, from which she releases a capsule, which contains the message she now reads to the watching world.

"It is my pleasure in this, my Golden Jubilee year, to declare the 17th Commonwealth Games open. All of us participating in this ceremony tonight, whether athletes or spectators, or those watching on televisions around the world, can share in the ideals of this unique association of nations, we can all draw inspiration from what the Commonwealth stands for, our diversity as a source of strength, our tradition of tolerance, and our focus on young people, for they are our future…"

Afterwards Chloe remembers David Beckham coming to speak to all the children who had taken part and signing autographs. She still has hers somewhere. He got them all to chant the motto of the Games back to him.

"Count yourselves…"
"In!"

This is what she remembers. That all this happened just six years after the city had been torn apart by the IRA bomb. The legacy of not just the major new venues – the Manchester Arena, the Aquatic Centre, the Velodrome, the City of Manchester Stadium, now the Etihad, home to Manchester City – but the Games Village, now a Hall of Residence for the University, and the more-than-twelve-thousand new houses built on what had been derelict land to the east of the city, on the site of the former Bradford Colliery. From *'One Nation Under a Groove Now We're On The Move'* to *'Aint No Stoppin' Us Now'*…

2013

"You're the one who's got this back to front," chides Petros later that evening. She has called him after she has walked the quarter-mile from the Library in St Peter's Square back to her home on Faulkner Street.

"Manchester's now a City of Culture to rival the best in Europe," she says. "Milan, Barcelona, Berlin…"

"I'm not doubting the Commonwealth Games played a part in revitalising the city," he says.

"A major part."

"OK. But who built on that legacy?"

"The Council. They had a plan for the regeneration of the whole region."

"But one which could only be realised with the support of the private sector."

"Enormous foreign investment from China and the Middle East?"

"From which we all of us benefit."

"Especially the private investors."

"Which is completely fair by the way."

"Why?"

"Theirs is the greater risk. They have the most to lose."

"I don't agree."

"For a small limited guarantee, the Council is able to leverage uncountably more funds, which they wouldn't otherwise be able to raise, not without massively increasing the council tax, or by making serious cuts elsewhere. That way they get to build the homes the city so desperately needs."

"Along with many more that we don't. Like penthouses for the super rich."

"That's the free market, Chloe."

"And it's fundamentally wrong."

"Why?"

"It puts too much power in the hands of a privileged few."

"But there are checks and balances. When Sheik Mansoor offered to buy the City of Manchester Stadium in the year after the Games had finished, he was only allowed to do so on the understanding that he built thousands of affordable houses in the immediate vicinity."

"Which he *has* done, I concede, but that merely opens the floodgates for other investors to dictate the terms. 'You scratch our backs, we'll clobber yours.' It gives them *carte blanche* to build whatever they like."

"Who, Chloe? Who are you talking about?"

Chloe pauses.

"My father, I suppose," she says at last. "What he doesn't understand is that I regard Manchester as my home. Mine, not his."

"I understand that," says Petros, in a tone immediately more conciliatory, "more than you might think."

"Oh?" Chloe's interest is piqued.

"A story for another time perhaps," he says.

"OK," she says, then picks up the thread of what she was saying before. "I suppose what really bothers me about all of this is the loss of control, the feeling of disempowerment, that somehow we, the common people, no longer count." She recalls David Beckham urging all of the children who'd taken part in the Opening Ceremony to 'count themselves *in*'. What had happened to that hope, that promise? "I – *we* – risk," she continues, "no longer having a voice. Or at least, not having that voice heard."

"Speak for yourself," laughs Petros. "Though I can't imagine for one moment you not making sure your voice gets heard." He hears her laugh down the phone. "As for me," he says, "I intend to throw my hat in the ring."

"Well," says Chloe, shaking her head, "good luck with that."

She hangs up. She looks at her grandmother asleep in the chair, the letter from her son-in-law, Chloe's father, lying open on her lap. No, thinks Chloe with greater resolve than she feels. Manchester *is* her home. She is committed to carving out her future here. Just as Queen Elizabeth had encouraged her to do all those years before. That is what her father will never understand. And perhaps neither will Petros. An accident of birth, no more than that. That is how her father views their connection to Manchester. For him there are loyalties and ties that stretch much further back, so that he regards the city differently, no more than a vessel, into which he can deposit the least he can get away with, and then squeeze from it every last drop he can, so that once he has emptied it, like the culverting of the rivers, drained and abandoned until all that is left of them is a stagnant ditch, he can move on. Out of sight, out of mind.

But that is not what Chloe wants, and she will fight her father as strongly as she can to hold onto it. What she wants is to throw herself into the thick of it, immerse herself in the push and pull of it, swimming against the tide if she must, navigating currents that may be rougher, but cleaner, towards a future that is fairer and more freely flowing. Here. In Manchester. Nowhere else. She will rehearse these arguments with Petros the next time they clash. It will be easier with him than with her father. There is less at stake. But it is less clear-cut, less black-and-white. There are more grey areas, more ambiguities to unpick. Petros, too, she suspects, has his own set of divided loyalties he must contend with. She folds her father's letter and puts it away, at the back of a drawer she rarely uses. But however hard she might try to forget it. She will know it's always there.

She needs a distraction. She decides to return to the article about the Queen gate-crashing the Town Hall wedding.

*

2012

Daily Mail

24th March 2012

HERE'S A ROYAL HOW-D'YOU-DO!

Frances, 44, a hairdresser from Prestwich, told our reporter, "The Queen called us by our first names – it was like she knew us! She said I looked lovely and she wanted to wish us all the best for the future. It was so lovely that she took the trouble to speak to us like that."

Later Her Majesty, dressed in a dusky pink woollen suit with matching horizontal boater, even agreed to join the happy couple for a photograph on the Town Hall steps.

"We learned a few weeks ago that the Queen would be in the building at the same time as us," confessed the groom, builder John Canning, "having lunch with the Lord Mayor. I'm a big fan of the Royal family, and so I thought I'd write and ask if she would like to attend. I said that I hoped she had a lovely day in Manchester, wishing her all the best for her Jubilee, adding that if she'd got any spare minutes, we were only next door! I'd never written a letter to anyone famous before, but I thought: 'What have I got to lose?' Even if we'd only got a reply, that in itself would have been marvellous. I never in a million years expected her to attend."

"It was the best wedding present we could ever have wished for," beamed the radiant bride. "She was just so lovely, so gracious…"

*

2013

You couldn't make it up, thinks Chloe. I'm not a Royalist, no matter what Petros might say, I never could be, but you have to hand it to her. The common touch.

But what does she think? Inside, in private, away from the crowds and the cameras? That's what Chloe longs to know.

How does she really feel when cutting a ribbon, unveiling a plaque, opening a building, like she'd seen her do at NOMA the previous week with such practised lack of fuss and ceremony? What does she say quietly afterwards to a man like Niall Booker, the Co-op's controversial CEO? Surely she must know of his reputation and his alleged misdemeanours? How does she square that with the ethics of fair-shares-for-all that lay behind the original vision of the Rochdale Pioneers who founded the CWS in the first place?

Or perhaps they weren't so squeaky clean themselves? Chloe scrolls further down till she finds the entry she's been looking for, when the Co-op opened their first Tobacco Factory in Angel Meadow one hundred and fifteen years earlier…

*

1898

Co-operative Wholesale Society of England & Scotland's Annual Report:

Item: Progress of Manchester Tobacco Factory

Two years ago, despite opposition from some anti-smoking voices in the Society, the Wholesale decided to commence the manufacture of tobacco, and, after mature consideration, the buildings of the former Arkwright Mill, abutting Miller and Sharp Streets with Ludgate Hill in the district known as Angel Meadow, were acquired. Given their proximity to our Manchester headquarters on Balloon Street, this was deemed a most suitable location. Very soon after work was started, it became apparent that significant extensions would be required, and accordingly additions have been made to the original premises.

The result of the first fifteen weeks' working was a profit of £351. This was a remarkably good beginning, as it is not always possible to show a balance on the right side of the account during the first period of a new product department. For the first year ending June, 1898, the profit realised was £3,312. At the present time nearly eleven tons of manufactured tobacco are sent out every week, and the factory has secured more than half of the trade of our other Societies.

These facts afford weighty testimony to the excellence of the varieties of tobacco blended, and it is hoped that all Co-operative worshippers at the shrine of 'baccas' will see that the incense they offer as a burnt sacrifice comes from the Miller Street Factory.

The Society now imports leaves from as far afield as Borneo, Sumatra, Brazil and Cuba. Our workers are paid above the minimum wage for just an eight-hour day. In addition they enjoy the services of a library and a welfare attendant. As a consequence our skilled workers can roll tobacco leaves into the finest cigars with the dexterity of classical pianists, which we are now exporting back to distributors around the world.

Staying with this musical theme, it has been decided to form the CWS Tobacco Factory Brass Band under the leadership of our Manager, Mr J.C. Cragg, who has raised £300 for the purchase of second-hand musical instruments. Take-up has been most encouraging and the band is already enjoying considerable local success.

*

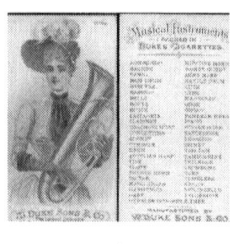

But not everyone is happy. Local residents of Angel Meadow are barred from applying for jobs in the factory. Instead the CWS employs people from what they describe as 'the better class districts', who daily run the gauntlet of the unemployed and the desperate, who must endure privations the brass-band-playing, cigar-rolling workers bussed in each day can scarcely imagine…

*

2013

Chloe shuts down the file. She knows that somehow she must learn to channel the skills of the aerial artist Lindsay Butcher if she is to perfect the balancing act she seeks.

After the Commonwealth Games Opening Ceremony, the eleven-year-old Chloe had managed to pluck up the courage to ask Lindsay whether she ever got frightened when performing at such a height. Up close Chloe could see that Lindsay's leotard was covered in lightly-coloured wing patterns.

"You get used to it," Lindsay had said. "Like everything. It becomes quite normal after a while. You see things so much clearer from up there. The city looks so different. Like a sleeping giant. A cocoon."

Before the adult moth breaks free and flies, thinks Chloe, recalling the moment more than ten years later.

She closes her eyes and tries to imagine it.

2

TRACING THE SOURCE

**2020 – 2013 – 2020 – 2005 – 1996 – 1852 – 1822 – 1852
1862 – 2010 – 2005 – 1996 – 1833 – 1996 – 2020 – 2005
2020**

2020

A hundred and twenty-two years later Petros is walking up Ludgate Hill. He stands outside the same Tobacco Factory, with its subsequent Art Deco extension, and takes a photo of it on his phone. It has recently been converted into desirable loft apartments, and he has bought the whole of the top floor, directly beneath the old CWS sign, and fitted them out himself.

Now they are ready for sale. They went on the market less than two hours ago and already he's been receiving calls from prospective buyers. He checks the time on his phone. He's due to meet one of them in ten minutes. Good. He likes to be early. In all things. It's always best to be ahead of the game, so he keeps his eyes and ears always open for the next opportunity. Like this had been.

He scrolls down to the Zoopla listing.

**Tobacco Factory, 30 Ludgate Hill, Northern Quarter
1 bedroom Apartment x 4
Asking price £250,000 each**

Features:
- Chain Free
- Duplex Apartment
- Factory Conversion
- Highly Sought After Development
- Ideal For Access To Northern Quarter
- One Double Bedroom
- Secure Allocated Car Parking
- Separate Kitchen With Ample Work Top Space
- Top Floor
- Vacant Possession

The former CWS Tobacco Factory, once part of Arkwright's original cotton mill, in Manchester's most highly sought-after quarter, offers residents the opportunity to enjoy a piece of the city`s Industrial Revolution heritage.

Occupying a prime site above Angel Meadow, the location offers quick and easy access to the new NOMA district, Victoria train station, Manchester Arena, the Printworks, an abundance of shopping opportunities, and walking distance to Manchester Piccadilly train, bus and tram stations.

Accessed via a secure communal entrance the development provides a lift service to all floors.

He is standing now beside that communal entrance, waiting for what he hopes will be his first sale of the morning. If he sells all four listed apartments by the day's end – which is his aim – he will have made himself a cool million. From an initial outlay of half that amount to purchase the floor from the property's owners, plus a further quarter million spent on fitting out what had been a completely empty husk – or a blank canvas, as he prefers to call it – he will have turned in a quarter million profit. Not bad for a morning's work. If it all goes well, that is. And he has no reason to doubt that it will.

He thinks back to his final year at uni, when his tutor would give him such a hard time, implying that he didn't possess the discipline necessary to hold down any kind of job, and smiles. Little did poor Clive realise that Petros had his whole future sketched out in full technicolour detail already. He had used his student loan to purchase his first property – a rundown, boarded-up end-terrace in the former Tripe Colony of Miles Platting, which, because of its semi-derelict status, he'd been able to snap up for less than £10,000. He smiles again, for it had been Clive who had unwittingly sent him down that path when, in their first year, he had shown them some photographs by George Wright. Clive was always going on about how brilliant they were, how they captured a lost age, depicting the city on the cusp of irrevocable change, with kids playing in the still-uncleared craters of Manchester's bomb sites before the slum clearances began. But where Clive saw those – to Petros' eyes – sentimental images as a window into the past, Petros viewed them as a gateway to the future. He still has the file stored on his phone - https://vimeo.com/76866293 - which he clicks on now to look at again, for old times' sake. Most of the streets were abandoned, but a few individuals still clung on, hoping for a miracle that never came. Some became squats but no one stayed for long. It was too grim. What Petros did was to use the rest of his student loan to make his property habitable, secure and safe. He lived in one of the rooms himself and rented the rest out at cheap rates to other students, providing him with a more-than-adequate monthly income until the inevitable compulsory purchase order popped through his letter box, offering less than the market amount, but more than double what he'd paid for it in the first place. He was on his way.

When he graduated, he talked his way into a job with Property Centric, who were rapidly buying up many of Manchester's former cotton mills and converting them into luxury apartments for young professionals, in the city's drive to encourage more people to live back in the centre once more. In an uncanny mirror-image of the CWS Tobacco factory when it first opened its doors for business as a new century dawned, these mill conversions were not for those workers who had been traditionally living in the less salubrious districts in which they stood – the Collyhursts, the Ancoats and, yes, the Miles Plattings – no, they were being driven further out to the margins of Harpurhey and Hulme, the damp-ridden 60s high-rises of Weaste and Salford.

But cities have always been crucibles of change, haven't they? Gentrification is a much-used, much-maligned term, but isn't that what everyone aspires towards, thinks Petros now, as he sees his first clients arrive, a young, casually but expensively dressed couple each on their own separate mobiles conducting their own particular deals, to keep on climbing that ladder towards a better, more prosperous life…?

*

2013

Final Presentation #2: Petros

Petros strides confidently into the Media Studio wearing a suit and tie to the predictable chorus of jeers and wolf whistles from the other students.

CLIVE:
All right. Settle down. Thank you, Petros. I'm delighted that at least one of you has made an effort to treat these presentations with the seriousness they deserve.

KHAV:
That's hardly fair, Clive. Lol and I haven't done ours yet.

CLIVE:
Fair enough. I'll wait till then and hope you'll not disappoint.

KHAV:
When have I ever done that?

CLIVE:
How long have I got?

KHAV:
And as for Lol, who knows who'll she be when it's her turn?

LORRIE:
That's right, Khav. (*She turns to Clive*). I like to keep you guessing.

CLIVE: (*raising a sceptical eyebrow*):
Well, looking at you today, I'd hazard a guess at either Blanche Dubois…

LORRIE: (*fluttering her eyelashes and adopting a southern belle accent*):
'I have always depended upon the kindness of strangers…'

PETROS: (*impatiently*):
Except that none of us are strangers…

CLIVE:
Or Bette Davis in *All About Eve*…

CHLOE: (*bursting in at the last moment*):
'Fasten your seatbelts, it's gonna be a bumpy night.'

LORRIE: (*with a disappointed pout*):
    Oh! I wanted to say that.

KHAV: (*flicking her fingers*):
    Wicked.

CHLOE:
    Sorry I'm late. Gran. Have I missed anything?

PETROS:
    Nothing of any consequence. I've not started yet.

CHLOE:
    What's the suit in aid of? Got an interview for a job straight after?

PETROS:
    Might have.

LORRIE:
    Job interviews are like first dates…

CLIVE: (*putting his head in his hands*):
    Please – not '*The Reader's Digest Guide to Successful Interviews…*'

LORRIE: (*ignoring him, standing on one side of Petros*):
    Good impressions count.

CHLOE: (*standing on the other*):
    Awkwardness can occur.

KHAV: (*standing directly in front of him*):
    Outcomes are unpredictable.

Although Petros knows exactly what is coming, Khav is too fast for him. She grabs his tie and yanks it tight, almost throttling him. The moment she releases her grip, she immediately launches into an energetic kung fu routine, complete with sound effects. When she finishes, she, Chloe and Lorrie, as one, sit on the floor before him expectantly. They hold up the handmade clapperboard and pass it between them.

CHLOE:
Petros Presentation...

KHAV:
Take One...

LORRIE: (*snapping it shut with a broad grin*):
Action!

Petros and Clive exchange a weary shrug of resignation.

PETROS: (*with practised formality*):
Thank you.

For my presentation today I intend to give a Lecture / Demonstration – a kind of role play, if you will – where I take on the part of a Famous Visiting Professor – hence the suit – and you take on the role of eager students, hanging on my every word...

CLIVE:
That'll make a change.

CHLOE:
Shh! I don't want to miss a word of what the Famous Visiting Professor has to tell us.

LORRIE:
But which Famous Visiting Professor are you?

KHAV:
Steve Jobs?

LORRIE:
That can't be right. If he was Steve Jobs, he'd be wearing a

black polo-neck jumper instead of a tie.

CHLOE: (*eyeing him narrowly*):
Marshall McLuhan.

PETROS: (*acknowledging*):
'*The Medium is the Message.*'

He taps on his phone. At once a film comes up on the screen behind him.

I'd like you to take a close look at this short clip. It's from *Charlie Bubbles*. Made in 1965. Directed by Albert Finney. Written by Shelagh Delaney – of *A Taste of Honey* fame – and shot just a few miles from where we're watching it today, in Salford, where Finney and Delaney both grew up. It's one of my all-time favourite films. Tell me what you see.

The extract begins with a high aerial shot. The camera swoops across a completely devastated, near post-apocalyptic landscape, one which appears to have been ravaged by some cataclysmic disaster – in this case, the bombed-out streets, which for years lay abandoned and were simply allowed to fall into further decay, until, with a zeal and fervour bordering on the religiously fanatical, the slum clearances began in earnest, just months before the shooting of this film, so that now hardly a house has been left standing amid the rubble of blown-up bricks, which lie in piles as far as the eye can see, knitted together by cobbled streets, criss-crossing where once whole communities stood like the warp and weft of some gigantic loom. Those few buildings that do still remain are either boarded up, or already roofless and windowless, poking through the cratered earth like broken bones.

As the camera draws nearer, a car can be seen driving along these deserted streets. On closer inspection, it is revealed to be an open-top Rolls Royce. The film gives the impression of being shot in a gritty black and white, but actually it's not, and the car is garishly, incongruously, gold. Driving the car is the film's eponymous hero, Charlie Bubbles himself, played by Albert Finney. Sitting alongside him, taking photographs of the ruined emptiness all around her, is, we assume, his girlfriend, portrayed somewhat surprisingly and not a little incongruously by a youthful Liza Minelli, appearing in her first feature. She is instantly recognisable, and this at once piques Lorrie's interest especially, who leans closer towards the screen to study her every movement and gesture.

MINELLI:

I think it's a shame they have to pull down all the old buildings. They have such character.

The car then drives past a line of old men waiting at a bus stop for a bus that will surely never come.

Where do your parents live now, Charlie?

FINNEY:

Oh – around here somewhere. I'll see 'em later, I suppose.

MINELLI:

A prophet is always without honour in his own land.

FINNEY:

What were you expecting? Bonfires in the streets, flags flying, and 'Welcome home, Charlie'?

Before she can answer, they are interrupted by the sound of a drum roll as around the corner appears a Marching Band of a Boys' Brigade or Lads' Club, led by a man in uniform comprising a white peaked hat and gloves, carrying a staff, which he whirls about him as he marches. They make their way surreally across the ravaged landscape, followed by Finney and Minelli in the gold Rolls Royce. The scene is shrouded in a Manchester fog. Broken telegraph poles stride towards the vanishing point, no longer laced together by the singing wires. In the distance, barely visible in the fog, towers of brand new glass-and-concrete flats rise up towards the sky.

Petros presses pause on this final image – the marching band, the gold Rolls Royce, the silent telegraph poles, the demolished streets, the high rise blocks of flats peeping through the mist.

PETROS:
Now – let me ask you again. What did you see?

LORRIE:
Liza with a 'Zee'!

KHAV: (*rolling her eyes*):
She's in love again, innit?

PETROS:
No. I think she might have a point.

KHAV:
Meaning?

PETROS:
Lol?

LORRIE: (*singing*):
'Money makes the world go around, the world go around...'

PETROS:
Precisely.

CHLOE:
Oh come on – that's such a cliché. I mean, it's practically a Morrissey wet dream up there. First of all it's written by Shelagh Delaney, who Morrissey not only adored but whose work he shamelessly plundered – the lyrics for *The*

Night Has Opened My Eyes are a straight steal from *A Taste of Honey*, while her photograph adorns the covers for *Louder than Bombs* and *Girlfriend in a Coma*. Next it's got Albert Finney in the lead, who attended the legendary Salford Lads' Club, outside of which Morrissey and the rest of The Smiths posed for their album *The Queen Is Dead*. Not that there's any evidence he ever went there – unlike Graham Nash, for example, who used to rehearse with The Hollies there – no, he merely stood on the shoulders of others who'd been there before him, while he shot the videos for *There is a Light that Never Goes Out* and *Stop Me If You Think You've Heard This One Before* in the conveniently named Coronation Street outside. So, Petros, I'm sorry to say that yes, we have indeed heard this one before, many, many times, and it doesn't improve with the telling. At the time the Lads' Club Committee were less than impressed, instructing solicitors to send out an official letter publicly condemning its use of their building by Morrissey without requesting their permission, which, they were at pains to point out, would not have been granted. 'The inclusion of the photograph of the exterior of our building,' they wrote, 'may cause anyone looking at the cover, or listening to the record, to attribute the material to the Club, its Committee, or Members, a claim we refute absolutely and unequivocally. We take particular exception to the reference in the song *Vicar in a Tutu*, for example, which implies that the singer, whose photograph would appear to imply was a member of our club, was engaged in stealing lead from a church roof.'

KHAV: (*shaking her head*):
How d'you know all this stuff?

CHLOE: (*witheringly*):
I research it. While thirdly, Petros, the Marching Band in

Charlie Bubbles is actually *from* Salford Lads Club. Morrissey must've wet himself when he saw it.

LORRIE:

I'm with Liza. I think it's a real shame they had to knock all those houses down.

PETROS:

You wouldn't've said that then if you'd had to live in one of 'em.

KHAV:

And you'd know, I suppose?

PETROS:

I would actually.

KHAV:

Ooh!

CLIVE: (*suddenly and decisively intervening*):
Sehnsucht.

KHAV:

What sucks?

CLIVE:

Sehnsucht. It's a term that means the opposite of nostalgia. Most of us are guilty from time to time of looking at the past through rose-tinted spectacles…

PETROS:

Not me.

CLIVE:

But when someone views the future through the same prism, believing that it's bound almost by the laws of nature to be better than anything that's gone before – that's *sehnsucht*.

PETROS:

In Greek we call it λαχτάρα – '*laktara*'.

KHAV:

I call it 'throwing the baby out with the bath water'.

CHLOE:

The Salford Lads Club Committee would agree with you. They embrace the fame that Morrissey has brought to it and now welcome fans to the club, encouraging them to pose for their selfies in front of its bottle green gates and doors.

PETROS:

And that's my point.

CLIVE:

Finally!

PETROS:

Before I showed you the clip, I asked you a simple question. What do you see? Lol saw Liza and the loss of the past. Chloe saw exploitation and myth-making. Clive saw *sehnsucht*, and Khav, you saw… what?

KHAV:

I'm still makin' me mind up, innit?

PETROS:

Very wise.

KHAV:

Keepin' me powder dry.

PETROS:

But Lol saw something else too.

LORRIE:

I did?

PETROS: (*singing tentatively*):
'*A mark, a yen, a buck or a pound…*'

LORRIE: (*catching on and joining in*):
'*That clinking, clanking, clunking sound…*'

PETROS & LORRIE (*together*):
'*It makes the world go round.*'

PETROS:

I anticipated this response, and so I'd like to continue my Lecture / Dem. with a little critique. Here's something I prepared earlier… (*He calls up to Tanya in the Control Booth*). All set, Tan?

TANYA:
Ready when you are, mate.

He taps once more on his phone and up on the screen behind him appears a sequence of photographs, depicting some of the changes Manchester has undergone in the last fifty years – photographs by Shirley Baker, Richard Davis, Peter Walsh and George Wright – children playing in bomb sites; gossiping women hanging out washing, donkey-stoning their doorsteps; solitary men, lost and out of work, standing on street corners; teenagers flirting in alleyways; rag-and-bone men with their horses and carts; tired, grimy faces, worn, exhausted figures, bent over bonfires scavenging for scraps; burnt-out cars, boarded-up houses; abandoned streets; the desolate walkways in the sky of Hulme's concrete crescents; Alsatian dogs prowling on the rooftop of Factory Records; crowds queuing in the rain outside The Haçienda, and the press of sweating bodies ecstatically dancing inside. Over the images, as they dissolve into each other successively, Petros signals to Tanya to cue in a beat-box backing track, which immediately has Khav dancing. On receiving a nod from him, she proceeds to embark upon a rap Petros has written especially for her to perform as part of his presentation.

KHAV:
>First it was cotton, canals, den coal
>But now dey all gone dey left a big hole
>We're payin' de price, it's takin' its toll
>So now we're all looking to find a new role
>
>What we're left with's a conflagration
>Disintegration in de conurbation
>Rumination for expiation
>Communication's de explanation
>
>Recreational innovation'll
>Bring a facial to brand new spatial
>Alignments, refinements
>Break free of confinements
>
>Explosions, extrusions
>Emotions, confusions
>De only solution's
>A street revolution
>
>I'm telling you all an' I'm telling you straight
>Pay heed to my call before it's too late
>We'll carry de torch from station to station
>Igniting a flame with our name for de nation
>
>Consecration, not desecration
>Celebration, unfettered elation
>Initiation leads to mass participation
>Convocation in de conflagration
>
>First it was cotton, canals, den coal
>Now this conflagration's gonna fill dat hole
>Gonna pay that toll, create de new role
>Conflagration's gonna make us whole…

She finishes to whoops and cheers from the other students. Even Chloe. Only Clive is silent. He stares, seemingly enraptured by the final image on the screen. It's a George Wright classic. In the foreground three boys climb a lamp post that leans at a precarious angle to the right of perpendicular, while, scissoring the sky behind, a derelict church spire teeters correspondingly to the left. Between where these two verticals intersect a tired, older woman squats on a pile of abandoned bricks, out of which, in the background, appears to sprout a high rise tower block in a shimmering mirage, its rooftop lost in a haze, which could be heat, but which is more likely to be smog. The three boys climb the lamp post oblivious. Their horizons seem limitless. The one who is highest, reaching a hand beyond the shattered casement, is Clive, ten years old at the time the photograph was taken. An ardent admirer of George Wright, as his students know only too well, this is a photograph he has not seen before.

CLIVE: (*very quietly*):

Can I ask you where you sourced this last image?

PETROS:

The British Culture Archive.

Clive nods.

PETROS:

Do you want me to send you the link?

CLIVE:

Could you please?

He decides to say nothing further. There's no point exposing himself to what would be certain to be merciless mockery, he thinks. Thankfully no one appears to have recognised him – though Chloe is staring hard at the image. But she speaks instead to Petros, not him.

CHLOE:
You're going to ask us again, aren't you?

PETROS:
I am.

CHLOE: (*grinning*):
Go on then.

PETROS:
What do you see?

LORRIE:
The old and the new.

PETROS:
And?

LORRIE:
The young and the old.

PETROS:
And?

KHAV:
It's just kids playin', innit?

PETROS:
Is it?

KHAV:
The one at the top thinks he's Spiderman. In a minute he's gonna try an' leap from the lamp post to the church spire.

PETROS:
Interesting.

KHAV: (*acting out as she speaks*):
'Faster than a speeding bullet…'
'More powerful than a steam locomotive…'

'Leaps tall buildings in a single bound…'

LORRIE:
That's Superman.

KHAV:
Yeah?

LORRIE:
You said 'Spider Man' before.

KHAV::
So?

LORRIE:
I'm just saying…

KHAV:
Whatever…

CHLOE:
'Heaven Knows I'm Miserable Now…'

CLIVE:
A girl after my own heart. But you'll have to explain, Chloe, for you've lost me completely now.

CHLOE:
Morrissey again. '*Dreaming.*'

CLIVE:
Of what?

CHLOE:
Escape.

PETROS:
Who's giving this presentation, Chloe? You or me?

CHLOE:
He couldn't get out of here quick enough.

CLIVE:
Who couldn't?

KHAV & LORRIE: (*together*):
Morrissey.

PETROS:
But *I'm* staying.

CHLOE:
Ah- ha! Now we come to it.

CLIVE: (*wearily*):
At last...

PETROS: (*with increasing passion*):
I'm sick to death of all this harking back to the old days – when things were better, smarter, more real, more sincere, more committed – when everyone had dreams, ideals, things they believed in – Give Peace a Chance, Power to the People, Take to the Streets, Man the Barricades – Rivers of Blood, Pillars of Fire. Oh, they say, if only you'd been around then, we all had a cause, something to believe in, something we could fight for. Stop the War – Ban the Bomb – Scrap the Poll Tax – Sunday Bloody Sunday. Black Panthers, Tamil Tigers. Anti-Thatcher, Anti-Blair. You should've been with us in the sixties, they say, or the seventies, the eighties in Hulme, in Moss Side. And my family's even worse – their grievances go back two hundred years – the Massacre at Chios – on and on and on... But you know, I'm not sorry I missed any of it. I don't want to drown in the past, wallowing in glorious failures, reminiscing about what might have been. I don't want to do any of that. I want to look forward. I don't want to run

away. I want to stay right here. This is where the future is, and we're going to make it for ourselves. That's what those boys are dreaming about when they're climbing that lamp post. We're going to go higher and higher, they think, and nothing's gonna stop us. And that one at the top – he's not looking down, he's looking up….

CHLOE: (*quietly*):

Or maybe he's just shit scared, that if he ever does look down, he'll fall in the rubble and never get up again.

PETROS: (*equally quietly*):

Better to be Icarus and die trying, than not to dare at all…

Chloe nods. She and Petros hold each other's gaze a long time. The others sense this and say nothing. Petros tries to read Chloe's expression but finds he can't. 'I don't agree with you,' it appears to be saying, 'but I respect your honesty.'

Eventually it is Clive who interrupts the silence. In truth he has been hardly listening to Petros's rant. He has been too caught up in so suddenly and unexpectedly being confronted by this image of himself as a small boy. He can't believe he has never seen this photograph before. Nor does he have any recollection of the occasion it was captured. It just looks like any other day he spent playing in the wreckage. The bomb sites were their playground, completely normal to him, and all the rest of the kids who played there. He looks again closely at the image. No – he has no memory of it being taken. George Wright was such a regular presence on the streets back then, photographing the city on the cusp of change, that he just merged into the background, doing a job just like anyone else, in the workshops, on the barges, in the demolition gangs, so that they simply paid him no attention. He never had to ask them to pose, they forgot he was there. No wonder then that he captured such singular moments. Like this one. In recent years Clive has become a collector. He has half a dozen George Wright photographs. They line the walls in his study, back at his home in Victoria Park, which he shares with Florence, his wife, their son and their daughter – when they're at home, which they rarely are these days – and their dog, Rafe, a lurcher-collie cross. He must look this particular image up on line. The British Culture Archive – wasn't that the site that Petros had mentioned? He'd see if he could order a print perhaps. Florence and the kids might get a kick out of seeing it. Looking at it now is rather like looking into a lost world, a time from another century, which of course it is, even if it's less than fifty years ago. He senses the students looking at him curiously. He really must get a grip. But more and more these days he feels that he's lost touch with them entirely. He shan't be sorry to be retiring next year. He feels his eyes begin to well up. No, no, no. This will never do. He hastily removes his spectacles and concentrates furiously on wiping them clean.

CLIVE: (*coughing awkwardly*):

Yes, yes, yes. All very fine, Petros. Year Zero and all that. You've told us in no uncertain terms exactly what it is you're against, but what is it you're for? What will you replace all this with? The Hulme Crescents have hardly been a recipe for success, have they?

He replaces his glasses, behind which he blinks rapidly.

Well?

PETROS: (*beaming, as if this has been the cue he's been waiting for*):

This. (*He calls up to the Control Booth*). Are you ready, Tan? (*She gives him a thumps-up to signal that she is*).

He taps his phone to bring up an image of the Beetham Tower. This immediately elicits a range of reactions from the students. Before he can prevent himself, Clive automatically groans.

PETROS:
You hate it, don't you?

CLIVE:
It's not my favourite piece of architecture, no

PETROS:
When it was built, it was the tallest building in Manchester and the tallest anywhere in the country outside of London. It still is. But it won't be for long. Just you wait. There'll be plenty more in the years to come.

CLIVE:
Heaven help us.

PETROS:
More than two hundred in less than a decade – you mark my words.

CLIVE:
You do realise, I suppose, that its appearance in the Manchester skyline robbed the city at a stroke of becoming a UNESCO World Heritage Site, for which it was under serious consideration because of its industrial heritage, the few buildings of which remain are now overshadowed by this – what's the word Prince Charles used…?

CHLOE:
Carbuncle.

KHAV:
It's not, though, is it? It looks more like a blade…

PETROS:
That's what they call it. 'The Silver Blade.'

LORRIE:
That's what they used to call Tonya Harding.

CLIVE:
Who?

LORRIE: (*experimenting with her hair*):
The American Ice Skater. Margot Robbie plays her in the film. I reckon I could do that look. (*She mimes an impressive triple salchow*).

PETROS:
In 2007 it was awarded 'Best Tall Building in the World' by the Council for Urban Habitat.

KHAV: (*still musing on its shape*):
…or maybe a UFO? Like the monolith in Stanley Kubrick's *A Space Odyssey*?

She re-enacts the scene where the apes dart back and forth towards it, gingerly touching the screen).

PETROS: (*ignoring her*):
You can see Jodrell Bank from the top. As well as the Pennines, Snowdonia, and ten English counties.

KHAV:
On a clear day. Not that we get many of those.

PETROS:
It doubles as a lightning rod.

KHAV:
Or maybe just a penis substitute.

She immediately launches into the Frankie Goes To Hollywood classic, 'Relax', which the rest of the students join in, while from her back pocket she takes out a condom, which she blows up as tall and straight as she can. Clive chuckles in spite of himself. Oh, the hubris of youth. While Petros, although he feels his presentation has been hi-jacked, still manages a wry smile. Let's see who has the last laugh, shall we, he thinks?

KHAV & LORRIE:
    '*Relax, don't do it, when you want to suck it to it*
    Relax, don't do it, when you want to…'

She releases the condom so that it farts across the studio until it lands on the floor deflated and spent.

KHAV & LORRIE:
    '*…come!*'

*

2020

Seven years later Petros loosens his tie, remembering the day. He's the one who's smiling now. He spoke more prophetically than he knew. The city is surrounded by a circle of glass and steel, with more than two hundred and seventy-five towers planned by 2025. Already there are more than twenty exceeding a hundred metres in height, with the South Tower in Deansgate Square becoming the first building anywhere in Great Britain outside of London to climb past two hundred metres.

    He looks around him now. As well as the South Tower, there's the East, West and North Towers. Over in Greengate, abutting the River Irwell is the Anaconda Cut. At the junction of Great Ancoats Street with Whitworth Street stands the Central City Tower. While just behind, at the far end of Miller Street where now he stands, is the old CIS Building, once the tallest building in Europe, and the new Angel Gardens Apartments, either side of NOMA's Egg Slice, all of them separate enclaves within the Co-op Group, the latest spawn of which is the Tobacco Factory, beside which he now waits for his next clients to arrive, for whom he has reserved a space in the NCP Car Park directly opposite.

*

2005

Fifteen years earlier Dr Grace Chadwick is standing in front of that same NCP car park. Except that it differs in one significant manner. The one Grace is standing by is derelict, awaiting repair and reconstruction, as it has been for almost a decade, an operation that has thankfully been carried out by the time Petros waits impatiently beside it. The reason for its sad, neglected state in 2005 is, in part, due to Grace herself.

In 1982 Grace was appointed the city's first Director of the Manchester Urban Heritage Park, a post she was awarded on the back of her role as one of the lead archaeologists overseeing the excavation and documentation of what remained of the Roman Settlement when *Mamucium* – as it was then – a minor outpost on the farthest fringes of the empire, was hastily abandoned in the fourth century. It was Grace, who, in 1953, when still only a student, had made the spectacular discovery of an entire skeleton of a slain soldier, the bones partly concealed by a riven oaken shield with the insignia of a bee crudely painted on it. Subsequent DNA testing suggested that the soldier was in all probability not part of the Roman Army, but from the *Settanti*, an ancient, early British tribe, who had harried the Romans as they retreated, later establishing a palisaded village close by, at the confluence of the Rivers Irwell, Medlock and Irk.

The discovery at the time made all the newspapers. Grace's photograph was on every front page. She was even interviewed on radio and television. But such early fame did not go to Grace's head. For one thing, her father, Jabez, the Head Gardener at Philips Park, would never have permitted it – "You know what they say about newspapers, Gracie? Today's headlines make for tomorrow's fish-and-chip wrapping." – and for another, Grace knew she had simply been lucky. The right time at the right place. It could just as easily have been any of the other undergraduates helping out with the dig instead of her. But it convinced her even more that this was how she wanted to spend the rest of her life.

And so she has.

The head of that first dig in Castlefield – Dr Mike Nevell, Professor of the University of Manchester's Archaeology Department – recognised in Gracie, as she was still called back then, something of the same passion that had first inspired him to embark on what for the most part is a thankless vocation, with weeks and months spent out in the mud and rain painstakingly scraping away at unearthed artefacts, which are, for the most part, mind-numbingly repetitive, with finds as spectacular as the one Gracie had uncovered as rare as a solar eclipse. "Things like that happen once, maybe twice only in a lifetime. Are you prepared for that?"

Gracie had answered that she was, and so Dr Nevell – or Mike, as she came to know him – invited her to join his team. She never looked back. As the years went by she came increasingly to enjoy those months of mindless mud-scraping. It was in the smaller discoveries, she felt, that the real insights were made – a clay pipe, a ceramic floor tile, even a scrap of hand-stitched cotton. These brought her quite literally within touching distance of the lives that had passed before her, on the very ground she walked on, and removed the surface of, inch by painstaking inch, layer upon layer, exposing the strata of history, upon which her beloved city had grown. Manchester. Her home.

It was perfectly natural, then, that her career would evolve seamlessly into the study of Manchester's more recent past, that she would specialise in *Industrial* Archaeology. Her father, as well as a gardener, was also a miner, as was her older brother, Toby. She felt a kinship with them, which had sprung from her childhood growing up in Philips Park, listening to her father explain how the bones from the paupers' graves that were washed away by the Great Flood of 1872, when the Medlock disastrously burst its banks, had gone on to enrich the soil in which each year he planted the thousands of bulbs for the annual Tulip Sundays. One of her earliest, most enduring memories was of their dog, Tag, unearthing a bone just beside the spot where her father was digging.

They were both dead now, Jabez and Toby, along with her mother, Mary, as well as her sister, Harriet, and Harriet's husband, Paul. Grace herself is seventy-two, but, despite having been born with polio, has never had a day's illness in her life. Her disability – a word she has never liked, and one she has never applied to herself – has, if anything, made her stronger. She has never, not once, used it as an excuse not to do something, even if others tried to prevent her. Like her mother, who was always worrying she might come to harm. And so Gracie had simply gone and done whatever it was she had set her mind on anyway, just to prove to people that she could. Like climbing trees, or riding a bicycle – which she still does today – and becoming an archaeologist.

Her life and career – for she has never separated the two – have been both successful and fulfilling. As well as becoming Director of the Manchester Urban Heritage Park, she was also appointed as County Archaeologist for Greater Manchester, in which she was frequently able to step in to temporarily halt any major new redevelopment in the city, in order to take advantage of each new piece of ground laid bare by their demolition and destruction, to comprehensively map and catalogue what had been revealed, before the construction of the new road, or shopping centre, or – as in this case today – car park could continue. Sometimes, if she was able to identify something of particular significance – a mosaic pavement, a medieval brick course, the cast-iron underpinnings of a bridge – these could be preserved and incorporated into the revised plans. But mostly what she found were smaller items, which were all meticulously recorded and sent to the Manchester Museum to be stored, and occasionally put on display. One of her favourite activities as part of her various roles has been to take some of these smaller artefacts to schools and ask the children to imagine the stories that might lie behind them. They never failed to surprise her, always coming up with suggestions, their imaginations bringing to life a shard of pottery, or coloured glass, a leather purse, a braided wrist band, a comb, a coin. Grace saw herself as providing the spark for these stories to come back to the light, after their years of being hidden underground in the dark.

She thinks back to the year 1953 once more. Just six months before her finding of the *Settanti* skeleton in Castlefield, there was an accident at Bradford Colliery, the mine where her brother worked. Nearly three hundred men were trapped. All but four were able to climb their way back to the surface by a series of ladders up a ventilation shaft, until one of the ladders came away from the rock wall. Toby was one of the four who were left behind when the ladder collapsed. He and the others had to find their way out by a different route, a much longer, more circuitous, more dangerous route, through a labyrinth of long abandoned shafts and tunnels, some of them going back as far as when the Romans had started to haul the coal from the earth from above. When he eventually made it back to the light, he told her how it had seemed as though they were ascending through layers of time. He had felt the eyes of miners from centuries ago had been watching them, their voices urging them on. At the point where the ladder had come away from the wall, it had created a cavity, a small hole into which Toby had put his hand, to save him from falling. Once he had managed to steady himself and find a foothold, he was able at last to extricate his clenched fingers. Inside the curled palm of his fist was an old coin, which he asked Grace to identify for him. She was able to confirm that it was Roman. "How did it get there?" he had asked her. "Who had put it there? Did he do so deliberately? Or did he just drop it?"

"Or she," Grace had answered, and the two of them had shared a smile.

That was how she saw her life. Unspooling a thread in the darkness so that she might enter places nobody had been to for centuries and not get lost herself, returning with treasure and stories. Then share these treasures and stories with children.

She wonders what has happened to Toby's coin. Was he buried with it? Or did he hand it down to one of his own children? Michael and Milly? Both grown and with children of their own. She hopes so. She must ask them the next time she sees them. She likes to think of things being passed on...

Grace herself has no children. She never married. There was someone who, for a time, seemed a possibility. Stephen. They'd been undergraduates together. He was a scientist, full of hope for a brighter tomorrow. He used to dismiss her passion for Archaeology as trivial and unimportant. "It's all dead and buried," he'd say, "best left where it is, no longer relevant in the modern world." They'd regularly spar over glasses of beer in *The Kardomah* on St Peter's Square, earnest in black polo neck jumpers and duffle coats, both of them enjoying themselves hugely, Stephen extolling the future, Gracie the past, but both of them knowing full well they were really just two different sides of the same coin. They'd go for drives sometimes in his open-top Triumph Vitesse, to pubs tucked away in the Cheshire lanes – *The Swan with Two Nicks, The Saracen's Head, The Bells of Peover* – and sometimes they'd go for walks, and he'd kiss her. She'd smile as he tossed back the lock of blonde hair that would fall so dashingly across his forehead, rather like a palomino stallion.

But it never amounted to anything. After he graduated, he went back south, to continue his studies at Oxford, and they lost touch. She would occasionally see a mention of him in a newspaper, along with the other boffins, whenever some new astronomical discovery was being announced, and speculate. Black holes. Dark matter…

Did he ever do the same if he ever came across a story about her, she wondered? Probably not. She did not think about him much. And in recent years, hardly at all. He'd be retired by now, of course. Like she was…

She retired nine years ago. In 1996, when she was sixty-three. But she still kept her hand in, and from time to time she was still asked to step in and lend her expertise to a particularly tricky site, in the capacity of a paid consultant. Like today.

Channel 4's *Time Team* has come to the city. After months of negotiation, permission has finally been granted to excavate the empty NCP car park for evidence of former occupation. It's thought that the original Arkwright's Cotton Mill once stood here. The first steam-powered mill anywhere in the world, its factory chimney was for almost a century the tallest structure in Manchester, until the watch tower at Strangeways Gaol was built, which itself dominated the city skyline till the construction of the Co-op's CIS Tower in 1962. Its shadow falls directly across Grace as she leans her bicycle up against a wall in Miller Street and waits to meet up with Tony Robinson, the presenter from *Time Team*, who has asked to interview her against the backdrop of preparations inside the car park, which has been screened off from curious spectators, while the top layer of concrete is being removed by volunteers.

As usual with all television shows, they're running late. Grace familiarises herself with the Dig's brief.

wessex archaeology

Wessex Archaeology, in partnership with Greater Manchester Council, have been commissioned by Videotext Communications Ltd to undertake a programme of recording and post-excavation work on an archaeological evaluation undertaken by Channel 4's 'Time Team' on the site of the former cotton mill of Sir Richard Arkwright, Miller Street, Manchester (hereafter 'the Site').

The Site occupies a position on rising land to the east and above the Rivers Irk and Irwell and is located within an open plan NCP car park centred on NGR 398984 384390, close to Victoria Station and Shudehill. The Site is bounded by Miller Street to the south and Angel Street to the north with Rochdale Road to the east and Dantzic Street to the west. The Site comprises four levels of car park. The factory is believed to have occupied the upper level. No remains survive above ground.

Prior to 1780 the Site had been in the possession of one John Pickford, who had used the site for the position of his brick works and yard. On his death an advert appeared in the Manchester Mercury in 1780 stating:

'To let, all that Close of Field, situated at the Top of the Shude-hill in Manchester late in the Occupation of John Pickford, deceased, containing upwards of two Acres, and used as a

Brick Yard, in which there is now a fine Breast of Clay upwards of two yards high, and Plenty of Water.'

Richard Arkwright (1732-92) leased the land, and with his partners William Brocklebank, John Whittenbury, John Simpson and Samuel Simpson constructed sometime between 1780 and 1782 a 'brick built and slated mill' 52.2m (171 ft) long by 9.1m (30ft) wide and five storeys high for the production of cotton textile…

So much, so obvious, thinks Grace. A young PA brings her a coffee, apologising again for the delay in starting. "Tony will be here as quick as he can," she explains, before being interrupted by her mobile phone. "Sorry," she says, "I need to take this." She steps away from Grace, pressing the phone close to one ear, while clamping her free hand to the other in an effort to shut out the incessant noise of drilling and hammering, the demands of TV schedules riding roughshod over the previous sacred rituals of silence and reverence that preceded the digs of Grace's youth. She understands completely, and sympathises. Time has always been money, and access to archaeological sites is typically reduced to just a few weeks, when ideally years are needed. Grace has had her fair share of battles in the past with the planners and developers over precisely how much time she can be allocated to carry out her work. Add camera and sound recording crews into the mix, and the costs quickly escalate.

While she waits for the PA to return, she sips her coffee appreciatively. That is one aspect of being on a dig, especially one that is close to a city centre, that has improved greatly since Grace first started out. The coffee. She remembers the dig in which she discovered the skeleton down at Castlefield, just one and a quarter miles away from where she now stands, being punctuated by all-too-frequent slurps of revolting instant coffee with teaspoons of dried, lumpy, powdered milk mixed in, from nasty plastic cups, that burnt her fingers and scalded her tongue.

She skims rapidly through the rest of the brief.

```
In September 1790 a six-horsepower, double
acting 'Sun and Planet' engine was ordered from
Boulton and Watt and installed in January 1791
in the new engine house. This was intended to
drive the mill machinery directly.
The Sun and Planet mechanism was patented by
Watt in 1781 and allowed for the development of
the rotative steam engine.
```

Grace likes this notion of the Sun and Planet engine. It couldn't have been better named. The lives of everyone connected to the Mill revolved around it.

```
The mechanism comprised a large gearwheel
fastened to the output shaft of the engine (the
sun), around which a smaller gearwheel (the
planet) rotated, held in mesh with the sun by
an arm. The planet wheel was fixed to the end
of the engine connecting rod, and as the piston
rod moved in and out of the cylinder, the
planet wheel described a circular path around
the sun wheel, causing it to rotate. The
configuration caused the sun wheel to make two
rotations for every cycle of the engine, thus
giving the output shaft a speed twice that of
the engine.
```

The PA, who, Grace learns from the name tag looped around her neck, is called Samira, returns to inform her that Tony's been held up in traffic, and that he'll be here in ten minutes. Grace thanks her and tries to find out what she can about her, without appearing to do so, a skill she has cultivated over her many years of recruiting assistants. Samira is from

Ethiopia, a Media graduate from MMU, and this is her first job. Her face glows with an eagerness Grace recognises from her own first days on a dig. Her skin irradiates it. She thinks *Time Team* is "just a terrific programme" and that Tony is "fantastic". She's "really nervous", but also "very excited", about the prospect of working with him. "As am I," confesses Grace, which puts Samira further at ease, so that she opens up more about hoping this opportunity "might just be the start". Grace sizes her up. "Is it television or archaeology that interests you?" she asks. "Both," says Samira at once, her senses immediately on high alert, as if this might be some kind of informal interview. She's heard of Grace Chadwick – who hasn't in this field? – and she's keen to make an impression. Which she does. Grace hands her a card. "These are the contacts for my successor as County Archaeologist. Robina McNeil. Give her a call. She might be able to help you." Beaming, Samira copies the details into her phone.

Just then Tony arrives. Leaping out of his car, he bounds over to Grace, reminding her of an enthusiastic puppy.

"Dr Chadwick," he barks, "I've been wanting to meet you for the longest time."

"Then you must call me Grace," she replies. "Everybody does. I insist upon it."

"Only if you call me Tony."

Samira fetches Tony a coffee, which he declares "a lifesaver", and then he and Grace head off in the direction of somewhere quieter, where they can discuss ideas for how Grace might contribute to the programme's introduction.

"You know the terrain," says Tony.

"I do indeed," she replies.

"So set the scene for us."

"Do you want me to use this?" she asks, brandishing the brief.

"Only as a last resort," says Tony with a grimace. "All very worthy, no doubt, but deadly dull. It's too dry. What we want are…"

"Stories," interrupts Grace. "Human stories."

"Exactly. What it was like to work here," he continues, waving towards the car park, "when it was still a mill."

"And what it was like to live in its shadow."

The two of them finish their coffee at exactly the same moment with a satisfied smile.

"I'm going to enjoy this shoot," says Tony.

"Likewise," agrees Grace. "Though I still prefer to call it a dig."

"Is that you telling me off?" laughs Tony.

"Only very slightly," says Grace, her eyes twinkling.

Samira, who has been hovering just out of earshot for the past few seconds, now steps forward. "They're ready for you now, Tony. Dr Chadwick."

She takes their empty coffee cups and watches the two of them walk back across the street to start filming, imagining a future.

"This unprepossessing car park," she hears Tony begin, in his opening piece to camera, "was once the site of the world's first ever steam-powered cotton mill, making Manchester the world's first industrial city. At its height four thousand spindles were in operation here. I'm joined by the esteemed Industrial Archaeologist, Dr Grace Chadwick, who's lived and worked in Manchester all her life. Can you imagine the noise of those four thousand spindles all turning at once?"

"*I* can't, no. But Samuel Bamford, the Manchester Radical, could, for he worked in a mill just like this one, and he likened it to the sound to thunder, the voice of God."

"Wow. It's no wonder so many of the cotton workers learned to lip-read."

"They had to. But even so, many of them still went deaf as a result of the long hours they put in here."

"No protective ear-phones back then."

"No, Tony. And it was even louder here in 1940, when the *Luftwaffe* rained down its bombs on Manchester during the Christmas Blitz. Arkwright's Mill was razed to the ground, and the land lay empty for the next forty years. Until this 'unprepossessing car park', as you so rightly called it, was built, and which is shortly to be knocked down and rebuilt."

"Which is why we're here today. To see what relics we might find, and what they might tell us about what life here at Arkwright's Mill was really like. Let's go and take a look."

The camera operator is happy with the take, as is the sound guy. Tony escorts Grace into the actual site.

"Of course," says Grace, "I know what you're really looking for."

"Oh?"

"It's what every dig hopes to find. Bones."

Tony's face breaks into a wide grin.

"Your reputation precedes you, Grace" he says, stepping aside to let her go on ahead of him. "After you."

*

1996

Manchester EveningNews

17th June 1996

CARNAGE IN CITY CENTRE

It is a day Manchester will never forget.

Two days ago, on Saturday 15th June 1996, the IRA singled out our city to be victim of the biggest bomb it has ever exploded on the British mainland, injuring hundreds and leaving no building within half a mile of the blast unscathed.

The day started in blazing midsummer sunshine. Just another sunny Saturday in Manchester. Or so we thought.

Two hundred miles south in London, anti-terror police were on high alert amid fears the IRA might target the Queen's *Trooping the Colour* parade. Just a few months earlier the Provisionals had ended a 17-month ceasefire by blowing up a lorry in Canary Wharf, killing two people.

But in Manchester things were more relaxed.

Nevertheless police were primed for trouble – as thousands of football fans prepared to pour into town to watch that afternoon's Euro 96 match between England and Scotland on giant screens set up in the city centre. TV crews from across Europe were in town to cover the next day's Russia v Germany game at Old Trafford. Thousands of shoppers were preparing to hit the streets too, many of them on the look-out for Father's Day gifts.

Unknown and unnoticed a white van had already begun its devastating journey.

Just before 9.20am, the streets were already filling up with crowds when two men in hooded anoraks and sunglasses left a heavily-loaded Ford Cargo van outside Marks & Spencer on the corner of Cannon Street and Corporation Street. It was parked on double yellow lines with its hazard lights flashing.

It contained 3,300lbs of homemade explosive, three times the size of the Canary Wharf bomb.

They walked away, ringing an IRA chief in Ireland to let them know the job was done. The pair escaped in a burgundy Ford Granada, later abandoned in Preston. Three minutes after the van was abandoned, a traffic warden slapped a ticket on it.

Some time after 9.38am a man with an Irish accent telephoned Granada TV, Sky News, Salford University, North Manchester General Hospital and the Garda Police in Dublin to warn that a bomb would go off in Manchester City Centre in one hour's time. He gave the location and used a code word known only to Special Branch.

On their CCTV camera in Bootle Street Police Station, officers watched in horror as footage was relayed showing people pushing up against and sliding along the side of the van, awkwardly parked on one of the city's busiest shopping streets. These officers then began one of the most extraordinary policing operations the country has ever seen: the evacuation of 80,000 people.

It was a Herculean task, aided by the luck of having extra police on duty for the football match. Gradually, grudgingly, people began to move, turning into a flood as word spread that the scare was real. The police cordon extended further and further out as far as a quarter of a mile, until there were no more officers to take it any further.

By 11.10am, the heart of Manchester city centre was deserted. The army bomb disposal squad – which had hurtled to Manchester down the M62 from Liverpool – was preparing to detonate the device from 200 yards away, just off Cross Street near Sam's Chophouse. Inspector Dave Comerford, link man between the police and the army, told colleagues over the radio that there would be two blasts – a smaller one as a remote controlled robot blew a hole in the side of the van, followed by the second, which would disable it.

At 11.16am, the first blast went off. At 11.17am, they ran out of time.

When the bomb exploded, the blast could be heard from 15 miles away. It issued a force so powerful it travelled around 90 degree corners, knocking people to the ground and blowing out virtually every window within half a mile, leaving a 15 metre crater around it. Glass rained from the sky, a fine dust followed by shards and eventually a torrent of rubble and debris. From his vantage point on Cross Street, Chief Inspector Ian Seabridge told us that "a sudden air of stillness descended on the city".

Then every alarm in Manchester started wailing.

In Bootle Street Police Station, the screens showing CCTV pictures of the army operation went black. At Belle Vue Ambulance Control they heard the boom and the telephone switchboard lit up. Within five minutes there were 60 calls from every street in the vicinity. 30 fire engines raced to the scene from across the region. 999 crews toured the city centre to pick up victims. At Manchester Royal Infirmary they were treating more than 100 casualties within minutes.

For hours afterwards dazed, confused people staggered out of the city centre to find transport. People as far away as Kendal Milne Department Store had been injured as the windows blew out, having wrongly believed they would be safe under the store's canopy.

Manchester's city centre now lies in ruins. Mannequins, initially mistaken for dead bodies, hang eerily from broken shop windows. Historic landmarks such as Manchester Cathedral, Chetham's School of Music, the Corn Exchange and the Royal Exchange Theatre are all severely damaged.

More than 200 people have been injured in the blast. Many are still bravely recovering in hospital. Yet one fact stands out – a testament to the heroic actions of the police in evacuating the city centre so rapidly. Not a single person was killed.

*

But behind the grim statistics lie the individual human stories. As she was to say nine years later to Tony Robinson, standing outside the NCP Car Park, it has always been the stories that have interested Grace the most.

As the police tried frantically to clear the city centre before the bomb went off, not everyone was keen to leave. Mancunians had become used to such scares and they felt they had better things to be getting on with.

One hairdresser refused to let her clients leave because they still had chemicals in their hair, arguing it would be "too dangerous".

A group of workmen wanted to stay put because they were on weekend rates.

PC Wendy McCormick found herself telling people in the Arndale, "I don't want to die because somebody won't finish their pizza."

But most people heeded the warning, and within minutes the whole of Manchester's city centre resembled a kind of orderly stampede.

A pair of women working in the Arndale, on their way out for a walk, were only saved because they nipped back inside to get their bags. Two minutes before the blast, they were standing on the bridge directly above it.

Most famously of all, Franklin Swanson and Amanda Hudson were part way through their wedding ceremony at the Manchester Registry Office, when they were ordered to evacuate. They had just declared, "We do," then had to flee without collecting their marriage certificate. They were caught on camera as they made their escape.

It's a photograph Grace has always kept a copy of, as a reminder, of when her life and work conjoined, when the past and present fused, for she too was one of the many individual stories to emerge from the smoke and ruin of that terrible day...

Grace has just retired. She has clung on for three years longer than she was meant to – all local authority employees are supposed to leave at sixty – but she has always been famous for her stubbornness, and she argued – successfully – that she was still more than capable of carrying out her duties. Then, when Greater Manchester Council decided to reorganise, Grace persuaded them to let her stay on till the new structure was in place. In the end that took three years, during which Grace was able to identify a potential successor – Robina McNeil – who had been acting as Grace's assistant during the changeover and was more than capable of stepping into Grace's not inconsiderable shoes.

Yesterday had been her last day. She had not wanted any kind of fuss. "For God's sake, don't give me a clock," she had railed.

In the event the Leader of the Council had presented her with a photograph album, filled with pictures of all the major digs she had been on, interspersed with newspaper cuttings detailing many of her most significant discoveries, beginning with that skeleton *Settanti* warrior unearthed at Castlefied more than forty years before. Grace, who was rarely, if ever, lost for words, for once was too moved to speak. She thanked everyone as quickly as she could, and, before the emotion of the moment might get the better of her, she told a few jokes about old dogs and new tricks.

But this morning Robina has asked to meet her for coffee.

"My treat," she says. "Just to say thank you."

"There's no need."

"I want to."

"All right. Where?"

"You choose."

"*Gander's*," she says decisively. "Do you know it?"

Robina smiles. Grace has never been one to equivocate. She's really going to miss her. "No," she says.

"I'm not surprised. It's tucked away in the Barton Arcade, just off St Ann's Square. They do excellent coffee. Also great Cajun food if you ever fancy eating there. And in the evenings they play live New Orleans jazz. It's wonderful."

Robina laughs out loud.

"What is it?" asks Grace.

"You," says Robina. "You're always full of surprises."

"I was quite the frequenter of jazz clubs in my youth, I'll have you know. Basement cafes, beatnik poets, that sort of thing. One likes to keep up."

"What time?"

"It's your treat, Robina. I'm in your hands."

"Ten thirty?"

"Ten thirty it is."

Now, at twenty-five past, Robina is sitting at one of the tables outside *Gander's*, beneath the fenestrated roof of the Barton Arcade, enjoying the way the sun is refracting through the glass atrium, making rainbow patterns, which dance upon the mosaic-tiled floor.

Grace arrives on the dot of half-past, breezily cycling right up to the table where Robina is sitting. The staff all seem to know her, greeting her by name. One of the waitresses takes her bicycle from her.

"Thank you, Josette," says Grace. "Now," she continues to Robina, "I recommend the Café Brûlot. Two please, Josette."

"Coming right up, Miss Grace."

The two friends spend an enjoyable half an hour telling stories and reminiscing. They order a second Café Brûlot, this time accompanied with beignets, a Creole version of French doughnuts, lightly dusted with sugar.

It is just as these pastries arrive that the order comes to evacuate.

At first, like everyone else, they don't believe it. They think it's just another hoax. There have been several in the twelve years since the IRA bombing of The Grand Hotel in Brighton, but none have amounted to anything. This time feels different. Already there are hundreds of people streaming past the Arcade, through St Ann's Square, away from the Arndale. There are police officers with loud hailers, urging people to leave the city centre immediately.

"Run," says Grace to Robina. "Don't wait for me. I'll phone you later, when we know what's been happening."

"But…" Robina is looking anxiously towards Grace's callipered leg.

"Go!" commands Grace.

At the same time, Josette is panicking. "Your bicycle, Miss Grace," she is shouting. "It's in the back. I can't get to it."

"Don't worry about it. Just do as the police tell you."

"Yes, Miss. Sorry, Miss."

Grace hobbles out into St Ann's Square and is almost immediately knocked down in the rush. Two young men help her to her feet, but then hurry on. She looks up at the clock in the tower of St Ann's Church on the opposite side of the

Square. It is just a quarter past eleven. She thinks she hears the bells toll the quarter but she can't be sure. The noise of the frightened, fleeing crowd is too great.

It is while she is making her way awkwardly towards the Church, weaving like a shuttle thrown across a loom when the ends have all been broken, that the bomb explodes.

Afterwards she remembers very little. The force of the blast lifting her off her feet and flinging her through the air. As if she had been catapulted from a trebuchet. A ringing in her ears so loud that she can hear nothing else. It's like being under water, everything muffled and far away. Then a violent whooshing as the sound roars back. Screams and cries. Fire alarms and sirens. The earth cracking as it tips and buckles beneath her. The incessant tinkling of glass shattering, cascading all around her, like a sharp summer shower. Her face, hands and arms a crimson pin cushion, speckled with blood where her skin has been punctured.

And a voice.

A desperate, lone voice, louder than everything else, piercing through the clamour like a needle in the ear.

A mother's voice, screaming for her child.

"Molly! Molly! Molly!"

Trying to pinpoint its direction, Grace scans the Square. But everything is a blur.

The voice comes again.

"Molly! Molly! Molly!"

This time Grace hears a second voice. Very close and very quiet.

"Mamma… Mamma…"

Grace looks down.

Clinging tightly to her legs, which are folded awkwardly beneath her, is a small child. A girl. A toddler. Except that she is too traumatised to even attempt to get to her feet. Instead, she grasps Grace's legs even harder, refusing to let go.

Grace now sees the mother, not ten yards away from her, frenziedly wheeling round, her arms like helicopter blades, slicing the air wildly just seconds before a crash.

"Over here!" shouts Grace. "This way!"

The woman freezes, her eyes trying to focus in on the source of the voice. Grace frantically waves, calling repeatedly. "Here! Over here!"

Finally the woman sees her. Then she sees her daughter. She hurtles towards them, heedless of the hailstorm all around.

Grace looks away while the tearful reunion takes place just inches away from her. Her presence feels like an intrusion, and she wishes she could leave them. But her right leg, her so-called 'good' leg is throbbing. Now that the aftershock of the explosion is beginning to fade, and people are starting to pick themselves up from the ground, examining themselves and the strangers they've been lying beside for injuries, Grace is becoming aware of the pain. She is sure she must have broken it.

The woman checks her daughter minutely for any cuts, but she appears to have survived the outrage miraculously unscathed, physically at least. She is unnaturally quiet. But then she spots the blood oozing from the top of her mother's head and immediately starts to cry.

That's better, thinks Grace. More normal. She points towards the cut. The mother raises her hand tentatively towards it and dabs gingerly, then looks at her fingers.

"I don't think it's serious," croaks Grace. She finds that her voice has lost its usual timbre. "Best to get it checked, though. There are bound to be ambulances here soon."

And there are. Though they are prevented from getting as close as they need because of the fallen masonry strewn across the streets by the blast. Their sirens wail like lost seagulls.

Eventually the paramedics pick their way through on foot, treating the casualties as they come across them, bandaging wounds, checking for concussion, organising relays of stretchers where necessary. The mother's head wound is cleaned and dressed. The daughter is looked at closely and declared to be fine. A blanket is draped around Grace's shoulders. The broken leg is confirmed and temporarily splinted.

"We really need to get you to a hospital," says a female paramedic, who, to Grace's eyes, looks frighteningly young, her face is pale with shock, her hair flecked with cement dust. "I'll try and get a wheelchair to you as quickly as I can," she says. "Then we can steer you between the rubble to the nearest ambulance."

Grace thanks her. "Make sure you look after yourself too," she says. The paramedic smiles thinly and hurries away. Grace turns to the mother. "You should go," she says to her. "I'll be all right."

"No way," says the woman. "If it hadn't been for you, I might never have found Molly. I'm staying right here till that chair arrives. I'm Jenna by the way."

"Grace. How old is Molly?"

"That's just it. Today's her birthday. She's just turned two. I promised to bring her into town to see the Bubble Man."

Grace knits her eyebrows together, not understanding.

"He has a giant wand and he blows these enormous bubbles. Molly loves them. Don't you, poppet? They're so big, some of them, you feel you could step right inside them. The water makes all these coloured rainbows…" She can't continue. It is as if all the strain and tension of the last hour has finally caught up with her. Her face crumples. "He wasn't even there," she says bitterly.

People are starting to leave the Square. By now they're beginning to learn something of what has happened.

"Bloody IRA," says a man passing close to Jenna.

"You don't know that," she hisses back at him.

He thinks about challenging her, but then decides against it. He shakes his head angrily, then hurries on.

"It bears all the hallmarks," says Grace very gently, fearing she may be entering tricky waters. There's something about this young woman that appears unstable.

"It's the IRA right enough," says the young paramedic returning with the wheelchair. "They telephoned the police and the BBC with a warning. Only they left the call till it was too late, didn't they? It's a bloody miracle there aren't hundreds dead."

Jenna falls silent. Her face darkens.

"Can I come with Grace to the hospital?" she asks.

"Sorry," says the paramedic. "There won't be room."

"I'll walk with you as far as the ambulance then."

She holds the chair steady, while the paramedic gently manoeuvres Grace into it They pick their way through the rubble. The city centre is unrecognisable. The devastation is appalling. Not a single building has been left untouched. The Arndale Centre, once the largest indoor shopping mall in Europe, is almost completely laid waste. Grace is reminded of her days in school, bent over a Latin primer, when she would much rather have been outdoors.

Barbari civitatem vastavant.

The Barbarians have laid waste the city.

Jenna is shaking.

"I'm a terrible mother," she says. "I nearly got my daughter killed."

"It was a random attack," says Grace.

But Jenna is not listening.

"You reap what you sow," she says. "I've been on marches, taken part in protests, helped organise rallies. I was even caught up in the Moss Side Riots. I've signed petitions, written letters to Parliament, campaigned to end direct rule in Northern Ireland. If I see an injustice, I have to call it out."

"It's good to be passionate," says Grace carefully, "to believe that what you're doing is right." This woman is teetering on the edge.

"I just want the world to be a better, fairer place for Molly to grow up in."

"That's what all parents want," says Grace.

"But this," says Jenna, swinging an arm wildly at the chaos and destruction all around her. "I never imagined that what I was doing would lead to anything like this." She is becoming hysterical.

"You need to calm down, Miss," says the young paramedic. "You don't want to upset your little girl now, do you?"

"No," replies Jenna, shaking her head from side to side.

"It's not as though you planted the bomb yourself, is it?"

"No, of course not," shouts Jenna.

"That's enough," says Grace, realising the need to step in firmly. "We all of us want to change things, but actions have consequences."

"I know," cries Jenna vehemently. "That's exactly what I'm saying."

By now they have reached the ambulance. Grace is lifted inside.

"I'm sorry," says Jenna. "Sometimes it's like I see a red mist."

"It's been a terrible day," says Grace. "Nothing can prepare us for something like this. Try not to be so hard on yourself. Rejoice in your daughter."

"Yes," says Jenna. "You're right. Thank you."

The doors to the ambulance close. Jenna watches it drive away from her. She looks about her. She has reached Piccadilly Gardens. She hardly knows where she is. The city looks so altered.

She feels a tug at her sleeve. She looks down. Molly is pointing. Jenna follows the direction of her outstretched arm.

It's the Bubble Man. He's there after all. He's dipping his wand into a bucket of soapy water. He is catching rainbows. He scoops them up into the ring at the end of the wand and blows a bubble large enough to encircle Molly completely, a globe so enticingly perfect but fragile, that Jenna is afraid to get too close to it, in case she should burst it.

She hoists Molly on to her hip.

"Shall we go and see Grandma and Granddad?" she says.

Molly's face beams with delight.

"Let's go and see when the next bus to Eccles leaves then."

She carries her daughter towards the Bus Station on the far side of the Gardens. Together they walk through a chimera of bubbles. Jenna's mind is made up. She will ask her mother and father, Nadia and Sol, if they will look after Molly instead of her.

"I'm not up to it," she mutters miserably under her breath. "I can't do this any more. Not on my own."

The bubbles bump against each other, until they become one, shepherding Jenna along the path she must take. The closer she looks, the more she comes to understand that it is she, Jenna, who is the chimera. Body of a woman, tail of a serpent, head of a dragon, breathing fire. A monster, conjured up to frighten children.

In the back of the ambulance Grace knows that she will probably never see Jenna or Molly again. In a city of more than a million, what are the chances? That they were, against all the odds, thrown together today is somehow miraculous. But that is the nature of city life. Every day she rubs up against complete strangers. Their paths cross, coincide, converge and then separate. In spite of the cataclysmic events of this day, she finds such random collisions generally more reassuring than disconcerting. We are all of us, she believes, individual atoms, single neutral particles, waiting to collide with another, to form a molecule, and then for these molecules themselves to combine to produce something more complex, until a whole chain reaction is set in motion, all of us bound to the body politic.

Looking out of the ambulance window on her way to the hospital, she surveys the devastation visited upon Manchester. This is the city she loves. Where she was born and where she will almost certainly die. But not today. It is the only home she has ever known, or wants to know. Forged from the fusion of the four elements, of which everything is constituted. The earth, which shook beneath her feet a couple of hours ago, the air, which choked the back of her throat, the water, which has turned rank and foul in the rivers, the fire, which burns in the streets.

But the earth will grow green again. The air will be sweet. The water will run clean once more at the confluence of the three rivers. And out of the fire the city will rise, replenished and reborn, stronger than it was before, ready to face whatever the future holds for her. Of this she is certain.

*

1852

Manchester Guardian

17th June 1852

FIRE DESTROYS ARKWRIGHT'S MILL

The fire broke out, about half-past nine, on Tuesday morning, at one of the smaller mills in Miller Street, occupied by Mr. J. A. Beaver, cotton spinner, close by Arkwright's original mill, the first to be built in Manchester, to which the flames rapidly spread. Both mills, which are very extensive, were in Mr. Beaver's occupation, though owned by Mr Richard Simpson, a partner of Sir Richard Arkwright's son.

The fire, which originated in the blowing-room, is thought to have been caused by the friction of the machinery. The hands were at work at the time, but mercifully most escaped without injury. From Information being conveyed to the police, Mr. Rose, with the Niagara Engine, and a party of firemen, was on the spot within ten minutes. At that time, the westerly end of the old mill was a complete prey to the flames, which, originating on the ground floor, had made their way through all the upper floors to the roof, a portion of which had actually fallen in before Mr. Rose's arrival, and the flames were rapidly spreading on every floor towards the upper or eastern end of the building. Nothing was left but to attempt to arrest their progress midway, and thereby save that portion which had not yet been reached by the fire.

To everybody but Mr. Rose himself, this seemed an utter impossibility; for the rooms were open from end to end, without any division-wall, or other means of cutting off the progress of the flames, other than by the exertions of the firemen. The result, however, showed what may be effected by judicious plans, courageously and skilfully worked out. Three other engines, the Water Witch, Neptune, and Thetis, having arrived, with their complement of firemen, branches were immediately introduced through windows in each of the five storeys at the same point, so that the water from the uppermost storeys, pouring down, aided the efforts made in the lower ones in the same line, and thus a very powerful and concentrated action was maintained.

The Niagara Engine was stationed in Miller Street, where also a branch and hose were attached direct to a fire-plug. The other three engines were stationed in the yard, on the north side of the premises, where a plentiful supply of water was obtained from one of the large reservoirs close by. Six pipes were laid – two from the Water Witch, two from the Neptune, and one each from the Niagara and the fireplug in Miller Street – and, in this way, the progress of the flames was completely intercepted by half-past eleven o'clock. By twelve, the firemen had subdued the flames at the westerly end of the building, which had continued to rage with great fury, a great quantity of cotton, to the value of between £300 and £400, which had been deposited in one of the cellars at this end of the building, having ignited, and contributed to the conflagration.

Notwithstanding the great attention necessary to preserve the easterly end of the building, the engine-house, and boiler-house, which, together with the large warping-room, adjoined the westerly or lower end of the mill, these were not neglected. The flames penetrated from below through the roof of the engine-house, but were eventually extinguished. Every practical effort was made to save the cotton in the cellars, but with little success, the flames having spread so much before the arrival of the engines.

The exertions of the firemen were most praiseworthy. It was astonishing how the progress of the flames was stayed, for the windows in the whole of the building were black with smoke and heat, and in many cases the glass was shattered. The fire encroached most in the upper storeys. But little of the roof now remains. Of the fifth storey, the length of six windows on one side has been preserved, along with all the machinery, which however is old and not of much value. In the next lower storey there remains a length of flooring of nine windows, beyond which there is a chasm open to the sky and to the ground. Indeed, the preservation of this portion of the premises seems most remarkable. The engines remained playing on the embers for some hours afterwards.

Three cheers for Mr Rose and the plucky fighters of the Manchester Municipal Fire Brigade, the first such service anywhere in Great Britain. *The Manchester Guardian* gives heartfelt thanks to the Town's Fathers for their rare insight in this matter, an insight not shared by

Mr Simpson, the owner of the historic mill, which, we understand, was not insured. No compensation will be forthcoming, therefore, to the thousands of industrious Mancastrians, who, as a result of such carelessness, have lost both their employment and their livelihood.

*

Superintendent William Rose scanned the scene unfolding before him with the practised eye of someone who had attended more than a hundred such fires in his dozen years of service. The trouble was, as he well knew, that in their scramble for building the mills to meet the seemingly insatiable demand world-wide for Manchester cotton – where less than half a century before there had been but one, now their number exceeded a hundred and thirty – the owners had paid scant regard to health and safety, and had crammed their chimneys and factories too closely together, so that now they marched cheek by jowl like ill-regulated soldiers. If one should fall, it would like as not tumble directly into the path of another, causing a veritable stampede of falling, burning masonry. As was the case now. At the heart of the conflagration lay that very first progenitor of all the mills, Arkwright's of Shude Hill, which was all but razed to the ground already, in spite of his brigade's best efforts. What concerned him more was the mill's – and therefore the fire's – immediate proximity to a number of courtyard dwellings, hunkered in the mill's shadow beside the foul and stagnant River Irk, which, in its current foetid state, offered his officers hardly any running water with which to curb the seemingly unstoppable spread of the blaze, now being fanned even further by a rising wind.

He looked about him wildly through the choking smoke and saw that a capable-looking woman had already begun to marshal local people into a chain of buckets, pans and kettles in a long line stretching from the parsimonious Irk to the nearby rows of houses.

"Who's that?" he demanded of a scurrying passer-by, pointing towards the capable woman.

"Miss Stone," coughed the passer-by. "Teacher at Sharp Street Ragged School."

Excellent, thought William. Teachers, in his experience, were eminently sensible and knew better than anyone how to establish order out of chaos. She had, he could now see, involved all of her charges as part of the water chain, so that, by being so busily occupied, they did not become frightened and start to panic, thereby hampering his brigade's efforts.

He quickly gave orders to one of his deputies to employ the Grand Fire Elevator – a mechanical ladder of his own devising – to carry out the rescue of the dozens of men and women still currently trapped on the upper floors of the mill before it collapsed to the ground beneath them, while at the same time sending another to instruct Miss Stone to re-direct her energies away from the sluggish, unforthcoming Irk to the more free-flowing marl-pits in the Daub Holes higher up the hill above the Meadow. He observed with satisfaction her nod to his deputy that she understood the logic of this fresh direction, wipe her soot-streaked forehead determinedly with the back of her hand, before re-forming the line as instructed. Immediately William dispatched half a dozen hand-drawn Tilley pumps to assist with the operation.

An hour later the flames are under control. The mill has been evacuated, most of the adjoining dwellings saved, and Miss Stone is now ensuring that her various charges are being safely reunited with sobbing, relieved and grateful parents or harassed older siblings before permitting them to leave her side, where they have gathered, like fledgling chicks in a nest. Superintendent Rose is just on the point of personally thanking her for her calm, authoritative clear-headedness, when he is interrupted by a frantic, screaming mother.

"Evelyn!" she is crying. "Has anyone seen Evelyn?"

The query ripples through the crowd more quickly than any flame as they all begin at once to search and scrabble in every corner and under every heap of fallen brick.

"What does she look like?" demands William.

"She's just a baby," answers Laurel, looking suddenly pale. "Barely two months old. If she's still alive, she'll be crying somewhere. What we need is for people to stop panicking and be quiet."

This teacher impresses me more and more, thinks William, and immediately commands the crowd to silence.

An agonising few minutes pass as everyone strains to catch the sound of a baby crying somewhere. In the absence of noise from the people all huddled together beside the still-smouldering building, there are still other sounds to try and filter out. Wooden beams cracking in the heat. Crows alighting on rubble and cawing into the wind. Water dribbling from the hoses.

Then, so faint that at first those who hear it think they might be dreaming it, it comes, the plaintive mewing of the lost child.

Everyone instinctively tenses and huddles together, almost as if they are a single, unified beast, which, if it draws itself as closely as it can, might more clearly identify the source of the cry.

"Shh!"

"Wait!"

"Listen!"

"There it is again!"

"Where?"

"There!"

As one, the beast points towards a nearby heap of bricks, piled so precariously that none dare venture upon it, for fear of disturbing its fragile balance and thereby risk crushing the infant.

"What are we to do?" they murmur.

"Evelyn!" cries the child's mother, rushing wildly towards where the baby's cry now grows stronger and more fretful.

At once William places himself in the path of the desperate mother to prevent her from wreaking even more harm.

"You!" demands Laurel, pointing to one of the small boys closest to the bricks.

"Yes, Miss?" says the boy.

"Think you can squeeze through without damaging a single brick?"

The boy, whose shoulders are so bony they might pass unimpeded between the narrowest of railings, quickly and quietly assesses the situation. He looks at the pile of bricks. Then he looks down upon his skeletal frame.

"Yes," he says. "I reckon I can."

"Then off you go," says Laurel. "And don't be tempted to hurry. Think of the tortoise, not of the hare."

"Yes, Miss." And off he goes.

For the next interminable few minutes, the crowd holds its breath, not daring to breathe, as the small boy agonisingly makes his slow, torturous way between the mountain of bricks, wriggling between each nook and crevice, until he disappears completely. The crowd gasps involuntarily as one, then holds its breath once more while they wait for him to return to the surface. The baby too has stopped crying, as if she has somehow sensed that even that most delicate of movements from her bird-like chest might disturb the nest she lies in.

After what feels like hours, the boy emerges, covered from head to toe in brick dust, tentatively holding the baby girl in his stick-like arms. The cheers that greet him threaten to bring the last remaining roof beam of Arkwright's Mill crashing to the ground, but disaster is averted. The baby Evelyn is reunited with her now hysterical mother, each outdoing the other in contesting the loudness of their lungs, while the bony boy brushes himself down and blows out his cheeks, showering all those who are near him with brick dust. Superintendent Rose shakes him by the hand, and Laurel quietly asks him his name.

"Frank, Miss. Frank Wright."

"Well," says Laurel, "that was a very brave thing to do."

"Thank you, Miss."

"How is it that I don't know you? You don't come to Sharp Street School, do you, Frank?"

"No, Miss. I go to Eggington Street Methodists."

"I see. And why aren't you there today?"

Frank looks down, shamefaced.

"Well?"

"Well, Miss, I wanted to see the Fire Bobbies..."

Laurel laughs. "Thank goodness you did, Frank. You saved the day."

"What's the baby's name again, Miss?"

"Evelyn."

"Eve-lyn..." Frank runs the name over his tongue and lips, savouring its sound. "It's a lovely name."

"Yes, it is. Do you know what it means?"

"No, Miss."

"It's French. A tiny bird. The wished-for child."

Frank's eyes widen in wonder. He looks back in the direction of where the mother holds and rocks this wished-for child, who is quiet now and sleeping, almost as if nothing at all has happened.

But it had. And Frank would never forget it.

*

"That boy's got the makings of a fine young man," says Laurel, watching Frank rejoin his friends, who clap him on the back, the hero of the hour.

" 'Appen," says Superintendent Rose, " 'appen not."

Laurel eyes him sharply. "What do you mean, William?"

"It depends on the company he keeps."

Laurel looks back to where Frank is surrounded by a knot of dark-haired boys.

"I don't follow," she says.

"They're Greeks," says William.

"So?"

"They've been arriving in ever larger numbers these last twenty years."

"I know. Mostly they are from Chios. They've been fleeing persecution from their oppressors. There's a terrible civil war raging on the island. Is it any wonder they should try to escape it? Wouldn't you want to do the same if you found yourself in such straits?"

"Ay. P'raps I might. But as an officer of the Law, I've 'ad occasion to break up too many quarrels between 'em since they arrived. It seems like they've brought their civil war over 'ere wi' 'em."

Laurel falls silent. There is truth in what William is saying. There have been increasing numbers of incidents between rival Greek factions in the town, especially in the Strangeways area, where mostly they have settled. Laurel considers the situation further. There is an undoubted pattern. Each successive wave of new arrivals into Manchester from overseas tends to conform to it. At first, for understandable reasons of security and comfort, they will stay close to one another, taking solace in the company of friends, refuge in the continuation of customs from the lands they have left behind. Different enclaves have formed across the city – the Huguenots in Newton Heath, the Dutch in Spinningfields, the Jews in Shudehill, the Germans in Denton, the Italians in Ancoats, the Chinese in Alport, the Irish in Angel Meadow, and now the Greeks in Strangeways – but over time the boundaries between them have become blurred. Increasingly their populations mix, as people begin to consider themselves first and foremost as Mancunians. There will always be tensions, traces of tribalism, but in the end a striving for harmony and understanding will prevail, an instinct to belong. Laurel fervently believes this. There is far more that binds us than divides us. This is her creed, which she sees being reinforced daily all around her as Protestants and Catholics, Gentiles and Jews, Methodists and Moravians, Hindus and Muslims, all rub shoulders together in the city's crowded streets and squares. She hopes that it will not be long before the Greeks feel similarly settled, certain of their welcome.

The three dark-haired boys, who currently surround Frank, do not share this same long view with Laurel. Their concerns are more immediate. Christos, Stefanos and Vassily live from day to day. Not even that. Moment to moment. They've learned from their fathers to choose their friends wisely. Which is why Frank is prized so highly. He is their first non-Greek friend. None of the other children who attend the Greek school on Waterloo Road have made any such friends. As far as they know. They intend to keep it that way.

"That was brilliant," says Christos, meaning the fire.

"Did you see the way the Niagara raced to the rescue?" says Stefanos.

"I'd like to be a Fire Bobby," says Vassily.

"So would I," says Stefanos.

"Me too," says Christos. "What about you, Frank?" He hands his new friend a piece of gum.

But Frank is quiet. He pops the gum into his mouth and chews carefully and deliberately. He's no longer thinking about the Fire Bobbies, even though smoke is still smouldering through what remains of Arkwright's Mill. His thoughts are all turned to the baby girl he rescued from the rubble. Evelyn. Such a pretty name. Her sweet face and kind demeanour, seemingly untroubled by her ordeal, as she lay there so trustingly in his arms, has stayed with him. Something has shifted inside him. Frank, who is not yet twelve years old, suddenly feels he is becoming a man. The gum begins to release its intoxicating flavour of mint and pine, which makes Frank think of far horizons.

"What shall we do next?" asks Stefanos, jigging from foot to foot.

"Let's go down to the Canal," suggests Christos.

"Or jump aboard a train," offers Vassily. "Frank?"

Frank shakes his head.

"Sorry, lads. I've got to work. My Dad'll have errands for me to run, deliveries to make."

The other boys nod, understanding. Frank's clever. Frank's Dad has a trade. He's a printer. He operates a press from an outhouse at the back of where he lives. Frank knows how to work it already. His brother, Gordon, taught him. The two of them will inherit the business when their Dad retires. Then they will expand it till it covers the whole of Manchester. The boys know this because Frank has told them.

"I've got plans," he says. "Just you watch."

They intend to, Vassily especially. Even though they don't quite know what he means.

They part and go their separate ways, Frank to Cheetham Hill, Christos, Stephanos and Vassily back to Strangeways.

The Greek boys don't expect they will ever have a trade. Their fathers are all labourers. They endure long hours in the Mastic Factory close to the River Irwell Railway Bridge, manufacturing glue, bone-grinding, mind-deadening work, which saps the soul.

"This is a bitter pill to swallow," Vassily hears his mother lament to his father at the end of each day, when he returns home at night, his clothes, his hair, his skin, his breath, all reeking of fish oil and animal fat.

"Yes," says his father, scrubbing himself as clean as he can with a cut of blood-red soap. "But it's the price we must pay for freedom."

It was not always so…

*

1822

Thirty years earlier.

Chios is the fifth largest of the Greek islands. It is also the wealthiest. This is due entirely to it being the only place on earth where the mastic tree grows naturally. So the legend has it.

The resin secreted from the glands of mature trees is collected in droplets, known as the 'tears of Chios'. It was Hippocrates, the Father of Medicine, who first coined that epithet. He prescribed it for colds, digestive problems and as a breath freshener. The Romans mixed it with honey, pepper and eggs to produce the spiced wine *konditon*. The Byzantines made the trade in mastic the Emperor's monopoly. By the time of the Ottomans it was worth its weight in gold. The penalty for anyone caught stealing it was execution by order of the Sultan, who harvested much of the island's entire crop for use as perfumes and essential oils for the concubines in his harem.

Lying in a favourable position in the north-east corner of the Aegean Sea, and separated from Turkey by a narrow strait of less then five miles, Chios found itself at the cross-roads of the world's trading routes. Its merchants grew rich, and so did its people.

But for all its wealth it has never been wholly independent. Homer was born there and knew well what it meant to be at the mercy of marauding invaders, the years that would be lost in exile or enslavement. First it was the Minoans, then the Persians. Then came the Peloponnesian Wars, when Chios was subjected to both Spartan and Athenian rule, the island changing hands several times. Then it was Alexander's turn to raid from Macedonia. After Alexander came the Romans, who garrisoned Chios and placed it in the province of Asia. St Paul visited it, but wrote no Epistles there. When Rome was divided, Chios was gifted to the Byzantines, who held it for seven hundred years, until the sacking of Constantinople during the 4th Crusade, after which it fell into the hands of Venice. Following a brief second interregnum by the Byzantines, it was ceded to Genoa, who largely ignored it, so that it was subject to regular raids by pirates, each of whom would hold sway for a short period between skirmishes. Briefly Philip of France installed himself as His Lordship of Chios, before being usurped by Pope Benedict VII, until the Genoese seized back control after a year-long siege of the island's castle. They then stayed in power for the next two centuries, until, in 1566, Admiral Piali Pasha captured it for the Ottomans.

There then followed a period of stability and prosperity. In return for exclusive rights to the island's mastic harvest, the people were granted a good deal of autonomy and, for the most part, left alone. For two hundred years, although not free, they thrived.

Vassily's father, Konstantin, was born into a life that had changed little in that time. His days were dictated by the rhythms of the mastic, as his father's had been, and his father's before that, going back through seven generations. The sun rose, the sun set. The mastic trees grew. The tears of Chios fell...

Konstantin is twelve years old when he is first inducted into the secret arts of planting and, pruning, cleansing and purifying, and finally of embroidering and stinging. When he was younger, he had helped with the harvesting, collecting and packing, while a scattering of egrets circled overhead, but it is only when he reaches the same age as the trees themselves, when they attain that perfect ripeness, that he is deemed ready to learn these finer, more arcane rites of passage. His father will be the priest of these rites, and he, Konstantin, the novitiate.

The mastic is a hardy tree. It grows in rocky soil in the valleys and mountain slopes on the south of the island, the *mastichochoria*, dedicated to its cultivation and protection. Cuttings are taken from mature male trees, the *karposkina*, and planted in February and March to a depth of one and a half inches. These will need regular watering for two to three years, when they are ready to enter their next stage, the pruning, which must be repeated each year from then onwards, in order to protect the tree from the tinder fungus. Shaped like a horse's hoof, this can, if not prevented, drain the tree of its tears. But as the tree grows past three years, it will no longer require watering, for it is hardy and resistant to drought, and, if over-watered, it may attract the cottony scale coccid, a tiny, but voracious insect. The female of the species has disproportionately large mouth-parts, which can pierce even the most gnarled and twisted of branches in its quest for their saps and juices, for which she has an insatiable thirst. Keeping the young tree safe from threat and harm is not unlike raising a son, Konstantin's father tells him.

Before the tree is ready for harvest, there are some important preliminary tasks that must be performed first. The soil beneath the tree must be purified in order to make the collection easier. The surface of the soil must be prepared with a layer of white ash, derived from the grinding and sieving of bones. This will not in any way damage or diminish the purity of the mastic. Rather, it will ensure the sap does not lose its lustre or clarity, for then it will be untradeable, and years of work will have been wasted.

Now the mastic is ready for the harvest, which must begin, as custom dictates, on the 15th of July, for this is the Saint's Day of the Martyr Julitta, a young widow with a child, who was beheaded by the Emperor Diocletian for refusing to renounce her faith in the face of torture.

"We must sacrifice ourselves for the land, and for the children who shall inherit it," proclaims Konstantin's father, raising the knife high above his head, like an Old Testament prophet.

The embroidery can begin. Konstantin will guide his son's hand to make the first cut, like a circumcision. He must use the *makhaira*, a finely-grooved, razor-sharp stiletto, to score a series of narrow, vertical slits, not more than half an inch long and less than a quarter of an inch deep, into the crevices of the bark, where the knotted branches intertwine. The older the tree, the more cuts must be made. The embroidery is best carried out during the hours of morning, before the sun has reached its zenith, so that the incisions can harden in the heat of the day.

"Now," says Konstantin's father to his son, "the sap needs two weeks to thicken and clot. The ejaculation will be slow but satisfying."

The egrets bask beneath, their beaks wide and waiting.

Konstantin learns that the embroidering must be done sparingly, so as not to weaken the tree, which will produce its finest tears between fifteen and twenty years of age.

The tears hang in *fliskaria*, attenuated clusters, which are then ready to be harvested with a scraper, a *timitiri*, and collected in tightly woven baskets called *malathouni*, which are stored somewhere cool and dry and shady.

Then comes the sifting, separating the leaves and the soil from the sap. Next comes the cleaning, with a hard olive oil soap, and last comes the stinging, in which any remaining trapped impurities are removed with a series of small, sharp knives. Finally it is ready for the grading. This is the job of the women, who chant their guttural throat songs while they sift and sort. There are three basic variants – the 'pie', the 'fat', and the 'fine'. The 'pie' for the gum, the 'fat' for the glue, the 'fine' for the perfumes and liqueurs.

"You've done well, my son," says Konstantin's father.

Konstantin tries to stand tall in his father's eyes. But at night he wonders which will be the fate that will await him once he has become a man? The pie, the fat, or the fine?

The sun rises, the sun sets.

Thus is Konstantin's life as an embroiderer prescribed, stitched to the rhythm of the flow of tears, hemmed by the kidney-shaped borders of Chios. As it was in the beginning, is now, and ever shall be. Chios is home and the world to Konstantin.

But then the wind changes direction. It blows in news of discontent from beyond the borders. The world's axis tilts. The egrets depart.

A ship flying a never-before-seen flag sails into the port of Çeşme, on the eastern edge of the island. The sailors call it the *kyanólefki*, the 'sky-blue-and-white', signifying the collision between sea and sky. It has nine equal horizontal stripes, alternating between the two colours. There is a blue canton in the upper hoist-side corner bearing a white cross. The cross symbolises the Orthodox Church, Konstantin is told, and the nine stripes correspond to the number of syllables in the slogan *'Eleftheria i Thanatos'*. 'Freedom or Death', which was chanted when the flag was first raised at a revolutionary assembly in Epidaurus, in the ruins of the amphitheatre where once the plays of Aeschylus and Sophocles had been performed, *The Oresteia, Oedipus at Colonus, Iphigenia in Tauris*, proclaiming Greek Independence, awakening the *Eumenides*, the Furies.

"What does it mean?" asks Konstantin.

"Trouble," answers his father.

And, like the Blind Seer, Tiresias, the ancient Prophet of Doom, his predictions are proved true.

It is 1822.

The fledgling Greek flag is hoisted in January. But hardly has it left the nest than it is plucked from the air by the swooping Ottoman falcon. But more and more baby birds take to the skies. The falcon cannot intercept them all. The cry of *'Eleftheria i Thanatos'* is heard from island to island, eventually reaching Samos, just seventy-five miles to the south. By March an expeditionary force of five hundred armed revolutionaries reaches Chios and lands there, fanning the flames of rebellion just as the preparations for harvesting the mastic are beginning.

But not everyone on Chios is convinced by the call to take up arms. The island has enjoyed peace and prosperity for centuries under a mostly benign Ottoman rule. She receives almost complete autonomy from the Sultan, so long as she continues to supply his harem with her finest tears. There are many who want to stay loyal. But there are more, mostly younger men, who are fired up with dreams of an independent Greece, Konstantin among them. The nine stripes of the sky-blue-and-white, they claim, represent not only the nine syllables of *'Eleftheria i Thanatos'*, but the nine Muses of old. Songs will be sung of their victory; the stars will foretell their fate in the firmament; history will record their names in the pantheon.

"You forget, my son," says Konstantin's father, "that among the nine muses are five different forms of poetry. Yes, there is the love, the pastoral, the epic and the sacred. But there is also the tragic. Which shall yours be?"

The island is divided, the argument is fierce. In the end it is the voices of rebellion that sing the loudest. Konstantin's father shakes his head sadly but bows to the inevitable. "We must follow our children," he declares. "What else can we do? The future is theirs."

The *kyanólefki* is flown from the castle walls in Chios Town.

The response from the Sultan is ruthless and swift.

Before the month is out, the Ottoman Fleet, under the brutal command of Kara-Ali Pasha, lands on Chios with forces numbering in excess of forty thousand troops. Orders are given to burn and pillage the island. The flames rage unchecked for weeks. The troops are dispatched to kill all infants under the age of three, all males over the age of twelve, and all females over the age of forty, with all the younger women and girls to be rounded up and raped.

When the fleet finally departs, the island is still ablaze. Out of a population of one hundred and twenty thousand, more than fifty thousand are dead. A further forty thousand, mostly women, are enslaved. But twenty thousand somehow manage to escape, to hide, then flee, scattering across Europe. One of these is Konstantin.

Those few that are left behind remain divided. When the War for Greek Independence is finally won, ten years later, Chios, still reeling from the massacre, chooses not to join this new rag-tag federation, but cling instead to a state of abandoned, hard-scrabble subsistence, a vassal of the Ottoman's crumbling empire, the ailing sick man of Europe. It will not become a part of Greece until the end of the 1ˢᵗ Balkan War in 1912, a full ninety years later. Throughout, the tears of Chios continue to fall in the wilderness.

Meanwhile the horrors of the massacre are roundly condemned. Delacroix depicts them in a searing painting that hangs in the Louvre. Lord Byron sells his estates in Hopwood Hall, twelve miles to the north of Manchester, to fund his Greek Brigade to fight alongside the rebels, while his great friend, Shelley, laments them in his poem, *Hellas*, with a hymn of hope for the future.

'The world's great age begins anew
The golden years return
The earth doth like a snake renew
Her winter weeds outworn…'

The sun rises. The sun sets.

For two years Konstantin wanders across Europe. He sheds his snake-skin many times. Each time it grows back, it does so more thinly stretched. It scrapes across his skull. There will be no returning home from this odyssey. No Penelope to wait for him, not even to weave his shroud. The tears of Chios are tears of blood.

He takes up with a small band of exiles. Fuelled by Byron's links with Manchester, they decide that that is where they will head for. Others have gone there before him. Strangeways. The name seems apt. For he is a stranger now everywhere, even to himself. Perhaps he might learn to find himself again there.

He boards a ship in Lisbon. It's a steam packet bound for Liverpool, part of the Red Star Line. It's called the *Hercules*. Konstantin takes this as an omen. He will work his passage through the storms of the Bay of Biscay. To add to the hero's twelve other labours.

During the crossing he comes to the aid of a young woman suffering with sea sickness.

"Keep your eyes trained on the horizon," he tells her. "It will give you a point of reference, allowing you to sense the motion of the ship, and your body's movement within it."

Her name is Thea. A gift from the Gods. She, too, is from Chios. She has a two-year-old child as a consequence of the rapes carried out under orders from Kara-Ali Pasha. She was shunned by some of the older ones who'd survived the massacre for deciding to keep the child, and so she too had left.

"It's not the child's fault," she says.

"No," says Konstantin, looking down at the infant, who opens her eyes and smiles trustingly up at him. "What is her name?"

"Amara. After my mother."

"Amara," repeats Konstantin quietly. "A bitter grace."

The three of them stare towards the horizon throughout the night, matching the movements of their bodies to each other. In the morning, Konstantin turns to Thea after she has finished feeding Vassily and says, "I will raise her as my own. If you will permit me, that is, and if it pleases you to do so."

Thea nods gravely.

"Yes," she says. "Thank you. That pleases me very much."

After they have disembarked at Liverpool, they walk to Manchester. It takes them three days. They follow the course of the Mersey & Irwell Navigation, walking the tow paths. Fiddler's Ferry, Sankey Brook. Howley Lock and Woolston Cut. Through the Lymm Loop and round the River Bollin. Past Sandywarp and Calamanco. Over the Barton Aqueduct, the locks at Sticklings, Mode Wheel and Throstle's Nest. Until they reach the Salford Wharf, Blackfriars Bridge and Strangeways. Their odyssey is at an end.

The streets are not exactly paved with gold, but there is work, a warm welcome, and a hope of home, their winter weeds outworn at last.

1852

Thirty years have passed since the Massacre on Chios. Thirty years since their arrival in Strangeways. The sun rises. The sun sets.

Amara is ten years a mother herself now. She has a son. But no husband.

"Do not worry," says Konstantin, the morning after the baby is born. "I shall look after him. Have you given him a name?"

She shakes her head.

"I thought I'd ask you," she says.

Konstantin regards the wriggling scrap that has been placed in his hands.

"Vassily," he pronounces. "A young prince."

Amara thanks the man who has been more than any father to her. She begins to cry noiselessly. Konstantin dries her eyes, then dabs his fingers gently on Vassily's brow.

"Let the tears of Chios flow once more."

The sun rises. The sun sets.

But Konstantin rarely witnesses either. He leaves the damp, one-roomed cellar they all share – Thea, Amara, Vassily and himself – before it comes up each day, returning long after it has sunk behind the Mastic Factory where he works. But he does not see it on a Sunday either, the one day of the week he does not work, for in truth the sun is rarely glimpsed down in the deepest recess of the dark courtyard where they must endure the days.

When they arrived in Strangeways, the Chian diaspora threw open their collective arms to embrace them.

"See they said," pointing to the soot-blackened factory chimney poking through the foul vapours rising from the foetid Irwell, "we even produce the mastic here too."

Konstantin frowns. He doesn't understand. How…?

"Don't worry," he is reassured, "the tree grows more widely than we thought. From its birthplace on Chios it has spread throughout the Mediterranean. From Syria to Spain. Malta to Morocco."

Konstantin shakes his head. The world shifts uneasily beneath his feet.

It does not take him long to realise that the same divisions he left behind on Chios, those who fought for independence and those who remained loyal to the Sultan, are to be found here in Strangeways too. Greece may have seceded from the Empire, but not so Chios. The old *status quo* from before the Massacre still holds sway here. Those with suspected allegiances to the *kyanólefki* are given the lowliest positions, the meanest tasks. Konstantin spends his years stirring the noxious mixture that makes up the glue the factory sells to the rest of the world. But Konstantin's world is even more circumscribed here than it had been on Chios.

The sun rises. The sun sets. Konstantin is bonded to the noose formed by the bend in the river. His days as an embroiderer are a forgotten shadow. No longer does he wield the *makhairi*, the razor-sharp stiletto, to carve the slits in the bark of the mastic tree, like a surgeon delicately incising with a scalpel. Nor the *timitri* to gently scrape away the hoof-shaped tinder fungus. Now he must wrestle with a rusting butcher's blade to hack away the horses' hooves for real, slicing away the rotting flesh to strip the bones from the carcass and boil them in enormous vats of lead, into which he has to climb at the end of each day's shift to scrub and scald away the collagen-coated scum.

These are not the attenuated clusters of dripping sap he remembers as a boy, but the bastard brood of gelatin and tallow. There is no calibrated gradient distinguishing the fine from the pie. There is only the fat here, the sweat and the grease. The tears of Chios are a bitter grace.

"A bitter pill to swallow," Vassily hears his mother lament to his father at the end of each day, when he returns home at night, his clothes, his hair, his skin, his breath, all reeking of fish oil and animal fat.

"Yes," says his father, scrubbing himself as clean as he can with a cut of blood-red soap. "But it's the price we must pay for freedom."

"*Eleftheria i Thanatos*," complains Thea wearily.

The ceaseless pounding of the machines in the factories shakes the walls of their cellar, threatening to bring it crashing down around their ears. In their relentless rhythm Konstantin hears an echo of his father's voice.

"We must sacrifice ourselves for the land, and for the children who shall inherit it."

Vassily runs outside, under the River Irwell Railway Bridge. He waits for a train to roar across it. He opens his mouth and screams as loud as his lungs will let him. He is determined one day to be heard. But for now the noise of the engine and the shriek of the whistle drown him out completely.

But the mastic is a hardy tree. It can survive in poor soil.

*

1862

The rains slams down like iron railings being hurled onto a roof, like nails that will need to be driven into the coffin lid after the funeral has finished. But for now the coffin lies open, in keeping with tradition, as the mourners scurry into the Greek Orthodox Church in Broughton, less than a mile and a half from Strangeways, to take shelter from the storm.

It is the 25th of March, the Feast of the Annunciation of the Blessed Virgin Mary, after which the Church is named, the first Greek Orthodox Church to be built anywhere in England. It is also the fortieth anniversary of the Massacre of Chios, and it is the day of Konstantin's funeral, Vassily's father, who died two days before from pulmonary fibrosis and a perforated peptic ulcer, which not even the beneficent chewing of mastic gum could staunch. The tears of Chios flow freely.

The mourners stand in line to view Konstantin's body.

"May your memory be eternal," they intone in turn.

The coffin is facing east, with Konstantin's feet towards the altar and his head towards the door, to signify he will shortly be leaving this place, having been placed there earlier by the bearers, after the *panikhida*, the procession led by the priest from Konstantin's home to the Church. The body lies directly beneath the high domed ceiling painted with a mural depicting Christ Pantocrator

Thea and Amara are dressed in black, standing beside the coffin. Vassily has the beginnings of his mourning beard, which he will keep for forty-nine days. He waits outside by the door, sheltering within the three-bay Corinthian portico topped by its modillion cornice made from dressed ashlar stone, to greet the people as they arrive, until everyone has entered through the polygonal apse, the pilastered columns, and passed the gabled pediments above the windows. Vassily is the last to approach the coffin. He pauses beside the body of the man he has always called *Pateras*, Father. His face wears an expression of such calm serenity that Vassily is stopped in his tracks. He cannot recall seeing his father look so peaceful while he was alive. Outside the storm still rages.

The priest begins the traditional Trisagion.

"Holy God, Holy Almighty, Holy Immortal, have mercy on us here this day."

Which he repeats three times, swinging his censer from north to south, east to west.

The Church is filled with the sweet smell of pine and cedar from the incense, ground from a mixture of charcoal and, appropriately, mastic, harvested from Chios itself for when the

Church first opened less than a year ago, designed by the architects, Clegg and Knowles, who stand respectfully at the back of the apse, as guests of Vassily. For Vassily's fortunes have taken a surprising turn for the better in the past twelve months, which he reflects on now, as the incense carries his thoughts and prayers up towards the icon of Christ Pantocrator, looming above them all. Perhaps it is this providential change that explains the transfigured expression on his father's face....

The sun rises. The sun sets. So, too, the moon. The seas ebb and flow. The tide in the affairs of men are indeed taken at the flood and lead to fortune, which subtly but discernibly switches away from those from Chios still loyal to the Ottomans towards those who now more confidently hoist the *kyanólefki* in Manchester's public places, Vassily among them, the azure blazon of the flag fluttering in a wind of change that is blowing stronger.

Then, one hot summer's afternoon, in the height of the dog days, when the stench from the Irwell is at its most ripe, the Glue Factory on its bank self-ignites in an act of spontaneous combustion and explodes. There are injuries, but no casualties. Konstantin escapes with minor cuts and bruises, but his lungs are thick with the fumes, the network of interstitial tissue choked and scarred...

The priest calls the people to prayer.

"In memory of the Martyr Julitta, Holy Mother of Sacrifice, we glorify and thank our Lord God in this, our obsequy, to commit the body of our beloved Konstantin. We beseech Thee, O God, to crown Thy departing servant, to relieve his suffering and to expel his fear. With the spirits of the righteous made perfect, we ask Thee to give rest to the soul of Thy faithful and preserve it in that Life Everlasting, which is with Thee, who loves all mankind..."

In the wake of the fire at the glue factory, prominent elders of the Chian diaspora contact the architects Clegg and Knowles, renowned for the excellence of their commercial buildings, to construct a warehouse at the junction of Mary Street and Julia Street, in the lee of the bridge at Great Ducie Street, close to Victoria Station. The architects duly oblige. Ducie Street Warehouse, as it comes to be known, is built from bonded red brick to the highest specifications. The elders take due note, so that when the time comes for them to be able to build their Church at last, they know who to contact...

The priest swings aloft the censer, filling the air with the fragrance of their homeland.

"Let us sing together the Funeral Praises, the *Evlogetaria*."

Vassily mouths the words, his thoughts elsewhere, grateful that his father sees from his coffin the sparks from his son's boots strike and catch hold as he takes his first unaided steps. Perhaps this is why his face is at peace.

The verses of the psalm drift in and out with the smoke...

The Warehouse is parcelled up into smaller, more manageable units, which are offered out at affordable rates, with loans available at favourable terms, for enterprising young businessmen with allegiance to the *kyanólefki*.

Vassily, together with his boyhood friends, Christos and Stephanos, is able to secure one of these units....

"Blessed are the undefiled in the way, who walk in the law of the Lord..."

"Blessed are they that keep testimony, and that seek Him with a whole heart..."

After watching the eleven-year-old Frank's heroics in rescuing the baby girl from the fire at Arkwright's Mill, Vassily has kept an eye on his friend, as he promised himself he would.

He has seen the way that he and his brother Gordon have expanded their father's modest printing company from the outhouse at the back of where they live into a much bigger, more professional operation, with their own premises on Portugal Street in Ancoats, where it is part of a larger industrial estate. Gordon, he observes, looks after the machinery, while the more entrepreneurial Frank takes charge of the business. He likes this notion of a division of labour. He, Christos and Stephanos will do the same. They will trade in mastic – what else, for that is what they know? – but they will specialise in sealants and adhesives only. Christos will oversee the manufacture, Stephanos the installations, while he, Vassily, will drum up the customers and secure the orders…

"I am a stranger in the earth. Open my eyes that I may behold things of wonder…"

"For I am become like a bottle in the smoke…"

"The proud have dug pits for me and have forged a lie against me…"

"Their hearts are as fat as grease…"

"The bands of the wicked have robbed me, but I have not forgotten Thy law…"

He goes to Frank for advice…

"Teach me good judgement and knowledge…"

"Teach me Thy statutes for they have been my song in the house of my pilgrimage…"

"You need proper publicity," his friend tells him. "A brochure, leaflets, advertisements."

Vassily nods, trying not to appear daunted by the enormity of the task.

"I'll help you," says Frank, "if you'd like me to."

Vassily declares he would like him to very much, and the two young men shake hands on it…

"I will keep Thy commandments with my whole heart…"
"And I will walk at liberty…"

"Let me pour you a glass of ouzo," says Vassily, sensing that now the tide in his affairs is changing and must be taken at their flood.

"No thank you," says Frank. "I'm a Methodist, and so teetotal. I'll join you with a glass of water, though."

They raise their glasses.

"To the Tears of Chios," says Vassily, before draining his ouzo in a single swallow.

"If you say so," smiles Frank, sipping his water more circumspectly.

At the conclusion of the *Evlogetaria*, the Priest calls upon them to join him in the singing of the *Kontakion*, the Hymn of the Eight Tones.

"O God of all Humankind
Grant rest to the soul of the departed
Now asleep in a place of light
A place of renewal and hope…"

The lid of the coffin is hammered into place. The nails resound like bells, ushering in a return of those lost golden days. The rain eases as the mourners retire to the Meeting Room at the back of the Church, where Vassily receives further expressions of condolence – from Messrs Clegg and Knowles, and from Frank. Thea and Amara serve out dishes of *koliva*, boiled wheat berries, nuts, raisins, pomegranates and spices.

After they have finished, and people have begun to drift away, Frank takes Vassily to one side.

"Look," he says, taking out a proof copy of a leaflet he is proposing be distributed door-to-door to advertise the new company. "What do you think?"

TEARS OF CHIOS

Does the wind whistle through your window?
Does the damp creep under your door?
Does the rain drip down from your ceiling?
Does heat escape through your floor?

Weep no more, for we at **TEARS OF CHIOS** will shed them for you
Bringing our experience and expertise to bear whatever the problem

No job too big or too small

Whatever the weather, you can count on us
Whatever the element, we've got you covered

Cracks in the plaster?   *Leaks in the roof?*
Holes in the floorboards?   *Gaps in the joints?*

We'll make you:
Air tight, Water tight
Damp proof, Fire proof

Contact Vassily Dimitriou: Manager

O LÓGOS MAS EINAI O DESMÓS MAS
O DESMÓS MAS EINAI I SFRAGIDA MAS

Our word is our bond
Our bond is our seal

Printed by F.G. Wright & Sons

*

2010

Alexis Dimitriou, known to all simply as Alex, stands in the Greek Orthodox Church on Bury New Road in Broughton on the exact same spot occupied by his Great-great-grandfather, Vassily, almost a hundred and fifty years before, for the funeral of Konstantin.

But this is a happy, not a sad occasion. Not a funeral, but a baptism. A *Christismós*, or Chrismation. Alex's daughter, Callista, has recently given birth to his first grandchild, a boy, to be called Yannis, 'by the grace of God', and, by the grace of God, Alex can take pride in the continuation of the line, stretching back as far as his ancestors, who, exiled from Chios, had to endure many years of wandering in the wilderness before finding their new home here in Manchester. He makes a silent prayer of thanks for his joy and good fortune before the rest of the family join him. They are all currently gathered in the octagonal apse at the back of the Church, making sure that Yannis is clothed in the traditional white *chiton*, the customary tunic worn for the *Christismós*, which is a combination of baptism and confirmation, a sacred mystery presided over by the priest.

Alex is happy for two other reasons. The business, which has been passed down father to son through five generations beginning with Vassily, is doing better than ever. It is no longer called *Tears of Chios*. Now they go by the less poetic, but more contemporary *TC Sealants*. Nor are they based at the Ducie Street Warehouse, which was bought out by the Manchester, Sheffield & Lincolnshire Railway in the decade after Vassily had first set up there with Christos and Stephanos. They've moved several times since then, but for the past five years they have enjoyed brand new purpose-built premises on the Arkady Industrial Estate on Briscoe Lane, Newton Heath, as part of the Council's massive regeneration scheme taking place in the east of the city, as well as an office on Peter Street in a prime central location. They have just won a prestigious three-year project to supply the structural glazing and mastic pointing for the Glass Walkway connecting the Manchester Town Hall Extension with the Central Library in St Peter's Square. Much of the credit for this success is due to Alex's Chief Engineer, Andreas, who has had to liaise closely with the architects Simpson & Haugh, who had bought out the descendants of Clegg & Knowles ten years before, wrestling with complex algorithms to persuade the City Council to accept that the seals they would install would be sufficiently weather-tight and strong to withstand the pressures imposed upon it by the groundbreaking designs. The fact that Andreas also happens to be Alex's son-in-law, Callista's husband, and father of Yannis, only serves to add to the satisfaction Alex feels this morning as he contemplates his lot.

The contract they have been awarded is to supply a series of one-and-a-half-inch-thick glass panels more than twenty-four feet in height, spanning more than sixteen yards in length, which will support a thirty-three-ton polished steel roof welded into an abstract undulating cloud, suspended above a clear, column-free space. The simplicity and purity achieved by the combination of the two elements of steel roof and glass façade appeals to Alex greatly. The structure is the form, the enclosure is the support. He pictures how it will look in his mind's eye, as he stands in the cool, still air of the Church.

Alex likes the elegance of this solution. It is how he likes all aspects of his life to be. Orderly, controlled, calm. He imagines the way the curved glass sliding doors will glide with a satisfying, barely audible hum as they open and close, open and close. The prospect of it fills him with immense pleasure and pride.

The third reason he has for the happiness he feels this morning is that it coincides with the eighteenth birthday of Petros, his son, who today officially becomes a man, when Alex will be able to offer him a position of importance in the company. Nothing with too much responsibility as yet, but one which will accord him the dignity and respect due to the son of the CEO, as well as enabling him to learn all aspects of the business.

Yes, he thinks, there is something deeply satisfying in the coming together of these three pieces of good fortune, like a rare conjunction of the planets. As a follower of the Greek Orthodoxy he believes implicitly in the triune, the three-in-one, a single God who is Father, Son and Holy Spirit, the undivided but distinct hypostases, who share one divine essence, the *ousia*, uncreated, incorporeal, everlasting, with none of it possible without the mastic sealant at its heart. An ancient root transplanted to modern soil.

And yet...

The side of his temple flickers and pulses slightly. The veneer of orderly, controlled calm that Alex prizes so highly begins to crack just the tiniest amount. He wonders what can have caused it. He notes it, but dismisses it. He will not let a single cloud spoil this sunniest of days.

He is roused from his reverie by the sound of the rest of his family and guests arriving into the Church. There is much excitement and anticipation in their echoing chatter, like the twittering of birds in a frenzy around the feeding table. He looks around. Petros is not there. The sound of the birds' clustering grows louder, raucous, more agitated, like an insistent tinnitus in his ear. He catches the eye of his wife, Sophia, as she is handing Yannis back to Callista, and mouths, "Where is he?" She smiles reassuringly. "Don't worry," she mouths back. "He'll be here."

The sliding curved glass doors of the yet-to-be-realised Library Walkway snag and stick. The pulse in the side of Alex's temple begins to throb.

Petros has been waiting for the post to arrive. The letter he's expecting should have arrived yesterday, but it didn't. He is on tenterhooks. When the rest of the family sets off for the Church, he tells them he'll be along in a minute. The silence when they all leave hangs heavily as he anxiously paces the hallway.

Just when he thinks he can wait no longer, or he would miss the *christismós*, for which Callista would never forgive him, he hears a van pull up outside. He waits nervously as the postman's footsteps approach the front door. A bundle of letters drops onto the mat. Petros seizes upon them. Adverts, junk, a few cards congratulating Callista and Andreas, some bills and... Yes. Here it is. The official logo of the university emblazoned on the front of the envelope. Petros tears it open.

Manchester Metropolitan University

9th March 2010

Dear Petros,

It is with great pleasure that I write to offer you a place to study for a BA in Media Studies at the Manchester Metropolitan University School of Arts & Humanities for commencement in September of this year.

This offer is conditional on you achieving 3 grades of B or above in your upcoming 'A' Level examinations. You should receive an official confirmation of this offer from UCAS within seven working days.

With warmest wishes,

Clive Archer, PhD
Department of Media Studies

Petros gives a whoop of joy before dashing out of the front door to catch up with the others, placing the acceptance letter securely in his inside jacket pocket.

He arrives in the Church just as the priest is inviting the family to gather round the baptismal font. Callista shakes her head in exasperation but smiles nevertheless. Sophia turns to Alex with an expression that suggests, "There – I told you he'd be here," then playfully pinches her son's hot cheeks. Alex merely frowns.

Petros tickles Yannis under his chin. Yannis giggles delightedly. He adores his Uncle Petros.

The service is to be carried out by Archimandrite Nikolaos Sergakis, in his capacity as Presbyter of the Church of the Annunciation, which sits within the Greek Orthodox Archdiocese of Thyateira & Great Britain, part of the Ecumenical Patriarchate of Constantinople. Father Nikolaos has the traditional long hair and knotted beard of the Eastern priests, worn, as custom dictates, to bear a physical resemblance to Christ, in accordance with Leviticus. *'Ye shall not make a cutting of the hair of your head, nor disfigure your beard.'* Then again, in Numbers, as a commandment given to the Nazarene. *'A razor shall not come upon his head, until the days be fulfilled, which he vowed to the Lord.'*

He smiles down on them all gathered around him, and signals to Callista to hand over Yannis for the start of the ceremony, which she does gladly. She has known Father Nikolaos all her life. He performed the Chrismation on her when she was a baby. He administered her First Communion when she was ten. More recently he married her to Andreas. Her eyes are drawn, as they have always been, to his thick, bushy beard, which reaches down to the middle of his chest. Dusted with grey, it has always reminded her of a hedge in winter, or a bird's nest built out of twigs and cotton wool. As a child she half-expected a baby cuckoo to poke out its tiny head at any moment, before flying out into the world. She wonders what Yannis must be making of it now, his large brown, moon-shaped eyes staring up at this venerable priest, who, to Callista, has always looked like the face of God. If he is frightened, he does not show it. Instead he merely chortles, as Father Nikolaos playfully sprinkles the holy water onto his button nose.

"*I sfragida tou dóurou tou ieroú pnévmatos.*" The seal of the gift of the Holy Spirit.

Father Nikolaos intones this eight times, making the sign of the cross each time, upon the forehead, eyes, nostrils, mouth, ears, breast, hands and feet. "*I sfragida tou dóurou tou ieroú pnévmatos.*" He anoints the recipient with the chrism, sacred oil distilled from mastic and myrrh.

"Let him be washed and anointed, as one who is baptised. Let him be counted among the worthy."

"Amen," say each of the rest of the family.

Petros feels the eyes of his father tunnelling through him, questioning if he is ready, weighing his worth in the scales. Can he be counted?

An hour later they are all sitting down to a celebratory lunch at *Rozafa*, on Princess Street in the heart of the city. Alex is well-known to them, and a private room has been arranged.

"A toast," he calls, when they have all finished dessert. He is already fairly well-oiled by this time. "To Yannis."

"To Yannis," they reply, and Yannis rewards them with a heart-stopping smile.

"To Andreas," continues Alex, "for winning the contract for the Library Walk, which means I am able to afford this lunch for us all today…" Everyone laughs approvingly. "And which, if we crane our necks, we might just be able to see where it will be built, round the corner from here, over the next three years. Thank you. Andreas, for being such an important part of our growing family."

"To Andreas."

"And finally, may I ask you to raise your glasses to Petros, my son, whose eighteenth birthday it is today. Now he becomes a man."

"He'll always be my sweet baby boy," jokes Sophia.

"And my annoying little brother," adds Callista, smiling.

"To Petros."

"As soon as you finish school," continues Alex, "you can join me in TC Sealants, learning every aspect of the business, as it has been through five generations, father to son, ever since Vassily, the first of us."

"To Vassily."

There is a momentary lull. Petros, sensing that his father has now run out of toasts, gets to his feet.

"Thank you." He coughs nervously. "I too," he says, "I too have some news." He takes out the crumpled acceptance letter from his inside jacket pocket. "This," he continues, brandishing the piece of paper in front of him, "arrived this morning. It was why," he adds, looking towards Callista with an apologetic shrug, "I was nearly late for Yannis."

Alex rises unsteadily from his chair. He is perspiring quite heavily. Sophia tries to intercept him, but he pushes her arm roughly to one side.

"What is it?" he slurs. There is a dangerous look in his eyes, which Petros fails to register.

"It's from the university," he says brightly. "I've got a place for next year."

The rest of the family burst at once into spontaneous applause.

"You're not as daft as you look, are you, our kid?" laughs Callista.

"Congratulations," says Andreas, shaking him by the hand.

"Just imagine," says Sophia, clasping her hands across her heart, "our son at a university, the first in the family ever to do so. I'm so proud."

Only Alex fails to join in. The others become aware of this and, one by one, turn towards him.

"Didn't you hear what I just said?" he growls. "When you finish school, you will be coming to work with *me*. It's all arranged."

"Yes, but… "

"You don't need a degree to do that."

"I want to be a student."

"You'll be a student with me."

"That's not what I mean."

"What's the course?" says Andreas suddenly, trying to lower the temperature.

"Media Studies," says Petros.

Alex explodes. "Media Studies? What's the point in that? If you'd said Business Studies, then maybe – just maybe – we might have discussed it, found a way you might be able to take it part-time, but Media Studies? It's not worth the paper it's written on."

"Oh, I don't know, sir," says Andreas in a further attempt to mollify. "We're conducting more and more of our business online, communicating with customers and clients via social media…"

Callista lays a restraining hand upon her husband's arm, and he fizzles out. She recognises the warning signs. She's seen her father like this before. There's nothing to be gained by arguing with him. Better to let the storm blow itself out. Andreas understands this and falls silent.

"My mind's made up," says Petros.

"Is it? And how are you going to pay for it? Because don't think for a minute that *I* will."

"I wouldn't want you to. I'll take out a student loan."

"And be paying back the interest for the rest of your life?"

"I think it'll be worth it."

"Why waste the time?"

"It's only three years."

"Think of the money you could earn in that time."

"That's not important."

"Easy for you to say when you've never lacked a thing."

"That's hardly fair."

"Isn't it? I'll tell you what's not fair – working every hour God sends just to make a better life for you, to provide you with something that's been built up over generations, something solid, that endures, only to have that flung back in my face."

"It's not that I'm not grateful. I am. I just don't want my future handed to me on a plate."

"It wouldn't be. You'd have to earn it."

"I want to do something that's *mine*, and mine *alone*, not something connected to the past."

"What's wrong with our past?"

"Nothing."

"You should be proud of it."

"I am. But not like this."

"Like what?"

"It's like you want to chain me to it. Like I'm some kind of dog in the yard."

Alex eyes Petros coldly. He speaks with a barely suppressed rage.

"I want you out of the house by the end of the week."

Sophia gasps.

"Why not today?" replies Petros defiantly.

The fuse that has been simmering in Alex's brain all morning now finally detonates and explodes.

"Go," he roars. "Now. I don't know you. I don't recognise you. You are not my son."

Petros looks helplessly at his mother and sister. Yannis begins to howl like a dog in distress, resisting all of Callista's efforts to quieten him. With a last determined look around him, Petros leaves.

"Cuckoo!" shouts Alex to his departing back, knocking over a still half-full bottle of wine in his fury.

Sophia watches in horror as the white tablecloth stains with red.

Alex reels away.

"Cuckoo," he cries again, less forcibly this time. He is aware, even as the word leaves his lips, that he has never actually seen a cuckoo, and he cannot remember the last time he heard one.

It will be three years before father and son come face to face again.

*

2005

wessex archaeology

```
Arkwright's Mill, NCP Car Park, Miller Street,
Manchester
Archaeological  Evaluation  and  Assessment  of
Results
```

Findings: (extract)

The primary aim of the evaluation was to identify the position of the original mill and the different phases of construction and alteration which occurred during its lifetime. The project also aimed to investigate the nature of the housing which existed along the south side of Angel Street to the north.

The evaluation successfully located the main building and enabled the identification of features associated with Richard Arkwright's original 1780-82 footprint. A further five phases of alterations were subsequently identified, associated with the introduction of new technologies, the replacement of failed machinery with old tried and tested methods, and significant rebuilding following the devastating fire of 1852, including what subsequently became the CWS Tobacco Factory.

Tony Robinson and Grace are poring over the findings at the end of the all-too-short four-week dig, with the ever-eager Samira in close attendance.

"Nothing very surprising," says Grace.

"No," says Tony, "but good to be able to confirm the fire unequivocally."

"I agree."

The evaluation also investigated one of the small cellar dwellings occupied to the north of the mill. It was clear that what had once been a small, two-room dwelling had been further divided into two separate one-room dwellings, most probably in the mid 19th century, a process seen across Manchester at this time to accommodate the increasing migration of people to work in the booming cotton mill industry.

"Well," says Tony, "what do you think?"

"All very meticulous and thorough. Though I would expect nothing less."

"The time constraints have been horrendous. There's so much more we could have done if we'd had another couple of weeks. I don't suppose your mate Robina might wangle us a bit extra?"

"No, I don't expect she can. You were probably lucky to get this long. The developers will doubtless be preparing to send in the Cavalry at first light tomorrow."

Tony sighs. "Twas ever thus."

He waves his empty coffee cup. Samira is instantly on hand to refill it.

"But did you find the stories you were looking for?" asks Grace with a grin.

He scrolls down several pages of the report on his i-pad until he reaches a passage he has highlighted for her especially.

"Take a look at this," he says, moving aside to give her more space.

"Hmm," says Grace with relish. "I think I'm going to need more coffee."

"No sooner asked for than delivered," says Samira, brandishing the coffee pot with a flourish.

```
Following the removal of the current tarmac
car park surface, large-scale rubble remains
were revealed, a very mixed deposit containing
considerable amounts of cinder, charcoal and
brick, which was shown to be the deliberate
backfill of a cellar, as well as material
dating from the 18th century through to the
20th century, including a ha'penny of George
III (dated 1775) lodged within a fragment of
mortar. The building had most probably been
```

demolished as a result of the Blitz in 1940, and the demolished material used to level the ground subsequently.

Following the removal of the backfill, it was clear this was in fact a cellar dwelling of a type similar to those inhabited by the mill workers and their families. Such cellars were originally built to relieve the damp in the poorly-built workers' housing of the late 18th and early 19th centuries, but inevitably became dwellings for sub-tenants. Whole families, or even more, might share a single cellar dwelling in extremely unsanitary conditions.

The area of living space was divided into two rooms by an internal wall. This wall was less than eleven feet long by less than a foot wide and survived to a maximum height of only two feet, constructed of hand-made bricks bonded with lime mortar. The bond of the bricks was unclear but appeared to be stretcher bond. The wall was keyed into and bonded to another, creating two smaller rooms within the dwelling, with Room 1 to the north and Room 2 to the south. The two rooms were connected through a doorway at the western end of the wall, and marked by a stone flag step in Room 2. The northern side of the doorway was not visible due to later alterations.

Room 1 was the smaller of the two exposed rooms, floored with large stone flags, the larger Room 2 being floored with randomly laid bricks. The floor has seen much alteration and relaying of bricks, with some basket-weave and herring-bone patterns discernible. Both rooms have the remains of hearths, identified through the considerable amount of charcoal and ash residue in and around the structures. It is scarcely to be imagined what life for a large family must have been like in either of these two low, tiny, sub-divided rooms.

Grace and Tony shake their heads in disbelief.

A later phase of alteration would appear to seal off Room 2, and thus prevent further access to it. The reasoning behind this is unclear and it is possible there was still a way of accessing the room which was not revealed by our excavations, but with the blocking of the light source into the room its use as a dwelling may have been discontinued. It is still uncertain when it, and others like it, was finally abandoned altogether, and in what form these may have survived when the site was bombed and levelled in the 1940s.

Grace leans back, rubbing her eyes.

"Reading on a screen always makes me more tired. Give me typed sheets of foolscap any time."

"Well?" says Tony, adopting his Springer spaniel pose once more.

"It's truly shocking," replies Grace. "The findings make it completely possible for us to visualise the appalling conditions the workers had to try and live in, but we can never truly understand what the reality must have been like. No wonder infant mortality rates were so high."

"And those that did survive barely made it past forty."

Grace shudders.

"Show me the list of the objects you found. It's those personal and domestic items that really bring a site to life. That's where the real stories lie.

Tony grins.

"Scroll down to Appendix 2."

Of the more than four hundred artefacts catalogued, Tony has flagged six for Grace's attention.

Category	Material	No.	Description
Personal	Clay	2	1 pipe with stem + bowl, 1 with stem only
Domestic	Glass	2	1 green bottle with dark blue stirring rod
Structural	Ceramic	102	Wall tiles decorative + plain
Personal	Brass	1	1 x George III ha'penny
Domestic	Animal bone	3	Possibly cat
Personal	Leather	1	Child's shoe

"The child's shoe is particularly affecting," she says, looking away from the screen.

Tony nods and sighs.

"But no bones," says Grace.

"Animal," protests Tony.

"It's not the same. A TV programme like yours needs a good skeleton," she says.

"I know," says Tony, shaking his head. "But there's still a cracking good story to tell here."

"There is," says Grace. "An important one. But it's always been about the bones…"

*

1996

It is the week after the IRA bomb. Grace is back at her home on Albion Road. She is chair-bound. Her right leg, which she broke in her fall during the blast, is plastered from ankle to thigh, while her left leg, her weak leg, is callipered, as usual. The hospital has lent her a pair of crutches to enable her to get around the house. At first she can barely hobble a few feet. But she perseveres. Like she has always done. In a few days she has mastered them. She can propel herself with a speed and a suddenness that alarms visitors, but delights Grace herself. She has always taken pleasure in subverting the expectations of others, in surprising them by how much she is capable of. She does not take kindly to being told what she can or can't do. Especially what she can't. It only makes her more determined than ever to prove them wrong, to show them that she can.

So that when she receives a call from Robina towards the end of that first week, she knows that there will be no lily-livered, mealy-mouthed platitudes from her. Robina has been well schooled. She knows better than to pussy-foot around, and so she comes straight to the point.

"I know you're meant to be retired," she says, "but we could really do with your input just now."

"I'm all ears."

"Apart from the obvious devastation wreaked by the bomb," she continues, "which is far more widespread than was at first thought by the way, there isn't a single building in the city that hasn't been affected in some way, windows blown out, walls knocked down, roof slates flung about like playing cards, paving slabs sticking up like drunkards – apart from all that, the explosion has revealed all manner of hitherto unknown finds, things that have been buried for centuries, suddenly coming to the surface…"

"Yes, I thought that might be the case."

"There's just so much of it I simply don't know how we're going to keep abreast of it all."

"You will," says Grace briskly. If Robina is looking for sympathy, she isn't going to get it. "We always have and we always will. It's what we do."

"I know. But there's not been anything on this scale since…"

"The Second World War."

"That's right."

"Not so long ago then."

"No. I suppose not. We just haven't the human resources to investigate and catalogue everything, that's all."

"We never do. That's just the way it is. All you can do is prioritise. Leave what you can't get around to for someone else in a generation or so."

"You're right. I know. It's all just a bit overwhelming at the moment. There's simply so much of it."

"What do you need me to do? I take it you've called for a reason."

"Yes," says Robina, sounding more business-like once more. "Sorry about that. There's something I want you to take a look at. Something particular."

"Explain."

"The row of buildings between the Corn Exchange and Hanging Ditch has been particularly badly hit."

"I'm not surprised. Some of them are very old. Behind the 19th century frontages there are still traces of medieval Manchester to be found. If you know where to look."

"Like The Shambles."

"Which were not where they are today of course."

"And they're talking about moving them again."

"How?"

"*The Old Wellington*, believe it or not, has somehow survived."

Grace whistles down the phone. *The Old Wellington* is the oldest surviving complete building in Manchester. The half-timbered pub was put up in 1552, six years before Elizabeth I ascended the throne.

"But its foundations are shot," continues Robina. "They're proposing to raise it up on hydraulic stilts and transport it three hundred yards to a new location, nearer to the Corn Exchange, creating a whole new shopping quarter."

"Don't tell me," interrupts Grace. "Called 'Shambles Square'."

"Got it in one."

Grace shudders at the thought. "Sounds like some ghastly botox job. Why can't they just let the old girl grow old gracefully?"

"Or *dis*gracefully," laughs Robina.

That's more like it, thinks Grace.

"Though I have hopes we might be consulted more this time around," says Robina. "While the Council is committed to rebuilding the Arndale…"

"They've got no choice, otherwise they'd be letting the terrorists win."

"Absolutely, but they also know that nobody really liked it how it was."

"A giant urinal wall."

"All those acres of yellow tiles."

"That kept coming unstuck and falling off."

"Which means now they've got a chance to redesign it, as well as rebuild it."

"And that's where 'Shambles Square' comes in?"

"They're even talking about a new Selfridge's."

"So what is it you want me to take a look at?"

"I'm coming to that. The area around the Corn Exchange has been designated a top priority, in that that's where they want to start the clean-up process first."

"But you've found something?"

"Yes."

Robina pauses. Grace can hear her take a deep breath.

"Well?"

"It's extraordinary," she says. "I've never seen anything quite like it before."

"Now you've really got me intrigued. I take it you must have found human remains."

"You could say that."

"A complete skeleton?"

"More than that."

"An undercroft? An ossuary?" asks Grace, becoming increasingly excited.

"No. It's not on that scale. It's more... intimate than that."

Something in the way Robina says 'intimate' makes Grace realise that this is something she has to see.

"When did you discover it?"

"This morning."

It is the urgency that prompts Grace into action.

"When do you want me to come over?" she says.

"When can you start?"

"How about now?"

"Are you sure? That would be fantastic. But what about your leg? Do you need me to send a car round?"

"I'll get a taxi, don't worry. I'll be there in an hour."

Robina gives her the precise details of the location, then hangs up. Grace does a three-hundred-and-sixty degree spin, balanced on a single crutch.

The site turns out to be a wine merchant's on Hanging Ditch. In the past hundred years it has been through many incarnations – a pawnbroker's, a taxidermist's, a watchmaker's, an ironmonger's, a bicycle repair shop – but before that, for almost a century, it was a Jewish tailor's by the name of Jacob's.

Robina has been able to find all this out through a thorough trawl of the Records Office. Above the shop are various small rooms, which have, over time, served as offices, store rooms and, in one case, as living accommodation. From one of these Robina has extracted a dusty glass bowl, decorated with hand-painted pink flowers, which has somehow survived the years.

"Campion," says Grace. "*Lychnis diurna*. One of my father's favourites."

"Of course," says Robina. "I was forgetting. Your father was a gardener, wasn't he?"

"That he was," says Grace. "Though Philips Park went in for ornamental borders mostly, municipal planting in regimented rows. There wasn't much space left for wild flowers. He let a few of these grow among some rogue tulips beneath the black poplars at the back of where we lived. My mother was especially fond of them."

"This is a lovely bowl actually," says Robina, holding it up to the light. "There's an engraving on the base." She holds it closer to her. "'*To L from L. Your dusky bell*.'"

"I wonder who L and L were," says Grace. "I'll guess we'll never know."

"Come and have a look outside," says Robina.

They make their way through to what was once a small courtyard at the back, now a heap of rubble from the blast. Robina reminds Grace it was formerly known as Omega Court, and that it might have been larger at one time, but at some point has been back-filled, possibly after the Blitz. But the aftershock of the bomb has revealed the particular find that Robina has brought Grace to cast her expert eye over.

At first glance it resembles nothing more than a brick wall. But the bricks are quite old.

"Late 18th century?" asks Robina.

"Earlier, I'd say. 1740s perhaps."

"Careful," says Robina. "What I've brought you to see is just the other side."

Grace manoeuvres herself with painful slowness, placing each crutch delicately between the rubble around the edge of the low wall, which is just a single course wide and less than six feet in height. The area has been screened off with what looks like Police Incident tape.

"Have Forensics already been?" asks Grace.

"They have," answers Robina. "They've done a quick preliminary examination and are happy for us to take a look before they come to take the bones away."

The bones.

Grace steadies herself.

"Have they given you a sense of how old?"

"Too early to say."

"Best guess?"

"Two hundred years?"

Grace nods. She edges further round until she is at last able to get her first sight what it is that has so excited her former colleague. What she sees takes her breath away.

Two skeletons. Complete and intact. Human. One male, one female. And – what is most extraordinary of all – they are wrapped together in a timeless, tender embrace.

Grace has uncovered numerous skeletons in her years as an archaeologist. Part or whole, they never fail to stir the blood, fire the imagination. They always excite the same questions. Who are they? Why are they here? In this place? How did they die? Sometimes she has been able to answer these questions, sometimes she hasn't. Her entire career has been waymarked by them. Right from that very first dig as a student when she had found the *Settanti* soldier crushed beneath the weight of a wooden shield painted with a bee.

But she has never before seen anything like this delicate dance of death. The intimacy of the scene is heart-stopping. It almost feels intrusive, even for a professional like her, to be gazing upon this couple's final moments, voyeuristic. As always, her mind is racing with theories, conjectures that might explain what has happened, and give a clue as to their possible identities. Speculations. Stories. Yes, for Grace it has always come back to stories. If we can discover them, she has said on many a platform when giving a talk or lecture, we can tell them. We can pass them on, so they can never be lost or forgotten.

She looks around for other clues that may help her solve the mystery. The single course of bricks that has, until just a few hours ago, kept the couple hidden from sight forms a tight ovoid. Four walls, slightly curved. Four elegantly-chamfered brick angle-corners. From what Grace is able to make out, they appear to have been constructed in haste, but sturdy for all that. They have withstood whatever time has thrown at it, even in the shape of the Luftwaffe, until last week's attack by the IRA.

There is evidence that there may have also been a roof at one time. Grace has to step carefully between a layer of smaller, broken bricks that lie scattered at her feet.

As well as the two bodies, the walls enclose a sculpture, from the same brick type, exquisitely fashioned in a bas relief. Grace has seen others like this before, in and around the city. A person could live in Manchester all their life and never see one. Unless they were shown. Grace has stumbled upon several. A bare-chested man atop a factory roof, hammer in one hand, chisel in another; a pair of compasses over a surveyor's office, scales balanced with coins, above a bank; a shoe stretched over a last at a cobbler's; a pair of shears and a tape measure over what was once a tailor's. She has seen weavers, miners, coopers and wheelwrights, farriers, foundrymen, lacemakers and lamplighters. And, in the graveyard behind St John's Church, an angel.

But this one is finer than any that Grace has seen before. It has been carved with such a fierce love and devotion. It depicts a handloom weaver, sitting at his loom, reaching out towards something beyond it, something only he can see. In his other hand is clasped a Cap of Liberty, a home-made cotton flag, which, miraculously, has survived, in all probability, thinks Grace, because of the air-tight, walled-up tomb that has held it for two centuries. With her gloved fingers she painstakingly unfurls it. On it is a hand-stitched inscription.

'Unity is Strength.'

It is almost too much for Grace to bear. There is no doubt in her mind that this was carried onto the field of Peterloo in 1819. She looks back towards the embracing couple with even more reverence.

'Unity is Strength.'

She tries to picture what happened, to excavate their story…

*

1833

Jem waits till he's sure Laurel is fast asleep. Then he wheels barrow after barrow of bricks from one of the nearby Hulks.

When he feels he has enough, he immediately sets to work.

Cutting, slicing, shaping.

His hands are strong and sure, nimble and quick. In scarcely any time at all he has built what looks like a high wall that encircles the weaver, his father, completely, so high that he becomes invisible. Invisible but still there.

Next, inside this wall, he tips out another barrow load of bricks, seemingly at random. They resemble a ruin, where something that once stood tall and proud has now come tumbling down, without shape, or order. But out of this chaos he fashions a new figure, basking on its surface, lightly, leaving neither shadow nor imprint, a moth. A Manchester moth, emerging from her pupa, her camouflaged cocoon of spun silk, whose gossamer-fine threads connect her to the handloom weaver's loom.

Jem looks at what he has created a long time, as if trying to make a decision. He waits until the last of the light has left the Yard. Then he leaves.

It is almost an hour later when he returns. He is carrying something heavy in a sack over his shoulder. With some relief he drops it to the ground. It splits slightly as he does so. A sliver of sand spills out.

He straightens himself up, puts his hands in the small of his back, closes his eyes, opens them, then leaves a second time, trundling his empty wheelbarrow before him.

When he next returns, the wheelbarrow is full. He has been to the Daub Holes and piled it high with a mixture of clay and lime. He slides it off the barrow onto the ground. Then he fills a bucket with water from the pump and begins to mix together a lime mortar, to which he adds handfuls of horse hair, which he takes from his pocket.

As soon as he is satisfied that the mortar is of the right consistency he carries in a third, much lighter sack, which he painstakingly arranges in a corner with the utmost delicacy and care, lest he should disturb a single atom of it. Then, having completed this task, he works quicker than ever. First he tapers the circling wall to form a dome, rather like a giant bee hive, over the grouping of the weaver, the loom, the nest of bricks and the moth, the cocoon and the thread. He does this until it is completely obscured from view, with what remains of the bricks, the lime mortar, and the third carefully-placed sack, all inside the hive.

He then proceeds to wall himself up entirely.

It takes him nearly three hours.

He waits.

He waits until he senses the dawn beginning to break

outside.

But no light penetrates this tomb he has built for himself. The darkness is absolute. He sees nothing. But in the emptiness of the space his fingers seek out his companions. They alight upon the finely wrought gossamer thread. They trace the line between the loom and the pupa. They settle upon the impossible lightness of the moth, which, although it leaves neither shadow nor imprint upon the nest of bricks, settles its weight upon his own skin, till they are perfectly bonded, each to each.

He waits.

He feels the wings open, then close.

Open, then close.

Beneath him, waiting for him, is the space vacated by his father, Henry, and by his father before him, Edwin.

Come, they say. Join us. The line is taut, the line is stretched. But it will not be broken. Pity will see to that.

Pity.

He carefully unwraps her fully-clothed body from the sack he has carried her in. Her face is unspoiled. She could almost be mistaken for merely sleeping. But she will never wake again Her skin is like paper, like cotton. He lovingly arranges her arms about his neck and places his own around her waist. He sets them both down beside the Cap of Liberty and patiently waits.

He waits a long time.

The last breath of air leaves the chamber. It empties him. So that he can now begin to be filled with all that she has given him.

Pity.

A bottomless well.

A tear slides down each cheek, scoring his skin. He gently fastens his lips against hers in a goodbye kiss.

Omega Place.

'And God shall wipe away all tears from their eyes; and there shall be no more death, neither sorrow, nor crying, neither shall there be any more pain: for the former things are passed away...'

*

1996

Grace and Robina tiptoe away. On her way out, as she picks her way through the rubble with her crutches, Grace almost stumbles on a loose piece of brick. She bends down to pick it up. It is chipped and damaged, but there is no mistaking that it was once the carving of a moth.

*

2020

If Petros ever pauses long enough in his hectic daily schedule to consider just how far – or little – he has come in these past seven years, he is likely to decide that his glass is half-empty, rather than half-full. Yes, he makes a good living, earns more money in a month than his father does in a year; and yes, he has established himself as a player in the Manchester property market, but not a significant one. He looks around at the ring of skyscrapers orbiting the city like the latest high-tech satellites – which is where the really major stars shine in the firmament – and all too quickly realises that he currently comes nowhere near their sphere of gravitational influence. Those realms belong to the overseas investors – the pension funds and oligarchs from Russia, the Middle East, and, increasingly these days, China. He ploughs the sub-orbital routes of the loft, mill and warehouse conversions, for young professionals wanting their first taste of city centre living before they are ready to launch into the more stratospheric heights of the Beetham,

Deansgate and soon-to-be-completed Trinity Towers, a pathway he had first taken with Property Centric, an independent firm specialising in these kinds of development, who'd taken him on as an assistant even before he'd left MMU, impressed by his entrepreneurial zeal that had seen him make a killing with the student squats in the Tripe Colony. But the position had turned out to be little more than a glorified runner, so he'd cut his losses and decided to run for himself, instead of someone else. That was five years ago.

He takes a sip of flat white from his biodegradable, eco-friendly, compostable, take-out coffee cup, and contemplates just how far he has travelled on his voyage so far. He lives in a loft conversion himself, in the old Ducie Street Warehouse, where his great-great-great grandfather's sealant business first started. There's an irony in that from which he derives a certain grim satisfaction. Though he's not sure why.

As he had stepped out of the coffee shop, he had overheard two older men disparagingly commenting to each other.

"This isn't Manchester any more. It's 'Starbucks Central'."

"Soon there'll be no room for real Mancunians here."

At first Petros had been dismissive – he wouldn't be seen dead in a Starbucks – but their bitterness had lingered, and, like the dregs of his coffee, had grown cold and unpleasant.

What does that mean? A real Mancunian? Someone who drinks pints of Boddington's, went to school with Ken Barlow, got wasted at *The Haçienda*, had a walk-on part in *Shameless*, talks like Liam Gallager, supports City (because no one from Manchester supports United)? Is it really that reductive? Surely not. Take *him* as an example – Petros. He drinks locally brewed *Turing, Engels* or *Marx* from Satanic Mills. He's never watched a single episode of *Coronation Street* – or *Shameless* when it comes to it. He thinks the whole *Haçienda* thing is boring. He'd much rather go and watch a film at Danny Boyle's *Home*. He prefers The Courteeners to Oasis, and he most definitely supports United. He smiles fondly at the memory of The Courteeners singing *Not Nineteen For Ever* in Albert Square the night United paraded the Premier League trophy after winning it for the twentieth time. That had been such a magical night. More than a hundred thousand people rocked up to welcome home their heroes, Sir Alex Ferguson's last hurrah. They had to peel me off the pavement, recalls Petros fondly.

But that was seven years ago. The same year Petros graduated with a two-one from MMU, certain that his future was assured just as surely as was United's. Little did he know. He should have paid better heed to The Courteeners' song.

"You're not nineteen for ever, pull yourselves together
I know it seems strange, but things, they change..."

The best United can hope for now, it seems, is a place in the Champions League by the ignominious back door of coming 4th in the Premier League – if they're lucky. The prospect of lifting a trophy again – any trophy – seem as remote as the chances of Petros orbiting with the big boys. It's City's star, with its Middle Eastern billions, that is rising now, in whose penumbra, Petros, like United, must mark time.

Time. He's twenty-eight now. Another two years he'll be thirty. Then it's downhill all the way. Born last century, he muses. 1992. He'd always liked the notion of comparing himself with United's Class of '92. But which one? Not for him the interstellar glory of a Beckham or a Giggs. No multi-million pound transfer deal to make him one of the Galacticos. Nor the grace or artistry of a Paul Scholes, or the in-your-face passion of a Gary Neville. No – a more accurate comparison for him would be Nicky Butt? Nicky *Who*, he hears people ask? Never heard of him. True. Not many people have, but didn't Pele say of him once he was England's best player? Man of the tournament in the 2002 World Cup? There's some compensation in that, thinks Petros. But immediately he recognises just how foolish he sounds – even to himself. Nicky Butt is yesterday's man, just as he, too, Petros, is in danger of becoming, if he doesn't close this deal today. At precisely that moment, a black BMW 320 Coupé, not dissimilar to one Petros himself had looked at in longing a couple of weeks back and no doubt conveying his next clients to him even as he tips out the last of his flat white, pulls up on the double yellow line directly outside the converted CWS Tobacco Factory, not bothering with the inconvenience of the NCP Car Park.

*

2005

Having said her goodbyes, Grace collects her bicycle from inside that Car Park, where already the developers are moving in with their JCBs. In a few days' time all traces of the *Time Team* dig will have disappeared. The remains of Arkwright's Mill will be concreted over. Its surrounding dwellings of Angel Meadow will once more be buried and hidden away, like a shameful secret, which is how they have always been, thinks Grace. But they will not be forgotten, just as the skeletons she uncovered in Hanging Ditch will not now be. Nor that of the Celtic soldier she unearthed more than half a century ago. They will be photographed, documented, exhibited, broadcast. A memory of them will survive in the stories that are told about them and be passed on.

She looks across to the old CWS Tobacco Factory, which lies empty and up for sale. No doubt this too will undergo a transformation, metamorphosing from pupa to imagine in the form of some swanky new apartments for young professionals, with the communal areas decked out in atmospheric sepia-tinted photographs of when it was a working building, complete with compulsory cobbled streets, wooden hand-carts, men with cloth caps and moustaches, women with clogs and shawls, children with a skipping rope, the whole scene bathed in the glow of gas lamps, shrouded in fog, smoke rising from rows of chimneys, while inside, the conversions will be equipped with every contemporary convenience, under-floor heating, fitted kitchens, designer bathrooms, cheek-by-jowl with tastefully restored original features, such as sanded bare floorboards, exposed and pointed brickworks, cast iron joists. Not that she has anything against this. She'd much rather see these magnificent old buildings be given a new life, re-imagined and reborn, rather than being demolished, which so many have been. She'd live in one herself if she could afford it. Not that she ever will. Nor is she discontented in the terraced house on Albion Street in Fallowfield, next to Platt Fields, that once belonged to her parents, but which has now passed down to her.

She is still musing on this matter of inheritance when she is assailed by Samira, who is gushing with gratitude. "It's just been terrific working with you," she is saying. She's "simply learned so much." She doesn't know how she "can ever thank" her, especially for "the introduction to Robina," who has invited her "to drop in for a chat," as soon as she's "finished with *Time Team*", which is something she's hoping "to go back to in the autumn," or "maybe next spring." They'll "let me know," she says, "as soon as they know themselves." Then she laughs. In the meantime she must "see what else pops up."

Grace smiles. The life of a freelancer. She never had to navigate such uncertain waters, being invited to join Mike Nevell's team even before she graduated. It was easier back then, more straightforward. She wonders how she would have managed, whether she could have so successfully embraced the reality of the modern portfolio career, as Samira so clearly does. Who knows what opportunities she may have missed as a consequence? The roads not travelled. On reflection, she thinks she would probably have made a good fist of it. At least Samira doesn't have to face the same prejudices of being one of very few women in a predominantly man's world as she had to when she was her age. She contemplates these little victories like stepping stones, which now younger women like Samira can follow – if they choose to. Somehow Grace imagines that Samira will succeed in forging her own path, one that has already led her from Ethiopia to Manchester, from Addis Ababa to Angel Meadow.

She wishes her *bon voyage* and watches her walk down Miller Street. By the boarded up entrance to the Tobacco Factory she sees Samira pause. She is talking to someone. It is a homeless woman asking for change. Instead of walking on by in awkward embarrassment, she has stopped. She is fishing in her purse for a pound coin. She is handing over what's left of her coffee. The homeless woman murmurs something that Samira can't catch. She leans in closer so that she can hear what she's saying. She listens. She nods. Then she turns and waves to Grace. A scrap of starlings skitters overhead. Grace looks up to follow their course, the way they all change direction at once, without any single bird appearing to lead, as if they are all hard-wired to work as one, in pursuit of food and shelter. The late afternoon sun flecks their black wings with iridescent blues and greens.

When Grace looks back, neither Samira nor the woman is anywhere to be seen.

*

2020

The two years Petros spent at Property Centric were not entirely wasted. He'd watched and he'd listened. And he'd learned. He saw how they took over what was little more than a red-light area of appalling squalor and degradation, and rebranded it, turning it into 'Picadilly East', with its cobbled, canal-side walkways and private courtyards planted with shrubs and hanging baskets, the bricked-up railway arches now opened up as bars and florists.

There were casualties, of course. Some of those mills had been home to artists' studios – Crusader Mill and Phoenix Mill – who had had to make way when the cranes and bulldozers arrived. But artists will always find somewhere. Take *Rogue*, for instance. They'd been the driving force behind the creative hub at Crusader Mill, but they'd quickly found new, better premises in the fifty-seven and a half thousand square feet of the old Victorian Varna Street Primary School in Openshaw, taking most of their stable of eighty-five artists with them.

"Hi," says Petros, extending his hand to the young couple snapping shut their mobiles. But just before he can greet them, he feels a tug on his jacket sleeve. He turns round. A wretched homeless woman, who he had not noticed before, is gripping him sharply by the wrist. "Any spare change?" she asks.

Petros looks down at her. Now that he comes to look at her more closely. He'd assumed she was old, but now he realises she could be any age. Maybe younger than *he* is, even. It's difficult to be sure. Life on the streets has given her a worn-out, weathered appearance, like the pupa of a moth stuck to a piece of rusted iron railing. He sees what might be the tattoo of a pair of angel's wings scratched into her shoulder.

"Here," he says, thrusting a ten pound note into her fist. "Now go and find yourself a different pitch," he adds, more roughly than he intends. She smiles. Her eyes now seem ageless. Like a lost child. She shuffles painfully to her feet. She is muttering what sound like incantations under her breath.

" *'And after these things I saw four angels standing on the four corners of the earth, holding back the four winds of the world, that the wind should not blow on the earth, nor on the sea, nor on any tree. And I saw another angel ascending from the east, having the seal of the living God. And she cried with a loud voice to the four angels, to whom it was given to hurt the earth and the sea, saying, 'Hurt not the earth, neither the sea, nor the trees, till we have sealed the servants of our God in their foreheads'."*

Petros pays her no heed. He turns his attention back to the advancing couple, who appear not to have registered the raving woman at all.

"Welcome to the Tobacco Factory," he says, surreptitiously removing the piece of chewing gum from his mouth behind the ubiquitous face mask, and extending his hand towards them once more. At the last moment he remembers to retract and replace it with the requisite elbow-bump, which is the *de rigeur* opening gambit of choice these days when conducting any kind of business venture. Damn this virus, he thinks, but then hastily dismisses the thought. House prices have been largely unaffected by Covid. If anything, they've continued to rise. At a time when the world feels trapped by lockdown, what better antidote than to change the setting of the gaol? What with the government's most generous cut in that pesky stamp duty, the property market is booming.

"Welcome," he says again, more brightly this time, accompanied by the obligatory fist pump, "to Angel Meadow, to the Northern Gateway, to your new home."

*

"Someone looks pleased with themselves."

Petros stops in his tracks. He recognises the voice and looks around. It's Chloe. She's waving to him from across the street.

"Oh," he says, momentarily flustered, "hi. I didn't see you."

"I know," she says. "You had this big grin across your face. That's not your usual expression when you see me. Usually you try to avoid me."

"Not true. I just…"

"Look the other way? Cross to the other side?"

"No, I…"

"You've an excuse now, though, haven't you? Now that we're all wearing these things..." She briefly pulls down the mask from her face before quickly replacing it. "Where's yours by the way?"

"Oh, I..."

"You're not immune, you know?"

"No, I..."

"What?"

"I forgot, that's all."

"Why's that then?"

"I was distracted."

"At the thought of meeting me?"

"Hardly."

"Charming."

"I mean, I didn't know I was going to run into you."

"Or I you. But see..." She indicates her mask once more. "I came prepared."

"Like a good Girl Guide."

"Actually no. I was a Scout."

"How come?"

"Girls were first allowed to join the Venture Scouts when they turned sixteen in 1976..."

"Really?" He is smiling now. This is typical Chloe.

"This was then extended to all age groups in 1991."

"Was it?"

"But it was only optional. It didn't become compulsory till 2007."

"The Last Bastion of the Male Only Preserve."

"Which is when I joined. I was thirteen."

"I never joined. Though I might have if I'd known there'd be girls."

"Even girls like me?"

"Dyb dyb dyb."

"Dob dob dob."

"*Scouting for Girls.*"

"*The Trouble with Boys.*"

"*This Ain't A Love Song.*"

"*Everybody Wants To Be On TV.*"

"You already are."

"On and off."

"Like these face masks."

"Put yours back on, then let's go and have a coffee, shall we?"

Petros instinctively checks his phone. Chloe raises her eyes.

"If you've got time."

"I've got time. It's just…"

"What?"

"Are you sure you want to?"

"I wouldn't have said."

"You might be just being polite."

"I'm never polite."

Their eyes smile at each other above their masks, his a plain white, hers all black with the words *'I Can't Breathe'* emblazoned in white across it.

"Black Lives Matter," he says.

"They do."

"I thought *all* lives did."

"Don't be naïve, Petros."

They're standing at New Cross, at the junction of Swan Street with Great Ancoats Street and Tib Street with Oldham Road.

"There's a place just near here," says Chloe, all brisk and business-like now. "Follow me."

"In all things."

"At exactly two metres distant."

Laughing, she ducks left into Luna Street, right into Henry Street, left into Blossom Street, right again into Cotton Street, then sharp left into Hood Street.

"Here we are," she says and gestures grandly towards a sign which reads, *'The Colony'*.

Petros nods. He's passed the place before but never been inside. He recognises the sign. *The Colony*. He's seen it somewhere else.

As if reading his mind, Chloe says, "There are three of them. One on Aytoun Street, another further down Great Ancoats Street, and this one, which I prefer. It's more tucked away, so you can usually find a space."

These creative hubs are springing up all over the city, especially here in the Northern Quarter. Ideal for hot-desking, networking. Petros tends to avoid them. He distrusts them. They're far too arty for his tastes. He's not surprised Chloe uses them. He prefers the old city pubs to conduct his business – *The Sawyers Arms, The Britons Protection*. He finds them more authentic. But since lockdown their atmosphere has changed. More and more people are uncomfortable about venturing inside them. He's known for some time he needs to find a new base. Somewhere like this might be the answer.

Chloe can see what he's thinking and smiles.

"The one at Aytoun Street, nearer to Piccadilly, is probably more to your taste."

"Oh?"

"More corporate."

He shakes his head. She always has been able to read him like a book.

"But we're here now, so you'll have to make the best of it. It's pissing it down outside now. We got here just in time. I take it you'll have a flat white?"

Before he can answer, she has already tapped their order into her phone and removed her mask.

"So," she says, "are you going to tell me what you were looking so pleased about that you almost walked straight past me?"

He grins and looks around. Although he's never been here before, nothing about its ambience surprises him. The usual exposed bare brick juxtaposed with steel joists and pillars. It could almost be one of his own conversions. On one of these pillars a tasteful sign in an old typewriter font – New Courier, if he were to hazard a guess – informs him of the building's history.

```
'Jactin House. Built in 1881, formerly a
place to stay for local mill workers during
the   Industrial   Revolution.   Completely
refurbished as part of our growing Colony,
2016.'
```

"Why 'Colony'?" he asks.

"You tell me."

"Either we're all of us busy bees loyally working away at Her Majesty's pleasure…"

"For the common good…."

"Or we're all part of some brave new world…"

"But as what? Are we the colonised or the colonising…?"

"Or maybe just merchants, peddling our wares between the two."

"And what wares might those be?"

"Dreams."

"You with your properties…"

"And you with your twenty-four hour news…"

They both laugh as their coffees arrive, accompanied by two glasses of iced water.

"This is like old times," smiles Petros.

"What would Clive make of it?"

"Oh, he'd wring his hands and hang his head, no doubt."

"But secretly he'd be proud of us."

"Do you think so?"

"Yes. I do."

They pause, remembering. Petros looks back towards the sign on the pillar.

```
'Overlooking the Cutting Room Square, Jactin
House is home to a new breed of productive
pioneers…'
```

"Is that what we are?" says Petros. "A new breed of pioneer."

"No, I don't think so. We're a very old breed. We just wear different clothes."

"Which are no longer made in buildings like these."

"No."

She picks up her phone once more and prepares to pay the bill.

"Here," says Petros. "Let me. Text it across. I've just closed a particularly lucrative deal. I reckon I'm good for a couple of coffees."

"I was wondering why you were channelling the Cheshire Cat."

"Though it doesn't feel quite the same when you can't shake hands on it. A fist pump just doesn't cut it. I need to look a person in the eye." He holds Chloe's gaze as he says this.

"In China," she says, not looking away, "we generally don't shake hands. But if we do, as a sign of respect, we lower our eyes." After a few moments she does so.

Petros looks down too, then pays the bill on his phone.

"Beware Greeks bearing gifts," he jokes.

"Should I?" she says.

"What?"

"Be wary of you?"

He laughs. "What's there to be wary of? I'm an open book."

"Yes," she says. "You are."

She smiles.

He smiles back.

Neither speaks for a long time.

Petros is on the point of saying something that has been on his mind for years when Chloe's phone pings on the table between them. She snatches it up, frowns as she checks the message that has just arrived, then grins.

"Sorry," she says. "Got to dash."

"Where?"

"Broadhurst House. Andy Burnham's just called a press conference. It's showdown time with Boris, I reckon. We must do this again some time. See ya." And she is gone. Petros feels himself momentarily caught up in her whirlwind vortex but then drops to the earth with a thud. The quarter of a million pound deal he closed less than an hour ago seems hollow and meaningless.

Just as he is about to leave the now-deserted Colony, he feels his own phone buzz and vibrate. He clicks it open. It's a message from Chloe.

"Don't be a stranger," it reads.

3

WALKING THE TIGHTROPE

2018 – 2019 – 2017 – 1947 – 2017 – 2013 – 2017 – 2019

2018

Eighteen months earlier, one of the *Rogue* artists not relocating from Crusader Mill to Varna Primary School is Molly. After the success of her *Thin Blue Line* installation at *The Etihad* she had needed her own studio. Up until then she had managed to work out of her and Michael's flat in Little Lagos on Moston Lane in Harpurhey, but now she needed more space. She realised that the kind of conceptual work she desired to make required it, and, once they had moved in with her grandmother Nadia in Patricroft and Blessing had started to walk and was into everything, she knew she needed to try and keep her work life and her home life more separate. The studio space at *Rogue* was perfect, and, being centrally located near Piccadilly, was commutable by tram.

"Take it," her grandmother had said. "I'll look after Blessing."

For a year this arrangement had worked perfectly. But then along had come Property Centric with an offer to buy up the whole mill for redevelopment. It was an offer *Rogue* could simply not match. When the Varna School in Openshaw became available, with the added attraction of a funding partnership with the local authority, *Rogue* did not have to think twice. All their existing artists were given first refusal on equivalent space in the new studios, Molly included, but Openshaw was twice the distance and the commute would be simply too much, and so she had turned them down.

"Not to worry," said Nadine. "We've plenty of space here. We can turn Ishtar's old room into a studio for you."

Ishtar. Esther. Molly's great grandmother, who had died long before she, Molly, was born, but whose presence was everywhere still. She fingered the white *qurqash* tied around her head. That had been hers too, given to her by Nadia to wear at her first installation, and which she had worn many times since. She traced the pattern of moths caught up in the weft, alighting upon laurel leaves.

"Thank you," she said, "but only till I can find somewhere else. Somewhere close by."

She did not have to wait too long. It was Michael who found it. One Sunday afternoon, after he had returned from cycling along the recently-opened Salford Trail with Blessing strapped into her special seat just behind him, he dropped the leaflet he had picked up while he'd been out onto the kitchen table where Molly and Nadia were preparing the supper.

Last Remaining Artist's Studio Available

**Islington Mill
1 James Street
Salford**

Call for more details or pay us a visit

"It's only four miles away," said Michael. "Less than half an hour's cycle ride."

Nadia and Molly shared a look.

"Sounds perfect," said Nadia. "Why don't you take a look?"

"I think I will," said Molly. "What do you think, Poppet?" she added, picking up Blessing in her arms, who rewarded her with the broadest of smiles.

Later, after putting Blessing to bed and waiting with her till she finally fell asleep, Molly checked out the website.

'We have worked with more than five thousand artists from thirty-five countries across six continents,' it read. *'We are home to fifty small businesses. Might you be another?'*

"Look at the size of the studios," exclaimed Michael. "You could really spread yourself out there. What's the rent like?"

"Reasonable," said Molly. "Only about three quarters of what I was paying *Rogue*."

"And more square footage."

"And closer to home."

"Sounds like a win-win."

"Here. Look. What do you think?"

She passed her laptop across to Michael, anxious for his reaction. She did not have to wait long.

"Wow!" he said. "It's perfect."

'Whilst being firmly rooted in Salford, we see the importance of going beyond our walls, reaching out to form creative links with organisations from across the world.'

But that was before Covid. After which the gates would be resolutely closed, locked and bolted, keeping the world away.

*

2019

But that was all in the future. Less than two weeks after first checking out their website, Molly had moved in.

Now, each day, she cycles the four and a half miles there and back along Section 8 of the Salford Trail from Barton Bridge to Media City. She begins by Pocket Park, a patch of green from where she has a clear view of the Ship Canal, the Swing Aqueduct and Road Bridge. She cycles along Barton Lane, underneath the Bridgewater Canal, passing *The King's Head*, with its sneering portrait of Charles II, looking supercilious rather than merry – perhaps he has a whiff of the nearby sewage farm assailing his nostrils – in the direction of Eccles, before swinging left into Grand Union Way and then right into Havenscroft Avenue. She wonders whatever must have happened to the original croft that provided such a haven, and from what? Another left turn into Caldon Close takes her directly alongside the canal, where she skirts the nearby Lankro Way until she reaches the Coronet Flour Mill beside the hydraulic Centenary Bridge and its graceful sister, the Lowry, which arches across the water towards the Imperial War Museum. Every time she passes this she recalls to herself that that is where her present journey first began – not just this cycle route that she now takes daily, but her pathway as an artist. It was there, in the Imperial War Museum, where she had first researched the visit of King Amanullah of Afghanistan to Manchester some ninety years before, how her great-grandfather, Hejaz, had travelled along the canal to meet him, only to be publicly humiliated as he flung himself in front of the King, somehow finding himself in possession of a lump of coal hewn by the King from the new seam at Bradford Colliery; how, forty years later, his son, Sol, Molly's grandfather, had recreated that same journey by foot in order to try and retrieve both his father's and his own sense of who he was, as well as reclaiming the piece of coal too, only to be thwarted at the last moment by the pit's untimely closure, and how ten years after that he had captured that whole glorious failure with a mural conceived on an immense scale, which he had fastened, with the help of his tutor, the photographer George Wright, to the walls of the then abandoned Pomona Docks, only for this too to be smashed and broken up by Peel Holdings as they laid waste to the site, all of it gone, save for one piece of wood, a fragment of an old piece of skirting board, which Molly quite literally stumbled across while in search of the lost mural, whose paint had all but flaked off, but of which enough survived for her to make out the merest trace of a small child holding out an umbrella to a taller man. That child was Jenna, Molly's mother, and the man was Sol, Jenna's father and Molly's grandfather, who had allowed Jenna to paint this final piece of the jigsaw, which Molly had rescued and which now hung on the wall above where her own daughter, Blessing, slept.

Now Molly finds herself recreating a part of that same journey herself, following the line, the thin blue line of the draughtsman's pencil marked out by Hejaz on a map of Manchester's waterways, which had served as a guide to Sol and as an inspiration to her own first installation the previous year. It is another, more fundamental reason why the decision to rent a studio in Islington Mill seems so right.

At Salford Quays she passes between the new gleaming BBC offices at Media City and the Blue Peter Garden till she reaches the bridge across the Mariner's Canal, which links the

Erie and Ontario Basins, from where she leaves the Canal and heads north-east along Ordsall Lane, which, in less than ten minutes, brings her to the entrance of Islington Mill.

Built in 1823 by the self-taught architect David Bellhouse, (who was also responsible for Manchester's Portico Library and its first town hall on King Street, later dismantled and rebuilt at Heaton Park), by 1900 it had become a *doubling*, as opposed to a *spinning* mill. Doubling, Molly learns, is a textile term for combining. It can be used in various ways. During the carding, several types of roving – the long, narrow bundles of fibre produced by spinning yarn from raw cotton – are doubled together to remove variations in thickness. After spinning, yarn can be doubled for many reasons. It might be doubled to create warp for weaving, or make cotton for lace. Sometimes it is used for embroidery and other sewing threads. Two threads of spun cotton are twisted together, and then three of these doubles are braided into a cable, which is subsequently mercerised, flamed and then wound onto a bobbin, having been stiffened into a fine, almost translucent silk-like lustre, reminiscent of parchment. Until the Mill finally closed in 1960, Islington specialised in producing an extra-strong nine-cord yarn. To produce the necessary rovings they followed a four-way process. First came the willowing, where the fibres were stretched and loosened. Next came the lapping, in which all the dust was removed to form a flat sheet, or 'lap', of teased fibres. This was followed by the carding, which combed the tangled lap into a thick rope, or 'sliver', half an inch in diameter, the removal of the excess shorter fibres creating a stronger, smoother yarn, known as the 'tow'. The machines they used for this stage at Islington consisted of one large roller, surrounded by several smaller ones. All of these rollers were covered in small iron teeth, which were spaced progressively closer together as the cotton progressed through them, so that it left the machine in the form of these 'tows'. Finally, in what was called 'drawing', four of these tows were combined into one, having first been evened out for greater consistency. They were then separated into rovings, or 'slubbings', as they were more frequently called. It was these slubbings that were then used for spinning. Each roving was about the width of a pencil. They were collected in a drum, from where they proceeded to the slubbing frame, which added twist, before being wound onto large bobbins, using a doubling winding frame not dissimilar to Arkwright's original water frame, through a series of rollers, a spindle and a flyer. At Islington they adopted the alternative 'twiner' method. This required a modified spinning mule and was chiefly used for the doubling of high quality warp thread, dependent on keeping the tension correct while feeding the produced thread evenly and tightly through flangeless paper tubes.

Molly discovers all this in her first weeks in the studio. She finds scraps of paper with old diagrams marking out the flow of cotton around the vast floors on which the different machines would once have stood. She imagines she hears the echoes of the shuttles flying across the looms in the rattle of the ill-fitting windows in her studio. She conjures the faces and voices of the long gone spinners and weavers like ghosts out of the air. She sees them turning with the dust motes in the diagonal shafts of light that slice the now-deserted, vaulted machine rooms. And it gives her an idea.

Downstairs, just inside the Mill's entrance, she starts up a conversation with the young woman who works on Reception. Behind her desk, hung on the stone wall, is a giant-sized framed print of one of Islington's most famous alumni – The Ting Tings, who began their career there in one of the basement studios. Jules de Martino and Katie White, whose helmet of artfully dishevelled blonde hair and short skirt, so reminiscent of Debbie Harry, is self-consciously mirrored by the young receptionist, who, Molly finds, looks strangely familiar.

"Do I know you?" she asks one evening just before she is leaving for the day. "Have we met before somewhere?"

The receptionist smiles in a demurely bashful, cat-like way. "I was at MMU," she says, looking away. "You probably don't remember me. Different year, different course. I'm Lorelei. Lorrie."

"Of course I remember. But we've not seen each other since….when?"

"The night of the Stone Roses concert in Heaton Park."

"Really? Has it been so long? I guess it must be. How are you?"

"I'm fine, thanks."

"So Lorrie is short for Lorelei? I'd no idea."

"After one of my grandmas."

"One of the Rhine Maidens?"

"Actually, that's not so far from the truth. She was part of an all-female circus troupe, who performed a kind of water ballet to Wagner's *Lament*, while suspended from a trapeze."

"It sounds amazing. Did you ever see her?"

"Unfortunately not. I've seen photos, though. There were three of them. They were dressed like mermaids, with flesh-coloured body stockings, and long, fake hair covering their tits."

"It sounds very daring."

"It was."

"Do you take after her?"

"I don't really know. I like dressing up."

Molly regards her more closely and can see that this is so. Today she has quite self-consciously made herself up to look like Uma Thurman in *Pulp Fiction*, complete with black wig.

"I used to dress like *that*," she says, pointing to the photo of Katie White from The Ting Tings on the wall behind her.

"Really?" says Molly, her eyes lighting up. "I came here to see them once about ten years ago."

"Me too."

"I thought they were great. Mainly to piss off my mum, who thought they were rubbish. She thinks all music stopped in the 80s. She was always going on about *The Haçienda* and the bands that played there – she still does."

The two young women laugh companionably with one another.

"I might dress up as that other Lorelei next week."

Molly raises a quizzical eyebrow.

"You know – Marilyn Monroe's character in *Gentlemen Prefer Blondes*."

"I haven't seen it."

"You could be Jane Russell. Then we could both sing '*We're Just Two Little Girls from Little Rock…*' "

"I… er – don't think that's quite my scene."

Lorrie shrugs. "Fair enough."

"Do you still see any of the others?"

"You mean Chloe, Petros and Khav?"

Molly nods.

"Chloe occasionally. She's the best of us at keeping in touch. Khav not so much. Petros not at all. You?"

"I see Khav quite often. You know she's at the Arts Council now?"

"Yes, I'd heard."

"She's a keen supporter of my work. I couldn't do half of what I do without her."

"That's great."

"Yes, it is. She's really found her niche, I think."

Molly heads for the door. Lorrie watches her.

"Why did you change your name?" she calls out suddenly towards her retreating back.

"I got married."

"No, I don't mean that. Congratulations by the way."

"Thanks."

"I mean – Wahid…?"

Molly halts, turns, then walks back.

"My great-great-grandfather – Yasser – who was the first of us to come here – from Yemen – when he arrived, his name was anglicised. I thought it was time to reclaim it."

"Yes. I see."

There is an awkward pause. Molly can tell that there's something else Lorrie wishes to say, so she waits to see if she will.

"Actually," she begins, I *have* seen you since Heaton Park. Once.

"I'm sorry. I don't remember..."

"My hair was blue at the time, if that helps at all."

Molly shrugs, then shakes her head.

"I wore it blue in honour of your installation. *The Thin Blue Line*."

Molly now frowns. This girl is seriously weird.

"There's no reason why you should remember me," continues Lorrie, rolling a pencil between the fingers of her left hand. "There were so many of us."

Realisation dawns on Molly's face.

"Oh – I see… Were you…?"

"One of the volunteers, yes. I unwound one of the blue tapes of cotton along one of the Metro stations."

"Which one?"

"Abraham Moss."

Molly nods. "Well – thank you. I didn't travel that line myself, so I wouldn't have seen you. Michael organised all of that…"

"But then I travelled in to *The Etihad* the next day to see *you*."

Molly spreads her hands. "There were thousands there that day, so…"

"I know. I couldn't get near you. I thought you were... magnificent. So brave."

Molly says nothing. She hadn't felt especially brave at the time. It was simply something she had to do, as a way of honouring her grandfather, tracing a line that began who knew where, but which somehow had stretched down to her, and a realisation that now it was *her* turn.

"I stayed till everyone had gone," continues Lorrie. "The cairn that you'd built with all those pieces of coal had been knocked down and scattered to the four winds. Crows had gathered to pick through the litter left by the crowds. The place seemed full of ghosts. It started to grow dark. I decided to come back early the next morning and try to collect all the pieces of coal and build the cairn back up again. But when I got there, someone had beaten me to it. It was all back in place, neatly stacked and shining. I looked around, to see who might have done it, but there was nobody there."

"Well – it wasn't me. But thank you for the thought."

"You're welcome."

Molly pauses. She really wants to leave but there's something about this girl that she finds oddly compelling.

"I did wonder," she says falteringly, "if you knew whether any textile artists were using any of the studios just now?"

"Not at the moment," the girl replies, becoming instantly more business-like, "but there've been several during the time I've worked here. I can give you a list of names if you like."

"Thanks. That'd be great."

"Any particular reason?"

"Actually..." says Molly slowly, wondering whether to answer this strange girl or not, before finally deciding that she will. Why shouldn't she? She's only trying to be helpful after all. "I'm looking for a loom."

*

After Molly has gone, Lorrie straightens her desk. A place for everything and everything in its place. That's how she likes it. Having first run a wet wipe along its stem and then made sure that its ball-point has been clicked back in, she places the pen that Molly used to sign out as she left back where it belongs, in a glass jar along with five others. Six is a good number for pens, she believes. The way they fan out symmetrically gives a most pleasing effect. From time to time she experiments with colour – silver, black, yellow, clear – the important thing being that they are all the same. Currently they are white, which has not been a success, for they attract smears far too easily. She shan't be ordering this batch again, but they were on offer, and she has to be mindful, always, of keeping down costs. The Mill has to watch every penny. That's what Bill says. Bill Campbell, Islington's Founder and Co-Director. He's great. That's what Lorrie thinks. Or Lorelei, as Bill calls her sometimes. Apart from her family, he's the only person who calls her that. Hardly surprising – it's a bit of a mouthful. She was Lol at uni. She's Lorrie here.

"I'm putting you in charge of stationery, Lorelei," says Bill to her one day. "I reckon you've an eye for that. I'm giving you a completely free hand – you know what our house style is like – just so long as you stick to the budget."

And she has. They may get support from the Arts Council, as well as the local authority, but for the most part they rely on the rent the artists pay for their studios.

"And I don't want to put that up," says Bill, "except as a last resort. That's why we're here. To support the artists and help them make the best work they can. And we all of us have a part to play in that," he adds.

Lorrie has taken those words to heart, and she knows that her efforts haven't gone unnoticed. Having sorted out the jar of pens, she now turns her attention to the various flyers in front of her, advertising future shows by the various different artists.

She makes sure that each pile is neatly aligned with the one next to it, that each stack is of the same height, and that each is in parallel with the edge of the desk. Then she checks to see who's in today. She keeps meticulous records of each artist's schedule. She knows which days each is in the building, and which times each prefers to work – some like to come in early in the morning, while others prefer not to show till after sundown and work through the night. She knows what each of them is working on, whether they're photographers, painters, ceramicists, musicians; poets, choreographers, graffiti or conceptual artists – like Molly, who'll fit right in. Lorrie is certain of that. She has a feel for which ones will and which ones won't.

When she first started out here at Islington Mill, she saw the position as just a stop gap. Receptionist. That was her official job title. She was straight out of uni, and she thought, well – at least it's in the same world, who knows what opportunities might open up for her? That was six years ago, and she's still here. The front desk is still her domain, but she's no longer called the receptionist. She's the Studio Manager now. And a good one.

"I don't know what we'd do without you," says Bill. "We should think about giving you a raise." She'd been pleased when he said that. Flattered. Valued. Now, her opinions are sought, her input appreciated. She is even allowed to curate some of the group shows, when several artists show their work collaboratively...

"Have you ever thought about being a producer?" Bill had said to her one day.

She had, but a nagging thought troubled her. What was it they said? 'Those who can, do. Those who can't, produce.' She'd always secretly harboured being an artist in her own right. The trouble was, she could never settle on what it was she wanted to focus on. But now that was starting to change. An idea had begun to form. And so she had gone to Bill one day and said, "You know that raise you mentioned…?"

"Yes," he said. "I wish we could. How about we include it in our next bid to the Arts Council?"

"I've got a better idea," she said.

"Oh?" said Bill, listening more carefully now.

"Why don't you let me have the use of some studio space – for free – when one of them's standing empty for a while. I know everyone's schedules. I can make sure that none of our resident artists are inconvenienced in any way."

"Do you know," he said, "that's not a bad idea."

"Thank you."

"When do you want to start?"

"Right now."

He'd looked at her and smiled. "OK then, Lorelei. I'll leave it to you to organise. What do you have in mind?"

She tapped the side of her nose. "It's a secret," she said. "I'll let you know when I'm ready to share it."

"Great," he said. "I'll look forward to it. Good luck."

That was typical of Bill, so generous, so encouraging. There were no hierarchies at Islington Mill…

That had been six months ago, and Lorrie had slowly been exploring her ideas ever since. She'd got back in touch with Khav, who had encouraged her to apply for a small R&D grant, which she'd got. Now she feels almost ready. She pictures the looks of surprise on the other artists' faces when she invites them along to see her first show and smiles with cat-like pleasure. She goes to the mini fridge at the back of her desk, which she opens to reveal an immaculately stacked shelf of identical yoghurt pots, from which she takes out one, automatically rearranging the row so that it is equal once more, before closing the fridge door. Then, with delicate precision, she peels back the foil lid, picks up her gleaming spoon in which she can always see her constantly changing appearance perfectly reflected back from its sparkling oval, before dipping it into the heart of the yoghurt, which she proceeds to eat slowly from the centre to the rim. Its taste is delicious, right until the last spoonful and the pot has been picked clean.

*

To: molly.wahid@gmail.com
From: studios@islingtonmill.com

Subject: Loom

Date: 17th June 2019

Hi Molly,

It was good to see you again earlier. Welcome to the Islington Mill family.

Please find attached a list of textile artists associated with the Mill, together with their contact details as requested.

If you're still looking for a loom, why not try Helmshore Textile Museum in Rossendale, or The Weaver's Cottage in Rawtenstall. They're both specialists in the field. (Details attached).

Good luck!

Kind regards
Lorrie

Lorelei Zlatan
Studio Manager
Islington Mill

*

At five minutes before six o' clock, Sunanda, Lorrie's replacement for the evening shift, arrives. She's been well-trained. She knows that Lorrie likes to leave on the dot at whatever time her shift ends. Not a minute before, nor a minute after. But not that well-trained. Outside, clearly it's been raining. Without thinking, Sunanda, as soon as she steps in, shakes out her umbrella. Almost at once she realises her error, but it's already too late. A pool of droplets has begun to form on the wooden floor just inside the front door, and before she can even say she's sorry, Lorrie is at her side.

"Don't move," she commands, then proceeds to mop all around where she stands. "Shoes," she says, whereupon Sunanda, like a dog with her head bowed low, removes her shoes one by one and holds them aloft while Lorrie carefully lays a sheet of newspaper at her side, onto which Sunanda can then place the offending articles. "Umbrella," concludes Lorrie, stretching out a marigold-clad hand, into which Sunanda meekly places the still-dripping parapluie. Holding the article away from her at arm's length, almost as if it might be contagious from which she might catch an unpleasant disease, Lorrie pokes it directly back through the front door, where she vigorously shakes it dry, then returns inside, handing the now no-longer-dripping umbrella back to Sunanda, who has remained rooted to the spot.

"Sorry," she says, removing a piece of gum from her mouth.

Within a nanosecond Lorrie is holding out a waste bin towards her, into which Sunanda drops the gum.

"Sorry," she says again.

It reminds Lorrie of when Sunanda first arrived at the Mill a couple of years before…

*

2017

Lorrie looks up at the large old Works Clock, rescued from when Islington was still fully operational as a cotton mill, that hangs behind the desk, next to the framed photograph of The

Ting Tings. 6.01, it reads. Lorrie frowns, then collects her coat and bag and leaves without a further word.

"Sorry," calls out Sunanda forlornly a third time towards Lorrie's retreating back.

Lorrie does not deign to reply. She merely lifts her hand, more of a dismissal than a wave, then steps outside, shutting the door firmly behind her.

It's less than two miles to where she lives and normally she walks. She wears a fitbit on her wrist, which counts and records the number of steps she takes each day. If she doesn't walk home, she won't reach her daily target of twenty thousand steps. But the rain has come on harder now, so by the time she has reached Salford Cathedral, less than three hundred yards away, she is already soaked. She havers, wondering whether she should wait for a bus. Fortunately, one arrives at exactly that moment, making the decision for her. It's the Number 100, heading for Shudehill. She steps aboard and finds herself a seat towards the back. Six minutes later she arrives at Victoria Station, Stop NW, from where she crosses to Stop NP, The Printworks, to pick up the 135 bus towards Bury, which, in just another six minutes, will drop her off at Derby Road, from where it's less than a quarter mile's walk to the home she shares with her extended family.

The 135 is more crowded than the previous bus, and there are no seats available. From where she's forced to stand, she can't help but see what the young man sitting close by her is reading in his newspaper. It's the picture that catches her eye first.

It's a nondescript photograph of a street lined with mobile homes and caravans. Most people would barely give it a second glance. Except that Lorrie would recognise it anywhere. It's the street where she lives.

She looks away, then immediately looks back. There's no mistaking it. She knows every building, every car, every landmark. She feels herself getting hotter and hotter. Her skin prickles. Why is her street in the newspapers? Then she catches sight of her own name. What...? How...? Why...? The next moment the young man gets up – the bus has reached his stop – and he leaves the newspaper behind him on the seat. In an instant Lorrie edges towards it, desperate to pick it up, but how can she? It's been touched by another person's hand. It lies there, crumpled and creased, taunting her, the photograph of her street flashing like a beacon before her. Agonisingly slowly, with the utmost care and concentration, she manages to sidle her way into the seat without touching or disturbing the paper. Taking up as narrow a space as she can, she balances her bag on her knees, flicks open the clasp with her right hand, then lets the thumb and forefinger of her left bore their way inside like a slow motion lunar probe, scarcely breathing, tensing her elbows so that they do not make contact with either the woman sitting beside her or the man standing above her, until finally she reaches what she'd been hoping to find, a pair of hygienist's gloves she always carries with her, in case of emergencies just like this, which she extracts millimetre by millimetre. Once they are clear of the bag, she slips them onto her hands with practised dexterity before picking up the newspaper and folding it neatly at the page she requires.

A year from now, when the coronavirus really begins to take hold, Lorrie will be unperturbed. It will be as if she has been preparing for just such a disaster all her life, which in a way she has. She will completely reorganise the way Islington Mill will operate to ensure it becomes Covid-compliant, and she will do so with an unflustered, clinical relish, remaining utterly calm while others flail and flounder all about her.

But now, she calculates, she has exactly three minutes before she reaches her stop in which to read the article. Breathing more calmly now, she scans it, paragraph by paragraph.

Manchester EveningNews

17th June 2017

THE HIDDEN CHEETHAM HILL NEIGHBOURHOOD WHERE ONLY FAIRGROUND WORKERS ARE ALLOWED TO LIVE

Chloe Chang visits a unique neighbourhood that's reserved exclusively for fairground workers both retired and current

Collingham Street is lined with trucks, trailers, stalls and mobile homes. But there's nothing temporary about this Cheetham Hill neighbourhood. Most residents have lived here for years and many plan to spend the rest of their lives here.

Founded more than 40 years ago, it was created by the Showman's Guild of Great Britain - and it's reserved exclusively for circus and fairground workers, both retired and current.

Built on the Queen's Road tip, a former rubbish dump, and rented out by Manchester Council, most of the 52 homes belong to older retired showmen and their families for whom an itinerant lifestyle has now become more challenging.

It's a close-knit community with a unique shared history.

Retired fairground ride operator, Pavel Zlatan, 89, is in his shed where he builds miniature motorised versions of the real thing. His models of waltzers and roundabouts are works of art worthy of a museum celebrating a bygone era. Every last detail is depicted in intricate paintwork on carved wood, including the cogs and wheels to make them move. He honed his skills building, fixing and managing his own rides on fairgrounds across the north west.

Showing us around sheds piled high with tools, Pavel says he's lived here on Collingham Street for 30 years

"All showmen used to do their own repairs," he says, "but it's all computerised now."

Pavel followed his Polish-Ukrainian father and Mancunian mother into fairground life aged just 14, when he joined Silcock's Travelling Fair & Circus.

"I've never known anything else. We moved around. Leigh, Atherton, Tyldesley, Chorley, Burnley, Blackburn. You name it, we visited it. Folk used to love seeing us, especially in the War years when everyone holidayed at home. Everyone would come out to meet us with jugs of tea and tell us they were glad to see us. 'It must be January,' they'd say, or whatever the month was, 'cos Silcock's are here.' There were no televisions or computers back then, you see. We were the only entertainment. That's changed so much. Now I build fairground models for each of my grandchildren. But I don't think they're that interested."

Traditionally, showmen used lay-bys or found accommodation with sympathetic farmers. But stricter planning and trespass laws led to settlements like these at Collingham Street, and there are now nearly 400 traveller sites across the north-west provided by councils, who charge low, affordable ground rents.

The prevalence of communities like this one is as a result of the need for both a comfortable retirement and a more formal education for the children of showmen and women.

While they might once have been regarded as 'winter quarters', much more time is now spent on sites like these. They have become permanent homes for most.

"I was born in a caravan in 1924"

It certainly suits Krysztof, 83, a former children's ride operator, like his older brother, Pavel, who spent much of his career at Silcock's Fun Fairs. He's also a *bona fide* War hero who took part in the Battle of Britain. As we arrive, Pavel's daughter-in-law Agniewska has just brought his dinner.

Proudly showing off his War medals, he says: "I was born in a caravan in 1924, in Jaroslaw, just east of Krakow, not far from L'viv, just the other side of the border with Ukraine. We got out just in time and came here to Manchester. My parents worked for Silcock's and we travelled all round Lancashire, Blackpool, Belle Vue, lots of places. I was 18 when I got called up, there were lots of us showmen in the forces, and a great many of my friends died."

Afterwards, the father-of-five ran children's rides, just like his parents before him.

Agniewska, 73, lives a few doors down with her husband Vitaly. Retired 12 years ago from their candy floss and toffee apple stall, she blows dust from a box of old photographs. A treasure trove, it tells a fairground family history dating back at least five generations, many of whom had been forced to flee from Nazi persecution in Poland during the thirties. Smiling out from a crumpled black-and-white photo she can be seen standing proudly by her coconut shy.

"It was hard graft," she says. "But worth it."

Stanislaw, 71, who used to run a hook-a-duck stall, is Agniewska's brother-in-law. He lives further down the street.

"There's lots of show people that come from round here. It's all we've all known since we were born. It's changed a lot - the rides have changed, the lifestyle's changed."

Agniewska's husband, Vitaly, is loading a truck. "People here never really retire properly. If you retire you corrode. My uncle retired and he was dead eight months later. We like to keep busy."

Vitaly introduces me to his father-in-law Pavel's wife, Lena, 79, who was a member of *The Rhine Maidens*, an aerial act, who performed acrobatics on trapezes in circuses all around Europe. She worries about the current generation. Lena's grandson, Stanislaw's boy, Milosz, 47, runs a bungee ride in the summer and in winter sells Christmas decorations and Bavarian goods at the German Market in Albert Square, while his daughter, Lorrie, is a Media Studies graduate, now working at Islington Mill Art Studios in Salford. "Soon all of this," says Lena, indicating the framed photographs of *The Rhine Maidens* on the walls of her neatly-furnished mobile home, "will be forgotten. My grandchildren barely notice them."

"That's not true," says granddaughter Lorrie. "But I've never lived the life of my grandparents. Collingham Street's all I've ever known. Even so, I know I'm from a circus family. It goes back nine generations on my mum's side. I'm never allowed to forget it. But for me, it was difficult at school. Friends' attitudes would change when they found out where I lived. It made me question who I was. We do face prejudice and I do think about whether I want my own children, if I ever have any, to grow up with that."

Who knows what the future will bring for the inhabitants of this remarkable community, survivors of a bygone age, as they re-imagine themselves in these changing and uncertain times?

*

Lorrie reaches her stop just as she finishes reading the last sentence. She is seething with rage and indignation. She pushes her way through the melee of standing passengers, still grasping the newspaper tightly in her sanitation-gloved hands, until she reaches the exit doors, which stick and complain as they reluctantly slide open. She feels uncomfortably hot and perspiring. When she steps outside she lets the rain fall upon her face and arms unimpeded, drinking in great gulps of traffic-polluted air. The bus pulls away, the other passengers who have either alighted or got off with her have all dispersed. She stands at the entrance to Collingham Street, but before she goes any further, she takes out her phone and angrily sends a text to Chloe.

"WTF!!!"
Within seconds a reply pings back.
"???"
"I told you those things in confidence. I never expected you to print them."
"What things?"
"*******"
"I only attribute one quote to you."
"Which makes me sound like I'm disowning my family."
"Rubbish. They couldn't be prouder of you."
"You make them appear quaint."
"How?" texts Chloe.
"Like you want people to be sorry for them."
"Not my intention."
"Survivors of a bygone age?"
"They are."
"That's patronising."
"Heroic."
"Fuck off!"

Suddenly the phone rings.
"Let's talk instead of text," says Chloe.
"There's nothing to talk about."

"I think there is."

"Go on then. I'm listening."

"Are you?"

"What?"

"Listening?"

Lorrie says nothing. The silence hangs in the ether between them.

"Well?" she says at last.

"What?" says Chloe.

"I'm listening now."

"Good. Your family love the article."

"They do?"

"They do."

"How do you know?"

"Because I've spoken to them, that's why. I showed them the proof first before I submitted it. They were delighted."

"You didn't show it to me."

"Because it's not about you. It's about them."

"You still quoted me."

"Are you denying you said it?"

"No, but..."

"But what?"

"I thought we were just talking. I didn't know you were working."

"I'm always working."

"So it seems."

"You know that about me."

"I don't know you at all."

"Listen, Lol..."

"Stop calling me that. No one's called me that in years."

"What *do* you want me to call you then?"

Lorrie says nothing. She is contemplating her name. Her names. Lorrie. Lol. Lorelei.

"I don't know," she says at last. She hears Chloe sigh down the line. "Listen," she says again, "I've got to go. It's pissing down. I'm soaked to the skin."

"Go home then," says Chloe kindly. "Get changed. Talk to your family. Then call me back."

She hangs up. Get changed, she thinks, looking at her bedraggled Uma Thurman get-up. Yes, she can do that. It's one thing she's always been good at, getting changed, but who will she be next?

She reaches the mobile home where she lives, runs up the three steps leading to the front door from the street, then pauses. From inside she can hear singing. Evidently her grandmother is having one of her parties. She's renowned for them. Any excuse and she's scurrying round with a few cans of *Żywiec* lager from the *Rodyna Deli* around the corner. To Lorrie's ears they already sound three sheets to the wind. Perhaps they're trying to drown their sorrows after reading Chloe's article. She thinks about turning back round and not going home tonight, but it's raining harder than ever now, and where would she go? Maybe, if she's quick, she can dash through the crowded living space and through to her own room at the back before anyone notices? Taking several deep breaths, she opens the front door and steps inside, where she is met with a fug of cigarette smoke. The windows are all steamed up from the electric heater, which is turned right up, and the contrast with the temperature outside makes her feel she might faint. She lowers her head and makes a determined dash for her bedroom door but her path is blocked. It's her grandfather, Vitaly, who is already benignly drunk and red-faced.

"Here she is," he beams, "*Lorelenka*, the heroine of the hour!"

"*Lorelenka*!" they all cry, tipping their cans once more to their lips.

"Join us for a drink," calls her father, Milosz, tossing her an unopened can. "We're celebrating."

"That's right," agrees Vitaly, placing a bear-like arm around his granddaughter's shivering shoulders. "Thanks to you, we're famous."

"Leave her alone," laughs Lena, her grandmother. "*Mój Boże, Wnuczka*, you look like a drowned rat. Go and put some dry clothes on."

Lorrie disentangles herself from Milosz and Vitaly, and escapes into the sanctuary that is her bedroom. It's a tiny space, only ten feet by eight, but it's hers. Inside all is as it should be, with everything in its place, the small chest of drawers and dress rail above for her clothes, the low table that serves as all-purpose desk and make-up bar. The meticulously aligned, evenly spaced framed posters of her various movie icons – Monroe, Minelli, Madonna – line one wall, while behind her, above her head, is a photo of Rita Hayworth, the famous one, from *Gilda*, the one Tim Robbins used in *The Shawshank Redemption* to cover up the escape tunnel he was digging each night in his prison cell. Lorrie likes to imagine that behind Rita lies a route for her own escape.

She steps out of her wet things, wraps a towel dressing gown around her and darts into the tiny cubicle next to her bedroom, where she takes a long, necessary shower. She turns the temperature up as high as she can stand it and lets the water warm her up completely, until she is surrounded in a miasma of steam. When she's finished, she wraps the dressing gown around her once more, winds a separate towel around her head, to prevent the last of the black dye that she has now washed out of her hair from spilling onto the floor. Then she scoots back to her bedroom and puts on an old T-shirt and jogging pants. Only her family ever see her dressed like this.

In the living room the celebrations are now in full swing. They're singing all the old favourites – *Bogurodzica, Pałacyk*

Michla, Warszawianka, Siekera Motyka, Gaude Mater Polonia, Żeby Polska Była Polska. Lorrie recognises them but she doesn't know them. She can't really speak Polish, apart from a few words and phrases, but she gets the gist. They're all of them songs of yearning for the old country. Her grandmother Lena knocks on her door.

"Come and join us," she urges. "This is your day as much as ours."

"I thought you'd be angry," says Lorrie.

"Why on earth would we think that? We couldn't be more proud of you."

Lorrie says nothing. She doesn't understand how they can possibly think that of her. She herself thinks she has disappointed them, betrayed them even, but they will have none of it.

"Come and join us," says Lena again, popping her head round the door this time. "We're proud of where we come from," she says, "but that doesn't mean we want to go back there. Our home's here now, in Manchester. Come." And she extends her hand towards her, which Lorrie takes. She has always loved her grandmother's hands. The twisted, gnarled fingers look so brittle they might break, the skin as thin as paper, but their grip is like a crow's, fierce and proud.

Lorrie allows herself to be led into the living room, where the singing has progressed to *Hej Sokoly*, to which her father, Milosz, and her aunt, Agniewska, are dancing a slow mazurka, full of love and longing.

"*Hej, tam gdzieś z nad czarnej wody*
Siada na koń kozak młody
Czule żegna sie z dziewczyną
Jeszcze czulej z ojczyzną…"

Lorrie has always liked this one. Milosz used to sing it to her when she was small. She had asked him what it meant, and he had told her with tears in his eyes.

"Lo there, somewhere from above the black waters
A young Cossack mounts his horse
Sadly he parts with his girl
But even more sadly with his homeland..."

And then he had lifted her high above his head and swung her round as he sang her the chorus.

"Hej, hej, hej sokoły
Omijajcie góry lasy, doły.
Dzwoń, dzwoń, dzwoń dzwoneczku,
Mój stepowy skowroneczku..."

Which he tries to do now, but she intercepts him, allowing him instead to dance her round the crowded living room, while the rest of the family, wreathed in smiles and tears, applaud and encourage.

"Hey, hey, hey, falcons
Fly past the mountains, forests and valleys
Ring, ring, ring little bell
My little steppe skylark..."

"We nearly called you that, your mother and I," says Milosz drunkenly, " '*Skowreneczku.*' Our little skylark..."

"I'm glad you didn't," laughs Lorrie. "Lorelei's enough of a mouthful."

"That was your grandmother's name on your mother's side," says Lena.

Here we go, thinks Lorrie, back down Memory Lane. And she's right. Vitaly is already getting out the photograph albums.

"This newspaper article by your friend..." says Pavel.

"She's not really my friend," says Lorrie. "I hardly see her these days."

"Then you should," interjects Stanislaw. "She spoke very warmly of you."

"Did she?" Lorrie is stunned.

"Of course she did," says Milosz, opening up another can of *Żywiec*, which Agniewska niftily takes from him before he can even begin to take a swallow.

"You've had quite enough for one night," she adds, raising a warning finger in that way she has that brooks no argument.

"This newspaper article," says Pavel again, holding it up, "means that we're not forgotten. People remember us. Perhaps those models I make of the old rides have made their mark. Do you still have the one I gave to you, *Kochanie*?"

"Yes," says Lorrie. "Of course." She feels a lump rising in her throat. He's not called her '*Kochanie*' for years. No one has. *Liebchen. Tesoro. Chérie.* Sweetheart.

"Only I never see you with it these days."

"It's in my room," she says. "On my shelf. With my other treasures. I keep it safe."

"Good. But it's a toy. It's meant to be played with."

"She's too old for toys," says Agniewska, tousling her hair.

"She's saving it for when she has children of her own," grins Lena.

Agniewska throws her mother a warning look

"I don't want to break it," says Lorrie.

"Oh," says Pavel, "you don't want to worry about that. It'd soon mend."

"Here we are," says Vitaly, emerging from the back of the cupboard where he has been rummaging these past few minutes. "I knew we had it somewhere."

He triumphantly holds up a reel of 8mm cine-film. He is immediately met with groans of protest, but Lorrie, almost surprising herself, asks, "What is it, Uncle?"

"Home movies," says Milosz. "Of your grandmother."

"Oh," gasps Lorrie, "I've never seen them."

Lena at once takes control. "Vitaly, find the screen. Stanislaw, set up the projector. Agniewska, put the kettle on. Make some *gorąca czekolada*."

Lorrie's eyes widen. *Gorąca czekolada* is a childhood favourite. One and a half cups of milk, half a cup of cream, five ounces of dark chocolate, three ounces of milk chocolate, a tablespoon of corn starch, half a teaspoon of vanilla, topped with rum or brandy, and heated together in a pan. Saved for special occasions. Like birthdays. Or if she had a cold.

Lena catches her look of surprise. "You need it," she says. "You got soaked to the skin earlier."

In a few minutes the whole family is huddled together on the sofa or the floor, sipping their *gorąca czekolada*, watching in rapt silence as the reel of home movies found by Vitaly spools back time, to when the world was a grainy black-and-white, peopled by smiling, jerky marionettes...

*

1947

The film has no sound. Scenes interrupt each other seemingly at random, as if the operator simply switched the camera on and off just as an image caught his attention before quickly losing interest.

"It's true," says Krysztof, who has just woken up after having slept through the singing earlier. "I'd just left the RAF and I decided to stay on. I was very much smitten with your grandmother, Lena, so I followed her here, only to discover she was already spoken for."

"What can I say?" laughs Pavel. "I was younger than you were. And better looking."

"At least you put in a good word for me," says Krysztof, "so I was able to get a job."

"That was me," interrupts Lena. "I felt sorry for you."

"Tell them what you did, *Wujek*," urges Agniewska.

"Whatever they asked me to," says Krysztof. "Jack-of-all-Trades..."

"Master-of-None," chime Pavel, Vitaly and Milosz in unison.

"I'd been an engineer in the Air Force, so whenever anything went wrong with one of the rides..."

"... which was often..."

"I'd be called in to try and fix it. Then I'd help put up the Big Top, rig the lighting, check the trapezes were secure...

"I used to help him with that," throws in Vitaly.

"Luckily for me," winks Agniewska.

"I'd even look after the animals," continues Krysztof, "if there was no one else on hand..."

The film appears to bear this out. Lorrie catches tantalising, fleeting glimpses of different aspects of circus life, both inside and out of the ring, but nothing is ever captured for more than a few seconds.

Krysztof sees her frowning. "It was Mr Barrett who suggested it."

"Who?"

"Norman Barrett," says Pavel.

"The Ringmaster," explains Vitaly.

"And the boss," adds Lena.

"He handed me the cine camera one day and said to me, 'Krysztof, you're a technical man. I expect you know how to operate one of these things. I'd like you to keep a record. Who knows how much longer we'll be able to keep all this going for?' "

"He spoke truer than he knew," recalls Lena.

" 'So – anything you see' he said," continues Krysztof,

" 'anything at all, just record it. But go easy on how much film you use. Make each reel last as long as you can.' Which I did. As you can see."

"Or not," complains Agniewska. "You can't tell who's who, or what's what with all this jumping about."

But you can, thinks Lorrie. As her eye becomes accustomed to the sudden, random cuts from one image to another, she starts to tune into the rhythm of it. It's like looking through a kaleidoscope. You never quite know what you're going to see next, except that it will always surprise and delight.

"Why have you never shown me this before?" she asks.

"We didn't think you'd be interested, *Kaczuszka*," says Lena.

"Oh, but I am…"

"Watch this next part then," says Vitaly. Watch it closely…"

Lorrie turns back to face the screen. A parade of elephants is marching along Deansgate. Astride each one sits a pretty girl, smiling and waving to the crowds lining the city streets. The girls wear flesh-coloured body-stockings so that they appear to be naked, with long, blonde wigs whose flowing, golden tresses cover them strategically. Like the slave girls choreographed by Busby Berkeley in Eddie Cantor's *Roman Scandals*, thinks Lorrie. She loves those thirties musicals – *Gold Diggers, 42nd Street, Footlights Parade* – and their iconic songs – *We're In The Money, I Only Have Eyes For You, Remember My Forgotten Man*…

"Is that …?

"Your other grandmother? Yes. And that's me on the one just behind her…"

Lorrie leans as close to the screen as she can so that her eyes are filled with the grainy image of the woman she's been named for. Lorelei. Her father, Milosz, surreptitiously wipes away a tear.

The picture then switches abruptly to inside the Circus Tent. The same elephants are lined up in the centre. In front of each a bucket of water has been placed. The Ringmaster…

"Norman Barrett?" asks Lorrie.

"The same," answers Lena.

…appears to be calling for volunteers from the audience. A man in an overcoat and trilby reluctantly stands up, urged to do so by his domineering wife.

"Is that you, Uncle?" asks Lorrie.

"The same," answers Vitaly.

"And that's me as his wife," chips in Agniewska. "Before I actually was."

"It's what gave me the idea," grins Pavel.

"But what are you doing in the audience?" asks Lorrie, confused.

"Plants," they answer together.

"Watch," explains Lena, "what happens next."

"The Elephant Barber," announces Vitaly, pointing to his younger self on the screen, where he sits on a stool in front of one of the elephants, while one of the clowns proceeds to cover his face with shaving foam. When he's finished, he steps back. Vitaly mimes that he needs some water to wash off the soap. The clown signals to Lorrie's grandmother Lena, sitting astride the elephant, who gently taps the top of its head, whereupon it places its trunk into the bucket of water before proceeding to squirt water directly at Vitaly's face, rinsing off the soap and knocking him off the stool in a single movement. The audience roars with laughter, while Vitaly pretends to look aggrieved.

"It was always cold," he recalls, "that water. I kept asking for them to make it warmer, but would they listen?"

"Of course not," laughs Agniewska.

"At least you were spared having to shovel up the elephant shit afterwards," moans Krysztof.

Next, the image switches to Krysztof leading a kangaroo into the ring.

"My big moment," he announces.

"Even bigger than shovelling elephant shit?" says Vitaly.

"Even bigger. A genuine *tour de force*."

"Be quiet, you two," scolds Lena.

Lorrie watches as on the screen Krysztof proceeds to tie on a pair of boxing gloves to the kangaroo's paws, which, as soon as they are firmly attached, begins to bounce around the ring, throwing out punches, as if challenging all-comers to a bout.

One of the clowns holds up a placard.

'Ten Shillings To Anyone Who Can Last One Round!'

Nobody is forthcoming until, once again, Vitaly, differently disguised now, with a moustache and a bowler hat, harried again by Agniewska, wearing a headscarf tied like a turban and shaking her rolling pin at him, reluctantly volunteers. No sooner has he stepped into the ring, shaken the clown by the hand, who, with his other hand, rings a bell, than he is immediately pursued by the fiery boxing kangaroo. A second clown trips up poor Vitaly, so that he falls head first into the sawdust. The kangaroo races past him, Vitaly gets to his feet with a sigh of relief, dusts himself down, only to turn back in the opposite direction at exactly the same moment as the kangaroo has completed yet another circuit of the ring, arriving just in time to deliver a knockout blow. While Krysztof leads the bouncing kangaroo away before it can inflict further damage on any other hapless 'volunteers', the two clowns drag a prostrate Vitaly out of the ring, before being chased back into it again by a furious Agniewska with her rolling pin.

The image fades, and, with it, the laughter.

When it returns, it is with a close-up of fountains throwing up cascades of coloured water into the air. All of the family fall silent.

"Now we come to it," whispers Lena, taking Lorrie's fledgling fingers into her own falcon's talons. "The Dancing Waters. Imagine the colours. Reds, greens, blues and golds. Can you picture them?"

"Yes," says Lorrie. "I can."

"The Circus Orchestra would play the opening bars from Wagner's *Lament of the Rhine Maidens*," explains Lena, "before switching to *By A Waterfall*..."

"Sammy Fain and Irving Kahal," says Lorrie before she can help herself.

"...which the audience would whistle along to, while we girls would climb up to the trapezes..."

"...lowered by me," Krysztof reminds her.

"...which would then be raised up into the roof of the tent..."

"...while Pavel and I made sure that the net was in place and secure..."

"...not that we ever had need of it..."

"...but we checked it nevertheless..."

"...and the dancing waters continued to rise and fall in time with the music. Look."

And Lorrie does look. She sees Lena and Lorelei, her two grandmothers, smiling and waving as they ascend skywards, now wearing sparkling swimsuits, glittering with sequins and diamantes."

"They were an iridescent green," says Lena, following Lorrie's gaze, "with gold trim."

"Like Gina Lollabridgida as Lola in *Trapeze*, when she first sees Tony Curtis," whispers Lorrie breathlessly. "Or do I mean Betty Hutton as Holly in *The Greatest Show On Earth* when she falls, literally, for Cornel Wilde?"

"You and your films," says Lena, smiling.

"Sorry. I can't help it."

"Forget about what it reminds you of, just watch what's here in front of you instead. This was real, not make-believe."

Suitably chastened, Lorrie allows the silent, out-of-focus images of her grandmothers, Lena and Lorelei, Queens of the Rhine Maidens, performing their death-defying acrobatics, suspended on the narrowest of horizontal, wooden bars, hanging by just two lengths of locally spun cotton rope, more than forty feet up in the air, smiling throughout. Lorrie watches entranced…

*

2017

Finally the film runs out. Lorrie's grandmother, her namesake, stands before her now, frozen in time, smiling and waving to her directly down the years, until she too fades. The silence inside the mobile home on Collingham Street lingers, broken only by the insistent, rhythmic flapping of the reel of film as it transfers from one spool to another and keeps on flicking round and round, like a bird's wings beating against the bars of a cage. Milosz, his eyes swollen and red, gets up and busies himself elsewhere.

"After Lorelei died," says Lena, "I tried to carry on the act on my own, but it was never the same. For one thing, I was never as good as she was."

"Don't say that, *Kochanie*," says Pavel. "You were just different. We all of us have something we're good at, just us, and nobody else."

He gives his wife a kiss, while Lorrie wonders just what it might be that she will be good at…

One by one the family disperses. Agniewska helps Krysztof down the steps to his own place next door, before heading back with Vitaly to their own home further along the street. While

Milosz covers his now-snoring father, Stanislaw, with a blanket on the sofa. Lorrie helps Lena stack the mugs, glasses and plates in the dishwasher, while Pavel packs away the screen and projector.

After bidding them all "Goodnight," Lorrie retreats once more to the sanctuary of her bedroom, feeling lighter than she has done in years. Her phone vibrates. Chloe has sent her a new text.

"R.U. feeling better?"
"Yes. Thank U."
" 😢 "
"It's OK."
"Check this out…"
She pings across a new emoji.

"A long time ago," texts Lorrie.
"Not so long."
"4 yrs!!"
"The blink of an eye."
" 😊 "
" 👀 "
"Click on this link… 🔊
It's suitably retro, I think xxx"

Lorrie does so. She places her tiny headphones inside her ears, lies back and listens. She recognises it at once. She smiles, remembering…

"What do you see when you turn out the light?
I can't tell you but I know it's mine…"

The years slip by. The walls of her bedroom dissolve and fall away. The music shifts from within the space inside her skull to the full-throated roar of her tutor group leaping as one in the Media Studio, arms joined, backs turned away from the control booth, all of them enthusiastically engaged in doing a *Poznań*, Lorrie included.

> *"We'll get by with a little help from my friends*
> *We're gonna try with a little help from our friends*
> *Yes we'll get by with a little help from our friends*
> *With a little help from our friends..."*

*

2013

Final Presentation # 3: Lorrie

The four friends continue to bounce up and down, singing in time to Ringo and The Beatles. Clive enters the studio, wearily shaking his head, but smiling nevertheless.

CLIVE:
Alright, settle down. Term's not over yet.

STUDENTS:
Shame!

CLIVE:
I agree. We still have another final presentation left.

STUDENTS:
Ooh!

CLIVE:
So are we ready?

STUDENTS:
We've been ready all our lives, Clive!

CLIVE:
Lorrie?

Lorrie gulps, swallows hard, looks up to Tanya in the Control Booth, who signals that she's ready, then nods

STUDENTS: (*counting down*):
 5 – 4 – 3 – 2 – 1…

LORRIE: (*nervously closing the clapperboard*):
 Action.

Instantly the introduction to the song 'Private Life' by Grace Jones crashes into the studio as Lorrie is caught in a tightly focused overhead spotlight, into which she looks up. Emulating the original MTV promo she peels off a mask that is a perfect replica for her own face, so that she is then able to mime in perfect synch with the song's opening lyrics.

LORRIE: (*as Grace Jones*):
 "J'en ai marre with your theatrics…
 Your acting's a drag…
 It's OK on TV cos you can turn it off…"

Lorrie is wearing a dark, hooded cloak, similar to that worn by Grace Jones in the video, which she now wraps around herself, so that she almost disappears inside it. She turns her back on her audience and walks slowly away from them, revealing three white envelopes on the floor.

The song continues.

 "Your private life drama, baby, leave me out
 Your private life drama, baby, leave me out…"

Clearly rehearsed, Chloe, Petros and Khav individually step forward. They pick up in turn one of the envelopes, take out a card from inside it and read what is written on it. The music continues more quietly underneath.

CHLOE:
 'Neoism.' (*She smiles*).
 'Neoism is a parodistic –ism.'

PETROS:
'It refers both to a specific sub-cultural network of artistic performance and media experiment, and, more generally, to a practical underground philosophy.'

KHAV:
'It has created multiple contradicting definitions of itself, quite deliberately, in order to defy categorisation or historicisation.'

CHLOE:
'It operates within collectively shared pseudonyms and identities…'

PETROS:
'…pranks and paradoxes…'

KHAV:
'…plagiarisms and fakes.'

CHLOE:
'The art and science of imaginary solutions.'

PETROS:
'Futurist…'

KHAV:
'Dada-ist…'

ALL THREE:
'Neo-ist…'

The song continues.

LORRIE: (*as Grace Jones*):
"You ask my advice, I say use the door…
But you're still clinging to somebody you deplore…"

Lorrie covers her face with the replica mask once more, before she retreats to the back of the studio. Chloe, Petros and Khav place their cards on the floor in a line along the front of the designated performance space, then move as one towards her, shielding her from general view. They remove the dark cloak and hood and turn it inside out. It is now entirely white.

As the song begins to fade, Chloe, Petros and Khav withdraw to the edges of the studio, from where they each place the tips of their fingers and thumbs together to form a kind of parallelogram, through which narrow beams of white light are directed towards the completely white form of Lorrie.

CHLOE:
'In a very dark chamber, at a round hole…'

PETROS:
'…about one third part of an inch broad…'

KHAV:
'…made in the shut of a window…'

CHLOE:
'I placed a glass prism…'

PETROS:
'…whereby the beam of the sun's light, which came in that hole…'

KHAV:
'…might be refracted upwards…'

CHLOE:
'…towards the opposite wall of the chamber…'

PETROS:
'…and there form…

KHAV:
'…a coloured image of the sun.'

The song has faded completely.
Tanya directs the three beams of thin white light to meet and join in a prism, refracting into a myriad of rainbow colours

onto the white form of Lorrie, who, still concealed behind the white cloak, plays a rapidly rising drum roll.

As this reaches its climax, she throws off the cloak to reveal herself dressed as an American Cheerleader. She wears bright blue leggings, trainers, a red mini-dress and white T-shirt, her blonde hair tied in bunches. Petros takes over from her on the drum, providing a steady rhythm to which she, together with Chloe and Khav, each now sporting pom-poms in their hands, launches into the familiar Toni Basil chant, the three of them performing an ironic cheerleader routine.

LORRIE, CHLOE, KHAV:
"Oh Mickey, you're so fine
You're so fine, you blow my mind
Hey Mickey, Hey Mickey..."

No sooner have they begun, than they toss it all away. Lorrie replaces the bunches in her hair with a jaunty grey cap and holds a microphone above her head in a pose reminiscent of the Statue of Liberty. She freezes. On the screen behind her is projected the opening frame of the YouTube video by The Ting Tings for their song 'That's Not My Name'. Lorrie's pose and costume exactly match those of the lead singer, Katie White.

LORRIE:
Neoism.
The art and science of imaginary solutions.
Ting, Ting.

The sound of a light bulb going off in your brain when you get a new idea.
Ting, Ting.

Cantonese for 'Listen, listen.'
Mandarin for 'an old bandstand.'
Ting, Ting.

Everything old is new again.

Neoism.
The creation of multiple definitions of oneself.
Paradoxes and pranks.
Plagiarisms and fakes.

I'm openly plagiarising Godley & Crème.
10cc. Manchester's finest.
Cry.
Acknowledging their influence.
Channelling their energy.
Ting, Ting.

Music begins. 'That's Not My Name.'

But instead of Katie White upon the screen, it's Lorrie herself, dressed as she is in the studio. Her face is in extreme close-up. She lip-synchs the lyrics. As she does so, her face is replaced, digitally dissolving into a series of other faces, in a clear homage to Godley & Crème's 'Cry'. Each of these faces is a different avatar of Lorrie herself. She transforms completely, from one to the next, all the while mouthing the words.

"Four letter word just to get me along
It's a difficulty and I'm biting my tongue
And I just keep stalling, not keeping together…"

The changes are rapid. Lorrie has meticulously made herself up to resemble as closely as possible her favourite movie icons, then filmed herself, with Tanya's help, one take after another. Marlene Dietrich in 'The Blue Angel'; Vivien Leigh as Scarlett O'Hara; Lauren Bacall in 'To Have & Have Not'; Lana Turner in 'The Postman Always Rings Twice'; Barbara Stanwyck in 'Double Indemnity', raising her foot to the side of her head to reveal the notorious anklet; Veronica Lake, her hair completely covering one eye in 'The Blue Dahlia'; Judy Garland in 'Summer Stock' – 'Sing Hallelujah, Come on, Get Happy' – with top hat, cane and black stockings; Audrey Hepburn in

'Breakfast at Tiffany's'; Kim Novak in 'Vertigo'; Marilyn Monroe in 'The Misfits'.

"Don't want to be a loner
Listen to me, oh no, I never say anything at all
But with nothing to consider they forget my name…"

And still they come. Thick and fast they appear and then vanish before they have barely registered. Now you see them, now you don't. Jane Fonda as Barbarella, Sigourney Weaver as Ellen Ripley, Jennifer Lawrence as Katniss Everdeen, Carrie Fisher as Princess Leia.

"They call me 'Hell', they call me 'Stacey'
They call me 'Her', they call me 'Jane'
They call me 'Quiet Girl'
But I'm a riot
'Mary', 'Jo', 'Lisa'
Always the same…"

Dorothy Dandridge in 'Carmen Jones'; Diana Ross as 'Lady Day'; Meryl Streep in 'The Devil Wears Prada'; Madonna as the 'Material Girl'; Keira Knightley in 'Atonement', wearing that green dress; Olivia Newton-John in the black leather jacket and skin-tight trousers from 'Grease', and Diane Keaton as 'Annie Hall' – well lah-di-dah.

And not just women, but men too. Bob Dylan on 'Highway 61', James Dean in 'Giant', in ten-gallon hat and cowboy boots, and Marlon Brando in 'On The Waterfront'. 'I could've been a contender, I could've been somebody…'

"That's not my name, that's not my name
That's not my name, that's not my name…"

Faster and faster the faces ripple up and down the screen. Lorrie is channelling the game she used to play at Christmas parties, where everyone would draw a hat on a piece of paper, fold it over, then pass it on to the person sitting next to them, and then draw a pair of eyes, before passing it on again, over and over, time after time, then a nose, followed by a mouth, then a chest with arms, then a pair of legs, and finally feet, with or without shoes or boots. When the piece of paper at last got passed back to her, she would unfold it, crease by crease, to reveal the composite figure who collectively everyone had drawn, that was somehow supposed to be her.

As the song builds towards its frenzied climax, the different faces become a blur, indistinguishable one from another, yet each somehow retaining a memory that lingers, permeating the composite.

'E pluribus unum'. Out of many, one.

She thinks of all the many streams and tributaries that creep beneath the city, out of sight, but still there, still crawling, however slowly, like blood through the veins.

Manchester. The confluence of the three rivers.

But there are so many more, culverted and hidden from view, like dirty secrets to be guarded before they can be released, waiting, biding their time, still flowing, till they can meet and join.

> "I miss the catch if they throw me the ball
> I'm the last chick standing up against the wall
>
> And baby can't you see that I'm so desperately
> A standing joker, like a vocal one-liner
> Instead of sing-along, this song is monotone
>
> That's not my name…
> That's not my name…

That's not my name…"

As the song repeats the last line over and over again, Lorrie covers the final composite face with the blank mask that is her own face, plain, unadorned, without make-up, beneath which all the other faces disappear.

She appears to be writing something. When she has finished she holds up a slip of paper to the camera, in front of her.

'Fecissemus patriam diversis de gentibus unam.'
From differing peoples we shall make one homeland.

Silence. Lights return in the studio. But Lorrie is nowhere to be seen. She has slipped out while everyone's attention has been on the screen.

CLIVE:
Where *is* she? I wanted to congratulate her.

KHAV:
She's channelling Garbo, yeah? I wanna be alone, innit?

At that precise moment each of the students receives a simultaneous text message.

LORRIE:
Thank U, Guys. I couldn't have done it without you. xxx

♥♥♥♥♥♥♥♥♥♥
*

Emerging from the darkness of the black box that is the Media Department's TV Studio, Lorrie is blinded by the sudden, contrasting fierceness of the light. As she walks through the campus, the people around her loom towards her, their torsos stretching and elongating like aliens in a mirage, as if none of them are real. She puts on a pair of dark glasses to allow her eyes to adjust. Gradually the figures begin to assume more recognisable forms, and she settles into a more comfortable rhythm. Devoid of all make-up and disguise, she feels herself disappearing in the anonymity of the noonday crowds. If she is not somebody else, she thinks, who is she? The dark glasses, rather than rendering her mysterious or enigmatic, merely serve to emphasise her sense of non-existence. She imagines the rest of her face being covered completely in a crepe bandage. Like Claude Rains in *The Invisible Man*.

The sun is at its zenith. It shines down on her like the narrow overhead spotlight had done in the studio, but here in the city there is no stepping outside of its beam, or switching it off. It is the hottest part of the day. Manchester is like a crucible, forging its future out of the fire. Perhaps Lorrie will simply melt, leaving nothing behind her but a puddle of water, which, in the heat of the day, will evaporate into air and disappear completely.

Just as she is leaving the campus and stepping out onto Oxford Road from the College Green at All Saints, her attention is caught by someone shouting from the steps of the old *Grosvenor Picture Palace* directly opposite. When it opened in 1913, it was the largest cinema in the city, seating more than a thousand people. It showed its last film in 1968 – *Attack of the Crab Monsters*. How Lorrie wishes she could have seen that! She's rather partial to fifties and sixties monster movies – *The Creature from the Black Lagoon, It Came From Outer Space, Tarantula, The Beast from 20,000 Fathoms* – in which a crudely animated monster, usually as a result of some misguided scientific experiment gone wrong, threatens to wreak havoc and bring about the end of the world – "Is this the end of civilisation as we know it?" – before some square-jawed boffin, aided by a plucky girl in glasses manage to save the day, so that the hero can remove the girl's spectacles and say, "Boy, but you're beautiful."

After 1968 *The Grosvenor*, rather like the rest of the city, fell into decay. It became a snooker club for a time, then a bingo hall, then a pub, before being boarded up for several years. But somehow it survived. Its green and cream faience tiles remained intact, together with the raised torch in white terracotta above its chamfered entrance, and it acquired Grade II listed status. Now it's a trendy student bar called *The Footage*, part of the *Scream* chain, occasionally showing late night screenings of cult classics, such as *The Rocky Horror Picture Show*, which Lorrie had naturally attended. Not, as her friends might have guessed, as Magenta, the French Maid in black stockings and suspenders, nor as Columbia, the Groupie, with her sequined leotard, gold swallow-tailed jacket and spangled top hat, though she was certainly tempted, but as Susan Sarandon's Janet Weiss, in her pink Peter Pan gingham little-girl's frock, complete with puffy white sleeves and collar, white belt with round buckle and matching cardigan, topped off with a white hair slide and a pair of white Mary Janes. Lorrie is always attracted to the idea of metamorphosis, the possibility of transformation and change, so that when Janet casts off this high school façade to uncover the temptress beneath, clad only in shiny silver lurex, Lorrie embraces the reveal with abandon.

"Let's do the Time-Warp again…"

But such thoughts are far from her mind just now, as the woman across the street continues to shout and rave, haranguing everyone, seeing no one.

" *'Instant kama's gonna get you'*," she rages.

She flails her arms about her wildly, lunging towards passers-by, who try to pretend she's not there, turning their faces away from her, stepping over her prostrate legs, crossing to the other side. But Lorrie is drawn towards her. Within her sound and fury, there is reason and logic.

" *'The fire consumes all in its path'*," she warns. " *'How rare the grasses that still remain green'*."

Lorrie has reached her now, and, for a moment, their eyes lock. The woman grabs Lorrie's wrist and grips it hard.

" '*I am purer than you, for I am created of fire, where you are born of dust*'."

"You're hurting," says Lorrie, trying to break free.

Immediately the woman becomes gentle, releasing her hold, and whispering softly to her.

" '*When thou walkest through the fire, thou shalt not be burned. Neither shall the flames kindle upon thee*'."

But then the passion takes hold of her once more, and she wheels away, crying out to anyone who might listen.

"Ting, ting!" she cries. " '*Behold, I bring fire, and, with it, good news, that you may warm yourselves*'."

The woman begins to tear at her clothes. She throws off her coat and flings it to the ground. Lorrie catches sight of an angel tattooed upon her shoulder, before the woman begins to whirl herself around in a Sufi-like frenzy, invoking the Koran, the Bible, the Baghavad Gita, the Guru Granth Sahib.

" '*Blessed is whoever is in the fire and all that is burned by its holy flame*'."

Lorrie tries to step within her orbit, to pin down her arms and bring her to a stop, but the woman's fist catches her full in the face, knocking her to the ground.

"'*And the angel of the Lord appeared in a flame of fire out of the midst of a bush*'."

And still the people pass her by. Nobody tries to intervene.

"'*And the bush burned with fire but was not consumed*'."

Suddenly, without warning, the woman ceases her dance and plunges to the ground. She pulls a whiskey bottle from the pocket of the discarded coat and pours it liberally in a circle around her. Then, before Lorrie can stop her, she takes out a match, lights it, then drops it onto the liquid, which at once bursts into flame, a ring of fire within which the woman falls. Her body twists and arches. Like a scorpion, appearing to try and sting herself, to avoid unnecessary pain and bring about a speedier death. But that is not what happens at all. The body, in heating up so quickly, rapidly dehydrates, provoking a series of sharp, uncontrolled spasmodic jerks. But even *in extremis* the scorpion's sting cannot penetrate the hard shell of the exoskeleton that protects it, and, in the unlikely eventuality of the sting piercing between the separate segments of this shell, scorpions are immune to their own poison. Instead, what happens is that the ring of fire sucks out all the oxygen and the creature suffocates. So, as the woman writhes and jerks involuntarily, she seems to be aware of what is happening to her. She looks directly at Lorrie through the curtain of flames and smiles.

This is more than Lorrie can bear. In a single desperate motion, she picks up the woman's discarded coat and throws it over the fire, stamping out the flames, before dragging the woman clear.

" *'Did I not say'*," she croaks, " *'that thou shalt not be burned. Neither shall the flames kindle upon thee…'* "

By this time, paramedics, alerted by someone from inside *The Footage*, have arrived on the scene, and the woman is carried away. The flames have all been put out, and people are continuing about their daily business once more, as if nothing has happened. Another homeless person has taken the woman's pitch on the steps of the old cinema already. Lorrie drops what change she has into her cup and walks on. She catches sight of herself in the shop window of *On the Eighth Day* and stops. Her hair, face, arms and legs are covered in ash and smoke. Like a penitent. She walks the two miles back from All Saints to Collingham Street like a pilgrim, each familiar landmark she passes a wayside shrine, a station of the cross, on the road towards the Lorelei Rock that is her home, with the words of the woman with the tattoo of an angel still ringing in her ears, rising above the crackling of the flames as Lorrie pulled her free, the last chick standing up against the wall.

" *'Götterdämmerung'*."

A summoning of the twilight, a darkness as thick as the black box TV studio she left behind not half an hour before. With the burning comes renewal.

Ting, ting.

*

2017

Four years later, back in the mobile home on Collingham Street, after the screen and projector have been put away, after the final blurred images of her grandmother, Lena, have dissolved, together with the other three Rhine Maidens, Woglinde, Wellgunde and Flosshilde, rising like mermaids from the dancing waters of Silcock's Circus, up towards the roof of the tent, where, surrounded by a circle of fire, they had soared through the air on the flying trapeze, after all of these have flickered and faded for the last time, Lorrie takes the scrunched up ball of newspaper, which had so enraged her just a few hours before, and carefully smoothes away its folds and creases, until she is at last able to lie it flat. She clears a space on her desk, just in front of her mirror, where she carefully places it, weighting it down with her Record of Achievement folder, in which she also keeps a copy of her degree, a two-one, on top of which she then balances the model of the fairground ride made by her Grandpa Pavel. She turns the handle in the side. At once the ride whirs into life. Round and round it goes, undulating up and down as it continues. Round and round, up and down, until the green and gold stripes painted on its side begin to blur. The Caterpillar…

*

2019

Now, another two years after that, when Sunanda arrives at five minutes before six o'clock, and thoughtlessly allows her umbrella to drip all over the entrance floor, Lorrie does not head out into the rain as she did so crossly two years before. Instead she heads down to the Basement Studio, which she now has free access to in lieu of a raise whenever it's free.

She heads down the iron staircase to it and unlocks the metal doors. It's another windowless black box, and that suits her fine, as does the fact that this is where The Ting Tings gave their first few experimental gigs.

Lorrie gets changed into her studio clothes. Today she's been dressed as Uma Thurman from Pulp Fiction. She cringes at the memory of the awful joke she attempted with Molly earlier in the day. She still gets nervous around new people, and dressing up as someone else helps her cope with this sometimes. But she alters her appearance far less these days. It's like being a member of something like Alcoholics Anonymous. "Hi, my name is Lorrie and I like dressing up as other people." Until today she'd not done that for nearly six weeks, and not for a couple of months before that. Since that day when Chloe had written that article, which at first had made her so mad, but which afterwards she came to realise had been done out of love, she's done it less and less. Though at times she will still occasionally fall off the wagon. Like today. But it no longer worries her so much when she does. She just channels Scarlett. '*Tomorrow is another day…*'

Now that she's changed, she sets about getting the studio ready. She fetches a length of rope from where she keeps it in a locker in the far corner. It's a cotton rope with a steel core. In most ropes the lay, or coil of the fibres, is the same in all of its constituent strands, but this can cause the rope to twist back on itself, which would be disastrous for Lorrie. That's why she uses this particular type, with the steel core laid out in the opposite direction to the outer layers, so that the twists can balance each other out. She attaches it to an iron ring attached to one of the girders supporting the stone roof, using a constrictor knot. It's a knot her father, Milosz, has taught her. It's similar to a clove hitch, but with one end passed under the other, forming an overhand knot under a riding turn. It has the built-in advantage of tightening further the harder she pulls the other end of the rope, which she loops through another ring attached to a second girder on the opposite side of the studio. Once secured the rope quivers taut and tensioned approximately one metre above the floor. As soon as she is satisfied that the rope is fixed, Lorrie uses a chair to step up onto it, initially holding on to the girder for support and balance. She's ready.

She will walk across it barefoot, so that the rope can be grasped between her big and second toes. When walking on the ground, Lorrie's feet are positioned side by side, so that the base for supporting her is wide in the lateral direction but narrow in the longitudinal, from front to back. Once she is on the wire, she has to reverse this. Her feet are still in a parallel position, but now one in front of the other, so that she must pitch her weight further forward. The ankle becomes the pivotal point. She stretches her arms out wide, not only for greater balance, but in order to redistribute mass away from the pivot. This increases the moment of inertia just before she takes her first step, which requires greater torque to propel her across the wire. The result is less tipping.

She edges slowly along the stretched length of the rope. She keeps her eyes on the opposite girder at all times, never on her feet, which she continues to lift and then place, one in front of the other, one sure step at a time. She has been practising for more than a year now. She has yet to make it to the other side in a single, unbroken walk, but she knows she will do so. If not today, tomorrow. She is walking her way back towards herself, towards who she wants to become, and she knows that person is waiting for her there to catch her, out of the blurred grainy film of her past, to guide her towards an as yet unimagined, unrecorded future.

4
EX MACHINA

2014

Chloe is early. She tries always to be. She hates the idea of keeping people waiting. She'd rather be kicking her heels for twenty minutes than having to scramble to be there in the nick of time. The thought of dashing in at the last possible moment, arriving hot, bothered and flustered, fills her with an almost physical dread. It reminds her of her Final Presentation at Uni, for which she had been so very nearly late, and how stressful that had been, causing her to nearly lose her thread. Since then she has always made sure to allow herself plenty of time to get anywhere. She never regards the accumulation of all these minutes spent waiting for her next appointment to arrive as lost or wasted. Far from it. She enjoys the feeling of calm and control it gives her. The chance to suss out her surroundings, to prepare what she might say first, which questions to ask and which to leave out.

But today is different. Her surroundings could not be more familiar. She's in the Grosvenor Building of the main MMU campus. She knows exactly where she's going. She's here to interview her old tutor, Clive Archer, who is retiring at the end of the month, for *aAh!*, the university magazine. He has specifically asked for her, she has learned, and asked her to meet him by the Holden Gallery, which is just along the corridor from his office. The days of male lecturers inviting their female students for a one-on-one in their office are long gone, thank God. Not that Clive would ever try anything. He's always been far too principled. The kind who invites trust and confidence, but always at a professional distance. Besides, he's happily married. To Florence. A jazz trumpeter, whose photographs adorn his desk, and whose music can frequently be heard emanating from behind his door, providing the tempo for his days.

Even so, Chloe has still arrived early. It gives her chance to have a quick peek at the Degree Show from this year's graduates. It's good. Bold and eclectic. Just as it should be. She likes its optimism.

A few minutes later, she hears a few bars of up-tempo jazz as a door opens.

"Pack up all your cares and woe
Here I go, singing low
Bye bye, Blackbird..."

She can almost imagine Clive walking briskly in time to its beat, before he closes the door for the final time and the music pauses mid-phrase.

"Oh what hard luck stories they all hand me..."

Did we, she wonders? Pile all our cares and woes upon his shoulders? Probably. Isn't that what students have always done...?

"There you are," he says. "Am I late?"

"No," she smiles. "I'm early."

"Old habits..."

She nods.

"Well," he says, looking around at the exhibition, "what do you think?"

"They're good," she says.

"Not bad for my last hurrah," he agrees, "but – between you and me," he adds, furtively looking over his shoulder, "they're a bit tame for my tastes. Not as feisty as your year."

Chloe raises and eyebrow. "Feisty?"

"Challenging."

"Bloody impossible, more like."

"Not at all. I enjoyed the cut and thrust."

"Even from me?"

"Especially from you."

"Thank you."

"For what?"

"For agreeing to this interview for a start."

"I helped set up *aAh!* to begin with."

"Did you?"

"Back in the day when it was all gestetners and roneos."

"You sound nostalgic."

"Not a bit of it. We used to get covered in blue ink. Well I did. I was always ham-fisted. It was the same when I was at school. I'd get in a right mess with my fountain pen. Every time I had to change a cartridge…" He makes the sound of an explosion, which he mirrors with his hands spreading apart.

"Thank goodness for biros," says Chloe, taking out one of her own. "Mind if I take notes?"

"Not at all. But aren't you just going to record what we say on your phone?"

She shakes her head. "I thought I'd be old school today."

"In deference to my great age?"

"Actually," she says, putting the pen away again, "I'd prefer to just listen and soak it all up."

"Aren't you afraid of missing any sudden pearls of wisdom I might utter?"

"Don't worry. I'll commit them to memory."

"Now it's my turn to thank you."

Chloe frowns.

"For assuming I might actually come up with any," he explains.

"Oh, I'm sure you will."

"Well, we'll see. But not on an empty stomach, that's for sure. Mind if we go and have lunch?"

"Might this be my chance to experience the Staff Canteen at last?"

"No such luck, I'm afraid," he says, already beginning to move on. "The company's dull and the food duller. Let's go to *On the Eighth Day* instead. Will that be acceptable?"

"Absolutely. I love the it there, but shouldn't I be treating you? Isn't that how these things happen?"

"It is. But I don't imagine *aAh!* stumps up for lunches, does it?"

Chloe shakes her head. "No," she smiles.

"And nor does a student loan run to such extravagances, even for a retiring ex-tutor."

"It doesn't. But it does stretch to paying for myself."

"I should bloody well hope so. You're talking to a soon-to-be-pensioner here."

Laughing, they cross Oxford Road to where their destination awaits. *On the Eighth Day*.

"I remember when this place first opened," says Clive, as they make their way downstairs to the Basement Café. It was nothing like the enterprise it is now. "In fact, I helped to build it."

Chloe's eyes widen. "I didn't know that," she says. "And you know how thoroughly I do my research."

"I do," he replies, with a twinkle of mischief in his eye. "I'm delighted to be able to surprise you at least once."

"Tell me the story."

"It's nothing, really. It was while I was a student myself."

"Here at MMU."

"It was Manchester Poly back then. I was doing an Economics degree. Only my own economics were not working out so well."

"Why's that?"

"I grew up less than ten minutes away from here. In Moss Side. You know this of course – if you've done your research properly?"

"At 246 Upper Lloyd Street. Near Whitworth Park,"

"Which back then was a complete no-go area."

"Gangs?"

"Partly. Mostly it was just a dumping ground for used syringes."

"Ugh."

"I wanted to leave home."

"Why?"

"Live a more student kind of life, I suppose."

"Was that the only reason?"

"If you're implying that I was trying to escape an abusive home life, you're barking up the wrong tree. True, my parents both died before I was four. My sister had to bring me and my brother up all by herself – until we were adopted, that is. But you know all this, surely?"

"Yes, but I'd rather hear it from you."

"I could have gone off the rails, I suppose. It wouldn't have been surprising. It was what my brother did." He pauses briefly. "But that was later. When I started at the Poly, he was already at what was euphemistically called the University of Life. Not working, that's for sure. More dubious forms of employment, I'm sorry to say. He didn't come home half the time. I did a lot of covering for him, I can tell you. So when it came to starting my degree, I thought – it's *my* turn now. I'm not my brother's keeper. Maybe if I had been, things might have turned out differently." His voice trails away as he loses himself in memories.

"That must have been hard on your step-mum."

"Yes. It was. I see that now of course. She was amazing. But then – I was only eighteen and champing at the bit. So I left home and tried to find myself a bedsit. The trouble was, because the Poly was so close to home, I wasn't entitled to a grant, so I couldn't afford to pay any rent. I could've gone home, I suppose, with my tail between my legs."

"Why didn't you? Too proud?"

"Too stupid. So…"

"What?"

"I dossed where I could. Friends' sofas. Tried to talk my way into various girls' beds. When that didn't work, I'd sometimes try and stay in the library overnight – you know, hide while the security bloke went round checking that everyone had left…"

"*I* did that!"

"Really?"

"Yeah – but not for the same reason as you. I'd just be so into my work – my research, my essay, my dissertation, whatever – I didn't want to stop."

"I can imagine."

"So what happened?"

"Well – sometimes I'd just try and snatch some kip in a doorway. One time I huddled in the one here."

"*The Eighth Day?*"

"Yeah – only it wasn't called that then. It wasn't called anything. It was boarded up. On one side was *Johnny Roadhouse*…"

"Even back then?"

"Oh yeah – *Johnny Roadhouse* has been here for ever. And always will be, I hope. It's still a Mecca for musicians. And on the other side was *Black Sedan Records*, where you could get the kind of records you couldn't get anywhere else."

"Such as?"

"Reggae, mostly, ska, dub, all imports."

"Was that the kind of music you listened to?"

"Still do. When Florence lets me. We used to hear it at *The Reno Club*."

"Where was that?"

"On the corner of Princess Parkway and Moss Lane East."

"Close to your home then?"

"Too close. If my Mum ever got to know I was there, especially when I was still at school, I'd be in big trouble. And once I started here, I'd have to make sure I went there by a circuitous route so as not to risk bumping into her."

"That's very sad."

"Yes, it is. But I wasn't thinking straight back then. That's what sleeping in shop doorways can do to your brain."

"I suppose."

"One morning, just before it got light, I was woken up by a gang of lads and girls trying to step over me to get inside this boarded-up shop. They called themselves a Workers' Cooperative. I didn't know what that meant at the time…"

"And you an Economics student?"

"This was still my first term, remember."

"OK, you're forgiven."

"They'd somehow managed to get enough money between them to pay the rent on this place for a few months. The trouble was, it was completely wrecked, and so they had to fit it out from scratch, using any scraps of wood and metal they could lay their hands on. Some of them lived in a commune out at Blackstone Edge, between Littleborough and Hebden Bridge. They grew their own food, shared all the labour between each other."

"Even looking after the children?"

"Yeah, they did actually. I became friendly with one of them in particular. John, his name was. He was a carpenter. He said that if I helped him out with the woodwork, when I wasn't in classes, they'd let me sleep there at nights, as a kind of caretaker, in lieu of rent, you know? So that's what I did for the next three months till the shop was ready to open."

Chloe looks at him sideways.

"Are you winding me up?"

"The cynicism of youth! Check this out if you don't believe me." He brings up a website on his phone.

'As the 60s rushed to a psychedelic close with a blaze of love and chemicals, heralding the dawn of a New Age of Aquarius, a right-on group of friends had their stab at creating a new order. They wanted to establish a way of trading goods that broke away from the ideas of money and commerce, and to that end founded On the Eighth Day.'

"So if you couldn't pay for something, you would barter, or offer to do something in exchange."

"It sounds very hippy."

"It was. But its heart was in the right place."

"Why the *Eighth Day*?"

"You've seen the graffiti all around the city? 'And on the 8th Day God created Manchester'?"

"Of course, but…"

"Where do you think that sprang from?"

"Here?"

He taps his phone once more.

'On the 7th Day God rested, and He, She, or It created something better.'

"Yes, but it also says a little further down," interrupts Chloe, having now brought the site up on her own phone, "'*It was a great place to tune in and drop out, but, as an attempt to escape the clutches of capitalism, it was less successful, and, in order to survive, it soon had to become a shop in a more conventional sense*'. Voila."

"Now you're sounding like Petros."

"Actually, I think I'm sounding more like my father."

"Oh. Is that something you want to talk about?"

"I think *I'm* supposed to be interviewing *you*, not the other way round."

"OK, but…"

"It's fine." She looks around. "I'm glad this place survived. It still has a groovy vibe."

"It's a sign of the times."

"Oh?"

"It's still a co-op – a real co-op, not like the one you so witheringly tore apart in your presentation…"

"Which is also a sign of the times…"

"Sadly, yes. But this place manages to be a Manchester Institution, while retaining its sense of being a genuine alternative to the mainstream."

"Vegetarian-vegan, ethically sourced, ethnically diverse, politically left-wing, culturally avant-garde…" She makes imaginary quotation marks with the first two fingers of each hand.

"Now you're making it sound like a brand."

"Which is exactly what it is."

"Please," he says, raising his arms in mock surrender, "no more. Don't shatter the idealism of my youth."

"I wouldn't dream of it," she laughs.

"Shall we order?" he says. "I'm starving."

"Fine."

He picks up the menu.

"I think I'll have a burger," he says.

"Vegan, I trust?" says Chloe.

"Naturally.

"Back when it first opened you were lucky if you got anything other than really heavy, stodgy brown rice."

"Sounds more like penance than pleasure."

"It was. We thought we were somehow showing our solidarity with the Vietcong by eating the same food as them."

"You can survive on just brown rice if you have to."

"So I'm told."

"But not perpetually."

"Not even temporarily. I used to betray my principles with a Chicken Biryani at *The Plaza*."

"*The Plaza*?"

"On Upper Brook Street. It was legendary. I was living in a squat by then, just round the corner on Dickenson Road…"

"This would be after your period in residence on the front step of *this* place?"

"Right. It was run by a Somali guy called Charlie Ali. It stayed open till 4am every morning, sometimes later, and it was incredibly cheap. The Biryani came with yellow rice…"

"…which would make a nice change from the brown…"

"…with raw onions in a tomato paste, topped with their special sauce."

"Special?"

"Yeah. It came in three strengths – hot, very hot and suicidal. It was considered a badge of honour to go for the suicidal."

"Yet here you are – you lived to tell the tale."

"Just about. Apparently they did a beef version, but I never tried that. There were rumours about the provenance."

"The provenance?"

"For beef, read dog."

"No!"

"Alasatian."

"Stop it – that's disgusting."

"I don't think it's true. More of an urban myth really. Anyway, it's not there now."

"What? The dog or *The Plaza*?"

"Both. Neither."

"Actually, I'd've put you down as more of a beef jerky and chips kind of guy."

"I used to be."

"Till your wife took you in hand?"

"Someone had to. We used to go there after a couple of hours dancing at *The Conti*."

"*The Conti*?"

"Short for *Continental*."

"More tales from your misspent youth?"

"It wasn't as glamorous as it sounds."

"You surprise me."

"The décor was like a public toilet. Skanky tiled walls, pools of sweat – and worse – puddling on the floor. Condensation dripping down the walls."

"Sounds irresistible."

"The beer was cheap."

"Please don't tell me that's where you met Florence?"

"No, no, no – she was always much classier than me."

"No?"

"Actually, it's still there."

"*The Continental*?"

"Just along the road from here. Squeezed under a railway arch at Oxford Road Station. It's called *The Zombie Shack* now."

Chloe's eyes light up. "Oh yes – I know it. I mean, I've passed it by, on the opposite side, giving it as wide a berth as possible."

"You've not been inside then?"

She gives him the most withering of looks. "Give me *some* credit."

"Ah well. Happy days."

"They don't sound like it."

Clive turns away, remembering. "They were actually."

"Well – sorry to tear yourself away from Memory Lane, but I'm starving."

"Sorry." He slides the menu towards her. "What will *you* have?"

"This, I think." She points to the menu mischievously. "'Chunky tofu, pak choi, aubergine, baby corn and green beans in a fragrant coconut sauce with lemongrass and kaffir lime leaves served on a bed of couscous with vegan prawn crackers'."

Clive opens his mouth to speak, but before he can say a word, Chloe continues. "Followed by the 'Medjool date and tahini energy bomb'."

"Now you're taking the piss."

"*Moi*? I wouldn't dream of it, Clive."

While they wait for their food to arrive, Chloe pours them each a glass of water, while Clive scrolls through his phone.

"Look at this," he says at last. "Circa 1970."

He passes the phone across. Chloe looks and smiles.

"'Pottery, incense, clothes'," she reads.

"Yes," he says, taking back the phone. "There were always a lot of joss sticks and incense, I recall."

"Very useful in masking other smells, I imagine. Certain chemical substances…"

"You're not wrong," smiles Clive.

"The people in the photo seem to be puzzled. Some are looking in at the window, but most are walking past. No one's going in, I see."

"Unlike today."

They look around and every table is full, every chair taken.

"You were ahead of your time," says Chloe.

"Now you're teasing me again."

"Not really. It must have been good to feel yourself at the start of things."

"It was."

"That's what Petros says."

"Oh." Clive looks away.

233

"You don't like him, do you?"

"I make it a rule never to dislike any of my students, past or present. It's his values I'm disappointed in. Unless he's changed? I've not seen him in more than a year. Not since he graduated. I take it you have?"

"A little." She looks down. "Not much."

"And?"

"You know me, Clive. I take no prisoners. I take him to task constantly over these values you take exception to."

"And how does he defend himself?"

"He doesn't. He just says he's trying to make his parents proud. Which he says by way of being sarcastic, but actually I think he means it."

"By building apartments that only the very rich can ever hope to afford?"

"He doesn't do that. Not yet. Though I think he'd like to. He converts buildings that would otherwise fall into rack and ruin if he didn't intervene."

"But he still charges outlandish prices, way beyond the reach of the ordinary working man or woman."

"He would say he's merely responding to market forces. As a former economist, I'm sure you can understand that."

"I can understand it, but that doesn't mean I'm in favour of it."

"Neither am I actually. But it's what *he* thinks. For now at any rate."

"You think he might change?"

"I have hopes. But which way? Right now he has his eyes fixed on those glass palaces encircling the city."

"And this is making his parents proud – how?"

"Isn't that what all parents want? For their children to have better lives than they did?"

"By which you mean making more money."

"Petros would say, 'What other yardstick is there?' "

"The Law of Perpetual Progress."

Chloe frowns. Clive continues before she can interrupt..

"As you so rightly pointed out, you're talking to a former economist."

"Except that it's no longer perpetual, is it? We millennials are probably going to be the first generation *not* to earn more than their parents."

"Generation Z."

"Like everyone I know, I'm finding it increasingly difficult not to be scared about the future and angry about the past."

"But you're still only young. Life for you is just beginning. You've everything in front of you."

"As opposed to you, who's got most of his life behind him?"

"I don't happen to agree with that, but yes, I suppose so."

"I've a cousin – Suzy – she turned thirty this year. She's much smarter than me. She trained as an architect, but ever since she graduated, she's been fobbed off with a series of unpaid internships for the most part. She'd love to design the kind of socially affordable housing units I'm sure you'd approve of, Clive, but she's light years away from even getting her foot in the door. I met her last week and she was at her wit's end. She lives in a flat the size of a shoe box in Fallowfield. Her rent consumes more than half her income, she hasn't had a steady job since Pluto was a planet, and her savings are dwindling faster than the ice caps you baby-boomers have melted."

"I'm sorry to hear that. What will she do?"

"I'm not sure. She might even go back to China. My father has promised to use his influence to help her get started."

"D'you think she'll go?"

"I hope not."

"Why d'you say that?"

"It's a Faustian bargain. I wouldn't want her to be beholden to my father in any way, that's why."

"That's the second time you've mentioned your father, and both times negatively. Are you sure you don't want to talk about him?"

"No," she says, shaking her head vehemently, as if trying to shut him out of her thoughts. She returns to what she was trying to say earlier. "We all know the statistics. More millennials live with their parents than with room-mates – look at me, I still live with my grandmother above a Chinese take-away that belongs to some anonymous chain – we are delaying partner-marrying and house-buying and kid-having for longer than the previous generation, yet, according to you..."

"Not me, Chloe..."

"...people like you, Clive, it's all our fault. We got the wrong degree. We spend money we don't have on things we don't need. We haven't learned to code. That's all Petros is doing – learning to code."

"You've not got the wrong degree, Chloe. Listen to yourself – all that passion, all that righteous indignation – you were born to be a journalist."

"That's if anyone'll hire me."

"They will. I'm certain of it."

"Nothing is certain. Not even the Law of Perpetual Progress." She bites viciously into her tahini energy bomb. Clive finishes his vegan burger.

"I'll tell you what *is* certain," he says.

"What?"

"The Matthew Effect."

"Is this another of your economic theories?"

"Not mine. It's a term that was first coined by Robert King Merton, an American sociologist back in 1968..."

"The Stone Age then?"

"That's right – when we still wrote in runes."

"And what did he carve, this Robert King Merton?"

"He came up with the theory that the rich get richer and the poor get poorer."

"That's hardly rocket science."

"Not in the slightest. He got it from the Bible. *The Parable of the Talents*, in the Gospel according to Matthew…"

"…hence its name…"

"…which says, '*For unto everyone that hath shall be given, and he shall have abundance. But from him that hath not shall be taken away even that which he hath*'."

"So?"

"What Merton did was to test this out, scientifically, based on painstaking, documented research, and then to calculate it."

"And?"

"He calculated that 7% of the population owned 84% of the wealth of the nation."

"I've got news for him. He's way out of date. The latest figures indicate the richest 1% now own more than the poorest 90% combined."

"I know. But back in the seventies this was a revelation. There was this theatre company, very agit-prop, very angry, but utterly brilliant, who called themselves after this statistic to draw more people's attention to the inequality and injustice of it."

"7:84?"

"That's right. They were based in Scotland, directed by John McGrath, who hailed originally from Birkenhead, but we won't hold that against him. They came to perform in Manchester once while I was a student. *The Cheviot, The Stag & The Black, Black Oil*. It was heavily influenced by Brecht – actors playing multiple roles, never letting you forget that what you were watching was a play, inviting you to judge, make comments, take sides."

"What was it about?"

"Nothing less than the history of the class struggle. Although it was set in Scotland – the title referred to three pivotal moments in Scottish history – the Highland clearances, the subsequent use of the land by English overlords for shooting, and the American exploitation of the discovery of North Sea oil – it transcended borders and applied to the class struggle everywhere. It was my Damascene moment."

"In what way?"

"It lifted the scales from off my eyes. I switched from Economics to Liberal Studies. And then to Photography. I came to realise that it was the arts which could bring political theory to life, make it more palatable, give it a far wider reach. John McGrath began writing scripts for television."

"You mean he sold out?"

"Far from it. Like Brecht himself said, *'Erst kommt das Fressen, denn die Moral'*."

"First comes food, then morality?"

"Precisely so. We need food to survive, and I felt the arts could provide it. I still do."

"Like this place here?" says Chloe, suppressing a smile.

"Scoff if you like," replies Clive, but the idea of an eighth day has always held a certain apocalyptic resonance."

"The Epistle of Barnabas."

"You'll have to enlighten me."

"One of the so-called disputed texts that were omitted from the Bible. In it, he says, '*I will make a beginning of the eighth day, that is, a beginning of another world*'."

The two of them look around the crowded café and smile.

"Actually, I was thinking Hazel O'Connor," says Clive.

Now it is Chloe's turn to look blank.

"One hit wonder of the punk era."

"I expect Lorrie would recognise the reference."

"I expect she would."

"Well?"

"Something about how, on the eighth day, the machine stopped. How did it go?" He starts to sing, quietly and rather tunelessly, "'*No time for flight / A blinding light / Nothing but a void / Forever night...*'"

"Cheerful."

"It sounded better when she sang it."

"Is that where you think we're heading – a forever night void?"

"Not at all. I'm an optimist. I always have been. That's why I became a teacher. It's like gardening. Planting seeds. You can't do that without a feeling of hope, that, come next spring, something new will grow."

"Can I quote you on that in my article?"

Clive smiles. "There's an old Irish folk tale in which the Fianna-Finn are discussing music. One of their elders, Fionn McCool, asks his son, Oisín, 'What's the finest music in the world?' 'The cuckoo calling from a tree,' answers Oisín. One by one Fionn asks the rest of the Fianna-Finn. 'The belling of a stag,' says one. 'The sound of the lark,' says another. 'The laughter of a girl.' 'The whisper of a loved one.' 'The lapping of water on stones.' 'Yes, yes,' says Fionn, 'these are good sounds, all.' 'What do *you* think, Father?' asks Oisín. Fionn looks around him and says, 'The music of what is happening...'"

Chloe taps this story onto her phone to remind her for later, when she will come to write up the article. When she has finished, she looks up. "And does this music of what is happening also apply to the sounds of the cranes and the bulldozers demolishing buildings outside?"

"Yes it does. For it's also the sound of new buildings going up in their place."

"Even those glass palaces ringing the city that you despise so much?"

"In theory, yes. Even those."

"In theory?"

"We're creatures of flesh and blood in the end, aren't we? Imperfect, irrational, inconsistent. My brain tells me over and over that change is a good thing, a necessary thing, replenishing, stimulating. Our eyes follow the rise of these steel and glass towers up into the sky and we can't help but be thrilled by the prospect of climbing up them, right to their summits, to look down on all the rest of the city toiling below us. But it's down there, among the noise and the bustle of all those teeming masses, where the creativity really starts. People talk about 'blue sky' thinking, but then they forget that in order to reach those cloud-capped towers, we first have to roll up our sleeves and get our hands dirty. And when we do that, we leave traces of ourselves behind, all of us, generation after generation, century after century, marks on the land, palimpsests, to prove that we were here, that we mattered, and that we still do."

Both are silent for a while. It is Chloe who is the first to break it.

"I went to Hong Kong once. On my way back from Shenzen after spending some time with my father. I stayed in Kowloon. I was fifteen. The day after I arrived, my hosts, distant relatives of my father, took me from Tsim Sha Shui, the southernmost tip of the peninsula, across Victoria Harbour to the northern shore of Hong Kong Island. From there we travelled by a series of covered walkways in the sky, elevators and underpasses right into the heart of the Central District. My feet did not touch the actual earth once during the entire journey. My hosts purred with such pride and pleasure as they showed me all this, and it's true – there was something intoxicatingly futuristic about this brave new world. But the next day I went by myself and took a different route, one which allowed me to get myself lost in the labyrinth of narrow streets and alleyways. Far from being futuristic, the city now felt positively medieval, with its bird markets and live snakes in tanks and unrecognisable fish being hauled in nets from the harbour and tipped right in front of you. These two worlds existed side by side, cheek by jowl. It was thrilling, exhilarating. A bit like *Blade Runner*, to be sure, overcrowded, polluted, but full of life, real. It kept you on your toes. And I liked that. So let them redevelop all they want here in Manchester – in Spinningfields and Deansgate and Angel Meadow – but let them keep Tib Street and Shudehill and Withy Grove as well."

"Bravo," says Clive, applauding. "Well said."

"Now *you're* taking the piss."

"Not a bit of it. I love your passion. Hold onto it. It will get you into trouble. But never let go of it. It's a gift."

Chloe looks down. "Thank you."

Clive checks the time on his phone.

"I'm sorry," he says, "but I have to go."

"Oh," says Chloe, making no attempt to disguise her disappointment. "Is the Vice Chancellor presenting you with your clock, or whatever it is they give people nowadays when you retire? I don't suppose I shall ever retire. Our generation won't. That's if we get a job in the first place."

"What *are* your plans now that you've finished your MA?"

"I've got an interview next week at *MCR Live*."

"That's great. Congratulations."

"I did some features here on *Hive Radio* as part of my MA, so I thought, why not?"

"Why not indeed? Good luck."

"Thanks. And I'm always pitching ideas for articles."

"A portfolio career."

"That's the new reality, innit, Clive, as Khav would say."

Clive smiles. "Are you still in touch with her?"

"She's working as an arts admin assistant at Z-Arts in Hulme. She also runs after-school classes for kids there in the holidays. 'Digital Discoverers'."

"That's great."

"Yeah – it is. Shit pay, though."

"That's the arts for you. Florence always says that if it's not for you, do something else. Like *I* did. Those who can, do. Those who can't, teach. As it happens, I think teaching is a noble profession."

"I agree."

"But if you're an artist, a true artist, like Florence is, then you don't have a choice."

Chloe pauses a moment. She wonders whether to ask this next question or not. What the hell, she thinks. He doesn't have to answer if he doesn't want to."

"How did you and Florence meet?" she asks. "If you don't mind me asking?"

"Not at all. Which version would you like?"

"How many are there?"

"There are always more than one, aren't there?"

"I suppose."

"I like to say that I discovered Florence."

"Really?" says Chloe, raising a rather rueful eyebrow.

"While she would prefer to say that she rescued me."

"In that case," laughs Chloe, "I think I'd like to hear *her* version."

"Very well, but I should warn you that it comes with a disclaimer."

"Oh?"

"In that it's my inevitably biased re-telling of her version."

"I'm sensing some prevarication here. You'd best begin, I think."

Just then a bell rings from the counter informing them that their coffees are ready. Clive waits while Chloe goes to collect them. When she returns, he says, "OK. Here goes." He takes a sip of his espresso and slowly starts.

"I'd moved. Again. I was no longer in the squat in Dickenson Road. I was now in Hulme. John Nash Crescent." He scoffs. "Imagine – naming those rat-runs after the architect who designed the Royal Crescent in Bath." He shakes his head. "It's hard to believe, but when they were first built they won several awards. They were quite fashionable to begin with. The French actor Alain Delon lived in one of them with his girlfriend Nico, the singer."

"*Très chic*," laughs Chloe.

"Oh yeah," sneers Clive. "Very *à la mode*." He brings up a couple of photos on his phone. "Look."

"These are good," says Chloe appreciatively.

"Thank you," says Clive. "I can say that because I didn't take them. They're Richard's."

"Richard?"

"Davis."

Chloe nods.

"You've heard of him?"

"You mentioned him in a lecture once. *No Place Like Hulme*."

"I'm glad that someone was paying attention."

"I hung on your every word, Clive."

"Of course you did, Chloe." He spears a last recalcitrant chip with his fork. "Here's a couple more he took."

"They're amazing."

"They are." He chews thoughtfully. "Now – where was I?"

"John Nash Crescent."

"That's right. Walkways in the Sky." He shakes his head. "They were a disaster on so many levels. They were the first council houses in Manchester to have in-built under-floor heating."

"That's good, isn't it?"

"In theory. The trouble was, none of the tenants could afford the extra bills, so they went entirely unused. They became home to cockroaches and rats, but because the piping was all encased in asbestos the council weren't able to repair them."

"So the vermin multiplied?"

"You could say that, yes. The highest walkways were the worst. Which is where our squat was, Richard and me, and a few others. They became no-go areas, the sole domain of drug runners. They smashed all our windows and kicked down the door. There was no point calling the police. They never ventured that high. So we simply boarded it all up completely."

"It sounds awful."

"You got used to it. It made for a good dark room."

"Is that what you were at that time – a photographer?"

"Trying to be. I wasn't that good, to be honest. I always saw what would have made the perfect photo a few seconds too late. But Hulme back then – we're talking the late seventies, early eighties – was home to all manner of underground artists trying to make their way – poets, punk bands, guerrilla film makers – all taking advantage of the fact that the Crescents were becoming increasingly derelict and abandoned, so that, if you didn't mind having no heating in winter, or sharing your squat with legions of mice, you could get by."

"It sounds as much a political choice as an artistic one."

"I've always believed the two are inextricably linked. But I'd say it was more 'anarchist' than 'political'."

"What were you agitating for?"

"I'd say it was more about what we were against."

"Which was?"

"Just about everything. Like Marlon Brando says when he's asked the same question in *The Wild One*."

"What are you rebelling against?" says Chloe, assuming the role of the sheriff from the film.

"Whadda you got?" replies Clive as Brando.

They both laugh.

"Actually, it was what got me started as an academic."

"*The Wild One?*"

"The Hulme scene back then. The squat was just across the road from these two revered institutions." He brings up two more photos on his phone.

"*The Factory* and *The Aaben*?"

"A club and a cinema."

"They look derelict."

"Appearances can be deceptive. *The Factory* was where Tony Wilson set up his first club, before he moved to *The*

Haçienda, but it still hosted the occasional rave or free gig, while *The Aaben* was the only place in the city where you could get to see European Art House movies. I remember going to see Bergman's *The Seventh Seal* there – you know, the one where Max von Sidow plays a game of chess with the figure of Death on the edge of a Nordic sea. It was a Monday afternoon. I was the only person in the whole cinema."

"You say that like it was a good thing."

"It was. It got me thinking."

"What about?"

"How all of it seemed to be connected. Hulme, the squat, the poverty, the crime, the riots in Moss Side, the anger towards Thatcher, how run down and shitty Manchester had become, yet here was this vibrant, energetic, dynamic, chaotic, leaderless art scene going on, especially music – 'Madchester' and all that – and I wanted to see how it all might fit together."

"Like a game of chess?"

"I suppose."

"The stakes were pretty high – you against Death?"

"I didn't think of it that way."

"So what did you do?"

"I applied to the Poly to do an MA in Critical Studies. That morphed into a PhD – New Media for a New Age – yeah, I know, it makes me cringe too when I look back, but at the time it felt important, necessary…"

"It still is. More so than ever now with the rise of social media."

"I agree. Meanwhile I kept going to *The Haçienda* for further research."

"Research?" says Chloe sceptically.

"Naturally."

"And there was I thinking you were going there just to get wasted."

"Oh for the cynicism of youth."

"You cut me to the quick, Clive."

"The truth was that Manchester was pretty grim back then. When you went to *The Haçienda* you could forget all about that for a few hours and lose yourself in the music and the dancing."

"Yes," says Chloe, "I can relate to that."

Clive is struck by the seriousness of this revelation. He wonders briefly whether to pursue it, but decides it's not his place to do so.

"Anyway," he says instead, "that's a roundabout way of answering your question."

"What do you mean?" frowns Chloe.

"*The Haçienda.* That's where I met Florence."

"Oh," smiles Chloe, "I see."

"She was still a student then. At the Royal Northern College of Music. I bumped into her by chance. She was with another guy. They played in a brass band together. He was a trombonist, I think. They'd just won a competition at *The Kings Hall* in Belle Vue, the night they began to demolish it, she was the last person ever to perform there, and they'd come to *The Haçienda* to celebrate, and to hear New Order, who were playing that night. Only the guy was off his face and had more or less abandoned her. She'd latched onto this other couple and become friendly with the girl. Jenna, her name was, who began pouring her heart out about how her boyfriend mistreated her too, so the two of them, Jenna and Florence, decided to drown their sorrows together, bemoaning their luck in love and denigrating the entire male sex while they were at it. Then Jenna's boyfriend came back and the two of them started a fight. Fights at *The Haçienda* weren't that unusual, but this one was threatening to get out of hand. Jenna was giving as good as she got, but in the end it was all beginning to get too heavy, so Florence tried to summon up some help. I happened to be heading in that direction. As it turned out, Jenna's boyfriend was my nephew, my sister Anita's boy, Lance, so I thought I should try and step in."

"Wow – it sounds like an episode from Corrie."

"It was."

"Anyway, after we'd calmed everyone down, Florence and I started talking. We hit it off straight away."

"Luckily for you."

"Oh yes. I've a lot to thank New Order for. They came back on to play their second set just then and did an early version of *Blue Monday*. When I heard Bernard Sumner sing those lyrics, *'I can see a ship in the harbour'*, I knew I'd found my safe haven…"

Clive falls quiet, remembering. Chloe feels almost intrusive, simply by being there. After a few more seconds have passed, she clears her throat and asks nervously, by way of a slight change of subject, "What happened to Jenna and Lance?"

"Oh," says Clive, smiling, "that's a much longer story, with many more cliffhanger episodes. For another time perhaps…"

He finishes his burger and orders another coffee.

"And you?" he says to Chloe.

She shakes her head and pours herself another glass of water.

"I thought you were pressed for time."

"I've a few minutes yet."

"OK. Good. So?"

"After that, Florence and I were never apart. I'd go and see her play at the College of Music, then, after she graduated, in various jazz sets at *The Band on the Wall*. And she'd come with me to *The Reno* and play there too sometimes…"

"The Caribbean Club your step-mum objected to?"

"The very same. Only she no longer minded me going there. Not now I was a lecturer at the Poly, not when she realised that other quite respectable folk used to frequent the place. She adored Florence. 'Is he treating you well, girl?'

she'd ask her. And Florence would smile and say that mostly I was a good boy and behaved myself. 'I'm glad to hear it,' my step-mum would laugh, then turn to me and say, 'You're lucky to have this girl, Clive, she's far too good for you.' Then the two of them would link arms and hoot with laughter. Those were good days. Florence made it her mission to keep me clean from drugs, eat more healthily, even take up exercise."

Chloe splutters at the thought.

"I know. *The Reno* had this football club. The only qualification you needed to play was an Afro hairstyle..."

"You didn't?" laughs Chloe, her eyes widening in disbelief.

"You better believe it," says Clive, bringing up another photo from his phone. "Afro Villa, we called ourselves. Check this out."

Chloe squeals with delight when she sees it.

"Which one are you?" she asks.

"Back row, second from the left," he says.

Chloe studies it closely, shaking her head and smiling, as Clive now adopts the same pose, arms folded, head casually cocked to one side.

"Where did you live?" she asks.

"We stayed in the Crescents."

Chloe expresses surprise.

"Not in the squat. On a safer level, lower down, with windows and a front door. There was already talk that the Council were considering knocking them all down. In which case, she argued, they'd have to compensate and re-house us. Which they did."

"Wise woman."

Clive nods. "She still is." He pulls up yet another photo. "Here," he says, handing it across.

Chloe takes the phone. It shows Florence as she was back then, in the eighties.

"She looks like Siouxie from the Banshees," says Chloe, passing back the phone.

"I'll tell her you said so," says Clive. "She'll like that."

"She looks strong."

"She is. She's the daughter of a miner. Five generations of them."

"It's a good photo. The reflection of the church in the window, the trees. A sign of things to come?"

"I suppose. Leafy Victoria Park feels a long, long way from the Crescents of Hulme."

Clive falls silent again. After a few moments, he continues.

"I would never have got through what happened next without her."

Chloe looks up, but says nothing. She senses Clive might be about to mention something important and she doesn't want to push it, so she waits.

Clive takes a deep breath.

"It was around this time that a serious turf war broke out between the drug-related gangs of Cheetham Hill and Moss Side. There'd always been rivalries between them, going right back to the days of the Scuttlers. But in the eighties they really peaked." He pauses, takes a sip of his coffee. "I've mentioned my brother, Christopher, to you a few times before." Chloe nods tremulously. She knows what's coming.

"Well," says Clive, "he was always on the fringes of trouble, but never anything serious. Shoplifting, possession, nicking the odd car. Nothing violent. Ever. Then one day…"

Clive stops. He finds he cannot continue.

"It was a drive-by," he says at last. "He was just caught in the middle of something that was nothing to do with him. The wrong place at the wrong time. Something he had a talent for. Christopher was deaf. He simply didn't hear the car or the gunshots. He died instantly. My step-mum never got over it. 'Try to think of him as he was,' I'd say to her. He was always such a happy kid. Here – look," he says, showing Chloe a last photo. "Christopher's on the right."

Neither say a word for a long time.

"Thanks," Clive says at last, "for listening."

"It was a privilege."

"You'll not use any of that in your article, I trust?"

"Of course not."

Clive nods, then collects himself.

"I'm sorry," he says. "I really do have to dash."

"OK," says Chloe, relieved to be back on safer ground. "So – where are you in such a hurry to be off to, if it's not to get a clock?"

He takes an A6 postcard from his jacket pocket and places it in front of her.

Arthur Lewis Centenary Public Lecture

6.30pm 23rd Sep 2014

Lecture Theatre A: Arthur Lewis Building, Bridgeford Street
Guest Speaker: Prof. Jim O'Neill, Honorary Chair of Economics
School of Social Sciences, University of Manchester
Introduction: Dr Clive Archer, Head of Media Production, MMU

Admission: Free

"Impressive," says Chloe. "Such august company."

"You know who Arthur Lewis was, don't you?"

"Only what it says on the plaque erected to him near the university. Otherwise, I don't think I'd have heard of him."

"The first black professor in a university anywhere in the country."

"Another first for Manchester. You'd think they'd be shouting it from the rooftops, wouldn't you?"

"I know. Shameful, isn't it? Every October they have Black History Month, then they forget all about us for the rest of the year."

"Did you know him?"

"No. I was too young. But I heard him speak once, and met him afterwards. He changed my life."

"How? I'd love to hear about it. If I come part of the way with you, can you tell me while we walk?"

"Good idea."

They pay their separate bills, then climb the stairs away from the Basement Café and step out onto the busy Oxford Road in the late afternoon sunshine. The leaves have begun to assume the start of their autumn colours in the small square across the way at All Saints. It's a Corot sky, with high, white scudding clouds, below which a low sun has slipped, slanting down on the rooftop of the John Dalton Building opposite. Chloe and Clive walk briskly in step towards the university campus, which has changed almost beyond recognition since the time Arthur Lewis was there.

"Though he'd still recognise the Museum and the Whitworth Hall," says Clive as they approach Bridgeford Street. "He was born in St Lucia, part of the British Windward Islands back then. Originally he wanted to be an engineer, but St Lucia, like the colonies in general, refused to hire you if you were black, so he switched to Economics and in 1937 he applied to study at the LSE, who, perhaps not aware of his background, accepted him. He was the first person of colour to go there. After graduating, he stayed on as a researcher for seven years, before eventually applying for the position of Chair in Economics at Liverpool University, who turned him down."

"Don't tell me – because he was black."

"Ten out of ten. But luckily for us, Liverpool's loss was Manchester's gain. In 1948 he was made Professor of Political Economy here, and he stayed for nearly ten years. It was while he was here he developed his theories in Development Economics, which would win him the Nobel Prize three decades later."

"A black Nobel laureate here in Manchester? Why don't I know this?"

"That's why – belatedly – they named a building on the campus after him, and partly why they've decided to hold this lecture today, to mark his centenary year coming up, in the hope that it will become a regular annual, high profile event."

"You said you met him? Have you time to tell me about that?"

"He stayed in Manchester nearly ten years. Then, in 1957, when Ghana gained independence, they invited Professor Lewis to be the country's Economic Advisor and help them to draw up their first Five Year Development Plan. Which he did. First and foremost, you have to remember that Lewis was a Fabianist and an idealist. These were the prevailing doctrines of the LSE. He maintained that the key to the transition from colonial rule towards fully-fledged independence was to be found in the redistribution of land – and therefore of wealth – from the white minority to the black majority."

"7:84 becomes 84:7."

"Precisely. And he worked out what came to be known as the Lewis Model to implement it."

"How?"

"In his theory, a 'capitalist' sector develops by taking labour from a non-capitalist backward 'subsistence' sector. The 'unlimited' supply of labour from the subsistence economy means that the capitalist sector can expand for some time without the need to raise wages. But – if these higher returns to capital are reinvested in training and raising the skill levels of workers, instead of merely being siphoned off as profits to be given over to share holders, the process becomes self-sustaining and leads to modernisation and economic development. The point at which the excess labour in the subsistence sector is fully absorbed into this new free enterprise sector, and where further capital accumulation begins to increase wages – that is the tipping point, and it is this that lies at the heart of the Lewis Model. After his five years in Ghana, he returned to England and was knighted for his contribution towards the establishment of these fairer labour practices – which were still profitable, let's not forget – and sometimes, during the sixties, he would come back to Manchester to give lectures. One of these was for schools. I was fifteen at the time. The idea of having to sit in the Whitworth Hall, just across the road from where we're now standing, listening to some boring old fart go on an on about Economics didn't appeal that much, but if it meant missing half a day's school, I was willing to give it a try. You have to remember, Chloe, I really didn't like school all that much, I was always getting myself into minor scrapes, mostly from trying to keep my brother out of even bigger ones, and at the time I had no idea what I would do when I left school, which I was due to do in just a few months' time. I remember sitting in that Hall, with all its stone carvings and stained glass windows, thinking, what has any of this got to do with me? Nothing. Then onto the platform walked this imposing figure, with his huge, domed, bald head, like a giant egg that seemed to be pulsing and vibrating with all of the ideas that were waiting to hatch out of it, and his strikingly clear eyes that stared out from his large glasses, which appeared to magnify them many times over, so that they looked like enormous searchlights beaming out in search of just me, or so it seemed. But more than any of this, he was black. Black guys did not speak from university platforms. None of our teachers were black. There was no one black on television, except for the Black & White Minstrel shows, so I wasn't prepared for this. We had no role models back then. Then, when he spoke, out poured these rich, mellifluous, honeyed Caribbean tones. I was spellbound. He had me right in the palm of his hand."

"What did he talk about? Not Dual Sector Economic Models, surely?"

"No. He talked about change. That nothing is fixed or immutable. Just as water will wear away a stone, so change is the natural way of things. Then he said something I've never forgotten. He said, 'And where this change begins is here,' and he tapped his chest with his fist. 'Inside each and every one of us. So if you don't like the way things are, then it's your duty to try and change them. Don't wait for others to solve your problems for you. Only you can do that. And believe me, you can'."

"Yes we can…?"

"Yes we can…"

The two of them stand in silence outside the Whitworth Hall, one of them remembering that moment, the other imagining it.

"And so," continues Clive, "instead of leaving school the next term like I was going to, I stayed on, much to the surprise of my teachers, and the delight of my stepmother. Two years later I got the 'A' levels I needed to start an Economics Degree at the Poly, and the rest you know…"

"Thanks," says Chloe. "I wish I was staying to hear your introductory speech at the lecture this evening."

"You've just heard it."

They both smile.

"But you're more than welcome to come along. It's open to the public and it's free."

"I can't. I've got to finish the article tonight."

"Of course. Good luck with it. You'll not be too hard on me, I hope? Remember – it's my last day today."

"I've not made my mind up," she says, but Clive can see her eyes are twinkling. "What will you do next?"

"Go home. Florence has a surprise planned for me, which I'm not supposed to know about."

"I mean afterwards – now you've retired."

"Oh, I've a few irons still left in the fire. I'm not quite dead yet. I sit on a few Advisory Boards, I might curate the odd exhibition or two, I might even…"

"What?"

"Try and write a book, maybe several."

"Really? What about?"

"This place, this whole convulsive, tumultuous miracle that is Manchester. Constantly reinventing itself."

"Like *you* did?"

"Like we all still do."

Chloe nods, taking this in.

"Stay in touch," he says. "Let me know how you get on."

"Don't worry," she says. "I will."

"Good. Well…" He goes to shake her hand.

"Actually," she says, ignoring his hand, "what you've been saying has given me an idea. Or rather, it's given me the confidence to go with something I've been thinking about for a few weeks now."

"Oh?" he says, awkwardly retracting his arm.

"Yes," she says. "It's this." She scrolls down her phone. "As well as writing this article about you, I'm also co-editing the whole of the issue – my last before I leave myself – and I've been wondering about proposing that in future each issue should focus around a single specific theme and design all its content around it. Like this," she says, holding out her phone. "What do you think?"

Clive looks. What Chloe is showing him is a mock-up for a front cover. It contains just a single word: 'yes'.

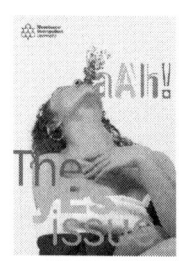

He hands her back the phone, smiling.

"Yes," he says. "Perfect."

Now, at last, she does shake his hand. Then she turns on her heels and walks swiftly away, back towards the other, younger university, MMU. In no time at all she is swallowed up by the crowds of students bustling between the two adjoining campuses until she is just a dot. In less than a minute he can no longer see her at all.

The sun has dipped lower in the sky, which is beginning to turn a crimson red. He raises a hand to shield his eyes from its glare. Silhouetted against it, a giant crane is hoisting a heavy demolition ball. Clive watches it, following its inexorable course, mesmerised.

They're pulling down the seventies halls of residence tower block that was first being built when *he* was a student here, he remembers.

Over four years he watched it grow, mushroom the sky, blot out the sun, shrug off its concrete pupa, until, unshackled from its scaffold chains, it released, from its unpinned peppered moth carapace, folded wings of plated glass, transporting him to those higher realms via perpetually self-propelling stairways above congested underpasses.

Climbing from these lower depths, he recalls, he'd sometimes rise up on the escalator, convinced of someone following him, a shadow on the stair, a whisper in his ear, but every time he turned around, no one was there. He'd glide towards the book shop on its first floor mall, along with discount travel agents, exotic fruit and flower stalls, the lure of far away places, poster destinations gliding either side the moving walkway.

Now this skeletal hulk stands delineated. Birds and clouds sail through its roofless, windowless edifice. Outlines of one or two single rooms remain intact, scraps of flapping posters, torn and charred memories. Marches and sit-ins, endless earnest debates, Mao and Ché and Joni Mitchell benignly smiling down…

"I am on a lonely road and I am travelling, travelling
Looking for someone – who could it be…?"

There was a girl he used to visit there, he remembers, before he met Florence. Her room, high up on the seventh floor, looked out across the city, street lights burning beneath invisible stars. That empty shell above him – concrete posts like jagged fists, protests wilting in the rain – might have been the exact spot where once he kissed her. She had a strawberry mark that bloomed on her cheek when she smiled.

I haven't thought of her in years, he thinks now. Not since Florence…

The demolition wrecking ball swings and smashes through the last remaining bones, crashing to the ground, scattering as cement dust clears. The sunset spreads like spilt paint. It streaks the chrysalis sky with red. A slow suffusing strawberry mark. Light tapping on his shoulder.

He turns round. He sees Florence floating up the escalator out of the past. She had always been there, waiting for when he would turn and see her at last. Unlike Eurydice, she does not fade as he looks on her. Instead she glides ever closer towards him until she can take him by the hand.

The Law of Perpetual Progress…

…which is what Chloe decides will be the title of her article – with the addition of a question mark at the end…?

After leaving Clive, she heads straight for the Geoffrey Manton Building, home of *aAh! Magazine*, situated midway between the Royal Northern College of Music and the Manchester Fashion Institute, diagonally opposite *On the Eighth Day*. Within ten minutes of hearing Clive declare her idea for the front cover as 'perfect', she has pitched the idea to the rest of the team, who enthusiastically support it. She then has less than an hour to meet her deadline for completing her article, and, true to form, she submits it early.

She steps back outside and breathes in deeply. It is early evening. A Friday. Already there is that anticipation in the air of the night ahead. The weekend about to start. The sky has reddened deeper. Chloe looks at it, as did Clive, through the skeletal silhouette of the partly demolished, former hall of residence. But unlike Clive, she does not see the past. Nor does she reminisce about anyone she might once have kissed. Instead, when she looks at the sunset, it doesn't make her think of spilt paint, or a strawberry mark on someone's cheek. It makes her think of the red dress she's going to wear for her date tonight.

It's a first date, which always fill her with a frisson of excitement and hope, for there's no way of knowing beforehand how it might turn out. As a general rule, she doesn't often do second dates. She tends to intimidate them that first time, and they don't usually ask her out again. She's tried both boys and girls, but in either case she ends up disappointed. Even when she dances, or, perhaps, especially then, for that is what she likes to do best of all on a first date – not for her the romantic candlelight dinner – she scares them off. Chloe aspires to the Sonoya Mizuno School of Dancing, the Tokyo-born English actor, as perfected in her role of Kyoko, the unnervingly lifelike robot in the film *Ex Machina*. She's even been known to send her dates a link to the YouTube link – youtube.com/watch?v=b7C69HqnV8s – so they might prepare themselves, but no one has so far come up to scratch. Mizuno dances again for The Chemical Brothers' video of *Wide Open*, in which motion capture is used to more accurately replicate her moves. Chloe thinks that would be the perfect solution to her dating issues. If she could dance the night away with a motion capture robotic version of herself, like Kyoko, everything would be fine.

Tonight she'll arrive early – as she likes to do – so she can be on the look-out for when her date arrives. She'll suss them out as they enter the bar, looking around to try and catch sight of her. She'll know at once whether the evening is going to work out or not. Probably it won't. But if she sees them first, she can quickly make her decision, then head off onto the dance floor on her own, clear a space for herself, let the music and the movement release those delicious endorphins and set them flooding through her veins. Perpetual motion, if not progress.

By the time Clive leaves the inaugural Arthur Lewis centenary lecture, the sky is dark, illuminated only by the reflected glow of the city's street lights. The night is cold but clear, and he feels invigorated by the liberation of his imminent retirement, excited by the prospect of just how much there is still for him to do. He selects a playlist from his phone, dons his headset and walks briskly in time with the music.

"Make my bed and light the light
I'll be home late tonight
Blackbird, bye-bye..."

By the time he reaches home, one and a half miles away in Victoria Park, the music has finished, the streets are quiet, and the house is dark. Perhaps Florence is not holding that surprise party for him after all. He turns the key in the front door and steps into the hall, where he is greeted by the reassuringly familiar hush of the house, punctuated only by the perpetual tick of the grandfather clock, which they bought with the proceeds of Florence's first paid gig more than thirty years ago.

But no sooner has he hung up his jacket on the banister at the foot of the stairs, than the lights are switched on, the door to the kitchen flung open, and two dozen voices sing out to greet him.

"Sur-pri-i-se!"

At once he is engulfed by friends congratulating him, hugging him, handing him bottles of wine, even his two kids are back for the weekend, while his dog Rafe waits patiently to be scratched behind the ears. From the living room the driving syncopated rhythms of Florence's band begin to ring out. Her unmuted trumpet punches out the melody, followed by the rich, dulcet tones of her voice as she starts to sing.

"Out of the tree of life I just picked me a plum
You came along and everything started to hum
Still it's a real good bet the best is yet to come…"

Yes, thinks Clive, catching Florence's eye between verses.

Yes, thinks Chloe, putting on her red dress ahead of a night of dancing.

5

IMITATION GAMES

2019 – 2013 – 1952 – 2019/1954 – 1951 – 1952 – 2020
1819 – 2020 – 1955 – 1956 – 1957 – 1958 – 1930 – 1958
1963 – 1964 – 1959 – 1964 - 2020

2019

To: molly.wahid@gmail.com
From: studios@islingtonmill.com

Date: 17th November 2019

Subject: Loom

Hi Molly,

Are you still in search of a loom? If you are, you might be interested in the attached. Once it became clear that neither the Helmshore Mill nor the Weaver's Cottage were able to help you, I've kept my eye out for anything that might be suitable, and I found this on Gumtree. If you need me to investigate further, please don't hesitate to ask.

Fingers crossed this is what you've been looking for.

Kind regards
Lorrie

Lorelei Zlatan
Studio Manager
Islington Mill

*

Molly smiles. Lorrie is nothing if not persistent. Molly doesn't think she's ever encountered anyone quite so efficient. Her attention to detail is almost frightening. The front desk at Islington Mill is a wonder to behold – practically a work of art in itself, with everything laid out so neatly, nothing out of alignment. It's not surprising, then, that so many of the artists-in-residence call on her to assist them when they are preparing for a new show. Her eye for detail, both in curating and hanging, has become the stuff of legend, and even the most macho of artists will defer to her judgement.

Molly has not had need to call upon this expertise yet. Nor is she likely to, for Molly's art, being conceptual, is more about the arrival of the idea, which will then dictate what must follow as a consequence. For her *Thin Blue Line* installation, it was Michael who had overseen all of the organisational details, but he is much busier at the university now than he was when they first met, and she doubts whether he will have the capacity for any future event, especially if it has a similar scale and ambition, which is what she intends. Michael will say yes, she knows, to whatever she asks of him, but she also knows that wouldn't be fair on him. He's currently in line for tenure, a permanent position, which, if he is successful in securing it, will require him to work even longer hours. Perhaps Lorrie might be able to step into Michael's shoes? Molly decides she will consider this in the coming weeks, as her ideas begin to coalesce. The loom might just be the final piece in the jigsaw.

To be fair, Lorrie's email is not wholly accurate. In one small detail it is incomplete. The Helmshore Museum have been as helpful as they can be, but, facing the possibility of cuts from their local authority that threaten its very survival, their resources have been stretched almost to breaking point. Even so, they have replied to Molly's requests with enthusiasm and good wishes, while explaining that at the present time they are not actively seeking new artefacts for their premises, but that if anything suitable for Molly's needs comes up, they will be sure to contact her. But they have not as yet done so. Lorrie's email, therefore, is both timely and welcome.

She looks around her studio. It is incredibly messy, which is just how she likes it. One of the advantages of not having to work from home any longer is that she can leave things where they lie, without fear of a curious three-year-old stumbling upon something sticky, or tasty, or sharp. But there is method in her mayhem. She knows precisely where everything is and can lay her hands on whatever she needs within seconds. But, looking round now, she knows she will have to make some changes, establish a bit more order, especially if she is going to create space for a loom. She wonders about asking Lorrie for help with this reorganisation. She has no doubt that Lorrie would rise to the occasion and, in no time at all, have a place for everything and everything in its place. But that is not what Molly wants. It is precisely the random, haphazard juxtaposition of objects that normally should not be lying next to one another that can throw up the kind of surprise she delights in. The surgically precise tidiness Lorrie would impose would only serve to limit such happenstance and stifle her creativity. Besides, she's not sure she can withstand the look of horror that would be sure to pass across Lorrie's face, however fleetingly, if she were to walk in now and find Molly wallowing in all this mess as happily as a pig in clover.

She clicks on the email once more and opens up the attachment.

⌬ Gumtree

Posted by: Tom
Date: 17/11/19

What: Antique Frame Hand Loom
Where: Elton, Bury, Lancs

Condition: In Need of Repair & Restoration

Price: £250
Delivery: Buyer must collect

Call: 07916 343644 for more details

The clock on the studio wall says ten past four. She needs to be making her way back home in another five minutes. She tries to get back before five each day if she can. Michael, too, is finishing a little earlier today. He had his meeting with the new professor this afternoon, and she wonders how he feels it went. She decides she'll text him quickly before collecting her bike and setting off.

> "How did it go? Been thinking of U :)
> ☺ ☺ ☺
> Text me from the train. I too might have some news.
> Love you xxx..."

The moment she sees it's been sent, she dials the number at the foot of the Gumtree posting.

"Hi. Is that Tom? I'm calling about the hand loom. Is it still available…? Great."

*

MANCHESTER 1824
The University of Manchester

19th January 2019

PRESS RELEASE

DAVID OLUSOGA OBE BECOMES PROFESSOR AT THE UNIVERSITY OF MANCHESTER

Historian, broadcaster and film-maker David Olusoga has joined The University of Manchester as a Professor of Public History.

David, who presented the BBC's landmark series *Civilisations* in 2018 alongside Simon Schama and Mary Beard, is one of the UK's foremost historians, whose main subject areas are empire, race and slavery. He was made an OBE in the recent New Year's Honours List.

Born in Nigeria to a Nigerian father and British mother, he migrated to the UK with his mother as a young child. He grew up in Gateshead and later attended the University of Liverpool to study the history of slavery.

"I got into history because I wanted to make sense of the forces that have affected my life," he says. "I'm from that generation who would look at Trevor McDonald on television – his gravitas and authority – and see hope and potential."

After leaving university, Olusoga became a television producer, working on programmes such as *Namibia Genocide and the Second Reich*, *The Lost Pictures of Eugene Smith* and *Abraham Lincoln: Saint or Sinner*. He subsequently became a presenter, beginning in 2014 with *The World's War: Forgotten Soldiers of Empire*, about the Indian, African and Asian troops who fought in the First World War, followed by several other documentaries. His most recent TV series include *Black and British: A Forgotten History*, *The World's War*, *A House Through Time* and the BAFTA award-winning *Britain's Forgotten Slave Owners*.

David is a prize-winning author of many books. He also writes for *The Observer, The Guardian, The New Statesman* and the *BBC History Magazine*. In the Queen's New Year's Honours list, announced earlier this month, David was awarded the OBE for services to history and community integration.

"For me, history has always been a public activity," he maintains. "It's about reaching out to as many people as possible. I've spent my career working with institutions similarly committed to making history inclusive, expansive and diverse. Joining the University of Manchester is to continue in that tradition."

Professor Alessandro Schiesaro, Head of the School of Arts, Languages and Cultures at the University of Manchester, said this of the appointment: "David Olusoga's insightful and inspiring research addresses some of the thorniest issues of human history, and his passion, clarity and depth set a very high standard. His appointment as Professor of Public History at Manchester further strengthens our commitment to broadening the diversity of our curriculum and to playing an active role in the public's engagement with historical studies."

*

The meeting between Michael and David could not have gone better.

Since his appointment earlier in the year, David has been making a point of sitting down one-on-one with each of his colleagues within the department and finding out about the priorities and aspirations of each. With the more senior members of the team there has been the usual cagey sparring, with few of them willing to play too open a hand for fear of putting their current positions at risk, but with Michael the atmosphere was open and friendly from the outset. For the first twenty minutes they discussed their shared passion for a re-examination of Britain's imperial past, with both of them agreeing that Post-Colonialism should be brought more centrally into the curriculum and made a compulsory component for all undergraduates. Next, David wanted to hear more about the subject of Michael's recently completed doctorate concerning the covert role of the Wilson government in the Biafran War.

"I'm Yoruban," said Michael. "I hold both Nigerian and British passports, and I feel ashamed of both countries. Their treatment of the Igbo bordered on genocide. But I'm also an optimist. I believe the future will be better than the past. History can help us understand our mistakes and learn from them, so that we don't repeat them. But first we must shine a light on what happened, no matter whose sensibilities we may offend, so that we can understand things better."

"I can see now why you're so popular with your students," said David, smiling.

"Thank you," said Michael. "I do my best. I want them to be as passionate and excited about History as I am."

They had much in common. David, too, had been born in Nigeria, in Lagos, like Michael. He, too, was Yoruban. But only on his father's side. His mother was British, and, when David was just five, she had taken him with her back to Tyne & Wear, a council estate in Gateshead, where he was one of only a handful of mixed race people. By the time he was fourteen, their house had been attacked on more than one occasion by members of the National Front, and his mother had been forced to seek police protection. David had wanted to know why this tension and distrust still existed in small but significant pockets in his adoptive country, and so he had gone to Liverpool to study the History of Slavery.

"Did you happen to attend the *Bittersweet* exhibition at *The Portico Library* on Mosley Street a couple of years ago?" asked Michael.

"No," said David, "unfortunately not. But I read about it. I take it you went."

Michael nodded. "It attempted to shine a light on the numerous ways in which Manchester and its inhabitants, particularly those who had a connection with the Library in its earliest years, were connected with the history of slavery and its abolition."

"Wasn't Lubaina Himid involved?"

"Yes," said Michael, smiling broadly. "It was the same year she won the Turner Prize, while still lecturing at the University of Central Lancashire in Preston, so the timing couldn't have been better. She invited a number of artists to make personal responses to *The Portico*'s collection of artefacts. One of them, Mary Evans, a British-based Nigerian artist, created a series of cut-out silhouettes built around the classical tradition of portraiture to question ideas around identity, representation and cultural change. The use of paper cut-outs was simultaneously brutal and delicate."

"You speak very eloquently about it. Your wife's an artist, I understand?"

"She is," answered Michael proudly. "She was one of Lubaina's assistants on the exhibition. A volunteer intern. It was one of her first projects after she graduated."

The conversation turned effortlessly to more personal matters. Michael learned about David's partner's work with the BBC Natural History Unit in Bristol, and how they were still undecided about where they would live, whether they would uproot to Manchester, or try to manage the two households simultaneously. They had a daughter, who was happy at school in Bristol.

"Do you have children?" asked David.

Michael beamed. "A daughter," he said. "Blessing. But she's only two. We're not thinking about schools just yet."

The two men smiled and shook hands.

"Well," said David, "I think I can safely confirm that your position here in the department is as secure as such things ever can be. I'm recommending your current temporary role be upgraded to a permanent one with effect from the next academic year."

Now, an hour later, Michael is cycling back from the old Arts Building on the University Campus to Piccadilly Station, where he will take the Northern Rail service for Liverpool's Lime Street, which will deposit him after just fifteen minutes at Patricroft Station, from where it is just another five minute cycle ride to their home on Stanley Road with Molly's mother, Nadia. He wants to surprise them all with his good news.

It's a cold, sharp evening. The street lamps glow like amber flowers, each surrounded by a halo of moths clamouring towards the light. His breath freezes in statues as he cycles, their shapes constantly evolving before evaporating altogether.

He cycles quickly. It's a route he knows intimately and he is familiar with all the alleyways and cut-throughs to keep him away for the most part from the busy rush hour traffic. In the nearly ten years he has been at the university, either as a student or, more recently, as a lecturer, he has been witness to its constantly changing surroundings, as the campus has continued to evolve and metamorphose before his eyes, with buildings being torn down and replaced by new ones on a seemingly weekly basis. They emerge from their hard casing of sheet metal scaffolding, unfolding their wings of glass and steel and testing them out in the sunlight. Somehow he has managed to navigate a path between all these changes, adapting his route to accommodate them. Unlike the moth mistakenly drawn to an overhead street light, thinking it is the moon, which, by a system known as transverse orientation, it uses as a kind of compass in its search for pollen or a mate, Michael has learned not to be distracted by all these newer, shinier beacons that light his way, but to steer a path between them. It strikes him that he, too, is evolving. He knows the labyrinth of Manchester and can recognise its ever-changing terrain of landmarks better than his home town of Lagos, where, if he were to be suddenly uprooted and transplanted there, he would quickly be lost. This is his home now, and he is glad of it, but he is acutely aware that, with the passing of another ten years, he might be in danger of losing that sense of where he has first come from altogether, unless he makes a conscious effort to stay connected. Which he intends to. He must take Molly and Blessing on a trip back to Nigeria to visit his family there, especially his mother, who continues to design and produce the most dazzling of textile prints, which Molly adores. They speak each month by Skype, but the virtual is no substitute for the actual.

He cycles down Brunswick Street, quickly crossing Upper Brooke Street, before turning left into the quieter, narrower Kincardine Road, where a few of the city's once-trademark redbrick terraced houses still survive. This takes him to Gartside Gardens, which he cycles through the centre of, from where he follows Statham Road, then Penfield Close, before cutting through to Clare Street, which leads to a pedestrian underpass directly beneath the roaring Mancunian Way. He is now back within another part of the campus, what used to be UMIST – the former University of Manchester's Institute for Science & Technology, once a separate entity, now merged with the university. To his left is the Ferranti Building, an uncompromising three-storey concrete block clad in ribbed aluminium, with an equally Modernist sculpture alongside, comprising three high-voltage ceramic compressors, known as the Insulator Family, while to his right stands the Barnes Wallis complex, named for the designer of the legendary bouncing bombs from the Dambuster raids on the Ruhr Valley during World War II, which were carried by Lancaster bombers manufactured just a couple of miles away in Trafford Park, worked on by Molly's great-grandfather, Hejaz. Once a student refectory, and in its heyday host to memorable gigs by Jimi Hendrix, The Yardbirds and The Who, it is now largely given over to computer clusters and work stations. The white stabbing vertical funnel on its roof casts a long shadow across the open space at its front, which Michael now cycles along. He skirts the MSS Towers, brutalist, windowless cuboids in white concrete rising more than fifty metres high, topped now by mobile phone antennae, until he reaches the Green beside the Dalton Institute and Joule Library, where there are six apple trees, carefully nurtured and protected. These trees, of the 'Flower of Kent' variety, are scions of the original tree beneath which Sir Isaac Newton sat while conceiving his theory of gravity. None fall on Michael's head as he cycles past them, although he never fails to be conscious of all these pioneers of innovation who have passed this way before him in the city he now calls home, and whose voices propel him along Echo Street towards Granby Row.

He passes another small park. The quirky, eccentric wooden sculpture of a soda bottle, surrounded by giant renderings of grapes, raspberries and blackcurrants, rises surreally in the penumbra of the early evening street lights. It's a monument to that much-loved, invigorating cordial first manufactured on this very spot as 'a tonic to restore the customer's vim', or Vimto, as it came to be called. 'The Ideal Beverage,' it declares on the bottle, and so it has proved for more than a century. It has in more recent years become the go-to drink for Muslims round the world during Ramadan, being licensed for production and distribution in Yemen. Michael smiles, as he always does, as he cycles past it. What would Yasser, Molly's great-great-grandfather have made of it, he wonders? "Oh," he hears Nadia saying, "he'd have loved it. He swore by it." Michael and Molly never knew Yasser of course, but they feel as if they do, for his presence still dominates the house they share with his granddaughter-in-law, Nadia. His influence is everywhere, being the first among them to settle here. Above the fireplace in the sitting room hangs a drawing made by his son, Sol, Nadia's late husband, of the Hejaz Mountains of southern Arabia, which he drew while he was on National Service there. "It was Yasser's pride and joy," Nadia tells them. "He would look at it every day and imagine himself there."

Michael tracks these half-forgotten back ways like a warp threading the weft, his bicycle a shuttle flinging him now into Sackville Gardens. A light shines in the domed window of the Godlee Observatory atop the old Sackville Building, home of the city's first Science Institute. The observatory was a gift from Francis Godlee more than a century before. Godlee, a self-taught Quaker and cotton magnate, and an enthusiastic star-gazer, donated considerable funds towards the setting up of the Institute, and then installed the observatory on its roof. The dome, improbably, is made of papier-mâché, which nevertheless somehow survived the Blitz, despite all of its neighbouring buildings being destroyed by the Luftwaffe, and it still houses its original reflective telescope, much like the one used by Newton. Despite being relatively small, it was able to assist the first American moon landing, sending the astronauts a warning about a potentially dangerous crater. Michael knows this because he has taken one of the tours of the dome, which the Manchester Astronomical Society occasionally carries out. He is drawn compulsively to these landmarks and arcane facts about his adoptive city with the same unstoppable zeal of a magpie in pursuit of something shiny to take back to his nest.

As he cycles through the heart of Sackville Gardens, with less than a third of a mile to go before he reaches Piccadilly Station, he hears his phone ping. It's from Molly. He leans his bike against the bronze bench that forms part of the Alan Turing Memorial sculpture in the heart of the green.

"Hi," she says. "How did it go?"

"Hi."

"Well?"

"I've got some news."

"So have I."

"You go first."

"No. You."

They pause, each trying to picture the other, comfortable in the silence that ensues.

"Where are you now?" asks Molly.

"Actually," says Michael with a smile, "I'm sitting on a bench next to Alan Turing…"

*

2013

BBC
NEWS

Local – North-West – Manchester
Long Reads

24th December 2013

ALAN TURING: MANCHESTER CELEBRATES
PARDONED GENIUS
by
Chloe Chang

The decision to pardon wartime codebreaker and computer pioneer Alan Turing has been roundly welcomed, but in Manchester, where the campaign began to clear his name, it has been especially celebrated.

Alan Turing is credited with cracking Nazi Germany's Enigma Code, in the process shortening World War Two, and saving countless lives.

He was also a mathematical genius, the father of the modern computer and much of his ground-breaking work was conducted at the University of Manchester. Today, mathematics students at the university attend lectures in the building bearing his name.

Turing was gay in a time when homosexuality was regarded as a criminal offence. In 1952, despite his outstanding War record and his groundbreaking academic achievements, he was arrested on a charge of gross indecency and prosecuted. This ended his career, and two years later, in 1954, he was found dead in his flat by his cleaner, having poisoned himself with cyanide, which a subsequent inquest deemed to be suicide.

The fact that such a "national hero" was treated by the state in such a "barbaric" way was described as a "terrible blight on our history" by Justice Secretary Chris Grayling yesterday, who had requested the Royal Pardon.

The decision has been welcomed by Manchester's gay community, who have strived for years to get Turing's story a wider audience. "It's great news but something that is long overdue," said Rob Cookson, Director of The Lesbian and Gay Foundation (LGF), based in Manchester. "It is testimony to the range of people involved in fighting prejudice. It is another step towards equality."

Re-Naming of part of the A6010

The original petition calling for a posthumous pardon was begun by William Jones - also a computer scientist and a gay man living in Manchester - which eventually reached 37,000 signatures.

Mr Jones said, "In Manchester he's not as well known as he should be."

Back in 1994, when the city's leaders renamed part of the Inner Ring Road 'Alan Turing Way', which now runs close to Manchester City's new stadium at *The Etihad*, some people living nearby did not recognise the name, but Graham Stringer, the Council Leader at the time and himself a mathematician, was "determined to put that right."

Over time the simple fact of renaming it meant people got to know more about him.

Statue Unveiled to a Local & National Hero

Calls for a permanent memorial followed, and a statue of Alan Turing sitting on a bench in Manchester's Sackville Gardens, close to the city's Gay Village, was unveiled in 2001. The statue depicts Turing holding an apple because it is thought that it is this that contained the cyanide which resulted in his death. Underneath is an inscription, written in quasi-Enigma code, 'IEKYF RQMSI ADXUO

KVKZC GUBJ', which, roughly translated, means, 'Founder of Computer Science'.

Sculptor Glyn Hughes said it is now a popular tourist attraction, but, when the idea for a prominent memorial was first put forward 13 years ago, funding was hard to come by, and in the end the statue had to be made in China for a fraction of the cost.

"I am absolutely delighted by the news of the pardon," Mr Hughes told us. "It will be a landmark case," he said.

As Turing's story gained traction. A petition started by computer programmer Dr John Graham-Cumming led to an official apology in 2009 from the then Prime Minister Gordon Brown.

His efforts were backed by Mr John Leech, Liberal Democrat MP for Withington, who tabled a motion in Parliament last year calling for this posthumous pardon. He said: "Alan Turing's contribution to Manchester was enormous, as well as his efforts in bringing the War to an early conclusion. He is both a local and a national hero."

'One of the Most Significant Scientists of His Generation'

The decision to pardon Dr Turing means attention can once more be focused on his remarkable academic achievements, which are now studied at the University of Manchester, where he spent the last six years of his life working. In that time he helped create the world's first modern computer, the Manchester Mark 1, and also invented a test for artificial intelligence.

Professor Dame Nancy Rothwell, President and Vice-Chancellor of the University, said: "His legacy will live on as one of the most significant scientists of his or any other generation."

The city council and the LGF last year launched the Alan Turing Memorial Award to recognise people who have made an important contribution to the fight against homophobia. Many campaigners are calling for Dr

Turing's case to set a precedent enabling further pardons for others who had similar convictions.

Pat Karney, the current Leader of the City Council, said: "Lots of other lives were destroyed. We will be righting their injustice in a symbolic way."

On 31 March - the date he was convicted - the City Council will hold an Alan Turing Pardon Day, when the names of other Mancunians convicted of the same offences will be read out in a ceremony before the statue of the great man.

*

1952

Lily Warner – formerly Wright – and, before that, Shilling – is getting ready to go out. She sits at the dressing table in her bedroom of the house on Lapwing Lane in Didsbury she lives in with her husband Roland and – currently – the three children they are providing temporary foster care for until somewhere more permanent can be found for them. The latest three – two boys and a girl, siblings – have been with them for six weeks so far, which is about the average, but it is proving to be more difficult than usual to place these, for, being siblings, they very much want to stay together, and Lily is adamant that their wishes should be respected. Anita, Christopher and Clive, aged twelve, six and four years old.

Anita asks Lily the same three questions every day.

"Have you found us somewhere?"

"You will make sure they keep us together?"

And: "Why can't we stay here with you?"
To which Lily always answers:
"Not yet."
"I will."
"Because there will be other children needing to stay here."
But Anita is not easily put off.
"We'd be no trouble, Mrs Warner. I'll make sure the boys behave themselves, Mrs Warner. You'd hardly know we were here, Mrs Warner."
Mrs Warner.
Lily still finds it strange when people call her that. Even after having been married to Roland for nearly four years. And Warner's not her husband's name anyway. Not his real name. When he was finally able to stay in England, after serving out his time as a German prisoner-of-war, and after the Atlee Government had finally put through all the necessary legislation to allow him to apply for naturalisation, the clerk processing his papers at the Town Hall in Albert Square in his haste mistook his surname – Werner, pronounced 'Vairner' – and promptly Anglicised it.
"Welcome to Manchester, Mr Warner," he said, as he officially stamped the last of the literally dozens of forms Roland had had to fill out. "I hope you'll be very happy here."
"But…" Lily had begun at the time, before Roland quickly intervened to cut her off.
"Thank you," he said, "I'm sure I shall be."
Afterwards, as they scurried outside, blinking in the watery sunlight, Roland took hold of Lily's hand.
"Warner," he said. "I prefer it. It's more English. Like I am now. It will be less trouble for both of us."
"Both of us?" Lily said with a smile.
"Yes," he said. And then he kissed her, before going down on one knee, right there in front of the statue of Prince Albert in the centre of the Square, and proposing to her.

Lily smiles at her reflection in the dressing table mirror. She couldn't be happier. Except for one thing. They have no children.

"Not yet," Roland would say if pressed. But they both know that it is highly unlikely.

As well as having had several names, Lily has lived a number of lives already in her relatively short span.

Today is her birthday. Roland has arrived home from work at Ferranti's earlier than usual and presented her with a bunch of her favourite flowers – yellow tulips – which she has placed in a vase and put on a window-sill next to the model of a toy boat, named after the flower, which was carved by her grandfather while he was interned on the Isle of Man during the 1st World War, just before he died, and which has been the only link to her natural family, handed down to her from her mother, who died while giving birth to her. Lily had then been placed in the orphanage of St Bridget's, at Trafalgar House in Audenshaw, where she had been given the first of her names – Shilling – by the kind Sister Clodagh. Her only possession had been the toy boat, *The Tulip*, which she then took with her when she left St Bridget's, when she was fourteen and a half, to become a maid for a Mr Godwit of Globe Lane, Dukinfield, where it soon transpired that her duties as a maid extended to entertaining Mr Godwit and his so-called gentlemen friends, Messrs Snipe and Crake, in their weekly parties in ways that went far beyond serving them coffee. Eventually, when she could take no more of it, she made a daring midnight dash for freedom, taking nothing with her except for *The Tulip*, as she plunged down the rabbit hole of homelessness, where she was picked up by the Twins, a pair of vicious pimps, who threw her back out on to the streets to fend for herself. It was there, one foul and stormy night, that George Wright had found her, half-naked and left for dead on the pitiless flagstones of Angel Meadow, clutching a wet bundle closely to her. That bundle had been *The Tulip*, wrapped in sodden brown paper. George had scooped her up in his arms, put her on the back of his DOT Racer motor cycle, looped her thin arms around his waist, then tore across Manchester in the pouring rain until he reached his parents' home in this very house, where she now sits in what had once been their bedroom, remembering all this, nearly two decades before, when she was still only sixteen. George's mother, Annie, had taken her in, looked after her until her broken body was healed, and eventually adopted her, so that Lily Shilling became Lily Wright, and Lily could not have been happier about it.

But then came the 2nd World War. Annie stepped on to an unexploded bomb after the Christmas Blitz on Manchester of 1940, and Lily was an orphan once more. She fell into a second rabbit hole after that. She shut herself away in this house on Lapwing Lane for weeks, seeing nobody, not even George, who by that time had become a reconnaissance photographer with the RAF, afterwards a *camoufleur*, designing and building decoys to hoodwink the *Luftwaffe* into thinking they were bombing the factories of Trafford Park, only to be wasting their explosives on the uninhabited Manchester Moors.

It was Pearl who had rescued her, another girl from St Bridget's, who Lily had helped place when she left, as a companion to Annie's ageing mother-in-law, Mrs Evelyn Wright, and who now roused her from her lethargy and took her to Sunlight House to enrol for War Work. First Lily became a plotter, working in the underground tunnels beneath Manchester Town Hall to mark on a giant map where the enemy aircraft were. Next she became a dispatch-rider, taking messages across the unlit city in the blackout on George's old DOT Racer. Then she became an ack-ack girl, aiming the huge searchlights into the sky above Levenshulme, close by the German Prisoner-of-War Camp on Melland Road Playing Fields. That was where she met Roland.

She first saw him planting vegetables in the camp allotment, a simple action that seemed to Lily to be infused with such hope for an imagined future that she struck up a conversation with him. After that she had to run the gauntlet of disapproving local women each time she went to visit him, their fingers touching through the wire fence, while her ears were assailed with taunts of "Camp Whore" and worse. She had told Roland all of this, on their wedding night in *The Queen's Hotel*, and he had not spurned her as she feared he might. Instead he had folded her in his arms and told her he had never known such courage. And now, each year on her birthday, he brings her a bunch of yellow tulips to place beside the toy boat.

She doesn't think she will ever be able to have children of her own. Not after all her body had to endure at Globe Lane and then afterwards while on the streets. That's why she fosters other people's. She got the idea from seeing the film *Blossoms in the Dust* at the *Levenshulme Palace* during a break between her shifts in the War as an ack-ack girl. It starred Greer Garson, and it was about one woman's attempts to find homes for children who, through no fault of their own, did not have one. I could do that, she thought. I know what it's like to be alone and friendless. And so she had turned the Wrights' home on Lapwing Lane into a temporary refuge and shelter for orphaned children, and called it '*Blossoms*'. There were so many children needing to be re-housed after the War, and scores of them had passed through her doors.

Children like Anita, Christopher and Clive.

Though, in truth, not so many like them, for Anita, Christopher and Clive are black, and there are fewer couples ready to take on the additional challenges which that brings, and fewer still who have sufficient space to take in three. In the worst case scenario they will be placed in a care home, but Lily will do everything she can to avoid that. She knows what it is like in an orphanage, and she will not wish that on anyone, least of all these three adorable children, especially Anita, who is already older than her twelve years, who looks at the world through eyes that have experienced more than they should have, and who sees in Lily a possible last chance to escape the system, and who will fight to stay here, to protect her two younger brothers with all the fierceness of a tigress.

Lily makes herself a promise. She will make sure they will not be thrown back on the mercy of the state, which does its best, but which has limited options and even more limited resources. She will find them somewhere, somewhere safe, where, like the seeds planted by Roland on the day that she first met him, they can grow healthy and strong, and thrive. All of her charges are blossoms, and she will not let any of them wither or fade.

She looks back at her reflection in the dressing table mirror and whispers to it, "I promise."

And as she does so, she hears the same whisper come back to her over the years. Lily has her faults. Lily has made mistakes. But one thing Lily has always done is to keep her promises. And she will do so this time.

"I promise," she mouths once more, "I promise," before applying the finishing touches to her lipstick.

"Are you ready?" asks Roland, popping his head around the door.

"Almost," she says. "Can you do me up at the back?"

Roland duly obliges, and she turns to face him. At once he leans in to kiss her.

"Not now," she smiles, "you'll muss my hair."

"Later then," he says.

"If you're good," she laughs.

"Aren't I always?"

She frowns.

"What is it?"

"Your tie, Roland. Honestly, you're hopeless. Here – let me."

She proceeds to undo the bow and start again.

"I'm sorry," he says. "I hadn't realised tonight was formal until Freddie mentioned something about having to get his dinner jacket from the dry cleaners."

"I'd have thought his wife did that for him?"

"Gladys – yes. Normally she would, but she's away for a few days, visiting her mother, I think."

"So she won't be there this evening?"

"No. 'Fraid not. Nor will Tom's Irene. Nor Geoff's Pamela."

"Oh."

"And Alan's not married."

"Isn't he?"

"No, so I expect everyone will make a great fuss of you."

"I hope not. I should hate that." She finishes fixing Roland's tie. "There."

"Thanks. I'm hopeless at these things. What would I do without you?"

"You'd manage." She turns away crossly.

"What is it?"

"I wish you'd told me earlier about none of the other wives being able to go this evening. Then I shouldn't have gone to all this trouble to get ready. You could have gone by yourself and had a night out with the boys."

"I'd much rather you were with me. But if you'd prefer to stay at home, I'd understand. I could tell them you weren't feeling too good."

"I wouldn't want you to cover up for me. Not like that. I'd been looking forward to meeting your colleagues from work – and their wives – having heard you talk about them for so long."

"There'll be other occasions."

"Yes, I'm sure."

"And at least you'll get to meet Freddie, Geoff, Tom and Alan."

"But I don't want to. Not like this."

"Like what?"

Lily looks at Roland long and hard.

"Do I have to spell it out?"

Roland realises what she means and looks down.

"No. I'm sorry. I didn't think."

Lily turns away. Involuntarily she shudders. She can feel her skin begin to prickle and burn. Beads of sweat glisten on her brow and neck. She is thinking back to her days at Globe Lane, when frequently she would be the only female for dinner, surrounded by Godwit, Snipe and Crake and their cronies, each of them leering at her lasciviously, pressing themselves upon her, standing uncomfortably too close to her, placing a hand upon her arm, or neck, or back, and leaving it there too long. And after dinner there'd be dancing, when each of them would demand their turn around the floor with her, and after that they'd take their turn in other things…

Roland knows that she is remembering those things.

"It won't be like that tonight," he says. "You know that. They're decent chaps, all of them."

"I'm sure they are."

"But if you'd still rather not go…?"

"No. It's too late now. I'm all ready, and Delphine will be here in a minute. The children have been looking forward to her coming. I can't inconvenience her or disappoint them. I expect I'll be fine. I just wish you'd warned me earlier, that's all."

Just at that moment the doorbell rings.

"I expect that'll be Delphine now. You know how she is – punctual to the second."

"I'll let her in, shall I?"

Roland hurries downstairs. Lily turns back to her reflection, which is now distracted. She quickly re-applies her lipstick, then realises it is now overdone, so she wipes it clean. She is just about to start again when she hears excited shrieking emanating from the children's bedroom. She opens their door in time to see all three of them jumping wildly up and down on their beds.

"Is Miss Fish here?" lisps Clive, the youngest of them.

"Indeed she is," says Delphine before Lily can speak. In an instant all three are silent and still, sitting on the edge of their beds, their hands neatly folded on their laps.

Lily has to prevent her jaw from dropping.

"How do you do that?" she whispers to Delphine back out on the landing.

"You forget, my dear, that I was a teacher for many years before I joined the University."

Yes, thinks Lily, and I bet you were quite magnificent, the sort who never has to raise her voice in order to maintain calm in the classroom, who the children can see at once will brook no nonsense, so there's no point even trying, yet at the same time they adore her and will do anything to gain her approval.

"Now," continues Delphine, "don't worry about what time you get back. Stay out as long as you wish."

Yes, Miss, thinks Lily instinctively, but instead says, "Are you sure?"

"Of course I'm sure. It's a night to celebrate."

Lily frowns in puzzlement.

"Hasn't he told you?" says Delphine.

"Told me what?"

"He probably thinks you know already. It's been the talk of the University all day."

"What has?"

"This," declares Delphine, and she waves a copy of today's *Manchester Guardian* in front of Lily's nose.

Manchester Guardian

23rd January 1952

A MADAM WITH UNPREDICTABLE TENDENCIES

**A Machine Able to Multiply
Two 12-Figure Numbers in 0.003 seconds
Officially to Open at Manchester University**

To think of two twelve-figure numbers and write them down and then to multiply them together would involve considerable mental effort for many people, and could scarcely be done in much under a quarter of an hour. A machine will be officially "opened" at Manchester University on Monday which does this sort of calculation 320 times a second. Provisionally named "Madam" – from the initials of 'Manchester Automatic Digital Adding Machine' and because of certain unpredictable tendencies – it is a high-speed electronic computer built for the University Mathematics Department, and paid for by a Government grant. It is an improved version of a prototype developed by Professor F. C. Newman and Dr. T. Kilburn of the Electrical Engineering Department, and Mr. A. Turing of the Mathematics Department, (pictured above), in partnership with a team of Computer scientists from Ferranti's led by Mr Roland Warner...

"Deplorable headline, I know," says Delphine, whisking the paper back from Lily. "Sign of the times, I suppose."

"And there was I," sighs Lily, "thinking we were going out to celebrate my birthday."

"And so you shall, my dear. You just have to share it, that's all."

"I suppose so."

"No suppose about it. It's another remarkable first for Manchester. Now – off you go and enjoy yourselves. I shall be quite all right here. The children will be off to sleep in no time, and I have brought my book with me. Am I staying in the spare room as usual?"

And before Lily can answer, Delphine has swept back into the children's bedroom, where all three have been waiting for her with the patience of Job.

"Now," she says, shutting the door behind them, "we've time for one quick game of *Snakes & Ladders* before I turn the light out."

"Yes, Miss Fish," they chorus obediently.

"Come on," calls Roland from downstairs, "we don't want to miss our bus."

Lily recalls that moment when she fled from Globe Lane all those years ago, how she flung aside the bracelet in the form of a snake that Mr Godwit had fastened around her arm, and how she had then fallen down to the bottom of the rabbit hole, from where it had taken many ladders to be finally able to climb out, back up into the light.

She pats the side of her hair, gives herself a reassuring nod in the hall mirror, collects her coat and links her arm confidently through her husband's, determined to wrest back control of the evening that lies ahead and enjoy it.

As the evening unfolds, Lily quickly realises that she has been worrying unnecessarily. They are booked in for a Chinese banquet at the recently opened *Ping Hong* restaurant on Oxford Street. It is the first Chinese restaurant in the city, and Roland's colleagues are keen to try it out.

Ping Hong Restaurant
Chinese Banquet
1ˢᵗ Course

Crab Wonton Soup (for tradition, in honour of ancestors)
Strips of cold beef (symbolising close familial ties)

Freddie, Geoff and Tom are charmingly old fashioned throughout. They address her as Mrs Warner at all times, even after she requests them to call her 'Lily'. They rise from their chairs when she needs to go to the bathroom. They include her in their conversations. They listen to what she has to contribute without being overtly patronising. She surprises them when it becomes clear that she understands the basics of binary computation.

"As you can see," jokes Roland, "my wife and I have no secrets from one another."

The gentlemen all laugh warmly and Lily is able to banish the memories of Globe Lane almost immediately. Their repartee is quick, shot through with mild teasing. They appear to have their own secret codes between them and frequently finish off each other's sentences. They remind her of *The Three Musketeers*, with Tom as the scholarly Athos, Geoff the more refined Aramis, and Freddie as the genial Porthos, which must make Roland their D'Artagnan, she supposes, eager to join their club, but who can never quite hide the difference of his accent. Alan on the other hand seems content to be the outsider. He is far too busy trying to impress the friend he has brought with him – Arnold Murray, who is much younger than the rest of them and undeniably pretty. That Alan is completely besotted with him is immediately apparent to her, even though Arnold makes little effort to pretend to be interested in what the rest of them are talking about. She wonders if Alan's attraction to Arnold is as obvious to them as it is to her. They appear to be blithely unaware of it. Or perhaps it is merely their impeccable good manners that prevent them from drawing any attention to it. Arnold looks bored, out of his depth, and Lily almost feels sorry for him. Or she would do, if he wasn't so dismissive of Alan's attempts to make him feel included. She finds that she likes Alan. He reminds her of some of the small boys she has fostered as part of *Blossoms*, so desperate to be accepted, to fit in, to please. At this moment, between courses, he is expounding on what his colleagues affectionately refer to as his 'hobby horse'.

"A simulation," says Freddie, "a poor substitute for the real thing."

"For now," he concedes, "but wait a few years. You'll see. The important thing is to prove the theory, establish the principle. Then wait for you engineers to catch up with the idea."

This remark is met with predictable jeers. This public school banter appears to lie at the core of how they continue to deal with each other as grown men, though only two of them – Geoff and Alan – actually attended public school, King Edward's and Sherborne respectively, while Freddie and Tom were Grammar School boys, at Stockport and Wheelwright's in Dewsbury, but they all of them went to Cambridge subsequently. Perhaps this is where they obtained their veneer of confidence and entitlement, thinks Lily. She wonders how Roland keeps up with them all, but somehow he does, appearing to give as good as he gets.

"What's the point," he is saying now to an increasingly besieged Alan, "of spending so much time trying to teach the Manchester Baby, or Madam, or whatever comes next, to play bridge or chess, when we should instead be focusing on more important, practical applications?"

"No," groan the others as one, "please don't get him started on that again?"

"Algorithms," he declares, pouring himself another bottle of *Tsingtao* beer, "are our hope for the future."

"They're boring," says Arnold, blowing a smoke ring directly at his friend, perfectly framing his face.

"They're beautiful," replies Alan, meeting Arnold's gaze directly.

"And why is that exactly?" asks Lily, purposefully intervening between them.

"Because they are always unambiguous," says Freddie emphatically, wafting away the smoke that has settled over the table like a pall. "Forgive me, Mrs Warner, if what I am about to say is too simplistic. Given the lack of any secrets between you and your husband, night-time discussions about algorithms might be your customary pillow talk."

"I doubt that very much," laughs Lily.

"In that case, the easiest way to explain an algorithm is that it is a clearly defined, finite sequence of basic instructions designed to solve a problem or perform a calculation, one that can readily be implemented by a computer."

"Alan's far too modest to say so himself…" begins Geoff.

"Really?" chips in Arnold. "I hadn't noticed."

"There's even a machine named after him…" continues Geoff over the laughter that has greeted Arnold's remark.

"The Turing Machine," adds Tom.

"…which would be capable of performing any conceivable mathematical computation…" concludes Geoff.

"…if it were representable as an algorithm," corrects Alan.

"And if such a machine could ever be built," Freddie reminds them all.

"I thought that was what you were all celebrating this evening," says Lily frowning.

"The 'Manchester Madam' is just a small step towards it," says Geoff.

"But a significant one," says Tom.

"It only demonstrates what I predicted more than a decade ago back at Cambridge," says Alan crossly.

"*Der Entscheidungsproblem*," whispers Roland to Lily, who merely frowns.

"Meaning what exactly?"

"Must we?" says Alan, taking another swallow of his beer.

"Patience, dear boy," says Freddie, affectionately patting his young deputy on the arm.

2nd Course

Whole Chicken (served complete with head)
(Unity & Wholeness, the Dragon & the Phoenix)

"*Entscheidung* is German for 'decision'," begins Roland. "And the 'problem' was posed by two German mathematicians…"

"Hilbert and Ackerman," interjects Tom.

"They sought an algorithm that would consider any statement that was put to it," continues Roland, "and then answer it 'yes' or 'no' in a way that was definitive, that's to say is universally valid and correct for every conceivable situation."

"And it was Alan who found the answer to it?" asks Lily.

"It was," declares Freddie.

"Who's a clever boy?" says Arnold.

"But not in the way anyone had predicted," says Roland.

"Oh, he's full of surprises," says Arnold again.

"I think someone has had too much to drink," whispers Lily to him, unheard beneath the general *bonhomie* around the table, so that Arnold blushes, stubbing out his cigarette in fierce embarrassment.

"What he proved," says Roland, "was that there was *no* solution."

"Oh," says Lily, "that's disappointing."

"On the contrary. It demonstrated just how powerful the Turing Machine is."

"I don't understand."

"It's not a real machine," says Alan at last, somewhat wearily, "at least, not yet. It's only an abstract."

"How does it work?" asks Lily. "This abstract?"

Alan regards Lily curiously. He sees that she is not teasing him, as he first suspected, but that she is genuinely interested. He likes her directness. She does not appear in any way cowed or intimidated by being the only woman present among all these men. Nor does she try to flirt with them, which would be understandable. Instead she holds her ground. She's strong-willed and independent, and appears very able to hold her own. She reminds him a little of Joan Clarke, who'd worked alongside him trying to crack German codes in Hut 8 at Bletchley Park, who he'd been engaged to for a while, until he'd had to confess his preferences for men. Joan hadn't been fazed in the least. She'd merely accepted that any marriage between them could hardly have much chance of success, and they had parted amicably. He thinks Lily is cut from the same cloth, and so he does not speak down to her, nor try to impress her, as his colleagues have been doing, though no doubt unconsciously.

And so he looks at her directly and says, "It manipulates symbols on a strip of tape according to a strict table of rules."

"Symbols?"

"Letters or digits from a finite alphabet."

"Finite?"

Alan smiles. She is already one step ahead of his explanation. "Yes," he says. "The machine 'reads' the symbol. Then it either writes a symbol of its own in response…"

"From the same finite alphabet?"

"…and moves on to another instruction, or…"

"Halts the computation…"

"Precisely so."

"Not unlike the way a loom reads a pattern before weaving it."

"Exactly."

"So what's all this about proving there was no solution?"

"It's a question of what we call the 'halting' problem."

"Go on."

"In order to prove whether the answer to a question is either 'yes' or 'no' in every possible circumstance, it is first necessary to show that the programme will eventually finish running, or will in theory run for ever."

"But to do that you first need an algorithm that is infinite, not finite," interrupts Lily excitedly.

"And as yet no such algorithm exists."

"And even if it did, theoretically each new input could contradict the one before it, *ad infinitum*…"

"So that the 'halting' problem is…"

"Undecidable!" choruses the entire party as one. All, that is, except Arnold, who scowls as everyone else applauds Lily and themselves.

At that point the waiters bring in the next set of courses, and everyone begins talking at once, pointing out the various dishes, heaping portions from each onto their plates. Lily overhears Alan apologising quietly to Arnold, asking him if he's all right, and Arnold replying that yes, he's fine, though to Lily his expression appears to belie this.

She delicately pokes her fork into the small helping of sea bass in front of her on her plate. The other gentlemen are still debating the more arcane points of *der Entscheidungsproblem*, but still seem no nearer to finding a decision they can all agree on.

3rd Course

Sweet & Sour Fish with Vegetables
(for prosperity & abundance)

Followed by Noodles
(for longevity)

"Where did you too meet?" she whispers to Arnold at one point, while leaning across to light his cigarette. He looks up sharply at her, like a child who has been caught out in a lie, before quickly recovering himself. Damn it, he thinks. She knows. But instead he merely says, "Rather like this, actually. We were both coming out…"

Lily raises an eyebrow ruefully.

"…of *The Regal* on Oxford Road," he continues, "and I asked him for a light."

"And did he oblige?" asks Lily, holding the flame from the lighter up towards the young man's handsome face. "I believe he did," he says.

He draws deeply on his now-lit cigarette, then breathes the smoke from the corner of his rather sensuous mouth away from Lily's face.

"I understand from Roland that it's your birthday today?" says Alan.

"It is."

"Many happy returns. I don't imagine this is how you envisaged you'd be celebrating it?"

"How old are you?" blurts out Arnold.

"Arnold, really," scolds Alan. "Don't you know it's rude to ask a lady her age?"

"Lily doesn't mind, do you, Lily?"

"Arnold, that's enough."

"She can ask me my age any time she likes."

"Very well, how old are you?"

"Please don't encourage him."

"Why don't you guess? That's much more fun."

Lily has decided she has had quite enough of Arnold.

"Evidently not old enough to know better."

"I'm nineteen," he declares defiantly, jutting out his down-like chin.

"Then little boys should be seen and not heard."

Arnold pouts and looks away.

Dessert

Fruit
Oranges (for wealth & good fortune)
Apples (for temptation)

Warm Tea
(for respect)

"But why teach a computer to play chess?" asks Lily.

Before Alan can answer, Arnold interrupts him.

"A computer beating a Grand Master at chess is about as interesting as a bulldozer winning an Olympic weight-lifting competition. It's just high speed calculation. It has nothing to do with intelligence."

Alan shakes his head with an indulgent smile towards his friend, before turning once more to Lily.

"Do you play chess, Mrs Warner?"

"Not well. My brother George used to let me beat him sometimes."

Alan peels himself an apple. "Arnold here likes to play chess, don't you?"

"I like to win."

"But you're too impatient. You need to learn to play the long game."

"Delay the gratification?"

Alan and Arnold share a look, which does not go unnoticed by Lily. Alan offers Arnold a slice of the apple, which he declines.

"You take too many risks," says Alan.

"I like to live dangerously," says Arnold.

Alan places the cut apple into his mouth, savours the juice as it runs over his tongue.

"But what kind of game would a machine play?" asks Lily.

"Whichever it decides."

"So it has a choice?"

"If programmed with unlimited possibilities, yes."

"But does it make these choices consciously? Intuitively?"

"It doesn't make them at all at the moment," sneers Arnold. "It's like everything else with Alan. Just a theory."

"But that is my aim, Mrs Warner."

"I do wish you'd stop calling me that. It makes me sound positively ancient. It's Lily – please."

"Well – Lily – the question I ask myself constantly is a simple one. It is this. Can a machine think?"

"And how do you answer yourself, Alan?"

"That's not so simple. I believe – in time – they may be capable of it, but I have no very convincing arguments of a positive nature to support my views. However, I do believe the onus should be on the sceptics to prove that the idea of a thinking machine is impossible, rather than relying solely with us scientists to prove that it isn't. Bertrand Russell says – you've heard of Bertrand Russell…?"

Lily rolls her eyes. "Of course I have."

"Well, he ridicules the possibility. He says that it is like asking a sceptic to disprove that a China teapot – rather like this one…" He holds up the decorative pot that the waitress has just placed on the table in front of him. "…is revolving around the sun while at the same time insisting the teapot is too small to be revealed."

"He has a point, don't you think?" asks Lily.

"No I don't," replies Alan hotly. "The entire edifice of scientific discovery is based on just such a conjecture. They are of vital importance, for they suggest possible useful lines of enquiry. That is the scientist's job. To dream the impossible, and then find a way to prove that it's possible."

Lily pours them both a cup of China tea and places a slice of lemon in each.

"So how are you going to do that?" she asks him gently.

"Don't get me wrong. I understand the need for empirical evidence as well as the next scientist. What I propose is a simple test."

"Go on."

"It's an adaptation of an old Victorian parlour game."

By now the others have begun listening to him once more.

"Is he telling you about the Imitation Game, Mrs Warner?" calls Freddie from across the table.

"I was just about to," says Alan, stubbing out his cigarette crossly.

"Why don't we play it?" suggests Freddie.

"What – now?" moans Tom.

"Must we?" complains Geoff.

"I'm intrigued," says Lily.

"Very well," concedes Roland. "It is your birthday after all."

"And what would a birthday be without a party game?" says Arnold, who has now visibly perked up.

A cloud passes briefly across Lily's mind, transporting her to a particular evening in Globe Lane, her last one there, when certain games had been played. She doesn't like party games. But this seems harmless enough. And they are in a public place, rather than a private house.

All eyes are fixed on Alan. He shifts uncomfortably in his chair, takes a sip of tea, then reluctantly turns to face them.

"The rules are quite simple," he says. "I need two volunteers. One of them must be you, Lily."

"Why?" she says.

"One volunteer must be female, the other male."

"Let Arnold be the other," says Freddie. "We've all played the game before."

"How exciting," says Arnold, rubbing his hands together. "What do we have to do? I'm warning you, Lily, I'm terribly competitive."

"It's not that kind of game," says Alan patiently.

"Oh," says Arnold, momentarily disappointed. "What kind is it?"

"It involves me asking you both a series of questions. Only you don't shout your answers out loud. Instead you write them down. I have my back turned, so I can't see which of you is writing what. Only use block capitals, then I shan't be able to guess at your handwriting. And when you've finished, hand your answers to someone else, who then gives them to me."

"What happens then?" asks Lily.

"That's the crux of the experiment. I have to try and ascertain from the answers each of you has written down, which have been written by a man, and which by a woman. Your role is to try and deceive me, so that I can't easily distinguish between you."

"It sounds very devious," she says.

"Doesn't it?" agrees Arnold. "I love it. Can we start right away?"

Alan turns his back, while Lily and Arnold are given a pen each with which to write their answers on the back of two of the *Ping Hong*'s menus.

"At the top of the paper," says Alan, instead of writing your names, one of you write 'A', the other 'B'. Decide between yourselves now, while I cover my ears, which one of you is which."

In dumb show, Lily agrees she will be 'A' and Arnold 'B'.

"Now," says Alan, "I'll begin with a simple question. Do you play cricket?"

Grinning, Lily and Arnold each write down their answer.

"Second," says Alan, "how long did it take you to get ready to come out this evening?"

Lily and Arnold have to bite the inside of their cheeks to prevent themselves from giggling as they each separately answer this.

"And finally," says Alan, "write a sonnet about the Barton Aqueduct Swing Bridge."

This final question provokes universal uproar.

"I say, Alan," protests Freddie, "that's rather a tall order."

"The first line then," concedes Alan.

Lily and Arnold attempt something, then put down their pens. Lily then passes her menu to Tom, while Arnold passes his along to Geoff. Tom and Geoff then hand each solemnly to Alan with a mock bow. Alan turns around.

"Well," says Freddie, "read us the answers."

"To Question 1 – 'Do you play cricket?' – 'A' has answered 'yes' while 'B' has answered 'no'. Most people would draw from these the obvious conclusion that 'A' must be male and 'B' female. But since I asked both guinea pigs to try and hoodwink me, I might then assume that the opposite were true, whereas I happen to know for a fact, because Arnold is a friend of mine, that he did not in fact play cricket at school, and so he might, if he were 'A' answer truthfully just to confuse me further."

"How do you know I was telling you the truth in the first place?" quips Arnold.

"Indeed," replies Alan, while the others laugh. "Now we come to Question 2 – 'How long did you take to get ready to come out this evening?' " Alan can scarcely suppress a smile as he quietly reads each answer. "'A' has replied, 'Not long enough,' while 'B' has answered, 'Don't you know it's impolite to ask me that?' "

This last remark is greeted by loud guffaws around the table.

"Arnold is always late, and so that could point towards him being 'A', but he is more than mischievous enough to have answered as 'B'. So once again, determining who is who is far from straightforward. So let us turn finally to Question 3 – the first line of a sonnet. 'A' has written, 'Count me out on this one. I never write poetry.' While 'B', on the other hand, has written, 'Shall I compare thee to the Golden Gate…?' "

This is immediately followed by spontaneous applause and the rhythmic stamping of feet and the enthusiastic rapping of knuckles upon the table.

"Once again, my friends," says Alan, urging calm and order from the assembled company, "we are in tricky waters. For isn't poetry the traditional domain of the female, which would appear to indicate 'A' to be male? And yet both our willing volunteers here," he continues, gesturing magnanimously towards Lily and Arnold, "are capable of the sure-fire wit of the answer furnished by 'B'. And so, you see, I am, to coin a metaphor from Question 1, stumped. I am unable – with certainty – to be able to distinguish from this simple test, this imitation game, which is male and which is female. I could hazard a guess…"

"Please do," urges Roland.

"Hear, hear," chorus the others.

"Very well. If forced, I would say Lily was 'A' and Arnold 'B'."

"Correct on both counts," smiles Lily.

"But that is only because Arnold and I are friends, and I have some insight into the devious way his mind works…"

"You don't know the half of it," laughs Arnold.

"Otherwise, I would have been all at sea," admits Alan.

"And your point in all this is?" asks Lily.

"Now we come to it," says Freddie warmly.

"That if we were to replace 'A' or 'B' with a computer and set the same kind of test…"

"...pitting a human against a machine," interrupts Lily, the light beginning to dawn on her.

"It would be just as difficult to distinguish between them."

"Surely that depends upon the nature of the questions asked," says Roland.

"I don't believe it does," says Alan. "If, for example, we were to ask a strictly mathematical question – say, multiply 78.21 by 34.56 – we might initially expect that the computer would get this right and the human may get this wrong. But let us assume the human gets it right, he or she will need a certain amount of time to do so, while a computer will be able to provide the correct answer instantly. 2702.9376 in this case."

"Show-off," says Geoff, who has only just finished working it out on the back of his own menu.

"However," continues Alan, "if the machine is smart enough, it will delay its computed reply, and even then, if programmed according to the rules of the game, give an incorrect response. What we want is a machine that can learn from experience. The possibility of it altering its own instructions provides the mechanism for this."

A low murmur of disquiet ripples around the guests.

"And so, Lily," says Alan, "to answer your question, my point is that, while our computers are not capable of such sophistication yet, in theory, over time, they will be, and so yes, I believe that a machine is capable of thinking, and in ways that will make it extremely difficult to differentiate it from us mere mortals."

He lights himself another cigarette in the silence that has descended upon the table in the light of this last remark.

"And that is what we shall continue to strive towards," says Tom.

"And why tonight's celebration of our unveiling of the 'Manchester Madam' is so significant," adds Geoff.

"But we're still only at the very beginning of our journey," says Roland. "Speaking as an engineer," he continues, "I for one am most excited by what the next breakthrough will be."

Lily smiles fondly at her husband. He's a little drunk, she realises, and why shouldn't he be?

"I believe a toast is in order," says Freddie, rising somewhat unsteadily to his feet. "To the future."

"The future," they all reply, raising their glasses.

"And what better place to be to prepare for that future than here in Manchester, which has always been the crucible of new discoveries, of new ways of thinking, new ways of interpreting the world we see around us, and not just interpreting it, but shaping it. To change."

"I'll drink to that," says Alan, chinking his glass against Arnold's.

The waitress is hovering with a tray. Lily nods towards her. She waits until she has finished clearing away everyone's cups and plates, dishes and bowls, then turns once more to face Alan.

"I still have a question," she says. "Three, actually. For all these scientific breakthroughs we rightly honour this evening, will a machine ever be able to replicate human emotions? Will it ever be able to fathom the heart? And do we want it to?"

The others nod their heads sagely. Some chuckle, others simply say, "Hmm." They all of them look towards Alan expectantly. But before he can answer, he is interrupted by an enormous clattering and smashing of crockery, as the weighed-down waitress drops her tray, and shards of broken pot shatter all around them. It appears to take an eternity until the last broken plate stops spinning and a terrible silence ensues. All eyes are focused on the poor girl, who looks as if she is about to cry. But after what is nothing more than a second's stillness, everyone begins moving at once. The other waiters bend down to pick up as many pieces as they can, while the proprietor berates the girl loudly and angrily in Cantonese. The gentlemen have all risen from the table and are brushing away the debris from their suits, while Lily instinctively makes a bee-line for the girl and immediately begins to help her. The proprietor is still shouting at her furiously. Lily attempts to step between them, to intervene and try and calm him down, but he is not to be quieted. Lily fears he may even strike the girl, so she scoops her up in her arms and hurries her quickly away towards the Ladies' Room.

Several minutes later Lily returns. The men all regard her with expressions of concern on their faces.

"What happened?" they ask.

"Is she all right?"

"Are *you* all right?"

"What did she have to say?"

Lily waves them away. "A story for another time perhaps. I'm fine. She's not."

The waitress returns to the Dining Room clutching Lily's handkerchief. Ignoring the stern looks from the proprietor, she hurries across to Lily.

"Thank you," she says, holding out the handkerchief towards her. "Best you go now."

Lily presses it back firmly within the waitress's closed palm. "You keep it," she whispers quietly, then steps away.

"Well," says Freddie, after everything has been cleared up, the bill has been paid, and they have all stepped outside into the cold. "I think I'm going to call it a night. Gladys will be wondering where I've got to."

"Me too," says Geoff somewhat sheepishly.

"And me," adds Tom, equally abashed.

"But don't let our boring, predictable ways inhibit all of you from going on somewhere else."

"We don't want to be too late back for Delphine," says Roland to Lily.

"Nonsense," says Lily. "She's told us to stay out all night if we want to. There's a bed made up for her in the spare room. There's no need for us to rush back. It is my birthday after all."

"Very well," says Roland, who is never able to resist her, especially when she wraps her arms around the back of his neck, as she does now. "What do you suggest?"

"How about *The Queen's*? It's been ages since we were last there. George and Francis said they might pop along."

"It sounds to me like you've had this planned from the start," smiles Roland.

"And there was I, hoping to be as mysterious and enigmatic as one of Alan's machines."

"I'll never crack your code, Lily," says Roland.

"And why would you want to?" concedes Alan.

"George and Francis?" asks Arnold.

"George Wright," says Lily. "The photographer. He's my brother – well, adoptive."

"And Francis?" says Arnold pointedly.

"George's friend," says Lily, looking Arnold directly in the eye.

"That wouldn't be Francis Hall, would it?" says Tom, calling back from the door, where he has just finished putting on his coat.

"Yes," says Lily. "Do you know him?"

"Geoff and I do." He turns to Freddie now to explain. "He's the chap I was telling you about. Queer sort of fish. Albino. But quite brilliant in radio astronomy. He helped Bernard out over at Jodrell Bank when he was setting up after the War. What he doesn't know about sound waves isn't worth knowing. Lenses too."

Freddie nods. "Yes. I remember now."

"Wasn't he involved with *Radio Aspidistra*?" whispers Alan.

"I don't know," says Lily. "He might have been. It was all very hush hush. He's not supposed to talk about it. And nor should you," she adds, scolding him with a smile.

"Don't worry," he says. "I'm good with secrets."

"Not as good as he thinks," remarks Arnold, as the four of them – Roland and Lily, Alan and Arnold – step out in the cold, night air of Oxford Street, and say their farewells to Geoff and Tom, who climb into Freddie's 1948 black Austin 16, which is parked directly outside.

"Can we drop you anywhere?" calls out Freddie.

"No thanks," replies Lily before the others can answer. "We'll walk." And she strides quickly up Portland Street, so that Roland, Alan and Arnold have to hurry to keep up with her. Roland catches her first. He takes her arm and whispers in her ear. "Steady the buffs, old girl."

"Less of the old," she says.

He recognises these signs in her – the flush on the back of her neck, the hectic colour in her cheeks – which are a warning that she might be teetering on the edge of making a scene. She does this rarely now, but even so, Roland is constantly on the alert, especially in social situations like these, when she has a tendency to drink just a little bit more than she should. He is about to warn her and say something crass about the effects of the sudden cold air, but he can see that she is smiling, and so bites his tongue.

"Don't worry," she adds, sensing his concern. "I'll calm down once I see George."

"Let's hope he's there then," he says, more to himself than to her.

"He will be. He wouldn't want to miss my birthday."

Back in the *Ping Hong*, Xiu Mei, the young waitress, under the watchful eye of the proprietor, clears away the last of the debris. Much of the food from the various dishes has not been touched. She tries to squirrel some of it away for later, to have cold when she is once more alone, upstairs in her tiny attic bedroom, in which she will not sleep. She will close her eyes and try to recall images of her village back in China, in the wetlands surrounding Shenzen, which she knows she will never see again. Manchester is her home now, and she must learn to accept this. She thinks back to the unexpected kindness shown to her by the young guest whose birthday it was this evening, and how she had coaxed something of her story from her, whose name, she said, was Lily. Like the flower. Perhaps there will be more people like her here in this strange city. Perhaps she will learn to settle here after all. Eventually. She opens her hand. The tightly scrunched handkerchief that Lily had pressed upon her opens up before her like the petals of a flower. It is edged with delicately embroidered pink blossom from a tree she does not recognise. She will keep this, she decides, as a treasure, a keepsake.

"Here they are," says George as Lily and Roland arrive, and he waves to attract their attention.

"But who's that with them?" says Francis, placing the spectacles he only allows George to see him wearing onto his nose to be able to inspect Arnold and Alan more clearly, then hastily removing them as they approach. "Spring Chicken and Mother Hen?"

"Behave," whispers George.

"Ooh, I love it when you're masterful."

"It's Lily's night, not yours."

"Yes, Miss."

Lily runs across to greet them.

"George," she says.

"Happy birthday, Sis."

"Thank you. I love it when you call me that." She studies his face, the kind eyes, the modest smile. But there's a strain there, she notices, which has been with him more or less since the end of the War, when he'd decided that he and Francis would simply carry on as 'just friends'. "How are you?" she whispers in his ear.

"Fine," he says. "Keeping busy. Which is how I like it."

"I heard that," says Francis, coming over to air-kiss Lily. "Busy, busy, busy. That's our George. He's hardly any time for his friends these days, have you, George? Well, buzz if you like, but don't sting me."

As if on cue *The Queen's Hotel* Band strikes up the popular Arthur Askey song, and onto the stage steps Chamomile Catch, the Manchester Songbird.

"I like to be a busy, busy bee
Being as busy as a bee can be
Flying round the garden, the brightest ever seen
Taking back the honey to the dear old Queen..."

Her arrival is greeted with huge applause by *The Queen's* regulars. Introductions are hastily completed by Roland.

"George, Francis – this is Alan, Arnold."

"Thanks, Roland. How are you keeping?"

"Never been better. We're celebrating."

"Music to my ears," pipes Francis. "Giancarlo," he calls to a passing waiter, "two bottles of champagne."

"*Si. Grazie, Signor.*"

"Happy birthday, Lily."

"Not just my birthday, Francis. Tell them, Roland."

"My good friend Alan and I are celebrating the launch of a new computer. The Manchester Automatic Digital Adding Machine."

"That's quite a mouthful, Roland," smirks Francis, which causes Arnold to splutter into his glass.

"Sorry," he says. "The bubbles went up my nose."

"That's why we call it 'The Manchester Madam'," says Roland.

"Really?" says Francis, ostentatiously clearing his throat. "I feel the Muse is upon me." He rises to his feet and begins to orate.

"There once was a Manchester Madam
If you gave her two numbers, she'd add 'em
Her perpetual motion
Provoked such devotion
But she'd toss 'em aside once she'd had 'em..."

"Bravo," cries Alan. "It's true. She's a most demanding mistress. She always keeps us to task, our noses to the grindstone, doesn't she, Roland?"

"I'm afraid so."

"But we'll master her yet."

"Such busy, busy bees, all of you. Work, work, work. What are we girls meant to do, Lily? Sit at home and knit?"

"Not likely. But I'm busy too, Francis."

"Yes indeed. All your good deeds."

"Well, you know what they say?" says Arnold, breaking into the circle, so that suddenly all eyes are on him.

"No, Arnold," says Francis. "I don't. But I expect you will enlighten me."

"All work and no play..."

"Makes Jack a dull boy. Yes indeed. Well thank goodness he's not here. I don't see any Jacks in the vicinity, do you, Lily? Or knaves."

Lily, steadfastly looking at Arnold, says nothing.

The moment is broken by Cam once more taking to the stage. She is wearing a white gardenia in her hair.

"I thought I'd sing some Billie Holliday songs for you this evening," she croons. "Hence the flower. Do you like it, boys? At least I'm not wearing it to cover up the scorch marks in my hair, like Lady Day had to." She turns towards the band leader. "Ready, Prez?"

"Ready, Miss Catch."

"I say I'll go through fire
And I'll go through fire
If I have to hold up the sky
Crazy he calls me, sure I'm crazy
Crazy in love am I..."

"I believe you worked with Sefton Delmer in the War?" asks Alan in as disarming a manner as he can.

Francis looks up sharply. "And I believe you were at Bletchley?"

"Both of us cracking codes, trying to keep that one important step ahead of the enemy. In your case, as I understand it, by a matter of fractions of a second."

"It's not something I'm proud of," says Francis, suddenly serious.

"Oh?"

"It may surprise you to learn that an extremely red-blooded male, a former champion boxer no less, who I am proud to count among my friends, once told me that the one and only time he ever lost a bout he considered it to be his finest contest. Winning no longer mattered. He knew that he had never performed so well. It just so happened that his opponent that night boxed even better."

"And your point is?"

"We won the War, but we didn't always abide by Queensbury rules, did we?"

"History's written by the victors, Francis."

"That's funnier than you know. My boxing friend's name is Victor."

"Nevertheless…"

"Nevertheless we're still bound by the Official Secrets Act and so no one will ever know the full story of what we did."

"In time they will."

"Long after both of us are gone."

"I hate secrets. I hate having to hide in the dark, keeping things covered up, locked away, out of sight."

"But not out of mind, dear boy, not out of mind…"

Arnold has rejoined them. He looks unhappy, thinks Francis. He doesn't know where he fits in here. He sits always on the fringes of conversations, not sure what, if anything, he has to contribute to them. He tries on various different roles – joker, cynic, man of mystery – but none of them seem to fit. He's bored. Not with the place, but with us. Francis recognises all of this in less than a minute. He's met Arnold's type before – God knows he has – and they always spell trouble. Restless, impatient, but so pretty, they make him weak at the knees just looking at them. No wonder Alan is so smitten. He's going to get badly burned, thinks Francis, but, looking at Alan again now, he realises that Alan understands this, but will walk this path he's chosen regardless of the consequences. Arnold, he sees, is fascinated by the clientele here at *The Queen's*, and he's already made eye contact with several of the older regulars. Time to intervene, decides Francis, and play the game he's best at, the witty quip to puncture the tension.

Turning to both of them he gives a small, polite cough before treating them to another of his limericks.

"There was a young girl from Man<u>chest</u>er
Met a scientist who so impressed her
Each time she was with him
Each new algorithm
With random abandon undressed her…"

Alan chortles with delight. Even Arnold cannot suppress a smirk.

Codes and signals, thinks Francis. Codes and signals...

Cam steps up to the microphone once more.

"It's that ole Devil called love again
Gets behind me and keeps giving me that shove again..."

George and Francis swap places. Francis goes to catch up with Lily and Roland – "Darling, I absolutely adore your new eye shadow, so very Blanche Dubois, 'I have always depended upon the kindness of strangers' – while George has now joined Alan and Arnold.

"Roland tells me that as well as being something of a maths genius, you're also publishing pioneering papers on biology?"

"I'd hardly call them pioneering."

"Don't hide your light under a bushel, Alan," says Arnold, smiling.

"I don't suppose you've heard the term 'morphogenesis'?"

"No," says George, "But I assume from its name it's something to do with change and new beginnings?"

"Oh for a classical education," remarks Arnold coolly.

"Actually," says George, looking at him directly, "I left school early to become an apprentice sign writer, and after that I helped my father run a printing works."

Arnold looks down, somewhat abashed, but quickly recovers himself.

"I think education's overrated," he says.

"Don't listen to him," says Alan. "He's only trying to be provocative."

"He's succeeding," remarks George. "Tell me about morphogenesis."

"Biologically speaking, it's what happens to cause a cell, a tissue, even a whole organism to develop its shape. I'm particularly interested in more complex organisms in which cells can differentiate."

George frowns.

"When a cell changes from one type to another."

"Like a cancer?"

"Yes, but even normal, healthy cells have to go through a process of change in order for the organism to thrive. I just want to try and understand this process better."

"So you can cure diseases?"

"That would be beneficial, obviously, but it could also lead us down the path of eugenics and fundamentally try to alter what is natural, to regulate it against some perceived norm. But who decides those parameters? Who gets to say that this behaviour is acceptable, but that one isn't? Isn't that why we fought the War?"

"I'd like to think so, but I can't say I'm so sure."

"Me neither. Basically I'm interested in how patterns form – you know, stripes, spots, swirls?"

"Like camouflage?"

"Sort of."

"I know a bit about that, as it happens" says George laconically. "I painted decoys."

"One of the *camoufleurs*?"

George nods.

"I see. What I'm interested in discovering is whether it's possible to predict *how* they might change, whether the ability to do so is inherent or learned."

"Like the Manchester Moth?"

"Exactly so," says Alan, warming to his theme, "and then a mathematical formula to describe it."

"But isn't it entirely random? Like the pattern the wind makes in the sand?"

"That's precisely the kind of mathematics I'm interested in. To produce an algorithm that can capture those patterns even when it appears that there aren't any."

George tries to take this in. "I'm essentially a practical man," he says. "Like Roland, I'm an engineer. When I was a boy, there was nothing I liked better than to tinker, to take things apart then try and put them back together again, only better. Like the printing machines in my father's Works. A couple of nights a week I used to tune the engines of motor cycles at Belle Vue Speedway. They were quicker than any bike you could ride in the street, but it was my job to try and make them go quicker still. It was all about the timing, I discovered. Later I came to realise that the same was true when it came to taking photographs. It's an instinct, knowing when to press the shutter, and when not to. To an outside eye it can seem quite random, but, like you say, afterwards, when I'm developing the picture and the image begins to materialise, almost by magic, although all kinds of chemical processes are at work, emerging first as a negative, then finally as the finished photograph, I start to see within it what I must, on some level, have glimpsed when I decided to press that shutter, an undeniable pattern in the composition, the arrangement of figures within the frame, the juxtaposition of people with each other, the collision of unrelated objects. A happy accident, I call it, but, from what you're saying, I guess it's not entirely an accident, is it?"

"Now I think it's someone else's turn to be hiding their light under a bushel. We both of us, I think, in our different ways are simply trying to make some kind of sense out of the chaos all around us."

"But I don't see it as chaos."

"Nor do I."

They both sigh with a deep pleasure.

"It's like a dance," says George.

"Yes, and I am trying to understand the choreography better."

"But who's the choreographer? I don't take you for a religious man."

Alan smiles. "Hardly. We dance alone."

"That's all very well," says Arnold, "but it takes two to tango."

Alan and George both laugh, but not unkindly.

"Alone together, I was going to say," adds Alan, affectionately ruffling Arnold's hair. "Do we really want to stand out from the crowd?"

"I do," says Arnold.

"But look at the Manchester Moth," says George. "He nearly became extinct precisely because he did stand out from the crowd."

"So he changed," says Alan. "He adapted."

"But can a leopard change his spots?" says Arnold, looking hard at Alan, who in the end is forced to look away.

"I think he has to," says George. "If he's to survive."

Cam adjusts the gardenia in her hair and begins to sing once more.

"Like the wind that shakes the bough
He moves me with a smile
The difficult I'll do right now
The impossible will take a little while…"

Lily steps outside for some much-needed air. She's not used to champagne these days, especially coming on top of the Chinese beer from earlier. She feels the beginnings of a headache coming on, and she massages her temples with her fingertips, while staring up at the night sky above her. Roland, who knows the map of the stars and constellations intimately from his time as a pilot during the War, has taught her to recognise the more prominent of them.

"Tonight," he had said, "if the sky is clear, look for the constellation of Aquarius."

"My birth sign," Lily had replied, smiling.

"Precisely," Roland had continued. "If you're lucky, you might just catch a glimpse of Mercury."

"The winged messenger."

"Actually, she is very hard to see. Being so close to the sun, she gets lost in its glare. She's quite elusive." He had tapped her lightly on the tip of her nose, grinning. "She's best seen at this time of year, just after sunrise, or when the moon is in Aquarius. Like someone else I could mention."

"Like tonight?"

"In ancient times, scholars thought these were two quite different planets. They referred to the early morning version as Apollo. It was Pythagoras who first realised they were one and the same. So Mercury has always been regarded as something of a mystery, with a dual aspect."

"Not to be trusted?"

"No, no, no. Not at all. More of an enigma."

"That's better," she had teased. "I like the idea of being an enigma."

"Mercury is certainly that. She races round the sun in just eighty-eight days. That's why she is always associated with speed. But it takes her more than fifty-eight of our days for her to rotate on her axis. This means that she is both the hottest and the coldest of all the planets. She's full of contradictions – hot and cold, fast and slow, light and dark, hard to see, difficult to pin down..." He had held her in his arms then and kissed her. "Does she sound like someone we might know?"

Lily had raised a languorous eyebrow and slowly traced a finger round his lips after he had said this.

"That's what makes her so endlessly fascinating," she had said, playfully nuzzling his neck…

Now, as she looks up, she thinks she might have a final chance to glimpse the planet, just before it starts to dip below the horizon. Yes, she's in luck. The yellowish-orange tinge of it, crescent-shaped, half in light, half in shadow, crackles faintly, like the cartoon radio waves on the RKO mast just before the film begins. *King Kong, Citizen Kane, It's A Wonderful Life. When The City Sleeps.* She wonders what message it is beaming out tonight.

She shivers.

She becomes aware of someone behind her. A shadow cast by the light above the hotel door falls across her. She hears a small cough.

"*Scusa, Signora…*"

She turns round. It's the Head Porter, who had greeted them when they arrived.

"Yes?"

"I have a message from Signor Roland. He asks if you need anything."

"Tell him I'm fine, thank you. I just needed some air, that's all. Though I am starting to feel the cold." She smiles. "I'm sorry – I don't know your name…"

"Giancarlo, *Signora*," he says, accompanied by a small, neat bow.

"You remind me of someone."

"*Si.* Is what everyone says. *Zio Luigi.* My uncle."

"Yes, of course. Now I remember. He was here the first time I ever came here. The night Signor Roland and I were married."

A faint echo of Cam singing, while Lily and Roland made love in the honeymoon suite upstairs, comes back to her now, floating on the air.

> *"Chills run up and down my spine*
> *Aladdin's lamp is mine*
> *The dream I dreamed was not denied me…"*

"How is he," asks Lily, "your uncle?"

"*Va bene, grazie,*" replies Giancarlo. "Always he asks me who is staying, who is coming to hear *Signorina* Chamomile sing."

"Checking up on you?" smiles Lily.

"*Non*, he is just interested."

"Really?"

"Well – *si, magari, probabilmente* – maybe he checks…"

"Please remember me to him."

"*Si, Signora*, I will. Now I go and fetch your coat."

Lily turns back towards the city. And there it is. Mercury rising. Lily stands and watches for several minutes.

It's past eleven o'clock now and the pubs have all closed their doors, tipping out the midweek drunks onto the streets, who, one by one, disappear with the dying sparks of the last trolleybuses, some of them retreating into the more shadowy recesses of Piccadilly Gardens just across from where Lily now stands. She sees a man strike up a match to light a cigarette beneath a street lamp beside the bronze statue of Queen Victoria by Onslow Ford. Apparently Ford had wanted to carve it in marble, but it was Queen Victoria herself who'd vetoed this idea, fearing that marble would not weather well in Manchester's testing climate, and so it was decided to use bronze instead. But in the fifty years since it was completed, the bronze hasn't fared too well either. Its soot-encrusted grime that coats it is leavened only by the considerable amounts of bird-droppings deposited upon the old Queen's head down the years. No wonder she doesn't look amused, thinks Lily. Some say *The Queen's Hotel* is named after the statue, but in fact the hotel was built more than half a century before, as a home for the wealthy textile merchant, William Houldsworth, who bequeathed it to his nephew Thomas less than a decade later, a racehorse owner, who converted it into a hotel in order to help clear his debts, or so it was rumoured at the time. Lily knows all this because it is written up in the foyer, complete with old photographs and maps. She remembers it all too vividly herself from her years of living on the streets as a girl, when she used to sit on the steps leading up to Victoria in the hope that some kind passers-by might take pity on her and drop some coins into her collecting tin. It had been a battle back then just to stay alive. On the top of the statue, high above the throne on which the Queen sits, is another statue. It shows St George fighting the dragon. When Lily used to beg beneath it, she would dream that one day he might come down and rescue her. But it had been a different George who had done that.

She remembers one occasion when someone had found her, practically prostrate with hunger on these same hotel steps where she had fainted and collapsed, and had tried to offer her some reviving soup, but Lily had fled, not wanting to cause trouble or embarrassment. As she remembers that night, she realises that the woman who tried to help her was Cam. Not that Lily knew her then. It was more than twenty years ago. But it almost seems as if history is repeating itself, for here comes Cam now, stepping out of the hotel and walking towards Lily with her arms extended. But it is not soup she is offering on this occasion, but Roland's coat. It, too, will keep her warm.

"Lily?" she says. "Giancarlo asked me to give you this. It is your husband's, *n'est-ce pas?*"

Lily manages to utter a weak "thank you", for she is still partly inhabiting that previous memory and is in danger of confusing then with now.

Cam pulls her shawl tightly round her shoulders. "*Merde, on se gèle!*"

She takes out a packet of cigarettes. "Want one?" she says to Lily.

Lily nods, slipping her arms inside Roland's coat. Cam lights her own cigarette, which she then uses to light Lily's, and passes it to her. It feels extraordinarily intimate.

"Thanks," she says.

They stand close to each other in silence a while. The man who had earlier lit a cigarette beside the statue of Victoria is still there. He reminds Lily of the man from the advertisement for *Strand's Cigarettes*, the way he stands there so nonchalantly beneath the street lamp in his belted gabardine and trilby, which he now tips towards Lily and Cam, before leisurely moving on. 'You're never alone with a Strand.' Lily has wondered what that is supposed to mean, what the background narrative is meant to suggest. Mysterious? Enigmatic? The way Roland teases her?

She shivers again.

Cam turns towards her. "*Ça va, chérie?*"

Lily nods again, blowing smoke from the corner of her mouth.

"I was just remembering, that's all."

"*Ah oui?*"

"You were very kind to me once. I was homeless. You found me. Here on these steps. You tried to help me."

"Only tried?"

"I ran away."

"*Oui, je comprends*. But I'm sorry. I don't remember."

"There's no reason why you should. It was a long time ago."

Cam immediately begins to sing very softly.

"*Long ago and far away*
I dreamed a dream one day
And now that dream is here beside me…"

"You sang that on my wedding night."

Cam smiles broadly. "Now that I do remember. Francis insisted on it."

"Dear Francis. He's such a romantic."

"I know. He misses George terribly."

"But they still see each other. They're still friends. They're here together tonight."

"*Oui, je sais, mais...* It's not enough for Francis."

"Nor for George."

"I know. These laws they still have, they're – how you say? – *méchant, mauvais, inique...*"

"Wicked, yes."

They both fall silent, smoking their cigarettes. Mercury is stealthily slipping from view.

"It is entirely random. Without balance or fairness. *Moi, je peux emmener des hommes ou des femmes coucher avec moi, et personne ne pense rien, mais pour un homme, c'est différent...*" She shakes her head and shrugs.

"Are *you* married?" asks Lily.

"*Non*," smiles Cam.

"*Have* you been?"

"*Oui et non.*"

"What do you mean?"

"Not officially, not with a piece of paper from the Town Hall, but in every other sense." She smiles again, in that way she has that Lily has noticed when she sings sometimes, as if she's sharing something secretly confidential with her audience.

"What happened?"

"It burned itself out. Like passion does sometimes."

"Not always, I hope," laughs Lily nervously, pulling Roland's coat more tightly around her.

"No," agrees Cam, her voice softening, "not always. '*Them that's got shall have*'."

" '*Them that's not shall lose*'."

" '*God bless the child…*' "

"Has there *been* one?" asks Lily.

Cam inhales deeply on the last of her cigarette. She thinks about whether she will share this knowledge with Lily or not. She decides she will. She stubs the cigarette out on the pavement with the heel of her shoe.

"*Regardes*," she says, taking a much-thumbed photograph from her purse.

It shows a young man in an RAF uniform.

"He's very handsome," says Lily.

"*Oui*," laughs Cam. "He has his mother's looks and his father's courage."

"I reckon you're courageous too."

"I take risks and I'm reckless. I'm not sure that's the same thing."

"What's his name?"

"Richie," she says softly.

"Does he fly the planes or service them?"

"He flies them. 54 Squadron. He's a member of the Black Knights aerobatic team."

"Don't you worry about him?"

"Every single second."

"That's what Roland did during the War."

"*Oui, je le sais…*"

Lily looks at Cam curiously. "How…?"

But before she can say more, Cam carries on.

"He's never wanted anything else. *Rien*." She pauses, considering whether to continue or not. Once again, she decides she will. "I remember the day he first told me."

"You do?"

"*Exactement*."

She pauses again. The two women regard one another carefully.

"Well," says Lily, "when was it?"

Cam lights another cigarette. She is wreathed in blue smoke.

"It was the night of *Les Lumières du Nord*. The Northern Lights. When the sky turned green and danced, when the world turned inside out and upside down. I was here, at *The Queen's*, working. Richie was with his grandfather, my father, a blacksmith who lived by Buile Hill Park. It had been snowing. Richie had been sledging. Beneath a Bomber's Moon. On a sledge I had made myself when I was younger than he was then. He had found it at the back of my father's forge and my father had mended it for him. The park was white, the snow untrodden. Richie was the only boy still out so late. He sledged while the German planes flew overhead, following the silver ribbon of the River Irwell that guided them towards the factories of Trafford Park, picked out by the searchlights of the gun emplacements. Richie watched it all in wonder. Then, one of the planes was shot down. It fell from the sky above him and dropped like a stone. At the last second the pilot parachuted out. Richie saw him fall towards him like a dandelion clock. The pilot landed in the canopy of a tree, where he became stuck. Richie rescued him. He climbed the tree and cut through the strings of the parachute, one by one, so that the pilot fell in stages, not all at once, until he landed in the snow. He saved his life, I think…"

Lily snatches the cigarette away from Cam and draws on it deeply. Her whole body is trembling.

"The pilot was Roland," she says in a voice so low it is barely audible.

"*Oui, ma chérie*," says Cam kindly. "*Je sais… Je sais...*"

A late night trolleybus passes below them. The cables crackle and spark.

"Richie ran to get help," continues Cam after it has passed them. "*Enfin*, he spied an air raid warden cycling down the street. A woman. He flagged her down and took her back to Roland. She knew basic first aid. She fixed his broken arm and did the best she could for his injured foot."

"Yes," says Lily. "I know that part of the story. I never knew the boy was your son."

"While they waited for an ambulance, Richie spoke with Roland. He asked him…"

"Yes?"

"What he saw when he flew his plane high above the clouds."

"And what did Roland say to Richie? How did he answer him?"

"He hasn't told you this?"

Lily shakes her head.

"Well," says Cam, taking back the cigarette and inhaling once more, "he said… *'Ich sehe Die Engel. Les anges…'* "

"Angels…"

"Oui. Richie never forgot this. Never."

"I don't imagine he did," says Lily, who is shaking once more. "And does he see them too? Now that he's a pilot?"

Cam shrugs.

"I 'ope," she says. "I 'ope."

Lily tries to take in all that she's just heard. Roland had told her some of it, about a boy cutting him down from the tree, and the air raid warden, but nothing about the conversation concerning angels. He probably doesn't remember, she thinks. He was delirious with the pain in his foot, the foot that eventually he lost, so she is not surprised. She decides she will tell him – later, when it is just the two of them, alone together, in bed. He will want to know that his words back then meant so much to a young boy that they inspired him to become a pilot and take to the skies just like he had done.

She takes a deep breath. She is no longer trembling.

"*Tu te sens mieux maintenant?*" asks Cam, gently taking her arm.

"Yes," nods Lily, "I think so."

"Then perhaps we should go back inside, *n'est-ce pas?*"

They are just about to turn when they are halted by the sound of someone singing. It's a woman's voice. It sounds rasping and cracked, like someone walking over broken glass, but resolute and strong, determined to make herself heard. But they cannot see her. The song seems to be coming from the far side of Queen Victoria's statue. Mesmerised, they walk slowly towards it, careful not to disturb or frighten the singer, not wanting her to stop.

Lily remembers what is on the other side. It is the statue of *Motherhood*, also by Onslow Ford, depicting the Queen as an allegorical figure, the mother of the nation. But when Lily used to sit beneath it, she saw it merely for what it looks like, a gentle, loving woman, who cradles two infants, replete and sleeping. The figure wears a cloak over her head, which adds both mystery and a deeper sense of protection and nurturing, the kind that Lily herself did not know herself as a child.

This is where they find the owner of the voice, who continues to sing, regardless of Lily or Cam. She has a tattoo on her shoulder, Lily sees, in the shape of an angel. She holds out her hand. Instinctively Lily reaches inside her husband's coat pocket, from where she pulls out his wallet. She takes a ten shilling note and places it in the woman's outstretched palm and closes the fingers over it. The woman looks at her directly in the eye for just a brief moment, halting in mid-phrase, before returning her gaze toward some hidden, fixed point in front of her, resuming her song.

She sings in a language neither Lily nor Cam can recognise. It is filled with guttural, back-of-the-throat cries of pain, and wild, wailing, roof-of-the-mouth ululations, punctuated by tongue-against-palate clicks and ticks. Her voice swoops and soars through the octaves. It sings of great journeys, vast distances beneath vaulted skies, sailing oceans, crossing deserts, scaling mountains, seeking refuge and shelter, a safe haven in the glittering city. She reminds them of some new hitherto unknown species of bird, sometimes the hunter, sometimes the hunted, whose time is coming.

They listen to her entranced.

Then, just when they think they might be starting to recognise a pattern in the cadence of her song, she stops abruptly and flies off into the darkness. The winged messenger. In dual aspect.

A voice, calling from somewhere behind them, hauls them back to the present. It is Giancarlo.

"Five minutes, *Signorina Catch*, *per favore*."

"*Merci*," she calls back. She takes Lily's arm. "*Viens, chérie*. It's time we went back."

As they make their way, unseen by them, a young rat ventures cautiously from beneath the base of the old queen's statue, curiously nosing the air in the space vacated by the tattooed angel.

When Cam returns to the stage, she steps up to the microphone, and softly starts to croon, her gaze falling directly on Lily, whose eyes are still far away, seeking that last glimpse of Mercury before she slips from view .

"Them that's got shall get
Them that's not shall lose
So the Bible said and it still is news
Mama may have, Papa may have
But God bless the child that's got his own
That's got his own…"

"Hey," says George, plonking himself down in the chair next to Lily.

"Hey," she replies.

"Having a nice birthday?" he asks.

"Seeing you makes it so," she answers with a smile. "How are you?"

"Me? Oh, I'm fine. Same old, same old. It's you I'm more concerned about."

"There's absolutely no need. No need at all." She smiles rather too hectically.

"Methinks the lady doth protest too much."

"I don't know what you mean."

"Lily, I've known you twenty years. I've seen you like this before. Something's bothering you."

Lily bites her lower lip and looks away.

"That's always been your trouble," she says quietly. "You know me too well."

"Come on," he urges. "You can tell me. I'm your brother."

"You are," she says passionately. "I don't know what I'd do without you."

"You'd survive," he says. "You always do. So – what's troubling you? I know there's something."

"I've made a promise," she says.

"Ah."

"And you know how important that is to me."

"I do."

"If I make a promise, I…"

"…keep it, I know."

The two of them share a long look. Each are thinking back to the night twenty years before when George had found Lily, half-naked and destitute, semi-conscious in Angel Meadow, and he had offered to take her back to his mother's house in Didsbury, where she might shelter, be looked after and recover. She was like a wild cat, biting and scratching to try and break free from the grip he had of her wrist, until her weakness forced her to give in and acquiesce. But before he could take her there, on the back of his DOT Racer, she had asked him to let her retrieve a sodden bundle that lay a few yards away on one of the greasy flagstones, slick with rain and ruin. "It's all I have in the world," she had said. George had been reluctant to let go of her wrist. He felt certain she would simply bolt and that he would lose her, and he feared for her safety if he were to let that happen. "I promise," she had said then. "I'll come back." And before George could protest, she had added, "I never break a promise." Something in the way she had said that, something about the expression in her eyes, convinced George that she was telling the truth, and he released his hold on her. In an instant she was gone, and, for a moment, George was certain he had lost her, but within seconds she was back, clutching the wretched, pitiful, ragged object closely to her. "See," she had said. "If I make a promise, I keep it…"

"Do you still have it?" asks George now, remembering.

"Of course I do," she replies. "I'll never part with it. Unless I have a child of my own…"

She looks away again, picturing the toy boat in her mind's eye, the one thing that has tethered her down the years to her lost beginnings. Carved by her grandfather while he was interned on the Isle of Man during World War One, handed down to her mother after he had died there, her mother, Ruth, who Lily never knew, who died herself on the day Lily was born, the identity of her father unknown, it could have been one of several men who had attacked her mother on the night of the sinking of *The Lusitania*…

"So," says George finally, "what have you promised this time?"

And Lily tells George about the three latest 'blossoms' she is fostering in the house that George had taken her to all those years before on the night that he rescued her, Anita,

Christopher and Clive, how desperately Anita had spoken to her earlier that evening, pleading with her to make sure that the three of them are not split up from one another, to promise that she, Lily, would find them a place where they could remain together. And Lily had made that promise.

"Ah," says George again. He has lit his pipe while Lily has been spilling out the whole story before him. It's a habit he took up during the War, during his time at Farnham Castle with the Surrealist Roland Penrose, the Modernist Hugh Casson, the Magician Jasper Maskelyne, and Lee Miller, the remarkable American Aviatrix, with whom George had flown along the spine of England through a thick fog, watching the land unfold beneath him like a knot of teeming, conjoined, skeletal rats bent on survival at all costs, who had later taken such searing photographs of the liberation of Auschwitz. When Lily had first seen him go through all the various extraneous rituals required to light up his pipe, the tapping of the stem on the mantel, the tamping of tobacco in the bowl, she had teased him mercilessly about it. But he hadn't cared, simply carrying on until he had struck his match and the pipe had caught. Now she finds its low red glow in the half-light of *The Queen's Hotel*, in the pause between Cam's songs, deeply reassuring.

"Well?" she says at last, her voice tremulous and quiet.

"Did you say that Delphine was looking after them this evening?"

"Yes. She's staying the night."

George inhales once more. His face is surrounded in a haze of blue smoke. He waits till it clears. His almond eyes are pinpricks of light. They fix her with their constancy.

"Ask Delphine," he says at last. "She'll know what to do."

"Yes," says Lily. "Of course. I should have thought of that. Thank you." She breathes out deeply. All the tension she has been holding inside her throughout the evening leaves her at once. She links her arm through that of her adoptive brother and leans her head against his shoulder. "What would I do without you?" she says again, blinking back the tears.

And for the second time George answers her. "You'd survive," he says.

She looks at him now with such gratitude and love. Roland, about to rejoin them after a most enjoyable conversation he has just had with Alan about the ways in which they might continue to develop the capability of their Manchester computer to be able to think for itself more independently, pauses when he sees that look Lily bestows upon George. He smiles. He is not at all threatened by it. He recognises it as quite a different kind of love from the one she feels for him, which he knows she will hold true always, because she has promised him she would, and she always keeps her promises.

"Hello," he says.

"Hello," she says back.

She leans across to kiss him, long and lingeringly upon his lips. George puffs contentedly on his still-lit pipe. He couldn't be happier for her.

As the distant bell in the Town Hall clock, old Great Abe, tolls midnight, with all small talk exhausted, they sit in silence, separate in their own couples, Lily and Roland, George and Francis, Alan and Arnold, reflecting on the words that Cam sings to them in the last song of her set, wreathed in the blue cigarette smoke that circles around her in the overhead light, where a single brave moth dares to dance.

"I was a humdrum person
Leading a life apart
When love flew in through my window wide
And quickened my humdrum heart..."

Cam allows the moth to alight on the back of her hand and lets it settle there a while before lifting it back into the air where it takes wing and soars.

"What is this thing called love?
This funny thing called love?
Just who can solve its mystery?
Why should it make a fool of me...?"

Lily lets her head rest upon Roland's shoulder and closes her eyes. Francis, as he always does, becomes caught in the web Cam spins as she sings, seemingly just for him, and sits at her feet like an acolyte, while the light that radiates around her seems to pass right through his own translucent skin, which has always held George in its thrall so completely that he is forced to look away in case its brightness blinds him, as he does now, a gesture Lily notices in the last moment before she closes her own eyes, his sadness intermingling now with her joy. Only Alan appears ambivalent, almost as if, at last, the infinitely ambiguous, unpredictable algorithm, which can never be wholly computed, and which he has sought for a lifetime, hovers tantalisingly within reach. Arnold, aware of Alan's gaze, blows another perfect smoke ring, while at the same time bestowing upon him a smile so radiant that Alan is utterly lost, falling within the black hole of its penumbra, from which there is no escape.

"I saw you there one wonderful day
You took my heart and threw it away
That's why I ask the Lord in Heaven above
What is this thing called love...?"

After the last note has faded and the spotlight on Cam narrowed to nothing but a dot, and when that, too, has vanished, Lily and Roland, George and Francis, Alan and Arnold gather outside on the steps of *The Queen's Hotel* to say their goodbyes.

"It's been a pleasure meeting you," says Alan, shaking Lily by the hand. "I hope you've had a very happy birthday."

"Yes, I have. Thank you."

"You'll excuse us if Arnold and I take our leave. If we're very quick, we might just catch the last train to Wilmslow." And with that they dash off together up the London Road towards the station.

George is standing by his beloved DOT Racer. He has already donned his own crash helmet and is in the process of handing a second to Francis. Overhead the stars are bright and clear. Already a frost is beginning to form on the roads, and their breath freezes in statues around them as they speak.

"If you think I'm getting on the back of that with you tonight," says Francis, "forget it. It's freezing. I'm calling a cab."

"Please yourself," says George.

"I intend to," says Francis. "Roland? Lily? Care to share a ride?"

"We'd love to," says Roland, leaning slightly to one side. Lily can see that his leg is beginning to hurt him, as it often does at the end of a long evening, chafing where the stump joins the prosthetic foot, which he had to have fitted following his accident in the War, when he painfully fell to the ground, damaging his ankle irreparably. It was bitterly cold on that night, too. The Northern Lights had made a rare, almost miraculous appearance over Manchester at the height of the Blitz, bringing everyone out of their shelters after the all-clear had sounded to marvel at the twisting, dancing sky. Roland was taken away to the Prisoner-of-War camp on Melland Playing Fields in Levenshulme, which was where Lily first saw him, planting vegetables behind a barbed wire fence, an investment of hope, a belief that there would be a different future, a future that would lead them to this moment, almost a decade later, standing beneath another snow moon. But no lights were dancing tonight. Nor were any bombs falling. Only a sharp frost settling on the ground and in the air, and the pain in

Roland's leg returning, reminding them both of the journey they had made together since then.

"You go with Francis," says Lily.

"What about you?" says Roland.

"George'll give me a ride home, won't you, George?"

George grins. He hands her the second crash helmet and gestures towards the DOT Racer. "Your chariot awaits," he says.

"Are you sure?" says Roland.

"I'm sure," says Lily. "Whoever's back first gets to put the kettle on."

"Deal," says Roland, as Francis flags down a taxi coming down the Station Approach.

After they've gone, Lily climbs astride the motor cycle and loops her arms around George's waist.

"I believe we've been here before," he chuckles.

"I believe we have," smiles Lily.

"It was raining then."

"And it's freezing now – so get a move on."

He kicks the starter and together they roar off into the night.

Some time later, just as they are passing the University, past the Computer Building where Roland had helped Alan make his breakthrough discovery, she whispers in George's ear.

"You saved my life that night," she says. "I'd've been dead if you hadn't found me."

"But I did."

"What're the chances, eh?" The billions of stars in the Milky Way arch above them. The countless, unseen particles whirling in space. "Out of all the random possibilities, how did it happen that you and I collided on that tiny patch of bare earth in Angel Meadow?"

"Was it random?"

"How else do you explain it?"

"I was a student of Mr Lowry. He liked to paint St Michael's Church. It was situated in Angel Meadow…"

"Which is where girls like I was at the time went to conduct their business."

"There – you see? Not so random after all, not when you think about it."

"But not one either of us could've predicted."

"No. I suppose not." He smiles.

"What?"

"I was thinking of something else you said that night."

"So was I."

"After three?"

"After three."

"One…"

"Two…"

Then both together: "Three," after which they shout as one at the tops of their voices, "It's a long fucking way to Didsbury!"

The sound of the engine as George opens the throttle wider drowns out their cry of triumph and defiance, as they speed beneath the January moon on a near-deserted Wilmslow Road.

*

Walking along a different Wilmslow Road an hour later, Alan and Arnold make their way from Wilmslow Station, past the Park, down Cow Lane, towards Alan's home at Number 43, Adlington Road. Alan is eager to get back and tries to hurry, but he keeps being pulled back by Arnold, who points out a tawny owl hunting silently through the trees, or a hedgehog snuffling blindly across the road, or a fox rummaging in somebody's dustbin. He pulls him into the shadow of a large beech tree to kiss him, only to pull away again quickly as they hear a bicycle bell ringing as it rounds the corner. That it carries a rather burly Police Constable only makes Arnold more nervous and jittery than ever, and he is overcome by a near-uncontrollable fit of the giggles. In between all these actions, he is constantly checking his watch.

"What do you keep doing that for?" asks Alan crossly. "I'll tell you what the time is. It's late. I have to be up early tomorrow morning. Some of us have to work."

Arnold pouts and dawdles even slower.

Alan, a keen amateur runner, muses on the fact that he could have run the twelve and a half miles all the way from *The Queen's* to Wilmslow in less than the time it has taken them already by train and by Arnold's tortoise pace from the station. But then he looks back towards his friend's anxious face, the way a lock of his hair falls so invitingly across his forehead, and how his bottom lip quivers so appealingly, that he pushes all such mean thoughts aside.

"Do hurry up," he says gently. "My balls will drop off if you take any longer. I'm freezing."

Arnold smiles thinly, checks his watch once more, then saunters casually towards him. "Don't worry," he says. "I'll warm them up for you when we get in."

"If we ever do," laughs Alan, playfully punching his friend on the arm. He wants him urgently.

"Race you," says Arnold suddenly, and before Alan can register it, he has bolted off down the road.

He quickly catches him up, and together the two of them reach the gateway to Alan's drive, simultaneously breasting an imaginary tape.

Laughing, the air freezing around him in ever-shifting shapes, Alan fumbles with his key in the front door in his eagerness to get inside, while Arnold attempts one final surreptitious glance at his watch.

"Three – two – one!"

Alan bursts in, intent on laying siege to what he hopes will be Arnold's weak defences, but the moment he steps through the door he senses something is wrong. He flicks the switch in the hall, and at once the light that floods in reveals a scene of wreckage and devastation. Pictures have been pulled from the wall, furniture has been tipped upside down, drawers have been pulled out and emptied, their contents scattered to all corners, and his personal belongings taken. Thankfully there has been none of the accompanying desecration that he has read about with other burglaries. No piss has been sprayed on the carpets, no excrement smeared on the walls. But the violation feels no less invasive for all that.

Just as he is beginning to take in what has happened, he hears a noise coming from the next room. Without thinking he rushes towards the source of the sound and finds himself face-to-face with the intruder. He's a young man, not much older than Arnold, and, as they confront one another within the enclosed smallness of the kitchen, it is hard to tell which is the more frightened. They stare, motionless for a moment, before the burglar looks over Alan's shoulder towards Arnold.

"I thought you said you wouldn't be back till two."

"I tried to delay him – honest," says Arnold.

The awful truth of what has happened begins to dawn on Alan.

"You," he says, turning to Arnold, "know each other?"

"Yeah, we know each other," answers the burglar for him. "Arnold told me about your little love nest. Proper cosy, isn't it? You've not got much worth nicking, though, have you? Still, I helped myself to a few choice items, which I'd like to hang onto, if it's all the same with you. As insurance, like. I don't expect you'll be going to the Police, but if you do, I might just have to tell them about the kind of things you get up to when you're not trying to teach a computer how to play chess. Alright?"

Alan is seething with fury. "No," he says, "it's not alright. I think you're bluffing. I'm going to report your little game to the Police right now. Bishop's pawn to C4."

He makes a dash for the front door, but the burglar beats him to it, knocking him to the floor as he flings it open and hurtles off down the drive, only to run directly into the path of the Constable Alan and Arnold had seen pass them by on his bicycle not fifteen minutes earlier.

"Someone's in a hurry," says the Constable as he blocks the path of the burglar, who he hastily places into a head-lock. "But not any more, I don't think. It looks like you've got some explaining to do."

"He tried to rob me," cries Alan. "We disturbed him in the very act of it. I'd be most grateful for your assistance."

"We?" inquires the Constable, looking round.

"Tell him, Arnold," says the burglar, trying in vain to release himself from the Constable's vice-like grip.

The Constable takes in Arnold's appearance, then transfers his gaze back towards Alan. An expression of distaste passes across his face, which he makes no attempt to disguise.

"It looks like we've got ourselves something of a *ménage à trois*, gentlemen."

"If you'd allow me to explain, Officer," says Alan, stepping forward, "it's all perfectly simple and straightforward." His voice is confident, but his movements are awkward, almost as if he is contemplating some complicated castling manoeuvre, reversing his king for his rook, unwittingly backing himself into a corner, just so he can allow his queen more freedom to roam.

"It's not at all simple or straightforward to me, sir. Do you know this gentleman?" he asks, referring to the burglar still struggling to breathe in the headlock.

"No, Officer. I've never seen him until this very evening, when I caught him in the very act."

"*In flagrante delicto*, you might say, sir?"

"I don't know what it is you think you're implying."

"Oh, I think you do, sir. I think you know only too well."

The Constable now turns his attention towards Arnold.

"But it would appear that you and this gentlemen…" He indicates the burglar. "…are in fact acquainted?"

"Yes," replies Arnold. "His name's Harry. Harry Kinsella. But I don't know him very well. I met him in a pub."

"Do you make a habit of meeting men in a pub? Is that where you met this gentleman?" He now indicates Alan.

"No," says Arnold. "I met him in a cinema."

"I see." He turns back to Alan. "Are you the owner of this property, sir?"

"Yes, Officer."

"And your name?"

"Turing, Alan."

"Well, Mr Turing, if you'd like to press charges, you shall have to accompany me to the station, together with your cinema acquaintance, Mr – er…?"

"Murray, Arnold."

"But I don't expect you'd like to do that, Mr Turing, would you, sir? Not if you want to avoid other less salubrious information coming to light?"

"I'm not in the least put off by your threats, Officer."

"Threats, sir? I'm only thinking of what's in your best interests."

"Best interests, be damned. It's obvious what's happened here. It's a honey trap, and I am the victim." Alan has now brought his knight into play.

"I'd advise you not to say anything more, if I were you, sir. Do you want to report the burglary or not?"

"I do."

"Then I shall have to ask you more precisely about the nature of your relationship with Mr Murray."

Alan pauses. He recognises that checkmate is now inevitable. He knows only too well that it is a failure of etiquette to play the game to the end once you know its outcome. But it's too late now. He won't back down. He offers his queen for sacrifice.

"I have nothing to hide," he says.

In the back of his mind he hears an echo of Chamomile Catch, the Manchester Songbird, singing, the ghost of a sad smile dying on her lips, as she unpins the white gardenia from her black hair.

"Good morning heartache
Here we go again
Good morning heartache
You're the one who knew me when
Might as well get used to you hanging around
Good morning heartache, sit down

Stop haunting me now…"

*

Knutsford Crown Court

Regina vs Turing
Monday 31st March 1952
Judge J. Fraser Harrison presiding

Prisoner: Alan Mathison Turing

Particulars of Offence:
Between the 17th day of December 1951 and the 22nd day of February 1952, being a Male Person, did commit several and diverse Acts of Gross Indecency with one Arnold Murray, also a Male Person.

Prosecuting: Mr R. David
Defending: Mr Lind Smith

Plea: Guilty
Sentence:
In lieu of a two-year prison sentence, to submit for treatment with anaphrodisiac drugs, inc. stilboestrol, a synthetic form of oestrogen, to be administered over the course of one year by a duly qualified Doctor at the Manchester Royal Infirmary.

Prisoner: Arnold Murray

Particulars of Offence:
Between the same dates, being a Male Person, did commit the same several and diverse Acts of Gross Indecency with the aforesaid Arnold Murray, also a Male Person

Defending: Mr E. Hobson

Plea: Guilty
Sentence:
Conditional Discharge: bound over to be of good behaviour for a period of twelve months

"What does this mean?" Lily asks Roland when she learns of the sentence. "Anaphrodisiac drugs?"

"There's no nice way to say it, I'm afraid," replies Roland. "Chemical castration."

Lily shudders.

*

2019/1954

"Hi," says Molly. "How did it go?"

"Hi."

"Well?"

"I've got some news."

"So have I."

"You go first."

"No. You."

They pause, each trying to picture the other, comfortable in the silence that ensues.

"Where are you now?" asks Molly.

"Actually," says Michael with a smile, "I'm sitting on a bench next to Alan Turing…"

Lily is at the foot of the stairs, having just put down the telephone in the hallway of the house on Lapwing Lane. She is trembling with disbelief. She takes several deep breaths to calm herself. Then the phone rings again, causing her almost to leap out of her skin.

"Hello?" she says anxiously.

"It's me," says Roland. His voice immediately calms her.

"Yes?" she says.

"I've got some news," he says.

"So have I," she says slowly.

"Oh. You go first."

"No. It's all right. I can wait. Why have you called?"

"I've got tenure," Michael replies excitedly. "As good as. David was most complimentary."

"Oh, it's David, is it?" says Molly. Michael can hear the gentle teasing in her voice. But in the next instant she is full of congratulations. "That's wonderful," she says. "You've earned it. You've worked so hard. I'm really proud of you. No one deserves it more. I can't think why it's taken them so long."

"That's what David implied."

"Oh, it is, is it?" Michael can picture the huge grin spreading across her face as she speaks. "And what else did David have to say?"

"Actually, he was really interested to hear about your work."

"Was he? That's partly why I'm calling."

"Oh?"

"There's no easy way to say this."

"What?"

"It's Alan, he... He's dead, Lily. His cleaner found him this morning. There was a half-eaten apple by his side, next to an empty phial of cyanide."

Lily closes her eyes.

"The poor man," she says. "The poor, poor man."

Neither of them speaks for several seconds.

"I suppose they're calling it suicide," says Lily.

"I suppose so, yes."

"Well it's not," says Lily, opening her eyes wide. "It's murder. Murder by the state."

"I've found a loom. Or rather, Lorrie has."

"Fantastic. That's brilliant."

"The thing is..."

"Yes...?"

"It costs £250."

"That's OK," says Michael, calculating quickly. "You've still got some money left from the Arts Council's 'Develop Your Own Creativity' Fund. That should cover it."

"Would that be acceptable?"

"I'm sure it would. That's what it says on the tin. 'Develop Your Own Creativity'. You'd be learning new skills, wouldn't you?"

"Absolutely."

"Well then…"

"What was *your* news?" asks Roland gently.

"Oh," says Lily, collecting herself. "Are you sitting down?"

"What is it?"

Lily takes a deep breath.

"We're going to have a baby," she says at last.

Roland is too choked to speak. Eventually he says, "Are you sure?"

"Yes," she whispers.

"I thought you couldn't…"

"That's what I thought too. But it seems I can. *We* can."

Both fall silent again, as the enormity of these two pieces of news sinks in. Lily puts her hand gently upon her belly. She imagines the countless millions of Roland's sperm swimming so heroically upstream towards what she thought were her damaged fallopian tubes, doomed to perish once they reached there. But somehow one has survived to make it all the way through to fertilise the egg, to penetrate the outer membrane and reach the cytoplasm, where it has now released its own unique genetic footprint. Already the separate chromosomes carried by the sperm and the egg will have combined to form a microscopic zygote, which have divided, again and again, until an almost invisible ball of about a hundred cells has settled on the lining of her uterus and become implanted there.

Lily is remembering some of what Alan described when she met him that one time on her birthday two years ago, something about the pattern the wind makes in the sand, how it appears to be random, but actually it isn't.

"That's precisely the kind of mathematics I'm interested in," he had said. "To produce an algorithm that can capture those patterns even when it appears that there aren't any."

"Are you still there?" says Roland.

"Yes," whispers Lily. "I'm still here…"

"Where are you now?" asks Molly.

"Actually," says Michael, "I'm sitting on a bench next to Alan Turing…"

*

1951

Gorton Reporter

28th August 1951

BANK HOLIDAY PICNIC TURNS TO TRAGEDY

Two Die as House Collapses due to Colliery Subsidence

Hours after this happy, carefree scene, in which families enjoyed a Bank Holiday picnic beneath the shadow of Bradford Colliery in glorious late summer sunshine, tragedy struck a nearby street in Clayton Vale.

Children played blithely unaware in fields adjoining the Ashton Canal in plain sight of the mine's giant cooling towers, while factory chimneys belched out plumes of black smoke, not knowing that in less than two hours this idyllic scene would turn into a nightmare.

Less than a mile away, on Himley Road, a narrow side street leading to St Willibrord's Roman Catholic Church, just as the children were getting ready to return to their homes after the picnic, an enormous sinkhole suddenly opened up, causing the house at Number 43 to come crashing to the ground in seconds.

Terrified onlookers reported the incident to the Emergency Services, who arrived on the scene within minutes, but not quickly enough for Mr & Mrs Joel & Carmel Fredericks, who were crushed beneath the wreckage.

Distressed neighbours told *The Gorton Reporter* that the house came down like a pack of cards. "One minute it was there, the next it was gone."

Extraordinary Act of Bravery Rescues Children

Seconds after the collapse local residents heard the terrified screams of Mr & Mrs Fredericks' eldest child, Anita, who miraculously had escaped unharmed. She was shouting the names of her two younger brothers,

Christopher and Clive, who were still trapped inside the rubble.

Without thought for her own safety and heedless of the warnings of neighbours, 11 year-old Anita clambered over the smouldering remains of what had once been her house, frantically throwing aside any loose bricks she could lay her hands on, until she had found a way to squeeze her way back inside just as the first of the Fire Engines screeched into Himley Road.

A tense few minutes ensued, while everyone held their collective breath, until Anita emerged, triumphant. "They're here!" she cried. "I've found them! They're alive!"

The Firemen then took over, painstakingly removing further bricks until there was a passageway wide enough for two of them to squeeze through. Several agonising moments later they returned, carrying a brother each. They were covered in dust and their clothes were torn, but otherwise they were unharmed, save for a few cuts and scratches. Seconds after they had been brought out, there was a further collapse of what remained of the building, bringing down more ruin upon the tiny terraced street.

"If Anita had not acted as swiftly and bravely as she did," said Police Sergeant Ratcliffe of nearby Clayton Brook Police Station, "the two boys would not be alive today."

Tragically the same cannot be said for the children's parents, whose bodies were later recovered by ambulance workers.

Mr Joel Fredericks, 36 years old, was originally from St Kitts. He settled in Manchester after active service in the War, during which he was a naval gunner on board *HMS Wanderer*, which played a crucial role protecting the Atlantic convoys. His wife, Carmel, whose parents were from the neighbouring island of Nevis, was born in Manchester, and worked at the Metropolitan-Vickers plant in Trafford Park, stripping down the engines of

Merlin bomber planes. The couple met when Joel was on shore leave in 1940 visiting family in Stretford, and were married following a whirlwind wartime romance.

All that remained of 43 Himley Rd after the fatal sinkhole collapse

Further Distressing Scenes as Survivors are Separated

The three children have been placed in temporary care – Christopher and Clive in Summerhill, a hostel for boys on Palatine Road in Didsbury, and heroine of the hour, Anita, in Westdene, a hostel for girls 7 miles away on Kilmington Drive in Cheetham Hill. Neighbours said that the cries of Anita as her brothers were taken from her were even more heart-wrenching than those when she thought they had been killed by the collapse.

The Gorton Reporter hopes that a way can be found to reunite these brave, orphaned children once more.

St Willibrord, the Northumbrian saint after whom the local school is named, is the patron saint of children. We are confident that the prayers of all our readers will be directed towards him to intervene quickly and mercifully in this tragic case.

*

The following morning Lily reads the article from *The Gorton Reporter*, which has also been carried by *The Didsbury & Withington Observer*. As soon as she has read it, she picks up the telephone in the hallway by the front door of what had formerly been the home of her adoptive mother, Annie Wright, and calls her contact in the Children's Services Department of Manchester Council.

"I'm ringing about those three poor children from the Clayton Vale sinkhole collapse," she says. "I have space for them here. We've no one staying with us at the moment."

An hour and a half later it is all arranged. That evening she takes a taxi, first to Kilmington Drive to collect a near-catatonic Anita, next back to Didsbury, to pick up the boys from Palatine Road. The moment Anita claps eyes on her brothers, the expression on her face is transformed. Her smile is one of beatitude and bliss. Likewise the two boys are equally transfixed. The three of them look upon Lily with adoration. She has become their saviour and their saint.

Three months later, on the evening of Lily's thirty-sixth birthday, just as she is getting ready to go out for the Chinese banquet with her husband Roland, where she will meet his colleagues from work, Freddie Williams, Geoff Toothill, Tom Kilburn and Alan Turing, to celebrate the launch of their new computer, Anita will come to her and ask, as she has done every day since their arrival, the same set of questions.

"Have you found us somewhere yet…?"

And:

"You will make sure they keep us together…?"

The third question – "Why can't we stay here with you?" – she has learned is not one that can be answered.

*

1952

Anita sits on the edge of the dining table chair in Delphine's flat at Darbishire House on Upper Brook Street. Her back is straight, her hands are folded neatly on her lap. She is wearing her Sunday clothes, which Lily had put out ready for her the night before. Her shoes are polished so hard that she can see her reflection in them, which shows an anxious, but composed face, with a new yellow ribbon in her hair, yellow to match the bunch of tulips she has brought with her, which Delphine – Miss Fish to Anita – is now arranging in a vase on the table in front of her.

"These are lovely," she declares. "Thank you. Tulips are my favourite flower."

"That's what Mrs Warner says too."

"Does she?" Delphine turns to regard this serious young girl sitting so earnestly before her. "I quite agree," she continues. "They carry such hope." As do you, Anita, thinks Delphine, as she steps away from the vase. It is in every pore of your being, as you sit there waiting to hear what I am going to say.

Outside the window a pair of starlings noisily skrike and squabble over a patch of acorns on the grass in the small square that Delphine's flat looks out onto. Anita's gaze is drawn by the way they tug and tussle with one another. Not unlike her brothers, Christopher and Clive, who are always quarrelling, who Anita constantly has to watch over. They're probably out there now, with Lily – Mrs Warner – who marched them all here this morning because Miss Fish had Something Very Important she had to tell them, and that is was to be she, Anita, who was to go in on her own and hear the news first herself, while Lily and her brothers would wait outside in the square just below. It is what Delphine had requested, and so here Anita now sits, trembling, on the edge of her seat, straining to see if she can catch sight of her brothers among the starlings.

"Here," says Delphine, placing a mug of hot Vimto in front of Anita. "Drink this. It's a cold day."

"Thank you, Miss Fish," says Anita quietly, immediately taking a sip. Delphine is not a person you say 'no' to. She understands this without needing to be told. But she also recognises that she would not ever wish to. That this is someone who knows what's best for you, and so it is wise to do as she requests. She takes a deeper swallow of the warming crimson drink. It's not something she has had before. It's delicious, and she beams.

Delphine's eyes dance with pleasure at the sight of such an unguarded smile.

"Here," she says again, and passes Anita a napkin, pointing to the blackcurrant moustache above Anita's mouth, which Anita dutifully wipes clean. "I think we might risk a biscuit too, don't you?" says Delphine, reaching down a tin. "Let me see – what have we got? Bourbons, Fig Rolls, and – oh yes, my favourites – Garibaldis!" And she produces a couple like a magician conjuring rabbits from a top hat, handing one to Anita, while saving one for herself. Anita takes a tentative bite. Her gaze now lights upon a dry, brittle bird's nest, which has been given pride of place on the mantelpiece. It looks so delicate, as though it might break apart at any moment, so fragile, but strong, for it appears to have endured for many years. Which it has. Delphine takes note of Anita's curiosity.

"That belonged to my mother," she says. "It's the only thing of hers I have," she adds matter-of-factly, not a trace of sentiment in her voice. Anita nods solemnly and takes a second small bite of her biscuit.

"Now," continues Delphine in an altogether more serious tone, "let us begin, shall we?"

Anita instantly puts down the biscuit and nods, trying to sit even straighter and taller.

"I shall not beat about the bush," says Delphine. She firmly believes in never talking down to children. When a thing needs saying, it should simply be said, without sugar-coating it. A child will see through any dissembling or attempt at concealment at once. Better always to be truthful and clear. Honesty, she has found, is always the best policy, though at times it can be like an icicle, for once it melts, it is gone for ever. "Mrs Warner has asked me to intervene on your behalf, Anita, to see if there is a way to be found to keep you and your brothers together."

Anita's bottom lip begins to tremble. She bites down on it hard to try and stop it.

"I know a little of what you must be feeling at this time."

Anita looks up sharply. Her eyes flash briefly, as if to say, 'How can you possibly know that?', which she tries, too late, to curb.

"Oh yes," continues Delphine, observing that look of defiance. "My own mother was an orphan. She lost both her parents at around the same age that you did and had to learn to look after herself quite alone in the most difficult of circumstances. She did not even have a roof over her head." Anita's eyes soften and widen as she listens. "And Mrs Warner, too, is an orphan. Her mother died when giving birth to her, and her father was unknown. She was placed in an orphanage at just one day old, where she stayed until she was fourteen, when she had to leave and was forced to fend for herself all alone in the city. That wasn't easy, as I'm sure you can imagine. You're old enough to know something of the dangers a young girl on her own might have to face." Anita looks down. She understands what Delphine is telling her. But it's not just young girls who face these difficulties, but young boys too. That is why she has vowed never to be parted from her two young brothers, but to be there for them always, for as long as they need her, especially Christopher, who has trouble with his hearing. "That is why," resumes Delphine, "Mrs Warner – or Miss Wright, as she was then – set up her foster home in the first place, to take in children like you and your brothers, who, for one reason or another, are not able to be with their parents – that's if they even have any – so that they don't have to go through what she had to, and be forced to live a life on the streets. And so she called her home *'Blossoms'*, for that is how she sees all of you, as blossoms, full of promise and hope."

Anita cannot stop the flow of tears that slide silently down her cheek. Delphine discreetly looks away to allow Anita to wipe them away fiercely with the napkin given to her earlier. Once she has composed herself, she looks back towards Delphine, who then continues to speak.

Yes, she thinks, I will tell her the whole history of how the situation now stands, so that she will understand the decision we have come to, for she deserves to hear just how the law operates, and then I shall ask her for her opinion of what I am proposing, what I firmly believe will be the best outcome both for her and her brothers.

"When Mrs Warner first started taking in children, it was just after the end of the War. There were many orphaned children, and there were many destroyed buildings. People had lost their homes as well as their loved ones. There simply weren't enough places for all those who needed them, and so the Council was grateful for the kind of spontaneous acts of charity offered up by Mrs Warner and others like her. But it was far from satisfactory. It worked out for some children, but not for others. Not all foster parents were as kind as Lily – Mrs Warner. There had to be some form of system. So – in 1948, just four years ago – the Government passed what's called *The Children's Act*. Before that there was no proper, organised system across the country. How you fared as a child who needed care depended very much on where you lived. Here in Manchester it was better than most. In fact, the very first case of fostering anywhere in England was recorded here exactly a hundred years before, when a vicar, the Reverend John Armistead, who lived just outside Stockport, took some children who he thought were being cruelly treated out of a Workhouse and placed them with families to look after them. But even after this, it was still very much a case of pot luck what happened to you. Then, twenty years ago, the Boards of Guardians, who had administered the Poor Relief for those in need across England and Wales, were abolished, and responsibility fell to local councils. At the time Manchester had only two places where they could send orphans – in Styal, in Cheshire, which could look after seven hundred children, and Withington, just down the road from here, where there was room for nearly a hundred and fifty. Apart from those, there were the homes run by charities, usually attached to the Roman Catholic Church, such as the convent Mrs Warner was sent to, but not much else. Then the War came, and the Blitz, which made the need even greater, which was why *The Children's Act* I mentioned came into force four years ago. It required local councils to provide all children up to the age of fifteen with a proper education, and also to make sure that any child who lacked a normal home, for whatever reason, was catered for and looked after. I'm telling you this, Anita, for two reasons – one, because I know that you are clever and can understand what I'm saying, and two, because it helps me to explain to you in more detail everything that is involved in making sure that you and your brothers receive what is best for you."

"You're not going to split us up, are you, Miss? Why can't we stay with Mrs Warner?"

Delphine looks at the desperate expression on Anita's face with great sorrow. She is being exceptionally brave. No child should be unhappy. Each one of them deserves to be treated as if they are special, to know that they matter, which, to Delphine, they all of them are, and have always been, during her many years of teaching.

"Let me reassure you at once, Anita. You and your brothers will not be split up."

The relief which floods through Anita at the point manifests itself in a rush of emotion.

"Thank you, Miss."

"But you will not, I'm afraid, be able to stay with Mrs Warner."

"Why not, Miss?"

"That is what I am about to explain to you, Anita. Drink some more of your Vimto first."

Anita automatically obeys. The cordial spreads its warmth and calm immediately through her.

"I wrote a letter to the Head of Children's Services in the Council, a Miss Lorraine Courtenay, who replied at once and kindly granted me an appointment to speak to her on you and your brothers' behalf. She grasped the situation at once and agreed that you should not be separated from one another. The Council has, since the Act was passed, approved a number of houses around the city, which are eligible to take in children. The adults who live there have all had to supply references testifying to their good character, which have all been thoroughly checked and verified before their applications to be foster parents have been accepted. Next, their houses have been inspected to make sure that they meet the required standards of hygiene and cleanliness, and that no more than two children would be sharing a single room. The Council then categorises these houses according to different criteria. Some are labelled 'receiving' homes, which are for emergency, short stays; some as 'intermediate' homes, where children stay for several weeks until a longer term placement can be found, and some as 'family' homes, where children live for much longer periods, as part of the host families, and for as long as everyone is satisfied that everything is working out well for all concerned. The Council makes these distinctions on the basis of the facilities each potential foster parent's house has to offer, and they have decided that Mrs Warner's is best suited to being an 'intermediate' home, which is why she takes children to stay with her for a number of weeks until something more permanent can be found for them. That's how you, Christopher and Clive came to be placed with her in the first place. The problem that arose then was trying to find somewhere where you could all stay together. Most of the 'family' homes tend to take in just boys, or just girls. I'm sure you can understand why, Anita? But I spoke with Miss Courtenay at some length. I explained to her that it was vital in your case for you all to stay together, that it is what all three of you want, and that both Mrs Warner and I believed that you, Anita, would help whoever you were placed with to look after your brothers. I have observed that you are a most capable girl, Anita, and I pressed my opinion upon Miss Courtenay most forcefully, so that she has agreed to my request, and I can confirm that you will all be moving shortly to a house not far from where we are now sitting this morning."

"Thank you, Miss," says Anita. She is overcome with gratitude that she temporarily forgets herself and flings her arms around Delphine, who finds she is deeply affected by the gesture and is unable to speak for several seconds. Finally, when she has recovered herself sufficiently, she raises Anita's face from where it is buried against her chest, and says, "I trust you will not cause me to regret my recommendation?"

"Oh no, Miss."

"In fact, I am certain of it. The way you have looked after your brothers ever since you lost your parents has been nothing short of heroic. Now – time for another Garibaldi, I think, don't you?"

"Yes, Miss," says Anita, smiling happily as she helps herself.

"The name of the person who will take care of you from now on is Mrs Adams. She lives on Upper Lloyd Street in Moss Side. She has a daughter of her own, Chantelle, who is sixteen years old, and who might very well be like an older sister for you, Anita. She is training to be a nurse at the hospital just across the road from here. But you will have your own room, and your brothers will have a room they can share. You will all go to the local school at Greenheys, which is less than a five minute walk away. I know it very well, for I am on the Board of Governors there. It will be particularly helpful for Christopher, who I have observed has a little trouble hearing sometimes…"

Anita looks up from her biscuit back towards Delphine, open-mouthed.

"What is the matter, Anita? Are you a goldfish?"

"No, Miss. Sorry, Miss. It's just that I didn't know anyone knew about that but me."

"You forget that I have been a teacher of deaf children for many, many years. I recognise the signs. Your brother's condition can be helped, for they are most skilled at Claremont Road. They will make sure that Christopher sits where he can lip read, while I shall book an appointment for him at my clinic at the University. Between us all we shall make sure he is well looked after, so you needn't worry about a thing."

"I don't know what to say, Miss. I can't tell you just how grateful I am. Though I shall be sorry to leave Mrs Warner. She's been ever so kind."

"And she will be sorry to see you and your brothers go, but also happy that things have worked out so well. And she will come and visit you as often as she can. As will I."

Anita feels a hard lump in the back of her throat. At the same time, she feels all of the tension that she has held in her body for as long as she can remember begin to slip away from her.

Delphine, too, finds the emotion of the conversation she has just had, and Anita's reaction to what has been arranged for her, as strong as anything she can remember. She busies herself with the tulips in the vase and looks out of the window. She sees Lily and the two boys playing with a ball on the grass. They look up, catch sight of her and wave.

"It's such a lovely day, crisp and cold, just how I like it," she says brightly. "Let's go and join Christopher and Clive and tell them the good news. They're just outside with Mrs Warner."

After she has put on her coat and hat, she walks downstairs with Anita. As they reach the front door, Anita places her hand inside Delphine's. It feels like a bird's wing. Fragile, but strong.

*

Once outside Anita walks purposefully towards where her brothers cavort round Lily like yapping puppies. They see her entering the square, where the last of what was once an avenue of cherry trees clings on, its roots cracking the concrete all around it, as it puts on its defiant show of late winter blossom. They see that she is holding the hand of Miss Fish, who causes the boys, normally so unruly, to quell their noise and become calm in an instant without ever raising her voice, or, as now, without needing to say a single word. As their sister gets nearer to them, they see her face, wreathed in tears, break out into the widest of smiles. It is like the sun coming out, and in that moment they know, know for certain, that everything will be all right, they will not be separated, and at once they begin to jump at her, each of them clamouring to be scooped up in their sister's strong arms. Their joy is infectious, and, without any of them quite knowing how, the five of them, the three children and the two grown-ups, are dancing in a ring, an unbroken circle, oblivious of the stares they are causing among the various passers-by, who also find themselves caught up in the euphoria, and whose day now seems brighter as a result.

Afterwards, when Lily has said her goodbye to Delphine, she and the children wait at the stop just below Delphine's window for the 209 Trolleybus, which will take them back to Lapwing Lane. The overhead wires crackle and spark, signalling its imminent arrival. The boys are excited. "It's like a dragon," roars Christopher, swooping down towards Clive, who hides behind his sister.

"What happened to Miss Fish's parents?" asks Anita suddenly.

"Oh," says Lily, immediately becoming serious. "They died."

"Yes, I know. But what of?"

Lily pauses a moment before answering. How much should she tell her? Anita looks up at her with her large, dark eyes, eyes which have seen too much unhappiness already for someone so young, but she is not to be fobbed off with some fairy story.

"A long time ago…" begins Lily.

"How long?" interrupts Anita.

"Thirty-three years," says Lily, "to be exact. There was a great disease that spread around the world. It was like the flu, only much worse. Many people caught it and died…"

"How many?" demands Anita.

"I don't know precisely," says Lily. "But millions, I think."

That puts a quietness on Anita at last. The trolleybus now approaches, spitting out fire like a dragon. On its side is an advert for matches, matches once made in Manchester, in Newton Heath, but no longer.

"Has it gone," persists Anita, "this disease?"

"Yes," says Lily, gathering up the boys around her.

"Will it come back?"

"No," she says. "At least, not the same strain."

"Can you promise?"

Lily looks at Anita squarely as she is about to step aboard.

"No," she says at last. "That's not something I can promise."

Anita breathes out deeply. She knows Lily is being honest with her. That is all she wants from anyone...

Echoes of this will float down to her ten years from now, when a handsome but feckless man with whom she is in love is packing a suitcase.

"Will you be coming back this time?" she says.

"Sure, baby," he says, "don't I always?"

"When, Leroy? When?"

He shrugs before pulling her to him and kissing her as though both their lives depended on it...

Now, standing beside the Manchester Royal Infirmary, she sees Delphine looking down from her window and waves. The trolleybus-dragon pulls up to the stop. Anita watches the shower of sparks dance and crack in the air around her.

*

2020

theguardian

20th October 2020

ANDY BURNHAM BLASTS TORIES FOR 'PLAYING POKER WITH PEOPLE'S LIVES' IN FURIOUS SPEECH

Greater Manchester Mayor accuses the Government of walking out of talks after refusing to provide a £65 million bailout for ailing businesses and workers.

Chloe Chang reporting online

Andy Burnham has accused the Government of walking out on talks for a financial bailout for Greater Manchester before it goes into Tier 3 restrictions as a result of the rising number of Covid cases in the city.

The Greater Manchester Mayor savaged ministers for failing to provide the minimum sum of £65 million needed to avoid a "winter of real hardship" under Tier 3 restrictions, which would plunge the poorest into poverty and homelessness.

He said civic leaders had reduced their original demand of £90 million for stricken businesses and for workers to top up furlough payments.

Mr Burnham then reduced it again to £75 million, then £65 million but the Government refused and walked away, with reports it would only offer £60 million. By contrast, the Government has already spent more than £200 *billion* on the coronavirus crisis.

The Mayor learned of the Government's decision while in the middle of his regular daily press briefing on the steps of Broadhurst House, when one of his aides interrupted him to show news of the announcement via Twitter on her mobile phone.

Mr Burnham was visibly shaken and distressed, not only to learn of the latest developments, but in having to do so in such a manner.

"This is brutal," he said, "really brutal. The Prime Minister is playing poker with people's lives through a pandemic. Is this how they mean to run the country? By piling pressure on people to accept the lowest figure they can get away with? Is this what they mean by 'levelling up'? What we've seen today is a deliberate act of 'levelling down'. It's a disgrace."

For more details go to: guardian.co.uk

*

Chloe sends the article with a link to a video clip of Andy Burnham speaking recorded on her phone to Petros, who receives it just as he is leaving *The Colony* on Hood Street, where the two of them were having coffee a little more than half an hour before.

"I wish you could have seen it," reads the text.
"It was one of those 'where-were-you-when?' moments….
👻
OMG xxx"

Petros smiles. What he likes most about Chloe is her certainty, her clarity, the way she looks at the world through a particular prism head-on, that there is an essential difference between what's right and what's wrong, and once you've figured that out for yourself, you have to hold onto it, no matter what. That's what he thinks has drawn her towards him over the years they've known each other, first as students together and subsequently as emerging professionals, even though, for the most part, they have clashed and argued. He realises that he enjoys these arguments, he always has, and he reckons that she must enjoy them too. Otherwise why would she keep coming back…?

*

2015

Five years earlier.

magic 1152

Hi there. This is Chloe Chang from Magic Radio 1152, speaking to you from the heart of Manchester. Right now, on this busy last Saturday afternoon in March, I'm standing in the middle of Market Street, just below the outdoor escalator leading up to the Arndale Centre's Food Hall. It's an unseasonably warm, sunny day. People are out and about enjoying themselves, strolling leisurely from shop to shop, stopping to chat with friends, buying themselves a coffee or an ice cream. Everyone's wearing their summer clothes – T-shirts, shorts, flip-flops. In nearby Piccadilly Gardens children are running in and out of the fountains. A holiday atmosphere pervades. And talking of holidays, have you decided where you might be going yourselves this year? One of the Costas? Club Med? Or maybe you fancy one of the Greek Islands? Azure skies, sparkling seas, the sun bouncing off those whitewashed, cliff-top villages? Maybe you fancy a glass of ouzo in a beachside taverna? I know I do. Well – we might be in luck...

I've been given a tip-off that something quite unexpected is about to hit these unsuspecting shoppers here on Market Street. A little bit of Greece is about to invade Manchester. Intrigued? Then follow me as I walk towards Tessuti. No – I'm not about to indulge in some Armani perfume, try on the latest Calvin Klein swimwear, or be tempted by a Valentino bag. Instead, it's the distant strain of some familiar music that is drawing not just me, but stopping everyone who hears it in their tracks.

Have you guessed what it is yet...?

Chloe pauses and lets the air waves be filled with the instantly recognisable refrain from *Zorba the Greek*, which she allows to grow louder and louder.

Isn't it glorious? Doesn't it bring a smile to our faces? Doesn't it make us all immediately want to kick off our shoes and start to dance?

Well – that's what's happening right now here in the heart of Manchester on this busy Saturday afternoon. It's one of those joyous 21st century phenomena – the flash mob. Seemingly ordinary, everyday shoppers, right in the middle of Market Street, have suddenly placed their arms upon the shoulders of apparent strangers and begun to execute the familiar steps of Zorba's dance. They cross one leg in front of *the other. They dip down low, then rise up on their toes. More and more of them begin to take up the call. Pockets of twos and threes and fours are joining up to form whole chains of dancers, who snake their way in between the wide-eyed shoppers, inviting them to join in. Many of them do – and why shouldn't they? They're not in a hurry this glorious Saturday afternoon, are they? – and those that don't join in, those too laden with bags, or those encumbered with push chairs and children – stop in their tracks to clap in time with the music's familiar accelerating rhythm. But then they too cannot resist joining in, weaving their push chairs in crazy patterns. The mood is festive, the atmosphere infectious. More and more people are now joining in. The whole of Market Street, it seems, is dancing. The music grows ever louder, ever faster. It's impossible to resist.*

And so you must excuse me if I stop describing what is happening for you for a few moments, because I need to join in myself. It's just too tempting. So – wherever you are right now, listening to this, in your kitchens, your gardens, your cars – no, not in your cars! – stop what you're doing right now, and join in with me doing the Zorba Dance. Let's get the whole of Manchester dancing. Woo-hoo!

The music ratchets up even louder, mixed in with the sounds of laughter and happiness from the crowds. Eventually the song finishes, followed by huge, spontaneous applause. An out-of-breath Chloe resumes her commentary.

Wasn't that fabulous? I hope you all joined in at home? I'm now making my way through the still-milling crowds to try and speak to the organiser of this incredible event today – Callista Kyriakidis. She's surrounded by supporters and well-wishers, and I'm just reaching her now…

"Callista – hi. I'm Chloe Chang from Magic Radio, and I wondered if you might spare a little time to talk to our many thousands of listeners?"

"Yes, of course. Excuse me – I'm a little out of breath still from all the dancing."

"I'm not surprised. It was fantastic."

"Thank you."

"Tell me – where did the idea come from to hold this event today?"

"Well – today is the closest Saturday to March the 25th, which is Greek Independence Day, when members of the Greek diaspora right across the world celebrate the moment we became a free people. Including here in Manchester, where we have been welcomed ever since the first of us arrived here almost two hundred years ago after the Massacre at Chios. We wanted to do something that was surprising and fun as a way of bringing everyone together."

"You certainly succeeded. The whole city has a smile on its face. You said 'we'. Can you tell us more about some of the people who've been involved today?"

"*The Hellenic School of Manchester.*"

"For those listeners who don't know about it, can you tell them what you do?"

"We're a supplementary school offering evening, weekend and holiday classes in Greek language and culture for people of all ages."

"Can anybody join?"

"It's mainly for members of the Greek and Cypriot communities here, but yes of course, we welcome everybody. *Philotimo.*"

"What's that?"

"It's our guiding principle. *Philotimo.* '*Be* good and *do* good'."

"Well, you certainly did us all a great deal of good this afternoon. Callista Kyriakidis, thank you very much."

Chloe proceeds to wrap up her programme, handing over to the next presenter. Hoisting her equipment onto her shoulder, she then seeks out Callista once more.

"Hi," she says. "Thanks for that. It was great."

"You're welcome."

"Actually," says Chloe, a little less confidently now that she has dropped her radio persona, "I'm wondering if you might be the same Callista who's the sister of a friend of mine?"

"You know my brother? Petros?"

Chloe nods.

"We were students together at MMU. I've not seen him much since, though. I doubt he'd remember me."

Callista eyes Chloe keenly. "I've never met any of his friends. We don't meet up that often. I had to drag him here today."

"Petros is here?"

"Somewhere," says Callista. "Unless he's sloped off already. I put him in charge of the music. No – there he is. Look." She points.

Petros is bent over cables and speakers. As if aware he is being talked about, he pauses, then looks up. He sees Chloe at once. His face darkens.

"Oh," says Callista, smiling. "I can see from his reaction that he does remember you."

Petros and Chloe regard each other from a distance. Chloe beams. Petros continues to glower. His eyes are like coals. The expression on his face is that of someone who has been holding his breath for the longest time under water and has just surfaced to take in more air. Chloe's smile does not waver.

"That was great," she says, indicating the crowds without removing her eyes from his.

Petros says nothing.

"How've you been?" asks Chloe.

"Can't complain."

"That makes a change," she says, still smiling.

Petros swallows hard. "You?"

"Oh," says Chloe, more expansively, "you know me. A bit of this, a bit of that. Plenty of irons in the fire."

The air hums with the sound of a nearby tram.

"Well," says Petros at last, "I'd best finish packing up."

"That's OK. I've to be back in the studio for another interview in ten minutes anyway."

"Which minor celebrity are you putting to the sword next?"

"Meaning?"

Petros indicates around him. "All this," he spits dismissively. "A Zorba flash-mob? It's hardly cutting edge, is it?".

"Tony Lloyd," says Chloe. "In answer to your question." She looks at him hard. "Is that cutting edge enough for you?"

Petros gulps. "The Police Commissioner?"

"And soon-to-be Interim Mayor."

"What will you ask him?"

Chloe smiles. "Why he wasn't down here on Market Street dancing."

"Seriously?"

"Makes a change from knife crime."

Petros shakes his head.

"I mean it," insists Chloe. "We have to tell better stories. Look around you. Everyone's smiling, everyone's having a good time. You just helped that to happen. *Philotimo*."

"No. That was my sister."

He looks away. Chloe follows his gaze. He's seeking out Callista. She sees him and waves.

"You'd better go," he says. "I know how you hate to be late."

They each smile, remembering.

"Bye then," says Chloe, waving the tips of the fingers of her left hand. "Don't be a stranger."

*

2020

"Don't be a stranger… Don't be a stranger…"

Five years later, Petros hears her voice rising up to meet him as he restlessly pounds the city streets.

He is trawling back the years He has begun to lose that sense of certainty he once had, and he's not sure why. Or how, or when. Only that it has somehow crept up on him in the last year or so. The deals he makes – like the one he closed earlier this morning at the former Coop Tobacco Factory near Angel Meadow – don't seem to satisfy him the way they once did. Perhaps he should mention it to Chloe the next time they bump into each other? Perhaps he should even risk setting up a meeting between them in the first place, rather than leaving it to chance – or to her? No. He shakes his head. She might get the wrong idea if he did that. She might misconstrue his motives and think he's asking her for a date. Which he most definitely isn't. Not that she would say yes if she thought that he was. But he's not. He just wants… What? What does he want? He's no longer sure. In fact he's no longer sure about anything. It must be the pandemic. It's thrown everything into uncertainty. It's no wonder, then, that he's begun to experience such doubt.

Snap out of it, he tells himself. Get a grip. What's the matter with you? You've just pulled in a quarter of a million quid this morning. You should be celebrating. But no matter how much he berates himself, he can't seem to shake off this sense of unease and uncertainty that continues to tap him on the shoulder, causing him to stop in mid-stride, as it does now, so that he pauses to catch his breath.

He finds he is standing on the bridge at Baring Street, which passes over the River Medlock. Less than half a mile away from *The Colony*. His feet have automatically taken him there. He's on his way to look at a new development nearby, one of many planned for the regeneration of the Mayfield area behind the station, what the investors are referring to as 'Piccadilly East', the next hot spot for young entrepreneurs. Until recently a complete no-go area, the seediest of red light districts, where business was carried out hurriedly and squalidly in bricked-up railway arches surrounded by dirty needles, discarded syringes, and rats. Now, already, squares have been cleared, coffee shops are springing up alongside the gentrified Rochdale Canal, a mere stone's throw away from the city's bustling gay quarter, with its bars and night clubs, its drag queens and comics, its murals and window-boxes. Even the Medlock, too, is ripe for restoration.

It's certainly ripe, thinks Petros, as the stench of rank and foetid sewage rises up from beneath the bridge. But it will not be so easily reclaimed as the canals around the city have been. So much of it has been culverted, blocked up, dredged and diverted, hidden away from the millions who walk or drive or ride across it in the trams each day, like a dirty secret. It has, Petros realises, been a constant thread stitched throughout his life. When his Great-great-great-grandfather Konstantin first arrived here in the 1830s, he crossed the Medlock near Ardwick, which was at that time the southern boundary of the city. He settled in Salford, not far from where the Medlock still joins the Irwell at Potato Wharf in the Castlefield Basin. Konstantin's son, Vassily, set up the family Mastic Works in Ducie Street Warehouse less than a hundred yards away at its confluence with the Irk, and Petros's father, Alex, still has an office next to Peter House on Oxford Road, beneath which the Medlock flows via one of it many culverts. A muddy stretch of it is still visible at the back of MMU, where he was a student, and now, in this moment of self-examination, he stands on the Baring Bridge looking down into another tiny outflow of it. If it were not so murky, after more than a century of pollution at the hands of the tanneries, dyers and chemical works that have poured their effluent into it, he might just be able to make out his reflection in it, even on this cloudy, overcast day, but he cannot. No clues come to him from its stagnant waters.

But when he looks more closely, he can see that the river is not in fact as putrid as it is widely held to be. It doesn't exactly flow, but it does trickle – just. Signs of life returning to it have been noted by enthusiastic birdwatchers, who have left a record of their sightings on a temporary hoarding on the bridge, which Petros looks at now. Canada geese have been spotted, as have finches, robins and thrushes, along with dunnocks, wagtails and dippers – even a kingfisher and a sparrowhawk. As if to demonstrate the fact, a moorhen casually cruises from between the rusting iron grille that marks the point where the Medlock emerges from the culvert which carries it from what was once an old Gas Works, beneath a car park at *The Etihad*, before it disappears once more less than a hundred yards further on beneath the Science Institute on London Road. Petros watches the moorhen glide casually by, its unseen webbed feet paddling determinedly ahead of the current.

The river was once navigable for a considerable portion of its lower reaches, back in the 18th century, when James Brindley was constructing the country's first ever industrial canal for the Duke of Bridgewater, which finished at the point where the Irwell and the Medlock joined, allowing cargo to continue their journeys further up each river. Petros knows that the Council has a long-term vision to open it up completely again in the future – he knows this because he gave evidence to the Environment Agency responsible for compiling what became known as *A Ten Year Green & Blue Infrastructure Strategy for the City* as to how such a scheme might benefit potential future property development – but as yet there are no plans, or, crucially, funds, to implement it. Just pie-in-the-sky, as far as Petros was concerned at the time, but it suited him well to speak in its favour during the consultation process, good to have his voice heard, his face seen, his profile raised. But now he's not so sure. Now he thinks it would be better to open up a green space right in the heart of the city. Manchester has no real parks to speak of, not in its centre. Those that survive still are all on the perimeter, in the outer boroughs – ironic really, when you think that Manchester was the first city in the country to put aside land for public parks, for the benefit of its working people, as havens to breathe cleaner air, open spaces away from the factories, well-tended with flowers and fountains, plus added amenities such as tennis courts, bowling greens and ornamental ponds. Then they went out of favour. Many were neglected, or worse, becoming no-go areas, the last refuge of gangs and addicts, locked up, closed down, abandoned, concreted over, built on. But now they are valued again. Friends' Associations are springing up to reclaim them. Tow paths are being reopened along the canals. Trees have been planted. Tiny oases of handkerchief-sized pockets of green have begun to sprout in the city. Like Sackville Gardens, where the statue of Alan Turing sits on his bronze bench, just across the bridge from where Petros now stands, looking down into the slowly reawakening Medlock, like a slumbering serpent, which one day might rise up like a Chinese dragon, garlanded and bedecked with colour, spitting fire, as the City, if it can ever shake off the shackles of lockdown, might once more dance and party beside.

Petros looks back towards the giant hulk of Mayfield, which once was a mighty railway sidings, goods yard and engineering works, where welders worked through the night repairing locomotives, the night sky filled with their sparks arc-ing above the station's glass cathedral dome, which, having laid silent for a generation, now resounds to the incessant roar of wrecking balls, pneumatic drills and jackhammers, biting into brick, cleaving into concrete, watched over by the towering cranes that look down over the city like gods from Olympus, as they strive to build their new Jerusalem, their Elysian palaces of glass and steel, from which Petros will make his next quarter-million, then party the nights away in *The Warehouse Project*, voted the UK's coolest, hottest night club complex, deep within the as yet undeveloped belly of Mayfield.

He stops. He turns away. He is breathing heavily, panting hard. He looks back down to the thickly oozing Medlock gurgling below him like a drain, gulping for air, just in time to catch a final glimpse of the moorhen as it disappears from sight beneath the next culverted tunnel.

Enough.

He recalls those lines of Prospero's from *The Tempest*, after he has finally quelled the storm. Petros had studied and loved the play for 'A' level, and its vision of a brave new world had first set the fires of ambition burning within him. But now he feels those flames might just be starting to die down.

'*Our revels now are ended. These, our actors, as I foretold you, were all spirits and are melted into air, into thin air…*'

Is that what is happening to him now, he wonders?

'*And, like the baseless fabric of this vision, the cloud-capp'd towers, the gorgeous palaces… shall dissolve…*'

Surely not, he thinks, surely not…?

'*And, like this insubstantial pageant faded, leave not a wrack behind…*'

He reels away. Is this what people mean by a Damascene moment.

He looks back at the river. Seeping out of the shadow of the past, trickling towards an unseen future, but flowing still. It was here before we came, it will survive us after we've gone. The marks we make upon it are what we leave behind.

A wedge of egrets skewers out of the tunnel, white against the black waters of the river. An ancestral memory stirs within him.

He knows exactly what he is going to do. He knows it with a certainty that is ferocious in its intensity.

A sense of certainty, yes.

He will follow the course of the Medlock – not from its source in the Strinesdale Hills to the east of Oldham – but from where it enters the old city boundary, near Ardwick, where it plunges underground into the culverts, tunnels and drains that underpin the city, retracing the route of those that went before him, until it empties into the Irwell, just a hundred yards or so from where the River Irk also joins this confluence, where Manchester first began.

He will pursue this task alone, as a challenge to his resolve, to prove to himself that he can, to fly in the face of those who would say it is foolhardy. He will do this as a way of reeling himself in, of bringing himself back to a sense of who he really is, what he really wants from his life. Money may make the world go round, but it's not what makes it tick, or chime, or resonate with meaning.

Below him, underneath the bridge, crouching beside the muddy Medlock, he sees a figure. Although he cannot see the face, the form seems familiar, the way the body shuffles, doggedly, like a caterpillar trying to cross a road, a suicide mission, but somehow making it to the other side. Now he remembers. This is the same woman, who earlier had tried to cadge some change from him outside the Tobacco Factory, who Petros had tried to buy off with a ten pound note, to shoo her away, so that she wouldn't tarnish the frontage of his investment, lower the tone of the neighbourhood, or cause a scene or embarrassment. Now it is *his* turn to feel embarrassed. He watches her squat beside the water's edge and sprinkle some bread crumbs at her feet. At once she is surrounded by the ever-present starlings, who strut fearlessly towards her, their beaks pecking straight from her hand. Undeterred she starts to sing, a guttural drone from the back of her throat, simultaneously overlaid with ancient wordless melodies, which swoop and soar and plunge, with squeezed vowels and clicked consonants, producing sounds that are as ageless as the running of water over stones, the spitting and crackling of flames in a fire, the roaring of wind through the trees, the marching of feet underground. But it is a song of the city as much as it is a song of the earth. Petros understands this, as does a colony of rats emerging from the culvert to scent the rise and fall of its notes on the air. Another ancestral memory stirs in Petros. He sees the tears of Chios hang in their attenuated clusters from the branches of the mastic trees. He knows he needs to harvest them before they stretch too far and break, before they fall to the ground and are lost and trampled on in the stampede. He will become an embroiderer.

But first he will need to thread himself through the needle of the Medlock's tunnels, pass through their pupa of concrete and brick, until he can emerge at last on the other side, fully imagined, face to face with who he has become, in the fierce glare of recognition.

He reels away from the bridge. The city reels along with him. He looks down at his feet. Which way will they take him? He begins to understand. This is not the road to Damascus after all, but to Delphi, where his father waits for him at the crossroads…

The woman has stopped singing. She is nowhere to be seen. The rats have retreated back into the sewer. The starlings have scattered to all corners of the city. The egrets fly across the face of the sun.

Without pausing to consider why, the action outpacing any thought, he picks up his phone and rapidly punches out a text.

"Are you ready?" it reads.

Chloe, picking it up, smiles and texts back.

"I've been ready all my life."

"So am I," he replies.

"Are you sure? Are you certain?"

"Yes," he texts. "I'm certain. I'm ready."

"Hold on to that thought. We go into Tier 3 from tomorrow."

Tomorrow...

And tomorrow and tomorrow...

Petros has always been impatient. The petty pace from day to day has always crept too slowly for him. But he understands that this time he will have to learn the art of patience. He will have to put his plan on temporary hold.

"The river will still be there when this is all over," says Chloe, when next they meet at *The Colony*.

"I suppose," he says.

"Lockdown can't last for ever.."

"Can't it?"

"When the first Queen Elizabeth was on the throne, they were always having plagues and pandemics. They were forever shutting down the playhouses. Only they didn't call it 'lockdown'. Instead, the people were 'sequestered'. That's a much gentler word, isn't it? Less externally enforced, more self-imposed. There's a kind of cloistered monasticism about it that sounds more reassuring somehow. Don't you agree?"

Petros says nothing but continues to listen carefully.

"It's also quite ascetic, quite self-disciplined, which is kind of appropriate for the task that lies ahead of you, don't you think?"

"Possibly."

"I can just see you in a monk's cell, can't you, stripped bare of all but the essentials, as you get ready to go on your pilgrimage?"

"Are you teasing me?" he says, but without a hint of rancour.

"Only a little," she says.

He closes his eyes and smiles. He rolls the word around his tongue, savouring the sound of it. "Sequestration."

"That's better," she says. "Think of it as meditation."

"Ommm," he chants, and they both laugh.

"In France," she continues, "they call it *'le confinement'*. Like the old-fashioned word for pregnancy. I prefer that best of all. It's more hopeful. It makes you think that something bright and new will be born because of it."

He opens his eyes and looks directly at her. "Yes," he says. "Yes."

They are silent for a while.

"What's that word your sister used?" asks Chloe some time later.

"*Philotimo*," he says.

"*Do* good, *be* good?"

"That's right."

"*Philotimo*," she repeats.

"*Philotimo*," he echoes after her.

*

Seven months earlier.

To: All Resident Artists at Islington Mill
From: Lorelei Zlatan

Date: 23rd March 2020

Subject: New Lockdown Measures

! This message is high priority

Following the Prime Minister's announcement that the country is to go into a lockdown to help combat the spread of the coronavirus, with all non-essential shops and services to close and everyone to work from home if possible, we have no alternative but to close all facilities here at Islington Mill, including the artists' studios, until further notice.

We understand what a bitter disappointment this will be to you all, for we all of us believe that there is a strong argument to be made for declaring the arts to be an essential service for the health and well-being of the nation, but for the moment we see no alternative but to close.

In order to combat the undoubted isolation this may cause for many of us, we are proposing a series of weekly Zoom conversations, in which we might all remain connected and offer ourselves mutual support.

Take care. Stay safe.

Lorrie

Lorelei Zlatan
Studio Manager, Islington Mill

(My pronouns are she/her)

*

Three months later.

To: All Resident Artists at Islington Mill
From: Lorelei Zlatan

Date: 23rd June 2020

Subject: Relaxation of Lockdown Measures

! This message is high priority

Good news!

In line with the Government's decision to ease the National Lockdown, we are delighted to announce that we are at last able to re-open the artists' studios, but with the following key restrictions remaining in place.

- Hours of opening will be restricted from 10am to 6pm
- Artists must work in their studios alone

- Artists will need to book an Arrival Slot with me beforehand in order to avoid congestion in the Entrance Hall & Reception Area. (Typically this will mean coming to the Mill in 15 minute intervals)
- All communal areas – the Bar, Café, Green Room and Main Exhibition Hall – will remain closed to the public for the time being
- These areas will be accessible for artists to arrange private meetings with gatherings of a maximum of three people at any given time. Social distancing of two metres to be observed and face coverings to be worn in respect of safety
- Unfortunately this means the kitchen, too, will not yet be available. Please ensure you bring any drinks or food with you, and then take what is left away with you when you leave
- Sunanda and I will be working a rota system at the front desk from behind the recently installed perspex screen

We look forward to greeting those of you who feel able to return.

During lockdown there have been so many creative responses to the restrictions imposed by the pandemic. This is what artists do. Following the success of our *Masks for Life* scheme, we are excited to launch our new *Memories for Living* project, with funds generously donated by the Arts Council, in which we invite you to give an account of your own unique experience of the pandemic using whatever medium you choose.

Please follow the link below to find out more:

http://www.islingtonmill.com/memories-of-living/

Take care. Stay safe.

Lorrie

Lorelei Zlatan
Studio Manager, Islington Mill

(My pronouns are she/her)

*

Memories of Living x 5: Molly Wahid

Entry on the Islington Mill website:

Molly has been a Resident Artist at Islington Mill for twelve months. She makes outdoor interdisciplinary installations, as well as regularly exhibiting drawings in galleries across the north-west. She has responded to her experience of lockdown by making five short films. Click on each link to view them.

1. Prepositions
2. Lists
3. Learning to walk by day
4. Learning to walk by night
5. Making it up

Each film consists of a single shot for its entire length, taken on a mobile phone, held by Molly. The shot depicts a simple, everyday action, lasting however long it takes. Over the image Molly speaks. The words do not describe the action. Rather, they sit alongside it. They act as an invitation for the viewer – and listener – to make what connections they choose.

Film #1: Prepositions

The image is of a kettle being filled with water from a tap. It is then switched on. We watch it slowly come to the boil.

VOICE OVER: (Molly):
Lately I've been thinking about prepositions
and the differences between them.
Something about the relationships they hold
between time and space
and the things they're attached to
fascinates me.

I think it's to do with the attraction of opposites –
in, out, on, off, to, from, with, without

under, over, beneath, above, before, after.
Take these –

Lock *down*.
Lock *up*.
Lock *in*.
Lock *out*.

I don't accept any of them.
Let's try putting different verbs with them instead.

Climb down.
Reach up.
Breathe in.
Speak out.

There's plenty more.
Just substitute your own.

The kettle boils.

Film #2: Lists

The image is of the same tap. From it a droplet of water forms extremely slowly. It swells until it drips and falls into a bowl in the sink below, already filled with water from previous drips. As the droplet lands, it sends out a series of ripples in widening concentric circles, which gradually settle so that the surface of the water is once more still, before another droplet swells and falls from the tap.

VOICE OVER: (Molly):
 I start each day writing a list.
 I like lists.
 I've always liked them.
 Especially when I can tick the things off I've managed to complete.

It's my dream that one day I'll tick off every single item from it.
I haven't done that yet.
I don't think I ever will.
But it doesn't stop me trying.

But then came lockdown.
Suddenly there was more time.
Or so I imagined.
But it hasn't worked out like that.
I've taken to writing different kinds of lists.
Not 'to-do' lists.
Not 'bucket' lists.
But lists that read more like poems.
Like –
The different birds I've seen in a single day.
Or the familiar landmarks I pass on a walk.
Or like this one –
The books on my shelf that I've still not read
Which I always said I'd get round to
Once I had more time.

The Order of the Day
The Gathering
An Episode of Sparrows
The Museum of Innocence
House of Spirits
The Light Years
How I Live Now
A Little Life
The Accidental
Private Life
Family Life
Preparation for the Next Life
How to be Alone

But there they sit still – unopened…
I've no excuse at the moment.
But somehow I can't seem to get started.
It's as if now that we suddenly have all this unexpected extra time
I want to make the most of it.
So I make a new list –
A much shorter one.
Here it is:

1. Go for more walks.
2. Learn a new skill.
3. Write fewer lists.

With additional notes to self –
When walking:

Take advantage of there being less traffic on the roads.
Notice things more –
Especially the ordinary, everyday things
The kind you normally just ignore.
Like rust on railings.
Stains on concrete.
Marks on the land.
Drawings.

Here goes…

A final droplet of water drips into the bowl. The screen blacks out.

Film #3: Learning to Walk by Day

The image depicts a pair of feet walking. Molly is directing the phone with her right hand. A couple of fingers have slipped partially across the lens. In her left hand she holds a small circular mirror. The fingers from this hand hold the edge of the mirror's frame. In it can be seen reflections of the sky above Molly's head, but which appear almost super-imposed above the image of her walking feet upon the ground. Disconcertingly it is almost as if she is walking in the sky. The reflections change rapidly as she walks. Sometimes there are clouds, sometimes trees, sometimes birds flying across.

VOICE OVER: (Molly):
    I'm walking.
    I'm not following a route.
    Either on a map or in my head.
    I have no plan or direction.
    I simply let my feet decide.
    I focus instead on what I see in the sky,
    The sky which is now below me instead of above,
    So that it feels like I am walking in the air.
    Almost. But not quite.
    My feet tether me.
    The sound they make as I plant them
    On tarmac, concrete, mud or grass
    Anchors me.

    I've walked these streets all my life.
    As did my mother, grandmother and great-grandmother before me.
    Where they lead
    I follow.
    But I also forge new paths of my own.
    I don't just mean those that were not here then,
    That have been built since,
    But those which I make for myself.

    I look at the birds that are always flying past,
    Scudding across the sky in the mirror I hold in my hand,
    Restless, always on the move.

Rarely do I see any of them land –
The occasional blackbird tugging at a worm,
Or wood pigeon paddling in a pool of sunlight,
Its tiny head a hammer
Pecking at some unseen foe…
Instead I watch them wheel above me
(Or below me now in the glass)
Tossed like leaves on the wind
Intent on some hidden purpose,
Always on the look-out for somewhere new,
Somewhere different, somewhere better.

As a child my father would take me to the city
To watch the starlings in their nightly murmuration,
Thousands of them, each clamouring to be heard.
I'd marvel at their aerial acrobatics,
The way they'd twist and turn, swoop and swirl,
In endlessly changing, shape-shifting configurations,
As if bound by a single unifying thread
That would steer them this way, then that,
Until, as one, they'd fall like arrows
To their own particular customised roost.

There are fewer of them now.
They must have gone somewhere else.
The new skyscrapers of glass and steel
Offer less inviting places to perch,
No cranny, nook, crevice or ledge
On which they might find purchase.

My grandfather used to draw them for me.
I tried to do the same.
I still do.
I find I always come back to them
Whenever I'm between things.

They're good mimics, he'd tell me.
They impersonate other birds,
Their different calls,
To stake out territory
Or attract a mate.
They've learned to fit in,
Even if that means hiding their iridescent plumage,
The shiny blues and greens,
Beneath an oily grey-black sheen,
Turning brown in winter with whitish speckles
That fade in the spring,
Their feathers worn and ragged.

I like them, I always have.
They're cheeky and scruffy,
They skrike and they scrap.
They're commonly thought of as vermin, as pests.
Their droppings discolour buildings,
They can decimate a field of corn within minutes,
But they are faithful partners
And devoted parents.
They shimmer and sparkle like constellations.

I walk in the air,
Watching them scud across the sky
That I try to hold in my hand,
So that I might become a mimic too
And learn to be more like them…

My feet have taken me to Pomona Island,
The former docks of the Port of Manchester,
Now a wasteland, waiting to be built on.
Planning has been granted
But as yet there's still no plan.
The owners – Peel Holdings –

Want to occupy every last inch,
While others yearn for parks and open spaces,
Cycle tracks and tow paths
Beside the cleaned-up Ship Canal,
Walkways in the sky…

I was first here four years ago.
It was the start of my journey as an artist.
My grandfather had just died
And I went to Pomona in search of him,
Some last vestige of the Great Mural he painted there,
Depicting not just his own journey,
Of how he came to be the man he was,
But everyone's, mine too,
Of who we are and where we've come from,
How we got here and where we might go next.
It had all gone.

Or so I thought at first.
But then my foot snagged on something
Buried in the undergrowth,
A piece of skirting board.
Flaked with paint it showed
A young man with his daughter –
My mother, *her* father, my *grand*father
The girl was handing the young man an umbrella,
Once lost, now reclaimed,

I have that painting still.
It hangs upon the wall above my own daughter's bed.
A blessing, a birthright.
We pass it on.

Now, as I return to Pomona,
I no longer recognise it.
It's not the same place.

It's been dug up by bulldozers,
Laid bare by diggers.
A crane hovers over it
Like some giant praying mantis.

But as I walk across it
The layers strip away.
Mighty ships docked here from all across the world.
My great-great-grandfather, the first among us, alighted here.
Before that a Great Exhibition was held here,
Michaelangelo's *Manchester Madonna*,
With waiting-to-be-filled-in angels…
And before that wild beasts once roamed the island.
A tigon escaped from its captors.
Nobody knows where it went
But people claim they hear it sometimes.
I hear it sometimes…

The land does not forget.
It holds these memories buried
Beneath the present devastation,
A mirage of the brave new world
The planners hope to build here.

Locked in by lockdown,
My walking will unlock them.
A straggle of starlings buffets against the wind…

The image freezes on a blur of starlings in the mirror held in Molly's hand, her feet having left deep prints in the mud beneath her, like drawings.

Film #4: Learning to Walk by Night

The image appears to be completely black, as if the phone has not been switched on. Only the occasional blur of movement betrays the fact that this film has been shot in complete darkness, as Molly moves through the familiar terrain of the internal landscape of her home, so that the viewer, like Molly herself, begins to discern recognisable shapes as they emerge.

VOICE OVER: (Molly):

>Comfortable shape of my husband hunched in a letter 's'
>Cat lying in the dip of the quilt between two bodies
>(deliciously stretching, purring)
>Interloper
>
>Sharp edge of bed-frame on easing back the quilt
>Dark gap by floorboard just beside the door
>(too loudly creaking, betraying)
>Sentinel
>
>Thick sleepy feel of air in the passage between bedroom and bathroom
>Yellow rug, still bright even in the almost darkness, befuddling my eyes
>(dimly adjusting, dilating)
>Conjuror
>
>Milky snuffle of my daughter's breathing as I pause to listen
>Shape of the handle fitting my palm
>(fearfully entering, checking)
>Blessing
>
>Light-of-the-world globe lamp turning beside her
>Circling continents, oceans, a moth's wings
>(opening, closing, then opening)
>Moon seeker

Bark of a spindle tree softly pale by light from the window
Ink-black leaves coiled ready to open
(tightly budded, waiting)
Shadow dancer

Tired roof of building opposite hugging its windows close for the night
Silhouettes of church spire and minarets of mosque
(patient chess pieces, looming)
Sacrificer

Bottle-green lino on kitchen floor, not quite black, and cool underfoot
Hand finding, detecting table corner
(fingers walking, tracing)
Tightrope walker

Familiar weight of chalk-white beaker, next to docile snow-white sink
Gleam of glass water-container
(dreaming, slowly filling)
Libation drinker

Tiny pond of water's surface glistening
Quivering as the moon tries to pull it closer
(net-widening, noose-tightening)
Huntress

Diana, I drink down the moon
Ariadne, I wind in the thread
(retracing, returning)
Night walker

This final image of the dancing, refracted moon slowly sharpens into liquid focus.

Film #5: Learning to Start Again

For this final film the images are presented in a series of stills. They resemble polaroids in the way the colours feel unfinished, like old snapshots or frames from a home movie, which is exactly what they represent. Each time the image changes, it is accompanied by the familiar sound of a new slide being projected from a carousel. Each depicts almost exactly what is being conveyed by the text at the time.

VOICE OVER: (Molly):
    I'm trying to learn new skills.

Slide: Molly at the loom, frowning.

    As you can see, I'm still a beginner.
    I pass the shuttle through
    in and out
    under and over
    in and out
    under and over
    until... when?

    If I'm not following a pattern
    (which I'm not)
    if I'm simply making it all up as I go along
    (which I am)
    how will I know when I've finished?

    That's easy.
    I won't.
    I'll simply stop
    when I run out of thread
    or my hands get tired.

    Perhaps I'll pick it up again the next day or
    perhaps I won't...

Slide: Close-up of the loom.

    the loom is old, it looks it, it feels it
    countless hands have touched it before me
    their fingers have left their imprints in the wood
    I feel them as I rub my fingers down the grain
    ghosts, trace memories

    yes – this loom is old
    but it is also new, new to me

Slide: Michael sitting inside a van, smiling, thumbs-up.

    my husband fetched it in a van he borrowed
    from a barn where it had lain forgotten

Slide: The semi-ruined barn at Elton.

    covered in dust and cobwebs and mouse and bat droppings
    it lay in bits

Slide: the loom inside the barn as described.

    but somehow, miraculously, none of these bits were broken
    when we got it home we tried to reassemble it

Slide sequence: Michael & Molly restoring the loom.

    painstakingly, piece after piece after piece
    like doing a jigsaw
    when you don't have the picture on the lid of the box to guide you
    you have no clear idea what it's going to end up looking like
    until it's finished
    and it's right there in front of you
    in front of *me*

Slide: Molly sitting at the loom again, as for the beginning. The slide then animates and becomes video footage of her weaving.

> I thread it up, I make a tentative beginning, I'm starting to weave
> I sense those fingers which have been here before mine instructing them in what they must do
>
> I literally have time on my hands
> all I have to do is listen…
>
> listen…
>
> listen…

Video: Molly continues to weave. We hear the rhythmical sound of the shuttle being passed and pulled through.

*

2019

Six months earlier. The last day of the year.
 "Michael?"
 "Tom?"
 "You found us then?"
 "Your directions were excellent."
 "I've given them many times before."
 "Well – thank you."
 "Sat Nav's no use round here."
 "No."
Michael gets out of the van he's borrowed from a friend of Nadia's and immediately steps into deep mud.
 "Sorry about that," says Tom. "It's like that everywhere. Isn't that right, Apichu?"
 A young, visibly pregnant woman emerges from a caravan and joins Tom.

"It's been raining ever since we came here," she says with a shrug.

"Apichu?" says Michael. "That's an unusual name."

"It's Peruvian," she says. "Tom and I met there." She links her arm through his.

"Gap year," explains Tom, smiling. "After I finished uni."

"Which turned out to be three."

"I was travelling."

"Then he met me."

"So I stopped."

They beam at each other.

"And then I wanted to see where he came from."

Michael looks at the bleak, sodden moorland, with nothing for miles around, just the distant ring of towns in a rain-soaked haze. Bolton, Bury, Rochdale. The grey sheen of the M66 snaking back to Manchester.

Tom catches the look in Michael's eyes.

"Well – not exactly here. But close by. Summerseat. Beside the Irwell. My Granddad worked in the Joshua Hoyles Mill till it closed in the 1980s. Then my Dad ran *The Waterside Arms*, the pub on Kay Bridge. That's where I grew up. It was originally built as a crèche for the workers at the Mill to leave their children during each shift. I wanted to show Apichu."

"But it got washed away in a flood."

"2015."

"That was the year we met."

"We were in Lima when the news reached us."

"I said he should go home."

"But my Dad urged me not to. 'Finish your trip first,' he said."

"So you stayed."

"I stayed."

Michael looks from one to the other as they tell him their story. But it seems to him that his presence is unnecessary, as if they tell each other this story often, to remind themselves why they are here, to anchor them.

"So what happened?" he says.

"The next year Tom's father died," says Apichu.

"Nothing to do with the flood," adds Tom.

"But it can't have helped. He lost his home, his livelihood…"

"Prostate."

"So this time when I told him to go home…"

"I did…"

"And I came with him."

"For my mother's sake." He turns away.

"She's not well," explains Apichu quietly to Michael.

"She has dementia," says Tom loudly, then adds more quietly, "She doesn't know me any more."

"Yes she does," says Apichu, taking his hand. "Deep down."

They look around. More rain is threatening. A gust of wind blows Apichu's hair across her face.

"We'd best go inside," she says.

She heads away towards a small caravan, from which a washing line is strung out towards a bent hawthorn tree.

"Or do you want to see the loom first?" asks Tom.

Michael looks up at the glowering sky.

"Loom first, I think."

Tom nods.

"I'll make some coffee," says Apichu.

"This way," says Tom, and he leads Michael towards a roofless, windowless, semi-derelict stone cottage.

"Do you mind if I take pictures?" asks Michael. "My wife – Molly – she'll want to see."

"Fire away," says Tom.

"The loom's for her, you see."

"Is she a weaver?"

"An artist. She likes to work in as many different mediums as she can."

He pauses to take a picture of the cottage.

"What do you think?" asks Tom brightly. Michael sees at once how important it is for him to answer with enthusiasm.

"It's in a terrific spot," he says.

"Isn't it?" says Tom. He is like a puppy fetching a stick, jumping up for Michael to throw it again. He flings his arms in all directions, pointing out landmarks. "There's the Elton Brook," he says. "Starling Reservoir, Barrack Fold, Bentley Hall. Owler Barrow, Higher Spen, Daisyfield. Cockey Moor, Kiln Clough, Top o' th' Carrs."

"Yes, I see."

"As soon as I saw it, I had to have it. I know there's a lot of work, but I'm not afraid of that. I said to Apichu, 'We could really make a life for ourselves here, build a home that's ours, not just the two of us, but for our children'."

He pauses. He runs his hand along the stone wall beside the open doorway.

"This house has stood here for more than two hundred and fifty years. I know it's in a sorry state right now, but it's survived the worst that time and the elements could throw at it. Look at it," he shouts. "Isn't it magnificent?"

They step across the threshold and at once it becomes quieter. Even though it has no roof or windows, Michael can sense a stillness descend upon them, the weight of all those years, the lives lived within its walls, the hopes and disappointments, the loves and losses.

"What do you know about it?" he asks.

"Not much," says Tom, his voice almost a whisper now. "It's been empty for longer than people can remember. I've tried to look it up everywhere – parish registers, old maps, tithe records. It doesn't even have a name. It's simply marked on the Ordnance Survey as 'Old Barn'. During the Second World War pigs were kept here. And from all accounts it was already a ruin back then. But nothing since. I have a picture of it – look."

He takes an old, much-folded black-and-white photograph from his anorak pocket.

"Who are they," asks Michael, "the man and the child? Do you know?"

Tom shakes his head. "The farmer, I presume," he says, "from Nob Lane Farm a couple of fields away. I asked, but the people there now are relatively new." He puts the photograph carefully back into his pocket. "It will be good for a baby to be born here," he speculates. "It will help bring the old place back to life."

They look around it in silence for a while. Michael has already begun to filter out the sounds from outside – the wind, the rain which has started once more, the faint distant hum of traffic – and is tuning in to the interior voices of the house – an old beam creaking, a mouse scrabbling in a corner somewhere, a bird fluttering in the rafters. There are leaves and ashes in the stone hearth, a patina of dust that lifts and then settles again each time he takes a step.

"I agree," he says at last. "This place feels full of stories."

"Doesn't it?" Tom's face is shining. "Sometimes," he confides, "I think I can hear them. It was the loom that clinched it for me. Someone worked at it here, made things with it. I can imagine the sound of it, the click and the clack of it, measuring the years."

"Can I see it?"

"This way," says Tom, and he leads Michael up a narrow flight of weathered stone steps towards what remains of an upper floor. Most of the wood has rotted over time, but a section has survived. Tom edges his way towards it, encouraging Michael to follow him. "This part's quite safe," he whispers. "It'll take our weight."

In the farthest corner, beneath the one part of the roof that still remains, Michael perceives the dark shape of a length of tarpaulin thrown over what he assumes must be the loom protected under it. He looks enquiringly at Tom, who nods. Carefully he unties the rope that tethers it, then gently pulls the sheeting away. The loom emerges like a moth stiffly unfolding its wings after years of being encased in its pupa. Michael takes a photograph. The click of the shutter as he presses it on his phone sounds intrusively loud.

An hour later Michael and Tom have dismantled and transported it piece by piece to the white van parked just outside. Tom has laid out sheets of plywood for Michael to reverse the van over, in order to prevent it from getting stuck fast in the sea of mud surrounding the cottage. As soon as they have finished Michael picks his way as carefully as he can towards the caravan, where Apichu has brewed fresh coffee.

He leaves his shoes on the mat just inside and joins the couple at the pull-out dining table. The caravan is as snug and warm as the cottage is cold and exposed. The windows have all steamed up, and Tom wipes a section of one of them with the cuff of his jumper, so that they have a clear view of their future home. The rain has now come on much harder.

"She reminds me of a ship riding out a storm," says Apichu as she pours. "She's withstood far worse storms than this. We'll make a home of her again."

"How long have you been here?" asks Michael.

"We only moved in a month ago," says Tom. "As soon as we'd secured ownership of the land and the building. We plan to start work on the cottage in the spring."

Michael nods.

"We know it's a big job," says Apichu. "It will take us two or three years, we think, but we're prepared for that. We know it'll be worth it in the end."

Michael looks around.

"I know what you're thinking," laughs Apichu. "It will be difficult to manage in this caravan for all that time."

"Well," concedes Michael, "I don't expect it will be easy."

"We'll be fine," she says. "I grew up in Medalla Milagrosa."

Michael looks puzzled.

"It's one of the *pueblos jóvenes*," she explains, "one of the largest of the shanty towns that surround Lima. Migrants from all over Peru live there, mostly mestizo campesinos, like me, mixed race Amerindian and European. I'm used to managing in cramped conditions. But it's much easier here. For one thing, there's no overcrowding…"

"And for another…" interjects Tom, coiling his fingers through his thick, red beard and smiling, "we have each other."

"And another arrival soon," she adds, looking down at her belly, which she strokes contentedly. She looks back towards Michael. "Do you have children?" she asks.

"A daughter," he says and grins. "Here. Let me show you." He brings up some photos on his phone. Apichu smiles.

"What's her name?"

"Blessing."

"*Bendiciendo.*"

She is interrupted from her reverie by the sound of a ping from Tom's laptop.

"Sorry," he says. "Newsflash"

"He likes to stay connected," smiles Apichu indulgently.

"From when I was travelling," explains Tom. "And for my work?"

"What is it you do?"

"He's a journalist," says Apichu.

"Features, mostly."

"What does it say?" she asks.

"Something about a new, unidentified virus in the province of Wuhan in northern China."

"That's too far away to worry us here," says Apichu, closing her eyes and lying back.

"I'd best be on my way," says Michael. "The storm doesn't show any sign of easing up just yet, does it?"

He puts his shoes back on, then pauses at the caravan door.

"Goodbye," he says, "and good luck."

He steps outside, followed by Tom.

"Just in case your van gets stuck and you need a push."

"Thanks." He hands Tom an envelope. "£250," he says. "As agreed." Then, just as he opens the van door, he passes him his business card. "Let me know how you get on," he says. "The baby. The house."

"OK," says Tom. Michael wonders if he will. He hopes so. Molly and Apichu would get on, he feels sure.

Just as he is about to pull away from the field onto the dirt track that leads down to Cockey Moor Road, his eye is caught by something he sees in his wing mirror. It looks like a small wooden cross poking up from the ground at the back of the cottage.

"What's that?" he points.

"It's a grave, I think," says Tom. "There are six of them in all."

"Really? Can I see?"

"Help yourself."

Michael jumps down and hurries towards it. The rain is slanting horizontally now across the moor. Tom is right. There are six crosses, in various stages of decay, but still clearly visible, as are the slightly raised mounds of earth that each of them stands alongside. The crosses lean precariously, as if they have been buffeted by squalls such as these over the centuries, but somehow have managed to cling on.

"I agree," says Michael. "These do look like graves."

"We find them comforting," says Tom.

"In what way?"

"They show that people did live here once. It wasn't just a barn for keeping pigs. Families made a life for themselves here. As we will."

Michael shakes Tom's hand, "Happy New Year," he says, then drives away, down the dirt track, along Cockey Moor Road, Ainsworth Road, Bolton Road and Rochdale Road, towards Heap Bridge, which crosses the River Roch, a tributary of the Irwell, where he will take the M66 and M60 motorways, which will convey him the twelve miles to Molly and Blessing on Stanley Road in only twenty minutes, but it will seem half a world away, where already particles of infected air in microscopic respiratory droplets are mutating, dividing, replicating, its rate of reproduction already above one, randomly spreading, an indeterminate, indiscriminate, indiscernible pattern, an imitation game, woven on a loom by separate hands.

*

1819

> *"With Henry Hunt we'll go, my boys*
> *With Henry Hunt we'll go*
> *We'll mount the cap of liberty*
> *In spite of Nadin Joe*
>
> *On the sixteenth day of August*
> *Eighteen hundred and nineteen*
> *A meeting held in Peter's Field*
> *Was glorious to be seen*
>
> *Some females dressed in green and white*
> *Before the hustings stood*
> *But little did they think that they*
> *Would see such scenes of blood..."*

A fortnight has passed since the terrible day when Agnes lost both her husband and her son to the sabres of the Manchester Yeomanry Cavalry, who had charged amongst the thousands assembled there to hear Mr Hunt speak for Reform.

"I'll reform you," one of the soldiers had cried when he ran her poor boy Jack through with a cutlass.

Then, less than half an hour later, her husband, Amos, had fought with the man who had commanded the troops, one of the

Magistrates, who had stood and watched the carnage from his balcony window and smiled, then afterwards had ridden through the blood-soaked field upon a white horse. Amos looked at him then and saw what he could scarcely believe. It was like looking into a mirror, for this man – Matthew, Agnes has learned he was called – was his identical twin. Separated at birth, neither knew of the other's existence till that moment. Amos had dragged Matthew from his horse, roaring Jack's name, and together the two of them had fought, a raw and bitter eye-gouging, throat-squeezing fight, which had seen them rolling over and over, almost in a lovers' embrace, towards the Daub Holes, the Lime Pits, which had sucked them greedily beneath.

An hour before Agnes had been handing Amos an apple, while they listened with pride to Jack, a drummer boy not long come home from Waterloo, beat out a rapid, joyful burst of *Peas Upon A Trencher*, the signal for light refreshment. How happy they had been…

Now Agnes sits alone, back in the cottage above Elton Brook, which had been their home, and before them her Uncle Silas the Weaver's. His loom, which Amos had so lovingly restored after Silas had died, upon which he had woven the cloth for the banner they had carried to Peterloo, which she had stitched with the words '*Unity is Strength*', stands silent. There is no unity any more, and no strength left in her. She simply sits by the empty hearth and stares through the wind-eye where there is no glass, out across the bleak moorland beyond. Her eyes are fixed on the row of wooden crosses that stand there in the grass, a low, pitiful mound of heaped earth beside each.

Agnes has planted every one of these crosses. The first was for James, her brother, who drowned in Elton Brook when he was only seven years old, while salmon leaped all around him. He had lost his footing on a makeshift bridge made from a fallen branch that she, Agnes, had coaxed him to stand on, and then hit his head on a rock. She had been too frightened to go in and rescue him, so that by the time her cousins, Ham and Shem, Silas's boys, came looking for her, it was too late. James had drowned, and Agnes never forgave herself, not even a year later, when, forced to leave Silas by her father's missionary zeal for the Moravian Settlement he had helped to build in Fairfield on the other side of the city, they had passed right through the centre of Manchester on a day that was thronging with thousands of people who had gathered to watch James Sadler lift off from Haworth Gardens, close by Angel Meadow, in a hot-air balloon, the first ever Englishman to do so, and their cart had become stuck in the crowds right beside the foaming River Irwell. A small boy, trying to save a runaway cat, had been knocked aside by the surge of the crowds and fallen into the river. Immediately it was clear that he couldn't swim, and he too seemed destined to drown, but Agnes saw a chance for redemption. She would not let another boy perish as James had done. Instinctively she hurled herself into the Irwell and plucked the boy from the path of a huge revolving water wheel just in time. The boy was Amos, who had only the previous day escaped from the House of Correction, where he had been placed as a foundling, born just eight years before on the night Manchester had been struck by an earthquake.

Peterloo had felt like another earthquake. But there was no chance of rescue or redemption on that occasion. Amos and Jack had been taken from her. In the blink of an eye both had gone. In less than a heartbeat she was alone.

The second and third crosses were for Silas and Meg, who had died while Agnes and Amos had been lost and wandering after their midnight flight from Fairfield, when their request to be married had been rejected by the Lot, the Moravian custom for making important decisions, leaving them to God, or fate, or simply chance, so they had run away and plighted their troth under the stars beside a black poplar tree on Cockey Moor, where they had exchanged tokens. Amos had given Agnes an iron ring he had forged himself in the smithy at Fairfield, and Agnes had given Amos a Roman coin that had once belonged to her brother James. These had been their wilderness years. Amos had lost the coin and almost his life in the mines of Bradford when a gas explosion brought the whole hill down upon him. Then had come the brickfields of Harpurhey, where their daughter, Daisy, had been sucked beneath the wet clay of the kiln fields, after which they had fallen into the despair of Dimity Court, a rat-infested cellar beneath the rim of the foul and stagnant River Irk, where Agnes had worked in a glue factory, ripping out the guts and intestines from the carcasses of slaughtered horses, and Amos had worked the steam-powered looms of his twin brother's mill on Oldham Street, though fate contrived to keep them from meeting. That would not happen until Peterloo.

But eventually they found a way to leave – Amos, Agnes and Jack. They boarded a barge on the newly-opened Bolton & Bury Canal, jumping ashore by the Elton Brook, from where they gulped in lungfuls of clean moorland air as they ran towards the cottage that had once belonged to Silas and Meg, and which, overgrown with ivy and bramble though it was, now became their home.

On the night of their return Agnes planted the fourth cross – for Daisy.

And there, for several years, they were happy. Amos took up Silas's mantle and became a master weaver. Agnes worked as a dyer and a finisher of the pieces of cloth that Amos wove.

But then Jack ran away for a soldier. A drummer boy on the plains of Waterloo.

He survived – just – but he did not return home for another two years after the battle was won. During all of those years, the years of endless winter, when the sun never shone, Agnes sat in the exact same spot she sits in now, waiting, scanning the far horizon in case he should return. Like Penelope in *The Odyssey*, while Amos sat weaving. Until the day he did return, suddenly appearing at the open wind-eye. But when he did, he was silent. He had been struck dumb. The horrors of what he had seen had so traumatised him they had torn the power of speech from him. His tongue could no longer articulate words, only strangled sounds from the back of his throat. But his face would light up to the percussive rhythms made by Amos on the loom and Jack would accompany him on his drum, which he would never let out of his grasp. It became his way of talking to them, and Agnes had felt almost whole again.

Now Agnes finds their absence unbearable. The loom and the drum. Both of them silent. Except for when the wind whistles through the still-remaining threads of the warp. The drum is in the ground. With Jack. A fifth cross marks the grave. While a sixth cross stands for Amos. But there is no body. That lies lost in the Daub Holes. Back in Manchester, where, in the years that will follow, the lime pits will be drained, and gardens will be laid out for gentlemen to stroll through with their ladies. They will be called 'Piccadilly', after the 'piccadil', the high-frilled collar worn by men of fashion, men like Amos's brother, Matthew, for all the good it did him.

Agnes sits by the wind-eye at the back of the cottage, her eyes fixed on the wooden crosses, thinking over the events of her life that have led to their planting. Like Penelope once more. But there is to no more weaving, not this time, not even a burial shroud. From time to time she sings – the litany that has accompanied her through all of her wanderings.

"And though our son who marched to War
To Manchester has come back
There's nowt left for him here no more
Save the Cavalry's cruel attack

And as I sit by the fire at night
There's none to comfort me
To Heywood, Hooley, Heap and Hell
The Good Lord has delivered me…"

Two weeks later that is how Ham and Shem find her, still sitting by the glass-less wind-eye, her eyes open and fixed on the row of six crosses leaning in the direction of the prevailing west wind that blows constantly across the moor.

How long she has been dead they cannot say. But they can guess what has happened. She had asked to be left alone when she came back from St Peter's Fields, and they had respected her need for privacy. But she has not moved from the spot she now occupies, not for food or water, not for rest or sleep. She has simply waited for Death to creep up on her, so that she might join James and Daisy, Amos and Jack, and she has not had to wait long. Grief has led her willingly by the hand to meet him.

It is the 15th of September. The Day of Our Lady of Sorrows. And there she sits, the *Mater Dolorosa*. A moth, which has only that morning, flown inside the cottage from the fields outside, lays its casing of eggs upon the heddle of the loom, then flutters around the silent cottage before finally alighting upon Agnes's shoulder, where it folds its wings to settle there, watching over her, keeping vigil.

Ham and Shem bury her out the back, along with all the other graves, and place a seventh cross to mark the spot where now she lies.

"Let's leave her be," says Ham, "and shut the cottage up."

Shem nods. "Aye," he says. "It's been a happy place for t' most part."

"Aye," says Ham. "An' it'll be happy again, given time."

The brothers board up the wind-eyes to let her rest there undisturbed, in peace with her ghosts and memories. Inside it is dark and cool. Thin bars of light pierce the slatted boards, slicing the empty space left behind. The moth tentatively opens, then closes her wings, slowly, repeatedly, patiently, waiting for her eggs to hatch.

*

2020

To: Tom Johnson
From: Michael Adebayo

Date: 23rd February 2020

Subject: Loom Query

Hi Tom,

I hope this email finds you well? This is just a quick message to let you know that Molly and I have finally managed to put the loom together – we think! Molly has had her first stab at threading it and attempting a basic weave.

We have a question. Do you have any idea as to the loom's age? Now that we've cleaned it up, it feels very old. The grain is worn quite smooth in places and feels as though it's been touched by many hands. Is there a way of finding this out?

All the best
Michael

PS Any news yet re the baby? We hope that Apichu is keeping well…

*

To: Michael Abdbayo
From: Tom Johnson

Date: 24th February 2020

Subject: Re – Loom Query

Hi Michael,

Check the construction of the joints.

- Until the late 1600s handmade dowels or pegs held the mortise-and-tenon joints together and were slightly raised above the joints.
- In the 1700s glue was used on dovetailed joints. These types of joints became more refined throughout the 1700s and the first half of the 1800s.
- In the 1860s the machine-made Knapp joint was developed and is commonly called a half-moon, pin-and-scallop, or scallop-and-dowel.
- In the late 1800s a machine-made dovetail joint was perfected, completely replacing the Knapp joint by 1900.

The wood for furniture pieces was hand sawn until the beginning of the 1800s. Visible saw marks up to that time will be straight. After that most wood was cut with a circular saw and any saw marks will be round.

Cheers
Tom

PS Baby girl born last week. Mother & daughter both doing fine. Not decided on a name as yet…

*

To: Tom Johnson
From: Michael Adebayo

Date: 24th February 2020

Subject: Re – Loom Query

Hi Tom,

Congratulations! Wonderful news! Molly says please pass on her love to Apichu. Any photos of the new arrival yet?

Thanks for the information regarding how to tell the age of wood. From what you have told us, I reckon the loom is early to mid-18th century. Which would fit with when you say the cottage was built. Fascinating. My boss at University would find all this so interesting. His name is David Olusoga. You may have seen him on the BBC?

He does that programme *'A House Through Time'*.

Stay in touch.

Thanks again.
Michael

*

To: Michael Adebayo
From: Tom Johnson

Date: 25th February 2020

Subject: Re – Loom Query

Hi Michael,

'A House Through Time', eh? Maybe he should try and tell the story of this one? One in the country by way of contrast with all those in cities? Though I fear it would not fill a single programme, never mind a whole series. It has lain empty for so long now, home to mice and birds rather than people, though there are times when I'm in here by myself, working to repair the walls, that I fancy I hear voices in the wind and in the rain, children's mostly, their high, piping laughter like water running over stones, though sometimes I think I catch the distant echo of a woman crying…

I reckon I must be spending too much time on my own. When Apichu and I eventually move in here with the baby, we'll be able to fill the space with our own voices, and who knows…? Maybe those of more children. We'll make our own stories, new ones. I think the house will enjoy hearing those.

All the best
Tom

*

After the loom has been completely reassembled, the wood cleaned and waxed, Molly looks on it with joy and wonder. It stands in a corner of her studio at Islington Mill, where the morning sun falls on it from a north-facing skylight. She walks around it, surveying it from every angle. It has a quietness and dignity about it she finds compelling. That so much care and craft went into the making of what was, in its time, a humble everyday kind of object, moves her beyond measure. She compares it alongside her easel, also fashioned from wood, with clean, streamlined, functional lines. It is not in any way unattractive and has already begun to acquire a patina of time, the way it is becoming splashed with splodges of paint, a not unpleasing random accumulation of different colours and pigments. But it pales into insignificance next to the loom. She knows it will never endure for so long. Nor will it acquire the same grace, or suggest the possibility of such a rich narrative. Probably only *her* hands will touch it. Unlike the loom, which has been stroked and caressed by who knows how many?

She runs her own hand along its contours now. It has that intensely satisfying, physical pleasure that only old wood can evoke, the feel and smell of it, which she breathes in deeply, as she continues to try to get to know and understand it by touch as much as by sight.

She closes her eyes. Her fingers slowly, minutely, explore every nuance of it, the direction of the grain, the way the dovetail joints hold fast to one another, yet still allow the loom to breathe. Her hands pass along the rods and shafts, the pedals and lambs, the heddles and horses, the whole castle of it, until they reach an indentation she has not noticed before near the base of the frame. Something has been carved there. She opens her eyes, gets down on her knees and presses her face as near to it as she can, in order to inspect it more closely. Its shape gradually reveals itself to her, as much in the negative space as in the carving itself, and, once she has grasped what it is, it will not leave her. It is a laurel leaf. The likeness is uncanny. More than that, it is extraordinary. She knows she has seen it before. When she stands up she is shaking.

The next day she returns to make sure. She has brought the white *qurqash* with her, first given to her by Nadia for her *Thin*

Blue Line installation at *The Etihad* two years before, which she'd worn again for her TEDx talk at Manchester Central Library one year after that on the bicentenary of Peterloo, in which she'd told as much of its story as she knew, how it had been worn by great-great-grandmother Rose on her wedding day to Yasser, and how after that by Esther, Rose's daughter-in-law, on the occasion of Yasser's funeral, but that it had a much older story than that, how Rose's schoolteacher, Laurel Stone, recognised it as being of special significance to her mother, Pity, back at the time when the first railway service anywhere in England set out from Manchester to Liverpool as long ago as 1832, and that it had passed through many others' hands in between.

She holds it up to the light, which almost passes through it. She studies its pattern of moths caught among laurel leaves. She places a single leaf of it against the carving at the base of the loom. She gasps. There is no mistaking it. The leaf on the cloth matches exactly the one etched into the wood of the frame.

She squats down on her hands and knees, then lies face down on the floor of the studio, crawling as close to the loom as she can. She takes a small magnifying glass she has brought with her from the back pocket of her jeans and holds it up to the carving. There, in the heart of it, is what appears to be no more than the tiniest speck of white embedded within the grain. Without the magnifying glass she would not be able to see it – a filament of cotton fibre. Her breathing has become shallow. She can feel her heart beating, hear the sound of its pulse in her ears. Her fingers tremble. Somehow she manages to steady them sufficiently to allow one nail to gently scratch away a flake of this fibre, which now she holds in the palm of her hand and looks at for a long time.

Carefully she puts it inside an envelope, which she seals. She will show this to Michael. He will know what to do. Maybe a colleague from the university?

She stands before the loom, beholding it with even more reverence, almost as if it is a shrine. She holds out the length of white muslin before her, allows the light to pass through it once more, feels the weight of all the memories held in its lightness, its legacy passing down the ladder of years, hand over hand over hand, connecting her, and all the lives that have led her here, to this place, this moment, this growing sense of who she is.

*

To: Dr Michael Adebayo
From: Dr Arune Balaikaite

Date: 20th March 2020

Subject: DNA Enquiry
Dear Michael,

The ability to differentiate between different mature cotton fibres according to their varietal origins used to be a complicated, not to mention expensive process. But more recent developments have made it much more possible, that is to say affordable, to isolate intact genomic DNA from individual fibres using a modified CTAB protocol (Cetyl Trimethyl Ammonium Bromide). Using this protocol, a cationic detergent allowing me to separate polysaccharides from the original plant material, I have been successfully able to retrieve DNA information from the sample you provided, by performing a PCR procedure, (to obtain a rapid Polymerase Chain Reaction) using specific DNA bar-coding.

The technology was initially developed to prevent fraud, to deter unscrupulous cotton traders from claiming their product to be of a higher quality source than it in fact was. By a rigorous application of these procedures, we are now able to verify, with almost 100% accuracy, whether a particular fibre is of Egyptian, Peruvian, Brazilian, Indian, American or Australian cotton, or from anywhere else in the world where it may be grown.

Most frequently our expertise is called upon to assist the Police in their criminal investigations, when the forensic examination of different fibres may be required to place a suspect at the scene of a crime by matching the DNA from a detailed analysis of microscopic fibres.

Unlike fingerprints or human DNA, fibres are not specific to a single person. However, they can form a vital form of what is referred to as 'trace evidence'. They may originate from one source – say, a carpet, item of clothing, or, as in your case, a piece of cotton and an object of furniture, which is how we would categorise the loom – and then be transmitted to a person or other material by what is known as direct or secondary transfer. By comparing the transferred trace with its original source, we are able to determine a match. Such forensically acquired evidence is now generally regarded as conclusive.

To determine whether there is in fact a match, we generally deploy one of two methods – polarising light microscopy and infrared spectroscopy. In the former, we use a microscope fitted with a special filter that allows us to examine the fibre using specific light wavelengths. How the fibre appears tells us the precise type of fibre it is. Natural fibres, such as wool or cotton, normally only require an ordinary microscope to view the characteristic shape and markings. Infrared spectroscopy, by contrast, emits a beam that bounces off the material and returns to the instrument. How the beam of light changes reveals individual details and characteristics of the chemical structure of the particular fibres under investigation, making it immediately apparent if there is a difference between them.

Having carried out both methods on the samples you provided us with, I can now state with absolute authority that the fibres from the loom and the fibres from the piece of cloth are identical. In my view this renders it almost certain that the cloth was woven on that particular loom.

I trust you find my conclusions satisfactory, and I thank you for the opportunity of this welcome change from the more grisly investigations we are usually tasked with. It would appear that the hitherto usually separate departments of Chemistry and History within the University have more in common with each other than might have been suspected, for we are both, are we not, sifting through evidence in search of a greater truth.

With best wishes
Arune

Dr Arune Balaikaite, MSc, PhD
Research Fellow
Department of Chemistry
University of Manchester

*

These findings only serve to strengthen Molly's resolve to pursue an idea that began to form from the moment she received the original email from Lorrie with the links to Tom's advert on Gumtree that the loom was up for sale and when she phoned to tell Michael the news, on the same day of his interview with David Olugosa for tenure at the University, as he sat down next to the bronze statue of Alan Turing in Sackville Gardens.

Contingency and confluence.

Happenstance and synchronicity.

The convergence of random particles.

She thought back to those dot-to-dot picture books she had enjoyed as a child, when the image, buried within the virus of seemingly meaningless and indiscriminate speckles and spots, began to coalesce, revealing itself at the last moment, creating a pattern where none existed.

Or a scratch card. When paper-based card has hidden information printed on it, like a PIN number or Lottery Ticket, and is then covered by a film of opaque latex. You take a coin and, with the edge, scratch away the latex film to reveal the mystery secret.

She will find a new way of weaving.

She reads everything she can find about it, how the early powered Jacquard looms learned to read punch cards containing the patterns recorded onto them, or how pianolas appear to play recognisable tunes completely by themselves when a paper roll is pulled across a metal cylinder, similarly punched with holes, so that the correct hammers strike the required keys. Like a basic, binary computer programme.

But more than the mechanical processes involved, it's the conceptual framework that fascinates her.

The aesthetics of algorithms.

*

TEXTILE

Cloth and Culture
Volume 15, 2017· Issue 2

Weaving Codes/Coding Weaves
by
Emma Cocker

Drawing on my experience as 'critical interlocutor' within the research project *Weaving Codes/Coding Weaves*, I will reflect on the human qualities of attention, cognitive agility and tactical intelligence activated within live coding and ancient weaving with reference to the Ancient Greek concepts of *technē, kairos* and *mêtis* – experience, rhythm and touch. I will explore how the specificity of 'thinking-in-action' cultivated within improvisatory live coding relates to the embodied 'thought-in-motion' activated whilst working on the loom.

Echoing the wider concerns of *Weaving Codes/Coding Weaves*, I will attempt to redefine the relation between weave and code by dislodging the dominant utilitarian histories that connect the computer and the loom, instead placing emphasis on the potentially resistant and subversive forms of live 'thinking-and-knowing' cultivated within live coding and ancient weaving. Intuition and immersion.

I shall seek to address the Penelopean poetics of both practices, proposing how the combination of *kairotic* timing and timeliness with the *mêtic* act of 'doing-undoing-redoing' therein offers a subversive alternative to—even critique of—certain functional technological developments (within both coding and weaving) which, in optimising efficiency, risks delimiting more creative possibilities, reducing the potential for human intervention and invention in the seizing of opportunity, accident, chance and contingency.

*

Opportunity, accident, chance and contingency.

Molly seizes the moment. She will thread the loom. She will make a beginning. She will seek out an algorithm so elusive that at first it will seem there is no detectable pattern, but eventually, unexpectedly, it will start to repeat itself. Like history.

*

1955

The Didsbury & Withington Observer

17th **January 1955**

ANNOUNCEMENTS: BIRTHS

Mr Roland Warner, Electrical Engineer at Ferranti International of Wythenshawe, and his wife, **Lily**, Manager of *Blossoms*, a Receiving Home for Orphaned Children, are delighted to announce the birth of their first child, a daughter, to be named **Ruth**, after her maternal grandmother, the late Ruth Kaufman. The baby was born at home last Tuesday, 11th January, shortly after midnight, and weighed 6lbs 9oz. The christening is to take place at St Paul's Methodist Church, Wilmslow Road, Didsbury, on the 3rd Sunday of next month, 21st February, immediately after Morning Service.

*

A week later an envelope drops through the letter box of the home of Mrs M. Archer – "Call me Merle, everyone does!" – of 246 Upper Lloyd Street. Merle's daughter, Chantelle, picks it up and, with a puzzled expression, takes it into the kitchen, where Anita, Christopher and Clive are finishing their breakfast before setting off for school at Greenheys Primary.

"It's for you," says Chantelle, tossing the envelope towards Anita, narrowly avoiding landing it in the butter dish.

"Who's it from?" asks Anita, immediately anxious. "I never had a letter before."

"There's only one way of finding out," replies Chantelle, her curiosity piqued.

"That's right," says Merle more kindly. "I'm sure it's nothing to worry about."

Anita looks from one to the other, then back down to the envelope, which she holds between the tips of her thumb and forefinger, almost as if it might explode in her hand. By now her two brothers have also become caught up in the mystery and temporarily leave aside their pieces of toast.

Slowly Anita begins to open it, barely able to breathe. What if the letter says that she is to be taken away, removed to some other institution, far away from her brothers? She slits the back of the envelope, then carefully removes what lies inside.

But it's not a letter. It's a printed card, an invitation, from Lily, requesting her, Christopher and Clive, as well as Mrs Archer and Chantelle if they so wish, to attend the christening of baby Ruth.

Anita, Chantelle and Merle purr with delight, while Christopher and Clive roll their eyes and return to the more pressing matter of an extra slice of toast.

*

CERTIFICATE OF ADOPTION

1. Entry No: 30804
2. Date: 25th NOVEMBER 1940 and place: ASHTON and country of birth of Child: ENGLAND
3. Name and surname of Child: ANITA FREDERICKS
4. Sex of Child: FEMALE

5. Name and surname:
              MERLE ARCHER
 	
Address: 246 UPPER LLOYD STREET
              MANCHESTER
and occupation
of the adoptive
parent(s) of Child:
              TEXTILE WORKER

6. Date on which adoption was effected:
              9th SEPTEMBER 1955
and description of Court by whom effected
              MANCHESTER MAGISTRATES COURT
              FAMILY DIVISION

7. Date of Entry: 23rd SEPTEMBER 1955
8. Signature of Officer Deputed by Registrar-General to attest the entry: *Peter Ridgeway*
CERTIFIED to be a true copy of an entry in the Adopted Children's Registry maintained at the   GENERAL REGISTRY OFFICE. Given under the seal of the said office on: 30th SEPTEMBER 1955

Similar certificates are produced for Christopher and Clive. Anita can breathe a little easier. Now that Merle has adopted them all, no one will be able to split them up. They can remain together always.

*

1956

23rd August 1956

Dear Anita,

Congratulations on passing your 'O' levels. It is a just reward for all your hard work. I imagine Merle must be very proud of you.

I am pleased to hear of your intention to pursue a Secretarial Course in Shorthand & Typing at St John's College on Byrom Street. I shall be delighted to provide you with a suitable reference.

Such a qualification will always be useful. There are an increasing number of opportunities for suitably qualified young women as legal, medical, academic and financial secretaries, as well as the more standard types of office jobs.

Good luck. I shall look forward to receiving regular reports of your progress.

Yours sincerely,

Delphine Fish, AuD

*

1957

Moss Side Weekly Review & District News

Saturday 8th June 1957

ANNOUNCEMENTS: WEDDINGS

This afternoon, Saturday 8th June, the wedding will take place between Miss Chantelle Archer, spinster of the parish of Manchester, and Dr Henry James Brennan, bachelor of the parish of Ashton-under-Lyne, at Christ Church, Lloyd Street North, Moss Side at 2 o'clock. Described by Pevsner as 'the finest of its kind in the city', Christ Church was designed by W. Cecil Hardisty in the Arts & Crafts Perpendicular style, where, says Pevsner, 'a bellicote sits roguishly on the north shank of the western gable'. For bride-to-be Miss Archer it has been her home church. She was christened there, confirmed there, went to Sunday School there, where later she taught, and now she will be married there.

Dr Brennan, known as 'Harry' to family, friends and colleagues, is a junior doctor at Manchester Royal Infirmary, where he has been working as part of Dr Michael Johnstone's pioneering team investigating the properties of Halothane, which has been heralded as a major breakthrough in the field of Anaesthetics. First synthesised six years ago by ICI Pharmaceuticals in Widnes, Dr Johnstone and his team have successfully made the necessary improvements to render Halothane safe for use in hospitals across the world.

Dr Brennan first met Miss Archer at the hospital, where she works as a State Registered Nurse.

Miss Archer will be given away by her mother, Mrs Merle Archer, a widow, who works at the historic Barracut Clothing Factory on Manchester's Chorlton Street, where she makes the famous Harrington jacket, recently seen being worn by none other than Elvis 'the

Pelvis' Presley on the sleeve of his latest disc, *Love Me Tender*.

Miss Archer will be attended by her adoptive sister, Miss Anita, as Maid of Honour, with her adoptive brothers, Masters Christopher and Clive, carrying out the important function of Chief Ushers.

Afterwards there will be a reception at *The Reno* night club on Princess Road.

*

Three months later, in September, Anita commences her second year at St John's College. From its humble beginnings two hundred years before, when it was at the forefront of the early Sunday School movement in Manchester, it became one of the country's first 'Continuation' Schools, offering provision for adults to carry on with their education at the same time as working in the nearby factories and mills. Now, in the 1950s, in conjunction with their partner establishment in Openshaw, they have become pioneers of the Technical College, offering vocational courses for civil servants, post office workers and secretaries.

Anita has successfully passed her Basic Pitman's, and now, with the encouragement of both Merle and Delphine, she has embarked upon her Advanced. But since Chantelle's marriage to Harry, there has been one less wage coming into the house. Anita is acutely aware that, in the normal course of events, she would be working somewhere herself and so contributing towards the ever-rising weekly outgoings. Christopher has just started at secondary school, so there has been his new uniform to buy, and, at the rate he is growing he is even outpacing Merle's skills as a seamstress to keep letting down the sleeves of his blazer or the turn-ups of his trousers, so that he might need another one before the year is out.

And so Anita works on Saturdays in the Food Basement of Littlewood's, on the ham and cheese counter, where she has to learn to operate the dauntingly intimidating 'Slicer', which threatens to slice off her fingers as well as the ham or cheese if she is not extra careful. Some of her customers are most particular about wanting the exact weight they have ordered – even a third of an ounce out either way will not satisfy – while at the same time she likes to let the pensioners have a little extra, so long as her supervisor is not watching.

But the one pound she earns for that single eight-hour day is barely sufficient for her own needs, let alone allowing her to help out with the housekeeping for Merle.

She is pondering this conundrum one Friday evening as she sits in *The Kardomah Café* on St Peter's Square. It has become something of a weekly treat and tradition among the girls at St John's College to go there on their way home at the end of each week. They usually have a single espresso and a cigarette, while they talk about their plans for the weekend. Occasionally they might yield to temptation and stump up for beans on toast, then feel guilty afterwards. Mostly the talk is about boyfriends. They seem always to be causing concern, so that Anita, listening to her friends' dissection of the particular failings of the latest Stuart, Clifford or Terry, wonders why they still persist. She's seventeen and hasn't had one yet. She supposes she ought to toss her hat in the ring at some point. But she's in no rush. She is only half-listening to the others' current tales of their latest trials and tribulations, thinking instead that she will have to stop these weekly get-togethers, for they're becoming expensive, when a small notice by the counter catches her eye.

WANTED

Waitress
Three Nights Per Week
5 shillings an hour plus tips
Apply Within

"Excuse me," she says to her puzzled friends and crosses to the counter to enquire of the barman.

"Sorry, love," he says . "It's gone. I should've taken down the notice but I forgot." Then, seeing the look of disappointment on Anita's face, he leans across and says, "But I happen to know of a job going at *The Queen's*."

Immediately her expression brightens. "Are you sure?"

"Positive. And they haven't even advertised it yet. Be quick, mind. Once word gets round on the grapevine, there'll be a queue a mile long."

Without a second's hesitation, she collects her bag, leaving her friends gaping like goldfish in the wake of her departure.

"What's up with her?"

"I've no idea, but she's been acting queer ever since her sister got married…"

*

The following week she starts at *The Queen's*. A cocktail waitress in the Lounge Bar, three nights a week – Thursdays through Saturdays – the nights when Cam is singing.

"Oh it's a long, long time
From May to December
But the days grow short
When you reach September…"

Anita is entranced by her. Cam is past sixty now, but she doesn't look it. She has lost none of her allure. The dresses she wears still cling to her figure. Her hair, whether piled high or tumbling loose about her shoulders, is lustrous and dark, snaking its way down her bare back, her skin like golden honey. Her voice is deeper these days, huskier, more gravelly, made even more so by the cigarettes she is never without, not even when she is singing, so that she is always wreathed in coils of blue smoke.

"When the autumn weather
Turns the leaves to flame
One hasn't got time
For the waiting game..."

She steps away to the side, yielding the stage to one of her musicians, a young man who plays the trumpet as though she is his lover, and he is kissing her, softly, as if for the first time. The delicately muted notes are stretched out so long and taut, so thinly attenuated, gossamer fine and fragile, as though drawn from his lover's lips with a glass pipette, it is as if he is spinning a cocoon, each slow continuous note a silver thread he wraps them both in, until Cam steps back into the light.

"Oh the days dwindle down
To a precious few
September, December..."

Anita, watching this night after night, is mesmerised. She cannot take her eyes off the young man with the trumpet, whose sinuous fingers, when they caress the curves of his horn, seem to be playing across her skin.

"And these few precious days
I'll spend with you
These precious days
I'll spend with you..."

She cannot believe her girl friends in *The Kardomah* have ever experienced anything like this with their Stuarts, Cliffords or Terrys.

His name is Beauregard. Or Roy. Or Leroy. Or King. All of these, or none.

"And what's your name, Princess?" he asks her one night, between sets, when it is quiet and she is not so busy.

And she finds that she has no voice with which to answer, as if his trumpet has sucked it from her.

Princess will do just fine.

"*Wah gwaan*?" he says to her one night just as she is leaving.

When she doesn't answer, he links her arms through his and tucks her under her chin.

"*Mi deh yah*," he laughs, answering his own question.

She knows exactly what he means.

Cam watches their dance from the wings, the way her moth is drawn to his flame, and remembers when she too danced with a beautiful boy, who would conjure notes from the air like petals from a daisy.

"He loves me, he loves me not…"

Oh, he loved her all right. There were nights when he couldn't have enough of her, when he lost himself completely in the fluttering of her wingbeats, two imagines caught in the grip of the concentration gradient, when all molecular particles above absolute zero fused in their coming together. But he didn't love her as much as those other notes calling to him from his trumpet to conjure them into existence. There was always one more, and another, and another, waiting to be discovered. Over the hills and far away.

Cam laid only a single egg. But it was enough. A tiny caterpillar of her own. Richie. He hatched with several lives. Born on the Adelphi Bridge when Cam was casting her vote in the first election available to her. Buried in a pile of rubble in the Blitz, but pulled out unscathed. Felled by a fever after rescuing a German pilot from a treetop, riding his mother's mended sledge beneath a bomber's moon and the Northern Lights. She cut him a chain of dancing cats from a newspaper, one for each life, in memory of her own mother, the runaway slave.

"Sur le pont d'Audubon
L'on y passé, l'on y danse
Sur le pont d'Audubon
L'on y dance toutes en rond..."

Time is a circle for her these days.

She looks at the way this new girl, Anita, who reminds her of herself when she was that age, cannot take her eyes away from Leroy Beauregard King. Oh, how his name becomes him. How finely he regards himself. He looks into Anita's eyes seeking only his own perfect reflection mirrored back. Leroy. *Le roi*. King. And she is his willing Princess. His captive, his slave.

Cam takes her aside one night and tries to warn her.

"Do you not have agency of your own, *ma petite*?" she chides. "*Tu n'es pas une demoiselle en détresse qui attend d'être sauver, n'est-ce pas?* If you place that boy any 'igher on 'is charger, like some knight of old, *il va tomber*, and come crashing down on top of you."

Anita looks pityingly at Cam then, and Cam understands that she's got it all wrong. Anita doesn't see Leroy as St George, some dashing Moorish knight, but as the Dragon. She is not afraid of him. No – she welcomes the lick of his flames upon her skin. She will learn to harness their heat. She will absorb their power and return fire for fire. She will not let them consume her. Unless they consume both of them. Cam clicks her tongue. *Quelle catastrophe...*

Anita is singing.

She sings when she walks through the door. She sings while she pours the cocktails. She sings while she wipes the glasses. She sings when she leaves at night.

"You got a fine voice," Cam says to her one evening. "Stay behind after we close and maybe I'll teach you."

Cam never leaves the hotel these days. *The Queen's* is her home now. She has a suite there. Luigi's old quarters, which Cam has customised with shawls and throws, pictures and flowers. There's a small upright piano in the corner.

"Come," she says to Anita the first night she invites her up there. "Sit beside me on the stool. Let me teach you."

And Anita learns. But the songs are always sad.

"*Les chansons ne sont pas tristes*," corrects Cam. "They're true. It's the blues, *Chérie*. You want to learn to sing, *il faut commencer par le Blues*."

And she does.

*"I'm feeling mighty lonesome
I haven't slept a wink
I walk the floor and watch the door
And in between I drink..."*

Then both of them sing,
"Black coffee..."

Before Cam takes over.
*"Love's become a hand-me-down brew
I'll never see a Sunday
In this weekday room..."*

Allowing Anita to finish the song for her.
"Black coffee..."

"You 'ave poured yourself some strong black coffee with Beauregard, *Chérie*," says Cam. "*Il va te garder éveillé la nuit*. He'll keep you awake at nights."

It will be some years before Anita understands there are always two meanings to everything Cam says,

Cam feels her own fires are beginning to burn low. She recognises the signs. She knows what they portend.

She can no longer sing two sets each night. Her voice can no longer perform the same pyrotechnics they once could. But she understands this, the inevitability of it, the slow decline. It's like when Richie performs his latest aerobatic display. He has tried to explain it to her several times, when she has asked him what it is that drives him to dance with death the way he does.

After you have flown so close to the sun, wing-tip to wing-tip, after you have fanned your vapour trails across the sky, there is that moment when you know you must come back to earth, that slow, decreasing circle till you touch down on land once more, when you can just let everything go, then sleep, recharge, till you are ready to go again.

She knows exactly what he means. It has been exactly the same for her. The dull but necessary periods of waiting between shows, itching to get back up on stage once more, behind the microphone, stepping into the light, opening her mouth to sing, not knowing quite where it would take her, only that it would be somewhere. Like she imagines what it must be for someone stepping out upon a high wire.

Except that now she feels she's been everywhere she can. It's been a wild ride, but it's coming to an end. Tonight, she decides, will be her last song. No encore. No announcement. She will just finish her set, and that will be it. She does not need to tell anyone. It's enough that she knows herself.

"Oh the days dwindle down
To a precious few
September, December..."

Her voice is barely a whisper.

From the corner of her eye she can see Roy and Anita making long, slow love in the wings. When Roy enters her, Anita opens her mouth to sing. She has found her voice at last to answer him note for note.

Its surge of joy pours through Cam, lifting her for one final take-off.

"And these few precious days
"I'll spend with you…"

They fill, then empty her.

"These precious days
I'll spend with you…"

*

1958

The funeral takes place at the Manchester Crematorium in Southern Cemetery on Barlow Moor Road, three miles south of the city centre. Hundreds of people are there, too many to fit inside. Scores of her admirers stand outside in an iron frost. A thick fog shrouds the graveyard. A pale sun is trying but failing to disperse it.

Among them are Lily and Roland, George and Francis, Anita and Roy. Lily has not brought Ruth with her. It's a week day, so she's at school, which is a good thing. She's only just started and she loves it. She would hate the thought of missing a minute of it, let alone a whole morning.

It allows Lily to look around her. She has been to this place just three times. Once for Hubert, once for Annie, and once before either of them, when she fled from the nightmare of Globe Lane, when she ran the length of the Nico Ditch, not knowing where she was going, until she ended up here, in this place of the dead, sheltering from the cold beneath the statue of an angel, in whose shadow she watched a pregnant rat give birth to a litter of pups, licking them all clean, trying to protect each one as it was born from the penetrating cold, covering them with her body.

She would do the same for Ruth.

She hears the voice of the priest drifting out to her from inside the Crematorium, caught in the tendrils of the mist, still gathered thickly about her.

"For the life of man is but a span
And cut down in its flower
Here today, tomorrow gone
The creature of an hour…"

And the memory of that time comes hurtling back to her. Nowadays, if that happens – and mercifully it does so less and less – she tries to shut it away as firmly as she can, but today she allows it to return, to wrap herself up inside it, like this dense, unremitting fog…

*

1930

Lily runs.

She follows the course of the Platt Brook as it dribbles away into Hough Moss. A mist hovers above it. It creeps towards her like a living thing. It swirls and gathers round her legs, making it difficult for her to decide where to place her feet. The earth remains solid, an ankle-wrenching, bone-breaking, hard-rutted grid, as unyielding as granite, the frozen ground a razor of splintered glass.

She picks her way across the dead marsh.

The Nico Ditch has disappeared. Some say this is where it ended, a thousand years before, a last skull-splitting axe on the edge of the city. Others claim it limped on another mile or two, the final drops of blood a sticky ooze staining the land brown before dripping into the River Mersey.

In the distance Lily sees a dark tower, its clenched fist punching up towards the fallen sky. Crows fly from it as she approaches, circling overhead, cawing, nails in a rusty tin. A grove of obelisks, needle sharp, stab the air. Ivy-clad gravestones rise up through the mist leaning precariously, drunkards ready to fall. Some are surrounded by nine inch high spiked railings, a mace of black filed teeth, ready to snap. Forgive us our trespasses and those who trespass against us. Some are completely overgrown, neglected, forgotten, the lichen eating away the leprous stone. But some are watched over by statues, winged marble angels, guarding, protecting, beckoning.

Lily stops.

After seven miles hard running Lily has reached this Great Southern Cemetery of Manchester, the largest burial ground in all Europe, more than two hundred acres of bones picked clean by a century of worms, the avenues of mature trees fed by the ashes of the burned. She stumbles towards the tallest of the angels just as the last of what little light there has been this grey steel day is leaching away. She hears a low whimpering, not ten yards distant. Dimly through the mist she makes out an old, retired soldier, wrapping his arms around himself and rocking back and forth. She walks nervously towards him. A wound of medals ribbons his chest.

"I'm not who once I was," he says. His hands tremble. He tries to clutch a scarf to this throat. "I lost myself somewhere. I can't remember now." He coughs. Once he starts, he can't stop. His body wracks, convulses. Lily puts a hand upon his shoulder. Finally he stops. Beads of blood speckle his chin. He is silent a long time. The frost hardens on the moss. In the distance a dog barks. The old soldier begins his rhythmic rocking once again. He speaks in time to it, the words barely audible.

> " 'What matters it how far we go?' his scaly friend replied.
> 'There is another shore, you know, upon the other side.

The farther off from England, the nearer is to France.
Then turn not pale, beloved snail
But come and join the dance...' "

*

1958

We are none of us who once we were, reflects Lily.

She feels a hand upon her shoulder, wrenching her awake, back to the present moment. It is Roland, her husband. He bends over her, his face full of concern.

"They're coming out," he says. "Will you be all right? There's something I have to do."

She sees the procession leaving the Crematorium. At the head of it is someone she has never seen, but who she thinks she recognises. She guesses what it is that Roland feels he has to do, and why he has to do it alone.

"Yes, of course," she says. "I'll be fine. Don't worry."

She watches Roland thread his way through the mourners until he reaches a young man in an RAF dress uniform of blue-grey, with a light blue shirt and navy tie. He is just in the moment of replacing his peaked cap back on his head when Roland intercepts him. Lily sees him introduce himself. She imagines the words he might be saying.

"You are the eleven-year-old boy who rescued a German pilot from a tree in Buile Hill Park when his parachute got caught in its branches, the same boy who ran off to get help and brought back with you a most capable female ARP Warden, who set my broken leg with a length of wood that you had found for the purpose, the same boy who probably saved my life. I am that German pilot, and I want, as well as offering you my most sincere condolences for the loss of your mother, to thank you."

Lily sees the look of disbelief pass across the young pilot's face, an expression which changes in rapid succession to one of incredulity, then amazement, then gratitude. She sees the young man shake the hand of her husband with such deep warmth and affection.

"You will never know," she imagines him saying, "the full significance and impact of your words upon me. Without them I would not have become a pilot. I would not be wearing this uniform. You spoke of seeing angels. I did not understand you properly at the time. But once I began to fly myself, ascending so high that the sky turns black, I knew the truth of it. For I have seen them too."

And Lily wants to go over to him and hold him tightly to her and say, "Your mother – she sang like one of those angels, a dark angel perhaps, one who knew the ways of the world, whose voice could heal the demons we pretend are not there, and when she sang, it was with love and understanding."

But she doesn't. She does not wish to intrude upon this private meeting between Roland and Richie, who now are shaking hands and parting.

Roland returns to her.

"Thank you," he says. "I feel as though a weight has been lifted from me now, a debt repaid."

Lily nods. She knows all about such debts, such weights and measures.

They go back to *The Queen's* for the wake, those who knew her there. Francis and George, Anita and Roy. Giancarlo is there, waiting for them. He has brought his father, Luigi, with him. He sits in a wheelchair by the front entrance, welcoming all the old familiar faces. He has a special word for each of them.

Inside, after several toasts have been drunk and speeches made and songs sang, people begin to drift away, until only the last few diehards are left.

George sits down at the piano. He begins to pick out the first few notes of a song that Cam had made her own over the years. He proceeds tentatively at first, but gradually grows in confidence. He does not often play these days. Roy saunters across to join him. He adds a few melancholy embellishments on his trumpet. Then Anita, emboldened by her lover's smile, quietly starts to sing, barely more than a whisper, so that to hear her, everyone must pause and hold their breath.

"The angels on high
Have broken their wings
The loneliest tears I cry
My heart never sings

I'm in disarray
My heart's on the floor
Laughter and dark for the day
Who's minding the store?

I silently call your name
But no one is here
My heart sadly hopes in vain
You might soon appear

But you slipped away
Remote ever more
Who's warming the chill every day
And who's minding the store...?"

*

Three months later.

3rd April 1958

Dear Anita,

I believe that further congratulations are due. I hear from Merle that you are to be married next week, the first Saturday after Easter. It is all very sudden, and I suppose that this means you will be finishing St John's earlier than envisaged. I can only assume that something more urgent compels you to marry in such haste. Do not think that I am expressing disapproval – not in the least, I believe we far too often abase ourselves before the altar of convention – it is only disappointment that you will not be able to complete your Advanced Pitman's, which would have stood you in such excellent stead in terms of possible future career opportunities. Still, you can always return to your studies when circumstances permit you once more. Your year and a half at technical college will not have been wasted.

There is nothing to be gained, I believe, in mincing words, or beating about the bush. You have always desired people to be honest with you, Anita, a most admirable trait, and so I intend to speak the truth to you now, the truth as I see it myself, which I readily admit is based solely on my own empirical observations.

Although I have never married myself, I have nothing against the institution per se, though there must be, I believe, more to recommend it than the mere legitimisation of sex. Sex is an entirely necessary activity, and one which can be highly pleasurable, so long as it is consensual. I myself have had first hand experience of this. But I did not consider it necessary to be married in order to do so. I have received more than one proposal of marriage – one suitor was particularly pressing – but I always said no, fearing that I might lose a certain amount of independence and liberty, were I to have accepted. That did not prevent us, however, from continuing to enjoy one another's company. But with him, and with all my sexual partners, I always insisted on the precaution of birth control. I understood well enough from my observations of others the difficulties facing a woman trying to raise children out of wedlock. The man by and large tends to avoid the kind of prejudice and rejection we women must endure in such circumstances.

Hypocrisy, of any sort, has always been something of a red rag to a bull, as far as I am concerned. The love expressed between two consenting adults should be sufficient for the world in my opinion, without recourse to signed pieces of paper. Especially when, as in certain circumstances, no such signed piece of paper is legally available. I speak here of 'that love which dare not speak its name', a most lamentable phrase in my opinion, for all love, of whatever complexion, should be allowed to proclaim itself. I have always thought society's hostility towards homosexuality to be so very unchristian. Does not the creed of 'live and let live' sit at the very heart of Christ's teachings of tolerance? 'Let each person lead the life that God hath assigned him, and to which God hath called him.' Paul's Letter to the Corinthians. But, as I am sure you don't need me to tell you, Anita, for every Bible quote in favour of one opinion, there is another to be found advocating its opposite. That is why it is so important for each of us to follow our own path. There is a Greek word I have always been particularly fond of. Philotimo. Roughly translated, it means 'do good, and you will be good.' Not unlike the words Jesus is meant to have said in his Sermon on the Mount. 'Whatsoever ye would that men should do to you, do ye even so unto them.'

Please do not think I am in any way trying to dissuade you from your decision to marry. For some couples, it is the ideal arrangement. Take Lily and Roland, for example. No couple could be better suited to one another. All I ask of you, Anita, is not to rush into something, merely because you feel it is what is expected of you by others.

I understand that your husband-to-be is from the Leeward Islands of St Kitts & Nevis, the same as your late parents. I wonder if that is what drew you to him to begin with. Merle also informs me that he is a musician. I'm sure you are already discovering that the artistic temperament brings its own particular challenges, but I am confident you will rise to meet these.

Good luck, my dear. Please write and let me know how you get on. If I may be permitted to give you one small piece of advice, it is this, from Mr Shakespeare:

'To thine own self be true.'

Yours equally truly,

Delphine

*

1963

After five years Roy leaves for the last time.

There have been many break-ups, many quarrels, many nights when Anita has thrown him out onto the streets, hurling his trumpet through the window after him. But she has always taken him back. Sometimes they have fought each other like alley cats, yowling and scratching and tearing at each other's hair, but, like as not, these turn into couplings of an altogether sweeter nature. Their fights have been fierce, but their loving has been fiercer.

The times have been tough for Roy. She understands this. After Cam died, *The Queen's* decided to dispense with a house band and the musicians were all let go. They have a DJ there now who spins discs – US imports, but it's not the same. Anita left too. She would have had to anyway once Lance was born.

Lance.

When the nurses presented him to her after they'd cleaned him up, wrapped in one of Cam's old shawls, Roy understood that from now on he came second in the pecking order of Anita's affections, so he quietly withdrew.

Actually he loves his son. He can't wait to teach him the trumpet when he gets older. But he doesn't know what he's meant to do with babies. They leak all the time. He hands him back to Anita with a shrug and a grin, the kind of disarming gesture she once found so irresistible. Less so now. She's tired all the time. She tries to keep herself awake with black coffee.

Black coffee.

She sings the song Cam taught her not so much as a lullaby to Lance, but to herself.

"I'm talking to the shadows
From one o'clock to four
And Lord, how slow the moments go
When all I do is pour
Black coffee...

Since the blues have caught my eye
I'm hanging out on Monday
My Sunday tear's too dry..."

But Roy must play his music. It's more than a job, it's a calling. He could no more give it up than breathing.

The Manchester Jazz Scene is good, but it's small. There's *The Sportsman's* on Market Street, *The Grosvenor* on Deansgate, *The Bodega* on Cross Street, and *The Post Office Club* on Spring Gardens. But there are too many players chasing too few spots, so he goes where he must. Leeds, Sheffield, Nottingham, York. Then further afield. Bristol, Gloucester, Oxford, London. Sometimes he's back in a couple of days, other times he's away for weeks. She never knows.

Then, he gets a winter slot at *The Mardi Gras* on Liverpool's Bold Street.

"Liverpool," he croons. "It's not far. I'll get the train home on my nights off."

But it's 1963. The worst winter on record. Even worse than the one in 1947, which even though she was only seven, Anita remembers. But this is even colder. The lead pipes freeze in their bed-sit on Kippax Street. Then they burst. The flat is flooded, then freezes again. The power is cut. Outside the streets are piled high with snow. Cars and buses have to be dug out. No trains run anywhere in the country. Roy does not come back from Liverpool on his rare nights off.

"I'm mournin' all the morning
Mournin' all the night
And in between it's nicotine
And not much hard to fight
Black coffee

Feelin' low as the ground
It's driving me crazy just waiting for my baby
To maybe come around..."

This is no good. She can't keep mooching around like this, waiting for him to get in touch. She must take matters into her own hands.

She has no phone, so she has to risk life and limb to make it to the call box on Great Western Street. Several time she slips and falls. She keeps Lance warm by bundling him up inside her own coat. But he doesn't seem to mind the cold. He's just turned four now. He doesn't like to be carried. "I'm a big boy," he says. But he still likes to taste the snow as it falls on his tongue. Like he did when he was a baby.

When they reach the call box, there's a queue. They stamp their feet to try and keep some sense of feeling in them. There are snowmen in Whitworth Park, but they have no faces. People cannot spare coal or carrots for eyes or noses. This is no Winter Playground. It's about survival. While they wait, a coal lorry is heroically trying to make it through the ice with chains on its wheels. Everyone cheers as it inches forward. But then it too gets stuck. Some people try to help the driver to release it, by scattering dirt beneath the wheels to give them traction, but their efforts are hampered by others who see a chance to help themselves to sacks of coal from the back, while the driver is distracted.

Eventually Anita and Lance reach the front of the queue. They squeeze inside the red call box, which is all steamed up from the breath of previous users and smells of its customary piss. She takes the scrap of paper with its hastily scrawled number on it and dials. No one answers for a long time. Finally someone picks up. It's a woman. Anita asks to speak to Roy. He's asleep, the woman tells her. She'll try and wake him. A few more seconds pass. Outside the queue is getting restive. A man angrily hammers on the glass. How much longer is she going to be? She holds up her hand to indicate just five more minutes. The man turns away, stamping his feet and cursing. Finally Roy comes to the phone. He sounds drugged, or hung over, or both. He slurs his words as though his tongue is too thick for his mouth.

"I can't come home, baby," he says. "We're holed up here for de duration."

Anita says nothing. She's thinking about that other woman's voice.

"I got news," says Roy. "Ronnie Scott's offering me dis residency. When de thaw finally comes, he says, all I gotta do is get myself down there."

Anita feels her mouth go even drier.

"London?" she manages to croak at last.

"I know, baby. This is de break I been waitin' for."

"London?" she says again.

"You an' Lance can join me soon as you ready."

"What's her name, Leroy?"

When Anita calls him by his full name, he knows he's in trouble. He has to think fast. But he's always been good at that.

"Who you talkin' about, baby?"

"The woman who answered the phone."

"Oh her? She de landlady here at de club. I forget her name."

The pips then go on the phone. Anita has no more change. She and Lance manoeuvre themselves back out of the kiosk.

"About bloody time," says the angry young man.

Back in the bed-sit Anita goes over what Roy has said. Or rather, what he hasn't said. It's entirely possible that he doesn't know the name of the woman he's been sleeping with. He'd have asked her and she'd have told him. But he'd have probably forgotten it immediately. He calls all women "darlin'", or "honey", or, as in her case, "baby". She doesn't so much mind his affairs as his pathetic attempts to deny them, to pretend they haven't happened. Like Delphine pointed out in her letter to her on the eve of her marriage, what she values above all else is the truth. She wants people to be honest with her. That's all she's ever wanted. Lily understood this. Merle. Delphine. But Roy has simply never grasped it. He tap dances around the truth so much that he probably believes the lies he spins. He lives entirely in a world of make-believe. He's feckless, a dreamer, his head in the clouds. But she has always known this. Right from when she first laid eyes on him and he called her his Princess. She found his charm quite irresistible. Cam had warned her from the start. "Don't you be believin' a single word he tells you, child. That tongue of his is drippin' with sweetness. Trouble is, he keep puttin' it back in the honey jar." He'd laughed when she'd said that, but Cam was not fooled. "Beauregard is a good name for him. Fine lookin', fine talkin', but it's all smoke and mirrors, *Chérie*. One day you're gonna look, and you're not gonna see him no more. He'll have vanished in a puff of smoke. *Disparu, ma petite*."

Anita looks around. There's no trace of him left anywhere. He's always travelled light. Now nothing remains. Not a suitcase, not his clothes, not his trumpet. Just the echo of him playing it, so sweet and mellow. And Lance. Lance is unmistakably Leroy's son. A true *'beauregard'*. He looks at her fearfully. He senses something important is about to happen.

"Is Daddy coming home soon?" he asks.

"No," says Anita. "He's not."

"Will he come when the snow melts?"

"No," she says again. "Not then either. He won't be coming back at all."

Lance looks down. His bottom lip begins to tremble. But then it stops. He looks back up again. "I'll look after you," he says.

She picks him up and holds her closely to her, swinging him round their tiny one-roomed bed-sit with its bathroom down the hall.

There is no way Anita will go to London. She promised her brothers, Christopher and Clive, that they would never be separated, she will not leave them behind. She sets Lance down on his feet. She will never abandon any of her boys. She will not let them down.

"Let's go and see Merle," she says brightly.

Lance, sensing the possibility of a treat, a piece of his Grandma's home-baked Black Cake perhaps, jumps up and down. "Yes," he cries. "When?"

"Now," says Anita.

*

1964

A year later the snow has finally gone. Anita sent a postcard to Roy, care of Ronnie Scott's, unsigned, with a simple message written on the back.

'Good luck. No hard feelings.'

Since then she's found a new place. On Raby Street. Just around the corner from Merle. Lance has started school at Greenheys. Where she and the boys had gone. Clive is still there – in the Upper School. He's fourteen next birthday. Christopher has left. He's coming up to nineteen. He's training to be a welder at Turner's Sheet Metal Works on Alexandra Road. It's less than a half mile walk from Merle's on Upper Lloyd Street, where he still nominally lives. He has to pass right by Anita's, so he sometimes pops in for a mug of tea.

That's how she gets to hear that he sometimes stays out all night with his mates. He's on a slippery slope, she can tell. He's always been a handful, like the time a few years back when he climbed up into the Bell Tower above Greenheys School and started shouting at all the people passing by below....

*

1959

Insults, mostly. Rude words. He had no idea why he was so angry. He just was. He was thirteen years old. Alone against the world. At least, that's what it felt like sometimes. At first he thought it would be a laugh. He'd only done it for a dare. He'd be like Jimmy Cagney in the film *White Heat*.

"Look at me, Ma! I'm King of the World!"

That's how it had felt at first.

Then, when he tried to climb down, he found that he couldn't. He lost his nerve. Clive tried to talk him down – bless him – but in the end he had to go and get help. He ran to the Library further up the road and got there just as a lady was locking it up for the night. Clive was so frightened he spoke too fast, and she couldn't make out what he was saying.

"Slow down," she said. "Take a deep breath. What's your name?"

"Clive," he panted.

"Good. Now Clive, tell me what's the matter."

Her voice was kind but firm, exactly what Clive needed.

"My brother… Christopher…The Bell Tower… Can't get down"

Grasping the seriousness of the situation at once, she hopped onto her bicycle and rode straight there.

"Call the Fire Brigade," she instructed over her shoulder as she cycled away. "Ask them to come as quickly as they can."

Feeling terribly important, Clive rushed to the phone box on Great Western Street – the same one that would be used by Anita at the height of the Big Freeze in 1963 – and dialed 999. By the time he had run back to Greenheys, it was already there. While the firemen were putting their ladders in place, the Librarian kept talking to Christopher, trying to keep him as calm as she could.

"Try not to look down," she said. "Look out instead. Tell me what you can see."

Christopher picks out the few buildings he can recognize that are visible to him.

"The chimney at Hyde Brewery, Miss… The Tootal Tie Factory… The Refuge Building… The Tower at Strangeway's Prison…"

"Can you really see all that way?" the Librarian asks.

"No, Miss. Not really. But I know it's there."

I'm sure you do, she thinks, but not from the inside, I hope.

As if reading her mind, he says, suddenly sounding very young and frightened, "They'll not send me there today, Miss, will they? When they get me down?"

"I don't see any police cars, do you, Christopher? These kind firemen are only interested in getting you down safely. Isn't that right, Officer?"

"Yes, Miss," said the one nearest to her, raising his forefinger up to tap his helmet. "But I understand," he continued *sotto voce*, "that he's been throwing stones at people passing by and calling them names." By this time quite a crowd had gathered on the pavement below. Those within earshot of the fireman confirmed that this was indeed what had happened.

"If he were my lad," said one of them, "I'd give him a good hiding the moment they get him down."

"But he's not yours, is he?" said another voice loudly, so that all could hear. It was Merle, fetched by Clive.

"Are you his mother?" asked the Librarian.

Merle nodded grimly.

"Do you mind if I keep talking to him while they try to reach him?"

"Be my guest. Just try not to frighten him any more than he already is."

"Thank you. I shan't be cross with him. I promise." She stepped away from Merle, who held Clive closely to her, and began to call back up to Christopher.

"My name's Miss Cotton," she said. "But you can call me Nancy. Can you still hear me, Christopher?"

"Yes, Miss."

"I beg your pardon?"

"Yes, Miss Nancy."

"That's better. Are you still looking out instead of down?"

"Yes, Miss Nancy."

"Good." She speaks slowly, enunciating each word with careful deliberation, so that he can hear what she is saying.

"Now try to stay exactly where you are, Christopher. The firemen will be with you shortly. They're just securing the ladders now. Don't be frightened."

"I'm not, Miss. I'm not afraid of owt. Anyone who says different is a liar, Miss."

"Now, Christopher, that will do. Nobody's saying anything of the sort."

"Sorry, Miss. Nancy. I didn't mean nothing."

"I know you didn't, Christopher. I almost wish I was up there with you, looking out over all the city. You may find this hard to believe, but once, when I was not that much older than you, twenty-one in fact, I flew in a hot air balloon."

"You never!"

"I did. It was a Sunday morning. I flew from one side of Manchester right across to the other."

"Wow. That must've been amazing."

"It was."

"Weren't you scared, Miss?"

"Not at all. I was exhilarated. Do you know what that means, Christopher?"

"I think so, Miss. Is it the same as 'excited'?"

"That's right, yes."

"Why? What were you doing up there?"

"Have you heard of the Suffragettes, Christopher?"

"Votes for Women an' that?"

"Exactly. I was flying across the city showering people with leaflets, encouraging them to support us."

"And they did, didn't they?"

"Some of them."

"You won the Vote, though?"

"Yes. We did. But not right away. It took quite a few more years."

"I don't think I could wait that long."

"Sometimes you have to."

"I might be dead before then."

Nancy looks sharply across to Merle, who covers her face. Why is this boy so unhappy, she asks herself? When it's clear he's loved and cared for?

"He's going to be fine," she whispers to Merle. "Look – the first of the firemen has reached him now."

Things happen quickly thereafter.

The fireman grabs hold of Christopher and lifts him safely out of the Bell Tower, passing him down to two of his colleagues, who, between them, carry him down. The crowd on the pavement all applaud, then gradually begin to disperse.

Christopher is reunited with Merle. Sheepishly he ruffles his younger brother's hair. "Well done, our kid," he says, then turns to Merle. "I'm sorry," he says. "Can we go home now?"

"I think you've a few other things to say first." She indicates the firemen.

"Sorry," he says.

"No need for that, son. We're just glad we got you down safe and sound."

"Thank you."

"It's not me you should be thanking." He gestures towards Nancy.

"Thank you, Miss. Nancy."

"You're welcome, Christopher. I enjoyed our conversation. Perhaps you'd like to have another one some time?"

He looks back towards Merle, who nods.

"I work at the Library," says Nancy. "Here – take this card. It has my name on it – there, see? Nancy Cotton, Moss Side Library – and the times we're open. Why don't you pay me a visit on your way home from school one day?"

Christopher beams. Merle mouths a silent 'thank you'.

"Yes, Miss. I will. I'd like to hear more about that flight of yours in th' hot air balloon."

"And so you shall. Now – I think it's time you went home, don't you? I expect you're hungry."

"Starving," he says, looking hopefully at Merle, who smiles and shakes her head.

"Some things never change," she says.

*

1964

And nor does Christopher, thinks Anita, watching him drink his tea, listening to him regaling her with tales she'd rather not be hearing about what he gets up to with his work mates. She tries to picture him in the sheet metal workshop at Turner's, the welder's helmet on his head, concealing who he is, bathed in the eerie glow of the blow torch, surrounded by the jets of sparks that arc in a halo of fire above him.

He did go back to see Nancy. Several times. She was almost the making of him. But after a year she retired and moved out to New Mills on the edge of the High Peak. It was less than twenty miles away, but it might have been the moon. She invited him to visit her there, but he never went. Merle heard later that she'd died.

But Anita has her own life to worry about these days.

Now that Lance is at school, she can think about getting a job – at least for the hours while he's there. But it's easier said than done. She would like to do what Delphine advised and finish her Advanced Pitman's now, but a job that pays is the first imperative. Although there are plenty of vacancies for typists, they are generally looking for younger, unmarried girls. She's only twenty-four, but already she feels old, as if life is passing her by. Merle could get her a position with her at the Barracut Clothing Mill, but they're only seeking full-time workers, and so, as an interim, to get herself back on her feet, she takes several different jobs. Five mornings a week she cleans at the school before the children and teachers arrive, taking Lance with her. Then she does a couple of hours at Atlas Dry Cleaner's on Oxford Road, packing up the items ready for the afternoon pick-up. From there she cuts through Santiago Street to *The Claremont Chippy*, where she does the lunch time shift till two o'clock, after which she has just got time to pick up what she needs for their tea before collecting Lance from school. After tea, she helps get Lance ready for bed before Clive comes round to keep an eye on him, while she heads off on his bike the one and a half miles to *The Trocadero*, a cinema at the junction of Wilmslow Road and Moor Street, opposite Rusholme Grove, where she works as an usherette for the first house each evening. Then on Saturdays she has managed to get back her old job in Littlewood's Food Basement, where she works all day, while Merle looks after Lance. On Sundays she spends the day washing and cleaning before collapsing, exhausted, into bed, ready for the whole whirligig to start up again on the following Monday.

This is the pattern of her weeks. Although it's tough, she finds she doesn't begrudge it. It is the choice she has made, the price she has paid for leaving Roy, about which she has fewer and fewer regrets as each month passes. She pays her rent on time each week. She puts food on the table each day. Lance thrives at school. He learns to read. He makes friends. He doesn't seem to miss his Daddy at all.

By September she feels secure enough to ditch one of the evenings at *The Troc*, as the cinema is familiarly known, in order to return to night school. She goes back to St John's to complete her Advanced Pitman's. A year from now, she thinks, she might begin to raise her sights a little higher. But in the interim there is Christmas to be got through. She is determined that this year she will try to make it as special as she can for Lance and her brothers.

She sees an advertisement in the window of Khan's Newsagent's on Claremont Road, which catches her eye.

> *For One Week Only*
> *Kendal Milne Department Store*
> *Seeks Casual All Night Staff*
> *to put up this year's*
> *Christmas Decorations*
> *27th Nov – 1st Dec inc*
> *6pm – 6am*
> *10 shillings an hour*
> *Apply in Store*
> *First Come, First Served*

Anita is stopped in her tracks. The hourly pay rate is twice what she gets in any of her other jobs. She does some rapid calculations. For just a single week's work she will earn thirty pounds! Unheard-of riches! She'll have to take time out from *The Troc* – but she's owed a week's leave in any case – and she'll have to work something out for Lance. Clive can't be expected to sit for him right through the night. Perhaps Merle will take Lance for a week? Perhaps he could have her – Anita's – old room? She'd still be back in time to take him to school each morning. OK – she'll have practically no sleep for a week. So? She's still young, she'll cope. It's only a week after all. Less than that. Five days. Yes. She'll work it out somehow.

She hurries to Kendal's in between her shift at *The Claremont Chippy* and collecting Lance from school. She's in luck. She gets the last vacancy there is. She will start at the end of the month.

*

But within the first hour she quickly realises that she's not as young as she thought she was. Everyone else working there is younger than she is. Students, mostly, who regard the whole idea as a bit of a lark, a chance to earn a few extra quid for partying, rather than the make-or-break difference it will mean to Anita.

She finds she has little, if anything, in common with any of them, and she a student herself not so many years ago, in the time before Roy, who, though she's not seen him in almost two years, still acts as a waymark in her life, a series of forks in the road. There was pre-Roy and post-Roy, and now there is no Roy, whereas all of the students working by her side to roll out the scenes of cotton wool snow and plastic reindeer appear to be paired off in a constantly changing merry-go-round, with everything still before them. Dave is with Jackie but then he's with Julie, and Jackie's with Brian, who used to be with Julie.

Then, on the second night, she meets someone the same age as she is, in similar circumstances, with similar dreams, haunted by similar doubts. Her name is Nadia, and they are drawn towards each other like moths circling the same flame.

Nadia, too, she learns, is looking after a child by herself, a daughter. But whereas Lance is nearly five, Jenna is only just one. And though she is bringing her up alone, this is not, unlike Anita, through choice. Her husband, Sol, she discovers, is in prison, not for anything violent, but for his part in a betting scam at a greyhound track. He's been sent down for a minimum of four years. Nadia confesses this on their third night of constructing their Winter Wonderland, while they lingered over a coffee and cigarette during one of their allotted fifteen minute breaks, which they take outside, leaning against the fire escape, shivering in the night's hard frost. She's tired and tearful and has let down her guard. Anita has it easy compared to Nadia. She finds herself singing again the old song from her time at *The Queen's*, the one that Cam had taught her.

"Now a man is born to go a-lovin'
A woman's born to weep and fret
To stay at home and tend her oven
And drown her past regrets
With just black coffee and cigarettes..."

"I don't accept that," says Nadia, after Anita has finished.

"No," says Anita. "Neither do I."

"Come on," says Nadia. "We'd best get back, or Miss Gresty will have our guts for garters."

They laugh and head back inside the store.

Miss Gresty. The Shop Window Designer, who they are all rather afraid of, who is always dressed from head to toe in black, with black bobbed hair, black lipstick, theatrically held cigarette holder with a black *Sobranie* permanently attached, black tights and black ballet pumps, who has cultivated a Russian accent – though rumour has it she's from Bury – and calls everyone "Darling."

For the most part, though, they simply work, packing bolts of brightly coloured material into wicker hampers to be transported up and down the elevators to whichever floor they are needed, unrolling yards and yards of cotton wool snow to be spread across every available surface, or carrying various mannequins up and down the stairs waiting to be dressed as angels, Santas, elves or snowmen, or tableaux of happy, smiling families.

All through each night piped music plays the latest hits from the Top Twenty. To Anita and Nadia, in their current hyper-sensitive state, when every sound makes their head spin and their body feel like broken glass, each song seems to carry a message just for her, freighted with meaning.

"When you're alone and life is making you lonely
You can always go

Downtown..."

*"I walk along the city streets
You used to walk along with me
And every step I take reminds me
Of just how we used to be
How can I forget you
When there is always something there to remind me...?"*

*"The dogs begin to bark, hounds begin to howl
The dogs begin to bark, hounds begin to howl
Watch out, strange cat people
Little Red Rooster's on the prowl..."*

*"All day and all of the night
All day and all of the night
All day and all of the night..."*

Over and over, on an endless loop, these tunes fill every floor of the store. Anita and Nadia find themselves singing along with them too, just like everyone else does, even though they are driving them both mad.

On the final night, with emotions running high and time running out, boxes are spilled, tinsel is torn and Christmas trees tumble, as tempers and temperaments fray. But it isn't Little Red Rooster who's on the prowl, it's Miss Gresty, who claps her hands to bring them all together for one last motivational speech.

"Darlings, tomorrow we open. In few hours time, when customers queue to see Christmas Grotto, we must be ready. No second chances, no wait till next day, so please – no more this bish-bash pell-mell helter-skelter."

Anita and Nadia have to bite the inside of her cheeks to stop themselves from giggling, but Miss Gresty is unstoppable.

"Take deep breath. Relax. Ten minute break, then start again. But first..." She flings open one of the emergency exits behind her and waves an arm theatrically. "Follow me."

They all troop behind her, up a back staircase, which leads all the way up to a narrow landing and another set of double doors.

"Up," she says, "up, up, and away. Watch out, strange cat people," and she gently pushes the two doors outwards, from where a final couple of steps lead everyone out on to the roof of the department store.

It's approaching half past three in the morning. A sharp frost has already formed on the rail that runs around the top of the flat roof. Overhead the stars in the Milky Way arch above them, hard and glittering. From the other side of Deansgate they can hear the bell of St Ann's Church toll the half hour. Everyone falls silent, their breath forming statues in the clear, crisp air. Someone sees a shooting star and points. Then nothing. They stand, singly or in small clusters, awestruck, not moving, holding their breath so as not to break the spell, the whole city stretched out before them, empty and sleeping in a sparkling moonlit monochrome. This is the true winter wonderland, not the pastiche they've been labouring to create in the store below them, and even Miss Gresty, for once, is lost for words.

Then, as if someone has lifted the tiniest corner of this blanket of silence that lies across the world, Anita thinks she detects the faintest of sounds, like when she would wake sometimes in the middle of the night just seconds before Lance had made even the slightest murmur, when he was a baby. Some of the others have heard it too, their heads turning in the direction of what now begins to resemble an infinitesimal squeaking. Like a fingernail gently scraping down a rusty kettle. This grows. The squeaking becomes many-voiced, high pitched, ultra-sonic, on the very edge of human hearing, like a hundred wine glasses singing when moistened fingers circle their rims, then a thousand, then a hundred thousand. The air begins to tremble, the whole sky alive with the sound, which has now become so loud that it seems to be right inside Anita's head, like a shaken tin of six-inch nails, as she, like everyone else, stands transfixed, straining to see where the noise can be coming from. Even had any one of them spoken, by now they could not have been heard. Instead Miss Gresty merely gestures, sweeping out an arm, her long black fingernail pointing down towards the street. As one, everyone looks, craning their necks, leaning over the rail.

There, below them, spanning the entire breadth of Deansgate, writhing, rolling, in wave after wave, boils an entire sea of rat. Thousands upon thousands of them, tumbling over each other, climbing, scrabbling, crawling, layer upon layer, several feet deep, so that had any of those watching been unfortunate enough to have been standing where now this seething mass of skin and fur, tail and snout bulges and surges, they would be wading waist deep.

Behind them, like giant locusts, two City Corporation lorries, with snow ploughs the width of the street, their huge headlamps raking the sky like search lights, herd the rats with mechanical efficiency the entire length of Deansgate. Anita hears someone say that the city's sewers, built more than a century before, in Queen Victoria's time, are starting to collapse, and that in order to begin the repairs, first they must move the rats to a different sewer in another part of the city.

It takes almost half an hour for the whole convulsive wildebeest of rat to pour beneath them, as they swarm towards Shudehill and the slimy granite flagstones of Angel Meadow beyond. The silence that they leave behind is like the one to be found on a battlefield, when the last few survivors crawl through an early morning mist, across the piles of stiff corpses, in the vain hope of finding a loved one still alive.

Anita hears in that hungry silence Lance's urgent cry, demanding to be fed. She is certain Nadia is experiencing the same primordial tug about her daughter. Jenna. Whose name means a bird in flight, Nadia has told her. She feels her hand upon her arm. They turn and head back down to finish their shift.

*

Just before 6am the work is finally finished. The Winter Wonderland of Santas and sleighs, Nativities and Noëls stands completed. Miss Gresty thanks everyone for their hard work and wishes them a "Merry Christmas, Darlings."

Anita is one of the last to leave. She says goodbye to Nadia just as the security staff are switching off the lights in the store and locking the doors behind her. The sky is inky black.

She crosses Deansgate. In a doorway opposite she thinks she sees a darker shape restlessly turning over. She sighs. This is a hard time to be homeless, a cold night to be sleeping rough. She approaches warily. She wants to reassure herself that the person is safe. But, just as she reaches the doorway, a hand thrusts out of the dark and grabs her by the wrist.

"Who's minding the store?" croaks a voice, like a rusty kettle.

Instinctively Anita turns back to look over her shoulder towards the now dark and silent Kendal Milne.

"Not there," says the voice. "Here." The figure jabs a bony finger into Anita's chest. Anita can just make out the figure's face, streaked with grime and dirt, plastered across with thickly matted hair, eyes like a crow's.

Anita perceives the shape of the figure, beneath the layers of coat and cardigan, to be that of a woman. The hand that jabbed her in the chest now reaches into one of her pockets. It pulls out a rat, its sharp pointed snout questing the air. Its slick fur quivers with curiosity. Not an atom of it is still, pulsing.

With her free hand, the one whose wrist is not still in the woman's vice-like grip, Anita fishes out a coin, which she's been saving for her bus fare back home, and holds it up before the woman's face. The woman puts the rat back inside her pocket and takes the coin from Anita. She slowly releases her fingers from Anita's wrist and struggles to her feet. In doing so, her coat slips briefly from her shoulder. She pulls it roughly back – but not before Anita has had chance to catch sight of a tattoo etched into her skin. It reminds her of an angel's wings. Their eyes fuse for a moment, then the woman lurches away in the direction of Shudehill. Anita thinks she hears her sing, a tuneless rattle in her chest, or it might just be a memory slipping down the years, a skrike of starlings taking off in their thousands from all the rooftops and ledges in the city, as they wake from their overnight roosting.

"As doubt settles in
And closes the door
It's only to hide what's happened inside –
Who's minding the store…?"

*

When she finally gets home, Anita collapses in her bed and sleeps for more than twelve hours straight. It's noon on Sunday by the time she drags herself awake. Her head pounds. Her body feels pummelled, as though she has been in a boxing ring. She is still weighed down by dreams of that teeming colony of rats being herded and corralled along Deansgate. Of the woman with the angel tattoo. There's a message in there somewhere that for the moment is still eluding her.

She heaves herself out of her bed to discover her stepsister Chantelle is bringing in a tray with a couple of rounds of toast and a mug of strong, sweet tea.

"What…? When…? Where…?"

"Don't you worry about a thing, sweet pea. Between us Merle and me have got everything covered. Lance is playing in the park with Clive. While you've been asleep, I've washed and cleaned. You've deserved your lie-in. I don't know how you've stuck it all week. I know what it's like when you do nights at the hospital. Your whole system gets completely messed up. But at least I get the chance to rest during the day, whereas you…"

"It'll be worth it. I know it will. I may not think so right this minute. But in a day or two, when I've caught up with myself."

"That's the spirit. Have some more tea."

Chantelle pours. Anita smiles.

"Thanks," she says. "You look done in yourself. Hard week?"

"You could say that," says Chantelle. "The usual rise in cases of winter flu. Only this year appears to be especially bad. A new strain apparently. A particularly virulent form of the virus. From Asia. The Ward's practically overrun. Harry says we should immunise everyone over sixty routinely. That way we could free up the hospitals for other things."

"But isn't that what the hospitals are for?" says Anita. "To look after the sick?"

"Of course. But Harry says it would be better to prevent them getting sick in the first place."

Anita nods.

And then it comes to her. The meaning of her dream. In spite of what it looked like, maybe the rats were not being corralled at all. Maybe they were not prisoners in chains. But an army on the march. A whole people on the move. Their weapons were not guns, but songs. Seeking new lands where they could begin to make their mark, somewhere they could begin to tell a different set of stories. Where, if they were sick, they would be routinely made better. She sees a long queue of people, stretching as far as she can see, like those rats on

Deansgate, all waiting to be vaccinated, developing a herd immunity.

And it seems to her that she has, for several years now, been living a lie, trying to be what others have wanted her to be, rather than simply being herself. She recalls the final words of Delphine's letter: 'to thine own self be true.' It's as though she is only now beginning to wake up. As if she has been asleep under the influence of one of Chantelle's husband Harry's new forms of anaesthetic, not really feeling anything at all, except a distant kind of numbness, a desensitised torpor, moving through the days like an automaton, not minding the store, not really, just remotely.

She rubs her eyes, yawns and stretches. She walks to the window and tries to look out. But the light hurts her eyes, which she narrows to slits. She forces herself to peel back their lids and open them wide. A low winter sun is slicing the sky. A hard frost glitters on the railings of the park across the street.

I need to get outside, she thinks, to feel the cold, sharp air in my lungs. I need to wake up.

"Thanks, Sis," she says to Chantelle. "I think I should go check on the boys."

"Are you sure?"

"Yeah, I'm sure."

Chantelle nods. "I'll get back to Merle then," she says. "We might join you later."

After she's gone, Anita throws on some clothes and hurries outside. It feels like she's stepping out from under the shadow of a prolonged period of quarantine, of solitary confinement, shaking off the shackles of self-isolation.

When she reaches the park, Lance is sitting on Clive's shoulders, roaring with pleasure. Christopher is there too. His cheeks are red and glowing. He asks them all to gather sticks and twigs, and bring them to him. He will build a fire, he says, and a few minutes later they are all standing together, warming their hands in front of the crackling flames, Anita and her boys.

Beneath their feet, protected from the frost, warm in the winter soil below the surface of the ground, hibernating pupae of the black peppered moth feel the heat from the fire reach down to them. Inside their hard, leathery outer casings, the nascent imagines begin to stir.

*

2020

To celebrate the gradual relaxation of the lockdown and the introduction of the rule of six, Lorrie decides to open up the Courtyard at the back of Islington Mill for a Midsummer Party for all the artists, staff and tenants of the studios to attend in relays of five at a time.

First she decorates the space. She hangs lanterns from nails affixed to the brick walls enclosing it. Next she demarcates separate areas for each person who might attend, creating five circles, each two metres in diameter, sketched out on the ground with night lights in individual terracotta pots. Finally she marks two discreet walkways through the Reception area and out towards the Courtyard, one for arriving, the other for leaving, both strung with ribbons of fairy lights, green for the way-in, amber for the way-out.

There will be no refreshments on offer, she tells people, but they are welcome to bring their own, so long as they keep these with them within their own dedicated space at all times, and then take them back home again afterwards to deposit with the rest of their own household recycling. She installs hand-sanitisers at frequent intervals, and, if any of the guests need to avail themselves of the toilet facilities, they are asked to clean up after themselves, wiping down all surfaces. Disposable gloves, cleaning materials and clearly visible instructions are all provided.

She hopes there is nothing she has overlooked. Lorrie hates the thought of segregation, but she has always liked the idea of rules and regulations. They simplify. They clarify. So long as they are for the mutual benefit of all. Which she believes these she has put in place for this first tentative step back towards people being able to gather together once more at the Mill have delivered.

She stands back to inspect her handiwork and smiles. Yes, she thinks. This should do nicely.

Because they are all artists, each has been asked to bring something small they have created during lockdown to act as a focal point for the party, a kind of mini-exhibition collaboratively curated, with each *objet d'art* to be placed on a table Lorrie has positioned specifically for the purpose at a point they must all of them pass on their arrival in the Courtyard. This, too, she has framed with candles and a mirror, taken from the Bar and leant against the brick wall, to reflect back each exhibit.

She has put together a playlist on her phone comprising pieces of music requested beforehand by everyone planning to attend, and so it is suitably eclectic, appropriately unpredictable and surprising, from garage and grime, to Tibetan bells and Buddhist chants, from hip-hop and rap to drag queen divas, from Northern Soul and Cool Britannia to Phil Spector's Wall of Sound – The Crystals and The Ronettes, (Lorrie's personal choice). She checks the bluetooth connection to different speakers strategically placed around the Courtyard until she is satisfied with the balance and volume. Now she has just one final task to complete.

She collects the wire rope from the Basement Studio on which she has been practising while the Mill has been all but closed. She attaches it to two iron hooks placed at diagonally opposite ends of the yard, which allows it to be suspended a couple of feet above head height. She tests its purchase for the desired balance between tautness and elasticity. Yes, she decides, it is perfect. She will walk along it once for each set of five who attend. That will be her own personal artistic contribution to the evening. Then, at the end of the evening, she will do something special, she will add something extra.

Fire.

The evening is a great success. Everyone follows Lorrie's rules to the letter, but there is no sense of awkwardness or constraint about this. Instead people feel relieved, reassured, that their safety has been so carefully considered and that they have not had to think of it for themselves. There is banter and bonhomie, there is pride and pleasure that, in the midst of the pandemic, they can come together like this, to celebrate the healing, transformative power of art. People bring paintings on pebbles, sculptures crafted from found objects, things that are playful, things that are poignant, pieces of glass, arrangements of feathers, mosaics from broken shards of pottery, poems, songs, each other. They wear home-made face masks, which they surreptitiously remove to drink the bottles of beer they have brought and then replace immediately afterwards. They smile, they wave, they dance, separately, but together.

At the very end of the evening, just before the final set of five gets ready to depart, Lorrie performs her *pièce de résistance*. Having walked across the tightrope above their heads to whoops of incredulous applause – "Bravo!" they have cried. "Encore! We'd no idea you could do this," a reaction she has hoped for – she has prepared a special additional treat. She will not only walk across the wire a second time, she will do so while at the same time performing poi, and not just traditional poi, but fire poi.

Poi.

Poi involves the swinging of tethered weights held in each hand through a variety of rhythmical, geometric patterns around the body and above the head. Lorrie taught herself to begin with by placing a tennis ball into a sock tied to a length of string, which she looped round the fingers of each hand. Once she had mastered the technique of continuously rotating each wrist so that she could keep the tennis balls in an even perpetual motion, she swiftly progressed to fire poi. This requires her to replace the weighted socks with wicks doused in Kevlar, a flame resistant material, which she soaks in fuel, then lights, so that once she starts to spin them, they leave behind a tracery of fire, surrounding her in an orbit of flame.

She waits until it is completely dark. She encourages the people standing on the ground below her to point their phones as torches up towards the night sky. The beams are filled with a million motes of dust, which twist and turn like tiny dancers. The occasional moth is drawn towards the light. Unseen, Lorrie begins to ululate. The eerie cry is picked up and amplified by the other women present, Molly included. Their cries bend the flames of the night lights in the linked lanterns. Slowly all the phone beams pan towards Lorrie, where they meet and conjoin. The million dancers tumble from the dust motes, reassembling like crystals in a kaleidoscope, to form the single, shifting figure that is Lorrie.

She is performing poi.

Her wrists delicately revolve, almost as if she is spinning an invisible, three-dimensional web around her, as though an entourage of fire-flies accompanies her in a glittering figure of eight, wrapping her head, arms and body in filaments of silver, when she steps out onto the wire, taut and quivering, and starts to dance, laughing and leaping, in and out the lacy loops of light. The people gather beneath her, drawn like an uprising of moths to her flame, reckless, transgressive, edging as close as they dare. But she dances on oblivious, completely lost to the moment, surrendering herself to the rhythm. Her body arches, a scorpion caught in a circle of fire, on and on till the last embers have burned themselves out, where they hang like a necklace of stars, till they too flicker and fade, leaving a jewelled palimpsest, sparkling on the ground beneath everyone's feet, picked out by the light from each phone, a balancing act, footprints, guiding each of them home, and Lorrie towards the far edge of the wire, a wire she imagines stretching out beyond her, beckoning, limitless.

*

facebook.com/molly.wahid/photos

Molly's Photos
(Lorelei Zlatan performs poi while walking the tightrope, 20th June)

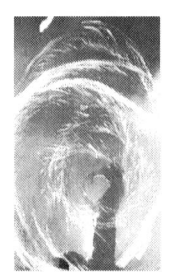

*

The following day, a Sunday, is the Summer Solstice. The longest day of the year. Michael borrows Nadia's sister Farida's car to drive himself, Molly and Blessing to Elton to visit Tom, Apichu and their baby daughter for the afternoon. He has not been back since the day he collected the loom, but they have stayed in occasional contact. Molly and Apichu have shared photos of their daughters on WhatsApp. Apichu has named her baby Samancha. Quechua for 'Blessing', having been taken by the name of Molly's child. "Quechua is the language I spoke growing up," she texted.

Today Molly is bringing a gift. It is the first item she has completed using the loom. It is a small, seemingly abstract design of blue thread meandering between irregularly shaped patches of greens and browns and greys. Some of the lines picked out in blue disappear from time to time, under a sleeve of dark grey. She has followed no pattern to achieve this effect, leaving what has randomly emerged in the fibre apparently to happenstance or chance, with the prospect of any of it ever being repeatable distantly remote. But this is not the case. The algorithm she has used to produce the sample is deliberately complex and has been carefully worked out. Over time, and with a sufficiently long enough piece of cloth – covering several hundred feet or more – the observant eye would be able to detect a pattern, albeit an unpredictable one.

She is wearing the white *qurqash*. Molly now knows that it was actually woven on the loom that had lain unused for two centuries in a corner of the derelict cottage Apichu has been renovating with her husband Tom, and she wants to show it to her, along with this new sample piece she has woven on it herself, after she and Michael had so painstakingly reassembled and restored it.

The day is clear and bright, sunny and warm, a marked contrast with the day when Michael had driven there to fetch the loom. Then it had been lashing with rain, and he had almost drowned in an ocean of mud. Today the clouds are high and white, like cotton wool, and the midsummer sun is shining down unimpeded. It is a child's drawing of a day, the picture completed when they arrive in Elton, by the sight of washing blowing on the line stretched between the caravan and the hawthorn tree, which is decked with the last of its pink blossom, while the cottage, although it is yet to have windows and a door, now has a new roof.

Tom proudly shows them round. They marvel at the progress he has made, while Apichu, carrying Samancha in a Peruvian sling on her back, is enchanted by Molly's woven cloth, which she lays out on the dry grass to inspect more closely.

"Did you really make this up as you went along?" she asks.

"To begin with," says Molly, "but I always had an idea in mind."

"Which was…?"

Molly shakes her head and playfully taps the side of her nose with her finger. "Tell me what you see in it first."

"The land," says Apichu. "The sky. Green fields. Rivers."

"And the patches of grey?"

"Buildings, people?"

Molly smiles. "You see it all so instinctively. I wish everyone saw my work that way."

"Now it's your turn," says Apichu. "Tell me what I'm missing."

"Nothing. That's exactly what I was trying for. Except perhaps…"

"Yes?"

"Do you see where the blue threads disappear beneath the heavy squares of grey?"

"Yes."

"I was thinking of the way the city has tried to force the rivers underground, to bury them, so that we don't see just how filthy and polluted they've become, so that we might forget about them."

"But they keep reappearing, don't they? Here… and here… and here. Water will always find a way."

"Yes. It will."

"Just like we will."

"I hope so."

Blessing has never been on moorland before. She has never seen so much empty space, so much open land, so much sky. She totters about as fast as her tiny legs can carry her, trying to run in every direction at once, so that she keeps tumbling over her feet in her hurry. But she never cries. She simply gets back up on her feet and tries again, only to fall over once more, prompting a giggling six-month-old Samancha to chortle with delight, so that Apichu is forced to unwrap her from the sling and let her try to crawl after Blessing as quickly as she can, as she tries to keep up. This maze of whirling, rolling, spinning, falling, tumbling, running and jumping is added to further by Tom and Apichu's dog, Ralph, another recent addition to the household, who tries to join with the two girls by chasing his own tail and barking with pleasure.

Tom fetches a kite he has made from inside the caravan, and soon they are all of them chasing it along the top of Cockey Moor, watching it climb high into the sky to dance with the cotton wool clouds, caught in their collective bubble, their own rule of six.

Afterwards, Apichu treats them to a picnic of *encanelado*, a Peruvian cinnamon cake made with eggs, sugar, flour, condensed milk, vanilla essence, baking powder, pisco – a South American brandy distilled with fermented grape juice – and three cinnamon sticks. Blessing insists on having a piece too, which she then proceeds to give most of to Ralph. She is enchanted by the caravan. "A house on wheels," she declares, smearing what's left of her *encanelado* across her face.

When it is time for them to leave, just as the sun is beginning to dip behind Winter Hill, at fifteen hundred feet the highest point along the West Pennine Moors, Tom takes Michael round to the back of the house.

"Look," he says, and points.

An eighth wooden cross has been added to the other seven graves that lie there.

"My mother," he says.

"Oh," says Michael, placing his hand on Tom's shoulder, "I'm very sorry for your loss."

"Covid," says Tom simply. "The worst thing was we weren't allowed to see her. We didn't even get to say goodbye."

Michael sighs.

"Her body's not here – obviously," says Tom. "But her ashes are. I always wanted her to see this spot."

He looks back towards the house.

"I'm hoping we'll be in by Christmas."

Michael's eyebrows shoot up in surprise.

"It won't be finished by then. But it'll be weather-proof, water-tight. I can keep working on the inside over the winter."

"When do you think you'll have completed it all?"

Tom grins. "Never, I don't suppose. You don't, do you? That's the thing with a home. There's always something."

Back by the caravan, Blessing is starting to grizzle.

"We'd best get a move on," says Molly. "She's getting cranky and cross."

"She's tired, that's all," says Michael. "She'll fall asleep as soon as she's in the car and I switch the engine on."

"Come again," says Apichu.

"We will," says Molly.

"Before there's another lockdown," warns Tom.

Apichu throws him a look.

"I'm just saying," he says.

She turns back to Molly, who is busy strapping Blessing into her car seat.

"Thanks for the sampler," she says.

"Thanks for the loom."

"What will you make next?"

"I don't know. I never do. But then somehow an idea arrives."

"Like a river emerging from underground."

Molly smiles.

"Something like that – yes…"

Tom and Apichu, with Samancha once more back in her sling, wave goodbye to Molly, Michael and Blessing, as they make their way along the dirt track down towards Elton Brook and the M66 motorway that glitters below them like a silver thread, arrowing towards Manchester as if hurtled from a shuttle across the warp and weft of the plain, spread out before them like a banquet, out of which the shimmering city rises like a mirage, its towers of glass and steel lining streets paved with promises they have yet to keep. They blaze like beacons dipped in gold by the last of the sun's rays, winking as the light bounces from them. On, off. On, off. Like a binary code.

They watch them till they become nothing but a speck on the land, while Molly looks back up the hill towards the spot where she imagines them still to be and pictures them there. Blessing is already asleep, just as Michael predicted she would be. He drives on, staring into the darkness as it gathers around them. Even if they can no longer see, or be seen, and their destination remains hidden from them, they know that it's out there, waiting for them. They continue to make their hidden way towards it, until they can emerge back into the light once more.

6

AMRIT SANSKAR

2013 – 2007 – 2013 – 2007 – 2013 – 2007 – 2013 – 2009
2007 – 2005 – 1955 – 2005 – 1966 – 2005 – 2013 – 2007
1976 – 2007 – 2011 – 2007 – 2013 – 2007 – 2013 – 2011
2010 – 2011 – 2012 – 1993 – 1992 – 2013 – 1999 – 2013
2012 – 1995 – 2012 – 2005 – 1947 – 2005 – 2013 – 2020
2013

2013

It's the day of Khav's final year presentation. It's already been postponed twice. The first time was when her grandmother, Urja, suffered a stroke and died. The second was when she had an argument with her father that was so fierce she was in no fit state to deliver it. Only Clive from outside Khav's family knew the full extent of what had happened, and it was he who had advised her to postpone it a second time.

"You'll not do yourself justice," he had said.

"But today's the last day I can take it," she had replied.

"Don't worry about that," Clive reassured her. "I'll sort out the necessary paperwork and permissions."

And he has. Clive has been true to his word. He has managed to persuade the Verifications & Assessment Board to make an exception in Khav's case, on combined compassionate and medical grounds, and grant her an extension of a further one week. As a result Khav is giving her presentation on the last Saturday morning in April. The campus is unusually quiet. Even for a Saturday. Most students are not back after the Easter break, and so there is something of a 'behind-closed-doors', 'cloak-and-dagger' atmosphere about the arrangement. The presentation has been scheduled for midday. At half-past eight Clive waits at the entrance to the Grosvenor Building to hand over the keys of the TV Studio to her. They arrive at the same time. Clive sighs with relief. He has really gone out on a limb for her, and he's been dreading another last-minute text saying she wouldn't be coming after all. But here she is, weighed down by what looks like a ton of props and equipment, much of which she carries in several bags on her back, while pulling along a suitcase on wheels in one hand and struggling with a canvas hold-all in the other.

He smiles. She grins sheepishly back.

"It looks like you've brought everything but the kitchen sink," he says.

"That's in here," she laughs, indicating the hold-all.

Clive unlocks the studio and turns on the lights.

"Right," he says. "You've got three and a half hours to get yourself set up and ready. Do you think that'll be enough for you?"

"Fingers crossed."

"Well, it'll have to be," says Clive. "I've got to hand in my assessment to the board, together with the video of your presentation, by half-past four this afternoon."

"Thanks, Clive," says Khav, suddenly serious. "I know you must have had to pull God-knows-how-many strings to make this happen, and I want you to know just how much I appreciate it."

"You don't know the half of it," says Clive. "But like I told them, if we're not here to enable our students to produce the best work they can, what's the point of us?"

"I'm really grateful."

"Just don't let me down, that's all."

"I'll try not to."

"I'm sure you won't. I'm looking forward to it. Tanya'll be along in about an hour if you need any technical help."

"Great."

"And I'll be back at eleven. Just make sure you're ready."

"What is it we say?" she grins. "I've been ready all my life, innit?"

*

2007

Six years earlier. Another Saturday morning.

Khavita is fifteen. Or Khav, as she prefers to be known. Though not by her father, who thinks Khav sounds more like a boy's name.

"What has happened to my little princess?" he moans to his wife the evening before in an aggrieved tone. "What have we done to deserve this cuckoo in our nest?"

Geetha, his wife, raises her eyes skywards and carries on preparing supper. Khavita has just stormed off upstairs to her room because her father has found out about her passion for break dancing and has forbidden her to continue with it.

"It's not natural," he now says to Geetha. "How is she going to attract a husband?"

"She's still a child. Let her have some fun."

"You spoil her, that's your trouble."

"It's just a phase. She'll grow out of it."

"It's not lady-like, all that wearing of boys' clothes and rolling about on the floor."

"I've taught her to make full Sunday dinner," says Geetha, "full vegetarian. Isn't that lady-like enough for you?"

"I blame the school. They are too lenient with her. They encourage her in all this nonsense."

"She comes top in all her subjects, Vikram – English, Maths, Science. What more do you want from her?"

"That's what I'm saying. What husband wants a clever wife?"

Geetha throws the wooden spoon she has been using to mix the chickpea flour for the *roti* directly at her husband in exasperation, hitting him squarely on the forehead with it.

"When last I checked, the teachings of Guru Nanak still had not changed. Women have the same souls as men. We have equal rights and equal chances. We can take part in the recitation of scripture, we can perform the singing of hymns, we can read from the Holy Book."

"But I don't remember it saying anything about girls dancing in the streets. It was bad enough when she insisted on learning bhangra, but at least that takes place at weddings, or festivals, where we can keep an eye on her. But now she wants to parade herself in public, heaping shame upon all of us."

"You're the one bringing shame upon us with all of this foolish carrying on."

"Why should she want to dress the way she does? She used to be such a pretty, sweet-tempered child."

"Nonsense. She's always had a mind of her own. You should be proud of her. You'll only drive her away."

"My sweet princess…"

Upstairs in her room Khav shuts her ears to the sound of her parents quarrelling about her. At least her mother has taken her side for once. But she knows that when it's just the two of them alone together afterwards, she'll only say, "Khavita, Khavita, why do you have to wind your father up so? You know what he's like. Why can't you be more like your sister Priya? She smiles sweetly whenever your father speaks to her. 'Yes, *Bapu*,' she says, 'of course, *Bapu*, whatever you say, *Bapu*,' then goes out and does exactly what she wants to anyway."

It's true. That's exactly what Priya would tell her too if she were here. But she's out. She's four years older than Khav and goes out with her boyfriend every Friday night, even though she's not supposed to, even though their father would kill her if he found out, but Priya never does get found out. She holds her tongue. She lowers her eyes. She's his true princess, not her. Not that Khav wants to be her Daddy's princess. She doesn't want to be anyone's princess. She knows that that's what her surname's supposed to mean – Kaur, in common with most Sikh girls – but it also means 'lioness'. That's much more to her liking.

She creeps towards her bedroom door, opens it the tiniest crack, then listens. Her parents have stopped quarrelling. She can hear the more familiar sounds in the silence that hangs between them – her mother chopping garlic and onions, her father impatiently rustling his newspaper. All is back to normal once more. She tiptoes back to her bed, opens the drawer in the table next to it, and pulls out a pair of scissors.

She separates her hair into two bunches, the hair that has never once been cut, not even trimmed, since she was born, which now grows down past her waist. Then she holds one of the bunches firmly in her left hand at a level with the tip of her ear lobe, and decisively cuts. When she has finished the first bunch, she systematically sets about performing the same set of actions with the second.

Her head immediately feels so much lighter and freer, almost as if she is floating. She scoops the shorn tresses from the floor surrounding her and stuffs them into a bin liner. Then she lies back upon her bed and closes her eyes, a broad smile upon her lips.

"A lioness," she whispers, before falling instantly asleep.

*

2013

Back in the TV Studio of MMU's Media Department, Khav begins to unpack the first of her cases filled with the props she needs for her presentation. The first thing she pulls out is a pair of scissors.

*

2007

The morning after she has cut her hair, before her father is awake, she steals downstairs and out of the house. Only her mother, who hears everything, detects her. She goes to the bedroom window and peels back the curtain the narrowest of cracks, so as not to risk waking her husband. She is just in time to see Khavita in her break-dancing clothes, her hair covered by a scarf under one of those back-to-front baseball caps, running down the street in that characteristic ungainly way she has. She looks to Geetha like a pirate. She smiles and closes the curtain, thinks about returning to bed, but changes her mind. Instead she slips on her dressing gown and pads downstairs. There, prominently placed on the centre of the kitchen table, is a note from her errant daughter.

"Meeting Abila in town. I'm helping her choose something for her sister's wedding coming up, and she's helping me do the same for Priya. I'll be back in time for tea. Love you, Kxxx."

Geetha half-wonders about calling Abila's mum to check. Khavita and Abila are best friends at school, so it's quite plausible the note is true, and that she has simply left early to avoid incurring her father's wrath once more. She decides to let it pass. Let's all have a quiet Saturday, she thinks.

By the time her mother has made this decision, Khav is boarding the 147 bus just round the corner on Cawdor Road, which will take her to Piccadilly Station.

She has no intention of meeting Abila, but Abila has agreed to cover for her. She knows that Khav will do the same for her one day.

*

2013

The second item Khav takes out of her case is a large glass jar, sealed with an air-tight stopper. Inside is one of the lengths of hair she cut herself when she was fifteen, now braided and preserved.

*

2007

Khav arrives on the concourse of Piccadilly Station just after half-past eight. Light streams through the glass atrium in diagonal bars. Among the shoppers and commuters Khav begins to pick out fellow breakers. She doesn't know their names, but she recognises some of them by sight and others by their clothes – the *de rigeur* hooded top, baggy trousers, trainers and baseball cap worn backwards. She is wearing the same. She fits right in. They none of them speak to one another, just the briefest of nods, the folding of arms across the chest, the flick of the fingers.

They're all of them waiting for Teniel. Without him they know they can't begin. He's the unelected, but nevertheless undisputed leader of them. He's also the best of them. Until someone new comes along to knock him off his perch. Khav would like it to be her, but she knows she's nowhere near ready enough to do that. They each of them know instinctively their rank within the pecking order and size up those who are nearest to them, both above and below, as their most immediate threats.

Just before nine Teniel casually saunters up the Station Approach, boom-box on shoulder, acknowledging no one. His mere presence carves a path before him between the shoppers and commuters. The bush telegraph signals his arrival to the rest of the breakers, who are all on instant high alert. Some of the boys' legs immediately begin that nervous tic and judder. Khav herself is not nervous. Just excited. She tries not to let it show. She's the only girl there, she realises. Sometimes there are one or two others, never more, but today there's only her. She wonders if the guys have clocked her yet. Under the baggy clothes it's not obvious. She raises her head and stares directly at Teniel. Keep it cool, she tells herself, keep it real. He ignores her. Excellent. That's his way of saying okay, you're in.

He places the boom-box down in the centre of the concourse like a dog defecating defiantly. He strikes up a pose. Don't fuck with me. Once he's sure he's got everyone's attention, he switches on the machine. The rhythms of Rock Master Scott & The Dynamite Three hit the air. *The Roof is on Fire, The Roof is on Fire.*

"Let battle commence," commands Teniel. "May the best breaker win."

The throw-down begins.

Immediately the waiting crew leaps into life. They fill the space with their separate, carefully honed and customised versions of Top Rock, Knee Drop, Spin Down, Hook Drop, mixing Indian with Cross Step, Six Step, Three Step, Shuffle, before each of them hit their perfect freeze – Hollowback, Baby, Elbow, Chair.

Khav bides her time, watching from the sides, patrolling the perimeter, a panther on the prowl. She doesn't want to show her hand too soon.

They all of them do a variant of this, sussing each other out, checking what's new, what's tried and tested, what works, what doesn't. Teniel conducts them all, the ringmaster to the circus, his eyes on all of them at once, who's making moves worth noting, who's not, who's on the rise, who's on the wane.

Finally Khav sees her chance. She leaps into the arena with a series of pretzels and sweeps before launching into her own distinctive set of dynamic power moves. She propels her whole body forward in a continuous rotational motion, alternatively balancing on her hands and elbows, back and shoulders. The Caterpillar. She throws in some head spins, air flares and windmills, plus the occasional breaker flip just for good measure. She follows these with her own unique tricks, hopping air chairs, handstand jumps, and, for her *pièce de resistance*, leg-threading while simultaneously hand-hopping, ending with a power freeze.

The rest of the crew cheer her on.

"Go, B-Girl," exhorts Teniel from the centre.

Khav flicks her fingers and exits from the ring with a nod and a scowl, but she can't completely hide the smirk that threatens to spread across her face.

But her triumph is short-lived. A posse of Transport Police march into the concourse, despite the boos from the applauding onlookers who have been enjoying this free throw-down performance, and the entire crew melt into the crowds, as if they have never been.

Just as Khav is about to leg it down the Station Approach, she is held back by an admiring Teniel.

"That was some throw down, B-Girl."

"Thanks."

"We could do with more sisters like you. Know any?"

Khav shakes her head.

"Then you'd better rustle up a few," he says, before tossing her his own cap. Then he too is gone like a puff of smoke.

*

2013

Khav takes the cap from her case of props and places it with a certain reverence among the other seemingly random objects gradually spreading around her in the TV Studio.

*

2009

Khav is seventeen years old. She attends the sixth form at Trinity High School on Cambridge Street, less than a five-minute walk from MMU, to which she will transfer in less than eighteen months' time. It takes her twenty minutes to get there by bus each morning. Its Ofsted report is 'outstanding'. Her father is immensely proud of this fact, and he will quote it to anyone and everyone. "My daughter's at Trinity High," he'll say. "An outstanding school." Then he will say to his wife, "Only the best will do for my little princess." And then he will add as a warning to Khavita herself, "Make sure you don't waste this opportunity." Not that he has any reason to fear that she will. She continues to shine in all of her 'A' levels. Vikram begins to imagine a future career for her as a lawyer. "She's always been a good talker," agrees Geetha. "Argumentative, you mean?" points out Priya, while fixing and setting her mother's hair. And this appears to be born out in Khavita's mid-year reports. 'Excellent, if challenging,' is the theme running through them. Then, when she indicates that it is her intention to apply not to Oxbridge, or even to Manchester, but to MMU to study Media Production, Vikram is apoplectic. "What is this Media nonsense?" he rails. "You must study Law." But when, the next year she turns eighteen and shows no sign of changing her mind, he plunges into despair. "What is she doing wasting her time with this second class degree? MMU is not even a proper university. In my day it was called a

Polytechnic, the place you went to if you weren't clever enough to go anywhere else." Geetha tuts and reminds him that they are now living in the 21st century. "Times change," she says. "MMU is one of the best places in all of UK to study Media, and it's right on our doorstep. She can stay at home, save money on rent. Just think, *Bapu*, we might see her reading the news on BBC one day." This mollifies Vikram a little. "Perhaps you are right, *Nona*. She might be the next Ranvir Singh. She is from Lancashire too, I think."

Khav knows when it's best not to push her luck. To keep her father sweet – and therefore off her case – she agrees to go to the Trinity Youth Centre nearby, just the other side of Platt Fields, as a volunteer helping the younger girls in various after-school activities. She attends what is called 'Girl Talk' on Thursday evenings.

There are about a dozen girls there, all aged between twelve and fifteen years. They arrive in dribs and drabs, looking desultory and bored before they've even started. When Khav asks them what they usually talk about in these sessions, they shuffle awkwardly. Eventually one of them, quite a large girl called Showmi, puts up her hand and begins to speak. But before she can get very far, Khav interrupts her.

"Hey," she says, "I'm not your teacher. You don't have to put your hand up with me. My name's Khavita, but I much prefer to be called Khav. So – Showmi – just say whatever it is that's on your mind."

"Well, Khav," she says, "what we normally talk about is food."

"Food? What kind of food?"

It's as if she has opened the flood gates, for within seconds she is practically drowning in their voices, all of them speaking at once, all of them complaining.

"Whoa," says Khav. "What're you sayin'? That all you ever do here is cook?"

"That's right," says Showmi, who is emerging as the other girls' spokesperson. "It's bad enough being taught how to cook by our *Maas* at home…"

"Tell me about it," agrees Khav.

"…without havin' to do it again here."

The rest of the girls immediately go into impersonations of their various Aunties.

"The way to a man's heart is through his stomach, isn't it?"

They all of them fall about laughing while they try to outdo each other in their mimicry of their Aunties' excesses.

"Listen, girls," says Khav, after they've started to calm down. "I'm not knockin' cookin', right? But I'm sensin' that you wanna try somethin' different, innit?"

"Raz!" they cry as one.

"So," she says, looking each and every one of them directly in turn, "how about we form an all-girl break-dance crew?"

"Raz! They cry again.

"Trinity Hall Breakers," says one.

"Platt Lane B-Girls," says another.

"Nah," says Showmi, "I got a better idea."

They all turn towards her.

"Well," says Khav, "out with it."

"Seein' as how our parents think we come here to learn cookin', what if we call ourselves *Missi Roti*?"

"Raz!" they cry again, shrieking with delight.

"Right," says Khav. "*Missi Roti*, it is."

Three months later, when Khav arrives on the last minute, like she always does, she's no longer surprised to find all the girls already there before her, busily practising their favourite moves, working up small group routines. The transformation from when she first met them could not be more marked.

"Hey Khav," they call. "Watch this new move." Or, "Hey Khav, can you help us how to work out this?"

She claps her hands and calls them together.

"OK, B-Girls. Listen up. I got a surprise for you today."

She gives a whistle and in walks Teniel, or sidles, rather, his head swaying slowly from side to side as he finishes listening to whatever's playing on his phone. The girls' collective jaws drop as one. They know who Tenicl is of course, they've seen photos, though none of them have actually seen him up close before. They try to look as cool as they can but fail miserably. One by one, as he passes them by in his slow, measured walk towards Khav, they fan their faces with their hands and bat their eyes. When he and Khav then embark on an elaborately complex home-boy hand-greeting, they are beside themselves with excitement.

In the two years since Khav first showed off some of her moves to Teniel on the concourse of Piccadilly Station, the two of them have become firm mates. They've perfected their own unique mix of hip-hop/street/lockin' and lindy, which they now demonstrate in front of the now whooping and cheering girls.

"Yo, *Missi Roti*!" says Teniel after he and Khav have completed their moves.

"Yo, Teniel!" they chorus back.

Immediately they crowd around him, each of them wanting him to give them particular tips on how to pull off the various tricks they've been working on.

"No," he says. "It's not me you should be askin', but Khav. She's your teacher."

"Respect," says Showmi, and the rest of girls strike up a solemn pose and nod towards Khav, who's not felt so high since that morning two years before, on the concourse of Piccadilly Station…

*

2007

Khav is on cloud nine, but then remembers she needs to check in with Abila to make sure her alibi is still operational. She takes out her phone and begins texting.

"Hey?"
"Hey."
"How's it going?"
"Setback"
"❗❗"
"Shopping trip with sis cancelled."
" 🫣 "
"Plan B."
" ❓ "
"Meet me outside Nando's in 20 mins."
" 👍 "

She pulls her skate board from out of her backpack and sets off at a lick, weaving in and out of the Saturday shoppers, who have to leap out of her way if they are not to be mown down. She hops out of the path of a passing tram, before scooting down Market Street as fast as she can till she reaches the escalator entrance leading up to the Food Court on the Upper Mall of the Arndale. The lack of weight from her now-shorn hair is exhilarating.

Just as she steps off the top of the escalator, she feels the vibration of her phone buzz in her pocket. She flips it open, expecting a second message from Abila, only to discover it's from her *Maa*. Just five words, but they rob all the joy from her in an instant.

"I know what you did."

*

One hour earlier.

Finally, sighs Geetha, as she hears her husband call to say that he is on his way to the *Gurdwara* for a meeting to discuss the arrangements for next month's services to mark the beginning of *Chet*. Now she might have some peace and quiet at last. He has been finding fault with everyone and everything all morning.

She decides to make herself a mug of mint tea to settle her nerves. But first she decides to check on *Nani* to see if she needs anything first. Urja, Geetha's mother, known to all as *Nani*, lives in the annexe they built for her at the back of the house in what had once been the back garden. They did this five years ago, when she started having trouble managing the stairs.

"Oh good," said Priya when this was all first being discussed. "Does that mean I can have *Nani*'s room and no longer share with my snotty little sister?"

"Or maybe I could have it?" Khavita had countered.

"No," Geetha had said. "Nani's room is bigger. Your sister is older. She needs it more than you do. You can have it when she gets married and moves out."

"Which will be never," fumes Khavita. "For no one will want her."

"Well that's just where you're wrong, Little Miss Know-It-All, it just so happens that..."

"Yes, Priya?"

Priya immediately clams up. "Nothing, *Maa*." She glowers at Khavita. "Don't you dare say a word, or else..."

And she hadn't. Khav had been true to her word. She'd never spilled the beans on her sister, not once, not ever, no matter what kind of scrapes she got into. They got on much better once they each had their own rooms. If pressed, they might even admit to almost liking one another.

But that hasn't stopped Vikram from finding fault with both of them whenever he can.

Geetha had not imagined when she first was married that she would long for and relish these oases of quiet and calm quite so much. Vikram had been so handsome back then, so solicitous of her, so courteous towards *Nani*.

"Of course," he had said, when Geetha had asked him if, after they married, she might remain living in the same house she had grown up in as a girl. *Nani* had not been the same since her husband, Agrawal, had died, just a few days after Geetha's and Vikram's engagement celebrations. "I would not wish to break the sacred bond between mother and daughter," he had said. "Had I been fortunate enough to have a house myself, then the first thing I would have done is to have invited *Nani* to live with us. I should have insisted on it. And so, to begin with, let us make our home together here."

That had been more than twenty years ago. It had been convenient at the time. Vikram was only starting out as a bank clerk and could not afford to buy them a house on the meagre salary he was paid. But the house on Albion Road was perfect for a growing family. Why – hadn't Geetha herself grown up here?

And so what had begun as a temporary expedient gradually turned into a permanent arrangement, which suited everyone. Vikram had managed to save a tidy sum by not having to pay out on a mortgage – Agrawal and Urja had paid it off just before Agrawal had retired from his work with Manchester Corporation Transport – and so, when it became clear that *Nani*'s health was declining, he was able to use those savings to build the annexe on the back. Honour, he felt, had finally been satisfied.

Geetha knocks on *Nani*'s door. As usual she is already dressed and up and about, as neat as a squirrel in her ways. Each day she appears to Geetha to grow tinier and tinier. Her bones are so fragile and thin she resembles one of the sparrows which skitter in and out of the hedge that separates the end of their garden from Platt Fields beyond.

"How are you this morning, *Nani*?"

"Grateful to see another day, Daughter. God is good. But it is you I am worried about. You look worn out."

"I'm fine, *Nani*. I'm just a little tired, that's all. I expect it's the strain of Priya's wedding coming up, then Vikram and Khavita are always at each other's throats. Hardly a civil word passes between them. He's always finding fault."

"What is it this time?"

"He doesn't like her break dancing."

"It's only a phase."

"That's what I tell him. But does he listen? No. Then he criticises me for taking her side."

"Fathers and daughters," says Urja. "Your father was just the same with you."

"Was he? I've forgotten."

"Always so protective. So reluctant to accept that you'd grown up and were quite capable of looking after yourself."

"Khavita's only fifteen."

"Yes, but she knows her own mind."

"That's true enough."

The two women smile, remembering the tempers and the tantrums.

"But she's a kind heart.," says Urja.

"She thinks the world of you," agrees Geetha.

"I know it, and I'm grateful for it."

*

2005

Two years earlier.

The annexe is complete, the builders have left for the last time, and Urja can at last move in. Fifty years she has lived in this house on Albion Road. She and Agrawal managed to put down a deposit on it just one year after they married. Before that they had had to live in Agrawal's mother's house, which had been an unmitigated disaster. Nothing Urja did was ever good enough for her. She found fault with everything – the way she cooked, the way she dressed, the way she cleaned. She and Agrawal never had a moment to themselves. Only when they were in bed, and even there Urja felt that her mother-in-law was listening out for every sound, her ear pressed to the other side of the paper-thin wall. It was intolerable. In the end she had to give her husband an ultimatum…

*

1955

"Find us our own house before our first anniversary, or I swear I shall not be held responsible for what I might say or do."

This was accompanied with an expression on her face that Agrawal had learned to recognise already in their few months together. It said, 'Do not argue with this look.'

And so Agrawal had gone to his father and set out the situation that now faced him. His father was sympathetic. He liked Urja. He had seen at once that she was exactly what his rather shy, but well-meaning son needed if he was to make his way in the world. She would give him the steel and determination he lacked, and so he agreed at once. The year was 1955 and the house on Albion Road was available for £1850, which meant that a deposit of just under £200 was required, which Agrawal was determined to pay back month by month, together with the cost of the mortgage repayments. It had been a struggle, but he had managed. In less than two years he had paid back his father, and, by the time he retired from his job with GMPTE, the Greater Manchester Passenger Transport Executive, in 1987, at the age of sixty-five, he had repaid the mortgage.

On his last day, after he had returned home with his Retirement Clock, a replica of the wall clock that had hung in the office where he had worked loyally for more than forty years, against which he had helped construct, then supervise the bus timetables for the whole city, which had been presented to him by his colleagues 'with gratitude for a job well done', he had sat down with a contented, if exhausted look on his face, then fallen into an immediate sleep, from which he quite simply never woke up…

*

2005

Poor Agrawal. He would turn in his grave if he knew just how much the house was now worth, sighs Urja. There had had to be a valuation when applying for planning permission to build this annexe she is now in the process of moving into, and Urja had seen the letter from the Estate Agents. £270,000 for a three-bedroom terrace. It didn't bear thinking about. She shakes her head. Who can afford such prices? No wonder so many of them are being converted into flats. Such a pity, for they make perfect family houses. As this has been for her, and now for her daughter and *her* family.

What would Agrawal have made of all these changes, she wonders, looking round at the large, freshly-painted room at the back of the house that is now to serve as her combined bedroom and sitting room, with a small but perfectly equipped kitchen just off to one side and a bathroom to the other, each kitted out with the latest 'mod cons'? He would probably have taken it all in his stride. She can imagine him looking around and saying, "Well at least we don't need to worry about keeping the grass cut…"

She smiles. It was true. What had formerly been quite a long back garden has now largely been replaced with the annexe and a decked patio just beyond the back door. They were neither of them great gardeners. They didn't have time, for one thing – they mainly used it for the children to run about in – but she did like to plant her bulbs for the spring. She'd been greatly assisted in that department by Jabez, their neighbour, who had been the Head Gardener at Philips Park, where he'd been responsible for their Tulip Sunday each year, and who had come to live next door with his wife, Mary, when he retired in 1960. He'd introduced her to tulips, and she'd planted them every year since. She hoped she'd still be able to in what little was left of the garden.

And the bird table too has survived. Every day Urja would scatter a few crumbs upon it. The children used to like to help her, Geetha especially, and more recently Khavita has liked to do this with her, then stand back to watch for the sparrows and starlings to arrive. They would never have to wait for long. Soon the table would be full of the birds' squabbling.

"Hush," she'd say. "There's enough for all of you."

The birds had been alarmed at first by the upheaval caused by the builders with their diggers and scaffolding, but soon they had learned to adapt to their presence, and the workmen too used to scatter their own crumbs on the table for them after they'd finished their lunch of bacon sandwiches.

The birds will miss the men's bacon, thinks Urja now with a smile. "You'll have to get used to going back to just chickpea flour," she says to them. And she knows they will.

Yes – Agrawal would have embraced the change, like he had always done at work, which seemed to alter every five minutes. First it was Manchester Corporation, next it was SELNEC – South East Lancashire, North East Cheshire – whose buses were that cheerful orange colour, and then it was GMPTE, who promptly changed them back to red again.

"Well," Agrawal would say, "people expect their buses to be red, it's what they're used to."

"So long as they're on time, nobody cares what colour they are," she would reply.

"And that is what I spend each day doing," he would then say, smiling.

"So when I am waiting at the stop with my neighbours and they complain that the buses are late, I should tell them to hold you responsible, should I?" she would tease.

"Please don't," he would say, holding up his hands in mock-horror. "I have enough letters asking me that same question as it is."

"And what do you answer them?" she would ask.

"I tell them that I am only responsible for *setting* the schedules," he would answer, "all of which have been timed and tested many times. But then the variables intervene, the unknowables."

"What do you mean?"

"A driver may be sick and have to be replaced at the last minute. There might be road works, an accident, a tree may have come down. There may be unexpected traffic, more passengers than anticipated trying to board. The roads may be icy, or flooded, or cracking in the heat. There may be a fog. So many things. Only God sees everything."

"That is what I tell my neighbours," she would say.

"And how do they answer you?"

"Then God should set the timetable."

"If only…"

And then they would laugh warmly, while she would serve up their supper of *chana massala* with *puri* and *dahl*.

But it had not always been so.

When Agrawal had first joined Manchester Corporation Transport, he had wanted to drive the buses, or, at the very least, be a conductor. "Yes," he was told. "By all means this is possible, but..." He had known what was coming. "You will have to remove your turban."

"But I can't," he had said. "It's part of my faith as a Sikh."

"That may be," they had said, "but it's part of a bus driver's uniform to wear the Manchester Corporation peaked cap." They had spread their hands and shrugged when they said this, as if to say, "Sorry, but those are the rules." Except that Agrawal did not believe they were especially sorry.

By way of compensation, they had offered him the administrative job of setting the timetables, which was in the office, where he could retain his turban, and which was also better paid. Mindful of his obligation to his father for the loan on the deposit for their house, he swallowed his pride and accepted the compromise. He remained there for the rest of his working life. Had it been such a compromise? Not when he saw his children growing up in the house, or when his daughter, Geetha, had been engaged to be married to Vikram, which they had celebrated there.

But others had been bolder than he had been...

Now, as Urja begins to unpack the first of the boxes she has brought down to the annexe with her, she wonders how such a rich and full life can be contained within so few of them.

Khavita is helping her. She is twelve years old and such a chatterbox. Always she is asking Urja questions. "What is this, *Nani*?" "Or this?" "Or this?" And she will not be satisfied until Urja has told her the whole story.

It is Khavita who pulls out the old, faded newspaper clipping from one of the boxes.

"What's this?" she pipes up, her mouth opening and closing like a bird's beak.

Urja takes it, screws up her eyes to try and read it, then tuts when she is not able to.

"Pass me my specs, will you please, *Dohti*?"

Khavita finds them under a newspaper and hands them across. Urja puts them on, reads the clipping and smiles.

"Ah," she says, "this was a great victory. Look." She passes the yellowing clipping back to Khavita, who reads it avidly.

*

1966

Manchester Guardian

11th August 1966

WE DIE WITH IT, LET US LIVE WITH IT

Sikhs' Case for Turbans

By our own Reporter

Another fold in the long tale of the turban was unwound yesterday in Manchester, where the Corporation Transport Committee currently refuses to allow turbaned Sikhs to work as bus drivers or conductors. The committee has a rule that drivers and conductors must wear the department's uniform cap.

Seven leaders of the Sikh community in the city – a dignified delegation wearing turbans from pale pink, through patterned browns and greens, to dark blue – yesterday met the chairman of the committee, Councillor C.R Morris, to tell him why they think the ban on turbans is wrong.

Matter of principle

The chief spokesman for the Sikhs was Gyaril Sundar Singh Sagar, a university graduate and a leader of the Manchester community, who started the story last year by applying for a job as a bus conductor. He offered to wear the department's badge on his dark blue turban. After research and discussion, the committee decided to stick to its rule – wear a cap or no job as a conductor. Sagar wanted his turban, refused a turbaned job in one of the bus depots and, with his community, has since been pressing the committee as a matter of principle, supported by Mr Agrawal Singh of Albion Road, Fallowfield, a Sikh administrative worker for Manchester Corporation Transport.

The Committee's original ban on turbans was upheld in the city council last year by 41 votes to 31. A second debate on the issue was averted last month when Councillor Morris said he was prepared to meet leaders of the Sikhs in Manchester, and hear their case. Yesterday, after an hour's discussion, he described Mr Sagar as a "powerful advocate".

Points raised by the Delegation were that the Committee had ignored the general feeling in the city that turbaned drivers and conductors should be allowed to work on the buses; that the turban was part of a "proper" Sikh's life, and that it was already accepted as a recognised headdress in the British Armed Forces.

The Delegation produced impressive figures showing that in the two World Wars more than 82,000 turbaned Sikhs were killed, and more than 108,000 wounded. More than half the Victoria Crosses won in the British Indian Armies were awarded to Sikhs, and Sagar made the point that if Sikhs could die with the turban, they should be allowed to live with it.

Finally, the Delegation offered a guarantee that Sikhs employed as conductors would wear turbans of any colour chosen by the committee, and said: "Turbans would add variety to the scene of Commonwealth here ... and probably bring more passengers to see how hard and well we work."

After the meeting, Councillor Morris said he had been most impressed by the Delegation's case. It had been listened to carefully and would be placed before the next meeting of the Transport Committee, whose decision would come before the city council in October. He said:

"I want the Sikh community to feel that we are not discriminating against them on religious grounds and that we are taking a tolerant and reasonable attitude."

Councillor Morris declined to hazard any guess about whether his committee, after hearing the Delegation's case, would be likely to change its mind. Sagar, and other members of the Delegation, said the question of turbaned drivers and conductors was now a matter of principle.

Councillor T. Thomas who asked the council last year *not* to ban the turban, attended yesterday's meeting and said that he had suggested that Sikhs might be employed on a short-term basis, leaving room for discussion if any difficulties arose. Alderman Sir Richard Harper, Leader of the Conservative group in the City Council, accompanied the Sikh delegation. He thought it had provided the Transport Committee with more information than it had when the original decision was taken. Few people seemed to appreciate the significance of the turban, he said. "In the eyes of the Sikh it is the visible sign of his spiritual grace."

Editorial: Turbans on the Buses

Sikhs must, as a tenet of their religion, wear a turban: Manchester bus drivers and conductors must, as a condition of employment, wear a peaked cap. It follows that no Sikh can serve as a bus driver or conductor in Manchester, and a year ago, a Sikh who applied for a conductor's job was refused on this ground and no other. The city council will soon have the chance to reconsider its policy, and we hope it will do so when the question comes before the full Council again in October.

The objection to turbaned bus drivers and conductors does not seem to rest on anything more substantial than habit. It has been suggested that to admit the turban would be to open the doors to all kinds of eccentricities in dress. To that there is one short, simple answer. There are few, if any, garments which can claim the religious sanction of a Sikh's turban. In addition it is practical, smart and well-defined, and Sikhs are in general noted for their fine and noble bearing. This newspaper believes there is no reason why they should be denied the right to wear the turban while discharging all the duties required of a bus driver or conductor. Manchester has always championed tolerance and understanding. Let her once again show the way to the rest of the country by removing this outdated restriction from some of her most loyal and valued citizens.

There are some who claim, such as Mr Enoch Powell, MP for Wolverhampton South West, that such gestures serve only to fragment society and dilute what it means to be British. Here at *The Manchester Guardian* we wholly refute such antiquated, discriminatory and inflammatory opinions. They have no place in a modern, diverse and pluralist Britain, which we, like all right-minded citizens, regard as being only beneficial to the future of us all.

*

2005

"So what happened?" asks Khavita after reading through the news clipping at her customary lightning speed.

"They won. The Council overturned their former ruling, voting in favour of turbans being allowed to be worn by seventy-one votes to twenty-three."

"Wow! That's like three to one in favour. A landslide."

"It was a red letter day indeed. And to cap it all, your *Baba*'s cousin, Mukhtiar Singh, became the first Sikh bus driver to be allowed to wear a turban in England."

"Didn't *Baba* want to drive a bus himself?"

"I think secretly he did. But he was happy where he was. He'd made his mark there and was respected. He knew where every single bus in the fleet should be at any given moment. He'd travelled every route – from Whitworth to Wilmslow, Chorley to Cheadle – so that he could correctly coordinate all of the separate timings. Even on holidays, he would take out his pocket watch…"

"This one?" asks Khavita, pulling it out of another of the boxes.

"Yes, that's right, the one which had belonged to his own *Baba*, and he would flip it open and say…" Urja pauses, assuming Agrawal's typical pose, and mimes flipping open the pocket watch. "'10.45. The 257 from Piccadilly to Davyhulme should be just pulling in to Trafford Bar right now.' Then he'd smile, close the cover of the watch, and slip it back into his pocket."

The two of them laugh companionably.

"I wish I'd known him," says Khavita, suddenly serious.

"He'd have been very proud of you, *Dohti*. He'd've taught you to play chess."

Silently Khavita vows to learn.

"Look," says Urja. "Here's a photo of him from those days."

"I've not seen this one before."

"No. I'd forgotten about it. It shows him wearing the Manchester Corporation Transport badge pinned to the front of his turban. He was very proud of that."

Khavita studies the faded, black-and-white image.

"Look how handsome your *Baba* was, *Dohti*," smiles Urja.

Khavita puckers up her forehead and frowns. "I think I've seen that badge in another of the boxes," she says.

Immediately she begins to rummage through one, before triumphantly lifting it out. "There! I thought so."

She passes it across to her *Nani*, who looks at it fondly.

"Why don't you keep it?" she says, much to Khavita's amazement. "And the stop watch too. They should be passed on."

Khavita holds the two objects – badge and watch – carefully side by side, one in each hand, lifting them up to the light, as if they were precious jewels...

*

2013

...which is exactly what they are, she thinks, holding them up again now, as she lays them out in front of her in the TV Studio, in readiness for her presentation, which will be starting in just over an hour's time...

*

2007

"Aiee!"

The sound of Geetha screaming is so loud that Urja hears it right at the back of the annexe.

"Aiee!"

It comes again, louder this time, as Geetha hurtles down the stairs, along the hallway, through the kitchen and into the annexe, the like of which Urja has not heard since she had to break the news to Agrawal's mother that her son had died in his sleep.

"Aiee!"

"Whatever is it, *Dhi*?"

Geetha thrusts the bin liner she is carrying towards her mother, then falls to her knees, sobbing. Urja tentatively opens the bag, wondering whatever can be inside it that is causing her daughter such consternation and alarm? Is it a rat? Surely not. Geetha is not the type to be sequeamish. She looks inside. Now she sees what it is and involuntarily gasps, lifting her hand to her mouth immediately afterwards. Two long tresses of hair lie scrunched and coiled together, more like snakes than rats' tails. She can almost hear the spit and sizzle.

"Aiee!"

*

Vikram by this time is too far away to hear his wife's cries of distress. But even if he had only just left the house, he still would not have heard them, for they would have been drowned out by the sound of the engine of his bright yellow *Bajaj Chetak* 50cc scooter he imported from India seven years earlier. He knows his daughters laugh at him behind his back whenever he steps onto it, but he doesn't care. To him this scooter is like the son he has never had. Every Sunday afternoon, after they have returned home from the *Gurdwara* and had their lunch, he takes himself out into the small parking space directly in front of the house, where he keeps it in a small lock-up store that fits neatly underneath the ledge outside the dining room window. Religiously he takes it out, genuflects before it, anoints it with oil, before reverently polishing it until he can see his own reflection in its shiny surface. Manufactured by Bajaj Auto in

Pune, the *Chetak* is named after the legendary horse of the warrior Pratap Singh. Each time he turns the ignition and hears it putter sweetly into life, Vikram imagines himself as the famed Mewari Rana astride his trusted steed about to ride out into battle.

Which is how he feels now as he turns from Albion into Furness, Landcross then Wilmslow Roads, before turning right into Wilbraham and Withington Roads, until he turns sharply, diagonally left, almost doubling-back on himself down Upper Chorlton Road, where the current home for the *Gurdwara* temporarily resides. He passes all the familiar landmarks – the *Gita Bhavan* Hindu Temple, St Margaret's Church, My Lahore Marquee in the grounds of the British Muslim Heritage Centre, the *Jame'ah Masjid E Noor* Mosque, and all that remains of that other temple to more sporting heroes, Maine Road, the former stadium of his beloved Manchester City, demolished just three years before and now the site of some still-unfinished, nondescript modern flats and houses.

Vikram had been deeply distressed by the club's decision to leave Maine Road, and although *The Etihad Stadium* is an architectural wonder, it does not as yet hold the same place in his heart as Maine Road still does. He even considered boycotting the club, as disgruntled supporters had done back when the club moved from its original Hyde Road ground to Maine Road in the first place, back in 1923, with one of the Directors, John Ayrton, resigning from the Board in order to form the breakaway Manchester Central FC, which played at Belle Vue for three seasons in the Lancashire Combination before folding after successive bids to join the Football League were turned down. Die-hard City historians have always maintained that the club's spiritual home lies in the east of Manchester, so when the opportunity arose for them to move into the brand new stadium built for the Commonwealth Games in 2002 after the Games were over, they seized it with alacrity.

Vikram ponders this every time he rides past Maine Road. He smiles, conjuring up in his mind's eye an image of one of his most treasured possessions, a single blade of grass taken from the Maine Road pitch after the last match ever played there, against Sunderland, which City had fittingly won 3-0. He keeps this blade of grass in an air-tight test tube, which he has placed in a small shrine among the framed family photos in their sitting room.

He understands the importance of a spiritual home and asks himself this very question each time he returns to India to visit family connections who still reside there. How would he define himself if asked to do so? As British or Indian? Punjabi or Mancunian? As Sikh or City fan? If pressed he would say it's a combination of all of these, but even that can seem reductive. The last time he was in India the Hindu National Party, the BJP, was busily renaming the towns and cities and other landmarks across the country in a deliberate policy of reclamation. Bombay had become Mumbai, Madras Chennai, while the much-loved station in Bombay/Mumbai, Victoria Terminus, universally known as VT, had been officially redesignated as *Chaprapati Shivaji Maharaj*, named after a Marathi warrior chieftain, who'd used guerrilla tactics to defend a last stronghold on the Deccan plateau. Meanwhile everyone on the streets still referred to the exuberant old Gothic masterpiece as VT, and Vikram is convinced they always will. It's all very well to rebrand a scooter as a folk hero liberating the masses from oppression and enslavement, like his trusty *Chetak*, but if you must do that, then at least do so with a name that everyone can easily remember, pronounce and absorb. VT will not easily become CSM. Of that he is certain.

He waits for a gap in the traffic to steer the *Chetak* past the old Maine Road, which used to be called Dog Kennel Lane before the football ground was built there, its name changing due to a request by a local Temperance Society who had premises there and who did not wish their address to be tainted by the wild behaviour so often associated with those who followed the beautiful game. It's nothing more than a building site now, with wire fences screening passers-by from the twenty-four hour constant noise of cranes and diggers and pneumatic drills, which are removing every last vestige of what once stood there. But, as Vikram drives slowly past, their incessant noise cannot drown out completely the sounds of cheers and chanting crowds that greeted each goal that was scored there. He wonders whether there will more name changes to come now as the flats and houses of the new estates being built begin to mushroom into the sky. Colin Bell Court perhaps? Or Summerbee Drive? He's heard that the Council has decided not to rename anything after any of the players. Surely, thinks Vikram, there's a place for a Trautmann Close? Vikram has always had a soft spot for Bert Trautmann, the German goalkeeper who had to overcome suspicion and even some hostility when he first arrived at the club shortly after the end of the Second World War, in which he'd been a paratrooper before being captured and interned in a prisoner-of-war camp in Ashton-in-Makerfield, just outside St Helens, some twenty miles from Manchester down the East Lancs Road. That was before Vikram's time of course, but all true blue City fans, young and old, are steeped in the legend of Bert Trautmann, who broke his neck during the FA Cup Final against Birmingham at Wembley in 1956 but played on regardless, which City won thanks to Bert's heroics. Vikram likes to see similarities between Trautmann and himself, each of them strangers in a foreign land, but made to feel welcome, so that both could call Manchester their home and be proud to do so. British, Indian, Sikh – yes, he is all of these, but he is Mancunian first. The other three have all sketched his outline, but it is Manchester which has filled in the detail, picked out the specific details by which he can be singularly identified.

This is who I am. Vikram Singh. British-born of Indian parents. Resident of Albion Road, Manchester. On my way to the *Sri Gobind Guru Singh Gurdwara*, my local Sikh temple.

He rides the last few hundred yards along Upper Chorlton Road until he reaches the building at Number 61, which has served as the temple's temporary home for more than thirty years.

The *Gurdwara*'s first Manchester home was at 35 Rosamund Street in Chorlton-on-Medlock, when a small group of members were able to pool sufficient funds to purchase the house there, which was converted into a temple as the congregation grew. This was in 1961, the year Vikram was born. But when, ten years later, the Council began the massive redevelopment in Hulme and the surrounding area, Rosamund Street was earmarked for demolition, and the temple was temporarily rehoused above a row of shops on Upper Brook Street not far from the Manchester Royal Infirmary. They stayed there for four years, until their current premises became available, which in the thirty years since has been much altered and expanded, but which is no longer fit for purpose.

Then, in November 2003, almost exactly six years ago to the day, an opportunity arose for them to purchase a large empty building just two doors down at Number 57 for £320,000. This came with planning permission to extend and re-develop so that an entirely new complex could be housed there, comprising an education and cultural centre, as well as a function room, committee room and a larger temple to meet the growing needs of the ever-widening Sikh community across the city.

"It is essential," Vikram had argued to plan for the next generation. "Our focus should be on our children." No one had disagreed with that sentiment, and, the following February, plans were approved at the staggering cost of two million pounds. The *Gurdwara* pledged to raise just over a million, with the shortfall secured by an £800,000 loan from Lloyds TSB. Vikram, who had just been appointed as Deputy Branch Manager at the Longsight branch on Stockport Road, had played not an insignificant part in helping to secure that loan, and so was now an important member of the Fundraising Committee.

It is to a meeting of this Committee that he has now ridden on his *Bajaj Chetak*, which will follow on immediately from the business of arranging the upcoming services for *Katak* that is not expected to take more than a few minutes. The Sikhs use the *Nanakshahi*, a solar calendar based on the *Barah Mahi*, a poem roughly translating as the 'Twelve Months', which reflects on the changing seasons. The year begins with the month of *Chet*, with the 1st of *Chet* corresponding to the 14th of March. *Katak* is equivalent to the weeks spanning the middle of October to the middle of November, and the *Nanakshi* Calendar begins in 1469, the year of the birth of Guru Nanak, whose framed portrait hangs garlanded with flowers above the entrance to 57 Upper Chorlton Road.

Standing on the steps leading up to the front door are his fellow committee-members, who applaud him as he turns his bright yellow *Babaj Chetak* into the driveway. They try to do this every time. It has become something of a ritual. He knows they are making gentle fun of him, but he doesn't mind. Let them laugh all they like, he thinks to himself. Just like my two daughters, and my wife also when she thinks I cannot see, but what care I for their mockery? I will rise above it. For just inside the front door hangs another portrait, this one a photograph from *The Manchester Evening News* of 1976, when his other hero, even greater in his eyes than his current idols, Vincent Kompany and Kolo Touré, challenged the ruling that stated all Sikhs must replace their turbans with crash helmets if they wished to ride a scooter or motorcycle on British roads, Gyani Sundar Singh Sagar. Not content with winning the battle for Sikh bus drivers and conductors, he then took on no less a figure than Lord Denning, the Master of the Rolls.

*

1976

Manchester Evening News

16th November 1976

VICTORY AT LAST FOR THE 'URBAN TURBAN'

Landmark Legislation Exempts Sikhs

Yesterday saw a landmark ruling for Sikhs in Britain when The Motorcycle Crash Helmet Act of 1972 was amended to exempt turban-wearing Sikhs from obligatory compliance.

This is a great victory for Sikhs across Britain, but especially so here in Manchester, where the campaign to bring about this exemption was spearheaded by the highly esteemed local community leader Gyani Sundar Singh Sagar (pictured below) who formed The National Turban Action Committee to be at the vanguard of protest against what he and fellow Sikhs regarded as nothing less than religious persecution, for it is the Sikh's sacred duty to wear the turban at all times.

Gyani Sundar Singh Sagar on his release from Strangeways
Photo by George Wright

One of the most eye-catching aspects of the campaign saw Gyani-Ji, as he is affectionately known by his admirers, buy himself a moped, which he then proceeded to ride about the city's streets in a highly visible and public manner, leading to several fines and ultimately a custodial sentence.

Even though he was 57 years old and suffering from asthma and diabetes, Gyani-Ji was not afraid of going to prison, since it would further highlight the arguments he was making to amend the law, namely that if Sikhs had been allowed to lay down their lives for Britain during the Raj and two World Wars without any legal compulsion for them to wear helmets instead of turbans, then they deserved the right to choose what to wear when riding a motorcycle. He urged the recently introduced Commission for Racial Equality (CRE) to support his campaign on the grounds that Sikhs were being discriminated against on racial grounds in the prosecution of the Act.

Master of the Rolls, Lord Denning, however, disagreed, and, in a rare public intervention, commented:

"The Statute as it stands contains a clear definition of what constitutes a racial group. It means a 'group of persons defined by reference to colour, race, nationality or ethnic or national origins'. That definition is very carefully framed. Most interesting is that it does not include religion or politics or culture. You can discriminate for or against Roman Catholics as much as you like without being in breach of the law. You can discriminate for or against Communists as much as you please, without being in breach of the law. You can discriminate for or against hippies, moonies or skinheads, without being in breach of the law. But you must not discriminate against a man because of his colour or of his race or of his nationality, or of his ethnic or national origins. The question before us today is whether the Sikhs are a religious or racial group. If their objection to removing the turban is on religious grounds, then *The*

Motorcycle Crash Helmet Act cannot be deemed to be discriminating against them on racial grounds."

Gyani-Ji was duly sentenced to seven days in Strangeways Prison.

However, before he could serve it, the Lord Mayor of Manchester paid his fines to spare him this punishment. Nonetheless, Gyani-Ji carried on riding his moped while wearing a turban without paying his fines and was sentenced again and then finally served a week in Strangeways Prison in 1975.

Upon his release from prison, Gyani-Ji's sons and supporters met him at the gates of the prison with his moped and flower garlands. They were joined by the press and Gyani-Ji proceeded to ride home wearing his turban and was stopped and booked seven times. He was prepared to serve an extended stay in prison for these actions.

The CRE, responding to his tenacity and moral purpose, appealed to the House of Lords, which upheld their complaint unequivocally. Summing up, Lord Fraser of Tulleybelton declared:

"... a group is identifiable in terms of its ethnic origins if it is a segment of the population distinguished from others by a sufficient combination of shared customs, beliefs, traditions and characteristics derived from a common or presumed common past, even if not drawn from what in biological terms is a common racial stock. It is that combination which gives them an historically determined social identity in their own eyes and in the eyes of those outside the group. They have a distinct social identity based, not simply on group cohesion and solidarity, but also on their belief as to their historical antecedents."

In short, they held that Sikhs could be deemed a racial or ethnic group, leading to the coining of a new, recognised legal term, 'ethno-religious'.

This ruling has paved the way for yesterday's historic amendment, allowing Sikhs to ride their mopeds, scooters or motorcycles without recourse to crash helmets or the removal of their turbans. A grand parade of proud, turban-wearing, helmet-less Sikhs rode through Manchester's city streets last night to cheering crowds and well-wishers.

The Cause of the 'Urban Turban' has been vindicated.

*

2007

How Vikram wishes he could have been a part of that parade. But he vividly recalls the occasion, of standing with his father in Albert Square, in front of the Town Hall, aged just eleven years, as the dozens of motorcycles rode round and round the Square.

Now he thinks about that victory every time he sits astride his *Bibaj Chetak*, so that he can rise above the taunts and jeers and sarcasm, as he does now, walking up the steps towards the front door of the *Gurdwara* along the gauntlet of his teasingly applauding fellow Committee-members. It feels a bit like he imagines it must be to step out of the tunnel at Maine Road, up into the sunlight, while being applauded by the opposition team for having emerged victorious.

*

2011

He experiences something not too dissimilar four years later, almost to the day, when the new *Gurdwara* is officially opened on the 14th of November, the first day of *Maghar*, just two months after the tenth anniversary of when the world changed forever with the bombing of the twin towers.

Vikram had heard countless distressing stories already from Sikh friends in America, who, since the attack, had been targeted by bigoted, frightened people, who could not distinguish Sikhs from Muslims, and who regarded everyone with a brown skin as an enemy.

Mercifully that has not been the case here in Manchester, where the Sikh community has grown from just seven hundred families half a century ago to more than fifteen thousand today, and as many again line the streets to witness the two-mile procession through Old Trafford and Whalley Range in what is a feast of colour and music. A two-minute silence in remembrance of the victims of 9/11 is the deliberately chosen prelude for what will be a two-hour celebration of fireworks as the Holy Book, the *Guru Granth Sahib*, covered in the *rumalla*, a white silk cloth, is carried shoulder-high and showered from above with rose petals. Vikram, together with his fellow Committee-members, is allowed the great privilege to be one of the final bearers, who lift it up the steps leading into the new temple, the completely re-imagined *Sri Guru Gobhind Singh Gurdwara*, flanked on either side by a Guard of Honour of twelve elders, each holding aloft a drawn sword, one of the five sacred objects that a Sikh must always carry. This is even better than walking out of the tunnel at Maine Road.

Once inside, beneath the temple's domed roof, a complete reading from the *Guru Granth Sahib* commences, which will continue uninterrupted for three days. The Holy Book is placed upon the *manj*, a raised platform with a cushioned bed, known as the *takht*. Suspended above this is the *chanani*, a canopy beneath which sits the *granthi*, the elder appointed to read the sacred text, which is written in *gurmukhi*, the official form of Punjabi. He holds a *chauri*, a ceremonial fan made from yak hair, which the *granthi* whisks above his head as he intones the words to the congregation, the *sangat*, who must at all times remain seated below the level of the *Guru Granth Sahib* as a measure of respect.

There are prayers and more music, there is all manner of free vegetarian food, which has been prepared in the *langar*, the large kitchen at the back of the temple, by members of the community as an act of *sewa*, selfless service to others. Vikram spots Geetha and Khavita among the *sangat* in the *Darbar Sahib*, the Main Prayer Hall, together with Priya and her husband, Duleep. Even Urja has been able to accompany them. They all of them wave encouragingly, but he manages to keep his own expression suitably serious, befitting the solemnity of the occasion. They are all of them wearing the *siropa*, the saffron-coloured piece of cloth that each of the attenders has been presented with as they entered the temple, signifying joy and union.

A reporter from the BBC asks him afterwards what the day means to him.

"It's impossible to put into words," he says. "We've waited such a long time for this moment. Everyone has worked so hard raising the necessary funds. Now at last we have a building that can be a genuine facility for the whole community. As well as religious ceremonies, we can now offer English and Punjabi language lessons, as well as health and fitness classes. There is a library, a gym, a sauna and steam room, in addition to the main temple. Anyone of any religion is welcome here. Please – come and join us."

Afterwards, when they are back home, they watch footage of the day on the local news.

"We must record it," says Vikram, rooting among a drawer for a blank video cassette. "Which of these can we use?" he says in a state of increasing anxiety. "Why doesn't anyone label them properly?"

"You can't use that one," intervenes Priya. "Or this, or this, or this. They're all of Duleep's and my wedding."

"Do you really need all of them? There must be hours and hours of it. It's not as if we'll ever watch all of it, is it?"

"*Bapu!*" cries Priya.

"I'm only asking," says Vikram, spreading out his hands defensively as he backs away

"And you can't use this one," chips in Khavita.

"Why not?"

"*Missi Roti*'s performance at the Caribbean Carnival last year."

Before Vikram can say anything, Geetha throws him a warning look.

"We must have a blank tape somewhere," he says, whirling about as if one might suddenly materialise right in front of him out of thin air.

"How about this one?" says Priya, pulling out one from the bottom of the pile. "It says, *'Bapu on his Bajaj Chetak'*. Surely we can tape over this?"

Geetha and Khavita are trying desperately to suppress their laughter.

"We could always film you again," suggests Priya helpfully, simultaneously biting the inside of her cheeks.

"Very well," agrees Vikram. "Quickly now, or we'll miss it."

The tape is inserted just in time. Priya presses 'record' just as the familiar strains of the *Look North* theme tune begin.

Only a tiny clip of what Vikram said to the reporter is included, but it is dutifully recorded onto VHS nevertheless.

"We've waited such a long time for this moment," he says, before the camera cuts to someone else.

"Not as long as you've been waiting for City to win the Premier League," jokes Duleep, who, much to Vikram's chagrin and dismay, supports that other Manchester team, who play in red, whose name Vikram will not suffer to be uttered in this house.

"Aiee!" shrieks Geetha as her husband and son-in-law playfully tease one another.

Priya and Khavita attempt to distract them by performing a mock-Bhangra dance, each swaying behind their saffron *siropa*.

"Aiee!" they cry as one.

In six months' time Duleep will have cause to regret the rashness of his jibe, for City will literally snatch the title from United's grasp in the most dramatic fashion – "Aguerooo!" – with a winning goal in the very last second of the very last match of the season, and Vikram will not take off his blue and white City scarf for a week.

But even this unforgettable moment will be eclipsed. As the family finishes watching the coverage of the opening of the new *Gurdwara* earlier that day, Priya announces somewhat casually, "We're going to need a few more blank tapes soon."

"Oh?" says Geetha, her senses shifting immediately into high alert. "Why is that?"

"Look," she says, holding out her phone with almost impish shyness.

At once Geetha and Khavita gather around her, straining to see. There on the tiny screen is the blurred image of the twenty-week scan of a baby.

"Aiee!" cry all three women together.

Vikram goes across to his son-in-law, claps him on the back and shakes him by the hand, all football rivalries forgotten, as Duleep looks sheepishly down.

*

2007

"Aiee!"

Geetha is on her knees, rocking back and forth. Urja looks down on her distraught daughter, who holds up the cut hair in disbelief.

"Not Priya, surely?"

Geetha shakes her head. "Khavita."

Urja sighs. She should have guessed. Khavita has always been the wilful one, the reckless one, and she has loved her for her fearlessness.

"Why?"

"Does there have to be a reason? You know what she can be like."

"I do, and that is why I am asking you. Something must have prompted this."

"I told you. She and Vikram are always quarrelling. Last night it was about this break-dancing nonsense. She's done this to spite him."

She immediately punches out a furious text on her phone.

"I know what you did."

"But it's not about break dancing, is it, *Dhi*?" says Urja, trying to instil some logic into the situation. "You know this, I know this. It goes much deeper. He tries to protect her too much. He always has. Can't you see? This is her way of saying that she can make her own decisions."

"That's not how Vikram will see it."

"No. I don't suppose it is."

Urja goes to the tiny kitchenette at the back of the annexe to make her daughter a glass of mint tea. Geetha is right. Vikram has always looked on Khavita as something of a cuckoo in the nest, something other than he had bargained for, and has never known how to deal with her wayward, independent streak. If only he wouldn't try always to pigeon-hole her, mould her into something she's not. If Vikram had been *her* son, she might have been able to say something to persuade him to act differently, but he isn't, and so she finds she must always bite her tongue. By the time she returns with the tea, Geetha has begun to calm herself a little.

"You know," says Urja, "it's what we all of us have thought of doing one time or another."

Geetha looks up at her mother in surprise.

"Even you?"

"Especially me. When you were little and always clinging to me, twisting your sticky fingers in and out of it, there was nothing I wanted more than to hack it all off there and then."

"But you didn't."

"No. I didn't have Khavita's courage."

"Is that what you call it?"

"I do."

"But it's forbidden. It goes against everything we stand for, everything Guru Nanak teaches us." She inclines her head towards the framed painting of the founder of their faith, whose portrait hangs in every Sikh's sitting room. "What will her father say? How am I going to tell him?"

"How are you going to tell him what?"

Geetha and Urja turn sharply. It is Priya who has asked this question, and she stands now on the threshold of the annexe, still not fully dressed, her own hair uncut and uncovered.

"I heard all the commotion and came down to see what on earth was going on. Are you OK, *Nani*? *Maa*?"

"I'm sorry we woke you," says Urja soothingly.

"You did."

"I know how you like to lie in on the rare days you are not working."

"I do."

"And you deserve it, after a full week of work."

"I do."

"It's your sister," wails Geetha, holding out the bag of hair once more. "*Bapu* will be furious."

"Then he will have to be furious with me," says Priya, thinking on her feet as quickly as she can.

"With you?" say Geetha and Urja simultaneously.

"Yes. It's all my fault. You see, last night I wanted to try out my new curling tongs – you know, the ones I brought home from the salon the other day? I'd been thinking about a new style Khavita might try for when she's my bridesmaid at the wedding next month. So – I…"

*

Back in Nando's Khav's phone pings again.

"What's going on?" says Abila. "Talk about hot line, innit?"

"It's from my sister. I'll just ignore it."

"Don't do that, girl friend. Why would your sister text you if it weren't important?"

"That's exactly why I ain't gonna read it."

"Let *me* then." Abila snatches Khav's phone and flips it open. Her eyes widen on stalks. "You gotta read this, Khav. It's unreal, innit?"

She holds the open phone out in front of Khav, who, scarcely believing what she's reading, grabs back her phone and reads the text twice more just to make sure.

> "You owe me big time, innit? I covered for you, right? I told *Maa* we had to cut your hair cos I burned it by accident last night. Best get your ass back here pronto.
> 💀💀💀💀💀💀💀💀"

Khav picks up her backpack and skate board at once. "Gotta go."

"D'you want me to come with?"

"No, ta."

"Text me, right?"

"Will do."

Wow, thinks Abila, after Khav has dashed off back down the escalator. I wish I could be a fly on their wall tonight…

*

…which in the end would have proved something of a damp squib to her, had she'd been there. If she was hoping for a blazing row, like something out of *Coronation Street*, she'd have been sorely disappointed. Instead of tears and recriminations, there was only laughter and the shaking of heads.

*

Priya is in full-on hairdressing-salon demo-mode.

"Creating voluminous, shiny, curly hair is the easiest way to glam up your look, no question about it. But if you aren't blessed with naturally curly hair, it can be a bit of a gamble to try to bring curls to life with a curling iron or wand. Isn't that right, ladies? So – to take the guesswork out of how to use a curling iron and make the overall styling process easier, just follow these five simple steps. Trust me. With the right tool and styling products, like hair mousse, heat protectant, and hair spray…" She holds up a sample of each to demonstrate. "…you'll be able to confidently curl your hair in no time."

She holds up the index finger of her left hand as she commences her five-step process, leaving her right free for displaying each new item.

"One: Carefully Select Your Equipment.

"Before buying your curling tool of choice, take a few things into consideration. For starters, determine if you prefer a curling iron with a clamp or a wand. A curling iron with a clamp, as you can probably guess, features a clamp that helps hold your hair in place as you curl. A wand curling iron has no clamp. Instead, you wrap your hair around the barrel and hold it in place while the curl forms. Your choice is all based on personal preference and which you find easier to use. Personally, I prefer the wand."

She displays it now, as if before a camera on a 'Home Beauty' TV Channel.

"Next, think about how curly you want your hair to be. If you're looking to create tightly-wound coils, you'll want to choose a barrel size of three quarters of an inch or less. If big, bouncy, beachy waves are more your jam, pick up a barrel-size of one-inch or even more.

"As far as *types* of curling tools go, ceramic and tourmaline are always a good bet, as they can help minimize the look of frizz." She holds out both hands in horror and screams. "Aiee!" before continuing with her demonstration.

"Next, there's the 'manual labour' aspect to consider. If winding your hair around your curling iron barrel isn't for you, an automatic curling iron, like this one…" She duly holds one up, "… may be just what the Doctor ordered. Or, in this case, your stylist!"

She beams a radiant camera smile, then pauses while she puts aside the curling wand, and holds up the first and second fingers of her left hand.

"Two: Start Your Look With Freshly Washed Hair.

"To get the most out of your perfectly curled look, it's always best to start off with clean hair. So hop in the shower and use a mixture of your favourite shampoo and conditioner formulated to manage even the tiniest appearance of – that word again – frizz…!"

On this occasion Priya pauses to pull a face like she's been electrocuted, stretching her hair sideways. "Personally," she continues, releasing her hair and tossing it to and fro in her best Bollywood manner, "I like to use *L'Oréal Paris EverPure*

Frizz-Defy Shampoo together with *L'Oréal Paris EverPure Frizz-Defy Conditioner*. I follow this up by..." She mimes squirting some gel onto the palms of her hands, rubbing them together with her highly painted and polished fingernails splayed outwards, before massaging her hair as she continues, "applying a hair mousse, like *L'Oréal Paris Advanced Hairstyle Curve It Elastic Curl Mousse*. This really helps add volume, especially to wet hair, while I cash in my bonus for fulfilling my quota of super-subtle product placements. Thank you, *L'Oréal*."

She holds up three fingers while introducing the next process.

"Three: Blow-Dry Your Hair."

She picks up her hair-drier as she continues the demonstration.

"Once your hair is about halfway air-dried, blow-dry it the rest of the way using a boar bristle brush until it's completely dry. Make sure to apply a heat protectant first, though, like the *L'Oréal Paris Advanced Hairstyle BLOW DRY IT Thermal Smoother Cream*."

"Just how many more mentions are you going to give them?" laughs Khavita.

"You can never have too many," answers Priya.

"It's true," adds Vikram, now completely caught up in the advert. "Who knows? *L'Oréal* may sponsor your salon, *Dhi*."

"*Bapu!*" complain Priya, Khavita and Geetha as one.

"Four," continues Priya, ploughing on regardless, "test your curling wand's heat."

"Aiee!" cries Geetha in anticipation of what she fears will come next.

Priya waves a dismissive hand. "Now that you've blow-dried your hair, it's time to get to work with that curling wand, ladies. It's up to you to show it just who's in charge here. Who's the boss?"

"Not me," wails Geetha, waving her hands from side to side.

"Then watch and learn, Madam.

"First, find the proper heat setting for your hair. Typically, it's a good idea to test out the lowest heat setting possible to see what type of curl it creates. From there, you can adjust the heat as needed before you start. This is where we went wrong, Khav, innit?"

"Not so much of the 'we'," says Khavita, flicking her fingers. "I had nothing to do with it."

By now both she and Priya are so caught up in the play-acting, they have almost convinced themselves that this is what actually happened. Priya ignores the interruption and continues.

"And finally, Five…" She waggles all five fingers. The nails are painted an iridescent, shocking pink, to which she now refers. "*Aphrodite's Hot Pink Nightie!*"

Vikram roars with approval. Khavita inwardly shakes her head. Priya has got him completely wrapped around those five painted fingers. She's always been able to do that, so that she is able to get away with anything, whereas she…

"Curl your hair," commands Priya, as if giving out orders on a military parade ground. "Create a section of hair to curl. The smaller the section, the tighter the curl. The larger the section, the looser the curl. Now – you want to curl your entire head of hair—not just the top layers—because the more curls you create, the fuller your hair will look, so – it's time to reach for your curling weapon of choice."

She holds up her wand and strikes a new pose.

"Calling All Lazy Girls—The Automatic Curling Iron Is Your Dream Come True."

She now shifts her gaze away from the imaginary TV camera, back to her 'live' audience in the sitting room.

"Open the clamp of your iron, then place it toward the root of your section of hair, with the hair placed between the open clamp and the iron. Be careful not to burn yourself."

"This is where we went wrong," explains Khav, stepping out of role..

"Shh," hisses Priya. "We're not done with the demo yet."

"Sorry," shrugs Khav, becoming the compliant client once more.

"Lightly close the clamp, then slide it down the section of hair until it's at the very end." Priya then matches what she says next with an appropriate gesture, fitting the action to the word. "Close and slide. Close and slide. Then..." She takes a handful of what remains of Khav's hair in her hand and adds for extra emphasis, "Twist, twist, twist!"

"Ow!"

"Twist the wand up toward your roots, wrapping the length of the section around it in the process. Wait about fifteen seconds for your hair to heat up..."

"Then...?"

"...flip it over and give it a good shake to loosen up your look for a more natural-looking finish." Priya demonstrates this on her sister with a flourish.

"Except..." Khavita, with her head tipped upside down, tries to look back up

"Somehow I got distracted" admist Priya matter-of-factly. "The next thing I know I can smell burning and smoke's coming out of the top of Khav's head, innit?" She mimes flapping away the smoke and throwing cold water over Khavita's head. "There was nothing else for it, *Maa*. All of her hair was singed. I had no choice but to cut it off."

Everyone looks forlornly at Khavita, who hangs her head to avoid their concerted, sorrowful stares.

"Priya saves the day!" announces Vikram. "Not to worry, Khavita," he adds, ruffling the top of his younger daughter's feathered head, "the one thing you can depend on about hair is…" He pauses. She looks up at him, smiling down on her.

"It will grow again," choruses everyone else.

Later, when everyone has gone to bed, Priya comes into her sister's bedroom.

"Why?" asks Khav. "Why did you step in and rescue me like that?"

"It's simple, sis. It's my wedding in a month, innit? I didn't want *Bapu* going off at the deep end and grounding you, maybe even banning you from being there."

Secretly Khav thinks this mightn't have been such a bad idea. There's been talk of nothing else but her sister's wedding for months. She's sick of it, and the last thing she wants to do is have to take part in it.

"If you weren't there," continues Priya, "all the Aunties'd keep wanting to know where you were, and their attention'd be on you instead of me, innit? And we can't have that, can we?"

"Suppose not," grins Khav.

"No suppose about it," grins Priya back, rubbing her knuckles hard along the top of Khav's now-shorn head. "Look," she says, bringing out a magazine she's been holding behind her back. "There are all sorts of tips in here for tying scarves in interesting, exotic ways. We'll get you looking like *Bapu*'s 'little princess' after all."

Two days later, when Khav is getting herself ready for school and is on the last minute as usual, she goes into the annexe to say a quick 'Hi' and 'Bye' to her *Nani*. She has a plain scarf tied round her head, so that it is not obvious that her hair has been cut, which she is still trying to fix properly.

"Here," says *Nani*, "let me."

Khavita meekly acquiesces.

"You may have fooled your father," she says, "with that tom-foolery of a charade you and your sister gave us the other night. You may have even fooled your mother. But you don't fool me, young lady, not for one minute. What on earth possessed you?"

Khavita's eyes immediately begin to well up.

"Don't tell me," says Urja, more kindly. "It was *Bapu*, wasn't it?"

Khavita nods.

"You wanted to get back at him somehow, didn't you, for the way he always seems to disapprove of what you do?"

Khavita nods again.

Urja places her fingers gently under her granddaughter's chin and tilts it up.

"He doesn't disapprove of you. He just doesn't understand you. He's frightened, that's all. For and of you. You're not what he imagines young girls to be like. You speak your mind. You don't like to conform just because that's what's expected of you. You need a better reason than that. Don't you?"

"How do you know all this?"

"Why do you think? Because I was just like you when I was your age."

Khavita's eyes widen. She simply can't imagine her *Nani* as a young girl.

"Sometimes you just have to learn to bite your tongue and be patient. He'll come round, you'll see. Now – off to school with you, or you'll be late. And we don't want that, do we, not on top of everything else?"

"No, *Nani*."

"He's right about one thing, though, your father."

"What's that?" asks Khavita incredulously.

"Your hair. It'll grow back again."

*

2013

Khav continues getting ready for her presentation. Her hair, in the past six years, has now grown back from just below the tip of her ear lobes to the centre of her back, between her shoulder blades. She automatically tucks where it has come loose back beneath her scarf.

*

2007

Before she begins the ceremony, Geetha lights a number of incense sticks, which she places in a circle around her. She requires to give the ritual she is about to perform its due observance.

She carefully collects the cut hair from the bin liner, before sitting cross-legged in the centre of the circle. She lays it horizontally in front of her along a length of white cotton, the one that had been used for Khavita's *naamh karan*, her naming ceremony in the week after she was born, and teases it out as gently as she can. She does not want to risk snapping a single strand of it.

Once she has uncoiled it, she weighs it down at one end beneath a small but heavy ceramic tile. Then she combs it through as delicately as is possible to untangle where it has become knotted and caught. This takes her a long time. By the time she has finished Geetha is in a near trance-like state. Satisfied that it is as smooth and free-flowing as she can get it, she lifts the ceramic tile and dabs the end that has been held underneath with a small amount of glue, just enough to bind the ends together and prevent it from unravelling completely. She then leaves this for half an hour to dry.

When she returns, she brings with her a bowl, which she has half-filled with hot water, into which she has mixed some baby shampoo and conditioner. She doesn't want anything that might be too strong or too active. She dips the hair into the water an inch at a time, softly massaging the diluted shampoo and conditioner into it with her fingertips. It feels like an act of enormous love. It reminds her of when Khavita had been just a few days old and she had washed her whole body in this way, caressing and pouring, fearful that she might break her if she were to attempt anything more than the lightest breath of air.

Once she has washed the entire length of cut hair in this way, she transfers it to another bowl, filled with only hot water, no soap or shampoo, and rinses it in the same painstaking, loving way. She then lays it out upon the piece of cotton once more, where she leaves it, to allow it to dry a little. While it is still slightly damp and malleable, she slowly proceeds to weave it into a three-way braid. She is so anxious not to damage it that it takes her an inordinate amount of time to complete a task which, when the hair was still attached to Khavita's head, she could have undertaken blindfold in a matter of seconds. Now it takes her almost an hour before she has finished it to her satisfaction. When it is done, she dips the remaining tips of hair which protrude from the final braided tie with a tiny dab of glue, so that now both ends are secured and will not fray.

She has finished it.

She steadies her breathing. The incense glows in the half-light of the room. She lifts up the braid and holds it as close to her face as she can, letting its familiar, lost fragrance flood her with all of the memories it contains. She inhales deeply many times. She does not know how long she keeps it there. Finally she lowers it, lies it across her lap, and lets it linger there a while longer. When the last incense stick burns out and the smoke sizzles and dies, she stands up. Her knees and hips are stiff from the amount of time she has been sitting there in the same position, not moving. She fetches a large glass jar from the kitchen. With great care she places the hair inside it, coiling it carefully, so that it forms a spiral. She then seals the jar with an air-tight lid. This will preserve it for many years to come. She will place it on a shelf in the wardrobe in her bedroom, where, each time she opens the door, she will see it in front of her, and the spiral of hair inside it, and remember.

*

2013

Khav quietly takes out the last of her props. It is the length of saffron *siropa* given to her on the day of the opening of the *Sri Guru Gobind Singh Gurdwara*. It is five metres long and she carefully unfolds it so that it forms a continuous strip across the studio floor, which will act as a demarcation between herself and her audience for when she delivers her presentation. When she has finished laying it out, she stands back and studies it for a while in silence.

Yes, she thinks. It will serve.

*

Tanya the technician arrives just as Clive said she would at nine o'clock. She is humming wordlessly and tunelessly to whatever song it is she is listening to on her outsized headphones, which she somehow manages to fit expertly around her impressive Afro. She is carrying a takeaway coffee, from which she swigs the last few dregs before depositing the cup in the correct recycling waste bin just outside the TV Studio. On seeing Khav, she flips off her headphones, switches off the playlist on her i-phone and cheerfully gives her a high five.

"Yo, Khav."

"Yo, Tan."

Tanya regards Khav's array of rucksacks, backpacks and cases with a wry grin.

"Looks like you've brought everything with you except the kitchen sink."

"Oh," laughs Khav, "that's what Clive said. Don't worry, that's in here somewhere too, I reckon."

The two of them share a smile.

"I'm really glad old Clive's been able to fix this up for you," says Tanya.

"Me too," agrees Khav.

"Let's give you a hand then. Where d'you want all this stuff?"

"Have we still got any of the old thirty-five millimetre reel cases from before we all went digital?"

Tanya's smile broadens.

"We just might have," she says. "Never throw anything away, that's my motto. You never know when it might come in handy."

"They're worth a couple of hundred quid at least on ebay these days."

"Don't tell the Dean that, or he'll have me selling them."

"Nah – Clive'd never let 'im."

"Clive wouldn't, that's true, but Clive's not the Dean, is he? What d'you want them for?"

Khav outlines her idea to Tanya, who nods.

"I reckon I could make that work. Leave it with me."

"Cheers, Tan."

"No problem." She switches the playlist on her phone back on. Khav can hear the distant buzzing of the track.

"What're you listening to?" she asks.

Tanya passes the headset to Khav, who places it to one ear. She raises her eyebrows in surprise. It's not what she was expecting. Tanya is always so cool Khav imagines she only listens to hardcore indie rap – Misha B or One Da – but to her surprise she finds herself listening to Lisa Stansfield. *All Around The World, This is the Right Time.*

"Rochdale's finest," says Tanya, taking back the headset. "Retro, innit? Forget Gracie Fields."

"Who?" says Khav.

Tanya pops her headphones back on and heads off in search of the reels. Khav watches her head nodding in time, as she sings somewhat tunelessly to: *"This is the right time – I can see it in your eyes…"*

Tanya has been an ever-present throughout Khav's time at MMU.

"Been around the world and I,I,I…"

Khav realises she knows nothing about her. None of them do. She normally keeps herself locked away in her cubby-hole of a store-room at the back of the studio, surrounded by the insides of computers, which she is constantly taking apart and then putting back together again. There's nothing she can't fix. But normally they can never penetrate her mask of dark glasses and head set. Khav doesn't think she's ever known Tanya to be so loquacious as she has been already in the past five minutes.

"I don't know when, I don't know why, I, I…"

Before Khav has finished unpacking her rucksack Tanya is back with a couple of film reels.

"Explain again what you wanna do with these then?"

Khav goes through it a second time. Tanya listens intently, nods, then grins again.

"Yeah, I can definitely do that."

"Thanks, Tan. I owe you."

"Let's see if it works first."

"It will. I have every faith."

"In me or you?"

"In both of us."

They laugh, then each carries on with their own particular task.

"How long have we got?"

Khav checks her phone.

"Forty-five minutes," she says.

"Ample time," says Tanya.

Another period of quiet concentration passes. Once again it is Tanya, uncharacteristically, who breaks it.

"What happened then?"

Khav looks up, frowning.

"Why did you have to cancel this presentation before?"

Khav looks down, biting her lip.

"Sorry," says Tanya. "None of my business."

"No, it's fine." This new side of Tanya invites the sharing of confidences. "The first time," she begins."

"First?"

"I had to cancel twice."

"Twice? I didn't know that."

"Yeah."

"Man, you've been through it."

*

2011

Khav is lying in bed wide awake. She's trying everything she can think of to get to sleep. Counting sheep, in both English and Punjabi, listing in order the chapters in each of the first five books in the *Game of Thrones* series, or *A Song of Ice & Fire* to give it its correct title, *A Game of Thrones* is the title of the first book only, but hey – that's what everyone knows it by – next she tries to allocate which character's perspective is featured in each chapter – it grows from nine in the first novel to thirty-one by the fifth – then she goes on to the three prequels, which set out the events that took place some ninety years before what happens in any of the novels, and finally she tries to speculate what might happen in the sixth and seventh, which have yet to be published... but it's no use. Nothing works. The problem is that Priya and Duleep are having sex – loudly – next door in her sister's bedroom, and the wall between their two rooms is paper-thin, so that nothing is left to the imagination. Unlike in *A Game of Thrones*, in which you don't have to imagine a thing because it is all shown right there in front of you, up close and personal. Not that Khav wants to imagine any of what might be going on next door. The only thing that could possibly be worse is if it were her parents she was overhearing, instead of her recently-married sister and her husband. But surely her parents don't do it any more? Please no, she thinks. At least *they* are spared having to listen to what *she* is having to, for *their* bedroom is further down on the opposite side of the landing.

Suddenly there's a pause.

Have they finished?

Please God, I hope so, thinks Khav.

But no – Duleep seems to have found a second wind and has started up again. Normally he is very quick – thank heaven for small mercies – but tonight is different for some reason. Perhaps Priya is giving him more encouragement than she usually does. Khav wonders how her sister feels about this nightly ritual. She never talks about it – at least, not to her – though before she and Duleep were married she could talk of nothing else. It was different then, for there was always the risk of their being found out, which probably added a certain frisson of excitement as they would have to grab what opportunities came their way before they were discovered – if ever Geetha and Vikram were out for the evening, or if they were baby-sitting Duleep's sister's two boys and they had finally got them to go to sleep, or, if they were really desperate, in the back of Duleep's Honda Jazz. Perhaps, thinks Khav, now that it's permissible, the excitement has gone and it's become more perfunctory. She can well imagine how it might become some kind of chore, something to be slotted into each day's list of activities, like shopping for groceries or cleaning your teeth.

Khav has tried sex herself just once. In Freshers' Week at MMU at the start of her first year there. She thought she should see what all the fuss was about.

*

2010

The Manchester Sikh Society held a welcome party, for students from Manchester and Salford Universities as well as those from MMU. Strictly no alcohol of course. But afterwards Mahendra, one of the older students, invited anyone who wanted to go back to his house on Ladybarn Road in Fallowfield, so she went along. There were non-Sikhs there too. And so there was alcohol. Mahendra asked her if she'd like a glass of wine, and she thought why not? It's not as if she'd been baptised, which would have made it strictly forbidden, though *Maa* had been dropping frequent hints about it ever since she had turned eighteen. "Have you thought about taking *amrit* yet?" she'd say. "It would be most auspicious now that you've started university, isn't it?" But Khav had kept putting her off. "Later," she'd say. "When I'm ready." But *Maa* wouldn't leave it alone. "When will that be?" she'd ask. Khav said she'd let her know as soon as she knew herself.

Anyway, one glass of wine led to a second, and the next thing she knew Mahendra was kissing her. It was pretty clear what he wanted, and so once again Khav asked herself, why not? He was also extremely good-looking, which made the question even easier for her to answer. He took her upstairs to his room, put on what he assumed to be romantic music and then, without any further preliminaries, immediately pounced. After a few seconds of clumsy fumbling with various items of clothing it was all over. It was not at all unpleasant, though she could hardly claim that the earth had moved. She was grateful that he had at least remembered to put on a condom in time.

He fell asleep almost instantly and lay there heavily on her for some while. Eventually she managed to ease herself out from under him, readjust her clothes and slip out of the room without waking him. She walked downstairs as casually as she could, but no one took any notice of her, they were all too intent on pursuing their own liaisons, so she squeezed past various couplings and let herself out through the front door. It was a warm September evening. She walked the less-than-half-mile between Ladybarn and Albion Roads, trying to assess how she felt about what had just happened. She supposed she should be thinking that something momentous had taken place, that she had become a woman, had crossed the threshold from girlhood to adulthood, but in truth she felt nothing of the kind. It didn't come close to the kind of excitement and fulfilment she had felt when she had taken part in her first throwdown on the concourse of Piccadilly Station three years before. Or from *Missi Roti*'s first public performance at the Moss Side Caribbean Carnival just six weeks before…

*

Less than a year after their first tentative beginnings at Platt Fields Community Centre, and just nine months since the surprise visit by Teniel had so excited and galvanised the girls, *Missi Roti* are invited to take part in the Manchester Caribbean Carnival in the heart of Moss Side. They have played some small local gigs and appeared in one or two unscheduled flash-mob throw-downs, but this is an altogether bigger deal.

There is some doubt as to when the first Carnival took place. Some say the summer of 1970, others a year later, in 1971. What *is* certain, though, is that a group of locals, mostly from St Kitts & Nevis, decided to hold an impromptu procession through the streets, ending up with a party, just like they used to back home. It was a success. A Committee was formed. Organisation was placed in the hands of female elders, women such as Claudia Jones, Locita Brandy and Anita Beauregard King. Every year since, traditional steel bands, dance troupes and floats have paraded through the neighbourhoods of Moss Side and Hulme, converging upon Alexandra Park for a weekend of community events, serious sound systems and incredible soul food. From such modest beginnings, the Carnival is now the largest of its kind anywhere in the country outside of Notting Hill. *Missi Roti* are programmed as part of these community celebrations.

They rehearse solidly for weeks. Khav wants to use music that is current, edgy, like Kanye West's *Power*.

"I'm livin' in the 21st century…
Every superhero needs a theme tune…"

But Showmi urges caution.

"Something old school. Something our parents remember. We don't want this to be our first and only time at the Carnival. Something classic.."

"Like what?"

"Like this, girl friend." And she presses 'play' on her boom box.

Showmi's right. It *is* a classic. *People*. Jimmy Cliff.

"There comes a time when we must fight again
For what we know to be the truth
Here comes the day when we must rise again
To save ourselves reclaim our youth…"

And all the girls at once join in with the chorus, as if the lyrics, written before any of them were born, have somehow been imbibed in the womb.

"So people – let's get together
And show our power
All over the world…"

Khav doesn't need further persuasion. For their last rehearsal she brings in Teniel once more, who enthuses with encouragement. "Sisters, you gonna take the stage by storm."

And so it proves.

The day of the Carnival is hot and sticky, the atmosphere one of joyful celebration from first till last. Some years there have been sparks of unrest, sudden flare-ups of trouble after too much weed and alcohol, fuelling what tensions might be simmering just below the surface of the day. But not this year. It's party time all the way. The floats provide a riot of colour. The dancers, with their towering head dresses and glittering rainbow costumes, shimmer in the heat like exotic tropical birds. But *Missi Roti*, in their street-cred baggies, don't care. They join the Grand Parade with all the other community groups, lifting their many flags and banners high in the air, which sizzles with the smells of jerk chicken, stuffed plantain, mango shrimp, callaloo with saltfish, seasoned red snapper.

The crowds converge on Alexandra Park, already high and humming with reggae, calypso and ska. Shirt-sleeved police officers dance with Rastas and Queens in their turbans and tams.

The Park has always been a place where the people have gathered, along its lime walks, its cricket pitch, its sunken bowling green and around its lake carved from the former lime pits. Keir Hardy organised the first Labour Party May Day Rally here. Emmeline Pankhurst spoke to several thousand Suffragettes here, inspiring one who heard her, the Music Hall singer Kitty Marion, to plant a bomb here. More recently The Buzzcocks played a *Rock Against Racism* gig here.

Khav feels giddy in the conjunction of it all. She recalls the lines of T.S. Eliot, whose *Four Quartets* she has just finished studying for her 'A' Levels, the results of which she will be getting the next week.

'Time present and time past
Are both perhaps present in time future
And time future contained in time past...'

When their name is called to go up onto the community stage on the Round Lawn adjacent to the Lake, she feels no fear, only excitement.

Afterwards, when they have come off to the cheers and applause of the thousands of revellers, all of them singing the words of Jimmy Cliff at the tops of their voices, just as Showmi had predicted they would, she is ecstatic.

This feeling is immeasurably superior to what she experiences six weeks later after her fumbled encounter with Mahendra. It is made even better by two letters she receives in the post the following week, one confirming her place on the Media Studies course at MMU following two As and a B in her 'A' Levels, the second from Z-Arts asking her to come in and meet them to talk about the possibility of *Missi Roti* becoming based there.

Hi Khavita, it reads

We really loved the appearance of *Missi Roti* at the Carnival last weekend and would love to hear what your future plans for the group might be.

We'd also be keen to discuss other ways you might like to work with us at Z-Arts. We are always on the look-out for emerging practitioners, and it is clear you have a talent for inspiring young people, who remain at the heart of our mission.

Please give me a call to arrange a time that will be convenient for you to come and see what we do here.

Kind regards

Yemi Bolatiwa
Community Engagement Officer
Z-Arts

Khav is bowled over when she visits the Centre the following week. It is in one of the oldest buildings still standing in Hulme, after the War and the many subsequent demolitions. It stopped being a Church in the 1960s when congregations had dropped below twenty. For a while it housed the Hallé Orchestra and the Northern Ballet Theatre for their rehearsals. Pavarotti sang there. Warren Beatty filmed a scene from *Reds* there, his film about the Russian Revolution, with its outside steps at the front standing in for the Chicago Court House. Then, in 2000, it opened its doors as Z-Arts, a resource for local people to take part in a wide and eclectic range of arts activities. Courtney Pine and Nitin Sawhney ran workshops there, Damien Hirst exhibited his pickled shark in the gallery there, Lenny Henry and Johnny Vegas performed there, and, much to Khav's delight, Benji Reid developed his *Life of a B-Boy* there, before transferring with wide acclaim to the National Theatre.

Now they run a host of holiday and after-school clubs for local kids. It is these particularly which Yemi wants to talk to Khav about.

"Apart from *Missi Roti*, do you have any other ideas?"

Khav pitches something that has been forming in the back of her mind throughout the last year, tentatively at first, then with more confidence as Yemi encourages it.

"I'd like to work with young people to make short films using their mobile phones," she says.

"What kind of films?"

"Anything that interests them, the things that matter to them. There might be things they want to rant about, complain about, or simply want to get off their chest. They might want to interview their friends, or take pictures of where they live, where they hang out. Or they might just want to film themselves singing and dancing."

"Sounds cool."

"I was thinking of calling it '*Digital Discoverers*'."

When she excitedly tells her parents about this, and how Yemi has suggested they try it out as a pilot during the summer holidays, Vikram is less than enthusiastic.

"You'll not have time," he says. "You need to prepare for the start of your degree course."

But when Khav contacts her tutor – a Dr Clive Archer – who has invited all prospective new students to contact him if they have any questions before they enrol, and he replies that the opportunities being offered to her by Z-Arts sound too good to be missed, Vikram is mollified.

"Ah well," he says, "if Dr Archer thinks it's a good idea, then of course you must do it."

Khav and her *Maa* share a private smile.

Already she is becoming a fixture there.

Yemi, she learns, is also a singer. She performs regular slots on *Reform Radio*.

"That's another of the great things about working here," she tells Khav. "They really encourage you to keep developing your own practice."

Once term begins at MMU, she continues to run a Saturday morning session of *Digital Discoverers* at Z-Arts. Reluctantly, she has had to give up *Missi Roti*, handing it on to the more-than-capable Showmi. At her final session with them, they solemnly present her with a *Missi Roti* baseball cap, which she frequently, and proudly, wears.

*

She's wearing it now, as she is walking home after the party on Ladybarn Road. She's glad of it. A light rain has started to fall. She turns her collar up against it. She rubs the hip of her left leg, which aches from where Mahendra had been lying on it.

She's glad to have reached home. She takes out her key and opens the front door as quietly as she can.

But it is not quiet enough, for no sooner has she stepped inside than she hears *Maa*'s voice calling from the kitchen.

"Khavita, is that you?"

"Yes, *Maa*."

"I couldn't sleep so I came downstairs for some *chai*. Would you like some?"

"No thanks, *Maa*. I'm tired. I think I'll go straight to bed."

"Was it a good party?"

"It was all right."

"Are you sure? You look different."

"No, I'm fine."

How did she know, thinks Khav later? Was it written across my face somehow? I didn't think so at the time, but perhaps it was. All I remember is climbing the stairs, heading for the sanctuary of my own room and getting straight into bed, only to hear that familiar rhythmic creaking of Priya and Duleep at it again next door through the wafer-thin wall.

"What might have been and what have been
Point to one end, which is always present…"

*

2011

Khav runs into Mahendra a couple of times in the weeks that follow on the MMU Campus and it's fine. They say hello but they don't engage in conversation. If anything he looks the more awkward of the two of them. Later, she sees him walking with somebody else, a white girl, who appears to have his measure. Good luck to them, she thinks.

As for herself, she has no more one-night stands. She has neither the taste nor inclination for them. Nor does she look to form any close attachments of any kind. She has lots of friends – male and female – and prefers it that way. There's always someone to hang out with on campus. Chloe, Petros, Lorrie. They're good mates and she likes the banter between them. It's only in her room at home that she finds herself brooding on these things, when she's forced to listen to her sister and her husband's nightly shuntings.

She finds that she has more and more sympathy for Duleep.

At first it was embarrassing, learning to navigate whose turn it was to use the bathroom and having him see her in her pyjamas and dressing gown. He was for ever apologising and scooting in and out as quickly as he could. But things have gradually settled over the four years he has now lived there. Now they can josh and joke with one another. She can hammer on the bathroom door and tell him to hurry up, or complain about the way he has smeared toothpaste in the sink, or sing loudly on the landing whenever she hears him farting.

But the truth is that she likes Duleep. He's kind and funny and interested in what she does. He's unfailingly nice to her sister, who's never been the easiest of people to live with – Khav and Priya have always fought like cat and dog, and still do sometimes – though less so since Duleep's arrival, for he has a way of acting as peacemaker between them without appearing to take sides, and he gets on really well with her father, who he can gently tease about his football and his scooter without ever showing the slightest disrespect. As for Vikram, he thanks his lucky stars that at least one of his outspoken, wayward daughters has made such a good match.

"We must try and found someone for you now, *Dhi*," he says repeatedly to Khavita. "Perhaps Duleep has a friend he can introduce you to…?"

Khav cringes and is grateful when Duleep jokes that he would not dream of subjecting one of his friends to such a fate. "How could they withstand this ordeal by fire?"

"Aiee!" replies Vikram. "Must I be cursed by having her stay in my house for ever?"

Geetha shoots her husband a look, as if to say 'not your house, but no matter.' Urja, helping Geetha to prepare the supper, says nothing.

There's nothing Khav would like more than to have her own flat, her independence, but for the moment she knows that's not financially possible, not while she's still a student, and not if it means exchanging one overcrowded household for another as somebody's young bride. She simply can't envisage it, especially if it means having perfunctory sex with someone every night. Her experience with Mahendra was not entirely disagreeable, but it has not left her with a desire to repeat it any time soon, if ever. She just can't imagine that kind of comfortable intimacy.

Even if she could, it must be difficult, she thinks, to start married life in the same house as your wife's parents, as Duleep has had to do, with her little sister just a few inches away on the other side of your bedroom wall. But there's no alternative. They can't afford a mortgage, not even on what Duleep and Priya earn combined, and rents are even higher. This way they get the chance to save up for a deposit on a place of their own – that's the theory anyway, but, with inflation topping five percent and house prices going up by double that amount in the last year alone, the prospect of that is becoming more and more remote, especially if a baby arrives and Priya has to give up her work at the salon…

Khav tries to stop this constantly whirling carousel in her brain.

At the same time Duleep appears to have exhausted himself next door. The loud groan when he comes sounds born more of desperation than exaltation, while Priya's whimpers and cries seem more like disappointment than pleasure.

Perhaps that's what all this extra effort is in aid of.

Priya wants a baby.

And whatever Priya wants, Priya gets.

Except with something like this, it's not something she can make happen all by herself, much as Khav suspects she'd like to.

Come to think of it, *Maa* has been dropping obvious hints lately, mentioning how she's run into one of Priya's old girl friends pushing a pram, or another one who's expecting, or another who's had twins. Heaven forbid.

*

2012

Six months later, and one week after Manchester City have secured their first Premier League title – "Aguerooo!" – Priya gives birth to a healthy nine-pound baby boy. "Aiee!"

"Have you thought of a name?" asks Vikram, still wearing his blue-and-white scarf. "Might I suggest Sergio?" he grins mischievously.

"*Bapu!*" wails Priya. "We are not naming our son after an Argentinian footballer."

"What about Mahendra then? A good Sikh name that also happens to correspond to that of the captain of the Indian cricket team."

"No," says Khavita hastily.

They all turn to look at her.

"Why ever not?" asks Geetha, eyeing her daughter sharply.

Khav can feel herself blushing. "I just don't like the name, that's all."

"Neither do I," says Priya. "Though Dhoni's proper gorgeous, innit?"

"What about Dilsher?" says Duleep, looking down at his son, who he is now nervously cradling in his arms.

"One who is determined and strong," says Urja, nodding. "Lion-hearted."

There is quiet as they separately ponder this.

"Yes," says Priya decisively. "I love it. Dilsher it is."

Duleep hands Dilsher back to Priya, as everyone gathers round to coo over the new-born lionheart, who sleeps blithely unaware that he is the centre of all their attention.

"*Doctor* Dilsher," muses Vikram delightedly. "*Judg*e Dilsher," he continues. "*Prime Minister* Dilsher," he concludes.

"Just so long as he's happy and healthy," smiles Geetha, shaking her head indulgently at her husband. "Go outside and polish your scooter," she says.

Vikram bows his head contritely.

"I'll join you," says Duleep. "Let us leave all the ladies together."

"About time too," laughs Priya.

Duleep and Vikram close the door quietly on them all and make their way downstairs.

"It's times like these," jokes Vikram, "when I almost wish I wasn't a Sikh."

Duleep's eyebrows shoot up.

"Then," explains Vikram, "we might smoke a cigar and drink a whisky."

Duleep laughs.

"I've a better idea," he says, and he goes to a cupboard in the kitchen, from which he produces a can of Brasso Three-in-One.

Laughing happily, father and son-in-law carry it out together to anoint the sacred *Bijaj Chetak*, whose shiny chrome surfaces will reflect their faces swollen with happiness.

Upstairs Dilsher opens his eyes, trying to make sense of the blurred, swimming figures gathered around him, which in time will sharpen into focus into shapes he will recognise.

Khav looks around at these same faces as Dilsher is handed between them. Now he is with Urja, with *Nani*, spanning four generations.

Home and the World.

*

1993

Khavita is one year old.

There is something wrong with her left leg. Geetha knows this. She has sensed it almost as soon as she was born. But her conviction has hardened during the last few weeks, when Khavita has been struggling to get to her feet, then always falling. She tries to tell Vikram but he will have none of it.

"Happy and healthy," he says. "That is what the doctor told us, isn't it? And look at her, smiling away so happily."

"That's wind," says Geetha dismissively.

"Well listen to her then, always chattering away to herself in that made-up language of hers."

"She's cross, she's frustrated. She wants to walk but she can't. There's something the matter with her leg."

"What? I can't see anything," he says, tickling the sole of his daughter's right foot.

"The other one," says Geetha in exasperation.

"What about it?"

"It's shorter."

"Nonsense. Have you measured it?"

"Yes."

"She wriggles and fidgets so much it's impossible to tell."

"Nearly two inches."

"What? Let me. Pass me the tape measure."

Geetha tries to keep Khavita still while Vikram attempts to measure each leg in turn. After several failed efforts, he finally manages to come up with one that he is satisfied with.

"*Hā'ē mērē rabā!*" cries Vikram. "You are right. Why didn't you say something before. We must take her to a doctor immediately."

"That is what I've been telling you, isn't it?"

The next day they have an appointment with their GP, who refers them to Mr Haroon Majeed, a consultant at St Mary's Children's Hospital on Oxford Road, opposite the University, who sees them six weeks later. Mr Majeed's specialism is in foot-and-ankle deformity correction. Together with his female assistant, Dr Sonia Abara, he examines Khavita with scrupulous care and attention to detail. Geetha marvels at how much more still her daughter is keeping for them than she ever does for her or Vikram. Having first removed her shoes and socks, Dr Abara then places the palms of her hands on each of Khavita's hip bones. Next, she gently begins to massage them for several seconds in order to render the muscles as loose as possible. After one minute, Mr Majeed checks the alignment of her ankle bones. He then lies her down upon a mat upon the floor in front of him and observes the way she moves, the way she crawls, and what happens when she tries to raise herself to a standing position. Finally, he asks Dr Abara to support her while he places each foot upon the mat, lifting first one, then the other, before nodding.

Having completed his examination, Mr Majeed hands Khavita over to Dr Abara, who sits her on her knee, where she remains quite placidly, while he explains his diagnosis.

"Your daughter has a classic case of LLD. That's leg length discrepancy. In layman's terms, she has one leg shorter than the other."

"With respect, Doctor, we know this," says Vikram. "But what does it mean? How did she get it? Can it be corrected? What must we do?"

Geetha looks keenly at her husband in a way that is intended to calm his growing agitation, which Mr Majeed immediately notices and quickly intervenes.

"It is likely she was born with it. But it is something that can develop in the early stages of a child growing, so it is probably more advanced now, which would explain why it was not picked up at the time. There are two types of LLD – functional and structural. In Functional LLD the bones are of equal length, but something has occurred, possibly the birth itself, which has altered the alignment of the hips, making the legs appear to be unequal. This can usually be treated with physical therapy, massage and specific exercises to correct the areas of imbalance and to aid posture. With Structural LLD either the femur – the thigh bone – or the tibia – the shin bone – is shorter in one leg than the other. This too is something the child may be born with, or it can develop in the first twelve months. From my initial examination, I suspect Khavita has the latter type – the structural variant – but I won't be sure until I've carried out further tests."

"What tests?" asks Vikram anxiously.

"Standard X-rays of the hips and legs, a CT scan of the soft tissue. All of them routine and nothing to cause alarm. But they will help me reach a more conclusive diagnosis." He turns now to his assistant. "Can you arrange for these as soon as possible, Dr Abara?"

Sonia nods and hands Khavita back to Geetha, so that she can make the necessary notes.

"If you are correct, Doctor, what is the treatment?"

"The same as for Functional LLD – physiotherapy, massage, exercise – but it may also be necessary for her shoes – when she begins walking more sturdily – to be fitted with a specially manufactured lift, and…" He pauses.

"Yes?" asks Vikram anxiously, suspecting already what the answer will be.

"I cannot rule out the need for possible surgery."

Vikram gasps involuntarily.

"But we are not at that stage yet," says Mr Majeed hurriedly, "and we may never be. In most cases it is not necessary. The most likely scenario is that your daughter's gait will be affected, that's all, and she will probably tire quite quickly. She may walk with a slight limp to compensate for the difference in leg length, but, with the right type of shoe, it will hardly be noticeable."

"Yes, Doctor," says Geetha, before Vikram can interrupt further. "Thank you. We're most grateful. Now – we mustn't take up any more of your time." She hoists Khavita up on to her hip, collects her bag and is already halfway out of the door when Mr Majeed calls back to her.

"Sonia here will be in touch. We shall monitor the situation very closely. Every month for the next six months. Then we'll know more. You need have no worries, Mr and Mrs Singh. Thanks to your diligence we have caught this early. There is no reason why your daughter should not be able to participate in full and active life."

Once they are outside in the fresh air again, Vikram takes Khavita from his wife and holds her closely to him.

"My little princess," he whispers to her, his eyes shining with tears.

Khavita looks back at her father, quite unperturbed, and giggles.

*

1992

When the baby is born, Geetha and Vikram follow to the letter the Instructions for Ceremonies, as set out in the *Sikh Rehat Mariyada*.

Geetha whispers the words of the *mool mantar*, the special prayer composed by Guru Nanak, into the baby's ear, before placing a drop of honey onto the baby's tongue. Two weeks later they visit the *gurdwara*, the temporary one on Upper Chorlton Road, for the *Naam Karan*, the naming ceremony. The *Granthi*, the chief elder, opens the *Guru Granth Sahib* randomly and reads the first passage his eyes light upon. Then, Vikram and Geetha are invited to choose a name for the baby using the first letter of the hymn on the same page.

The letter is 'K'.

"Khavita," they say together.

The *Granthi* announces this to the *sangat*, the small congregation, who sit below the level of the Holy Book.

"Khavita," he repeats.

" 'Princess'," responds the sangat.

"And let her have the surname 'Kaur'."

" 'Lioness'," they answer.

Afterwards, the *karah parshad*, a sweet dish made from flour, semolina, butter and sugar, is distributed among the *sangat*.

Vikram proudly carries his wide-awake daughter around the hall.

"I will protect you always," he silently vows.

Khavita determinedly wriggles to be free of his smothering arms.

*

2013

In the TV Studio Khav takes off her built-up shoe and places it in front of her in the centre of the circle she has created for her presentation.

*

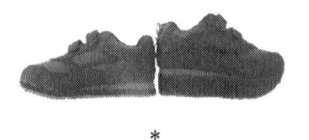

1999

Khavita is nearly eight years old. She has recently begun to think of herself as Khav. That is what some of the children call her at school. She has started to make several good friends. But there are still others who tease and bully her about her foot, the way she drags it sometimes, especially when she's tired.

"Khavita, Khavita, let's trip her up and beat her," they chant in the playground.

If Priya hears them, they stop at once. She'll box their ears if they don't. They know this because they've seen her do it. Afterwards Priya will croon to her sister, "Khavita, Khavita, no one will defeat her…"

But Priya will be starting secondary school in September, and Khav worries that, without her big sister there to protect her, the bullying will get worse. "You'll have to toughen up," says Priya simply. Khav nods. Her sister has her own worries now. From being the biggest fish in what has been a pretty small pond, she now faces the prospect of becoming a minnow in a very large ocean. But she's not deterred by this. She has her own circle of friends. They will look out for each other.

"You must learn to do the same," she tells Khav, so Khav has recently taken to being the class clown, a strategy that seems, so far, to be working, although her teacher has expressed some concern to Vikram and Geetha.

"You need to watch that tongue of yours," *Bapu* has said, while *Maa* says nothing. She just looks at her with a frown and raises a warning forefinger. That is usually enough to prevent Khav from answering back.

Today is the last Saturday of the summer holidays. *Bapu* has ridden off on his *Bajaj Chetak* to the temple as usual, while *Maa* has taken Priya off into the centre of town to buy her her new school uniform.

"Why must we always leave things to the last minute?" complains Priya. "Suba and Mayuri got theirs ages ago."

"Because you keep growing so fast, young lady," answers Geetha. "I don't want to be having to alter it before you even start."

Priya sees the sense in this, but she pouts anyway. She's been dying to get together with Suba and Mayuri, so that they can all three of them try on their uniforms and see how they might customise them to make them more fashionable. Now she'll have no time before their first day next week.

This means that Khav is being looked after by her *Nani*. Normally she likes this. She will do things for her *Nani* that she would never do willingly for her *Maa*, like cooking and baking, but her *Nani* is not feeling too well this morning.

"I can't seem to get going somehow," she says. "I think I'll just have a lie-down for half an hour. You go out into the garden for some fresh air. I'll be right as rain again soon."

And she will be. Khav knows this. Her *Nani*'s just old, that's all. Khav can't imagine ever getting old. She goes outside into the small garden at the back of the house, which is surrounded by a wooden fence on one side, some railings at the end, which separate it off from the park in Platt Fields, and a high hedge on the other side, which marks the boundary with next door, where Dr Chadwick lives. Dr Chadwick is old too, thinks Khav, but nothing like her *Nani*. For one thing, she insists on being called Grace. "It's my name," she says. "What else should you call me?" And for another, she still rides a bicycle. She goes everywhere on it, even to work down the busy Wilmslow Road in the middle of rush hour. Khav would like to ride a bike. But *Bapu* will not hear of it. Because of her foot.

She takes a football with her into the garden and begins to dribble with it. She's not very good, but she's getting better, she thinks. She decides to practise some free kicks. She wants to bend it like Beckham, only she's not allowed to mention his name in *Bapu*'s hearing, nor anyone's who plays for that other team in Manchester, the one in red, whose existence must not be acknowledged, especially this year, after they have won that impossible treble of Premiership Title, FA Cup and Champions League. "One day," *Bapu* had muttered as fervently as any prayer offered in the *Gurdwara*, "we shall do the same..." Khav says nothing. Nor does Priya. She thinks David Beckham's "proper gorgeous", regardless of which team he plays for.

Khav lines up her free kick. Her target is the hawthorn tree that grows up out of the high hedge. She decides to take a curved run-up. Like Beckham does. But just as she reaches the ball, her weak foot gives way from under her, causing her to balloon the ball high into the air. It still manages to hit the tree somehow, but right near the top, where it lodges itself in the topmost branches.

Khav frowns. She picks herself up. She's not hurt, just cross. She looks around. Her *Nani* is not in the kitchen. She still mustn't be downstairs yet. She can't leave the ball in the tree because *Bapu* will be cross if it's still there when he gets back. Khav knows she's not meant to play football unsupervised. She picks up the clothes prop that's used for the washing line and tries to use it to dislodge the ball from the tree, but it's not long enough. When she shakes some of the lower branches to see if that might somehow work it free, she only succeeds in making it become wedged in even more.

She decides she'll have to climb the tree and fetch it down herself. There's nothing else for it. If she uses part of the hedge to get a foothold, she should be able to make it. She mentally works out a route that she can follow. She wriggles her way through the middle of the hedge, which is full of sharp thorns that prickle and snag at her clothes. *Maa* will not be best pleased, but there's nothing she can do about that. She'll have to try and attend to that later, after she gets down. She reaches the first branch of the tree, onto which she manoeuvres herself carefully. She half-wonders, at the last moment, whether it will take her weight, but it does so easily. She sidles along it towards the trunk, then pauses to get her bearings. She looks down on the hedge. She's never seen it from this perspective before. She hasn't realised just how thickly it has grown. It is a source of much discontent for *Bapu*, a literal thorn in his side, one of many, for there is always something he finds to complain about.

"It is like the Great Hedge of India," he rails.

"What's that?" Khav has asked him.

"It's nothing," says her *Nani*. "Nothing at all. It's not even there any more."

"But this is," says her *Bapu*, pointing at it with a pair of shears, which he uses to attack his side of it with a will two or three times each year. "The Great Hedge of India," he explains to Khav between hacks, "was something the British put up right across India."

"Why?"

"To collect taxes on the salt being carried from one part of the country to the other. It was a way of keeping us down. Ghandi-ji knew this of course. It was why he led the Glorious Salt March."

Khav has no idea what her *Bapu* is talking about. "I thought *we* were British," she says.

"We are," he replies proudly. "But we are Indian also," he adds. "And Sikh."

"And Mancunian," chips in Priya, winking at *Maa*, who bites her lip to stop herself from laughing.

"More than a thousand miles it ran for," says Vikram, resuming his attack upon the hedge. "From Pakistan in the north-west, right through the Punjab, down into Maharashtra, then out towards Orissa in the east."

"What happened to it?" asks Khav.

"It became too expensive to keep up. It needed more than fourteen thousand soldiers to patrol it. *Jemadars*, they were called. Your great-great-grandfather was one." Priya gives a mock salute. Vikram frowns, then continues.

"The trees, which were all imported from England, didn't take to the Indian climate, and many of them withered away and died. Like I wish this would," he says, hacking at a particular recalcitrant branch with renewed vigour. "Eventually they abandoned it. I wish I could say the same about this one." He wipes the sweat from his forehead with the back of his hand. "Why can't we have a nice easy fence like the one on the opposite side?"

"Because," says *Nani* with unusual force, "Jabez planted that hedge when he and Mary first moved in from when they had to leave the Lodge at Philips Park. It was his pride and joy, that hedge. A haven for birds, full of white and pink blossom in the spring. He and Mary were such wonderful neighbours. There isn't a day goes by that I don't miss them, and Dr Grace does a marvellous job in keeping it up."

Vikram falls uncharacteristically silent. He knows there is nothing he can say to change his mother-in-law's mind. He only met Jabez and Mary a couple of times. They died shortly after he and Geetha were married. First Mary, then, a few weeks afterwards, Jabez, as if once one of them had gone, the other could not wait to follow on, like the pain a person still feels in a limb that has been severed. As for Dr Chadwick – Grace – Vikram has never been able to fathom her. She wrong-foots him at every turn. She is even more forthright in expressing her views than he is, and is never afraid of telling him exactly what she thinks on any given topic, especially if her view is contrary to his. Like her refusal to even consider the removal of the hedge. There is no doubting her tenacity and combativeness. Perhaps that is why she never married, he speculates. But she is a doctor of science, an esteemed archaeologist, and Vikram, whatever else he may be, is unshakeable in his respect and admiration for anyone with a university degree. He looks back at his younger daughter, who is always asking him questions, and who is so often dissatisfied with his answers, and wonders whether she might be the first from their family to achieve such an honour. He knows that such a route is not for Priya. Her head is too much in the clouds, if it is not to be found buried in her fashion magazines. But Khavita? Perhaps. And so he must protect her as best he can from the dangers of this world.

Khav considers this as she stands on the lower branch of the tree, looking down upon the hedge. She gazes back up towards the canopy where the ball remains firmly fixed. If *Bapu* caught her climbing trees, there'd be hell to pay. Best be quick then, she tells herself. She puffs out her cheeks and starts once more to climb.

At first all goes well. She progresses up the tree, branch by branch, until finally she is almost within reach of the ball. But not quite. She stretches out her fingers, which are tantalisingly close to it, but not so near that she can grasp it. She needs to climb a little higher. She tests the weight of the branch above her by pulling on it gently with her right hand. Yes, she thinks, if I'm careful, it will carry me. She tentatively hauls herself up towards it. She straddles it with both legs. It bows and bends beneath her, but it holds. Now, all that she has to do is to ease herself along it until she is able to reach out and collect the ball. She pulls her way forward, slowly, inch by agonising inch.

Then, just as she is about to make the last stretch towards the ball, she slips. Instead of straddling the branch, she finds herself hanging upside down from it. She desperately tries to right herself, but her actions are too sudden, too hasty. The branch bends down at an alarming angle. Her fingers are no longer able to maintain their grip. She feels the bark sliding through them, scratching her with their sharp burrs and thorns, and then, almost before she realises it, she is free of it, falling through thin air, the ball tumbling after her, bouncing on her chest and head on its passage towards the ground, which now rises up rapidly to meet her, only for the hedge, at the very last moment, to break her fall, cushioning her from the worst of it, so that in the end she plunges through it, until it dispatches her in a heap upon the pile of recently mown grass cuttings in next door's garden, softening her fall.

Grace, who has been watching Khavita from her kitchen window, is galvanised into instant action. The expression on her face, which, earlier, as she watched Khavita's determined progress up the tree, was one of pleasure and amusement, has swiftly turned to one of anxiety and concern. She hurries outside and is by Khavita's side before the girl has fully realised what has happened.

"Can you stand?" she asks.

Khav does so.

"Can you wiggle your fingers? Like this?"

Khav copies the actions.

"Did you hit your head?"

"No," says Khav. "I don't think so."

"Follow this with your eyes," says Grace, and she raises her index finger in front of Khav's face. Khav follows its progress seemingly without difficulty.

"You've been lucky," says Grace. "Come inside and let me get you a drink."

Khav hobbles her way towards the back door.

"Where does it hurt?" asks Grace.

"All over," says Khav sheepishly.

She tries to brush off the worst of the grass from her clothes before stepping inside.

"Don't bother about that," says Grace. "Here." She hands her a glass of water, which Khav drinks in a single swallow. She starts to go quite pale.

"You'd better sit down," instructs Grace, and she leads her into the front room. "You need some sugar. Wait here."

Khav sits in an armchair with a high back. She suddenly seems very small and young.

"I shan't be long," says Grace.

Khav looks towards the fireplace opposite her. Hanging on the wall above the mantelpiece is a framed child's drawing. It's of the skeleton of an elephant. It eyeless sockets appear to be staring straight at her. Khav finds it hard to look away from them.

"Here we are," says Grace, returning with a tray. "Eat this." She hands Khav a plate with a sandwich on it.

"Is it medicine?" asks Khav.

"Sort of," says Grace. "Think of it more as a reward for being so brave."

"What is it?"

"A sugar butty."

Khav's eyes widen.

"This is what my mother used to give me if I ever fell out of a tree."

Khav's eyes widen even further.

"Yes, I know it's hard to believe. But once I was the same age that you are now, and there was nothing I liked better than to climb trees. There was one in the Park just outside our front door. I've a picture somewhere."

She moves across to the sideboard where there are several framed photographs arranged together. While she is looking for the one she wants, Khav takes a tentative sniff of her sugar butty. It's made of white sliced bread, spread with thick slabs of butter, then sprinkled liberally with caster sugar, before being folded over in two like a doorstep. She cautiously takes a small bite. She feels at once the rush of sweetness and immediately takes another larger bite. It's the most delicious thing she's ever tasted, partly because she knows that somehow it's forbidden. She savours the crunchiness of the sugar dissolving under her teeth.

"Dr Chadwick," she whispers between mouthfuls.

"Now what have I told you about that? My name's Grace."

"Sorry – Grace – are you a real doctor?"

"I am, Khavita, but not of medicine."

Khav supposes this is all right, so she continues to munch her way delightedly through the rest of her sugar butty.

"Here we are," says Grace, picking up one of the photographs. "This is the one I was looking for."

She brings it across to Khav. It shows a young girl, dressed as a pirate, swinging from a rope looped around the branch of a tree.

"Is this you?" asks Khav, her eyes now practically on stalks. The thought that this old woman standing next to her now and the child in the photograph being the same person is something she finds hard to believe.

"A long time ago. I was seven, I think."

"The same age as me."

But what Khav can't take her eyes from is the calliper the child – Grace when she was just seven too – is wearing on her leg. Surreptitiously she tries to see whether she is still wearing one today, but it's difficult to tell beneath her trousers.

"I know what you're wondering," says Grace, smiling, "and the answer's yes." She raises the trouser covering her left leg to reveal the iron brace. "It's attached to the shoe and it hinges at the knee." She demonstrates. "That's how I'm able to ride my bike."

"My *Bapu* won't let me ride a bike."

"I don't see why you shouldn't."

Khav lowers her gaze.

"Because of your foot?"

Khav quickly looks up.

"I know about that," says Grace. "Your mother told me one time. She wondered if I might be able to help you."

"What did you say?"

"I said 'yes', of course, but only when the time is right. I reckon that time has come, don't you?"

Khav finds that there is a hard lump in her throat, preventing her from being able to speak, so she nods her head as seriously as she can.

"Have your drink first," says Grace. "It's hot Vimto. Just the thing after a fall from a tree."

"What's Vimto?"

"What's Vimto?! And you a Manchester girl born and bred?! It's a Manchester Institution, that's what it is. It's one of the things that's made us who we are. It's a cordial made from grapes, berries and spices. 'For Vim and Vigour!' They first started making it to a secret recipe nearly a hundred years ago in a shed at the back of a house on Granby Row. Now they've got factories right around the world. The biggest one of all's in Bangalore. Now drink up."

Khav does as she's bid and finds that this is another magical discovery. As soon as she's finished it, she puts down the mug with a huge smile on her face, made to look even bigger by the raspberry-coloured clown's grin she has acquired around her mouth.

"That's better," says Grace, laughing. She perches on the arm of the chair next to where Khav is sitting, looking up at her with a certain trepidation behind the Vimto smile. "You may find this hard to believe," she continues, "but you and I have quite a lot in common. We both have one leg that's shorter than the other. It's something we were both born with. In your case it was LLD, in mine it was polio. That's a disease that's easily preventable today. There's a vaccine. You take it on a sugar lump." They both smile. "And in your case, there are exercises and physio you can do. But there are differences. I have to wear this leg-iron, whereas you have to wear a built-up shoe. But we have to wear them for the whole of our lives, so there's no point complaining, it's just the way it is. But that's good, because they help us to do things we otherwise wouldn't be able to. Like play football and climb trees."

"But I can't do either of those things. Not well anyway. I kicked the ball too high, then I fell out of the tree."

"Phooey!"

Khav looks up, surprised. That's not the kind of thing she expects to hear an old woman come out with. But Grace, it seems, is full of surprises. She's not like any other old person she's ever met before. In fact, she's not like any other person at all.

"Do you not think I didn't fall out of trees when I was your age? I was always doing it. The same when I was riding my bike. I came off every day. But did it stop me? No Siree, Bob! When I saw other kids spin a one-eighty skid, I made sure I could do a three-sixty. When I fell out of a tree, I just found a better way to climb it next time. There's nothing you can't do, Khavita. Not once you set your mind to it."

Khav nods, trying to take this in.

Grace suddenly claps her hand in front of her mouth.

"Who's meant to be minding you today?"

"My *Nani* – why?"

"She'll be wondering where you've got to."

"She was having a lie-down earlier."

"Even more reason for me to go round and tell her where you are. Don't worry – I won't say anything about you falling out of a tree. I'll just say you came round to ask for your ball back. Pour yourself another Vimto. There's more in a jug in the kitchen. I won't be long." She lurches purposefully towards the front door.

Khav is about to get herself that second mug, when her eye is caught once more by the drawing of the skeleton of the elephant above the fireplace. She moves to take a closer look at it. It's been done with meticulous care, even down to the wires and steel rods that are holding it all in place. In the bottom right hand corner, she notices, is a small signature:

Grace Chadwick, aged nine years.

This is a day like no other. A day filled with surprise and wonder.

Grace returns, talking as she comes back though the front door, and lumbers down the hallway.

"Your *Nani* is fine. She says to stay as long as you like, but don't forget you promised to help her later bake the eggless cake with orange juice."

Khav nods.

"Mmm," says Grace. "Sounds delicious. Perhaps you might save me a piece?"

"I will. If my sister doesn't scoff it all first. It's her favourite."

Grace laughs as she comes back into the front room.

"Ah," she says, taking in where Khav is standing, "I see you've discovered Maharajah?"

"Maharajah?"

"The Elephant who walked all the way from Edinburgh to Manchester."

"Oh yes. My *Nani* talks about him."

"Well, this is his skeleton."

"And you drew him?"

"I did. It was in the middle of the War. Manchester had been badly bombed. We caught a bus that had to keep changing its route because of all the fallen buildings and craters. The skeleton was put on show in the Museum and there was a school trip to go and see him."

"Did you like school, Grace?"

"Yes. Mostly. Though there was one thing that made it difficult."

Khav automatically looks at her leg.

"No, not that. Everyone was used to that. Much more difficult than that was the fact that my teacher was my sister."

Khav's eyebrows shoot to the top of her head. The idea of Priya ever being her teacher is just too appalling to imagine.

"I know. It was totally embarrassing at first. Everyone assumed I'd be the teacher's pet, but Harriet – my sister – soon made it clear that there'd be no favouritism as far as I was concerned. If anything, she was tougher on me than anyone else. But that was fine. She knew not to make allowances, that I'd hate that. Whenever we had Sports Day, I just ran in the same races as all the other kids."

"Did you win?"

"Of course not, don't be silly. But I didn't come last." She grins, which then fades. "Harriet was a good teacher. I miss her."

"What happened to her?"

"She died, Khav – what do you think? She was a fair bit older than me. But she had a good life. She was happy." She pauses a moment, then carries on. "We all die, Khav. It's the natural order of things. But we leave something of ourselves behind. In the things we say and do, the people we meet, who have memories of us after we've gone, which are passed on down to those who come after us. We must try to make our mark then, mustn't we? Like Maharajah did. Just look at him.

Isn't he magnificent? The way he holds our gaze even when he's just old bones. I remember I drew this very quickly. I spent much longer just looking at him, the way his skeleton was put together. He was so big. He towered over me. If I'd stretched my arm up as high as I could, I still wouldn't have been able to reach even the top of his leg. Then I looked more closely at each one of those legs. And I discovered something really important. They're all of them different. Not one of them is the same length as another. Yet when he ran, he would have kicked up such great clouds of dust with every step. People would have been able to see him coming from miles around. And before they could see him, they would hear him. A deep rumbling rising from below the surface of the earth. And I could tell all of this just from looking at his bones. That was when I knew."

"What?" whispers Khav.

"What I wanted to be when I left school. An archaeologist. Someone who studies the past from the things that are left behind."

"Like bones."

"That's right, Khavita. Like bones."

Khav looks at the drawing a long time. Grace watches her with enormous pleasure.

"Can I ask you a question?" says Khav at last.

"Of course you can. Anything you like."

"Really? Anything?"

"That's what I said."

"Well – you know how you ask me to call you 'Grace' instead of 'Dr Chadwick'?"

"Yes."

"I don't want to be Khavita any more. Will you call me Khav please?"

Grace considers the question with proper seriousness. "Perfect," she pronounces. "Khav suits you much better."

Khav beams.

"But what about your father?"

"Oh," says Khav, laughing, "I'll always be Khavita to him, I expect."

"That doesn't matter. We're all of us different people, depending on who we are with." Grace ruffles the top of Khav's head. "Time you were getting back, I think. You've an eggless cake with orange juice to bake before your sister gets back. Come along."

Khav begins to head towards the hallway.

"And where do you think you're going, young lady?"

"To the front door."

"I don't think so."

"What do you mean?"

"You need to return by the same way you arrived." Grace puts her hands on Khav's shoulders and propels her towards the back door and the garden.

"But...?"

"Only this time you're going to climb the tree without falling out of it."

Khav looks up at Grace and can see that her mind is quite made up. There is no way she is going to change it.

"Are you sure?" she says.

"I couldn't be more so. I have complete confidence in you."

Khav looks up at the tree.

"Work out your route before you start. Where to put your hands and feet. Which branches will support you and which you think won't. Of course, there's no way of knowing for certain, not until you're actually up there. Trust your instincts. Believe in yourself."

Khav stares intently at the tree, the way it emerges in a series of twists and knots from out of the hedge, the way it all connects beneath the outer layer of leaves, like the bones of a skeleton.

She marches towards it. She reaches up her arm to find a secure hand-hold, which she grasps tightly. Then she raises her leg, the shorter one, and places the built-up shoe firmly into a cleft between two lower branches. It holds. She hauls herself up, then looks for where is best to make her next move.

That's my girl, thinks Grace, watching from below. You've started.

Soon Khav begins to find her rhythm, progressing smoothly and confidently from branch to branch, until finally she reaches a spot from where she can comfortably jump the rest of the way to the ground and a softer landing than the one she experienced just an hour before.

With a final flourish she gives a triumphant wave to Grace before disappearing behind the hedge. Grace tosses the ball back over.

"Thanks," Khav shouts back, "for everything." Then, a few seconds later, Grace hears her calling out cheerfully, "Hi, *Nani*. Here I am. Have you had a good rest? That's good. I'm home now."

*

2013

"Tanya?"

"Yes, Khav?"

"Do you have any drinking glasses?"

"What kind?"

"Any. They don't have to match."

"How many?"

"Ten, twelve?"

"I reckon I might be able to rustle up that many for you. I can raid the cupboard where we keep stuff for receptions."

"Great."

"What do you need them for?"

Khav takes from her rucksack a bottle of Vimto.

"I want to give everyone who comes a small taste of it right before I start."

"Cool. Leave it with me."

"Thanks, Tan. You're a star."

"I know it."

They share a deep smile.

*

2012

It's all change at Albion Road.

Dilsher is eight months old, as bright as a button. He's the apple of everyone's eye. With a smile that can charm the birds from the trees. But he doesn't sleep. Hardly at all. He cat-naps. Ten minutes here, half an hour there. Then he's ready for action. Priya and Duleep are exhausted. So too is Khav. She's no longer kept awake by her sister and her husband having sex, but by the product of it, who roars all night long. Lion*tongue* as much as lion*heart*. Occasionally she offers to have Dilsher for an hour or two, just to give them a break. But if he ever starts to cry or grizzle, Priya is back like a shot, like she's programmed.

So Khav decides to decamp downstairs to the sitting room, where there's now a sofa-bed.

"Let Dilsher have my room," she tells Priya, "and you and Duleep can take it in turns to keep him occupied through the night. He'll find a routine eventually, and then he'll need his own room anyway. I'll be fine downstairs, don't worry."

Priya is too tired to argue. She thanks Khav, then bursts into tears. She does that a lot these days. Her face is devoid of all make-up and looks washed out. She no longer bothers to paint her nails. Even her hair has lost its lustre and now hangs like limp rags on either side of her worn-out face.

There's no way I'm ever havin' kids, Khav tells herself.

It's much better downstairs. She should've done this years ago, she thinks. She can still occasionally hear Dilsher when his roars reach volcanic proportions, but mostly she can't. There are simply too many doors in between them now, and she sleeps better than she has since before Priya got married.

But it still only takes the slightest noise to wake her.

Nani, she learns, sleeps even more lightly than she does.

One night Khav hears her padding about in the annexe next to the sitting room. Wondering if she is OK, she slides back the connecting doors to discover her polishing her ornaments. It's just gone three in the morning and still dark outside.

"What are you doing, *Nani*?" she whispers.

"What does it look like I'm doing, *Dhoti*?" she answers. "Here – you make a start on the glass animals," she says, and tosses Khavita a cloth.

*

1995

Khavita is three years old. This is possibly her earliest memory.

It is the 23rd of October, the month of *Katak*. The family is celebrating *Diwali*, the Festival of Lights. Vikram, Geetha, Priya and Khavita are walking between the houses of various Sikh friends around Rusholme and Fallowfield, admiring each of the decorations that are on display. The oil lamps, or *diya*, in every window and on every step leading up to the different front doors, flicker and sparkle around the spectacular *rangoli*, hand-made patterns of coloured sand, rice, powder and petals, which cover the pavements with their abstract swirls. Moths dance around the flames, as do the passers-by of all faiths.

Khavita's hip aches but she refuses to be put in her pushchair, insisting instead on walking round with them unaided. As a result, their progress is slow. Priya, aged eight, chatters non-stop, asking her father question after question.

"I thought *Diwali* was a Hindu festival?"

"It is."

"Then why do we celebrate it too?"

"Do you really want to know?"

"Yes, *Bapu*," she says. "Or I wouldn't be asking," she adds sweetly.

"Well," says Vikram, declining the selection of *mathi*, sweetmeats offered by someone carrying a tray, from which, he notices, Priya takes a handful, "how many of those have you had already?"

"I don't know," replies Priya, barely intelligibly, her mouth stuffed with cake.

"No more," says Geetha, raising a warning finger.

"Sorry, *Maa*," says Priya reluctantly, as she swallows the last crumb.

"Well," resumes Vikram, "we share many beliefs and practices with other faiths. Like Christians, Jews and Muslims we are monotheistic."

"What does that mean?"

"We believe in just one God, one Creator, who permeates all things."

"Unlike the Hindus, who worship thousands?"

"Not exactly. They too worship one Supreme Being, but they do so through many different names. Though their main three – Brahma, Vishnu and Shiva – have strong similarities with the Christian Holy Trinity."

"Wouldn't it be simpler if we all practised the same thing?" asks Priya, frowning.

"That's what I think," sighs Geetha, as she wrestles with Khavita, who is now so tired she has flopped straight down onto the pavement, where her eyes have become drawn to another of the *rangoli* patterns. Taking advantage of her sudden absorption, Geetha quickly manages to scoop her up and strap her into the push-chair before she has chance to resist. Once installed, however, she sets up an immediate howl of protest, and Geetha hurries on to avoid further embarrassment. Vikram and Priya trail after her.

"But it's all this variety and diversity that makes life so much more interesting, Priya, don't you see? Like all the different spices that go together to make the best *chana masala*."

"Mmm, now you're making me hungry again."

"Onions, tomatoes, chickpeas, chillies," taunts Vikram.

"Stop it!" squeals Priya.

"Garlic, ghee, cumin, coriander…"

"I'm not listening," cries Priya, covering her ears.

"Ginger, turmeric, amchoor, lemon juice…"

"It won't be long till we get back home now," calls Geetha over her shoulder. The more she hurries with Khavita in her push-chair, the more she loves it, squealing to go even faster, so that she no longer tries to wriggle to get out of it.

"So what about *Diwali* then?" persists Priya, as she and Vikram quicken their pace, trying to keep up. "Why do we celebrate it too?"

"Do you want the long answer or the short one?"

"Both."

"Well, the long one is that we celebrate the day our sixth Guru, Hargobind, was released by the Emperor Jahangir from the Gwalior Fort, where he had been imprisoned for his beliefs for many years."

"And the short one?"

"Look around you – at all the lights shining everywhere. Why would we not want to be a part of such a festival?"

"And the fireworks too."

"Absolutely. If we hurry, we might arrive in Platt Fields just in time to see them."

"You two go ahead," calls Geetha. "I think I'll just take this one straight home. See you when you get back. Don't worry about the *masala*, I can always reheat it."

"That is the beauty of vegetarian food, isn't it?" smiles Vikram. "Come along, Priya, let's not miss the fireworks."

Geetha wheels Khavita back to Albion Road and home. Lying back in the chair, she watches showers of sparks fall from the sky. When she reaches where they live, she sees the *diya* dancing in every window. Geetha manoeuvres her around and through the complex patterns of *rangoli*, glittering like lit serpents.

Inside the house there are rows of terracotta pots, each with their own small candle, flickering shadows on the walls and ceilings. Her *Nani*, is there waiting for her, smiling as she reaches down to unstrap her from the chair, her face looming over her like a lantern, or the moon. She lifts Khavita into the air, swinging her high and round, so that she giigles with pleasure.

"More," she says. "Again."

These were her first two words and remain her favourites.

Nani takes her over towards the alcove beside the fireplace, where she keeps all of her glass animals on rows of shelves. The lights of the candles gleam and bounce upon them, reflecting endless mirages of themselves deep inside the glittering glass, like a hall of mirrors.

Khavita senses that they're coming alive in front of her. She hears all their different voices, the diverse cries and shrieks and trumpets and roars. Geetha pulls back the curtains at the back of the house just in time to see the last of the fireworks cascading in fountains of rainbow-coloured lights, caught in the prism of Khavita's eyes, where they imprint themselves for all time upon the back of the retina's nerve.

2012

Khav remembers this again as *Nani* throws her the cloth in the midst of her night-time wandering and bids her to dust and polish, even though there is not a speck of dust on them anywhere to be found.

*

2005

Seven years before, when Khav was just thirteen and was helping *Nani* to unpack as she moved downstairs into the just-completed annexe, the first thing she does is to put the glass animals back onto their shelves in their new, unaccustomed surroundings.

"How come you've got so many, *Nani*?"

Urja laughs. "I know. It's a whole menagerie, isn't it? It started when I was a child, younger than you are, and I would spend the school holidays with different Aunties. My parents both worked long hours and there was nobody close by to look after me, so I would spend a week with each of them in turn. It was quite complicated, let me tell you. Just before it was time for me to go back home, they would say to me, 'Don't forget to take something home for your *Maa*.' The first time one of them said this I didn't know what to get, and it was she who suggested a glass animal – this one." She picks up a doe-eyed Bambi. "My *Maa* was so pleased with it that I would get her a new one every time I came back from staying away. She always said she liked each new one the best, but really I know now that she was only saying that to please me, for one time I overheard her on the telephone to one of my Aunties telling her about it. 'There are so many of them,' she said, 'it's becoming like a zoo here. It takes me half the week just to dust them all.' But she was laughing when she said this, and I knew she didn't mind, not really. And as the years went by, it became one of those traditions that you just can't break."

"Like *Diwali*?"

"Exactly. But the truth was that I liked them just as much as *Maa* did. Probably more. So that when I got married to your *Baba*, she said I should take them with me to this house, which I did, because she was so sure I would miss them. And she was quite right, isn't it?"

"I'm glad you did," says Khav, picking up each one in turn, then placing it in the exact spot from her *Nani* instructs.

There is every animal imaginable – lions, tigers, giraffes, zebras, horses, donkeys, dogs, cats, as well as crocodiles, octopuses, whales and dolphins, plus swans, flamingos, ducks and geese.

"Which is your favourite, *Nani*?" she asks as they continue to unwrap them from tissue paper before arranging them carefully on the new shelves.

"This one," declares Urja without hesitation, picking up a glass elephant complete with tusks.

"Why?"

"It reminds me of how Guru Nanak raised one from the dead."

"Oh," says Khav, not really listening. She gets bored hearing these tales about the founder of their faith. She doesn't really believe in them.

But Urja continues undeterred.

"He was resting in a garden while visiting the Emperor in Delhi. He built a deep well and would offer water to weary travellers as they came by and distribute food among the poor. One day some people arrived who were grieving the loss of their elephant, which had recently died, and which they had left in the shade of a tree close by. 'He is not dead,' said Guru Nanak kindly, 'just sleeping.' The people thanked the Guru for his concern but assured him that the elephant truly was dead.

And so Guru Nanak went himself to investigate. He knelt beside the prostrate animal and whispered to it softly in its ear. Within seconds the elephant revived, climbed back to its feet and trumpeted its thanks."

Urja takes the glass version of the elephant back from Khavita and gives it an extra polish for good measure before giving it pride of place on her shelf.

Khav screws up her face.

"Sorry, *Nani*, but that's just a fairy tale."

"Is it indeed?" says Urja, smiling fondly at her frowning granddaughter, who always has to question everything. "In that case, let me tell you a different story. This is something that happened to me, so I can promise you it's true."

Khav is now all ears and sits beside her Nani on the sofa-bed, who has poured them each a glass of *lassi*.

"Now then," she says, "where shall I start?"

"At the beginning," laughs Khavita, "like you always do."

"Very well," she smiles. "It had been the coldest of winters…"

*

1947

Urja has experienced nothing like it before. She is so cold that every part of her hurts. If she ever has to step outside, she covers every inch of herself. Only her eyelashes remain exposed, and within seconds even they begin to freeze over. At night, in bed, she wears two pairs of socks. She heaps extra blankets and coats on top of the eiderdown, and wraps herself as tightly as she can inside Agrawal's warm embrace.

From 21st January to 14th March it snows somewhere in England every single day. On Saddleworth Moor the depth of the drifts is measured at seven feet. Cattle and sheep are later discovered quite literally frozen to death.

Outside Urja's window on Albion Road, Platt Fields look like a Christmas card, a glittering, sparkling white, but elsewhere the picture is far from festive. Children build snowmen with twigs for a nose and pebbles for eyes. Carrots and coal cannot be spared. Rationing in the Peace is even harsher than it was during the War. Delivery wagons cannot make it through the blocked roads to bring the desperately-needed sacks of coal, which remain stuck on goods wagons trapped by ice-bound railway tracks. Even the Ship Canal is frozen over, with ice-breakers required to force a way through the solid crust of ice upon its surface and free the cargo ships and tankers from the silent dockyards at Pomona.

Each day Agrawal tries to keep as many buses running as he can. The entire trolleybus fleet is out, with the overhead cables frozen solid, while several of the double-deckers have found themselves buried in huge snowdrifts massed in Manchester's outlying towns. Only the city centre remains clear, but there the streets and pavements have merged to become one single treacherous sheet of ice.

Manny Shinwell, Minister for Fuel and Power in Clement Atlee's increasingly unpopular Labour Government, is forced to cut rations even further, so that even the staff at Buckingham Palace must work by candlelight.

Urja dreams of the hot, dry, dusty village on the edge of the Thar Desert she only dimly remembers as a small child before her parents uprooted them here to Manchester. In her dreams she is happy there, but she knows the reality there is very different now, with talk of division, of separating Hindu India from Muslim Pakistan, with the desert forming a dangerous hinterland between the two. She thanks her parents every night in her prayers that they had the foresight to leave when they did and settle the family here instead. "It will be a bloodbath," her father tells them. "You mark my words. And where will we Sikhs be? Caught in the middle, that's where." So when she wakes up to yet another morning in which she has to scrape the ice from off the insides of the window panes, she resolves to banish those dreams of sun and sand to the basement of her brain and lock them away there. Manchester is her home now, hers and Agrawal's, and it has welcomed them into her arms, even if, for the moment, those arms are cold and trembling, chilled right through to the bone.

Then, in March, the thaw begins. The snow is replaced by rain, the wettest March in more than three hundred years. Rivers burst their banks. The Irwell, Irk and Medlock disgorge tons of built-up effluent into the city's streets and cellars. Rats scurry along pavements. They scuttle out of doorways, they slither up drainpipes, seeking the higher ground.

Finally, on 14th April, Easter Sunday, the 1st day of *Vaisakh*, when Sikhs celebrate the Creation of the Five Khalsa, the central tenets of their faith, the sun breaks through the grey blanket of cloud for the first time in months. Urja and Agrawal rush outside to greet it, along with, it seems, the entire population of Manchester, who throng the streets and gather in the parks.

It is then when they first see the elephants.

Or, rather, they feel them. The way the ground shakes, their feet pounding the earth.

Then they hear them. A deep rumbling, followed by a wild, unbridled trumpeting as the procession approaches.

There are six of them, linked trunk to toe, each of them ridden by a young girl dressed as an Indian princess.

They have come to advertise the Circus at Belle Vue, which is opening the following day.

"Let's go," says Agrawal excitedly.

Urja's jaw drops. It is not like her husband to be so impulsive.

"Yes," she says, caught up in the exuberance of the moment, "let's."

It feels like they have been at last set free from the long, hard yoke of winter.

The next day is even brighter and sunnier.

Urja and Agrawal set off early to join the Easter Monday Bank Holiday crowds. From their front door on Albion Road they head straight to Wilmslow Road, skirting the edge of Platt Fields, then cross over into Dickenson Road, from where it is a direct two mile walk to their destination, crossing the junction of Anson and Birchfields Roads, then over Stockport Road onto Stanley Grove, which takes them past the Greyhound and Speedway tracks to the Hyde Road entrance of Belle Vue Zoo & Gardens. They walk as if to a festival. Later they will learn that more than a hundred and fifty thousand devotes like them visited there that day, relishing the chance to walk free from the iron grip of austerity, if only for twenty-four hours.

People have removed their coats like the animals in the zoo shedding their winter fur. It strikes Urja as strange to see bare arms and hatless heads again after months of them being wrapped and swathed in so many layers. Everyone is in festive mood. On another impulse Agrawal buys them both an ice cream. They're not real ice creams of course – sweets won't come off rationing for another six years – but their post-war equivalent, using condensed milk, peanuts and carrots. But to Urja and Agrawal they taste delicious.

Belle Vue has come through the War largely unscathed. During the Blitz there was some minor damage to the Scenic Railway from an incendiary, which has now been repaired, and which Urja and Agrawal ride on together, enjoying the panoramic views of the city as their carriage reaches the summit of its climb, then shrieking excitedly as it plunges back down towards earth once more. The Reptile House was hit by the shell splinters of an ack-ack gun, which killed a bison caught within the ricochet, while interruptions in the supply of gas resulted in the loss of all the tropical fish. The monkeys could no longer be fed on bananas but developed a taste for boiled potatoes, while the sea lions had to make do with a shortage of fresh fish by feeding on strips of beef coated in cod liver oil. The Council was concerned about the possibility of the big cats escaping and prowling the city streets during the blackout, and so they replaced their keepers with soldiers armed with tommy guns. But, to everyone's relief, the thirteen lions, six tigers, two leopards, two cheetahs and one tigon all survived unharmed. In fact their population increased when one of the lionesses, called Pearl, gave birth to a litter of six cubs during the celebrations of V.E. Night.

Urja and Agrawal take pleasure in each one. Urja has glass versions of all of them – except the tigons. She looks at them closely now, these rare hybrids, which, to her, exhibit the best qualities of both species.

"They remind me of us," she says, linking her arm through her husband's. "British and Indian both, living here in Manchester."

They pose for a photograph beside the Moghul Temple and Grotto, inside which there are crocodiles and cobras, as well as hothouse flowers. When no one is looking, Agrawal plucks one and places it behind Urja's ear. She smiles coyly, before covering it with her hair as they walk back outside, where a queue is already forming for a surprise Agrawal has been planning from the moment they arrived.

"What is this?" asks Urja.

He points shyly to a sign.

Elephant Rides!
Adults & Children May Ride

She looks at him with wide eyes.

"Are you sure?"

"If we had been married in India, who knows? You may have ridden to your wedding on one, isn't it? Let's pretend, shall we?"

She lowers her eyes and pulls her scarf across her face.
While they are waiting in the queue, they get talking to a woman and her son, who are standing just in front of them.

"Hello?" says Urja, bending down so that her eyes are on a level with the little boy's. "What's your name?"

"Solomon," he says seriously.

"We call him 'Solly'," says the mother, smiling.

"And how old are you, Solly?" asks Urja.

"Six," he replies.

"Six?"

"And three quarters," he adds.

"Oh," says Urja, standing up straight once more, "then that makes you a very big boy, doesn't it?"

"Yes," says Solly. "My grandfather says I have to be very grown up and look after my Mummy now that Daddy has gone away."

"Oh," says Urja, "I see." She looks instinctively towards the mother, who is older than Urja might have expected. A late baby perhaps.

"He died," says the mother quietly. It's not clear whether the boy hears this or not, for he says nothing.

"The War?" asks Urja, as delicately as she can.

"No," says the mother. "This wretched winter. Pneumonia."

Urja lifts her hand involuntarily up to her mouth. "I'm so sorry," she says.

"Thank you."

"I like your hat," says Solly suddenly, pointing up at Agrawal.

"It's a turban," he replies, beaming down at the boy.

"Can I try it on?"

"It's too big for you," says Agrawal. "It would cover your head completely, then you wouldn't be able to see where you were going."

"I wouldn't like that."

"I'm sure you wouldn't. In my religion you have to be grown up to wear one."

"What do boys wear then?"

"It's interesting you should ask. They wear what's called a *patka*."

"A *patka*?"

"That's right. Like this." Agrawal pulls out a large, clean handkerchief from his pocket. "Would you like me to show you?"

"Yes please, Mr...?"

"Singh."

Agrawal takes Solly to one side, sensing that the boy's mother and Urja are keen to have a conversation. Solly lowers his head and passively allows Agrawal to tie the handkerchief around and upon it.

"Is Mr Singh your husband?" asks the mother.

Urja nods proudly. "Agrawal."

"I'm Esther," says the mother, holding out her hand,

"Urja."

Having introduced themselves the two women fall briefly silent, as if not quite sure how to proceed.

"I like your scarf," says Urja eventually.

"Thank you," says Esther, at once beginning to remove it so that Urja might take a closer look. "It belonged to my late mother-in-law. Rose. She wore it on her wedding day. Her husband is from the Yemen. He came to Manchester to help build the Ship Canal. Some of the men he worked with clubbed together to buy Rose this scarf. They got it from one of the early Penny Bazaars set up by Marks & Spencer, I believe."

She pauses and smiles. "I'm sorry. I don't usually talk so much."

Urja is examining the scarf. "It's beautiful," she says. "So delicate. Moths caught up in the leaves."

"Yes," says Esther. "I've taken to wearing it all the time since my husband died…"

Urja holds it up to the light. The sun is almost directly overhead. It bounces off the glass roof of the Reptile House, and its refracted beam casts a multi-coloured rainbow across the white cotton of the cloth. Urja looks around at the smiling faces of the crowds pressing on all sides, their skin every possible shade, all contained within the prism of this city they each call home. The moths flutter and then settle. She hands the cloth back to Esther, who ties it back around her head, a gesture Urja mirrors as she pulls up her own scarf. The two women smile warmly towards one another.

The moment is broken by Solly returning with Agrawal.

"Look, Mummy," he cries. "Mr Singh has given me a *patka*."

"Very handsome," says Esther.

"I want to see," he says, dancing round her.

She takes a compact mirror out of her bag and holds it up for her son to stand on tiptoe in order to peer at his reflection.

"I look like a pirate," he says, with delighted approval.

"Give the handkerchief back to Mr Singh now, Solly, there's a good boy."

"Let him keep it," says Agrawal. "It's quite all right."

"Are you sure?"

"Yes, yes. Quite sure." Agrawal inclines his head from side to side, smiling.

"What do you say, Solly?"

"Thank you, Mr Singh."

"You're most welcome."

Suddenly, they have reached the front of the queue, and it is Esther's and Solly's turn to ride the elephant.

"There's room for four," says Esther. "Would you like to join us?"

"Please say that you will," says Solly, tugging at the sleeve of Agrawal's jacket.

"Yes, sir, Cap'n, aye-aye!" replies Agrawal with a mock salute.

Once they are safely installed in the *howdah* upon the elephant's back and have accustomed themselves to the rocking, swaying motion as they are transported around the park and gardens, they fall back into easy conversation.

"Have you been on an elephant before?" asks Solly.

"No," says Agrawal, looking at Urja shyly, "this is my first time."

"Oh," says Solly, frowning, "I thought you must have done back in your own country."

Urja smiles. "We were born here," she says. "In Manchester."

"Oh," says Solly again, frowning even harder.

"Our parents came here from India. But even they had not ridden an elephant there. You have to be very rich to do that. Like a Maharani."

"What's that?"

"A Princess."

The man leading the elephant around Belle Vue now calls up to Solly.

"That is the name of this elephant," he says. "Rani."

At the sound of her name, the elephant promptly trumpets loudly, raising her trunk high into the air.

Solly is entranced.

"This is my first time too," says Esther. "In fact I've never been here before, even though, as a girl, I lived less than a mile away in Gorton. There were six of us – myself and five brothers – and my parents simply couldn't afford to bring us all. Sometimes, in the evenings, though, we'd sit on the wall in the yard at the back of our house and watch the fireworks. If I close my eyes I can still see them now, like shooting stars raining down from the sky…"

She closes them again now, remembering. After a few moments, she opens them again and continues.

"This is where my parents first met. They came here as children on a Sunday School outing. Just before my father started work down the pit and my mother began as a little piecer in the mill. Times were harder then. They too rode on an elephant that day."

"On Rani?" asks Solly.

"No. They rode on a much more famous elephant. His name was Maharajah. He had walked all the way to Manchester from Edinburgh with his keeper Lorenzo after the owners of Belle Vue had bought him in an auction there. He was meant to come by train, but he didn't like being locked up in the carriage, so he kicked his way out and walked here instead. It took him ten days. Everywhere he went the people came out to cheer him. By the time he reached Manchester thousands lined the streets. They heard him before they saw him, a deep rumbling, like thunder, coming from deep beneath the earth, and then a great cloud of dust kicked up by his huge pounding hooves. Then finally they saw him…"

*

2005

"Oh," says Khav, listening enthralled to her *Nani* recounting nearly sixty years later this story Esther had told her, "I would love to have seen that." She is thinking also of the time when Grace had shown her the drawing she had made of Maharajah's skeleton, and how all things pass, but out of their endings come new beginnings.

"Yes," agrees Urja. "The way Esther described it, I felt as though I was there."

"I'm not sure I like the part where you and *Baba* were riding on the other elephant, though."

"Rani?"

"No. It's cruel to ride on elephants like that."

"I know, *Dohti*, but we didn't think like that back then. And I don't believe Rani was mistreated."

"How can you be sure?"

"I can't. But I think you can tell how an animal is from looking into its eyes. Just as you can with people."

"They should be left to roam free in the wild."

"Who? People or animals?"

"Both."

Urja sighs. "I expect you're right," she says. "I don't suppose you want to hear the rest of the story then…?"

Khav considers this. She does and she doesn't. In the end curiosity gets the better of her conscience.

"I'd like to know what happened," she says at last. "It's all in the past now. It's not like you can change any of it."

I don't know about that, thinks, Urja. Just in the telling of it, a story gets changed, isn't it…?

*

1947

When the elephant ride has finished, Esther and Solly, Urja and Agrawal, go their separate ways.

"I don't like to leave Yasser too long," Esther explains. "The light has gone out of him since Hejaz died."

Urja watches them walk away until they become completely swallowed up in the dust kicked up by the thousands of pairs of feet in the holiday crowds.

They have an hour before the circus is due to begin. They decide they will find somewhere to sit on the grass in the gardens to eat the picnic that Urja has somehow managed to create for them from their meagre rations before going on one more ride until it is time for them to enter the Big Top. The ride they choose is the Caterpillar.

It trundles up and down in a wide circle, which gradually picks up speed – but not too fast, which is Urja's main concern after they have eaten – and which halfway through gets covered by a large green canopy, plunging the riders inside into semi-darkness, who sit in cars that can only fit two, so that it becomes the perfect excuse for courting, or newly-married couples to participate in some unseen, innocent canoodling. The outsides of the cars are decorated with tree and leaf designs – the maker's name skilfully intertwined between the foliage, *Pavel Zlatan* – so that when the green canopy automatically descends, much to the merriment and mirth of all, to conceal the riders inside, it does indeed resemble a giant caterpillar undulating its way through the greenery.

Urja allows Agrawal to place his arm protectively round her shoulders as the ride begins. Then, when the canopy has covered them, she permits him to steal a long, lingering kiss. During it, she opens her eyes. Sunlight filters dimly through the green canvas covering. The sounds, too, seem like they are submerged under water, all mixed together, surfacing slowly, re-formed, so that, from the inside, rather than resembling a caterpillar, it feels to Urja more as though they are chrysalids, trapped inside the pupa, waiting to emerge as moths, like those on Esther's cotton scarf, to rise up towards the light and settle, basking in the warmth, opening their wings to soak up the sun's rays.

Inside the Big Top the elephants return, four of them kicking up the sawdust in time to the Circus Orchestra playing Wagner's *Ride of the Valkyries*. The girls who sit astride their heads are dressed like exotic temple dancers, or *Kathak* brides. Vibrantly coloured saris with tightly-stitched pleats fan out over their legs and knees, while each top is in a different, iridescent green, or red, or gold, or sapphire, crossing over one shoulder in a tight, close-fitting way at the *pallav*, the end of the sari cinched at the waist, held in place by a sequinned belt, with jewelled *bindi* on their foreheads and their hair scraped back into a knot adorned with artificial, sparkling lotus flowers.

Once they have completed several circuits, the elephants rise up on their hind hooves, before kneeling on their front legs, allowing the girls to slide gracefully down their outstretched trunks and into the centre of the ring. The elephants leave the tent and the orchestra switches to the *Lament of the Rhine Maidens*, as the girls remove the flared skirts of the saris to reveal bare legs covered in glittering tights. Trapezes are lowered onto which they climb, to be hoisted towards the distant roof of the Big Top, where individual spotlights pick them out, as they soar and swoop over the heads of the disbelieving, open-mouthed crowds, Urja and Agrawal among them.

One by one the girls perform a series of aerobatic somersaults, leaping from one to another of the trapeze bars swinging in perfect synchronicity, before tumbling safely down into the net waiting for them below, until only one is left, flying higher than all of them. The Ringmaster introduces her as Lorelei, Queen of the Flying Trapeze, and explains that she will now perform her final feat, her *pièce de résistance*, her *coup de théâtre*, her death-defying feat never-before-seen anywhere in the world, while, to the gasps of the edge-of-their-seats audience, the safety net is cut down and removed.

Urja wants to cover her eyes but she dare not look away. She wants to cry 'Stop!' but is far too tense to speak. She holds her breath, she tilts back her head, strains her eyes to pick her out, high above, so tiny she can fit her completely within the circle of her finger and thumb which she holds up to her eye. She tries to picture herself up there at the top, to be looking down, instead of up, to see not just the crowds in the Big Top, but all those outside within the perimeter walls of Belle Vue, and beyond to the whole of Manchester stretching out widely in all directions, so that it appears to contain within it all the world, and imagine what it must feel like to be about to dive towards it, to plunge headlong right into the teeming, swirling mass of it, the beating, pulsating heart of it, a seething, molten crucible, then fly up out again from this cauldron, rising like a phoenix, rekindled, reborn.

The drum rolls, the lights fade to a single spot, Lorelei climbs to the highest platform, turns and waves to the waiting crowds below, takes hold of the trapeze, which, as she does so, bursts into a circle of fire, setting off a relay of flames igniting each of the other swinging trapezes. With a final crescendo of cymbals, she launches herself into the air. She swings beneath her trapeze, then neatly propels herself upwards so that she executes a perfect loop within its frame, enabling her to balance on the bar by her waist alone, slowly removing her hands, before appearing to lose control and fall, only to catch herself at last moment by hooking her feet around the junction of the bar and the ropes either side supporting it. She swings high and wide upside down over the audience. Then, pulling herself back up into a standing position with supreme control and strength, she prepares for her big finish. A series of five hoops are lowered into the space between her own trapeze and that of another, the last of the empty trapezes still swinging by itself.

Each of these hoops is then set on fire, like the Olympic rings. The whole arena appears to be a roaring ball of flame. Lorelei, using her legs as levers, powers the trapeze to a speed so great that, from below, to Urja she appears nothing but a blur, or perhaps several mirrored versions of herself, repeated endlessly through space, like reincarnated avatars.

At last Lorelei is ready.

With sudden decisiveness she launches herself towards the five hoops of fire. She coils her body into a tightly tucked position, then propels herself forward, as if fired from a cannon, passing through each one, until she reaches the empty swinging trapeze at the opposite end, which she catches one-handed only. The audience gasps in genuine fright, only for Lorelei to let herself dangle there, safe and unharmed, as the flames everywhere are doused, and the trapeze she now clings to, as though it were the easiest thing in the world, is lowered down to the centre of the ring, onto the back of an elephant waiting patiently for her, which then transports her on a lap of honour to the cheering, applauding, satisfied crowds, who are, all of them, in their own separate, individual, less spectacular ways, no less heroic than Lorelei has been.

Afterwards, as Urja and Agrawal make their way the two miles back home to Albion Road, surrounded on all sides by the tired but happy crowds dispersing from Belle Vue, radiating to all points of the compass as if from a pilgrimage, the sun has set and the stars are beginning to show in the early evening sky. Agrawal points out the more familiar constellations – the bear, the crab, the lion, the bull.

"Are there not any in the shape of an elephant?" asks Urja.

"According to ancient Vedic mythology," he replies, "there are four elephants holding up the world, standing on the back of a giant tortoise moving us slowly through space."

Urja leans into him and smiles.

"But actually," he continues, "there is one, here in the northern sky, in the constellation of Cepheus, named after an ancient King of Ethiopia. It's an enormous cloud of gas and dust, some twenty light years in length, known as the Elephant's Trunk Nebula, because of its snout-like shape."

"I like the sound of that," says Urja.

"The trunk is nursing new-born stars that have not yet matured to shine as brightly as one day they surely will."

Urja rests her head on Agrawal's shoulder.

"Where?" she says. "Show me."

He looks up at the sky to get his bearings. Then he moves Urja out of the way of the passing crowds and positions her directly beneath the *Ursa Minor*, the Little Bear. He stands behind her, placing one hands upon her shoulder and pointing with the other.

"Do you see the Little Bear?" he says.

"Yes."

"Now – follow my finger south. The next bright cluster of stars – fourteen if you count them all – is Draco."

"The Dragon?"

"Yes."

"I see it."

"Now – move your gaze to the left a little. Do you see the five stars forming a 'W' shape?"

"Yes."

"That's Cassiopeia, the vain queen."

Urja giggles as Agrawal explains.

"Now – do you see the cloud of stars between Cassiopeia and Draco?"

"Yes, I think so."

"That's the Elephant's Trunk Nebula."

"Oh," says Urja, a little disappointed. "It doesn't look much like a trunk."

"No," says Agrawal. "You need a telescope to make it out properly. If you really look carefully, you might just make out a star in the centre of it that's brighter and redder than all the others."

"Maybe," she says, screwing her eyes up tight, then declaring more certainly. "Yes – now I can."

"That's known as Herschel's Garnet. The composer William Herschel first noted it when on a walk from Halifax to Manchester one evening on his way to play a concert here. Later, when he became Royal Astronomer to King George III, he made a more detailed study of it, and it was named after him. Well – think of the garnet as the tip of the elephant's trunk."

Urja beams.

"How do you know all this?" she asks.

"My father told me. Back in India he built himself a home-made telescope, which he put on the roof of his home in the village near Chandigarh."

"Perhaps we should visit it one day?"

"No," he says, taking his wife's hand in his, "this is our home now."

They walk back to Albion Road beneath the winking garnet star in the centre of the Elephant's Trunk Nebula, while behind them, from the island within the Boating Lake in Belle Vue, the nightly firework display begins, sending shooting stars across the night sky. Urja recalls Esther telling her how, as a child, she and her brothers had watched these while sitting on the top of the wall in the yard at the back of their house, and she wonders if this is something her own daughter, if she has one, might be able to see from the house on Albion Road...

*

2005

"… and I did," says Geetha, joining Urja and Khav in the annexe, just as they are placing the last of the glass animals, the elephant, on the shelf that has been specially saved for it.

*

2013

Khav grows used to her *Nani*'s night-time wanderings. She no longer springs to her feet to check on what she's doing. Like as not she's making herself a drink. She catnaps for most of each day, twenty minutes here, half an hour there, then she's wide awake. Little wonder she has no kind of pattern or routine these days. Some nights Khav doesn't even wake up when she hears her padding about on the other side of the sliding doors that separate the annexe from the living room, where she herself sleeps.

But on this particular evening she does wake up. For some reason she's on an instant high alert. She strains her ears, listening for the slightest sound, while her eyes adjust to the darkness.

"*Nani?*" she half-whispers, half-calls out loud. "Are you all right?"

No answer.

"Can I get you anything?"

Again, no answer.

Then a tiny gasp, a stumble, and the tinkling of breaking glass.

Khav is on her feet at once and through the sliding doors. Urja is on the floor, surrounded by shards of shattered glass. Her body quivers in a series of short, repeated jolts. A sharp, bird-like croak rasps from the back of her throat. Khav drops to her knees beside her. The left side of Urja's face has dropped and gone slack. The whole of her left side has lost all power of movement. The fingers of her left hand have closed over something that Khav cannot make out Somewhere above her head she hears a panicked fluttering. She switches on the light. A moth is banging its wings against the bulb's dazzling glare.

Khav picks up her phone, dials 999, then rushes upstairs to wake her parents.

The ambulance arrives in just over twenty minutes. Immediately the paramedics stabilise her breathing, fit her with an oxygen mask and lift her onto a trolley. Geetha climbs unhesitatingly into the back of the ambulance to accompany her mother the short five-minute journey to Manchester Royal Infirmary, while Vikram gets ready to follow on his *Babaj Chetak*. Khav stays behind to let her sister know what has happened.

Just before the ambulance leaves, one of the paramedics manages to prise *Nani*'s fingers loose from what she has been clinging on to and hands it carefully to Khav. It is the glass elephant.

*

A week later Urja is dead.

She regains consciousness just once. All the family are gathered round her hospital bed. Even baby Dilsher is there, as good as gold. Her right eye sees them all, focuses on each one of them in turn. The one side of her face that has remained mobile attempts to form a half-smile. She appears to be in no pain. She looks at them all for a full five minutes. Her breathing is calm, no longer laboured. Imperceptibly she nods her head, raises her right hand to caress the baby's unblemished cheek, then, having said her silent farewell, she slips away from them.

Her face is at peace, the skin as translucent as a bird's egg, as fragile as delicately stitched thread.

One by one the family stoop to print the gentlest kiss they can upon her tissue paper forehead.

Vikram then reads from the *Sukhmani Sahib*, the Prayer of Peace for Joy of Mind. In keeping with the spirit of *hukam*, or the divine order of seeking spiritual oneness with God, they read at random, from where the Holy Book falls open, the opening stanza of a *shabad* composed by Ravi Das, the *Adi Granth*, literally the root and heart of their faith.

"When I existed, You did not.
Now You exist and I do not:
As a storm lifts waves from water
Still they remain water –
Water within water."

*

"Clive? It's me – Khav."

"Hi. Is everything all right?"

"No. That's why I'm calling. My *Nani* died this morning."

"Oh… I'm so sorry to hear that, Khav. Is there anything I can do?"

"Yes. As a matter of fact there is. That's why I'm calling. It's meant to be my Final Presentation tomorrow. But that's when the funeral is taking place now."

"So soon?"

"Sikhs need to hold them within three days of someone dying."

"I didn't know that. Then of course we must find a new date for your presentation. Leave it with me. Call me again when you feel ready."

"Thanks, Clive. I really appreciate it."

"Please pass on my condolences to your family."

"I will. Thank you."

*

Immediately after death has been pronounced, Urja's body is washed and prepared for cremation. Sikhs believe in reincarnation and the transmigration of souls, which never die. Cremation releases the spirit from the prison of the body, aiding it in its endless search for attainment, in the continuous cycle of birth, death and rebirth. Because she had been baptised and was thus an *amritdhari*, she is ceremonially dressed in the five articles of Sikh faith, the five 'K's, the *karkars* – the *kesh*, the uncut hair; the *kangha*, a small wooden comb; the *kachhera*, or undergarments; the *karha*, an iron bracelet, and the *kirpan*, the curved dagger.

Her body is then adorned with orange and white chrysanthemum flowers. It is taken first to the *Gurdwara* on Upper Chorlton Road, three and a half miles north-west of her home on Albion Road, for prayers and hymns. It is a private affair, attended only by close family and a few friends. The men wear black turbans, the women white headscarves. No eulogies are delivered, there are no outward signs of emotion or weeping, for this would be against their belief that the body is merely a vessel. Instead the *kirtan sohila* is sung, the traditional night-time hymn, followed by the *antim ardas*, the final prayer.

"I am the Sacrifice to the Song
Bringing Perpetual Peace..."

Afterwards they transfer to the Manchester Crematorium at Southern Cemetery on Barlow Moor Road on the eastern edge of Chorlton-cum-Hardy, two miles south of the *Gurdwara*. Geetha, as Urja's oldest surviving relative, presses the switch to commence the cremation.

Twenty-four hours later they receive the ashes, which, as is the custom, they release into the nearest body of water, the flood plain of the River Mersey in Fielden Park. They return to the *Gurdwara* to set in motion a continuous reading of the *Guru Granth Sahib* in Urja's memory, which will take ten days, at the end of which they will light *joti*, candles made from ghee and cotton, in the window of the house on Albion Road, the sweetness of their fragrance serving to cleanse and purify.

*

"Khav? This is Clive. Is now a good time to speak?"

"Yes. The reading of the Holy Book finished yesterday. All the traditions have been observed now."

"I see. How are you feeling?"

"Drained. But *Nani* would have been pleased."

"Good."

"Thank you."

"I've a new date for your presentation."

"Oh?"

"A week tomorrow. Two o'clock. Will that be OK?"

"It'll be fine. Thanks again for arranging everything."

"Don't mention it. I'm looking forward to hearing what you've got to say."

"So am I."

On either end of the call both of them smile.

"Do you think you'll be ready?"

"Don't worry, Clive." She pauses. Both of them know what she's going to say next. "I've been ready all my life."

*

In the almost three years she has been at MMU Khav has seen Mahendra on a number of occasions. It's a small campus and so it is inevitable that their paths will cross at times. They never refer to their somewhat anti-climactic one-night stand back in Freshers' Week of 2011. In fact Khav has all but forgotten it, and she suspects that Mahendra has done the same. Just one of those minor random collisions that happen sometimes, from which both parties can walk away more or less unscathed.

She has remained a member of the Sikh Society, through whom she has made several good friends. One of these is Vidhya – Mahendra's sister – who, if she knows anything at all about what happened, or, rather, didn't happen, between Khav and her brother, never lets on, and Khav has never mentioned it to her. She's never mentioned it to anyone, not to her sister, nor, even, to Chloe, with whom she has had no end of intimate conversations. Chloe tends to treat these like she would any other journalistic investigation, by asking difficult questions, but at the same time inviting confidences somehow. But with Vidhya, Khav's relationship is more politically focused – which is not to say it isn't also personal, the personal is political after all – and it usually includes four or five other young Sikh women, who have, between them, formed a small sub-group within the wider Society.

On this particular day, a week after the continuous reading of the *Guru Granth Sahib* for her *Nani* has been completed, and the day before her rearranged Final Presentation, Khav is meeting Vidhya for their monthly lunch in *On The Eighth Day*, together with Tanveet, Beesham, Lakshmi and Saroor. They all scurry in from an early summer shower, shaking their umbrellas, except for Khav, who has never owned one and who would, even if she did, be always leaving it behind somewhere, on a bus, or a tram, or in a café, so she merely shakes herself dry, rather like a wet dog.

After the kerfuffle of their arrivals has finally subsided, they order their lunch, then settle down for their customary group conversation, something they all of them eagerly look forward to. The topic under discussion today is *kesh*. The politics of hair.

"I'm thinking about wearing a turban," announces Vidhya.

"You should," says Tanveet. "You'd look very nice in one, I think. They come in such fashionable colours nowadays."

"That's hardly the point, though, is it?" says Beesham.

"It might be," says Vidhya, smiling. "What's wrong in wanting to look nice?"

"Nothing," concedes Beesham, "but you'd be making a statement, innit?"

"What does your *Maa* think?" asks Lakshmi.

"Or your *Papa-ji*?"

"I don't think he'd mind so much, but *Maa* would be furious." She giggles. "Just to see the look of horror on her face is temptation enough, I think."

"I don't believe you," says Beesham. "I think you've given it a great deal of thought. You know exactly what the significance of making such a gesture would mean. You're just teasing us when you pretend it's only a whim, or some fashion thing."

Vidhya smiles again. She half-closes her eyes at the same time, so that she resembles a cat.

"You're very quiet, Khav," she says. "What's your take on it?"

"I think you're still not answering Beesham's question."

"Fair enough."

"So?"

Vidhya regards the other women, who look at her expectantly.

"What is it Guru Nanak says? '*From woman man is born. Within woman man is conceived. Through woman future generations come. Without woman, there is no one*'. I take that to mean that women and men are to be regarded as equals. Two sides of the same human coin. If men can wear a turban, why should women not also?"

"It's what the Guru intended, why he first instructed his followers to cover their heads to begin with," interjects Beesham fiercely, "so that there would no longer be any divisions between people."

"No matter what their caste," adds Lakshmi.

"Or their gender," concludes Beesham.

"And yet," says Khav, shrugging her shoulders and spreading her hands.

"And yet," agrees Vidhya.

"I'm a *keshdari*," says Tanveet. "I've never cut my hair."

"I have," says Khav. "When I was thirteen, I tied it in two bunches and cut each one off with a pair of scissors just to spite my *Bapu*."

The others react in varying degrees of shock and amusement.

"But I've grown it again since," she adds.

"Well, I've never cut mine," continues Tanveet, "though I've often wanted to. It's so heavy for one thing. But I've never wanted to cover it with a turban."

"Why not?" demands Beesham.

Lakshmi looks down.

"You know very well why not," answers Vidhya quickly, saving Tanveet from further embarrassment. "For the same reasons you haven't, Beesham. Or any of us."

"It's not feminine," says Lakshmi, imitating one of her Aunties.

"You don't want to look like a man," says Khav, adopting a similar role.

"How will you ever get a husband?" they both chime together.

The others laugh, including Beesham.

"I'm sorry, Tanveet," she says. "I get carried away sometimes."

"The Guru says we must not cut our hair because it is a gift from God," says Tanveet, "but where do we draw the line? Do we wax? Shave under our armpits? Thread above our upper lips? I know I do."

"But will you continue to do so when you take *amrit*?" asks Beesham.

"I don't know," says Tanveet. "That's why I haven't taken it yet."

The others nod in sympathy.

"I *have* been baptised," says Vidhya, "but I still don't act consistently. Beesham's right. The way *kesh* is policed is specifically gendered. I have a cousin who has PCOS – polycystic ovary syndrome – which means that she grows excessive facial hair. When I last saw her, she had a full beard." The others gape in astonishment, but Vidhya counters their reaction. "It looked nice. More importantly, she was very happy with it. But she was coming under enormous pressure from her family to shave it off. 'It makes you look too masculine,' she was told. That's what my *Maa* and *Nani* would say to me too. So they encourage me to wax. But when I chose to pluck my eyebrows as well, they were appalled. We can't win, girls. Not removing our body hair makes us appear too masculine and harder for us to find a husband, but if we cut the hair on our head, we are morally loose. Even if we don't cut it, but we decide to leave it uncovered, we risk upsetting somebody."

"Unless we become famous and appear on TV," cuts in Khav.

"Like Pooja Bedi," says Lakshmi.

"My *Maa* loves Pooja Bedi," says Tanveet.

"Even when she did that ad about *Kama Sutra* condoms?" sneers Beesham.

"She pretends that never happened," says Tanveet.

"Exactly," continues Vidhya. "Look at Khav – even she wears her baseball cap, innit?"

"Yo," they reply, flicking their fingers in unison.

"Sikh men, on the other hand," says Vidhya, "especially in Canada and America, routinely shave their beards in order to improve their business prospects, while my brother swans about in shorts. Can you imagine the fuss if *we* did that?"

The others laugh as they tuck into their lunch.

"So what will you do?" Khav asks Vidhya quietly when they are readying themselves to leave. "Will you wear a turban?"

"Maybe," says Vidhya. "Maybe not. I'm not as PC as I pretend. Nor as honest as Beesham. But I suspect she's right. It'd be as much a fashion statement as any kind of manifesto."

"I don't believe you," smiles Khav.

*

After scrupulously dividing the bill evenly between themselves, the five young women part amicably, having enjoyed, as they always do, their lively lunch time conversation.

There's a welcome break in the rain. The sun is trying to break through the blanket of grey cloud that splinters in arrow-like shafts of diagonal light, bouncing off the puddles on Oxford Road, causing Khav to pull the peak of her cap lower over her eyes. She decides she'll risk trying to walk the two-and-a-quarter miles back to Albion Road, rather than catch a bus. If she hurries, she should make it in just over forty minutes. She wants to use the time to think. The topic of their lunch time conversation has chimed with some thoughts of her own she's been having recently, especially since *Nani* died, and she needs to go over her presentation for Clive the next day.

The hard fact is that she still doesn't know what she's going to say. She can't decide. She keeps having second thoughts. Then third thoughts. Then going back to her original ones. But none of them seem right. They don't gel with how she feels about things any more. She keeps thinking about that story her *Nani* told her about the elephant that walked all the way from Edinburgh to Manchester, how people would feel it coming before they saw it, the sound of its hooves rising up from deep underground, like an earthquake, after which nothing could ever be the same again. She pictures it in her imagination, emerging out of the dust, trunk raised and roaring, charging straight for her.

An idea dimly begins to form in her mind.

What if…?

I wonder…

She takes out her phone and calls Vidhya.

"Yes?"

"What does Guru Nanak say about tattoos?"

"Well…"

Khav can instantly picture the smile forming on her friend's mouth as she pauses.

"Permanent or temporary?"

"Either. Both. It's hypothetical, innit?"

"Well," says Vidhya again, "a permanent tattoo would require the removal of some body hair, and we know how contentious that can be. Your body is a temple, so treat it with respect, some would say, and don't desecrate it."

"Yeah, but adorning it's not the same as desecrating it, is it? It's art."

"An expression of devotion?"

"A sign of deference."

"Maybe. But I'm sure the Guru says somewhere that our skin is a gift from God and so cannot be improved upon."

"But doesn't he also say that as Sikhs we should be judged by our actions, not our appearance, by what we do, not how we look, accepting our differences, respecting our choices?"

"It sounds to me like you've already made your mind up."

"Nah. It's hypothetical, innit?"

She puts away her phone. She has just passed Devas Street, where Contact Theatre hauls itself awkwardly up behind the University Students' Union like some strange mythical castle built by Gaudi, with its octagonal brick towers like jagged fists and its zinc portcullis caught in the act of forever falling or rising.

A small crowd has gathered just in front of it. At first Khav thinks that some kind of impromptu performance must be taking place, but, as she gets nearer, she realises this is not the case. Instead a homeless woman is being asked to move on by some official, much to the anger of the passers-by, who are rallying to her defence. The woman herself appears to be haranguing them all, shouting angrily and incomprehensibly in a language known only to her.

Khav edges closer to her. As soon as the woman catches sight of her, she stops in mid-rant and fixes her eyes solely upon her.

"You," she says, pointing directly at Khav. "I have something for you."

Now that she has calmed down and appears to recognise someone, the rest of the crowd disperses and begins to drift away. The harassed official, relieved that the woman is no longer his problem, vanishes along with them. Khav approaches cautiously. The woman is rummaging in a plastic bag. The old, threadbare coat she is wearing slips off one shoulder. Khav notices a tattoo there. The synchronicity of this, following the call she has just finished with Vidhya, strikes her hard. She tries to take a closer look at it while the woman continues to search for whatever it is she's looking for. It's an angel.

'Do Sikhs believe in angels?'

This was the topic for one of the group's earlier lunch-time discussions.

Beesham, as always, had been clear and forceful.

"Sikhs deny the existence of heaven and hell," she declared. "In so doing we must also deny the existence of heavenly beings, such as angels."

"I don't think we rule out the possibility of them," Tanveet had ventured, before retracting somewhat in the face of one of Beesham's stern glares, "but because God alone is what we focus on, they wouldn't be of any importance."

"Not angels, nor devils. There is no duality for Sikhs, there is only the One," Beesham had then said emphatically.

"You don't believe that," said Vidya. "I know you don't. Things are never that clear cut."

"You're right. I don't. I'm just quoting my *Papa-ji*, that's all," replied Beesham, "who likes always to have the last word. Actually I believe things are much more complicated. There are two sides to everything."

"I seem to remember the Holy Book mentions them," said Lakshmi, chewing thoughtfully on some *naan*. "Something about an Angel of Death, a messenger of some kind..."

"That's right," said Tanveet, trying to recall the angel's name. "Azrael. That's it. He – or she – are angels male or female...?"

"Neither."

"Both."

"Bi."

"Trans."

"... crosses over from one world into another, carrying others with them..."

Khav considers all this while the woman with the angel tattoo continues to rummage in her bag, muttering darkly.

Behind her, pasted to the front of Contact Theatre, just below the falling, or rising, grey zinc portcullis, is a vibrant, multi-coloured poster.

CONTACTING THE WORLD
International Biennale

Bringing Together
Young People from Around the World
to create ground breaking new theatre

Share, Exchange Collaborate

Since 2002
CONTACTING THE WORLD
has featured companies from
Zambia, Nigeria, Rwanda, Somalia
Palestine, Poland, Pakistan
India, Sri Lanka, Bangladesh, Malaysia
Jordan, Syria, Iran, South Africa
Nepal, New Zealand, The Philippines
Germany, Turkey, USA, UK

With a cry of triumph the woman finds what she has been looking for and extracts it out of the depths of her bag like a magician conjuring a rabbit, which she raises aloft, clutched tightly in her grimy fist.

Except that it's not a rabbit. It's something else entirely.

With unexpected tenderness she uncurls her bruised and stained fingers to reveal something surprisingly delicate and fragile balanced upon her cupped palm. The object emits a translucent glow that lights the woman's face as she looks down into it. She slowly transfers her gaze from this object of wonder in her hand directly towards Khav, while her other hand beckons to her with a gnarled and crooked finger.

Khav approaches.

She knows before she sees it exactly what it will be.

Ever since 2005, after her *Nani* had told her about how she had acquired her menagerie of glass animals, each year Khav had bought her a new one for her birthday. She remembered the list of big cats that had survived the War at Belle Vue – the thirteen lions, six tigers, two leopards, two cheetahs, one tigon and six lion cubs born on V.E. Night – and has tried to find one of each. The lion, the tiger, the leopard and the cheetah she has been able to find, as well as a pair of cute lion cubs, but the tigon has so far eluded her. At first she wasn't even sure what one was, and so she had had to look it up. Tigon – a male tiger crossed with a female lion. As opposed to a liger – a male lion crossed with a female tiger. Some sources state that neither is found in the wild, that they are the products only of experimental cross-breeding with animals kept in captivity. Like zoos. Belle Vue Zoo is long gone, shut down in 1977. No loss there, thinks Khav, who is no lover of animals being kept in cages or behind bars. But the more she researches, the more she unearths stories of tigons and ligers being spotted in the wild. Some sources put this down to probable escapees from wild life parks, but there are other claims – unsubstantiated but compelling nevertheless – that go much further back, suggesting these hybrids occurred naturally and much earlier. She likes the idea of these, transgressors that have somehow survived against all the odds. Hybrids are generally hardier and tougher than thoroughbreds – that's what her *Nani* always said about wild dogs and roses – and Khav has always harboured the notion that she's something of one herself, a tomboy, with one leg shorter than the other, one foot in the past, the other in the future, a British Indian, a dutiful daughter, but at the same time a break-dancing B-girl. And so she tried to find her *Nani* a glass tigon to complete her collection, but she had never found one. She had haunted the flea markets, charity shops and bric-a-brac stalls across the city, but without success. She'd even gone as far as looking them up in Manchester Central Library, where she found a picture of one, made by the renowned artist Caitlin Mallone, who had produced glass objects of extraordinary grace and wonder that were now highly sought after. She had started out as the first female glass blower at *A World in a Grain of Sand*, the magnificent glass emporium on Great Ancoats Street, sadly no longer there. Khav had seen evidence of her work in the Whitworth Art Gallery & Museum, less than a hundred yards from where she is now standing. But not one of her glass tigons. Only a handful of these were ever produced and Khav has never seen one, not for real, only in old photographs.

Until now.

It is this which the woman with the angel tattoo now holds before her in her worn and weathered hand.

"You want?" she says. Her voice is more akin to a bird than a human, a half-strangulated croak from the back of the throat, not unlike a magpie or a rook.

Khav's own throat has gone so dry she finds she can't answer.

"You want?" the woman says again.

Khav nods breathlessly.

The woman rubs the thumb and fingers of her other hand rapidly together.

"You want, you pay."

"Yes," says Khav, finding her voice at last, "of course. How much?"

"How much you have?"

Khav fumbles in her pocket. She pulls out a ten pound note.

"Is that all?"

Khav nods.

"OK," says the woman, snatching the money. "Here. You take." She hands Khav the glass tigon, then scurries away.

Khav is lost in the wonder of it. The way it catches and holds the light. The animal seems almost alive. It is of an altogether different order from the usual mass-produced tweeness of the kind more usually to be found.

" '*To see a world in a grain of sand...*' " she hears herself whisper. " '*Hold infinity in the palm of your hand...*' "

When she looks up again, the woman has disappeared. A lone moth flutters against the bars of the railings running along Devas Street.

It is then that Khav receives her moment of revelation.

The sun, which has been constantly flitting between clouds this last half-hour, now breaks free completely. It strikes the glass tigon directly, which reacts like a prism, refracting the beam into a multi-verse of different colours. But only for a moment. Another larger, blacker cloud covers it once more. The afternoon light has taken on that ominous, bruised quality just before a storm hits, and Khav does not have long to wait. A crack of thunder splits the air. Instantly, as if someone has flicked a switch, the rain begins to fall, huge drops in bucketsful. Within seconds Khav is soaked to the skin. The water pours down in rivulets upon her cheeks and face, which she lifts up to let more wash over her. It feels like a baptism, a total immersion.

She knows with as much certainty as she knows her own name that the woman with the angel tattoo is the reincarnation of her *Nani*. Of Urja.

Khav comes from a long, unbroken line of Sikhs. She has been brought up as one. She has dutifully observed all of the customs and traditions. She has obediently accompanied her parents to the *gurdwara* each week. She has lit candles, offered up prayers, taken part in ceremonies and rituals. But she has never stopped to consider the meaning behind any of these. Mostly she has been simply doing what has been expected of her, what she's been told. She hasn't ever thought about whether she believes in any of it.

Until now.

She's listened to the readings from the *Guru Granth Sahib* without really taking in any of the words. Even when they've been aimed directly at her or her family, such as when Priya was married, or for Dilsher's *Naam Karan*, or even, more recently, for *Nani*'s funeral, the *Antam Sanskar*, when prayers for her next reincarnation were offered up by the *sangat*, the congregation. She's dismissed it all as nothing more than superstition.

Until now.

She's even spoken the words themselves along with everyone else, reciting them automatically, her mind somewhere else entirely.

'*Waheguru*, the Spirit of God lives inside everyone. Like a reflection in a mirror, or a fragrance in a flower. Through a long series of purifications, the seemingly eternal cycle of *samsara*, during which we go through many millions of reincarnations, in every possible form of life, we shall in time break free from the everlasting night of birth and death and rebirth, and our soul, the *atma*, shall look upon the divine light that only dawns within.'

But she has never paused to think about what any of this might mean. Nor the significance of *karma*, the consequences our actions in one life might have for our next.

Until now.

The thunder cracks over her head once more. The rain continues to fall in torrents. But she doesn't care. She feels the inspiration of this new knowledge and awareness surging through her, filling her with energy and hope. Without a second's thought she runs through the puddles and standing water as fast as her uneven legs can carry her, not stopping till her lungs reach bursting point, as she rounds the corner into Albion Road, fumbles with her key to fling open the front door, where she stands, dripping from head to toe on the mat, her silhouette backlit from the storm raging outside, like no less a figure than Azrael herself. The Angel. The Messenger.

"*Maa*!" she cries. "*Bapu*! I'm home!"

But when, half an hour later, she has finished telling them what she has witnessed, the storm no longer rages outside the house, but within. Vikram's fury is limitless. He rants, he raves. He rages, he roars. Louder than she imagines even than a tigon, whose manifestation in molten sand and ash she still clasps in her hand. His words hammer against her ears more loudly than the rain hitting the window pane. She feels as though her head will shatter and explode with the force of them.

"How dare you?" he cries. "How dare you insult the memory of *Nani* by suggesting she might be reborn as some homeless bag lady? How can you even think that such a thing is possible? Think of all the countless, selfless good deeds she did in her life. Always putting the needs of others before her own. The number of times she looked after you, her precious *dohti*. Is this how you repay her? Is this how you value her many acts of sacrifice? Do you know nothing of *karma*? Aiee!"

Vikram is beside himself. He keeps up this tirade for a full forty minutes. He bangs his fists on table-tops. He pummels the sides of his own temples in frustration. He storms about the house, slamming doors and knocking over chairs.

Geetha puts her head in her hands and wails. Dilsher begins to scream at the top of his voice. Priya charges downstairs and thrusts her face inches away from her sister's.

"Are you satisfied now?" she yells. "Now that you've turned the whole house upside down? Have you any idea just how long it's taken me to get Dilsher off to sleep? Listen to him!" Dilsher is becoming hysterical. "This is all your doing!"

She too now tears about the house, desperately trying to calm her inconsolable son, while Vikram continues his rampage unabated.

"Always you have been difficult, always you have tested us to the limit, always you have been determined to go your own way, trampling over everybody else's needs but your own."

"Aiee!" cries Geetha once more, rocking back and forth and ululating.

Khav, standing in the centre of the storm, the eye of this hurricane, swirling all around her, vainly tries to speak, to attempt to explain, but she is trapped within the vortex. She is standing close to the window where the candle for Urja is burning, which the family must keep lit for another three hundred and fifty days. It bends under the force of her father's anger. Khav looks at it long and hard. She tries to focus all her will upon it, to shut out the maelstrom reeling all around her. Then she looks at the glass tigon, then back to the candle once more. It comes to her in an instant what she must do. She leans towards the candle and blows hard, once. In an instant the flame is extinguished.

A terrible silence falls upon the house. The smoke from the snuffed-out candle coils around her.

Eventually Vikram speaks. His voice is like ice. Khav feels its fingers grip around her heart. His words are daggers.

"Go," he says. "I want you to leave. Immediately. You must not set foot in this house again. You are no daughter of mine."

With that he turns calmly on his heels and walks deliberately up the stairs. Khav watches his departing back, then turns to look at her mother. Geetha says nothing. She shakes her head and shuts her eyes. Khav opens the front door and steps outside. The rain has stopped. A pale sun bleeds through a bandage of cloud. A rainbow appears, mocking her. She limps painfully away from the only home she has ever known. Albion Road. She wills herself not to look back.

*

Chloe's phone pings. It's a text from Khav.

"Can I crash at yours for a few days?"
"Sure. Why? Are U OK?"
"Tnx. Tell U when I see U. xx"

*

Clive's phone pings. It's a text from Chloe.

"Call me when U get this. Urgent. Re Khav. Tnx."

*

"What is it? What's happened?"

"Khav can't do her presentation tomorrow."

"What? Why not?"

"Problems at home."

"Oh." A pause. "Can you be more specific?"

"Her Dad's kicked her out."

"Why? What's she meant to have done?"

"Take his side, why don't you?"

"I'm not. It's just…" Another pause. "Is she staying with you?"

"Yes."

"How long for?"

"As long as she needs. Till she can sort things out."

"Can I speak to her?"

Chloe looks across to Khav, who shakes her head. "Not right now. She's too upset. It's serious, Clive, what's happened. She's in no fit state to do her presentation."

"OK."

A deep sigh. "Thanks, Clive."

"The thing is – she's already had one postponement…"

"Yeah, but that was for her *Nani*'s funeral."

"I know – it's just that tomorrow is the last day she can retake it. I'm meant to send off all your grades for external verification then."

"But you're the Course Leader. Can't you swing something, plead mitigating circumstances? Which would be true by the way."

Clive thinks for a moment.

"All right – listen. If Khav can get a Doctor's note confirming that she's simply too unwell to take the presentation, and you can get that to me before midday tomorrow, I can then arrange for another delay."

"Thanks, Clive. You're a star. I'll make sure that she does, and I'll bring the note to you personally."

"Right. OK."

Chloe hears a sudden, sharp intake of breath from Clive on the other end.

"Shit."

"What is it?"

"I forgot. It's the 2nd Years' presentations all next week. The Studio will be fully booked."

"Oh." Chloe can almost hear the sound of Clive thinking on his feet.

"It'll have to be a week tomorrow. Early."

"Saturday?"

"It's the only free day. Otherwise she'll be too late, and she'll risk getting an 'ungraded', which I'm sure she doesn't want, not after all the hard work she's put in over the last three years."

"OK. What time?"

"Tell her to meet me there at around 8.30. I'll arrange for Tanya to be there by nine to help her set up."

"Thank you, Clive. I will."

"I'll still need that Doctor's note tomorrow."

"Sure. Don't worry."

"OK. Oh – Chloe…?"

"Yes?"

"Give her my best, won't you?"

"I will."

"I hope she manages to sort things out at home."

"I hope so too. But that's not going to happen overnight."

*

2020

It's all change once more at Albion Road.

Dilsher is now eight years old. He goes to Wilbraham Primary on Platt Lane just a ten minute walk away. He loves school and is doing well there. He's still a light sleeper, but he no longer demands attention when he wakes while it is still dark in the mornings. Instead he reads voraciously. Currently he's working his way through the books of Onjali Q. Rauf. *The Boy at the Back of the Class, The Star Outside My Window, The Night Bus Hero*. It was Khav who first introduced Dilsher to her, after she'd heard Ms Rauf deliver a TEDx talk entitled '*Making Herstory: Why Children Are Our Most Powerful Hope For Change*'. Khav believes this absolutely, and she wants Dilsher to also.

Dilsher now has a sister. Rukmini. Ruki for short. Ruki is five and has been at the same school as her brother for a term and a half. Sometimes, if Priya is too busy, Khav walks her there. Ostensibly she is walking Dilsher there too, but he maintains he is big enough now to walk there by himself, so she goes along with his stance by permitting him to walk fifty yards ahead of her and Ruki. "So long as you stay where I can see you," she tells him. Hearing herself say this, she is forced to smile. She sounds like her *Maa* when she was Dilsher's age. Dilsher reluctantly complies – an honourable draw – while Ruki chatters happily non-stop beside her, her hand automatically inserted into her aunt's larger paw. Is that what she now is, thinks Khav in disbelief? An Auntie? Will she soon be giving Ruki advice on how to prepare a full Sunday dinner, vegetarian only? Or asking her embarrassing questions about her boyfriends? She shakes her head and smiles.

"What is it, Auntie?" asks Ruki guilelessly.

"Nothing," says Khav. "And please stop calling me 'Auntie'. Khav will do just fine."

"Yes, Auntie Khav."

As soon as Ruki began sleeping through the night, which she did almost at once, being as unlike her brother in this as it was possible to be, it was decided she was ready for her own room. Much to the relief of Priya and Duleep, who had had enough sleepless nights with Dilsher to last them a lifetime. This meant another complete change-round in the house on Albion Road.

Vikram and Geetha decamped downstairs into what had been Urja's room in the annexe, so that Priya and Duleep could move into their former bedroom, allowing Dilsher to move into what had been *theirs* and Ruki to have *his*, the room which had originally been *Khav's*. Khav, who, since she had returned home after the argument with her father, had been using her *Nani*'s annexe almost as an independent, separate flat of her own within the house, now moved into the sitting room and slept on the sofa bed there, as she had when Urja had first moved into the annexe before she died.

The rift with her father has been repaired, if not exactly healed. Much to Geetha's relief, at least there is a semblance of peace in the house. Khav and Vikram are polite, if distant, civil, if cool, with each other, so that meal times, which are the only occasion when the whole family comes together, pass off without unpleasantness. Otherwise everyone goes about their own business more or less independently of one another.

When Covid really begins to take hold and the first lockdown is announced towards the end of March, Geetha is anxious that the enforced confinement, throwing them all unexpectedly back into close proximity with one another, might bring about a resurgence of all the old conflicts, which she has worked so hard to suppress, forcing them back into the open, but she is pleasantly surprised. By and large, they manage to navigate these potentially troubled waters more successfully than she had feared.

This has been helped by their particular individual circumstances. Vikram, who had now become Manager of the Longsight Branch of Lloyds TSB, still goes out to work each day. His hours there are reduced, but at least the banks are still open. Duleep, who does something unfathomable with IT, is able to work on his laptop in his and Priya's bedroom for most of each day, while Khav can also work from home. She has done well since she graduated from MMU, and secretly, Geetha knows, Vikram is immensely proud of her, though he will never say anything.

Khav works two days a week for the Arts Council, as part of their Assessment Team in the office on Balloon Street. This was how she had first come across the work of Molly, whose initial application for a GfA – a Grant for the Arts – to carry out some initial research into her proposed *Thin Blue Line* installation in 2018, had caught her attention. Its boldness and originality had stood out, and Khav had signposted it to her Team Leader as worthy of support. Then, after the initial research had been completed, Khav encouraged Molly to apply for a subsequent grant to fund the actual installation, which, when it finally took place, had created waves of significant interest. Here was an artist to watch, and Khav had felt a glow of satisfaction that she had played a small but influential part in enabling Molly's career to get the kick-start it needed.

For two other days each week Khav works as an Administrator for the Manchester International Festival, a fairly junior position, but one which allows her to coordinate some of the local participatory outreach programmes across the city.

One of these has been to work in partnership with Jane Parry, the Neighbourhood & Engagement Development Officer of Manchester Central Library, to plan a series of TEDx talks. It was as part of these she had first come into contact with Onjali Q. Rauf, and also how she was able to invite Molly to present one at the previous year's Festival to mark the 200th anniversary of Peterloo. Molly had given an inspiring performance tracing the story of a piece of white cotton cloth that she was wearing as a *qurqash* on her head, which had been passed down through various generations of her family, but whose journey also had a link to the day of the massacre itself. It, too, had caused further ripples, and Molly's reputation was growing. Khav had now begun working with Molly towards a possible commission for the 2021 Festival – providing the pandemic has been vanquished by then – and she has been in fairly regular contact via Zoom to discuss possible ideas. It is through these that she discovers that Molly now has a studio in Salford, at Islington Mill, where Lorrie is the Gallery Manager. It has been good to be back in touch with Lorrie again, albeit remotely, who really seems to have found her niche there. She confides in Khav that she has begun learning a new skill – to become a tightrope walker – and perhaps one day she might be able to perform at the Festival herself. Khav promises to keep her informed of any possible opportunities, and the two of them arrange to meet up, if ever the restrictions are relaxed.

Khav works these four days, spread across the two jobs, from a small table in what had once been her *Nani*'s annexe, where her parents now reside. Geetha insists upon it. Khav, even seven years after her *Nani* has died, still feels her presence in the room. The glass animals are still on the repaired shelves, the Caitlin Mallone tigon now among them. Where Khav got this from, or what it still signifies for her, is never spoken of.

She spends much of her time in front of a screen. As well as Zoom meetings with colleagues, she needs to keep abreast of the various digital offerings many of her artistic clients are creating online. Their imagination is typically fired by the current constraint of galleries and theatres being closed for the duration. Their capacity to respond to the new normal continues to inspire. She is reminded of her time as a B-girl, when she and Teniel would simply turn up unannounced at crowded, public spaces and begin a throw-down. Like guerrilla fighters. The thought of being in a crowded, public space now fills her with alarm. But artists have always found a way of subverting rules and restraints, of taking risks, and this is what has attracted her to them.

Lorrie sends her a link to the *Five Lockdown Films* made by Molly, which Khav watches with a growing sense of excitement. Especially *#4: Learning to Walk by Day*. The connections vibrate across the ether. We are all of us part of this circle, she thinks. Locked in by lockdown. But, like the tigon, we will escape. Set free by art, which Molly compares to the act of walking. Khav tries to take a walk each day, for thirty minutes, as prescribed by the government.

She still hopes she might once again catch sight of the woman with the angel tattoo, hunkered down beside some railings perhaps, her palm outstretched, hoping for some spare change, but she never does. Instead, like Molly, she sees straggles of starlings buffeting the wind. She wonders if, perhaps, her *Nani*'s soul might now have migrated to one of them. She watches the way they swoop and dive towards the window at the back of the house, through which *Nani* herself had scanned the skies for their coming each day. She hears in their skrike and squabble the voices of Dilsher and Ruki in the sitting room next door, where each day they do their home schooling, which neither of them enjoys, both of them missing their friends and their teachers. Sometimes it is Khav who takes their lessons, occasionally it is Duleep, but mostly it is Priya, who, forbidden by the new rules from carrying out her work as a hairdresser, must stay indoors with her children. Not even Platt Fields, which mock them with their close proximity, are available to them as a means of escape, being locked and shut by Order of the Council.

Priya is finding lockdown especially tough. She's a people person, and she desperately misses her clients. Just as they miss her. In between Dilsher and Ruki being born, she has left the salon and set up her own business, doing her customers' hair in the comfort and convenience of their own homes. Older ladies mostly, widows, who look forward to Priya's weekly visits, when she will shampoo and set their hair, while they put the world to rights, or confide their worries about their grown-up sons and daughters and their various children. She's as much their counsellor, confessor, therapist and social worker, as she is their hairdresser. If anyone's a key worker, she will argue, it is her. But now her bright green Ford Escort van, with its gold lettering on the side, *'The Salon In Your Living Room'*, decorated with a pattern of scissors and combs, lies parked and idle on the street outside.

Priya is going stir-crazy, and frequently Khav will hear her raise her voice with Dilsher and Ruki, who will grow fretful and fractious by turns, their mother's moods as contagious as the virus.

The situation is not helped by the difficulties Priya is experiencing in trying to draw down government support. As a self-employed worker, she has been told she is eligible for a grant, but that she must wait a further two months before she can claim. Khav, as a freelancer herself, is sympathetic and understands the difficulty. She helps her sister with all the numerous online forms she has to submit, or takes the children off her hands for an hour or two. Dilsher and Ruki love it when this happens. Unlike their mother, who follows the timetable of lessons sent to her by email from the school, Khav goes off-piste. She lets them paint, not worrying about the mess they might make. She plays chess with Dilsher, snap with Ruki, and ludo with them both. She tries to teach them the different strategies for finding their way home. Do they concentrate on just one counter at a time? Or do they race all of them simultaneously around the board, but risk none of them reaching their prized destination? How best to respond to each roll of the dice? Which choices to make? She even teaches them some basic hip-hop and break-dance moves, which they show off later to Priya and Geetha – but not to Vikram. To quieten them down afterwards, she reads them stories. Ruki's favourite is *Punchkin*, an Indian version of Rapunzel. Khav's hair has continued to grow back and is now more than half-way down her back. Ruki loves the idea of growing her own hair as long as Punchkin's, so that it might reach all the way down to the ground from her bedroom upstairs. She's not so much excited by the thought of a handsome prince wanting to climb up it to rescue her – she doesn't need rescuing, thank you very much – as by the prospect of being able to use it as a ladder to escape all by herself, and, perhaps also, if he's good and she's feeling particularly well-disposed towards him, her brother too, so that they might run off into the wilds of Platt Fields together, and then somehow climb back up it again afterwards. Home in the time of coronavirus – sanctuary or prison?

Khav enjoys these times with them, especially since the other job she used to do pre-Covid for the other two days of her typical working week, as a Children's Play Worker with Z-Arts in Hulme, has been suspended. What started out ten years ago as running *Missi Roti* there on Saturday mornings quickly grew to her being invited to run after-school groups, holiday classes and summer carnival projects. Now she has a temporary rolling annual contract to help coordinate Z-Arts' regular programmes of young people's workshops in every kind of discipline – not just street dance, but drama, puppetry, mask-making, singing, photography, film-making, game design and graffiti. Her

'Digital Discoverers' have gone through two or three generations of young people by now. They continue to thrive and have regular live screenings. At least they used to – before the pandemic struck. Now they must restrict themselves to making short films on their phones confined within the four walls of where each of them lives, which they regularly share on youtube. They're acquiring quite a following.

Khav sees all three jobs as mutually compatible, with aspects from one spilling easily into the others, so that, if asked how to define what she does, she will answer, "I'm a Community Arts Facilitator." And if she is then asked, "What does that mean?", she will simply say, "Come along and find out."

And as often as not, they do. Khav has lots of friends, but these, too, she can no longer see, except on Zoom or Skype or Facetime, which are all OK, but no substitute for the real thing. Especially with one of these friends, who is more special, who she has yet to introduce to Geetha or Vikram, despite knowing that she should have done by now, but who would simply not understand, especially *Bapu*. The peace that exists between them these days is a fragile one. Khav knows it would take very little to break it, and she has no desire to do this, for her *Maa*'s sake more than her own, for it is she who is the real heroine of the hour, she who is the glue that holds them all together in this time of lockdown, she who comes back each day from her trials and ordeals with the local shops and markets, exhausted by the never-ending grind to find rice, or flour, or toilet rolls, or whatever is the latest necessity to be in current short supply, causing stampedes that empty the shelves for all except the earliest riser.

It is not just her *Nani* that Khav sees glimpses of in the scrapping starlings' daily forays, but her *Maa* too. Her hair, which, five years before, still retained its dark, glossy, lustrous sheen, is now completely grey, her face thinner and more lined.

theguardian

16th June 2020

HIGHER COVID DEATHS AMONG 'BAME' PEOPLE NOT DRIVEN BY HEALTH ISSUES

ONS says greater risk is largely due to life circumstances.

Chloe Chang reports

Figures from a report published today by the Office for National Statistics (ONS) confirm that people from black and south Asian ethnic backgrounds have a greater risk of death from Covid than white people. The report further reveals that such differences are not driven by pre-existing health conditions, but largely down to factors such as living arrangements and jobs.

Among males in England and Wales, the rate for those of a BAME background dying from Covid is 2.7 times higher than that of white males, while for females the rate is almost twice that of white females

Ever since the pandemic began, it has appeared that people from BAME backgrounds are at greater risk from the coronavirus than white people. This official ONS report has now provided the figures to substantiate those claims.

The results reveal that in all ethnicities, males have a higher rate of death than females.

"Our statistical modelling shows that a large proportion of the difference in the risk of Covid-19 mortality between ethnic groups can be explained by demographic, geographical and socioeconomic factors, such as where you live or the occupation you're in," said Ben Humberstone, Deputy Director of the Health and Life Events Division at the ONS.

The fact of having confirmation of what has long been widely accepted and understood, however, while removing once and for all any potential racial or biological stigma, brings no comfort to those individuals, families and communities already so disproportionately affected by the pandemic.

"It's as though we are being punished for doing those important jobs that others may not wish to do, while at the same time looking after our elderly relatives in multi-generational households," one anonymous Sikh community leader told us yesterday.

*

Suddenly things begin to move very quickly. Events spiral out of their control. Like water emptying down a drain. Or the last few grains of sand trickling ever faster through the hour glass. In a year when every day has felt like Groundhog Day, endlessly repeating itself, so that it has been difficult at times to be sure of even what month it is, let alone what day, the experience has been not unlike looking through both ends of a telescope simultaneously. The year seems barely to have begun, yet at the same time it feels as though life has been like this for ever, suspended, frozen, on hold. Then something happens to set the hands of the clock spinning faster and faster. Khav wants to grab a hold of them to slow them down, but she can't. Where, before, the days had dragged, now they gallop all too quickly. The hours race by like seconds.

Vikram comes home one day from the bank in Longsight complaining of a cough. There's a tightness across his chest, he says. He must have caught a summer cold. But then, when Geetha serves up his favourite *palak paneer*, a spinach curry flavoured with garlic and ginger, with *jeera* rice and *lassi*, he pushes it away, saying he simply can't taste it.

That night he is unable to sleep. His breathing is laboured, coming in short, uneven, rasping gasps. Geetha creeps downstairs and wakes Khav on the sofa bed, asking her what she should do. Khav, instantly alert, calls 111, who advise them to monitor the situation closely. "It may indeed be just a summer cold," they say. "Give it twenty-four hours. If he doesn't begin to feel better, or if he starts to develop a fever, take him to your nearest hospital."

"But he already has a fever," says Geetha. "He's burning up."

"Right," says Khav decisively and immediately dials 999.

Twenty minutes later the paramedics arrive, by which time Vikram's breathing has become even more difficult. They assess the situation at once, carry him downstairs, lift him into the ambulance, where they put him on oxygen, then whisk him off the one and a half miles to Manchester Royal Infirmary, with siren blaring and blue light flashing.

When Geetha tries to climb into the ambulance to accompany her husband to hospital, she is told firmly, but not unkindly, that she is not allowed to.

"It's the rule," they say. "Covid. To protect you and the rest of your family."

Time freezes once again.

But also it rushes by all too quickly.

The last grains of sand plummet through the hour glass until all have passed through and the upper chamber is empty.

Three days pass.

Vikram has become a statistic, another of the thousands infected by the virus. Behind the full face visor he is unrecognisable.

On the first day Vikram is transferred to Intensive Care.

They are none of them permitted to visit him.

On the second day Vikram is put on a ventilator.

They remain forbidden from seeing him. They could speak to him via a mobile but Vikram is not well enough to answer.

On the third day Vikram dies.

A kind nurse from the ICU rings them up to give them the news. She sounds emotional and exhausted. Geetha feels sorry for her. She tells her to make sure she looks after herself. The nurse thanks her almost tearfully. She tells Geetha that Vikram regained consciousness briefly in the hours before he died. She wrote down what he said. She was to tell them he loved them, she says, to remember that this was just another part of his journey and they were not to be sad. He had been blessed, she tells them, to have such a loving wife as Geetha, and two such beautiful daughters. Priya, he said, you will be a fine mother to your son and your daughter. You already are. Finally, the nurse says, she was to tell Khavita that her father was immensely proud of her, her courage, her independence, her free spirit, and that he prayed she would forgive him for all the unkind things he may have said to her in the past. He was only ever trying to protect her, to do what he felt was best for her, for all of them.

A deep, profound silence hangs over the house on Albion Road.

For several days after the funeral and cremation, while the continuous reading from the *Guru Granth Sahib* is taking place at the *Gurdwara* on Upper Chorlton Road, nobody speaks unless they have to, and even then it is in hushed whispers with as few words as possible. Outside the weather is warm. The air has a drugged heaviness about it. Even the starlings are quiet, unable to shake themselves from their heat-induced stupor.

Dilsher plays endless games of chess with himself, trying to find new ways of avoiding the inevitable checkmate.

Ruki reads and re-reads *Punchkin*, hoping that she might change the story, so that her *Baba* might have been able to climb down her hair and escape, but she never can. Instead she winds her hair back up, wrapping it tightly around her head, like pulling up a drawbridge.

Priya locks herself in her bedroom and refuses to come out. Duleep does all he can to try and bring her back to herself but he simply cannot reach her, so he loses himself in the world of binary codes in his computer, a series of ones and zeros, endlessly reconfiguring themselves, switching from on to off, on to off.

Geetha busies herself in cooking, preparing *langar* for the *sangat* in the temple.

Only Khav feels the need for action, to step back out into the world and take up her place there once more.

As the lockdown restrictions slowly begin to ease, as shops and bars and restaurants reopen, as people start to take their first few tentative steps back towards whatever this new normal might look like, Khav knows with a sudden certainty what she will do.

She will become an *amritdhari*, an initiate of the *khalsa*, and enter fully into her Sikh life.

But first, she will take out her *Bapu*'s shiny yellow *Babaj Chetak* from its steel lockup in front of the house, and she will ride it into the city.

She will go directly to her special friend. Their relationship must be hidden no longer. No more secrets. No more evasions. No more delays.

She will tip the hour glass back up again. She will make the most of each grain of sand, each moment, seizing every one of them and making them her own.

She lifts the glass tigon from its shelf, looks at it directly in the eye, then smiles.

She sits astride the scooter, pulls back the brake with her left hand, switches on the ignition with her right, then releases the brake, but too quickly, and the scooter kangaroos forward. She tries again, more slowly this time. That's better. A moth lands upon the back of her hand. She looks at it closely. It seems in no hurry to take off again. It is the black-peppered

'Manchester' moth, the one which changed colour to blend in with its environment better. She brings it up closer to her, so that she might examine it in more detail. It slowly opens, then closes its mottled wings, before leisurely taking off again. It's time that she, too, was on her way, thinks Khav. She turns the throttle forward to increase the speed. Yes, she thinks. She's got this. She eases into the traffic on Wilmslow Road, fully in control of her balance now, and heads towards the city.

Through Fallowfield, Rusholme, Moss Side, All Saints.

The yellow scooter glides past, the sun bouncing off its bright yellow chrome, creating dappled circles of saffron light, which dance upon the pavements, dozens of *rangoli* patterns flickering with hope.

The future beckons like a beacon.

Manchester waits to welcome her, its glittering glass towers soaring into the sky like fireworks.

*

2013

Khav's phone pings. It's a text from Clive.

"Call me when you get this."

"Hi," she says.

"I've got a new date," he says. "For your presentation. A week tomorrow."

"Saturday?"

"It's the only vacant slot."

"OK. Thanks."

"I got your Doctor's note. That made it straightforward. A combination of compassionate and medical grounds."

"I could've done it yesterday, if I'd had to."

"No. You wouldn't have done yourself justice"

"I suppose not."

"That's what matters."

"Thank you, Clive. Not just for this, but for believing in me."

"It's my job." A pause. "Now just do yours."

"I'll do my best."

"You'll do more than that. Just go out there and smash it."

"I'll try."

"A week tomorrow. Saturday. Noon. Come along early. Half-eight. I'll be there to let you in. Tanya'll be along around nine to make sure you've got everything you need."

"Right."

"Right."

*

"Yo, Khav."

"Yo, Tan."

*

The clock in the TV Studio shows a quarter to twelve.

"Ready?" says Tanya.

"Ready," replies Khav. "I think."

"You'd better be. Clive's waiting outside."

"Just give me five more minutes, OK?"

"OK."

Khav surveys the studio. Everything is in place. Tanya has set up the old 35 mm film spool on a turntable, onto which Khav has placed all of her props, so that they can revolve on a continuous loop like a carousel. She's rigged a white cotton sheet in front of them, with a light set behind them, so they can be projected onto it, like shadows puppets.

These are all positioned near the back of the studio. In front, Khav has laid out an old oriental rug lent to her by Chloe, on which Khav will sit during her presentation. Around this she has placed a number of small terracotta pots, each with a candle inside, which she has yet to light. To the side of the screen, slightly right of centre, is a microphone, a loop machine, a *dhol* drum, a roll of plastic bubble-wrap, and a *shruti* box. Between her 'set' and the row of chairs that have been placed for her small audience the saffron *siropa* has been stretched across the studio.

She nods.

"Yes," she says. "I'm ready."

"It looks great," says Tanya. "Just give me the signal when you want me to switch on the carousel."

"I will."

The two of them stand by the studio door looking back towards the set one last time.

"It looks like the start of some kind of ritual," says Tanya after a few moments.

"That's exactly what it is," says Khav. "It's my *Amrit Sanskhar.*"

Tanya raises a questioning eyebrow.

"An initiation ceremony," explains Khav, turning her face towards Tanya.

The two of them are standing very close to one another.

"An initiation?" whispers Tanya very softly, looking directly into Khav's eyes.

"Yes," says Khav, equally softly, returning her gaze.

*

Two days earlier.

Vidhya's phone pings. It's a text from Khav.

"Does the Amrit Sanskar have to take place in the Gurdwara?"
"No. It can happen anywhere."
"How many people have to be present?"
"There's no fixed number. 5? 6? Why?"
"I'm thinking about becoming an *amritdhari.*"
"Great."

"But I want to do it my own way."
"As it should be. But…"
"But…?"
"It won't be officially recognised."
"That doesn't bother me. Will you come?"
"Love to."
"Ask Tanveet, Beesham and Saroor."
"Will do. What about your family?"
"No. Bapu would refuse and Maa would feel she has to stand by him."
"I'm sorry."
"Don't be. I'm not. This is for me."
"When?"
"Saturday. MMU. Grosvenor Building."
"We'll be there. Good luck. xxx"

*

Saturday. Just before twelve.

"Good luck," whispers Tanya to Khav, her lips gently brushing her cheek.

*

Final Presentation #4: Khav

It is exactly midday. High Noon for Khav.

Tanya opens the TV Studio doors and the small invited audience enters the space, filled with excitement and anticipation. Vidhya, Beesham, Tanveet and Saroor, followed by Chloe, Petros and Lorrie. None of them says a word. Tanya has lit the Diwali candles in their terracotta pots, which encircle the space where Khav is to deliver her presentation, but for the moment she is nowhere to be seen. Tanya indicates where they should sit, just the other side of the length of saffron cloth that demarcates the space between performer and spectators. Dutifully they all sit on the chairs that have been carefully allocated for them. The atmosphere is unusually decorous, a marked contrast to the casual informality of earlier

presentations. Tanya hands each of them a glass of Vimto as they arrive, which they sip in excited, giggling anticipation.
Clive, who is the last to arrive, picks up on this at once.

CLIVE:

Khav – before you start, I feel it is incumbent upon me to remind you that this is meant to be a Media Production presentation, not a theatre performance or gallery piece. What branch of the media are you focusing on here? It's not immediately apparent. Chloe, you may recall, gave us News Reportage, Petros used Documentary Photography, Lorrie a Music Video. You?

KHAV: (*answering unseen from a corner of the Studio not lit*): *Ravanachhaya.*

CLIVE:

You'll have to enlighten me, Khav.

KHAV:

That's what I'm here to do, Clive.

CLIVE:

Explain.

KHAV:

Ravanachhaya is the ancient Indian folk tradition of shadow puppets, Clive. Traditionally performed by peddlers, travelling from village to village, singing songs, telling stories. Shadow puppets are the earliest form of cinematography, innit?

CLIVE:

Yes, I see. Not unlike the work of Leni Riefenstahl.

KHAV:

To be honest, Clive, I was thinking more the Deathly

Hallows sequence from the last Harry Potter film, innit?

At once Chloe, Petros and Lorrie begin to hum the opening bars of the film's theme tune.

CLIVE:
Thank you, Khav. Consider me enlightened.

KHAV:
Whoa, Clive! Let's not be getting ahead of ourselves.

Chloe, Petros and Lorrie collectively whistle and applaud. Clive sits in his chair, shaking his head, but smiling, while Khav tosses the old clapped-out clapperboard to Lorrie.

Do the honours as usual, will you, Lol?

LORRIE: (*delightedly snapping it shut*):
Action.

Khav now signals to Tanya to switch on the turntable.

The carousel slowly begins to revolve. Onto the makeshift screen are projected the shadows of Khav's props – the baseball cap given to her by Teniel, her first pair of built-up shoes, the glass tigon, Agriwal's Manchester Corporation Transport badge. The audience watches them pass by in mesmerised fascination.

While they are thus engaged, Khav limps barefooted into the light cast by the Diwali candles in front of the screen. She sits cross-legged behind the microphone. She switches on the loop machine next to her, then picks up the plastic bubble-wrap, which she proceeds to pop beside the microphone. The loop machine instantly records, then repeats its atmospheric crackle and fizz. It sounds at once like a fire taking hold. To add to the illusion, Tanya releases a small amount of dry ice from a smoke machine, which rolls across where Khav is sitting, so that the fire appears to be emanating directly from her. Tanya now activates the colour wheel in front of the light behind the screen, so that, instead of the silhouettes being merely black against white, they are now infused with red, yellow and orange. Khav then picks up the dhol drum and begins a low, incessant rumble with her fingers upon the stretched skin of its surface, like the sound of something big approaching from far-off, feet pounding in the earth, getting nearer and louder. Next she begins to sing into the microphone, a rising, insistent, sacred Indian chant, the notes returning in a repeating, circular pattern.

KHAV: (*singing*):
  Bhand jammi ai
  Bhand nimmi ai
  Bhand mangan vi ahu
  Bhand mu a
  Bhand bali ai
  Bhand hovai bhandan

  So ki o manda akhi ai
  Jit jameh rajan
  Bhandahu hi bhand
  Upjal bhand ai
  Baj nah ko e

Round and round the chant repeats, mixed in with the sounds of the fire and the approaching feet. The smoke rises. Khav stands. She walks forward, into the centre of the circle. She turns so that she is facing away from the audience. A tight, narrow light shining upwards picks out her bare back. Etched delicately onto her skin in dark blue ink is a tattoo. It is of an elephant charging. The mix on the loop machine grows louder.

The sound of the approaching hooves increases in volume, drowning out the other tracks, so that it almost appears as if the elephant on Khav's back is about to leap from her skin and trample underfoot all who stand in her path. But just as it reaches its crescendo, it cuts out.

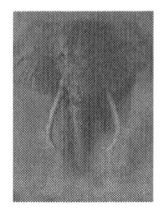

Silence. Blackout

Out of the silence the sound of the shruti box can be heard. The air passes through the bellows to produce a sustained drone, not unlike a harmonium. Unseen, Khav keeps this going by gently pushing the bellows in and out with her stronger right foot, keeping her hands free, so that she can operate the shadow puppets, which proceed to pass in turn from one side of the screen to the other.

A man praying in Amritsar. A ship crossing the ocean. The Manchester skyline. A double-decker Corporation bus.

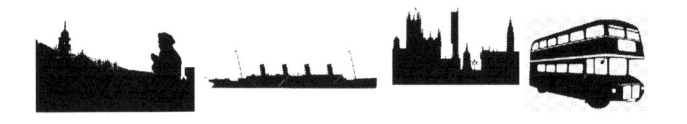

A sikh couple getting married. That same woman when she's older, with a granddaughter, who's looking up to her right, something having caught her eye. A moth laying her eggs. The egg, the caterpillar, the pupa, the imagine.

The drone of the shruti box fades. The parade of the shadow puppets is complete.

Khav returns to the circle in front of the screen. Her hair is loose and uncovered. She wears the traditional kachera, the white undergarments, a sleeveless chemise, a pair of loose cotton shorts.

Vidhya, Beesham, Tanveet and Saroor step forward. Between them they dress Khav in a white shalwar kameez and cover her head in a plain black cloth, which they just rest there, but do not tie. They place a small wooden board on the studio floor in front of her, which they decorate with a rangoli pattern in the shape of the khanda, a Sikh symbol depicting two swords, signifying the commitment to fight for what is right, framing a circle, showing that God is one, without beginning or end. Khav steps into the centre of it.

They then present to her each of the remaining khalsas. Vidhya gives her the kirpan, the ceremonial dagger; Beesham the kanga, the comb; Tanveet the kara, the iron bracelet, while Saroor sprinkles the amrit, the sugared water, from a bowl over Khav's hair, the kesh. They then together recite the Mool Mantar.

VIDHYA:
   Ik Onkar – there is only one God

BEESHAM:
Sat Nam – Eternal Truth

TANVEET:
Kurtah Purak – the Creator

SAROOR:
Nir Bhau – without fear

VIDHYA:
Nir Vair – without hate

BEESHAM:
Akal Moorat – immortal in form

TANVEET:
Ajooni – beyond birth or death

SAROOR:
Saibhang – self- existent

ALL:
Gurprasaad – by the Guru's grace…

They return to their seats. Khav picks up the saffron siropa that stretches right across the studio, folding it in on itself as she does, measuring it against the span of her arm, until she has concertina-ed it into a single four-foot width. While she is doing this, she translates the words of the chant that she sang earlier

KHAV:
From woman, man is born
Within woman, man is conceived
Woman becomes his friend
Through a woman, the future is born
To woman, man is bound

So why call her bad?
Why put her down?
From woman, woman is born
Without woman, there is no one...

She has now completed the process of winding and folding the siropa. She now adopts an entirely different, cheery tone as she addresses her audience directly.

KHAV:

Hi, folks, and welcome to KKYTC.
Khavita Kaur's You Tube Channel.
Today I'm going to show you how to tie a *pukka* turban, innit?

She signals to Tanya, who cues in the theme tune to Tony Hart's 'Vision On'. Immediately, Chloe, Petros and Lorrie hum along cheerily in time to it, swaying from side to side.

KHAV:

There are several different types of turban. First there is the *fifty* – a small piece of plain cloth, like this one here.

She removes the one that has been resting on her head and holds it up.

It got its name from the Sikh Regiment of the British Army. Sikhs requested a standard issue of five yards of cloth to cover their heads as custom dictates. The British wanted to dispense with turbans altogether. In the end a compromise was reached, and the Sikhs were issued with half the length they asked for – fifty percent. The *fifty* is generally worn under the turban proper.

She lays the fifty temporarily to one side.

It is not unlike the *patka* worn by young boys. Very handy for playing sports. Or break-dancing.

She grins, then picks up the folded siropa once more.

Next, there is the *keski*, a relatively short form of the turban about three yards in length. Then there is the *dastar*, four to six yards in length. Then the *pagri*, a double width of five to six yards, and finally the *domalla*, a double-length, double-width turban, ten yards by ten. Don't worry – I'm not going to try that one. I'd tie myself up in knots. Literally. Instead, I give you the *dastar*.

She displays the siropa to the audience, as if to a camera, then hands it Clive to examine, before encouraging him to pass it on for others to see.

First, I pull up my hair, right to the top of my head, as if I was making a pony-tail. Next, I twist it tightly together into a thick coil, like rope. I make a knot with it on the top of my head, near the front. See? I keep on wrapping it round itself, pulling a part of it through, a bit like a slip-knot, till it's completely secure.

Now I tie on the *fifty*. I place it over my forehead, take the two ends from the front at each corner, and tie these round the back. I pull the ends tightly, so that they become like strings. I cross one end over and round the knot on top, holding it steady with one hand underneath my chin. Then I cross the other end round in the opposite direction. I wrap both ends around the front of the knot, then secure them at the back.

So far, so straightforward, innit?

She collects the siropa back from Lorrie, who has been the last person to inspect it.

Now we come to tying the turban itself. Not so straightforward. First you place one corner of it in your mouth. Like this.

She attempts to continue to describe what she is doing without letting go of the end of the turban which is now held between her teeth.

This allows me to have both hands free while I wrap the turban in a series of figure-of-eight movements, crisscrossing the head, looping above and below the knot at the front. I try to keep layering it as I go, like stairs on an escalator, round and round, up and down, until nearly all of the cloth is used up. This might take a bit of time, so please feel free to talk among yourselves.

The theme tune for 'Vision On' continues louder, which everyone joins in with once again.

Finally, I tuck the end of the cloth into the topmost folds of the turban, making sure to pull it as tightly as I can so that it won't fall out. Then I take out the end that's been in the corner of my mouth all this time – phew! – pull it round the back, and tuck that into the back and lower folds of the turban.

Et voilà! The turban is complete.

She does a twirl to the great delight and appreciation of her audience, who all get to their feet and applaud.

Thank you. My name is Khavita Kaur.
And this has been my *Amrit Sanskar*.
Innit.

*

She strikes up her familiar B-Girl pose, which all her friends instantly mimic back to her, except for Clive, who is wise enough to know when not to push his luck. Instead he gives her a thumbs-up as he exits the Studio. The rest clamour around her.

"That was brilliant, Khav," says Chloe. "What say you to a celebratory night out dancing?" She launches into a quick rendition of her favourite Kyoko dance from *Ex Machina*, which Lorrie immediately joins in with.

"No thanks," says Khav, throwing a quick look towards Tanya. "I'm knackered."

Chloe, catching the look, smiles, then says, "Fair enough. But if you change your mind, you know where to find us."

She ushers Petros and Lorrie out with her. Vidhya, Beesham, Tanveet and Saroor have left already. Only Khav and Tanya remain.

"Are you really too knackered to celebrate?" asks Tanya quietly after they've gone.

"Why?" says Khav. "Did you have something in mind?"

"I might have," says Tanya.

They are standing very close to one another. Tanya slowly runs the tips of her fingers lightly along the side of Khav's cheek, stopping as she reaches her lips. Gently Khav enfolds them gently within her own hand, as if sheltering a moth that is cupped there, to protect her from damaging her wings.

7

The Glittering Prizes

2013 – 1949 – 1954 – 1959 – 1965 – 1975 – 1987 – 1992
2007 – 2013

2013

Professor John Brookes, Vice-Chancellor of Manchester Metropolitan University, sits alone in his office. He needs to put the finishing touches to his speech for the following day's Graduation ceremony at the Bridgewater Hall. Normally he would not invest so much time in it, but tomorrow's speech will be his last such address, for Professor John Brookes is about to retire, and so he wants it to count. What he says will form part of his legacy, and this has become increasingly important to him in these last weeks.

He asks Rick not to put through any calls unless they are absolutely essential. Rick is John's secretary. His colleagues had raised a collective eyebrow when he appointed him. All the other senior staff had women secretaries. Naturally. But why, thought John? Why should this still be the case? This is the 21st century. Surely things have moved on? Such prejudices belong in the Dark Ages, don't they?

Evidently they do not. John knows that the assumption has been that he must be gay. Not that there's anything wrong with that. As it happens, he's not. But he felt he somehow had to dispel such rumours by inviting his wife and two sons to as many functions as possible in his first few months in post. Such behind-the-hand remarks were counter-productive, They could only get in the way of the serious work he was planning to do during his tenure as Vice-Chancellor. He knew he brought no baggage with him and he wanted to keep it that way. There were no skeletons in his cupboard. He'd never been one of those professors who seduced his female students – though there were still plenty who did – nor had he allowed himself to be seduced by them. He understood all too well how such things happened. But he himself had never been tempted. Oh, he had patronised many, no doubt, and even though such occasions had been inadvertent, that was still no excuse. And he had probably touched a number of them inappropriately – of that he was certain. Nothing overt or unpleasant, just a tap on the elbow, or a hand on the shoulder. But these seemingly innocent actions could be so easily misinterpreted, couldn't they? He himself had learned this the hard way.

Once, when a female student had complained of feeling unwell and become somewhat tearful, he had offered her a tissue and rested his hand upon her arm sympathetically for a few seconds. She had gone ballistic and fled from his room, weeping copiously. Goodness knows what his secretary had thought at the time. That was back when he was still in Wolverhampton. His secretary was a woman then. Shirley. She said nothing. But he could guess at what she must have been thinking. He said nothing either. Whatever he might have said would only have sounded self-vindicating and defensive. Instead he immediately implemented a training course for all teaching staff on what was, and was not, appropriate verbal and non-verbal interactions between lecturers and students, and enrolled himself at the top of the list, by way of setting an example. He'd tried to be on his guard ever since, but he was conscious of not keeping pace with changing trends. He rarely spoke with students these days. His days were entirely taken up with endless committee meetings, one after the other, so that he was aware of being even more out of touch with what was current. The young women were all so self-possessed these days, so mature, so independent.

Take the one who came to interview him recently for *Aah!*, MMU's Campus Magazine. Chinese girl – what was her name,

Chloe Something-or-Other? – she scared him half to death, with her combative fierceness, her razor-sharp intellect, all concealed behind such impeccable politeness and that inscrutable mask of a smile. He pauses to remonstrate with himself. There he goes again, adopting the kind of lazy stereotyping that could so easily be misinterpreted as racist, however unintended. Exactly the kind of thing he has been so keen to root out since his appointment here eight years ago, when his application had been unanimously approved by the University's Academic Board and he had transferred to Manchester from Wolverhampton, an unquestionable step-up. Equality and Diversity have been his watchwords ever since. They run through every department's policy statements like water through a sieve, all the impurities collected and removed, at least in theory, but just as the City Council's attempts to clean up the canals and the rivers flowing through the centre of Manchester are routinely foiled by those self-proclaimed, self-congratulating Captains of Industry driving the current property boom exploding everywhere he looks, despite their protestations, their assertions that they are building a greener, cleaner city, then dumping excess waste in the still-polluted waterways, so his own drive towards a more equal, more diverse institute of learning have from time to time foundered.

"How," this young woman had wanted to know, "do you defend the University's eagerness to jump into bed with all these shadowy financial institutions, who want to see their name attached to the many new buildings that have gone up around the campus, yet cut corners when it comes to quality and responsibility?"

She was hinting – none too subtly – at the leaks that had been discovered at the recently built Halls of Residence on the new Birley Street Campus in Hulme.

"Yes," he had said, "that was unfortunate, and you can rest assured that we're doing everything we can to bring the builders to account and remedy the situation."

She had smiled when he said that, reminding him of the way a cat will purr while at the same time unsheathing its claws.

"But isn't that what happens when you sell your soul to the private sector, Vice-Chancellor?"

John had breathed a sigh of relief. Now that she had nailed her colours to the mast, he felt more confident in how he should respond. Like her question implied, he had throughout his career argued that education was the duty of the state. But he was a realist, which meant that he was also a pragmatist. Public/private partnerships such as the one she was referring to were the only way for the university to continue to expand, and expand they must, for MMU was now the sixth largest university in the country with in excess of fifty-four thousand students enrolled on nearly five hundred different courses.

"We're the fastest-growing university in the country," he said to her. "Expansion is happening at an unprecedented pace, there are bound to be some teething problems."

Ouch.

He shouldn't have said that. She was onto him like a flash.

"Is that what the students are, Vice-Chancellor, teething problems?" she pounced, flexing her claws. "And that if you throw them a pacifier, like cheaper cocktails in the Student Union, they'll be distracted from the pain for a while till they grow up and leave, and you hope they don't leave negative feedback on Facebook?"

If he hadn't been feeling a little bit rattled by the insistence of her questioning, he would have enjoyed being interviewed by her. Wasn't she the perfect embodiment of everything a university should want a graduating student to become? Reaping the benefit of a first-class education and now flexing the muscles of that learning by acting and thinking so demonstrably independently?

"The thing is Ms..." He peered a little closer to her to be able to read the name on her ID pass hanging round her neck, unfortunately giving the impression that he was staring at her breasts, causing him to lurch back so violently that he almost tipped over the chair he was sitting on.

"Chang," she said, relishing his discomfort.

"Yes, thank you. The thing is, Ms Chang," he attempted again, "like most Higher Education institutions, we've had significant cuts to our grant from Central Government."

Chloe nodded sympathetically.

"Which means," John had continued, "we've had to make some difficult decisions."

"Like cutting costs."

"Yes."

"By cutting corners."

"Yes. No."

"But isn't the truth of the matter, Vice-Chancellor, as our politicians are always so fond of saying, that MMU has slipped to 54th in the University rankings...?"

"4th if you rank us against the newer universities."

"And even lower when it comes to Research Outcomes?"

"That varies between Faculties."

"I know." She smiled sweetly. "I'm fortunate enough to be a student in one of those better performing departments."

"Really? Which one?"

"Media."

John smiled inwardly, despite the discomfort he was feeling. "Ah," he said, "one of Clive Archer's girls."

"Hardly, Vice-Chancellor."

Damn it – he'd put his foot in it again.

"Protegées then."

"I like to think that I'm here on my own merit, Professor."

"Quite so."

"Well, I think I have all I need. Thank you for your time."

John watched as she rose to show herself out, extending her hand for him professionally to shake, her claws now safely sheathed once more.

"One last thing," he said, just as she was reaching the door.

"Yes?"

"A word to the wise. When interviewing someone, try not to let your own opinions show."

"I don't believe I did that, Professor."

"What about when you implied I was selling my soul to the private sector?"

"Oh," she smiled disarmingly at him once more, "I was just playing Devil's Advocate."

She turned and walked confidently away. She had enjoyed herself hugely. She made a mental note to replay some of the more choice extracts of the interview with Petros, who would be sure to see things from the Vice-Chancellor's perspective. Especially that part about the leak at the Hall of Residence…

"Just suppose, Professor" she had put to him, "that the leaks turn out to be systemic rather than isolated, what would you do? Ask the students to vacate their rooms while you fixed the problem?"

"Only if absolutely necessary."

"Oh? So you'd be happy to let them live in damp, unsanitary conditions for a while?"

"Of course not."

"Just imagine all those texts to concerned parents."

"We'd find them alternative accommodation naturally."

"Except that that's not so easy, is it? You've already stated that MMU's the fastest-growing uni in the country, and, as you've also said, you've got to put us somewhere, haven't you?"

"Oh," replied John, looking distinctly uncomfortable, "you're not in…?"

"In Birley? No, no," she laughed. "But I could've been. I believe several hundred are."

"Yes, yes. I'm sure our Buildings Manager has it all under control."

"I'm sure he does. But let's take another scenario. What if the world was suddenly hit by a global pandemic? Despite imposing all kinds of restrictions on the free movement of people, shutting down the hospitality and leisure industries, wreaking who-knows-what damage to the economy, requesting people to work from home where possible, hospitals cancelling all but emergency operations in order to have sufficient beds to cope with the influx of patients sick and dying from the virus, the Government decides to keep schools and universities open? But – well, you know what students are like, Vice-Chancellor, they *will* insist on congregating in large numbers in close proximity to one another – so that you simply have no alternative but to suspend operations, send all the students back home, where they can spread the infection among their families and loved ones, and deliver all lectures online?"

"We could cope with that. Our IT Department's at the cutting edge of the newest technology."

"I'm sure it is, Professor, but you're missing the essential point here."

"Which is?"

"If the students were sent home, would they get a rebate on the rent they will have already paid up front for at least the term ahead?"

"Well, that's not something I can answer right now. It would have to be done on a case-by-case basis. Each student comes to their own arrangement with their own particular landlord. That's not something the university can interfere with."

"Not even for their own Halls of Residence? Like Birley?"

His mouth opened, then closed again. Like a goldfish. Chloe reminded him of a cat once more, eyeing him swimming round and round the bowl, just biding her time till she might plunge in her paw and scoop him out.

"It appears to me that universities these days are completely in hock to these private landlords, and that not to reimburse students for the rent they've paid, in advance and in good faith, when it is the university who sends them home, might be regarded as some kind of dereliction of duty of care, and that it – you – would therefore be liable, should a student, or a student's parents, decide to sue for damages." She smiled that cat-like smile once more. "Would you care to comment, Vice-Chancellor?"

"I think you're in danger of descending into the realms of science fiction, Ms Chang. We've not had a pandemic in this country for almost a century. Not since the Spanish Flu just after World War One. What are you suggesting? Some kind of outbreak of a new strain of SARS?" He laughed. "I hardly think so. This isn't China now, is it?"

He put his hand immediately to his mouth. He'd done it again.

"Please forgive me, Ms Chang," he stammered. "I meant no offence."

"None taken," she said passively. "I was born right here in Manchester."

"Yes indeed, but still…"

Chloe looked on as he continued to dig himself deeper and deeper into the hole of his own making.

Yes, she thought, as she exited through the Vice-Chancellor's door. She would enjoy recounting this to Petros when she next saw him. He'd probably agree with Professor Brookes as like as not, being a landlord himself these days, but might not wish to admit it. She'd enjoy watching him squirm...

John watched her departing back with considerable relief.

One of Clive Archer's students, eh? I wouldn't be surprised if he hadn't put her up to this in the first place, thought John.

"Give him a hard time," he can just imagine him saying. "He gets paid enough."

He and Clive had crossed swords on several occasions, usually over Clive's constant demands for more and better resources. John was a scientist. He'd studied Physics at Sheffield. He saw the value in traditional subjects like those, but he remained unconvinced by the academic merit of faddish courses like Media Studies. He found himself privately sympathising with those views popularised by the *Daily Mail*, that all students did in Media Studies was watch old films and deconstruct television programmes. Publicly of course he defended the Department to the hilt. It helped that they were one of the University's success stories, recruiting more applicants than any other Department, so that competition for places was high, ranking it in the top ten in the country in terms of subject, and the calibre of student extraordinarily high – witness Ms Chang just now – while their progression routes into meaningful professional employment after graduation – as opposed to including jobs as *baristas*, as some Departments had been known to do – were undeniably impressive. But even so. They'd be offering *Social* Media Studies next, with students submitting assignments via text and Twitter. Heaven forbid.

Sally – his wife – is right. Time to retire. Quit while you're still ahead. Spend more time with Digger, their Golden Retriever, and devote more energy to putting together a new Kit car, something he's been wanting to do for years now. Maybe a Dutton Sierra, or a Ferrari Daytona. Or possibly a Robin Hood S3 from their factory in Mansfield.

The thought of this cheers him up immensely. He sets himself back to the content of his speech to the Graduates tomorrow. The encounter with Chloe has got him thinking. Hers is a success story exemplifying everything he has tried to do during his time at Manchester. Equality and Diversity. Yes. He's feeling much more positive again now. What he needs are some well-chosen quotes about the value of education. Lighting fires in people's hearts, that sort of thing.

He presses the intercom on his desk.

"Rick?" he says.

"Yes, Vice-Chancellor?"

"Can you lay your hands on an *Oxford Dictionary of Quotations* for me?"

"Certainly, Vice-Chancellor."

Five minutes later, John is trawling through various possibilities.

'The future of the world belongs to the youth of the world, and it is from the youth and not the old that the fire of life will warm and enlighten the world.'

Thomas Mann. Yes, thinks, John, that's a good place to start. Then follow that up with the famous Yeats quote.

'Education is not the filling of a pail, but the lighting of a fire.'

A bit of an old chestnut, but no less true for all that.

And how about this from Victor Hugo?

'To learn to read is to light a fire; every syllable that is spelled out is a spark.'

John has never read Hugo, but he and Sally did go to see *Les Mis* once. He doesn't remember them saying this, though there was much storming of the barricades – which leads him to this one, rather surprisingly from the French General, Marshall Foch.

'The most powerful weapon on earth is the human soul on fire.'

Perhaps he needs something less stirring, less *agit prop*, to bring a certain lightness to the proceedings. The last thing the graduates want to listen to is some old fart giving them a lecture. This from Abbie Hoffman might fit the bill.

'Free speech means the right to cry "theatre" in the middle of a crowded fire.'

Perhaps not. A bit too clever for its own good. Something more sober, more serious.

This from Shaw, John learns, was delivered down the road at *The Midland Hotel*, when Anne Horniman was running her independent theatre there, and Shaw was still continuing to woo her, half-hoping she might marry him after all.

'Life is a flame that is always burning itself out, but it catches fire again every time a child is born.'

No. Too pretentiously self-important. Typical Shaw.

Maybe he might risk some Larkin?

'Kick up the fire and let the flames break loose.'

Yes, he likes that. But wait a minute – as soon as he acknowledges that it's Larkin – which he'll feel it incumbent upon him to do – all the parents in the Hall will immediately think, *'They fuck you up, your Mum and Dad...'* No, that will never do.

Better, perhaps, to fall back on Plutarch, the Old Faithful, like the geyser in Yellowstone Park, which John and Sally and the boys had once spent a glorious vacation camping beside.

'The mind is not a vessel to be filled but a fire to be kindled.'

Yes. That's the ticket.

He closes the book.

"Rick?"

"Yes, Vice-Chancellor?"

"Has my 5 o'clock arrived yet?"

"No, Vice-Chancellor. He's just called to cancel. He sends his apologies. Something came up apparently."

"Thank heaven for small mercies."

"But the Contractors at Birley are on the line."

John's shoulders sink. "What do they want?"

"Some problem with the glazed ceramic tiles and fritted glass panels cladding the Energy Centre."

"Which I expect they want us to pay for…"

"Yes, Vice-Chancellor."

"Oh well, better put them through."

As John listens to the architects telling him that this latest setback could in fact be a great opportunity to incorporate something they had always wanted to explore, he feels Chloe's cat-like claws scratching at his neck.

"Teething problems," she says. "Pacifiers." Then something about, "Playing devil's advocate and selling your soul…"

*

Helena Norwood, Awards and Conferments Manager for MMU, patrols the foyer of *The Midland Hotel* like a Field Marshall inspecting her troops just before they are about to go into battle, which is what the fortnight of Graduation Ceremonies that is about to commence in precisely two hours' time resembles. She is a known stickler for detail. She has the whole lay-out, not only of the hotel, but of the Bridgewater Hall opposite, where the ceremonies will take place, finely etched in her brain. But for good measure, and in order to leave nothing to chance – every last second has been meticulously planned to run like clockwork – she has charts and diagrams posted up on every available notice board in the hotel. She has also texted every member of her team a copy of each day's schedule a fortnight in advance. Her two trusty lieutenants – Tricia Boyce, her Lead Steward, and Tina MacLeod, Head of Robing Services for Ede & Ravenscroft, with whom Helena has forged a strategic partnership that is mutually beneficial to all parties – are standing by, awaiting their orders. Helena checks her phone, her watch and the clock on the wall of the hotel foyer, now serving as her Operational HQ. When the second digits of all three synchronise to inform her that it is precisely 09 hundred hours, she gives a calm, quiet, barely perceptible nod, but that is all the Lieutenants need to swing into their much-practised routines.

"Let battle commence."

With understated ceremony and importance, Tricia opens the doors. She and her team of gowned stewards glide silently across *The Midland*'s carpeted floors, indicating with the merest suggestion of a gesture which way people should go.

First up are those members of the University's academic staff who are taking part in this morning's formal procession, which will signal the start of the ceremony, and who will then take their places on the Bridgewater Hall stage behind the central platform. All the staff this year are known to Helena and Tricia. They have processed behind the Ceremonial Mace on numerous occasions before, they are old hands, there is even time for the occasional light quip, so they are quickly dealt with, which is just as well, for at half-past nine the doors are opened to the students – or the graduands, as Helena more correctly designates them.

The first cohort to be made ready for their passing out parade this year is the School of Arts & Humanities. Thank heaven for small mercies, thinks Helena, for these students are by their very nature potentially the most difficult. They are notoriously wayward and liable to do something unpredictable, such as breaking rank, subverting the uniform, indulging in unscripted improvisation.

To someone less experienced than Helena, this might present quite a daunting prospect, but Helena has seen it all before – from political protests to drunken stunts. Who could forget the year when one graduating Art student stripped off all her clothes and went up onto the stage wearing only her tasselled cap? Or the time when a troupe of Drama students decided to try and kidnap the Vice-Chancellor from the stage and hold him hostage until he agreed to give them all a first? These days the students seem better-behaved, more concerned about maintaining their various social media profiles than anything else, making sure that every second of their journey from the auditorium to the platform then back again is captured on smart phone and instantly uploaded onto Instagram.

And so Helena is secretly pleased that she will be getting the School of Arts & Humanities over and done with first. Best to get them out of the way now, rather than having the spectre of them hanging over proceedings like some carrion crow. It should be all plain sailing from there on for the rest of the Graduation fortnight.

The only potential wrinkle that she can foresee is that she has learned very late in the day that Professor Brookes has elected to put in a personal appearance at this morning's presentation. Normally he leaves all the ceremonies to his two Pro-Vice-Chancellors, attending only the one ceremony at which the Honorary Doctorates are bestowed upon whichever celebrity happens to be flavour of the month.

Last year, she feels, reached a new low, with awards being conferred on a fashion designer, a TV presenter and a rock musician. Sarah Burton, the fashion designer, had, it seems, created the wedding dress for the Duchess of Cambridge, as well as dresses for Michelle Obama and Lady Gaga. Poor Tina had been half-frightened to death at the prospect of what she might say when it came to having to robe her for the ceremony.

"She'll probably try to customise it in some way, I suppose," she had said.

"Let her dare," Helena had replied in that tone of hers that allowed for no dissent.

In the end she need not have worried, for the previous year Ms Burton had received an OBE at the Palace, and so knew what was expected of her on such occasions. The TV Presenter, however, was an altogether different matter. Gethin Jones, who had studied Geography & Economics at MMU and been Captain of the Rugby Team during his time there, had apparently made something of a name for himself as a contestant on *Strictly Come Dancing*. Why that warranted him being awarded an Honorary Degree eluded Helena. It was not as if he had even won. But her biggest fear lay with the rock singer. She imagined some gum-chewing, foul-mouthed, drug-taking fiend, who would probably be stoned and would need special chaperoning. Like The Beatles had allegedly been when receiving their MBEs from the Queen. But her fears had proved completely unfounded. Guy Garvey, from the Mercury Prize-winning band Elbow, could not have been more charming. She had not heard of him of course, but his dulcet Bury tones and his delightfully disarming manner won her over completely, so that afterwards she had made a point of looking him up and listening to some of his music, *The Seldom Seen Kid*, which she surprised herself by enjoying far more than she would have expected, one song in particular, *Weather to Fly*, which was a veritable ear-worm, going round and round in her head.

"Are we having the time of our lives?" he sang, which chimes so resonantly down the years as Helena regards each new batch of fledgling graduands flutter so eagerly before her, "spinning and diving like a cloud of starlings," as Guy Garvey sang in another of his songs. "Why shouldn't we try? Perfect weather to fly…"

Helena surprises her colleagues by spontaneously humming it, while the first of this year's outriders flutter their wings against the plate-glass doors, clamouring to be let in.

"I'm one of seven kids," Guy had told her, "and the only one not to go to a university," he later confided. "My mum was forced to put a picture of me singing with the band on the wall next to all the graduation photos of my brothers and sisters.

Now she'll be able to put one up of me dressed in the proper gear at last."

This year's list is a less contentious one, with the magnificent Joan Bakewell being the most high profile later in the fortnight, which is when she would have expected Professor Brookes to have put in his token appearance, but there is an actor to be honoured this morning to coincide with the Theatre School graduates who receive their degree immediately afterwards. David Threlfall. Helena remembers him as an unforgettable Smike in the RSC's *Nicholas Nickleby*, for which he won a most deserved Olivier Award, but she fears he is only known to most people as that incorrigible scallywag Frank Gallagher from Paul Abbot's *Shameless*. Shame*ful*, more like. Helena herself of course has never watched *Shameless*, but she has read about it and worries that Mr Threlfall might not be able to resist dropping into character when confronted with a captive audience. She knows what actors are like. He is likely to speak for a long time and indulge in anecdotes.

What with him and the decision by Professor Brookes to say what will doubtless be considerably more than the 'few words' he has requested, Helena is anxious that this morning's session might overrun. Although she can be surprisingly flexible in some aspects of each session's ceremony, there is one thing about which she is immovably adamant. There can be no running over time. Her schedule will simply not allow it. Each ceremony is meant to take sixty minutes. Experience has taught her that this will invariably mean more like seventy-five. Consequently she allows for ninety. But not a minute more. Ninety minutes will mean that this morning's ceremony, scheduled to commence promptly at eleven, will finish no later than twelve-thirty, which will allow her team just ninety more minutes to be ready for the afternoon ceremony that is due to start at two. The trouble with Professor Brooks – as with all Vice-Chancellors – is that they simply have no conception of the amount of work involved in executing such a complicated turnaround in such a short time. Not only is the Bridgewater Hall to be completely cleared, cleaned and re-set, but all the robes for the afternoon's graduands have to be laid out in the foyer of *The Midland Hotel*, while inside and out photographs of the morning's recipients are being taken and processed.

Fortunately, Helena has an ally. Professor Sharon Hanley. Professor Hanley – or Sharon, as she is to Helena – has been at the University since 1987. It was she who had first masterminded the transfer of the Graduation Ceremonies from the draughty but gloriously Gothic Whitworth Hall to the Bridgewater Hall in 1997, just a year after the city's new Concert Hall and home to the Hallé Orchestra had opened. Having its own distinctive venue for this highlight of each academic year had been an immediate unqualified success. It finally and irrevocably cut the last remaining ties MMU had with the older Manchester University, who had always tended to look down their noses at this upstart of a newcomer, when they no longer had to share the Whitworth Hall with them.

Professor Hanley knew the importance of the ceremonies needing to run like clockwork. She had already reassured Helena that she had instituted a digital equivalent of the old shepherd's crook used to hoik off Music Hall performers from the stage when they had overstayed their welcome. She has had one of the Hall technicians rig up a set of three lights on the front of the Vice-Chancellor's lectern. Sharon will be able to press a switch on her laptop that will enable these three lights to be turned on to alert Professor Brooks to the fact that he must wrap up what he is saying in just three minutes. Then two minutes. Then one.

"That should do the trick," says Sharon. "I'll keep him to time. And that actor-chappie too – there's no need to worry."

Helena agrees that there's not.

She checks all three digital timing devices one more time.

She looks pointedly towards Tina and nods.

This is all that Tina and her silently gliding ballet of stewards need to open up the glass doors once more. The starlings swoop in noisy murmuration.

Chloe, Petros, Lorrie and Khav have all arranged to meet outside *The Midland Hotel* ahead of collecting their gowns. It will be the only occasion during the entire day they will be able to get together as just the four of them. With their surnames respectively being Wang, Dimitriou, Zlatan and Kaur, they will be separated once they are in the Bridgewater Hall, and afterwards they will be having lunch with their families, before going on to the Faculty Reception in the Grosvenor Building back at MMU. Accordingly they had decided upon this pre-Ceremony meet-up.

Chloe is wearing her red dancing dress.

"You're not going to do your *Ex Machina* dance, I hope?" says Petros.

"I might," grins Chloe.

"I was thinking I might do the break dance from *Ghost World*," laughs Khav, indicating a pair of new trainers, in sharp contrast to Chloe's and Lorrie's high heels.

"Scarlett Johansson," replies Lorrie automatically.

"Cool," enthuses Petros.

The girls smile. Petros doesn't know about Khav's LLD. The built-up shoes mask the condition well.

"I don't want to do a Lizzie Maguire," shrugs Khav.

"And fall off the stage pulling down all the balloons with you," says Lorrie, covering her face in embarrassed delight.

"I don't think they have balloons in the Bridgewater Hall," says Chloe.

"Certainly not," says Tina, Head of Robing, who has been enjoying their banter. "Here – let me help you," she adds, turning back to Khav, who is struggling to fit the cap over her *fifty*. "If you tie the knot in your hair a little lower down, the cap will then sit easily on the top. You've got time," she says, indicating a small ante room behind the tables laid out with all the robes still awaiting collection. Khav smiles her thanks, then withdraws. Tina turns her attention back to Chloe.

"What a beautiful dress," she says. "That shade of red exactly matches the red of the gown, while the sky-blue lining of the hood will set it off perfectly. But the lack of buttons at the front is an issue. We need something with which to fasten the front of the gown to stop it slipping back over the shoulders. We don't want it strangling you, do we?" Tina laughs, as she always does, at this joke she must tell a hundred times each year.

"Sounds like a plan to me," says Petros.

Chloe throws him a look.

"Have you got some kind of brooch with you?" suggests Tina.

Chloe triumphantly pulls out a safety-pin from her bag.

"Always the Girl Guide," scoffs Petros.

"DYB, DYB, DOB," she laughs, holding up the three fingers of her right hand, while holding down the fourth with her thumb.

"*I* have a brooch," says Lorrie, stepping forward. "I picked it out specially." She is, as always, immaculately turned out. "I wanted to honour a famous movie graduation scene," she explains breathlessly, "but I couldn't decide which one. My first thought was *Mona Lisa Smile*, but I was torn between all three heroines – Maggie Gyllenhall, Kirsten Dunst, Julia Styles – I wanted to be all of them. Next I thought Reese Witherspoon from *Legally Blonde*. Perfect. Maybe I would memorise that speech she gives about believing in yourself, but then I realised I'd have to wear the Playboy Bunny costume, and I didn't think Ms MacLeod would be very pleased about that."

"Quite right," says Tina. "She wouldn't."

"So I settled on Buffy."

"The Vampire Slayer?" says Petros, shaking his head. "Have you brought your stake with you?"

"Shucks, I forgot. My bad."

"You can always borrow my *kirpan*," offers Khav, returning now with her fifty re-tied and the cap sitting snugly on top.

Tina looks from one to the other with an expression of alarm.

"Don't worry, Ms MacLeod," says Chloe. "I don't think she'll be needing it."

"I'm not sure," says Lorrie, gleefully relishing her role. "At the end of Series 3, the Principal at Buffy's High School transforms into a demon from the Underworld, complete with horns and a tail, but luckily Buffy saves the day."

"I don't think there's much chance of Professor Brookes turning into a demon," says Chloe. "Or a vampire. He's more likely to bore you to death than bite you."

"How long do you think he'll speak for?" asks Khav.

"We should run a sweepstake on it," says Petros.

"How long before he quotes Plutarch?" says Chloe.

"Plutarch?" asks Lorrie. "Like in *The Hunger Games*?"

"No, as in the Roman philosopher."

"I thought he was Greek," says Petros.

"Born a Greek," says Chloe, "but became a Roman."

"I love that dress Katniss wears that catches fire when she swirls it round," says Lorrie.

" '*Education is not the filling of a pail…*' " begins Chloe.

" '*… but the lighting of a fire*'," complete Petros and Khav.

" '*The mind is not a vessel that needs filling…*' " all three of them chant.

"Wait," squeals Lorrie, "I know this one." She screws up her eyes in an effort to remember. " '*But wood that needs igniting*'."

Fully robed and gowned, the four friends march with arms linked out into Peter Street, laughing and talking at the tops of their voices. They could not be happier. They turn right, pick up a takeaway coffee from the Starbucks on the corner, turn left onto Mount Street, left again onto Windmill Street, then right onto Lower Mosley Street, where the glass-fronted Bridgewater Hall awaits them, its pointed roof rising up like the prow of a ship, reflected in the waters of the Rochdale Canal, which flows alongside. The starling murmuration of students is now wheeling around the plaza in front of the Hall, landing excitedly, before frantically taking off again, all of them eagerly fluttering around the polished Italian Carrara marble sculpture by Kan Yasuda, the blue-grey Ishinki Touchstone, that the four friends now head towards and ritually tap for luck, taking each other's photos on their phones.

Just before they head inside, Lorrie and Khav catch sight of Chloe helping Petros to adjust the front of his gown, where the chevron collar of the hood has become caught up in his tie. Her fingers, as she smoothes and smartens the collar, brush against the university's coat of arms, which appears in a repeated pattern along it. A pair of gryphons breathing fire, with stags' antlers rising from their heads, hold up a helmeted shield, depicting six spade-irons symbolising hard toil, above a chequerboard representing the land, from which another fire springs. Chloe has seen these spade irons before. They all have. They adorn the tops of the railings that enclose the campus green at All Saints. How many times must she have passed them by without properly noticing them? Chloe will think of this moment the next time she walks beside them and runs her fingers along them, brushing against a pair of moths basking shyly side by side in their shadow, their wings opening, then closing, then opening again...

She looks back down upon the coat of arms decorating Petros's gown. Standing above the shield is a third gryphon.

This one has no antlers. Instead it holds up a globe containing a hive of bees, the emblem of the city, at the centre of the world.

Chloe takes out another safety pin from her bag, which she holds between her teeth, while she painstakingly straightens his attire, before pinning it secure. It is a moment of such rare intimacy between them that Lorrie and Khav feel they should look away, which they both do in silence. Neither of them says a word to the other about what they have seen. Had they looked a little longer, they would have seen Chloe lean in close to Petros and whisper in his ear, and had they been nearer to her, they might have heard her say,

"Remember – don't be a stranger…"

*

The Bridgewater Hall was opened by Elizabeth II in September 1996, just two months after the IRA bomb ravaged the city centre. Chloe smiles as she passes the plaque declaring this fact, recalling her rundown of the Queen's various visits to Manchester during her reign for her Final Presentation, rather like her Top Ten Greatest Hits. She wonders if she has ever heard an actual concert here. Or anywhere that she might actually have chosen to attend simply because she liked the music, rather than as part of some royal duty. Chloe speculates idly on what kind of music the Queen actually enjoys. She pities her having to sit through all those endless Royal Variety performances. Does she secretly enjoy the Sex Pistols' version of *God Save the Queen*? Is she a closet punk? Probably no to both of those. Rumour has it that she likes Musicals, with *Annie Get Your Gun* being a particular favourite. Chloe pictures Elizabeth and Prince Philip singing together the duet *I Can Do Anything Better Than You. "No you can't." "Yes I can." "No you can't." "Yes I can."* That and *Oklahoma*. Chloe smiles. She imagines the Queen playing charades at Christmas in Windsor Castle. "Song Title: eight words… *I'm Just A Girl*

Who Can't Say No." Apparently she's a fan of Gary Barlow too. I wonder, thinks Chloe now, if, when bestowing the OBE upon him earlier that year, she asked him for a verse from *Sing*, featuring voices from around the Commonwealth.

"There's a place, there's a time, in this life, when you sing what you are feeling..."

Is that what's happening here, she wonders, looking around her, as starlings from across the world are flocking together?

"The world is listening to the words we say..."

Tricia Boyce and her team of silent stewards invisibly corral the flock through the foyer, down the aisles, towards their individually allocated seats. Chloe, Petros, Lorrie and Khav wave their fingers to each other as they separate.

"See you later," they mouth.

Named for the 3rd Duke of Bridgewater, after whom the Bridgewater Canal was named, the Hall is built on a specially constructed arm in the basin of where the Manchester & Salford Junction Canal meets the Rochdale Canal, which in turn flows into the Bridgewater. The auditorium, where the four friends now walk to find their places, sits on an earthquake-proof foundation of steel springs that insulate it from the noise of the surrounding traffic and the Metrolink trams, which run right alongside. There's not been an earthquake in Manchester since 1775, when all the church bells for miles around rang by themselves unaided. Would that have caused the giant organ, with its five and a half thousand pipes that cover the rear wall with wood and burnished metal, the largest such instrument in the country, to have played by itself? Chloe rather hopes it might do so today, for anything would be preferable to the dirge-like hymns that someone invisible is inflicting on them this morning. *O God, Our Help In Ages Past*. What's that about?

She scans the upper tiers rising up behind her, the circles and balconies, where proud parents and family members are assembling, looking down from on high upon their offspring, about to fly their nests and launch themselves into the world. The lower half of the Hall is clad in a deep red sandstone that reminds Chloe of the inside of an egg, from which she will shortly hatch, towards the translucent light seeping through the glass and aluminium shell from above.

She spots her father immediately. There he stands, front and centre of the Dress Circle, her grandmother scarcely visible beside him, just the top of her head peeping above the guard rail. How typical, she thinks. Trust her father to get himself the best seat. He arrived last night, having flown Business Class from Shenzen, via Beijing and Frankfurt. He stands above her now in his expensive suit, not seeking her out, as other families are doing and waving excitedly as they spot their son or daughter, but as if surveying his domain, an eagle in his eyrie, eyes narrowed in pursuit of prey.

Is that what she is to him, she wonders? She shakes her head. She refuses to accept the role he has given to her, but it is a conversation she knows she must have.

"After ceremony," he said to her this morning as she got ready to go, "I take you to lunch. We talk. About what you do next."

She turns away and sits low in her seat. With their graduation caps on, all the starlings look the same. From behind, he'll not be able to recognise me, she thinks. She defiantly flicks her tassel, as if preening an errant feather.

Petros, Lorrie and Khav are simultaneously experiencing similarly conflicted thoughts about their parents. Petros is convinced that his will not be there. Why should they be? He hasn't even told them. Even so, he wills himself not to turn around to look for them just in case, to save himself any further humiliation or embarrassment.

Khav, on the other hand, knows that hers will be there. She's been back home a month now, after sleeping on various friends' sofas – Chloe, Vidhya, Beeshem, Tanveet – following the appalling argument with *Bapu* when she had told them of her conviction that *Nani* had been reborn as the Woman with the Angel Tattoo. Since she returned, there's been no mention of it, and Khav herself has no intention of raising the matter. She feels secure in her own belief and doesn't need her family's approval. But at the same time she has no desire to upset her *Maa*, who has found herself so painfully torn, caught between her husband and daughter, like Mohini, the female avatar of Vishnu, being pulled apart in opposite directions by the *Gajasuras*, the elephant demons. Khav knows how badly Geetha wants to attend this morning's ceremony, but she will only do so if Vikram consents to accompany her. He had, until this morning, still not declared his intentions, but one look at Geetha's imploring eyes at the breakfast table had decided him. "I go for your *Maa*," he had hissed to Khav under his breath. Priya, still consumed in the sleepless cocoon of broken nights with Dilsher, has barely registered Khav's return to the fold. Khav doubts whether she even noticed she was gone. Khav is desperate to turn around, to see if she can spot them among the thousand guests arrayed on the balconies above her, but resists the temptation. Somehow she fears that, if she does, they will vanish before her eyes, like Satyavan to her Savitri, Eurydice to her Orpheus.

Lorrie, however, is confident of her support, just uncertain of its precise make-up. There has been much excitement among the mobile homes on Collingham Street. Everyone wants to come – Pavel, Agniewska, Krysztof, Stanislaw, Vitaly, Lena, Milosz, all of them – but each student is limited to only three guests each, unless exceptional circumstances can be shown, or, as sometimes happens, the number of graduates taking part in a particular ceremony happens to be lower than usual.

The School of Arts & Humanities is one of MMU's largest, but the Bridgewater Hall can seat more than two thousand six hundred people, and so, by dint of judicious planning, with particular attention paid to precise seating allocations, it is sometimes possible to accede to occasional requests for additional places. Judicious planning is Helena Norwood's forte. There's nothing she likes more than demonstrating her capacity for squeezing a quart into a pint pot, where others would quail at the prospect and simply throw up their hands in despair. Such melodramatic gestures do not form part of Helena's demeanour. She is flexible but firm, accommodating but clear. If she can accede to a student's request, she will do so. But equally, if she cannot, she will inform them quickly but kindly.

"The difficult we do immediately. The impossible may take a little longer." This is her watchword, originally attributed to Charles Alexandre de Calonne, the ill-fated Comte D'Hannonville, who tried, but failed, to implement unpalatable tax reforms in pre-Revolutionary France. Helena knows this because History was her subject and this particular period the focus of her thesis. Unfairly judged by 19th century historians, Helena takes quiet pride in stealthily restoring his reputation with her not infrequent allusions to his legacy. As Calonne's contemporary, Nicolas Chamfort, Secretaire des Jacobins, so adroitly observed, "He was applauded when he lit the fire, but condemned when he sounded the alarm."

Helena has made it her mission that there will be no alarms sounded on her watch. She has been delighted to be able to find places for all of Miss Zlatan's extended family and has promised to accompany them personally to their allocated places in the right of the Upper Circle, where wheelchair access is more readily available via a specially designated lift.

Lorrie was thrilled. This would mean that Pavel and Krysztof, both in their nineties, Lena in her eighties, and Agniewska, Stanislaw and Vitaly, all in their seventies, would be able to attend after all, but then Milosz, her father, had announced that he had an important delivery to make in North Wales and was no longer certain he'd be able to attend. If he couldn't, then none of them could, for it would be Milosz who would be driving them...

Lorrie is inconsolable. She understands very well that the summer is the busiest time of the year for her father, delivering to all the travelling fairs across the north-west, but surely he could make an exception just this once, for the graduation of his only daughter?

Later, in her cubby-hole of a bedroom, surrounded by her movie posters of Monroe, Minelli, Madonna and the rest, she wraps herself up in her duvet, feeling sorry for herself. But not for long. Her family may no longer be itinerant, as they once were, but they remain ready to be back on the road at a moment's notice if they have to. Like the birds, they used to move with the seasons, and even now their bodies and minds are still hard-wired for change, seizing the moment, grabbing each of them while they can, never thinking too far ahead. Lorrie knows she has inherited much of this same restlessness. She has no idea what she will do the day after tomorrow, after she has graduated, only that she'll recognise what it is when she sees it. In the meantime she will not let the grass grow. But for now, this particular moment, what matters most to her is that she does not graduate alone tomorrow. The thought of it sits in her stomach like a stone.

She is roused from her reverie by a gentle knocking on the outside of her door.

"Come in," she says miserably.

It's her grandmother, Lena, in her eighties, but her eyes still bird-bright and clear, her body wiry and taut from her time as a trapeze artist.

"Each night," she says, "before I did my act, I'd look down from high up in the roof of the circus tent onto the audience below. They looked so tiny, little more than dots, so I could never see their faces. But I knew that, somewhere down there among them all, Pavel would be there, looking out for me. It didn't matter that I couldn't actually see him..."

She pauses. She lays her bony, shadow-thin hand against Lorrie's wet cheek.

"Don't worry about tomorrow," she says. "We'll be there. One way or another..."

And so, as she takes her seat in the Bridgewater Hall, she cannot resist taking a quick peek up and to her right to see if she can spot any of them there. To do that, she must first slip her glasses surreptitiously out of her bag and hold them up swiftly in front of her eyes before anyone can spot that she needs them. She really must do something about a prescription for contacts.

Tomorrow, she tells herself sharply, tomorrow.

But now a quick scan reveals that all of her family are there, the whole tribe of them, her father included. They spot her too and wave encouragingly.

The stone that had been sitting so heavily in her stomach is gone in an instant. She puts away her glasses and looks back towards them once more. Against the blur and haze of the lights behind them, she thinks she picks out her grandmother, her arm still outstretched in a wave, as if she is about to launch herself into the air at any moment...

At the same time, Tricia Boyce, Leader of the Silent Stewards, gives a signal to Dr Pete Dale, Senior Lecturer in Music, seated at the organ, watching out for her in the small mirror above his head angled towards the main door, that the Vice-Chancellor and members of the Academic Board have formed up outside and are now ready to enter the auditorium. Pete immediately launches into the fanfare he has selected especially for today's ceremony.

Pete, a loyal and devoted fan of The Clash and author of several distinguished papers and articles about them, his most highly esteemed being *Death to Traditional Historicism: Futuremania, the Avant-Garde & Post-Punk*, had toyed with the idea of playing *London's Calling* to accompany the Ceremonial Procession. It would certainly be a crowd-pleaser, but hardly fitting a graduation here in Manchester. Then he had considered – briefly – *Should I Stay or Should I Go?* Several of the students, he was sure, would appreciate the irony of that as they contemplated their next move, but, given the Vice-Chancellor's impending retirement, it might be misinterpreted as some kind of covert message directed towards him. Not that he would recognise it. Professor Brookes is not, as far as Pete is aware, partial to punk. He could be wrong of course – who knows what he might have got up to in his misspent youth? Except that Pete suspects the Professor's youth was probably not misspent – though Pete would argue, and has, that a youth spent listening to The Clash could never be considered misspent. But to be fair, the Vice-Chancellor has pretty much given Pete a free rein ever since he arrived from his previous post in Gateshead. Manchester had attracted him like a magnet, and not just because it has been a crucible for so much recent music – 10cc, The Buzzcocks, New Order, The Smiths, The Stone Roses, Oasis – but for its reputation for always being at the start of things. Pete has a passion for 20th century classical music, as well as punk, and, since his arrival at MMU, has unearthed some forgotten, neglected gems, several by Manchester-born composers, who he has proudly championed and showcased. Professor Brookes has been an ardent supporter of Pete in this, and so Pete has decided to mark the Vice-Chancellor's final Graduation Ceremony with his own transposition for organ of *Four Fanfares for Trumpet* composed by Charles William Eric Fogg in the 1930s, for which he now, quite literally, pulls out all the stops of all four manuals of the largest organ to be installed anywhere in the country for more than a century.

Suitably stirred by the enormous sound of Fogg's fanfare roaring through the Bridgewater Hall like the Day of Judgement, the entire auditorium rises to its feet, as the Ceremonial Procession makes its grand entrance. They make their slow and dignified way to the stage where Tricia Boyce hands the silver mace to the Vice-Chancellor, before withdrawing silently back into the shadows. Professor Brookes accepts it with a small bow before placing it on a stand in front of his lectern. Pro-Vice-Chancellor Sharon Hanley speaks with formal solemnity into the microphone before her own lectern to the left.

"*Aperta congregatione.* I declare this congregation open. Please be seated."

A great hush falls upon the roosting starlings.

Professor Brookes steps forward to speak.

"The Roman philosopher Plutarch once famously said, '*Education is not the filling of a pail, but…*' "

" '*The lighting of a fire*'," shout out Chloe, Petros, Lorrie and Khav from their individual seats.

Helena is on an instant high alert. However, it appears that this is no pre-arranged signal for some mass protest, but merely a spontaneous in-joke from a small group of friends. She recognises the Chinese girl in the striking red dress and smiles. The interruption appears to have thrown the Vice-Chancellor.

"Indeed. As I said. Though perhaps Plutarch is more famous than I realised…"

He is threatening to peter out before he has even begun. Helena, seizing the opportunity, catches Sharon's eye at her lectern and quietly nods in her direction. Professor Hanley, taking this as her cue, taps the laptop in front of her. At once, three lights begin to wink at Professor Brookes from his lectern. Disorientated and confused, he cuts to what had been intended as his closing remarks and completes his address in record time.

Helena is delighted. She can now feel more indulgent towards the actor when it is his turn to speak, knowing that this morning's ceremony should not now overrun. She makes a mental note to seek out the girl in the red dress afterwards if she can and personally congratulate her on her First – she knows that this is what she has been awarded from where she is sitting in the auditorium – as her way of thanking her for the most timely interruption. Not that she can be seen to be condoning such behaviour outwardly. She suspects that the girl will see through the pretence immediately. In fact, Helena rather hopes she will.

Sharon Hanley takes the opportunity of this unexpected hiatus to step towards her microphone.

"Thank you, Vice-Chancellor. Members of the Academic Board, Graduands, Ladies and Gentlemen, it is my great pleasure this morning to welcome the first of our honorary awardees this year to receive a Doctorate in Arts, Mr David Threlfall."

Warm applause greets his arrival onto the stage. A few young men, who, to Helena's keen eye, look as if they have begun to party rather too early, chant out in unison, "Make poverty history, cheaper drugs now!" No doubt one of the catchphrases associated with the disreputable Frank Gallagher. But a sharp look by her in their direction soon has them buttoning their lips.

"Vice-Chancellor, Pro-Vice Chancellor, it is a humbling honour to receive this recognition from the University where I myself was a student and began my actor training. Let me say at once that I still consider myself to be in training, and I expect I will be right up until someone decides to pull the plug. Which

I hope is not for a long while yet. I believe it's customary for someone receiving one of these to offer up some tasty bits of sage advice. Well, I don't know about that. What might Frank have to say on the subject?"

As one, as if primed, the students call back, "A word to the wise!"

"Exactly. Well – all I can tell you is that I regard myself as the luckiest person alive. I get up each day, go to work, where I pretend to be someone else, have fun, then go home again. Acting is about life. It's about getting to know how other people live, think, feel – and you can practise any time. It's about challenging yourself. There'll be some dark times, some rejections, but it's how you get through those that shape you and make you into the person you become. Good luck."

He steps down from the stage to even warmer applause than that which greeted his appearance on it.

Excellent, thinks Helena, smiling appreciatively as Tina guides him expertly towards the exit, where the Head of the School of Acting will be feverishly waiting for him. That is how to deliver an acceptance speech – with wit, self-deprecation, and, most important of all, brevity.

She follows Mr Threlfall out into the foyer, where already he is surrounded by admirers. Her work here is done. She can now return to *The Midland* to prepare for the afternoon's ceremony. One down, nineteen more to go.

There is little left to be done now except invite each of the five hundred students graduating from the School of Arts & Humanities up onto the stage in turn. Thanks to Tricia and her team of Silent Stewards, this proceeds like the well-oiled machine it has become over the years. The students leave their seats row by row, starting from the front. They snake down the left hand aisle back towards the rear of the stalls, along the back behind the last row, up the right hand aisle towards where

Professor Hanley announces them individually. When their name is called out, they mount the few steps up onto the stage – or, in the case of wheelchair users, proceed along the front – crossing it from right to left, pausing in the centre, where Professor Brookes waits to shake each one of them by the hand.

One by one they pass across to the cheers and applause of their families and supporters. Those awarded a First are followed by the rest, whose degrees are not differentiated publicly between Two-One, Two-Two and Third. Petros, Lorrie and Khav all receive a Two-One. Chloe, unsurprisingly, gets a First.

No misfortune or calamity befalls any of them. Lorrie, whose sight only troubles her when people or objects are far away from her, manages the steps comfortably, even in her high heels. Khav navigates her way across the stage with her limp barely perceptible. Chloe resists the temptation to launch into her Kyoko dance. The only incident of any note concerns Petros. When he reaches the Vice-Chancellor to shake his hand, just as he is about to continue his passage to the other side of the stage, he pauses, turns back, and appears to ask the Vice-Chancellor a question, who, somewhat nonplussed, repeats whatever it is he has previously said.

Afterwards, in the scrum of the foyer, when friends are all trying to reunite with one another simultaneously, before joining their families outside on the Plaza in Barbirolli Square, Chloe, Lorrie and Khav all want to know what it was that Petros and the Professor were talking about.

"Who's your new friend?"

"You and the VC bosom buddies now?"

"What did he say to you?"

"I don't really know," says a still-flustered Petros. "What was it that he said to us when he shook our hands?"

"No idea," says Lorrie. "I was too busy concentrating on not falling over."

"Something Latin, innit?" says Khav.

"I admit you," says Chloe.

The others look at her blankly.

"Now that we've graduated," she explains, "we're officially members of the university."

"What were we before then?" says Khav. "Unwelcome guests?"

"It's a tradition, that's all. So he says to us, 'I admit you to the University.' Only he doesn't. It's too much of a mouthful, and there are more than five hundred of us. So he shortens it. He just says, 'I admit you,' then shakes our hand."

Petros puts his head in his hands and groans.

"What is it?" they ask him.

"I thought he said, 'I'll *miss* you'."

"So?" says Khav.

Lorrie giggles. Chloe suddenly realises.

"No," she says, " you didn't?"

"I did," moans Petros, even more embarrassed.

"What?" says Lorrie, jumping up and down. "Tell us!"

"I was confused, so I went back to him and said, 'Oh – I'll miss you too…' "

The others howl, helpless with laughter. They clutch at each other, doubled up in delight, biting their cheeks, crossing their legs, shrieking to stop in case they wet themselves. Petros is mortified.

"Will you miss us too?" says Lorrie, batting her eyelashes.

"Fuck off," he says, but he's smiling in spite of himself.

"Don't worry," says Chloe. "Your secret's safe with us."

"That's what I'm afraid of."

"Innit?" says Khav.

Outside in Barbirolli Square, named for the conductor Giovanni Battista 'Sir John' Barbirolli, who saved the Hallé Orchestra from dissolution during World War Two, the student-starlings flutter excitedly. The Plaza is a constant whirl of movement, as they flock together, alighting in small groups, only to take to the air again before settling briefly somewhere else, pausing only for yet another photograph, the midday sunlight bouncing off the hundreds of mobile phones like shiny pieces of glass their eyes are constantly drawn towards. The air vibrates with the sound of their chirruping, drowning out the noise of traffic, humming like telegraph wires, sending out their song to all corners of the world. In one final, triumphant burst, they fling their mortar boards high above their heads, where, for a split second, they hang suspended, time on hold, the black tassels like wing feathers, a great murmuration, wheeling above the city. Perfect weather to fly.

Aperta congregatione.

*

The four friends temporarily depart. They go their separate ways for a post-graduation lunch with their respective families, Petros to *Rozafa*, a Greek taverna on Princess Street, Lorrie to *Platzki*, a Polish diner on Deansgate, and Khav to the *Rajdoot Tandoori* on Albert Square. Chloe remains at *The Midland*, where her father has commandeered a table in the French restaurant there.

"What about the *Yang Sing*?" asks Chloe. "I've made a reservation for us there."

"I cancelled it," says her father simply. "Why should I want to eat Chinese when the best French cuisine in England can be found right here?" He looks around proprietorially.

"But what about Guang Li and Jian? They'd been looking forward to welcoming you?"

"They won't mind. They've been paid."

Chloe looks away. She hates the way her father believes everything has its price.

Her grandmother beams.

"See what a success your father is, *Sunnu*. Such largesse he bring with him."

"Steak," says her father to the waiter hovering beside their table. "Rare."

Petros makes his way towards Princess Street accompanied by his sister, Callista. Both are aware that, without her presence, he would not be going.

"I've gone out on a limb to organise this," she is telling him, "so make sure you behave yourself."

"I always do," he says.

"Hmm," she grunts.

"I do," he says. "It's Dad who starts things, not me."

"No, it's never you, is it?" she replies witheringly.

He stops, mid-stride. They have just past the tram stop on St Peter's Square. "Maybe this isn't such a good idea after all," he says. "Tell Dad I had to go back early to the university to help with the Faculty Reception this afternoon."

"Tell him yourself," says Callista. "I'll not make excuses for you."

Petros sighs. They continue to walk side by side in silence. The truth is that Petros adores his sister. The last thing he wants is to hurt her feelings. While she still lived at home, she was able to maintain some kind of peace between his father and him. It was she who was the glue that held them together, not their father, in spite of him running a firm that manufactured mastic. But when she left to get married to Andreas there was no one to act as the peacemaker any longer. But even she has not been able to heal the rift that cracked open so violently on that terrible occasion three years ago, on the day of the Chrismation service for Callista's son Yannis, a day which also coincided with Petros turning eighteen, when he joyfully announced that he had received the offer of a place to pursue a degree in Media Studies at MMU, only for his father to explode with disappointment and a feeling of betrayal He had berated Petros that such a suggestion was preposterous, out of the question. He would instead be joining him in the Mastic Business as soon as he left school. That it was his duty, as well as his birthright. "If you renege on one," his father had shouted, "you sacrifice the other." With Callista no longer there to build a bridge between them, neither had backed down. Petros had left home at the earliest opportunity. He had rarely been back since; and never if he knew his father was likely to be there. They had not spoken for three years. Now he is returning to the same restaurant which had been the scene of that seismic eruption.

"At least be civil," his sister now pleas. "For my sake."

Petros agrees that he will. He can deny his sister nothing. He misses her calming influence still.

Chloe is telling her grandmother about what Petros said to the Vice-Chancellor. She's trying to lighten the atmosphere. She thinks her grandmother will enjoy the silliness of it, as well as relating to the misunderstanding. It is something she herself still does now, mix up words in that way, even after sixty years of living here. She's also trying to make the subliminal point that she too would miss Manchester if she had to leave, which she has no intention of doing any time soon.

"Did you notice?" she asks her father.

"No," he says. "I left."

"Oh." She feels as though he has punched her in the stomach. "Why?"

"It was you I came to see graduate. Why would I stay to watch all those failures with only a Second Class degree?"

Lorrie is delighted with her Two-One. There'd been times when she hadn't thought she would get any kind of degree at all. But what she may have lacked in flair or academic brilliance, she more than made up for her in application. Unlike many of the students, Lorrie has never shied away from seriously applying herself. 'A hard worker at all times,' her school reports had always said of her, a trait no doubt inherited from her family, who were all, without exception, hard workers. 'Steady and consistent,' was another oft-quoted remark. 'Her diligence and conscientiousness deserve to be rewarded.' And it has been. A Two-One. A fair reflection, she thinks now, as she hurries down Deansgate to meet whoever of her family has been able to make it today.

Her destination, is *Platzki*, the award-winning Polish diner, in what had once been the Great Northern Railway Warehouse, a place synonymous with hard work. Perhaps that's why her family had suggested it. More likely it's because Agniewska knows the proprietors. Long established or recent arrivals, the Polish community all seem to know one another, who's related to who back in the old country. Except for Lorrie. For her, *this* is the old country. She's never been to Poland. She's never been out of England. She's hardly ventured far from Manchester. Just the occasional trip with Milosz, her father, in his summer round of the fairs of Lancashire, Cheshire and North Wales.

Five minutes later she reaches the converted Warehouse. Its towering Victorian edifice, recently cleaned up, so that the polished red, yellow and blue bricks gleam in the early afternoon sunlight, is undoubtedly impressive. She's never really noticed it before, not properly. It's not a part of the city she visits as a rule, rarely straying from her usual route between the university and her home, which doesn't come this way. Perhaps, now that she's graduated, she might explore Manchester more. A blue plaque tells her that twenty-five million bricks were used in the warehouse's construction – shielding her eyes from the sun as she looks up at it now, she can well believe it – along with fifty thousand tons of concrete, twelve thousand tons of steel, and more than sixty-five miles of rivets. On the ground level were railway sidings where up to five hundred goods wagons at a time could be stored, while at a level below, barges moored directly underneath to load and unload from the Manchester & Salford Junction Canal using a complex system of lifts and hydraulics. More than a thousand men worked there, scurrying about the shafts and tunnels like an army of moles. To build the warehouse, the railway company had to demolish an entire settlement – the district of Alport – and displace a whole community. More than a thousand families lost their homes with the stroke of a pen. Earlier still, she reads, the area was nothing more than heathland, meadow and pasture, with the River Medlock winding peacefully through it, farmed by tenants on the Mosley Estate, till they too were turfed out, first by the Dissolution of the Monasteries, next by the Civil War. Now the Warehouse is no longer. After decades of lying idle and abandoned, it has metamorphosed into a leisure complex, housing a cinema, casino, fitness centre and a car park, as well as multiple shops, bars and restaurants, *Platzki* being just one of them.

Lorrie steps inside, looks around as she gets her bearings. There is a slippage in time. The army of moles shimmers and is replaced by the seamless choreography of gliding waitresses and sales assistants, bar staff and baristas, each separate yet conjoined in this twenty-first century ballet, the same uncrossable divide between the leisured and working classes, *eloi* and *morloch*.

Her eye is caught by a flurry of arms, frantically waving like flags atop a building. Her family. All of them. Pavel, Krysztof, Agniewska, Vitaly, Stanislaw, Lena and her father. Milosz too is there, his arms flailing like a windmill.

"I thought you said you couldn't make it," she says, her voice breathless and trembling.

"You didn't think I'd miss my daughter's graduation, did you?"

"I thought you had deliveries to make."

"I did," he says. "I do. Let them wait."

Lorrie beams.

"Let's eat," says Agniewska. "I'm famished."

"Me too," says Pavel.

"You never eat a thing," scoffs Lena.

"True," says Pavel, "but I like to look."

"The last refuge of the old," agrees Krysztof. "When we can no longer perform as we once did," he explains, "we can still watch."

"Take no notice of them," says Milosz to his daughter. "Order what you like."

"Really?" asks Lorrie.

"Anything."

"In that case, I'll have this," she says, pointing, "and this."

The others roar their approval.

And so, while they tuck into their *kopytka*, traditional Polish potato and spinach dumplings, Lorrie has everything on the dessert menu – blueberry cheesecake, followed by cherries with dark chocolate sauce.

Chloe's father devours his steak with relish. Chloe and her grandmother have barely picked at their own food. He puts down his fork and summons the waiter with a peremptory snap of his fingers.

"Coffee," he demands. Not waiting to check whether anyone else wishes to join him, he adds, "For one."

The moment the waiter leaves, he takes an envelope from the inside pocket of his jacket and places it in front of Chloe, who regards it suspiciously.

"Open it," he commands.

Reluctantly she does as she is bid. It contains two one-way air tickets from Manchester Ringway to Shenzen.

"For you and your grandmother," he explains unnecessarily.

"Yes. I can see."

"Well," says her grandmother, "you not thank your father? See how generous he treat you," she beams.

Chloe says nothing.

"There's more," he says, producing a letter written in official Mandarin.

She studies it in silence.

"Do you need me to read it for you? Have you forgotten your mother tongue completely?"

"I never knew my mother," she replies icily.

Her father looks down.

"So proud would she be," says her grandmother, "if she had lived."

"Well?" asks her father after a further pause in which Chloe has continued to offer no comment on the letter in front of her.

"Yes," she says at last. "I still read Mandarin. Though I don't speak it now. Cantonese only with *Lao lao*."

"Then you will do fine when you return," he oozes. "Most people in Shenzen speak three languages – Mandarin, Cantonese and English. You will soon fit in."

"Thank you, *Baba*, but…"

"But nothing. What is there to discuss?" He snatches the letter back from her. "The offer is in black and white. See." He points impatiently to the logo at the head of the paper.

深圳卫视
SHENZHEN TV

"A two-year training programme they are offering you. Twelve TV channels, four radio stations, *Shēnzhèn Guǎngbō*

Diànyĭng Diànshì Jítuán is third largest Media Group in all of China. Sport, news, entertainment. In five years you'll have your own Talk Show."

Chloe says not a word.

When Khav enters the *Rajdoot Tandoori* on Albert Square, she is faced at once with two surprises. The first is that her father, Vikram, her *Bapu*, is there. She hadn't known whether he would show or not, and she wasn't sure whether she wanted him to. Now that she sees him and returns his nervous wave, she finds she is both pleased and relieved.

The second surprise is that sitting on the other side of him, next to her *Maa*, is Dr Chadwick, her next-door neighbour, who has always insisted that Khav calls her Grace. "Everybody does," she says.

"I'm a stand-in for Urja," she declares.

Khav feels *Baba* looking down upon them with a broad smile on her face. She smiles back. Somewhere in the distance she hears the sound of something coming closer, a deep rumble, followed by a low roar, rising to a trumpet.

"I've been offered a scholarship to do an MA in Journalism next year," says Chloe, "and that is what I intend to do."

Bao seethes with a cold and silent fury.

Chloe has witnessed these moods before. Though not for many years. Not since he first decided to return to China when the news came through of the Central Committee's decision to compulsorily purchase the land surrounding the shanty hut he was born in, which his parents had fled from at the height of the Battle of Liaoshen, when both sides in the Civil War had begun operating a scorched earth policy, to seek a better life in England...

*

1949 – 1954 – 1959

Bao was just four years old when he arrived in Manchester. By the time he was nine, he was already working in the family laundry business, one which had been set up by Zhang, his father's Great Uncle, who had settled in the city after helping to build the Ship Canal. Over time the name *Zhang* was corrupted to *Chang*.

He worked long hours, in all areas of the business, and, while he worked, he watched. He watched and he studied. By the time he was fourteen he began making suggestions about how they might change certain aspects of what they did that would save them time, and time, he quickly came to realise, meant money. He developed a facility for figures that impressed even his father, who, it was assumed, had no equal when it came to the use of the abacus, but his prodigy of a son taught him that the old proverb that stated the impossibility of teaching an old dog new tricks was in fact a fallacy, and that it would be to the benefit of all to pay careful heed to this precocious young pup.

*

1965

By the time of his *Guan Li*, the capping ceremony, when a Chinese boy traditionally comes of age when he reaches twenty, the rest of the family were ready to defer to him in most matters of business. Bao's *Guan Li* coincided with the *Ji Li*, or Hairpin Ceremony, of Dai Tai, who had just turned fifteen. Dai Tai was the daughter of a neighbour of Bao's father, a neighbour and a rival, with whom Bao had been advising a possible partnership. Rather than competing with one another, they should, he argued, benefit from each other's trade. Together they could become bigger and stronger. Between them they could corner, then control the market. Astrological charts were consulted. Yes. The timing was auspicious. To cement the bond still tighter, Bao and Dai Tai would become engaged...

Xiu Mei was expected to have very little say in this, Dai Tai even less. She asked her mother what she should expect from a marriage. Respect, she replied. A recognised role. A position of some esteem within the two families. What else could Xiu Mei say? It was what her own mother had told her on the eve of *her* marriage. She omitted to mention that all of these dubious honours came with conditions. Respect? In public only. In private a wife was entirely dependent on whether she was fortunate to have secured a husband who was considerate by nature and patient in practice. To begin with, Xiu Mei was unlucky on both counts. Her husband regarded her as his personal property, her body a vessel to receive whatever he chose to deposit there. A recognised role? Slave, nurse, concubine. Esteem? Possibly. And also influence. If she was clever enough to produce a son. This was her trump card. If she succeeded in this, she would at once ascend to an altogether higher plane of existence. All other degradations would cease automatically. If...

Unfortunately, Xiu Mei had been unlucky in this also, as she had been in the character of her husband, Zhao Li, who was also considerably older than her. It was not that he was especially cruel. Rather that he lacked warmth. Also imagination. When she succeeded in producing only a daughter, and a rather plain one at that, he predictably shunned her. He sought other beds for consolation. In the end disappointment turned to indifference, indifference to acceptance – for both of them – that this was what fate – *mingyùn* – had in store for them. They found solace in the only ways open to them. Xiu Mei sought the company of other similarly neglected or deserted wives, planning grandiose schemes for their own daughters' hoped-for matches over endless games of *mah jong*, while Zhao Li simply buried himself in his job, as a lowly clerk with a firm of accountants, where his conscientiousness was noted, but, for the most part, unrewarded. He worked longer and longer hours, only returning home after he was certain Xiu Mei would have retired for bed, and rising to leave the next morning before she awoke.

This suited them both perfectly. Neither interfered with the daily lives of the other, while at night they slept in separate rooms. They both resigned themselves to living out their days in this predictable, if disappointing arrangement. Then three unexpected things happened.

First, Zhao Li stumbled upon a major accounting error made by one of his superiors. Zhao Li was able, by dint of a swift but unobtrusive action, to avert total disaster, saving the firm from potential losses exceeding tens of thousands of pounds, while at the same time sparing his superior from the personal shame, dishonour and humiliation that exposure of his error would undoubtedly have heaped upon him. Zhao's actions did not go unnoticed. They were rendered even more meritorious by his refusal to draw attention to them, or to expect any form of acknowledgement in return. Accordingly, his grateful superior invited him to become one of the firm's senior partners, in which position Zhao prospered further. In a few short years he became an extremely wealthy man. But he shared none of this success with Xiu Mei. He merely invested his good fortune – modestly and cautiously – for which he received unspectacular, but reliable dividends, while he and Xiu Mei continued to live quietly, separately and frugally.

While Zhao Li was sequestered in his office, Xiu Mei would fill her hours alone at home listening to the radio, the BBC Home Service. *Mrs Dale's Diary* and *Desert Island Discs* were particular favourites. It was not that she understood what either of them were particularly about, but they gave her the illusion that she was beginning at last to settle in her adoptive country. This brought her unexpected ease and comfort. Zhao Li indulged her in this pastime. She would twitter away about the latest goings-on at Virginia Lodge in the fictional suburb of Parkwood Hill almost as if they were her next-door neighbours. Zhao Li himself had little time for the radio, although he found the dulcet tones of Jack de Manio reading the morning news reassuringly comforting in this land where the Prime Minister continually attempted to persuade the nation that they had "never had it so good". Zhao Li believed him. He was equally struck by one particular element of *Desert Island Discs*. His wife would listen to it avidly while she prepared the Sunday lunch with Dai Tai. He himself paid it little heed, preferring instead, on his one day off a week from his work at the accountants', to go over the family finances. What intrigued him was the unquestioned assumption that each castaway would, as a matter of course, be delighted to receive *The Complete Works of Shakespeare*, along with the *King James Bible*. He decided therefore to devote what little free time he had in reading both, the better to understand the national character of the majority of his customers.

The second thing to happen was just as unexpected. Zhao Li was a man of regular habits. Each day he would take a forty-five-minute lunch break, during which he would walk the short distance from Charlotte Street, where the firm's offices were situated, to Albert Square, where he would raise his hat in deference to the statue of the Prince Consort, a man who Zhao Li admired greatly for his enterprise and vision. He would walk around the statue, which stood opposite Manchester's magnificent Town Hall, pausing at each of the four corners of the Gothic ciborium, topped by the ornate spire, beneath which the figure of the Prince stood proudly upon a marble plinth, facing west. Within the canopy were four allegorical figures, symbolising Art, Commerce, Science and Agriculture. Below each of these stood a further four secondary figures. For Art, there were depictions of Painting, Architecture, Music and Sculpture. For Commerce, there were the Four Continents. For Science, there were Chemistry, Astronomy, Mechanics and, Zhao Li's personal favourite, Mathematics, and for Agriculture, there were the Four Seasons. Zhao Li greatly admired the order and symmetry represented by the Memorial. He identified strongly with the Prince, a foreigner, who was at first regarded with suspicion by the British, but who came to be greatly revered by them. As he, too, hoped to be – if not revered, at least respected. He would find a place on the nearest bench he could to the Statue, where he would eat a cold lunch of bean sprouts and curd, after which he would settle to read a further extract from the Bible or the *Complete Works*.

On this particular day he was reading *Much Ado About Nothing*. The title especially appealed to him. He had just finished the line, *'Let me be that I am and seek not to alter me'*, when he suffered a sudden and massive heart attack, which killed him instantly.

Xiu Mei was comforted by the thought that this meant he probably did not suffer too much in the process. She did not like to think of him in pain. She mourned him as custom decreed. She and Dai Tai maintained a vigil beside Zhao Li's body for seven days. They wore white; they hung a white banner above the door; they lit odourless joss sticks – for it is the smoke, not the fragrance, which conveys the prayers up to heaven – and they laid out miniature replicas of Zhao Li's suits made from bamboo paper, which they burned, together with a suitcase full of rice paper money. On his headstone, after his burial in Philip's Park Cemetery, Xiu Mei had inscribed further lines from *Much Ado*.

'For it falls out

That what we have we prize not to the worth
Whiles we enjoy it, but being lacked and lost,
Why, then we rack the value, then we find
The virtue that possession would not show us
While it was ours…'

The third thing that happened, following directly on the heels of the second, was that, by becoming a Widow, which, in addition to restoring the Respect, Recognition and Esteem that had been so patently unforthcoming to her as a mere Wife, she had accordingly acquired Status, which was further enhanced by Wealth, for she was now in possession of a substantial Inheritance. Zhao Li had left her his entire fortune. This also meant that Dai Tai, the erstwhile 'plain daughter', was now a much sought-after Prize.

Xiu Mei was besieged by requests from all those families within the Manchester Chinese Community in possession of sons, nephews or cousins they deemed worthy of consideration as potential husbands for Dai Tai. The sole criterion for eligibility in this undignified cattle market was money. Naturally, Dai Tai was not consulted in the matter. Her own personal feelings were neither here nor there. Xiu Mei's response was more fatalistic. Her daughter's future husband, whoever he might be, would be kind, or he would not. Happiness did not come into it. Of course, Dai Tai would be furnished with a generous dowry, but the bulk of Zhao Li's fortune would remain with Xiu Mei while she lived. If Dai Tai's future husband, and, just as importantly, his family, wished to inherit it in due course, they would have to treat her daughter with due consideration and dignity. Pragmatism. This was the approach she adopted. Pragmatism had been Zhao Li's watchword, and Xiu Mei recognised the value of it.

It was about this time that Xiu Mei began to be visited by a stranger, a dirty, unkempt and bedraggled woman, who slept rough in Xiu Mei's doorway. Her first instinct had been to send her away, but something about the timing of her appearance, on what would have been Zhao Li's sixtieth birthday, made her pause. She recalled the way sometimes, late at night when he couldn't sleep, he would read to her from a passage he particularly enjoyed in the *King James Bible*. One of these returned to her on the morning she first encountered the homeless woman, whose overcoat had slipped from her shoulder to reveal the striking tattoo of a pair of wings.

'Be not forgetful to entertain strangers, for thereby some have entertained angels unawares...'

But Xiu Mei was also reminded of a time when she had only just arrived in this country, when she spoke little English and understood even less, when the uncle for whom she worked long hours in the *Ping Hong* restaurant treated her with such casual disregard, when she had nothing but the clothes she stood up in, which she must wash each night in the cold, bare attic room she slept in and put back on each morning even though they had scarcely dried, when the only act of kindness shown to her had been by a stranger, a young woman, who had found her weeping in the lavatory after she had spilled the tea and dropped the tray, smashing all of the crockery, because she was frightened and her hands were trembling, who had knelt beside her and taken out a white handkerchief edged and embroidered with delicate pink flowers, which afterwards the young woman had given to her, and which she had still to this day, in a drawer beside her bed, where she kept her few treasures, such as Dai Tai's first pair of baby shoes, and Zhao Li's copies of Shakespeare and the Bible.

The following day the homeless woman with the angel tattoo was again asleep on Xiu Mei's doorstep. But this time, when Xiu Mei bent down to wake her, to give her a bowl of noodle soup, she could see that the woman was ill. Her forehead was matted with sweat. Her lips were cracked and sore. Her chin was flecked with spittle. Xiu Mei took the white handkerchief edged with pink flowers and dabbed the woman's face with it, drying her skin and smoothing her brow. The woman opened her eyes and looked directly into Xiu Mei's. She tried to speak, but her words were little more than bubbles of air. Xiu Mei leant her ear against the woman's lips to try and catch what she was saying.

"Keep your friends close," she whispered, "but your enemies closer…"

Xiu Mei sat up, startled. These were the words of Sun Tzu. Another of Zhao Li's heroes, who had served as his guide when climbing up the accountants' ladder.

The next morning the woman had gone. Xiu Mei never saw her again. But she now knew what she must do with regard to choosing a husband for Dai Tai. She consented to a meeting with a young man, bristling with self-confidence. His name was Bao. His father had once been a rival of Zhao Li's…

After the traditional exchange of gifts between the two families – oranges for good luck, sesame seeds for fertility, rice sweets for prosperity, and a pair of scissors, shaped like a pair of moths, symbolising the couple's inseparability – a red banner was hung above the door of Bao's family's house to greet Dai Tai when she arrived by procession on the day of the ceremony. The day before Dai Tai's hair was washed in water infused with pomegranate leaves by Xiu Mei, before being ceremonially combed four times in front of a small hand mirror to signify the light of the moon. The first combing – *yàt sò sò dou méih* – was the hope for her to remain together with her husband till the end. The second – *yih sò baak nìhn hóu hahp* – was to be blessed with a hundred years of marriage. The third – *sàam sò jí syùn mùhn tòhng* – was for their house to be filled with children and grandchildren, and the fourth – *sei sò baahk faat chàih mèih* – was a wish for a long life. The following day Dai Tai arrived wearing a highly embroidered, long red silk dress, stitched with dragon and phoenix adornments. No expense was spared. Bao always remembered this.

To begin with, the signs were optimistic. The businesses grew, just as Bao had predicted they would. But in all other aspects the marriage was turning out to be less auspicious than had been foretold. Dai Tai, it seemed, could not bear children. She would conceive, but then she would miscarry. "Be patient," Bao's father advised. "She is still young. Let her recover her strength first before you return to the marriage bed."

*

1975

Bao took his father's counsel to heart. He focused all of his energies on the business, working longer and longer hours. By the time he came home each night, Dai Tai would already be asleep, and he hadn't the heart to wake her.

Ten years passed.

The business grew. Even without Zhao Li's steadying hand at the tiller. He had died disappointed never to have seen a grandchild. Isn't that what their exile had been for after all? To thrive and prosper in a far-off land, which, though suspicious at first, had grown to accept and welcome these strangers at their gate that they had come to depend upon them for their skills and services?

*

1987

As Zhao Li's widow, Xiu Mei had come to live with her daughter and her husband, as was the custom, and Bao was not a man to shirk his duty, whatever he might have felt in private. Xiu Mei's influence and status had by this time diminished, even if her wealth had not. She was now subordinate in rank to Bao's mother, with whom she did not get on. She was relegated to her own apartment within the building where they lived, rarely joining the rest of the family, and never seeing her daughter alone. Several years passed. This unsatisfactory but unavoidable situation prevailed. But if there was one thing Xiu Mei had learned from her late husband, it was the art of patience. So – she waited. She bit her tongue and bided her time.

Then, when Bao's mother died, Xiu Mei's position was immediately reinstated. She was once more invited to assist Dai Tai in her role as wife to the important businessman Bao had now become. She was appalled by what she discovered. She was shocked to see just how constricted her daughter's life now was. She hardly ever went outside the four walls of their three-floored flat on Faulkner Street, in sight of the recently erected *paifang*, the giant traditional Chinese archway, under which all the city centre traffic had to pass on its way to Piccadilly Gardens, in what had now become universally known as Chinatown, the largest enclave of its kind in the country after London. Its vibrancy and colour brought visitors to see it from miles around. But Dai Tai did not see it. She never lifted her eyes from the ground. If ever she did go outside – to buy food from the supermarket just a few doors down from her – she clung to the shadow of the walls, hoping to remain invisible. The arch, decorated with its dragons and phoenixes, mocked her with memories of the dress she wore for her wedding, which had been wrapped in tissue paper and put away, not seeing the light of day since.

Bao meanwhile had expanded the family business far beyond the confines of the laundry where he had started out into the financial markets of the city's banking district literally a stone's throw away. He spent most of his time in nearby Mosley Street in his office in the Bank of China, one of only four branches they had in all of England. When he was not in the bank, he played the tables at the *Genting Casino* round the corner on Portland Street, not caring whether he won or lost. Being a shareholder there too, it hardly mattered. If he lost, he won.

Xiu Mei decided to take matters into her own hands. She took down her daughter's wedding dress from the top of the wardrobe, where it had been abandoned and forgotten. The box was so dusty she almost choked when she touched it. She gingerly opened the lid. She delicately peeled back the outer layer of tissue. At once a moth that must have been trapped inside for who-knew-how-long fluttered up and past her, heading directly for the window and the light, where it banged its wings against the glass. Xiu Mei, anxious not to startle or damage it, gently opened the window and ushered it back out into the air, into the world once more.

She repeated the ceremony of the wedding. She washed Dai Tai's hair in pomegranate water. She ritually combed it four times. She dressed her in the red silk dress embroidered with fire-breathing dragons and phoenixes. They arose from the ashes of long, cold, forgotten years. Dai Tai awoke after what had seemed a long sleep. Dai Tai – meaning 'towards hope…'

*

1992

Bao is now forty-seven years old. Dai Tai is forty-two. Chloe is born. She is eight weeks premature. She is tiny but strong. She survives. But her mother does not. Dai Tai dies within twenty-four hours of the birth from a post-partum haemorrhage. At first the signs were not picked up – the increased heart rate, the feeling faint when trying to stand – but when her blood pressure continued to fall and more blood was lost, the doctors were alerted, but it was too late.

"The contraction of the uterus was poor," Bao is told. "Her red blood count was already low." But he does not hear them. "She was Asian," they tell him. "Over forty," they add. "All possible contra-indications. We are so very sorry for your loss."

Bao leaves the hospital without a word. He plunges himself deeper into his work. When Chloe is strong enough to go home, it is Xiu Mei who collects her.

It is Xiu Mei who gives Chloe her name. "She is English," she tells her son-in-law. "She should have a name that English people can pronounce and understand. It's becoming quite fashionable. Your cousin has named his daughter Suzy. It means 'be joyful'."

"Why Chloe?" asks Bao in a rare moment of apparent interest.

"The young green shoots of a plant in spring."

Bao looks down on his daughter's scrunched up face and grunts. "As you wish," he says. "I care not."

Xiu Mei picks the baby up. "Chloe," she coos. "I will look after you. Don't worry about your father. He's just sad, that's all. He misses your *Mŭqīn*, your *Mama*."

The truth is that Bao did not miss Dai Tai. Not really. She had for so long effaced herself that he had all but forgotten her existence even while she was alive. He knows that this is not how he ought to feel, and so he punishes himself by working even longer hours than he had before. He consoles himself with the thought that at least neither she nor her grandmother will want for anything materially. That at least will partially assuage his guilt.

And it does.

Time passes. Chloe grows. She learns to accept her father's distant, silent moods. He is never cruel or unkind to her. He's simply absent for most of the time, even when he is physically there. She doesn't question this. It's just the way things are.

*

2007

Chloe is fifteen. It's already clear how bright she is.

"You should think about Oxbridge," her teachers tell her. Her father's interest is piqued by this. A daughter at either Oxford or Cambridge would be an undoubted feather in his cap.

"But what about *Lao lao*?" says Chloe.

"Don't worry about me," says Xiu Mei.

"Actually I'd rather stay here in Manchester," says Chloe. "I want to study Media. They don't do that at Oxbridge. But they do at MMU."

"Then you are not as clever as your teachers say you are," says Bao.

He thrusts a copy of the Financial Times in front of her and points to an article on one of the inside pages.

Financial Times

24th March 2007

CHINA PASSES NEW PROPERTY LAW

After 14 years of labyrinthine debate the Central Committee of the Chinese Government yesterday created a new *Property Act*, which becomes law with immediate effect.

The 1982 Constitution of the People's Republic of China under the Chairmanship of Deng Xiao Ping provided for the 'socialist ownership' of land and property. In practice this took two forms – state ownership and public ownership. Yet at the same time deeds attached to former private ownership, though officially overruled, were never legally made invalid.

When Jhiang Zemin succeeded Deng, the whole debate was opened up for greater scrutiny, but became completely mired in red tape. It took a change of Leader to at last untie it. One of Premier Hu Jintao's first acts on becoming President in 2003 was to pass the 4th Amendment to the 1982 Constitution. Article 13 of this Amendment stated that: 'The lawful private property of individual citizens shall be deemed inviolable.' It further clarified this by declaring that the state would also provide a guarantee of protecting 'under law' any citizen's 'inheritance rights' in accordance with any aforementioned private property.

Yesterday, the Property Act has been further amended by Hu to clarify that: 'The country may, as necessitated by the public interest, expropriate or requisition a citizen's, or his descendants', private property and pay all due compensation thereof...'

"Pack your suitcase," Bao commands Chloe. "We leave for Shenzen tomorrow. You shall witness your inheritance first hand."

Chloe does not like Shenzen. It's not that it isn't exhilarating or stimulating. The rapidity of change is breathtaking, the sheer size and scale of the ambition quite awe-inspiring. No – it's the way in which it is so totally unregulated that she finds so disconcerting, the way all traces of its previous history have been swept away. Not so much clean slate as scorched earth. On the twenty-two hour flight she had read as much as she could about its past. It had enjoyed a rich and diverse heritage under the previous *Qin, Tang, Song* and *Ming* dynasties, trading in salt, tea, spices and rice. Nothing of that now remains, in spite of it being the second largest container port in the world. Shenzen is a designated 'Special Economic Zone', a mega-city with a population of twenty million and rising, focusing instead on international financial services, a globalised technology hub, dubbed the Chinese Silicon Valley. Situated on the Pearl River delta, it stretches forty-three miles from Huizou in the north to Hong Kong in the south.

Chloe takes a photograph of the area where her father's ancestral property once stood. No trace of the hut his family had lived in, the shack where he had been born, now survives. To Chloe it looks as though the land has been laid waste by an earthquake. But her father does not share this view. He sees only what, in less than a decade, will replace it.

"Out with the old, in with the new," he proclaims, stretching his arms out wide. "This is Year Zero."

Unlike Manchester, where the future is being layered upon the past like geological sediments, so that, for Chloe, there is always the sense of walking in the footsteps of those who went before her, of hearing her own voice caught up in the echoes of all those who preceded her, so that she feels part of a continuum, Shenzen is not standing on the shoulders of giants. Rather, it is trampling them into the dust and rubble of the endless building sites, so that a great fog descends upon it, obscuring it from view, like a conjuror distracting his audience from what is actually going on, until the veil can be pulled back when the conjuror is ready to amaze. But where Chloe can see no evidence of any form of guiding hand, Bao understands that there is no single magician, but a whole circle of them, of which he can see himself becoming a part.

It becomes evident within just a few days that claiming his compensation will not be straightforward for Bao. There are whole labyrinths of bureaucracy to navigate, each with their own library of forms to be filled in, taken from one office to another, to be stamped, copied, filed, cross-referenced. It is like a rigged game of Monopoly.'Do not pass Go. Do not collect £200.' Or, as in Bao's case, what he hopes will be closer to £2 million.

But rather than being daunted by all the hoops he must jump through, he appears to relish them. After less than a week, he declares he has decided not to return to Manchester until every 'i' has been dotted and 't' has been crossed. However long that may take. Meanwhile there are opportunities to pursue.

Chloe returns alone.

Her father does not come back for another six years. Not until the eve of Chloe's graduation. The week before, he whats-apps a photograph to her. It was taken, he says, from the exact same spot that Chloe took hers less than five years ago.

"Do you see the tallest tower?" he texts. "I'm part of the consortium that raised the capital to build it. I'm turning a profit on it already..."

2013

"If you insist on this foolhardy idealism of yours and refuse to accompany me back to Shenzen, where so many more lucrative media opportunities are there for the taking, then at least do me the courtesy of considering this."

Bao slides a folder across the table towards his recalcitrant daughter.

Chloe opens it and sighs. It is a Mission Statement from a Chinese Investment Company with an office here in Manchester.

YING DE GROUP
YOUR DIRECT LINK TO FUNDS

Our innovative service creates mutual benefits for both UK businesses and Chinese investors. Through our service, quality businesses can easily access funding from prudent Chinese investors who believe in their ambitions for growth.

"We are looking at several sites here in Manchester already," says Bao. "Deansgate Square, Castlefield. Angel Meadow. NOMA, Axis Tower, Anaconda Cut, The Blade. Next week our Paramount Leader, Xi Jinping, will make historic state visit to the city. I introduce you."

Xiu Mei, peering over Chloe's shoulder, points to the girl in the photograph, rocking with delight.

"That girl could be you, *Sunnu*. She even look like you."

Chloe shakes her head.

"I'm sorry, *Baba*. I just don't believe in it."

"Then you are no daughter of mine."

Chloe lets the force of this sink in before she answers.

"I have," she says, in a voice more composed than how she feels, "a friend, however, who would be intensely interested. Might he go with you in my place?"

"Did he get a First?" asks Bao.

Chloe looks down.

"Then what is the point?" he says. "Without China," he continues, "Northern Powerhouse is just Northern Poorhouse." He snaps his fingers and immediately the waiter is at his side. Bao proffers his credit card between the first and second fingers of his left hand, which the waiter extracts as delicately as if he is removing a wafer of gold, which, to all intents and purposes, he is. Bao does not deign to speak to him. Why should he? There is no need.

Once the bill has been settled, he rises to his feet immediately. "Xiu Mei will return to Shenzen with me," he declares, "whether you choose to or not."

"*Lao lao*," says Chloe, surprised, "are you sure? Is that what you really want?"

"I think," says Xiu Mei, "I should like to see my home again."

Chloe nods. "Yes," she says. "So would I." Bao and Xiu Mei turn to her with renewed hope. "But," she continues, "my home is here."

"So be it," says her father, helping Xiu Mei to her feet. "You may stay in Faulkner Street as long as you wish. I don't expect we shall see one another again." He turns on his heels and walks swiftly away.

Xiu Mei takes from her purse a small, neatly folded cotton handkerchief, edged with the embroidered pink blossom of a spindle tree.

"Here," she says, pressing it into Chloe's hand, "take this. For souvenir. Kind lady gave it me long time ago. I never forget. You and your father. Like two sides of same coin. Can never land at same time."

She turns and hobbles after her Bao, looking one last time over her shoulder at her stubborn granddaughter with a mixture of bewilderment and loss.

"So," says Alex, Petros's father, the moment their plates of *dolmadakia* – vine leaves stuffed with minced lamb, fresh dill, mint, parsley – have been cleared away, "what will you do now? What are your plans?"

No beating about the bush then? Well, thinks, Petros, no time like the present. Might as well get this over with.

"Well…" he begins.

Callista shoots him a warning look.

But before he can get any further, Andreas, Callista's husband, has already jumped in.

"We've been thinking," he says, "your father and me…"

You more likely, thinks Petros but doesn't say.

"…given your degree, you might want to join our Marketing Team, bring in some fresh ideas, design a new website, get to grips with social media – you know…? What d'you think?"

"Well…" says Petros again.

"You don't have to answer right away," interrupts Andreas.

"Yes he does," says Alex. "He's already turned down the chance to join the family business once before. This is his last chance. I won't be asking him again."

Petros breathes deeply. Then, looking not at his father, but directly at Andreas, he says, "No thanks. I appreciate the offer, but I have other plans."

"And what might those be?" sneers Alex.

"I'm starting up my own business. In fact I already have. Property Development."

"Really?" says Alex. "And who's going to finance this little enterprise?"

"Me actually."

His father looks up aghast.

"I've already done up and sold one. With the profit I made from that, I've been able to secure a loan that's enabled me to buy two more. I'm on my way, Dad."

His father says nothing. Nor does his mother, who simply looks down, kneading her fingers on her lap. Callista lays her own hand upon them, to try and still their agitation, while at the same time trying to indicate how pleased she is for her brother.

"Well," says Andreas, "that's great. You should've said earlier. Good luck."

"Thanks."

"If you ever change your mind," he continues, "the door here will always be open."

Petros's father bristles, but says nothing.

"But what will you do now?" says Vikram to Khav. "I've never really understood the benefits of Media Studies."

"No, *Bapu*," says Geetha hurriedly, before Khav can say something she might later regret. "A degree is a degree. They can never take that away from her. We're proud of you, *Dhi*," she adds, turning back to her daughter.

"Quite right," says Grace. "When I was a student I used to get asked that all the time. 'What's the point of a degree in Archaeology? What kind of job will that get you afterwards?' And I'd say, 'An archaeologist.' That was the only thing I ever wanted to do. Right from when my father taught me about the bones that lay underneath Philips Park after the Great Flood of 1872 had washed out half the graves at the nearby cemetery. From when I first came face to face with the skeleton of Maharajah the Elephant in Manchester Museum and I tried to draw it, to try and understand it better. And from when I first went to Central Reference Library and was shown maps of early Manchester. I wanted to know where we came from, how we got here, how we grew as a city. Then, when I found the bones and shield of an early British warrior from the time when the Romans left these shores, I was hooked. I knew exactly what I wanted to do. I had a passion, a cause, and nothing was going to stop me. That's what counts, finding something that matters to you. For me it was archaeology, who knows what it will be for Khav? But the one thing I do know about her is that she's someone who cares deeply about other people, about trying to help them discover just what it is that they can do that nobody else can, then encouraging them to follow their dream. Am I right, Khav?"

Grace takes a satisfying bite from what remains of her poppadom and munches on it triumphantly. That's one of the wonderful things about getting old, she thinks. Perhaps the only one. She can say whatever the hell she feels like, neither giving a damn, nor caring what anybody thinks, without fear of contradiction.

Geetha and Vikram look at Grace open-mouthed.

"Actually," says Khav, "I've already got a job."

Her parents turn from Grace back towards their daughter.

"Z-Arts have offered me a one-year position as a Community Arts Assistant."

"Splendid," says Gracie. "Congratulations."

"What does that mean?" says Vikram. "Community Arts? Spraying graffiti on walls? More of that hippy-hoppy nonsense?"

"It's not nonsense, *Bapu*. It's helping people find a voice, a way of expressing themselves. I'll be organising classes and workshops in a whole range of activities for people of all ages. After School Clubs, Tea Dances, Jewellery, Ceramics, Photography. Henna painting – you should come along and try it, *Maa*."

Geetha looks down. Grace can see just how important her parents' approval means to her.

"Put me down for that henna painting," she says.

"I will," says a relieved Khav.

"I might fancy a go at the Over 50s Hip-Hop as well, while I'm about it."

Even Vikram finds he can smile at the idea of that. But when he looks back at Grace, his expression falters. She is serious, he can tell.

"Think of it as a start, *Bapu*," says Khav, "a first step on the ladder, like when you began as a lowly clerk in the bank. The Arts Council have one of their main offices here in Manchester. They're always looking for administrators with a couple of years' experience behind them. Z-Arts will help me get that."

"The Arts Council?" says Vikram, sounding a little more mollified. "That's more like it. Then you would be a Civil Servant."

Unseen by Vikram, Grace eyes Khav directly. She puts her finger to her lips and winks, smiling. "Round One to you," she mouths.

"The trouble is," says Lorrie, after she has demolished the cheesecake and chocolate sauce, "I simply have no idea what to do next. No idea at all."

"Don't worry about it," says Milosz. "Something will turn up, you'll see."

"That's right," says Agniewska. "It doesn't do to plan. Who knows how long it will be before circumstances force you to have to pack up and move on."

"That's good advice, Lorelenka," says Pavel. "The talk of a traveller."

"But we don't travel," says Lorrie, "not any more."

"Not today," says Agniewska, "but tomorrow… who knows?"

"Keep your options open," says Milosz. "You can always work with me on the fairs through the summer."

"Actually," she says nervously, "I have an interview next week."

"Really?" says Agniewska. "Where? Why didn't you tell us?"

"In case I didn't get it, I suppose."

"Of course you'll get it," says Milosz, putting a huge bear-like arm around his daughter.

"What is it for?" asks Lena.

"It's at an Art Gallery in Salford. Islington Mill."

"I know this place," says Pavel. "It used to make calico. I remember buying yards and yards of it once to make the cover for the Caterpillar Ride at Silcock's. Years ago. I thought it had shut."

"It's a gallery now," says Lena impatiently. "Lorelenka just told us."

"What kind of job is it?" asks Vitaly.

"Only a receptionist," says Lorrie. "But it's a start."

"That's right," says Lena. "Who knows where it might lead? You'll be organising them all in no time, you'll see."

"I don't know about that."

"Listen," says Lena, gripping her granddaughter's arm. "When I first started work at the circus, I had no idea where it might lead. I looked around me, watched what everyone else did, had a go at this, tried a bit of that. Then, when someone asked me if I wanted a turn on the trapeze, I thought: why not? There'll always be a safety net to catch me if I fall. But I never did. I climbed higher and higher. Right up into the roof of the Big Top. But even then I never thought about where it was all headed. I just thought about the next moment. I swung in the air, forward and back, forward and back, just fixing my eye on the other trapeze bar opposite, waiting for me to fly towards it and grab a hold of it with both hands, which is what I did.

Chloe walks through the foyer of *The Midland Hotel*, where students for the afternoon's ceremony are already milling around. She walks through them, already not one of them any more. She steps outside onto Peter Street and looks up. The sun is shining in a Corot sky. A few high white clouds float like thistledown, or dandelion clocks perhaps, blowing away time. She walks purposefully back towards the University, not wishing to be late for the Faculty Reception, where Clive is apparently going to say a few words, before declaring the exhibition of all the final year students' work open to visiting family and friends, ahead of its press and industry opening a couple of hours later.

At the same moment Petros, Lorrie and Khav are separately making their way there too. Petros is heading down Princess Street before turning right onto Whitworth Street, which he will follow until he reaches *The Palace Theatre*, where Willem Dafoe and Mikhail Baryshnikov are starring in Robert Wilson's production of *The Old Woman*, written in the 1930s by Daniil Kharms before he was exiled to the Gulag, a play about an artist struggling to find some kind of inner peace. He turns blindly onto Oxford Road.

Lorrie proceeds by way of Great Bridgewater Street, Whitworth Street West and Tony Wilson Place, past where *The Haçienda* used to be, which is now a major construction site, with the building of Danny Boyle's complex of theatre, cinema and gallery, to be known as *Home*, well under way. She passes where new streets are being planned in honour of other Manchester luminaries – Jack Rosenthal, Anne Horniman, Isabella Banks. Finally she reaches *The Cornerhouse*, almost directly opposite *The Palace* where Petros now walks. The film now showing is the Baz Luhrman version of *The Great Gatsby*, with Leonardo DiCaprio and Tobey Maguire, which Lorrie has already seen, but which she pauses once more beside, to look at the posters and publicity stills. She's never read the book, and she didn't much care for the film, but she adores the fashions, and wonders if she might adopt Carey Mulligan's hairstyle as Daisy, the blonde kiss-curl on the forehead, before resolutely walking past and onto Oxford Road..

Khav is early. She decides she will stop by the City Art Gallery on Mosley Street, to which she cuts through directly from Albert Square after she has left the restaurant there. She is drawn to the new Grayson Perry exhibition like a moth to a flame. *The Vanity of Small Differences*. The title especially intrigues. Six giant tapestries which highlight tiny but significant shifts in attitudes towards class, taste and belonging. Nothing is quite what it seems. Rather like the artist himself. Or should that be herself, wonders Khav? She finds herself intrigued by the way Perry will sometimes present himself to the world as a man, but frequently as a woman, like when she went up to collect the Turner Prize ten years before. Khav wishes she had the same certainty about her own identity to be able to do the same. He? She? Pronouns are such slippery things. Perhaps new ones are needed. She will ask Tanya about this when she next sees her.

She ducks down Nicholas Street, right into Faulkner Street, scurrying beneath the Chinese Arch – she knows this area well now after her weeks of sleeping on Chloe's sofa – then left onto Dickinson Street, right onto Portland Street and left onto Oxford Street, just before it changes to Oxford Road, after she has passed between *The Palace* and *The Cornerhouse*, at just around the same time as Petros and Lorrie.

Chloe, almost from the moment she leaves *The Midland* and crosses St Peter's Square, has been walking in a straight line. She passes the turning to where she lives without even affording it a second glance. She fails to notice what is showing in the galleries, theatres or cinemas. Instead she keeps her eyes firmly fixed in front of her. She will not be distracted from her main goal, which is to prove her father wrong. She recognises this for what it is – the vanity of small differences – but she will not let that deflect her. In her father's eyes she may already be in exile, in a gulag of her own making, but this city is her home, even if it is still being built all around her. The sound of her footsteps is drowned by the ceaseless pounding of pneumatic drills and jack-hammers, subsumed within the constant traffic thundering beside her. She passes beneath a large billboard on the waste ground where the BBC once stood, before moving out to Media City in Salford, scraps of torn posters flapping in the wind. One of them is an old advert for *Vision Express*, a Gatsby pastiche. '*There's a revolution in sight.*' But Chloe does not register it.

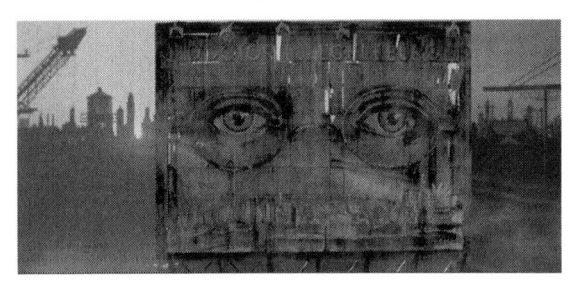

They are all four of them now walking along the same road. Separately but together. At times their paths will diverge. At other times they will conjoin. From time to time one or other of them will pick up a stick and run it along the spade iron railings that divide the campus they currently walk towards, possibly for the last time, and the city that holds their futures before them like a promise. A future that sometimes will shine bright and clear, but at others will remain stubbornly hidden. Not unlike the River Medlock, whose culverted, invisible watercourse their feet pass over on this midsummer afternoon, occasionally surfacing to surprise them, blinking in the sunlight. They none of them have any way of knowing, except the feeling that they are somehow bound up in each other, in this moment, in others that have gone before, and in who knows what others may come to pass.

*

Manchester Metropolitan University

**School of Arts & Humanities
Grosvenor Gallery
Graduates Show
+
Holden Gallery
George Wright Retrospective
July 2013**

Clive looks around the two adjoining galleries one last time. Yes, he decides, everything is ready. It's been a close-run thing, but they've managed it, with just half an hour before they are scheduled to open their doors to the friends, families and supporters of today's graduates, with the more formal press and private view to follow this evening.

Tanya stands by the door, waiting for Clive's signal.

He nods. "Yes," he says. "Open the flood gates."

"Hardly a flood," smiles Tanya. "More like a trickle."

"If we open it, they will come," he says, spreading his arms wide.

Tanya throws open the doors, and the first eager few step tentatively inside. Clive recognises a couple of the students, proudly leading their parents to where their own particular stand is situated.

"I don't know how to thank you," says Clive.

"You can buy me a beer later," says Tanya.

"It's a deal. Without you, this wouldn't be happening."

"Without the students, you mean."

"Yes, yes, obviously. Actually, I was thinking more about next door."

"I know," says Tanya. "It's a triumph."

"It is, isn't it?" He performs a neat cabriole, then trots off to introduce himself to various parents.

The Graduates' Show features final years' student work from all the departments in the school – Photography, Graphic, Product and Fashion Design, Fine Art, as well as Media Studies. Each student has an allocated space, an equal allotted square footage, in which to feature a selection of their work. There are more than a hundred of them to be accommodated. Somehow Tanya has managed to squeeze them all in. Being a Group Show, crossing several disciplines, there has been a fair bit of wrangling and horse-trading between the various Department Heads, egos to be massaged, compromises to be made. Tanya, as the Faculty Technician, has had to bear the brunt of the squabbles and politics, but, as she has done successfully for the past three years, she has been able to satisfy everyone's competing needs.

"You're a miracle worker," Clive has declared.

"All in a day's work," she has joked.

In truth, Clive, as the Senior Department Head, is no longer interested in the kind of in-fighting and point-scoring indulged in by his younger, more ambitious colleagues. He'll be retiring this time next year, and so he has persuaded the others to let him curate the accompanying Professional Show in the smaller Holden Gallery just along the corridor. The Professional Show has become an MMU tradition over the years. The School runs a regular Exhibition Programme throughout the year, mostly emerging or early career artists, frequently former graduates, but, for the End of Year Graduates' Show, they try to invite a more established artist with a wider national – sometimes international – reputation to exhibit alongside. It's an unparalleled opportunity for both the graduates and undergraduates to get to meet an artist of real standing, a chance for the invited artist to curate their own solo show without any commercial pressure or restraint, and a way for the staff to give their graduates a proper send-off, a show of appreciation for all their hard work over their three years there, and provide them with a launch-pad for the start of this next phase of their fledgling careers. Competition to select the invited artist is fierce among the staff, and this year that honour has fallen to Clive.

He has decided to break with tradition. Instead, as has become the custom within the School, of asking a contemporary figure to exhibit, one of the Young Turks, Clive has decided to curate a major retrospective of the works of the Manchester photographer George Wright.

He has made the decision for three reasons. First, because he can. Second, because 2013 marks the centenary of George Wright's birth as well as being thirty years since his sudden death in 1983 from a motorcycle accident, and third, because Clive happens to believe his work is in the front rank, ripe for reassessment. This exhibition, he hopes, will provide the platform.

There have been many fine Manchester photographers over the years. Clive has known many of them. David Gleave and Adam Pester, with their social-realist images of hidden Manchester. Amanda Window, who's been taking pictures of local bands and musicians for more than a decade, at out-of-the-way venues like *Jimmy's*, the *Night & Day Café, Band on the Wall*, where she took several shots of Clive's wife, Florence, a couple of which now adorn their sitting room wall. Paul Wright and Adam Burton with their photographic essays of Manchester in the eighties, Richard Davis and his signature *No Place Like Hulme* series, with whom Clive had once shared a less-than-salubrious squat, and Peter Walsh with his iconic images of *The Haçienda* in its heyday – Happy Mondays, New Order, The Charlatans, even The Stone Roses and Oasis. But there have, in Clive's opinion, been only two great ones – Shirley Baker and Martin Parr. He believes George Wright belongs in that pantheon.

Clive was a contemporary of Martin. They both studied Photography at the Poly, as it was then, at around the same time, Clive starting just one year before. It soon became apparent that Martin was destined for great things. With his pal Daniel Meadows he went off in search of the real Coronation Street, only to discover it had been demolished, so instead he directed his camera onto nearby June Street, where he persuaded the people who lived there to let him photograph them in their front rooms. It was a simple but brilliant idea, which immediately catapulted him into the limelight. This was followed by his series of portraits of drinkers in different Yates's Wine Lodges across Manchester and the north-west. Though undoubtedly brilliant, they made for uncomfortable viewing. What was Martin's purpose in exhibiting them? His motives seemed uncertain, ambiguous. Fears that he might have been exposing his sitters in June Street to potential ridicule for their taste in décor – though to Clive's eye Martin's images were respectful, even heroic – invoking criticism that the work was merely a pastiche, only intensified with the Yates's Wine Lodge series, which some regarded as further reinforcing northern stereotypes. Martin defended himself by saying that what interested him most were the things that distinguished the mythology of a place from the reality of it, a criticism often labelled at George Wright's work, particularly those images that portrayed feral kids playing on wrecked and abandoned cars dumped on demolition waste ground, which were labelled sentimental by some, nostalgic by others, yearning for some kind of lost Eden. But to Clive's mind this was missing the point. When George Wright took those photos, they were urgently contemporary. Context is all. Taken in the late sixties and early seventies, they showed bomb sites that had still not been cleared nearly thirty years after the War had ended. This wasn't mythology, but reality.

These tensions were clearly evident in Martin's next major show – *Point of Sale* – a collection of images of Salford supermarkets, for which Martin switched from black and white to an unforgiving, neon colour. He followed this up with the show that first brought him national attention – *The Last Resort*, Martin has always been good with titles – featuring dozens of photographs of holidaymakers at the working-class town of New Brighton on the tip of the Wirral peninsula, where the River Mersey meets the Irish Sea, less than an hour's drive from where Clive is standing right now, waiting to welcome his guests. These were once more in an eye-popping, saturated colour, but much more garishly crude, like over-developed holiday snapshots. They depicted obese men and women reminiscent of McGill's saucy seaside postcards, but in grotesque close-up, surrounded by the detritus of candy floss, ice cream, and discarded fish and chips, swooped on by ravenous gulls. Were they celebratory or exploitative? The critics were divided. Their warts-and-all Hogarthian exuberance clearly struck a chord, however uncomfortably, arriving as they did in the middle of Thatcher's Britain.

Clive remains ambivalent. Are the photographs cruel or affectionate? And does it matter either way? For Clive it has come to. There's no doubting Martin's importance as a chronicler of a certain type of Englishness – Clive resists the term 'northernness', for *The Last Resort* could just as easily have been shot in Southend or Clacton as it was in New Brighton – but he wonders sometimes whether his erstwhile friend has fallen foul of his own mantra. "I take serious photographs," he has said on many occasions, "disguised as entertainment," and, in so doing, he has become something of an institution, a factory, not unlike Warhol, though obviously not as well-known, mass-producing for commercial gain.

"And what's wrong with that?"

Clive can still hear Petros's voice in his ear now, asking that very same question when Clive had delivered his annual lecture on the topic six months ago. "Why can art only be regarded as serious if it's difficult? Why does it always have to be so elitist? What's wrong with being populist?"

"Nothing," Chloe had replied. "So long as it doesn't rest on its laurels. So long as it's not about getting cheap laughs. So long as it doesn't just appeal to the lowest common denominator. So long as it's not complacent. So long as it's not just about making a fast buck."

"Take the money and run," Petros had shot back.

Chloe had looked at him long and hard then. "You don't really mean that," she had said.

"Watch me," said Petros.

"I intend to," said Chloe, and Petros had not known how to reply.

Clive hears these echoes now as he looks around him at the exhibition, beginning to fill up with people. Chloe, Petros, Lorrie and Khav are all here, he notices, as they had promised they would be, helping to show people round. He catches their eye. They wave. They smile. They give him an encouraging thumbs-up.

Clive has lost touch with Martin now. Not that they were ever that close, being in different year groups. Martin was from Surrey, Clive from Moss Side, and the difference had always showed, and now Martin lives in Bristol.

"Not that that matters," Lorrie had said, when he had raised the question of whether in fact Martin could be truly considered Mancunian. "We all of us come from somewhere else originally."

"And he's a cocky bastard," said Khav, "innit? Right in your face the whole time. I think he's brilliant."

"Now who's reinforcing northern stereotypes?" said Chloe.

"Sorry – I left my whippet outside."

For a time Martin had lived in Hebden Bridge, just up the road from where Clive's friends from *On The Eighth Day* hung out. He took a series of studies of rural life while he lived there, which are not much shown these days, which is a pity, thinks Clive, for they retain a tenderness and dignity, a sense of quiet intimacy not so evident in his later works.

It is these qualities – tenderness, dignity and intimacy – which are, Clive believes, the hallmarks of George Wright's works. In these he has much in common with that other Manchester photographic great, Shirley Baker. She and Martin are like chalk and cheese. They couldn't be more different. He's practically a household name, while she's hardly known at all – though that is finally beginning to change. About time too, thinks Clive. To begin with, she tried to get a job as a Staff Photographer with *The Guardian*, but they turned her down on the grounds that women weren't suited for documentary social realism. *The Guardian*, for fuck's sake! Subsequently they reversed their position, but only after Shirley had begun to develop a fast-growing reputation as a street photographer to rival Cartier-Bresson, though unlike him she never asked her subjects to pose, or re-stage an incident she might have seen but just missed. On the back of these early shows she began lecturing part-time at Salford College of Art, part of the old *Mechanics' Institute*, which is where she first met George Wright, who was doing the same. They became good friends. They liked to work in the same way, immersing themselves completely in a neighbourhood, enabling the people living and working there to get to know them and, over time, trust them, so that when they were taking their photographs, they were practically invisible. This was how they both managed to capture moments of such candid spontaneity. They never regarded one another as competitors, for they scrupulously avoided each other's territory. Rather, they viewed each other as fellow-chroniclers. Later, when Shirley had begun giving the occasional guest lecture at Manchester Poly, Clive went along. He was at the time still trying to make a career for himself as a photographer in his own right, mostly of the thriving underground music scene, but he was beginning to realise he was never going to cut it. He knew what constituted a good photograph, he understood the context in which he was working, but his images were forced and derivative. It was not that he didn't possess a keen eye, but he wasn't good at capturing that killer shot that defined the moment. He would see it, but too late – afterwards, rather than anticipating it before it arrived. That instinct, which he could recognise in others, was what he lacked for himself, and already his mind was starting to turn towards the possibility of teaching, not just photography, but across a range of different media. It wasn't a case of 'those who can, do; those who can't, teach', but more a case of recognising that his own particular skills lay more in interpreting, contextualising, curating. Shirley encapsulated this difference in just a few words the first time Clive had spoken to her.

"I love the immediacy of unposed, unpremeditated photographs. Less formal, everyday images of local ordinary people can often convey more about the life and spirit of the time than any number of the great and the famous."

Clive found himself in complete agreement. What was he doing chasing after the likes of the Gallagher brothers and The Charlatans? He was in danger of becoming a charlatan himself.

It was Shirley who had first introduced him to the photographs of George Wright. He had just died and a Memorial Exhibition was being held at an eccentric little gallery out in Denton, just six miles to the east out along the

A57. *Hall & Singer*, it was called, a former optician's, under a sign depicting a giant pair of spectacles, which gazed out blindly over the city. The owner, a frail man in his eighties with the palest, most translucent skin Clive had ever seen, who wore a pair of dark glasses even though it was evening and indoors, spoke to him about George with enormous pride and love.

"I sold him his very first camera – a Foth Derby, with retractable viewfinder, lens in front combined with a backsight..."

"Collapsing panel with small bellows behind," interrupted Clive, "folding mechanism with scissor strut."

"A connoisseur?" inquired Francis.

"An enthusiast," corrected Clive.

"He was standing right where you are now," said Francis. "He was just eighteen. The late afternoon light fell upon his hair and shoulders. I can picture it still. Like it was yesterday..."

A moth had landed softly on Clive's shoulder. Francis cupped it gently in his palm and carried it outside. As soon as he let it go, it fluttered up towards the giant spectacles, where it settled once more, opening and closing its wings.

"Look around," said Francis, casually wafting his hand. "Take your time."

And Clive had. He became immediately smitten, entranced. He wandered slowly from one photograph to the next. At one he suddenly let out an involuntary gasp.

"What is it?" asked Francis.

"I believe it's me," said Clive, scarcely believing his own eyes. "When I was a child. Look."

Francis joined him in front of an image of two boys on a piece of bombed-out waste-ground. One of the boys was standing on the roof of an abandoned, rusty container, hands in pockets, looking anxious. The other was in the middle of executing the perfect swan dive down to where a heap of mattresses lay precariously on a heap bricks and rubble, an expression of unalloyed ecstasy on his face.

"Which one are you?" asked Francis, briefly removing his dark glasses to reveal an extraordinarily arresting gaze. Clive found himself momentarily thrown by the redness of the iris at the centre of each eye.

"The one looking worried, I'm afraid. I was always scared we were about to get caught."

"Who's the other boy?"

"My brother – Christopher. Nothing frightened him."

"So I can see."

"He died."

"Oh. I'm sorry."

Francis had put his dark glasses back on after that and allowed Clive a moment to himself. Clive had known at once that he wanted to find out everything he could about George Wright. This particular photograph he now stood before contained all the reasons why. It was a perfect example of the 'unposed spontaneity' that Shirley had spoken about. It spoke directly of what life was really like for children growing up in the so-called swinging sixties, the grinding poverty of rubble-strewn bomb-sites and partly-demolished streets, living next door to roofless houses with broken windows and boarded-up back-entries, what Martin had meant by the reality behind the mythology. It was at the same time a double-portrait of remarkable insight, capturing exactly the precise difference between himself and his brother, the heightened juxtaposition of joy and fear, certainty and doubt. It was the perfect example of the true artist's ability to predict a moment, then capture it, a moment loaded with hope and foreboding, a firework that would burn brightly but then die. And, until just a few seconds ago, Clive had been completely unaware of its existence. Unaware that it had even been taken. Yet here it was, captured and framed for all time, for future generations to look upon and think, 'Wish we'd been there,' whereas at the time he had been wishing himself anywhere else.

Now, thirty years later, these memories return as he looks around at the exhibition that he has, with Tanya's considerable help, been able at last to realise.

Tanya has excelled herself. Rather than simply hanging the photographs on the gallery walls in the traditional manner, it had been Clive's idea instead to create a series of environments, enclaves, like mini stage-sets, in which to display the various different facets of George's *oeuvre*, so that the viewers are taken on a series of journeys into separate self-contained worlds, each of them connected by cobbled walkways, tantalisingly lit and accompanied by discreetly atmospheric soundscapes – children's skipping rhymes, snatches of conversation between women gossiping while they donkey-stone their doorsteps, the tinkle of an approaching ice cream van, the distant, ominous rumble of the wrecking ball. Tanya has created each of these stage sets with flair and finesse, with a subtle and judicious use of actual three-dimensional props to demarcate the space – a bicycle, a ladder, the wheel from a rag-and-bone cart, a few carefully placed piles of bricks. She has separated sections of the exhibition from one another with suspended sheets of corrugated iron, onto which she has projected images of characters whose faces are frequently repeated in the photographs, as if they are still here somehow, tapping the viewer on the shoulder, as if to say, 'Look, that's me over there, and there too, but I'm still here as well, see? I haven't gone away...'

All the major periods in his long sixty-year career are represented. Here are the early portraits of individuals at work, poignant with youthful optimism, presented in an idealised heroism that is almost Soviet in the lighting and the poses, except that, instead of being shown as archetypes, George gives us the whole man or woman, complete with transcripts of their personal testimonies, the nuts and bolts of them – miners, milkmen, typists, tanners; coal merchants, car mechanics, cotton workers, road menders; ironmongers, greengrocers, railway porters, pump attendants; dyers; farriers and foundry men, fitters and firemen; French polishers, plumbers and plasterers, welders and window cleaners; seamstresses, laundresses, waitresses and actresses; tripe boilers, barbers, bargemen and bus conductors; electricians, lab technicians, dieticians, hair beauticians; shop girls, delivery boys, panel beaters, pattern cutters; butchers, bakers and candlestick makers – representing every walk of life, so that the viewers find themselves surrounded on all sides, just as they are across the whole of Manchester, by the ceaseless activity of work, work, work, the convulsive upheaval of all this constant change, witnessed through the eyes of everyone George has photographed, these faces of the city. The gallery pulses with them. The air vibrates. The earth shakes.

Over there are the sporting heroes. The fighter Victor Collins, shadow boxing in a ring, wreathed in sweat and steam beneath a single overhead light; the speedway champion Ivan Mauger, a multiple blur of speed, as he breasts the tape, his rear wheel throwing up a spray of cinders in a perfect arc; the footballer Denis Law, right arm raised aloft after scoring, saluting the crowd like a matador; the cricketer Clive Lloyd, bat like a toy in his huge hands, stroking the ball through the covers for four.

And always, always, the crowds – at the dog track, on the terraces, in the stands – enraptured as if for a religious ritual. George trains his lens upon the faces of the supplicants and captures their transfigurations, the triumph out of despair, the ecstasy out of anger, the stations of the cross, the sorrows and beatitudes, prefiguring Martin Parr by several decades.

The same heroic faces are picked out repeatedly, in different times, in different guises. George loved a public gathering, a meeting, a march, a rally, and photographed them all. Here Clive has placed George's epic portrayal of the Mass Trespass onto the Peaks alongside the Routing of the Blackshirts, in which Mosley is mocked and ridiculed and finally driven out by the outrage of working people, in spite of the efforts of the police to prohibit them. George is back with them again as Gyani Sundar Singh Sagar is greeted by cheering crowds on his release from Strangeways, only to be re arrested at once as he sits astride his motor cycle wearing his turban instead of his crash helmet. Gyani-Ji's triumphant return to the *Gurdwara* is captured by George for posterity when the right to keep the turban is finally won. Khav has passed this very same photo nearly every Sunday of her life where it hangs in the foyer of the temple on Upper Chorlton Road on her way into each week's service. She waves to Clive as she sees it exhibited here, now.

And George is standing outside Strangeways again, in 1964, waiting with the crowds when the last man in England to be hanged, Gwynne Owen Evans, is executed in a cold, grey dawn. He captures the quiet, pinched faces of the people, their gaunt cheeks and closed eyes.

Later, he is on hand to witness when passions erupt in the Moss Side Riots in the summer of 1981. But these are not angry images. Emerging out of the smoke and fire are gestures of hope and reconciliation. One in particular has always struck Clive with its compassion and kindness. A young female protester, her face black with smoke, blood trickling down the side of her head from a cut just above her right eye, is tending to a policeman, who has just been thrown from his horse, which rears up in panic on its hind legs, while the girl places her sweater underneath the constable's helmet-less head against a concrete kerb. Clive has also been drawn towards this photograph for he recognises the young woman. She was, for a time, friendly with Christopher, his brother, then, later, with his nephew, Lance. Someone else, it seems, has recognised her too. A young student, whom Clive does not recognise, wearing some kind of small *hijab*, is peering intently at the photograph, her face almost pressed directly against that of the woman in the picture.

"Excuse me," says Clive, somewhat tentatively. "Might I be of assistance?"

The young student instantly springs back, almost as if Clive's words have been a cattle prod.

"I'm sorry," they both say together.

"After you," says Clive.

"The woman in this photograph," she says. "I think it's my mother."

"Oh," says Clive, then falls silent as he lets the implication of this remark sink in. For Clive realises that, incredibly, this must make him and the student in some distant way related. Her great-grandmother must therefore be the Great-great Aunt of his wife, Florence, which must make the two of them – what? Third cousins? Several times removed? Clive is no good at this sort of stuff. He'll have to ask Florence later when he goes back home this evening. He would like to ask this young student her name, but before he can say anything, she is speaking to him once again in anxious, hushed tones.

"I'd rather my grandparents didn't see this if you don't mind? It would only upset them. That's them over there," she says, pointing to an older couple, hovering uncertainly by another of the photographs on the opposite side of the gallery.

Clive nods.

"I'll stand in front of it for a while," he says. "I've to give a short speech in a few minutes, I'm afraid. There'll be more people in here by then, so they shan't be able to get as close to it as you did, so maybe they'll not notice. I'll keep guard in the meantime."

He offers her a conspiratorial grin, which she returns gratefully, before leaving him to rejoin her grandparents.

Clive watches her discreetly, reflecting on the power of George Wright's photographs to touch people's lives so directly, even more than thirty years after the event. He signals to Tanya and briefly explains the problem.

"I get it," she says. "You don't want people getting too close to this picture. I should've thought of it before. Don't worry. I've got an idea. I'll be back in a sec."

And she is, in about forty-five seconds to be precise, during which time she has been rummaging in that Aladdin's Cave that is her technician's store cupboard, from where she returns with a length of blue-and-white police incident tape, which she stretches in a wide arc around the photograph, further heightening the drama of its image.

Clive waits as more and more people crowd into the gallery. Chloe, Petros, Lorrie and Khav have been instructed to guide the graduates' family members this way first, so that they will give more attention to the few words Clive will have to say to them, it being his turn this year to host the reception, before they can be ushered back towards the larger Grosvenor Gallery, where they can proudly be shown their offsprings' final year show.

There's already a bottleneck around the ramp leading up to a slightly raised platform in the far corner, which Tanya has screened off with flats painted to look like partially knocked-down brick walls, onto which are projected images of Manchester during the Blitz. Not the panoramic views associated with Humphrey Jennings of towering, hydraulic ladders and huge, shuddering water cannon gushing futilely onto the flames issuing out of burning buildings, but the more human, intimate dramas being played out in front of them, so typical of George's vision. An exhausted fireman sits on a broken heap of rubble beside the still-smouldering bones of a bombed-out building, sipping tea from a chipped enamel mug. A small child in her mother's outsized shoes pushes a toy pram towards the hole where once her house had stood looking for a lost doll. Someone has set up a gramophone beside an Anderson shelter, and a middle-aged couple dance amid the haze of a shower of ash still falling from a grey early morning sky. Children rummage for shrapnel beside a burst water pipe. A dog barks hungrily at the camera.

Once they have reached the top of the platform, the viewers are plunged into a near total blackout. Intermittently, out of the darkness, a series of timed images flash briefly below them. These are the few examples that remain of George's decoy photographs, taken from the belly of a reconnaissance plane, a Lancaster, built at nearby Trafford Park, which depict sudden bursts of flame from the 'starfish', the strategically-placed iron baskets lit to form a ring of fire around the fake ports and factories George and his team of *camoufleurs* had created to fool the enemy aircraft and lure them into dropping their bombs on this 'Manchester-on-the-Moors', instead of the real thing.

He looks around with pleasure and with pride. Everyone appears to be completely enthralled by George's photographs, as he knew they would be. His most famous picture, the one he is best known for and will be for ever associated with, attracts the greatest interest.

"Oh," he hears people exclaim, "I've seen this photo before. I hadn't realised…"

It's the one that made his name. A gaggle of scrawny boys, who have all been waiting with unbearable anticipation, at last get their reward. They are in Philips Park for the last Tulip Sunday ever held there, in the May of 1960. Two elephants from nearby Belle Vue, who have been giving rides to children all day, now rest near one of the ornamental ponds in the park. Their keeper is washing them down. When he sees the boys approach, he knows exactly what they're hoping will happen. He knows precisely because he was one of them when he was a boy himself. George also knows what is about to take place, for he too was one of the jiggling, giggling gang nearly forty years before, and so he has positioned himself in the perfect place. But even he could never have predicted the final outcome. At a signal from its keeper, one of the elephants dips its trunk into the waters of the pond, then sprays it directly at the boys, hitting them all firmly in the face. Bull's eye. Squealing with delight, they leap as one into the air, shaking their heads and bodies as they do like soaked and happy puppies, so that a thousand droplets of water cascade around them, caught by the afternoon sun. George has clicked the shutter of his camera at exactly the right moment, capturing the elephant trumpeting in glee, with trunk aloft, and all the boys jumping like salmon. It is one of those photographs that imprints itself directly onto the hearts and minds of everyone who sees it. It never fails to raise a smile of unfiltered joy on all who look upon it, the kind that Clive knows he could never have taken himself, for he would have seen it too late, one of those 'remember when' moments, which pass into the collective unconscious...

Like when The Beatles played before they were famous at Urmston Show on Chassen Park; or when Yuri Gugarin, the first man in space, drove through the pouring rain in an open-top Daimler, waving to the cheering crowds who lined the streets, many of them dressed in home-made space suits; or the silent, grieving throng, who stood, heads bowed in sorrow and disbelief, as the bodies of the Manchester United footballers killed in the Munich Air Crash arrived at Ringway...

George had photographed them all.

But there are private moments too. The laundry ladies at Old Trafford, who probably knew the players as well as anyone. George has captured them in all their smiling pride, hanging out football shirts on washing lines strung against the football ground. Clive has exhibited this to the accompaniment of the audio reminiscences of one such laundress, known to all as Auntie Joan...

I had a job helping out at a refreshment kiosk on match days. The club's secretary Walter Crickmer, who also died at Munich, told me the club were openin' a laundry an' asked if I might be interested in workin' there. That's how I started...

Back then most o' t' players trained at Old Trafford. It were a small staff. When I joined there were perhaps ten or eleven, that's all, plus the players, an' that was the entire club. You knew 'em all. You saw 'em every day. They'd come into t' laundry to cadge a cup o' tea, 'ave a cigarette, or borrow t' paper. They called me Auntie Joan... Bobby Charlton, Duncan Edwards – they all came in after they'd finished their training. I think they were sometimes a bit lost an' lonely, you know...? If they got a bit of lipstick on their shirt, they'd tek it to us girls an' get it washed. It were that kind of thing...

The players were not the big stars they are today, but would travel in to t' ground on t' bus or cycle. They'd go in t' same shops as us... We lived in Salford. Eddie Colman – another who died in Munich – lived in t' same street as us. A lot o' t' boys lived in Stretford, round Longford Park, close to Old Trafford. The players'd go dancing to t' Plaza on a Saturday night. The fans'd see 'em there, or in t' chippy... On Sunday afternoons you'd go into Longford Park an' find 'em playing football wi' t' kids. They'd be walkin' around an' someone'd 'ave a ball an' they'd join in. That's the way it was...

Fairly soon after t' crash the bodies started to arrive. They were brought straight to t' ground. The gymnasium, which were alongside t' dressing rooms, was turned into a temporary mortuary. That's where the bodies stayed for quite some time. We ended up polishin' t' coffins. Partly it was cos we were just wantin' to do summat – owt. I'm sure they din't need polishin' but there was this closeness wi' us, a genuine affection, caring' for 'em when they was alive an' carryin' that on. It always struck me that one week we were washin' their shirts, the next we were polishin' their coffins...

Just thirteen days later they took to the field again. Somehow they cobbled a team together made up o' young lads barely out o' short pants. Carried on a tide of emotion from across th' whole country, they won. Three-nil against Sheffield Wednesday. They never stood a chance. Then this same tide took 'em all t' way to Wembley, to t' Cup Final, where they lost in th' end to Bolton Wanderers. Though it were a victory just to get there. Just ten years later they won the European Cup. The first English team ever to do so...

Clive was there too on that swelteringly hot May night in 1968 when Bobby Charlton, Brian Kidd and George Best scored four goals between them to overcome the mighty Benfica and take the trophy.

It felt to Clive that the whole nation was behind United on that day, even City fans. As he made his way to Piccadilly to catch the special train to the old Wembley Stadium, with its legendary twin towers, his red-and-white scarf wrapped around his neck, everyone he passed stopped to wish him luck. "For Manchester," they said. "For the Busby Babes…"

The whole adventure had begun two weeks before. Tickets for the final were due to go on sale at Old Trafford at eight o'clock on a Sunday morning. Clive and Christopher decided they would need to get up well before dawn and walk the three miles to the ground to be there before the gates open, if they were to stand any chance of getting one…

But when the alarm clock rings, Christopher is too hung over from a Saturday night out with his pals and doesn't even stir, but Clive is undeterred. He walks the unnaturally quiet Moss Side streets alone, hearing the birds singing in Whitworth Park, something he has never heard before – or since…

It must be only half-past five by the time he reaches the ground, but already there's a huge crowd milling around excitedly, forming a series of queues at each of the turnstiles, where the tickets will go on sale. To qualify for a ticket, Clive has to produce a sheet of paper, provided in the programme for the first game of the season, onto which he has to stick tokens that are printed in every home match, both for the first team and the reserves. There are forty-two spaces and, if he is to have any chance of claiming a ticket, not only does he have to be early to secure his place in the queue, he has to have a full token sheet. But he only has forty-one tokens. He missed one of the reserve games – number twenty-eight, he can remember it still – and he's sure he'll have no chance, but he has a cunning plan. He has brought Christopher's token sheet with him too. Christopher doesn't have a number twenty-eight token either, but he does have a number eighteen, and Clive reckons he can risk putting this spare number eighteen in the place where the number twenty-eight should go, and alter the 'one' to a 'two' with a biro. He's counting on there being so many people there that the ticket seller won't check too closely, he'll just want to see a full token sheet. On the walk to Old Trafford, when Clive had hatched this scheme, it felt like an ace plan, but now he's actually there, approaching the ground in the early morning light, it feels stupid. He feels he's bound to get found out.

He walks down Matt Busby Way, where the scene is almost biblical. A series of make-shift stalls have sprouted outside the stadium. They're selling hot dogs, mugs of tea, or Oxo, or Bovril. One enterprising chap has set up a table selling individual tokens at exorbitant prices (more than a shilling each!), while another is even selling glue to stick the tokens in place – "a penny a dab…" The hell-fire preacher, who attends every match, week after week, year after year, whatever the weather, wearing a bowler hat and carrying a sandwich board with religious tracts painted on it, is there too of course. He stands on an old vegetable crate, from which he harangues the crowds cheerfully. "Where will YOU spend eternity?" he cries. "In the Stretford End," Clive chimes back, at which the preacher laughs hugely, before embarking on another sermon.

Clive leaves this bazaar behind him and makes his way towards the queues, his heart in his mouth. He checks he has the right money. The tickets cost ten shillings – that's four weeks pocket money for Clive, so he's had to borrow half of it from Anita. The sun rises, the turnstiles open, and the tickets go on sale. Clive seem to be miles away, as the queues snake around the ground.

An hour passes, then two.

Clive edges agonisingly slowly towards the front.

Then, suddenly, one by one, the turnstiles start to close as each one sells its allocation, until there are just two queues left open. He creeps a little closer, then the other gate shuts. He's in the last queue. There are seven people in front of him. Six, five, four, three, two – then it's just him. He squeezes through the turnstile, sheepishly presents his token sheet, certain he's going to be rumbled – it's going to be so humiliating – but the man selling the tickets is so exhausted he barely gives it a second glance. Clive pays his ten shillings. The man hands over the ticket, then, after just one more person, closes his gate. Clive has got the last-but-one ticket for the European Cup Final.

Clutching it tightly in his hot and clammy hand, he runs back out onto the forecourt in front of the ground. Immediately he is offered ten pounds for it, an unimaginable sum, a king's ransom. But there is no way he will consider selling it...

He has it still, in a clip-frame on his desk at home, a memento of an unforgettable night. Manchester United. Champions of Europe. Just ten years after Munich. A promise fulfilled...

Clive regards the whole exhibition as a promise fulfilled...

There are other private moments too. The intimate shots of the singer Chamomile Catch at *The Queen's Hotel*, wreathed in cigarette smoke, the rapt faces of her admirers, listening to her over a late night whiskey and vermouth, the coded glances, the covert smiles, the shared understanding, that here, at least for now, their secrets were safe.

Perhaps the most private and possibly most revealing series of all is one of his first. Taken each day over the course of a year, shortly after the death of his father, George pointed his camera at the same spindle tree, growing just outside his front door, in the cobbled Ancoats street where he lived, across the road from the Printing Presses where he worked before the start of the War. A whole way of life is captured in that simple, repeated frame, the same figures passing to and fro in the background, children chalking patterns in the pavement, clouds scudding overhead, the tree, changing so infinitessimally slowly through each season, the first tiny buds, the faintest hint of colour, the full leaf, broad, elliptical, serrated, a dark green in summer, with paler flowers in autumn, the capsular fruit, red, purple and pink, their four lobes splitting to reveal flame-orange seeds, then leafless again, dusted with frost and snow...

Tanya has set up a separate enclave for them. She has positioned a front door near a corner of the gallery, as if seen from the inside of a house. The viewer is invited to push open the door. Immediately she is greeted with a vista of a terraced street. Placed on a doorstep is a mock-up of a camera on a tripod. When the viewer stoops to look through the lens, she is treated to a time-lapsed sequence of each of these seemingly identical, but subtly different images, one after the other, taking her through the course of a year in just six minutes, all the while to the accompaniment of the deep rhythmic rumble of the printing presses close by.

Clive is pleased to note a small but interested knot of people are queuing to discover what lies behind that familiar-looking, reassuring front door, with its stained-glass fanlight. He would like to go and join them, to eavesdrop on the comments *A Year in the Life of a Spindle Tree* might elicit, but he is prevented from doing so just yet by Khav, who is waving to him from a photograph near the entrance, beckoning him to join her there.

It is one of two photographs that have never before been exhibited. Anywhere. They are from private family collections.

"I'd like you to meet my next door neighbour," says Khav, beaming. "Dr Archer – Dr Chadwick. Clive – Grace."

"Delighted," says Clive. "I know you by reputation of course. It's wonderful to meet you at last."

"Thank you," says Grace. "Khav has told me a lot about you," she adds, a mischievous glint in her eye.

"Oh dear," laughs Clive.

"Don't worry," says Khav. "Only the good stuff. Well – I'll love you and leave you."

Clive and Grace watch her rejoin the throng, each of them smiling.

"I can't thank you enough for the loan of your photograph," says Clive. "When Khav first mentioned you had a George Wright, I could scarcely believe my luck. Can you tell me more about it?"

"It's really just a family memento, a souvenir snapshot that just happens to have been taken by a world-class photographer."

"Do you really think he is? World class, I mean?"

"It's not my field, but yes – I do, for what it's worth."

Clive beams. "I'm so pleased. How did it come to be taken?"

"Well," begins Grace, "it was a surprise for my parents. That's them there." She points to the couple sitting on a bench front and centre. "It was organised by my sister, Harriet." Grace points again. "The setting is Philips Park. The last ever Tulip Sunday." Clive nods that he understands. Grace continues. "My father – Jabez – was the Head Gardener. We lived in the Lodge at the entrance to the Park. It was a wonderful place to grow up." She trails off, remembering.

"I'm sure it must have been," prompts Clive.

"Yes. He was also a miner. You can see the twin headstocks of Bradford Pit in the background. The Council had decided to finish with the tradition of Tulip Sunday and to discontinue the posts of each park having its own individual keeper. So this was my father's last day. At the same time the Coal Board was already starting to run down their operations at Bradford. Although there was a century's worth of coal at least waiting there underground, extracting it had become increasingly difficult and uneconomic, and so, for my father, this was a double blow. My sister felt that the day should be honoured in some way. She knew George Wright through her sister-in-law – Giulia Lockhart, the fashion designer. Do you know her?"

"I've heard of her, yes."

"She used to design costumes for the Manchester Film Studios on Dickenson Road – she'd appeared in films as an actress first and she was also a model, something of a pin-up for the men in the forces during the War. She was especially kind to me around that time."

Grace's voice trails away, as she looks down towards her left leg, on which, Clive can see, she is wearing a calliper, showing beneath the bottom of her trousers.

"Giulia agreed to ask George to take the photograph. He was only too happy to oblige. It was left to Harriet then to arrange it all, making sure that everyone arrived at the agreed spot at the agreed time. It must have been a logistical nightmare, especially with so many children involved." She points to several randomly on the photograph. "I nearly didn't make it myself," she adds. "I got held up with my work and lost track of the time. That's my bicycle there," she says, pointing to where she had flung it hastily to one side before breathlessly taking up her position on the bench next to her parents.

"It's a wonderful composition," says Clive. "It reminds me of those old grammar school photos, where all the pupils stand in massed ranks behind the seated row of teachers with the headmaster in the middle."

"It wasn't arranged like that," corrects Grace. "People just stood or sat where they could. That's George's friend, Francis, waving a bunch of tulips on the end. He arrived even later than me. No. It all somehow came together at the last second."

"But he managed to place you all in front of those looming pitheads, with that large circular bed of black and white tulips on the slope behind you."

"Yes, you're right."

"Why black and white for the flowers?"

"That was my idea," smiles Grace, remembering. "Coal and bones."

"I understand coal," says Clive, "but bones...?"

"The Park was built on what was once a paupers' grave. And the Philips Park Cemetery is just next door. Many miners ended their days there."

"Yes. I see. The end of an era."

"I suppose," says Grace, "but it didn't feel sad. Look." She points to a formation of aeroplanes flying overhead. "The Black Arrows – forerunners of the Red – were booked to do a fly-past as part of Tulip Sunday."

"The timing couldn't have been more perfect," enthuses Clive.

"Or more fortuitous. They just appeared, like dots at first. Then, when they were directly overhead, they released those coloured vapour trails. Our spirits soared. George didn't need to ask us to hold a smile. For that's what we were already doing."

"And that was the moment George captured," echoes Clive thoughtfully.

"Yes," agrees Grace. "So you see – it was as much about the future, as it was about the past."

Clive nods. "Thank you. I might borrow that phrase when I speak to all the students in a few minutes' time."

"Be my guest. But I'll not stay for that if you don't mind."

"Not at all. I wouldn't be staying myself if I wasn't actually giving it."

"No," she says. "It's not that. It's the standing. I get tired. Never used to. Time was my stock-in-trade. Now I'm in danger of becoming an old fossil myself." She laughs. "I'll be off then. I'm glad to have met you. Good luck."

Before Clive can even say 'thank you', Grace has slipped away. He looks across to the other photograph from a private collection on the opposite wall. The young student with the *hijab* is standing next to it alongside two people Clive presumes to be the grandparents she had alluded to earlier. He really should have gone and introduced himself to them by now. He catches her eye and waves. He is just about to cross the Gallery to join them, when he is intercepted by Tanya, who hands him a microphone.

"Time for your speech," she says with a grin. "I'll just turn down all the various soundscapes and raise the general lights."

"Yes, OK," says Clive, before turning back to the student and her grandparents with a helpless shrug. "Later," he mouths. She nods and smiles.

Clive taps the top of the microphone, which pops embarrassingly.

"Good afternoon," he begins. "Thank you all for coming. For those of you who don't know me, my name's Clive Archer, and I'm Head of Media Studies. Welcome to the School of Arts & Humanities on this most happy of occasions, when we all come together to celebrate the successes of this year's graduating students. I'm very much looking forward to meeting as many parents and family members as possible, having had the enormous pleasure and privilege of teaching your sons and daughters during their three years here with us." He turns to face those students he can see directly. "We shall miss you greatly when you are gone…"

Chloe nudges Petros with her elbow and grins. Petros, blushing deeply, looks down, abashed.

"You'll be relieved to hear," continues Clive, "that I shan't be speaking for long."

This remark is greeted by immediate whistles of approval, led by Khav.

"But it's a tradition we have here at MMU that a member of each School says a few words to their students and their families, before releasing you out into the world, and this year, I'm afraid, that dubious honour falls on me. I remember when I was a student here myself, back in the dim and distant days of the last century, having to listen to a similar speech by one of my erstwhile tutors, and now I can't recall a word of what he said. Whether that was because he had little that was memorable to say, or that I was simply not paying attention, I couldn't possibly say. No – I confess. I'm certain it was the latter."

Polite laughter greets this remark, and Clive feels encouraged to proceed.

"I know that you are all itching to go into the Grosvenor Gallery next door to see the final shows of all of your offsprings' work, and I can reassure you that the doors will open as soon as I have finished. But first, I'd like to thank you for coming to admire these truly astonishing photographs in here by the incomparable George Wright, whose centenary we are now celebrating, and who died when he was just seventy, thirty years ago this month. Sadly I never met George, but I have spoken to many who did, and some who knew him very well. Several of you here this afternoon know that my wife, Florence, is a musician, a trumpeter. There's a photograph of her over there, taken by George, when she was just seventeen. She was playing at the very last concert to be held in the Kings Hall, Belle Vue, before it was knocked down, and George was there to capture this historic moment, as he was able to do on so many occasions. Someone asked him once what advice he might have for a young photographer who was just starting out. He thought for a while, puffed on that pipe of his that he was never without, and said, 'The same advice I was given myself when I was still in short trousers. "Find tha'self a proper job".' The man who gave George that piece of advice was none other than L.S. Lowry, and George took him at his word. He worked as a teacher part-time at *The Mechanics' Institute* for much of his life. He had what we like to call now 'a portfolio career', by which we mean he had a number of irons in a number of fires. It's what I suspect most of you who are graduating this year are likely to do too. Keeping your options open, trying to stay flexible, fleet of foot, ready for whatever opportunities might come along. As well as teaching – evening classes, mostly, to men and women who also had other jobs, but who searched for that something extra in their lives that art and creativity can always bring – as well as that, George was also, at various times, a printer, a mechanic at the Belle Vue Speedway track, and a sign writer. For those of you who have been in the magnificent Reading Room of Manchester Central Library, with its astonishing domed ceiling, it was George who painted the inscription, which runs around the rim of it. And it's the words that are written there that I wanted to draw your attention to this afternoon."

He pauses. He takes a sip of water. He has his audience's attention now, and he does not want to lose it. He takes out a piece of paper from the inside pocket of his jacket, which he unfolds and raises with his left hand.

"This is what it says. '*Wisdom is the principal thing…*' The principal thing," he repeats. "It's from the Bible. The Book of Proverbs. Now, I have to confess, I'm not much of a bible reader myself, but this particular phrase has always stayed with me. '*Wisdom is the principal thing.*' It then goes on to say, '*Therefore get wisdom, and, with all thy getting, get understanding.*' Wisdom and understanding. They're not always the same thing, are they? Many times we argue over what they actually mean. 'Get a proper job'. That's what Lowry said to George Wright. And George took him at his word. But what did he mean by a proper job? One that made him a lot of money? Or one that made him happy and fulfilled? Hopefully one that did both."

Clive surveys the circle of faces looking back expectantly towards him. Chloe, Petros, Lorrie and Khav. None of them, he notices, has their parents with them. Why is that, he wonders? What undercurrents lurk in their absence?

"I imagine," he continues, "that many of you here today have been asking yourselves that same question. You've probably been asking it in different ways ever since you first applied to study here. Forgive me if what I'm about to say causes offence. It is not intended to, believe me. Think of it instead as a provocation. But I can picture a conversation that starts with something like this. 'What's the use of an Arts degree? What kind of job is that going to get you? Art's all very well, but it doesn't put food on the table'."

A laughter of recognition ripples around the Gallery.

"I could answer that by reminding you that the creative industries are currently the third largest contributors to the nation's economy, but that probably wouldn't cut much ice, even though it's true. For what is also true is that, for most of us, the jobs and careers our children do are not the same as the ones that we pursued. Many of them hadn't even been invented, and the same will be true for their children. We've got to learn to accept the wisdom of that, and, with it, get understanding. As Kahlil Gilbran famously said, '*Our children are not our children. They are the sons and daughters of Life's longing for itself.*' My wife, Florence, sings a version of it in her sets sometimes. '*Seek not to make them like you. For life goes not backwards, nor tarries with yesterday*'."

He observes the effects of these words passing across the faces of Chloe and Petros, Lorrie and Khav, like high clouds in a Corot sky.

"Manchester," he continues, "has been home to so many 'firsts' – the world's first industrial city, the world's first steam-powered cotton mill, bus service, train service, telephone exchange, the birth of nuclear physics, radio astronomy, the computer age – but there's another first we're understandably less proud of. Historians tell us that the English Civil War began here, or rather, the first casualty occurred here, when a certain Richard Perceval, a linen weaver from Levenshulme, was allegedly killed coming out of *The Bull's Head* on Hanging Ditch by one Thomas Tyldesley, a soldier from Astley. If you walk from the Reading Room in Central Library, having read once more the inscription written by George Wright on the domed ceiling, down the marble staircase, past the statue of *The Reading Girl* by Giovanni Ciniselli, the book she is holding now blank, but once thought to be a poem called *The Angel's Story*, the contents of which are now lost, then carry on down the connecting Glass Walkway between the Library and the Town Hall, and enter The Great Hall there, you will encounter another of the city's great hidden treasures, the Manchester Murals, painted directly onto the walls by the pre-Raphaelite artist Ford Madox Brown, who lived for a time in Victoria Park, less than a stone's throw from where Florence and I live today. Once you are there, stand in front of the mural depicting that infamous incident that heralded the start of the English Civil War. It shows the city defending itself from the Royalists, standing up for Reform and Change, as we have always done here in Manchester. It shows soldiers desperately fighting on the Hanging Bridge across the Ditch where the Irk joins the Irwell. In the bottom right hand corner, a young boy is attempting to venture onto it. But his path is blocked. He is holding the arm of an older man, who has just fallen in the battle. It looks as though he has deliberately placed himself in front of the younger man – perhaps his son – to prevent him from being hurt. The son, if that is who he is, has closed his eyes, knowing there's nothing he could have done to stop his father from making this sacrifice, from trying to protect him, so that he might have a future. For no parent wants to outlive their child. The only thing this father wants is for his son to have a better life than he has had, in whatever unknown form that takes. And so I will conclude my address with a plea to all the parents here to remember the words of Gilbran and recognise that your children come through you but are not from you, and though they are with you, yet they belong not to you, while at the same time I ask all the children to accept that, in this civil war that sometimes may take place between you and your parents, they act only as the bows, from which you are the living arrows that are sent forth. Who knows where you may land? For now all we can do is watch you as you arc your way across the sky. So remember – '*Wisdom is the principal thing. Exalt her, and she shall promote thee. She shall give to thine head an ornament of grace.*' Then who knows what you will write upon the waiting page of the statue of *The Reading Girl*? What new words will be needed to tell of your deeds in the next instalment of *The Angel's Story*? And so, good luck to you all. Find yourselves that 'proper job' we all of us seek."

"That was quite a speech," says the grandfather of the young student with the *hijab*.

"Sorry," says Clive. "I hadn't planned on saying half of what I did. It just sort of insisted on being said."

"Well," says the grandfather, "it certainly struck a chord."

Clive thinks back to the remark the young student had said about not wanting her grandparents to see the photo of her mother, their daughter, caught up in the Moss Side Riots.

Instead he says, offering his hand to shake, "We've not been introduced, have we?"

"I was just about to," says the girl. "My grandparents – Mr and Mrs Ward – Sol and Nadia. Dr Clive Archer."

"And you are…?"

"Oh – sorry. I'm Molly."

"Pleased to meet you. All of you. I can't thank you enough for the loan of your photograph. Or, rather, photographs."

"That's quite all right. We tend to think of them as just a single one too, don't we, Nadia?"

The woman nods. "But these are not our originals," she says, looking back at Clive.

"No," says Clive. "I hope you don't mind. We didn't want to risk any damage coming to them, for they're quite fragile, especially being so small, and so many of them. My assistant, Tanya here…" Clive indicates her as she now joins them. "She came up with the idea of digitally scanning them, retaining the exact same configuration of course, then enlarging them, so that we could attach the prints to these pieces of wooden planks and boards that you see today."

"I don't mind at all," says Nadia. "They look better when they're bigger. Don't you agree, Sol?"

"Yes," he says. "They're closer to the actual size this way. Though, if anything, the mural was even bigger."

"Much bigger," agrees Nadia. "You wouldn't have been able to fit the whole thing in here. There isn't a wall long enough."

"I wish I'd seen it," says Clive.

"So do I," says Molly.

"Can you tell me more about it?" asks Clive.

"It was a long time ago," says Sol.

"Thirty-five years," adds Nadia.

Sol shakes his head in disbelief. "I suppose it must be," he says, then breaks off, wracked with a series of painful-sounding coughs.

Nadia looks towards him anxiously. "Sorry," he says, after the fit has subsided. "I can't seem to shake it off."

Tanya hands him a glass of water.

"Thanks," he says.

After he's drunk all he needs, he continues.

"It was nothing less than an attempt to create a history of the world," he says. "My version of it anyway."

"It's got everything in it," says Molly proudly. "How we first came to this country. How my great-great-grandfather helped build the Ship Canal, how my great-grandfather tried to meet the King of Afghanistan, but he met my great-grandmother instead. How my grandfather recreated that journey in an epic walk to retrieve his birthright..." She has become increasingly animated as she talks, pointing to each episode as it has been depicted.

"And who's this?" interrupts Clive, pointing to a small vignette of a child handing what looks like an umbrella to a man standing over her.

"That's our daughter," says Sol, "Jenna. Giving me some last minute advice before I set off." He falls silent.

"Did you heed it?" asks Clive.

"I tried to," says Sol. "But I lost the umbrella. It was taken from me."

"That's why you asked her to paint it back in, just after the mural was unveiled," says Nadia, putting a hand on her husband's arm, "didn't you?"

Sol nods.

"I didn't know that," says Molly and scrutinises that section more closely.

"She's not here with you this afternoon then?" asks Clive, nervously looking around.

"No," explains Nadia. "She'd've liked to be. But she had to work. She's flying out to Yemen as a matter of fact." She looks at her watch. "She should be landing there just about now."

"Really?" says Molly. "I didn't know."

There is a pause. An awkward quietness hangs between them. Clive tries to lighten the mood.

"So Molly," he says, "are you a student here too? I don't remember seeing you."

"I'm about to be," she replies, brightening.

"That would explain it then. What course will you be on?"

"Fine Art," she says with a grin.

"Oh dear," he says. "I hope you weren't put off by what I was saying just now."

"Not at all. Being an artist is the most proper job I can think of."

"Good for you," laughs Sol, before lapsing into another spasm of coughing.

"George was Sol's teacher at night school," says Nadia. "At the Institute. He recognised his talent, and he encouraged him."

"Yes," says Clive, looking back at the mural. "What happened to it?"

"It was demolished," says Sol, "soon after Peel Holdings bought up what was left of Pomona Docks."

"I'm so sorry," says Clive.

"Don't be," says Sol. "George warned me that it was likely to happen. We only got permission to hang while the site was lying idle, before the sale went through. George arranged everything. I don't mind that it's gone. Honestly. This whole city's built upon layers of history, one on top of another, like sediments of rock. We each of us leave our marks on the land, even if they're so small sometimes that we don't get to see them. I expect bits of my mural are still scattered among the debris and the waste."

Molly looks up as she hears this. It has given her an idea, though she isn't quite sure what it is yet. It's connected somehow to what Clive had said earlier about wisdom being the principal thing, but she doesn't know how. She feels the idea slipping from her, like when she's sketching with charcoal and the marks begin to smudge, but she hopes some small residue of it will remain.

"Well," says Clive at last to Sol and Nadia, "thank you for the loan of your photographs."

"You're welcome," says Nadia.

"And for telling me your story."

"It's good that other people will get to see it," she says. "It deserves to be heard."

"At the time," says Sol, "George said something about taking lots of photographs, then joining them together…"

"Like David Hockney," adds Molly excitedly, "so that you could look at it in many different ways simultaneously."

"That's right," says Clive, smiling. "Then join them up in the way that makes sense to you."

They all take one last look at the mural together, each seeing it differently.

"Well," says Nadia, "I think we'd best be getting along. We've a bus and two trams to catch." She links her arm through Sol's to support him. "You can stay a bit longer if you like," she says to Molly.

"Thanks. I think I will."

After she has watched them go, she turns back to Clive.

"Thanks for not mentioning my Mum in the Moss Side photo."

"And now she's in Yemen."

"I never know where she is half the time."

"What about your Dad?"

Molly shakes her head. "I don't get to see him much."

Nor do any of us, thinks Clive of his recalcitrant nephew, but decides to say nothing.

"Are you looking forward to starting here next term?" he says instead.

"Very much," she says.

At that moment, Chloe, Petros, Lorrie and Khav come over to join them. The Gallery is thinning out. Most people have made their way to the Grosvenor Gallery next door to see the graduating students' final shows.

"Is there anything else you need us to do?" asks Lorrie.

"No, I don't think so," says Clive. "You've been marvellous. Thanks for all your help. This is Molly, by the way. She's doing Fine Art here next year."

"Hi."

"Hi."

"Hi."

"Hi."

"Come and have a look at the Degree Shows," says Khav. "See what you're letting yourself in for, innit?"

"Thanks. I'd love to."

An hour later Molly feels like she's known them all for ever.

"What're you doing tonight?" asks Lorrie.

"Nothing. Why?"

"Only we're all going to see The Stone Roses at Heaton Park. Come with us if you want."

"I'd love to. But I haven't got a ticket. And I bet they sold out months ago."

"They did," says Tanya, who now joins them. "But you can buy mine if you like."

"What?" says Khav, disappointed. "Are you not coming?"

"I can't, babe. It's the Press Night for the George Wright Show tonight. I got my dates mixed up when I bought the ticket."

"Dipshit."

"I know. So, Molly – it's yours if you want it."

"How much?"

"Fifty-five quid."

Molly gulps.

"I know," says Chloe. "It's outrageous, charging all that just to stand in a field."

"Except it's not just to stand in a field, is it?" says Petros. "It's the fucking Stone Roses 'reunion' tour, back here in Manchester, where it all started."

Chloe grins. "I know. I just like to rattle your cage, that's all."

"And you fall for it every time," laughs Khav.

"OK," says Molly. "I've been saving some money from my waitressing job."

"Where's that then?" says Lorrie.

"*The King's Arms*," replies Molly.

"Bloom Street? Salford?" asks Lorrie.

"That's the one."

"Paul Heaton's place?"

"He's my boss."

"Ex-Beautiful South?"

"Yeah, that's right."

"Wow! What's he like?"

"Come and find out. I'll introduce you if you like. I work Fridays and Saturdays."

"Beautiful South?" sneers Petros. "Good band, crap name. They should've called themselves the 'Beautiful North'."

"What?" says Chloe, arching an eyebrow. "And lose that delicious sense of irony?"

"Fuck off," says Petros. "Is that ironic enough for you?"

Molly laughs. She is enjoying herself hugely.

"Cash or BACS?" she says to Tanya.

Tanya texts Molly her sort code and account number. Within seconds the transaction is complete. Molly then texts Nadia to let her know that she'll be late back and not to wait up for her.

"As if we would," Nadia texts back. "Enjoy yourself."

"Let's grab a pizza," suggests Lorrie.

"Good idea," agrees Khav.

"We've loads of time before we need to be on our way," adds Petros.

"Yes," says Chloe. "All the time in the world."

Molly follows happily in their wake.

*

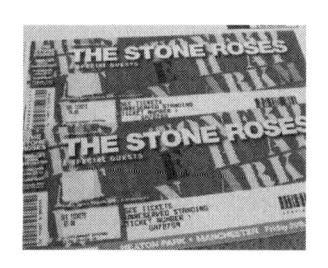

It's an "I-Was-There" moment.

"I was there when The Stone Roses played Heaton Park..."

"...when Liam Gallagher led his rag-tag Beady Eye onto stage as support..."

"...when he belted out old Oasis songs and we all joined in..."

"...*Morning Glory, Rock 'n' Roll Star, Champagne Supernova*..."

"...when the sun set and the lights went down and we knew it was about to start..."

"...when Ian Brown, John Squire, Gary 'Mani' Mountfield and Alan 'Reni' Wren finally shambled on with a cheery wave..."

"...Hello Manchester..."

"...when they launched into *I Wanna Be Adored*, and they were, and we all of us were..."

"...*Fool's Gold, Sally Cinnamon, Where Angels Play*..."

"...*Gold road's sure a long road*
Winds on through the hills
Gold road's just around the corner..."

"...when we crowdsurfed, feeling everyone's hands beneath us, guiding, supporting, passing us from the back to the front, floating, flying..."

"...*Rain clouds, oh they used to chase me*
Down they would pour

*Join my tears, allay my fears, sent to me from heaven
You're my world..."*

"...when ten thousand cigarette lighters and twice as many lit mobile phones were raised into the air, slowly swaying from side to side, like candles lighting the way home..."

"...*Come with me to a place no one has ever seen
A million miles from here where no one's ever been
I'm on the edge of something shattering
I'm coming through...*"

"...on and on through the night, till the fireworks exploded in a last hurrah..."

"...which we sat and watched till the last spark faded and was gone..."

"...*Below the country rolls like a mighty boiling sea
The warm red sun gives up and sinks into the trees
Take a look around
There's something happening...*"

After the crowds have begun to disperse, high on hope and happiness, Chloe, Petros, Lorrie and Khav decide they will stay all night in the park, Molly too if she'd like to. Molly thinks she'd like to very much.

Petros rolls a joint, which they companionably pass between them. They are sitting cross-legged at the top of the park, just below the Temple, an observatory built in 1800 by Sir Thomas Egerton, the 1st Earl of Wilton, from where he could view the full extent of his estate, from this, the highest point in all of Manchester at just over three hundred and sixty feet. But now the park belongs to the people, the largest municipal park in all of Europe, and the five friends survey their city stretching out below them like a golden promise.

The glittering towers of glass and steel are all lit up like the fireworks they've just been watching at the close of the gig. Petros takes immense pleasure in naming them all. Beetham Tower, Anaconda Cut, Deansgate Square, St John's, St Michael's, Angel Gardens, The Egg Slice, Spinningfields. Manchester will soon become a vertical city and he is thrilled by the prospect.

At the same time, they are all of them struck, as they look down upon this brave new world, that it is a scene that none of their ancestors would recognise. Not Yasser or Zhang as they were digging the Big Ditch, as the Ship Canal was affectionately dubbed. Not Konstantin and Vassily as they built the first Greek Orthodox Church in England. Not Urja's Agrawal as he drew up the timetables for the ever-widening spider's web of bus routes spreading across the city. And not Lena as she swung from the highest trapeze in the roof of the Big Top.

And nor would the crowds who flocked to the park a century before to marvel at the sound of Enrico Caruso's crackly, recorded voice emanating from a pair of what then seemed like enormous speakers, paltry by today's standards, when compared with the bank of more than fifty that were twice the size needed to carry the songs of The Stone Roses to the seventy-five thousand fans who had gathered like acolytes to worship at this Temple, which still holds in its ancient stones the echoes of that earlier concert, masterminded by Billy Grimshaw, the 'Gramophone King'.

And again, just a decade afterwards, when the park had been almost as deserted as it is now, those privileged few, who had listened in rapt wonder as Francis had seemingly conjured sounds literally from the air, when he had fashioned an oversized crystal radio receiver using the Temple's rotunda as a natural amplifier, summoning Beethoven out of the ether, miraculously, *musica universalis*, the harmony of the spheres, the movement of the celestial bodies, the *Prometheus Overture*, conjuring the gift of fire.

The five friends, like a dare of moths all drawn to the flame, continue to look down, passing the joint between them.

They are almost ready to hatch, to crawl, to take those first few tentative steps before they shrug off the weight of the hard leathery casings of their ancestors' skins, and become their fully formed independent selves, their imagines.

But not yet. There is time for another joint first, to sit and watch the glittering lights twinkling below them, more and more of them by the hour, it seems, mirroring the uncountable stars in the sky above them.

They lie back on the grass, trying to name as many as they can. But there are too many of them. They fall into a deep, contented silence, watching, as the Perseids begin to put on their nightly summer show of shooting stars and meteor showers. They count more than sixty in the first hour. Enough for each of them, plenty for all. It is a time of magic.

"Take a look around… Something is happening…"

But what?

As the joint is being passed between them, Molly, sitting slightly apart from the rest, looks down the line of her new friends. Less than twelve hours ago she did not know of their existence. Now they are sharing this moment she is certain none of them will forget. Such random collisions. She thinks back to the words Clive had spoken earlier at the Exhibition, standing beside the joiner-photograph of her grandfather's lost mural.

"...and with all thy getting, get understanding."

What will be the principal thing for her, she wonders, within so many chance encounters? What kind of understanding will drop upon her like gifts?

Another shooting star has traced an unpredicted line across the sky. Happenstance or design? What pattern or meaning might she extract from it? She has no idea and revels in the not knowing. She will make of it what she will. Perhaps that will be her principal thing? The ability to surrender to the chances of the moment.

She looks along the row of her new friends once more, following the journey of the joint, in much the same way that she watches the meteor till it finally disappears. Except that it never quite does. There is an after-burn it leaves behind. A palimpsest. The red glow of the cigarette's tip deepens and fades, deepens and fades...

One by one they fall asleep, dreaming of fool's gold, where angels play, and how they each want to be adored.

They wake as the dawn begins to streak the sky. Silently they stand up, stretch, brush the grass from their clothes, before beginning the slow descent of Heaton Park towards the city.

As they reach the gate, they quietly embrace. They stand in a circle, their arms on each other's shoulders, looking into each other's faces, smiling, not speaking. There is no need for words. They know they will remember this moment for the rest of their lives.

With a silent nod they break the circle. They part, charting their own separate ways back home. Like tributaries of a single river before they reach their confluence. Skittering threads under a blue morning as a new sun rises. Manchester widens its embrace to welcome them, its grey rooftops and silver towers dipped in flame.

Epilogue

Larvae

The larvae of the moth are fitted with two sharp mouth parts called mandibles. Working them from side to side they use these to eat their way through the membranous lining of the egg sac. Immediately after hatching, the caterpillars separate from one another, for resources are scarce, and each must consume what they can in as short a time as possible.

They move rapidly from one place to another, hiding among the leaves and branches of trees. They are instinctive twig mimics, varying their colour to match their surroundings, though sometimes they are known to announce their presence more boldly. Usually this is when they are preparing to assume their pupal form.

When they need to come to ground, they learn to spin tensile threads of gossamer silk, floating downwind, landing wherever they can. They do this partly by design, but mostly by luck. Not all will survive…

Moth continues in:
Volume 2: A Crown of Glory
(Ornaments of Grace, Book 12)

Glossary of Sikh Terms

Adi Granth: sacred text of Sikhism, (also known as *Guru Granth Sahib*, see below)
Amritdhari: individuals who have taken Amrit Sanskhar
Amrit Sanskar: initiation ceremony to become a Sikh
Antam Sanskar: Sikh funeral rites
Antim Ardas: final prayer of the funeral ceremony
Atma: soul, essence, breath

Baba: grandfather
Bapu: father
Barah Mahi: poems in the Punjabi folk tradition
Bindi: red dot worn in the centre of the forehead

Chanani: canopy above the Holy Book in a Sikh temple
Chauri: whisk, traditionally made from yak's hair, carried by the priest
Chet: first month in the Sikh calendar, coinciding between 14 March and 13 April

Darbar Sahib: inner sanctum of the holy temple
Dastar: type of turban
Dhi: daughter
Diwali: Hindu Festival of Light
Diya: oil lamp, usually made from clay
Dohti: granddaughter
Domalla: double length turban

Fifty: small head-covering worn beneath the turban

Granthi: ceremonial reader, male or female, of the Sikh holy book
Gurmukhi: traditional script of Punjabi used in the holy book
Gurdwara: a Sikh temple
Guru Granth Sahib: Sikh Holy Book (see *Adi Granth* above)

Guru Nanak: founder of Sikh faith

Hā'ē mērē rabā: Oh my God!
Hukam: a divine command

Joti: candle

Kachhera: traditional undergarment worn by Sikhs, one of the 5 K's
Kangha: comb carried by all Sikhs, one of the 5 K's
Karah Parshad: type of halva sweetmeat, made with wheat flour, ghee and sugar
Karma: consequences of actions
Karkars: the articles of Sikh faith known as the 5 K's
Katak: eighth month in the Sikh calendar, coinciding between 15 October and 13 November
Kaur: surname traditionally used by Sikh females, translates as 'princess'
Kesh: traditional Sikh practice of not cutting one's hair
Keshdari: one who follows the rule of kesh
Keski: short form of turban
Khalsa: 'to be pure, to be clean, to be free from' – applies to both the community that considers Sikhism to be its faith, as well as a special group of initiates
Khanda: sharp, broad sword or dagger
Kirpan: curved sword or knife traditionally carried by Sikhs, one of the 5 K's
Kirtan Sohila: evening prayer for Sikhs, sometimes translated as 'song of praise'

Langar: community kitchen in a Sikh temple

Maa: mother
Maghar: ninth month in the Sikh calendar, coinciding between 15 November and 15 December
Manj: raised platform with a cushioned bed on which the Holy Book is placed

Mool Mantar: opening verse of the Sikh Holy Book
Naamh Karan: naming ceremony
Nani: grandmother
Nanakshahi: Sikh calendar, based on the tropical solar year
Nona: wife

Pagri: type of turban
Pallav: one end of a sari
Patka: head covering traditionally worn by Sikh boys or young men

Rehat Mariyada: approved code of conduct for Sikhs
Rangoli: traditional Indian patterns made with coloured rice and powder
Rumalla: small square or rectangular silk used to cover the Sikh Holy Book

Samsara: period of wandering during the soul's reincarnation
Sangat: congregation in a Sikh temple
Sewa: selfless service
Shabad: hymn, or sacred song
Shalwar Kameez: traditional costume of tunic and trousers
Singh: traditional Sikh surname
Siropa: length of cloth presented at special ceremonies to be draped around the neck
Sukhmani Sahib: prayer of peace

Takht: throne, or seat of special authority, on which the Holy Book is placed

Vaisakh: second month in the Sikh calendar, coinciding with 14 April and 14 May

Waheguru: the one true God in Sikhism

Dramatis Personae

(in order of appearance)

CAPITALS = Main Characters; **Bold** = Significant Characters; Plain = Characters (who appear once or twice only)

CHLOE CHANG, student at MMU, later a journalist
PETROS DIMITRIOU, student at MMU, later a property developer
KHAVITA KAUR, known as **KHAV**, student at MMU, later an arts administrator
LORELEI ZLATAN, known as **LORRIE**, sometimes as LOL, student at MMU, later a Gallery Manager
DR CLIVE ARCHER, Head of Media Studies, MMU
Tanya, studio technician, MMU
Queen Elizabeth II
Prince Philip, Duke of Edinburgh
Homeless Woman with Angel Tattoo
Bao, Chloe's father
Xiu Mei, Chloe's grandmother
Asif, seven-year-old pupil of Blackley Primary School
Frances Canning, bride at wedding attended by the Queen
John Canning, groom at wedding attended by the Queen
David Beckham, footballer
Kirsty Howard, six-year-old girl suffering from rare heart condition
Lindsay Butcher, aerial artist at opening of Commonwealth Games
George Wright, photographer
Florence Blundell, trumpeter, Clive's partner
DR GRACE CHADWICK, archaeologist
Jabez, Grace's father
Toby, Grace's brother
Harriet, Grace's sister
Paul, Harriet's husband
Mary, Grace's mother

Tony Robinson, TV presenter of Time Team
Samira, Time Team PA
Robina McNeil, Grace's successor
Inspector Dave Cornerford, police liaison officer at time of IRA bomb
Chief Inspector Ian Seabridge, supervising officer at time of IRA bomb
P.C. Wendy McCormick, Arndale Centre
Franklin Swanson, groom married during IRA bomb attack
Amanda Hudson, bride married during IRA bomb attack
Josette, waitress at Gander's
MOLLY, student at MMU, later a conceptual artist
Jenna, Molly's mother
Young paramedic on scene after IRA bomb
Bubble Man, Piccadilly Gardens
Male passer-by, accusing IRA
Superintendent William Rose, Niagara Fire Engine
Woman passer-by at scene of fire at Arkwright's Mill
Laurel Stone, teacher at Sharp Street Ragged School
Evelyn, a rescued baby, later Frank's wife
Screaming Mother, of Evelyn
Frank Wright, boy who rescues, then later marries Evelyn
Christos, friend of Vassily
Stephanos, friend of Vassily
Vassily, adopted son of Konstantin, recently arrived from Chios
Gordon, Frank's brother
Thea, Konstantin's wife
Konstantin, refugee from Greek War of Independence
Konstantin's father, on Chios
Amara, Thea's daughter, Vassily's mother
Alexis, known as **Alex**, Petros's father
Callista, Petros's older sister
Yannis, Callista's baby son
Andreas, Callista's husband
Sophia, Petros's mother
Archimandrite Nikolaos Sergakis, Greek Orthodox priest
Jem, a brick mason

Pity, his common-law wife
Michael, Molly's husband, a history lecturer
Nadia, Molly's grandmother
Blessing, Molly and Michael's daughter
Yasser, Molly's great-great-grandfather
Bill Campbell, founder and director of Islington Mill Studios
Sunanda, Lorrie's assistant at Islington Mill
Pavel, Lorrie's grandfather, maker of fairground rides
Krysztof, Pavel's brother, retired rides operator
Agniewska, Pavel's daughter-in-law, former stallholder
Vitaly, Agniewska's husband, Pavel's son, former circus worker
Stanislaw, Vitaly's brother, former circus worker
Milosz, Stanislaw's son, Lorrie's father, fairground worker
Lena, Pavel's wife, Lorrie's grandmother, former trapeze artist
Lorelei, Stanislaw's late wife, Milosz's mother, Lorrie's other grandmother, trapeze artist
ANITA, Clive's older sister
Christopher, Clive's older brother
Merle, adoptive mother of Clive, Anita and Christopher
John, a carpenter from Hebden Bridge
Suzy, Chloe's cousin
Principal Trombonist, Florence's early boyfriend
Lance, Anita's son, later Jenna's boyfriend
Arthur Lewis, Nobel Prize-winner for Economics
Girl with strawberry mark on her cheek
David Olusoga, professor of history at Manchester University, TV presenter
Hejaz, Molly's great-grandfather
Sol, Molly's grandfather, Nadia's husband
Alan Turing, pioneer of artificial intelligence
LILY WARNER, formerly Wright, formerly Shilling
Roland Warner, Lily's husband, a computer engineer
Freddie Williams, colleague of Alan Turing
Tom Kilburn, colleague of Alan Turing
Geoff Toothill, colleague of Alan Turing
Delphine Fish, professor of audiology
Arnold Murray, Alan Turing's friend

CHAMOMILE CATCH, known as **CAM**, jazz singer
Francis Hall, owner of Hall & Singer, George Wright's friend
Giancarlo, Head Porter at The Queen's Hotel, nephew of Luigi
Luigi, retired former Head Porter at The Queen's Hotel
Richie Catch, Cam's son, an RAF pilot
Esther, Sol's mother
Harry Kinsella, a burglar
Joel Fredericks, Anita, Christopher and Clive's late father
Carmel Fredericks, Anita, Christopher and Clive's late mother
Police Sergeant Ratcliffe, Clayton Brook Police Station
Andy Burnham, Mayor of Greater Manchester
Tom Johnson, journalist, Apichu's husband
Apichu, Tom's wife, from Lima, Peru
Agnes, survivor of Peterloo, wife of Amos, mother of Jack
Jack, Agnes's son, a drummer boy
Amos, Agnes's late husband
Matthew, Agnes's twin brother
Silas, Agnes's cousin
Meg, Silas's wife
Ham, Silas and Meg's elder son
Shem, Ham's younger brother
James, Agnes's younger brother
Rose, Yasser's wife
Dr Arune Balaikaite, chemist
Emma Cocker, academic coder
Ruth Warner, Lily and Roland's daughter
Chantelle, Merle's daughter, a nurse at Manchester Royal Infirmary
Dr Henry 'Harry' Brennan, anaesthetist at MRI, Chantelle's husband
Girlfriends of Anita from St John's College
Barman at The Kardomah
Leroy Beauregard King, aka **Roy**, jazz trumpeter
Old Soldier in Southern Cemetery
Fireman attempting to rescue Christopher
Nancy Cotton, a librarian
Miss Gresty, shop window designer, Kendal Milne

Farida, Nadia's older sister
Samancha, Tom and Apichu's baby daughter
Ralph, Tom's dog
Urja, Khav's grandmother
Vikram, Khav's father
Geetha, Khav's mother
Priya, Khav's older sister
Abila, Khav's school friend
Teniel, a break dancer
Showmi, Khav's assistant with Missi Roti
Agrawal, Urja's husband, Khav's grandfather
Gyaril Sundar Singh Sagar, Sikh campaigner
Councillor C.R. Morris, Chair of Manchester Corporation Transport Committee
Alderman Sir Richard Harper, Tory Leader, Manchester Council
Lord Denning, Master of the Rolls
Lord Fraser of Tullybelton, House of Lords
Duleep, Priya's husband
Mahendra, early boyfriend of Khav
Yemi Bolatiwa, singer, community engagement officer at Z-Arts
Mr Haroon Majeed, paediatric consultant, St Mary's Hospital
Dr Sonia Abara, Mr Majeed's assistant
Urja's father
Elephant Keeper, Belle Vue
Ringmaster, Belle Vue Circus
Vidhya, Khav's friend at MMU
Tanveet, Khav's friend at MMU
Beesham, Khav's friend at MMU
Lakshmi, Khav's friend at MMU
Saroor, Khav's friend at MMU
Dilsher, Priya's son
Rukmini, Priya's daughter
Professor John Brookes, Vice-Chancellor, MMU
Rick, Professor Brookes' secretary
Helena Norwood, Awards & Conferments, MMU
Tricia Boyce, Lead Steward

Tina MacLeod, Head of Gowns & Robing
Guy Garvey, lead singer with Elbow
Professor Sharon Hanley, Pro-Vice-Chancellor, MMU
Dr Pete Dale, Senior Lecturer in Music and organist, MMU
Zhang, part of Yasser's team building the Ship Canal, great-great-great-uncle of Chloe
Dai Tai, Chloe's mother, Xiu Mei's daughter
Zhao Li, Xiu Mei's husband

The following are mentioned by name:

[Karl Ludwig, dress designer]
[Niall Booker, CEO Coop]
[Coop Customers]
[Rev. Paul Flowers, former CEO Coop]
[Rent boys]
[People who lost houses in mortgage sub-prime crisis]
[Workers at NOMA]
[Cheering Crowds to greet Queen at NOMA]
[Loyal Royalist]
[Robbie Williams, singer]
[Visitors to Vauxhall Gardens]
[Richard Arkwright, inventor, mill owner]
[Hermes Investment Group]
[Venture Capitalists]
[Friedrich Engels]
[Passers-by on Oxford Road]
[Crane drivers]
[Demolition workers]
[Jarvis Cocker, lead singer of Pulp]
[Late night drinkers in Chinatown]
[Students in Central Library]
[Retired soldier from British Legion]
[Chinese clarinettist, pupil at Chetham's]
[Puyi, Last Emperor of China]
[Chloe's great-great-grandfather]
[Queen Mother]
[Princess Anne]

[Peter Phillips, Princess Anne's son]
[Teachers & pupils of St Philip's Primary School]
[Weapons of Sound, junk percussion orchestra]
[Bhangra, hip hop, capoeira dancers at Commonwealth Games]
[S Club 7]
[Former Coronation Street stars]
[William Walton, composer]
[Band of the British Grenadiers]
[Royal Northern College of Music Brass Band]
[Bishop & Tyga, west coast rappers]
[Relay Runners carrying Jubilee Baton]
[Spectators at Opening Ceremony of Commonwealth Games]
[Sheik Mansoor, Abu Dhabi]
[Albert Finney, actor]
[Shelagh Delaney, playwright]
[Liza Minelli]
[Marching Band in 'Charlie Bubbles']
[Men at bus queue]
[Graham Nash, of The Hollies]
[Morrissey, lead singer of The Smiths]
[Chairman, Salford Lads' Club]
[Committee Members, Salford Lads' Club]
[Fans of Morrissey]
[Shirley Baker, photographer]
[Richard Davis, photographer]
[Peter Walsh, photographer]
[Boys in George Wright photograph]
[Rafe, Clive's dog]
[Clive's grown-up son & daughter]
[Stanley Kubrick, film director]
[Frankie Goes To Hollywood]
[Professor Mike Newell, archaeologist]
[Students on dig]
[Tag, Gracie's dog]
[Miners at Bradford Colliery in 1953]
[Children Grace speaks to in schools]
[Milly, Toby's daughter]
[Michael, Toby's son]
[Stephen, Grace's former boyfriend]
[John Pickford, original owner of site of Arkwright's Mill]
[William Brocklebank, partner of Richard Arkwright]

[John Simpson, partner of Richard Arkwright]
[Boulton & Watt, engineers]
[Samuel Bamford, Manchester Radical]
[Mill Workers in 19th century]
[Camera operator for Time Team]
[Sound recordist for Time Team]
[Saturday morning shoppers in Manchester]
[TV Crews for football match]
[Police in London]
[Driver of white Ford Cargo van]
[Traffic Warden]
[Garda Police, Dublin]
[Bootle Street Police Station officers]
[Army Bomb Disposal Squad]
[Belle Vue Ambulance Control telephonists]
[30 fire crews]
[Wounded Casualties from IRA bomb]
[Shoppers at Kendal Milne]
[Hairdresser, Arndale Centre]
[Pair of women collecting handbags]
[Reluctant workmen on weekend rates]
[Fleeing bridesmaid in photo]
[Leader of Manchester Council at time of IRA bomb]
[Mr J.A. Beaver, cotton spinner]
[Richard Arkwright Jnr]
[Richard Sampson, partner of Arkwright Jnr]
[Police at scene of fire at Arkwright's Mill]
[Municipal Fire Brigade officers at fire at Arkwright's Mill]
[Firemen at Water Witch, Neptune and Thetis]
[Manchester Town Fathers]
[Chain of volunteers with buckets at fire]
[William Rose's Deputy]
[Millworkers trapped by fire]
[Children from Ragged School]
[Parents of children]
[Huguenots in Manchester]
[Early Dutch settlers]
[Jews in Shudehill]
[Germans in Denton]
[Italians in Ancoats]
[Chinese in Alport]

[Irish in Angel Meadow]
[Greeks in Strangeways]
[Frank Wright's father]
[Hippocrates]
[Roman & Byzantine mastic traders]
[Sultan of Ottoman Empire]
[Sultan's concubines]
[Merchants of Chios]
[Homer]
[Minoans]
[Persians]
[Spartans]
[Athenians]
[Alexander the Great]
[Genoese]
[Philip of France]
[Pope Benedict VII]
[Admiral Piali Pasha]
[St Paul]
[Venetians]
[Pirates]
[Mother Julitta, a martyr]
[Emperor Diocletian]
[Greek revolutionaries from Samos]
[Nine Muses]
[Aeschylus]
[Sophocles]
[Eumenides, the Fates]
[Admiral Kara-Ali Pasha]
[40,000 Ottoman troops]
[Victims of Chios Massacre]
[Chios Exiles]
[Workers at Strangeways Mastic Factory]
[Mourners at Konstantin's funeral]
[Clegg & Knowles, architects]
[Priest at Konstantin's funeral]
[Simpson & Haugh, architects of Library Walkway]
[Jesus Christ]
[Henry Stone, Jem's father]
[Edwin Stone, Jem's grandfather]
[Young couple driving a BMW]

[Liam Gallagher, Oasis]
[Ken Barlow, Coronation Street]
[The Courteeners]
[Sir Alex Ferguson, manager of Manchester United]
[Ryan Giggs, footballer]
[Paul Scholes, footballer]
[Gary Neville, footballer]
[Nicky Butt, footballer]
[Pele, footballer]
[Boris Johnson, prime minister]
[Waiter in The Colony]
[Jules de Martino, founder of The Ting Tings]
[Katie White, founder of The Ting Tings]
[David Bellhouse, architect]
[Resident artists at Islington Mill]
[Passengers on No 135 bus]
[Man reading a newspaper on bus]
[Spectators at Silcock's Fair]
[The Rhine Maidens, female circus aerial act]
[Norman Barrett, Ringmaster]
[Busby Berkeley, choreographer]
[Eddie Cantor, Hollywood actor]
[Gina Lollobrigida, Italian film star]
[Tony Curtis, film star]
[Betty Hutton, singer and actress]
[Cornel Wilde, film star]
[Grace Jones, singer]
[Toni Basil, singer]
[Kevin Godley & Lol Creme of 10cc]
[Marlene Dietrich]
[Vivien Leigh]
[Lauren Bacall]
[Lana Turner]
[Barbara Stanwyck]
[Veronica Lake]
[Judy Garland]
[Audrey Hepburn]
[Marilyn Monroe]
[Jane Russell]
[Madonna]
[Rita Hayworth]

[Jane Fonda]
[Sigourney Weaver]
[Jennifer Lawrence]
[Carrie Fisher]
[Dorothy Dandridge]
[Diana Ross]
[Billie Holliday]
[Meryl Streep]
[Keira Knightley]
[Olivia Newton-John]
[Diane Keaton as Annie Hall]
[Bob Dylan]
[James Dean]
[Marlon Brando]
[Greta Garbo]
[Summer crowds in All Saints]
[Claude Rains as the Invisible Man]
[Susan Sarandon]
[Magenta, from Rocky Horror Picture Show]
[Columbia, from Rocky Horror Picture Show]
[Workers in On The Eighth Day]
[Customers in On The Eighth Day]
[Charlie Ali, record shop owner]
[Robert King Merton, US sociologist]
[St Matthew]
[John McGrath, writer and theatre director]
[Bertolt Brecht]
[Actors in 7:84 Theatre Company]
[Barnabus, from the Apocrypha]
[Hazel O' Connor, singer]
[Fionn McCool, mythological Irish hero]
[Fiann Finn, followers of McCool]
[Oisin, McCool's son]
[Chloe's relatives in Hong Kong]
[Digital Discovers, youth group at Z-Arts]
[Drug runners in Hulme]
[Police in Hulme]
[Tenants in Hulme crescents]
[Tony Wilson, TV presenter, Factory Records, Haçienda]
[Bernard Sumner, lead singer of New Order]
[Members of Afro Villa football team]

[Black & White Minstrels]
[Students of both university campuses]
[Mao]
[Ché Guevara]
[Joni Mitchell]
[Sonoya Mizuno, actress]
[Kyoko, role played by Mizuno]
[The Chemical Brothers, indie band]
[Chloe's occasional 'dates']
[Party guests for Clive]
[Florence's Band]
[Lubaina Himid, Tate Prize-winner]
[Professor Alessandro Schiesaro, Head of Arts, Languages & Culture, Manchester University]
[David Olusoga's parents]
[National Front members, Gateshead]
[Trevor Macdonald, newsreader]
[Simon Schama, historian]
[Mary Beard, historian]
[Harold Wilson, former UK prime minister]
[David Olusoga's partner and daughter]
[Barnes Wallis, inventor of the bouncing bomb]
[Jimi Hendrix]
[The Yardbirds]
[The Who]
[John Dalton, scientist]
[James Joule, scientist]
[Sir Isaac Newton, scientist]
[Francis Godlee, Quaker]
[US Astronauts on the Moon]
[Chris Grayling, Justice Secretary]
[Rob Cookson, Director of Lesbian Gay Foundation]
[William Jones, computer scientist]
[Graham Stringer, Leader of City Council 1994]
[Glynn Hughes, sculptor]
[Dr John Graham-Cumming, computer scientist]
[Gordon Brown, former UK prime minister]
[John Leech, Lib Dem MP for Withington]
[Professor Dame Nancy Rothwell, President & Vice-Chancellor, Manchester University]
[Pat Karney, Leader of City Council 2013]

[Mr Godwit, Globe Lane]
[Messrs Snipe & Crake, Godwit's friends]
[Pearl, Lily's friend from St Bridget's]
[Prisoners of War, Melland Road Camp]
[Clerk at Town Hall]
[Disapproving women at POW Camp]
[Gladys Williams, wife of Freddie]
[Irene Kilburn, wife of Tom]
[Pam Toothill, wife of Geoff]
[Male dinner guests at Globe Lane]
[Athos, a musketeer]
[Aramis, a musketeer]
[Porthos, a musketeer]
[D'Artagnan, a Gascon]
[David Hilbert, German mathematician]
[Wilhelm Ackerman, German mathematician]
[Joan Clark, associate and ex-fiancée of Alan Turing at Bletchley Park]
[Waiters at Ping Hong]
[Proprietor of Ping Hong]
[Guests at The Queen's Hotel]
[Resident Band at The Queen's Hotel]
[Prez, a band leader]
[Pythagoras]
[Apollo]
[Man lighting a cigarette in Piccadilly]
[Queen Victoria]
[Drunks in street after closing time]
[William Houldsworth, textile merchant, builder of The Queen's Hotel]
[Thomas Houldsworth, William's nephew, racehorse owner]
[Police Constable on bicycle on Adlington Road]
[Judge J. Fraser, presiding over Alan Turing's case]
[Mr R. David, prosecuting counsel]
[Mr Lind Smith, defence counsel]
[Mr E. Hobson, defence counsel for Murray]
[Neighbours of the Fredericks on Himley Road]
[Firemen rescuing Christopher and Clive]
[Ambulance workers, Himley Road]
[Picnicking families, Bradford Colliery]
[Board of Guardians for the Poor Laws]
[St Willibrord, Northumbrian saint of children]

[Reverend John Armistead, pioneer of fostering]
[Lorraine Courtenay, Head of Manchester Children's Services]
[Sammy & Eve, Delphine's parents]
[Victims of Spanish flu, 1918-19]
[Female Aide to Andy Burnham]
[Zorba 'flash mob' dancers on Market Street]
[Tony Lloyd, Chief Commissioner of Police and Interim Mayor of Greater Manchester 2015]
[James Brindley, engineer who built Bridgewater Canal]
[Prospero, The Tempest]
[Michaelangelo]
[Peel Holdings, property firm]
[Diana, goddess of the moon]
[Ariadne, daughter of King Minos]
[Tom Johnson's parents and grandfather]
[Joshua Hoyles, Summerseat mill owner]
[Farmer and child from Nob Lane Farm]
[Recent occupants of Nob Lane Farm]
[Amerindian migrants in Lima]
[Henry Hunt, orator at Peterloo]
[Joe Nadin, Deputy Constable of Manchester Police, 1819]
[Crowds at Peterloo]
[John & Caroline Lees, Agnes's parents]
[Members of Moravian Settlement, Fairfield]
[James Sadler, hot air balloonist]
[Crowds in Haworth Gardens]
[Penelope, wife of Odysseus]
[Peter Ridgway, Registrar, Manchester Magistrates Court Family Division]
[Elvis Presley]
[Clifford, Terry, Stuart, boyfriends of Anita's friends at St John's College]
[Priest at Cam's funeral]
[Mourners at Cam's funeral]
[Annie Wright, Lily's adoptive mother]
[Hubert Wright, Annie's husband]
[Man queuing for call box]
[People stealing coal]
[Woman answering phone at The Mardi Gras, Liverpool]
[Ronnie Scott, jazz musician]
[Crowd outside Greenheys School]

[Dave, Jackie, Julie, Brian, students working at Kendal Milne]
[Resident Artists at Islington Mill]
[Guru Nanak, founder of the Sikh faith]
[Abila's sister]
[Rock Master Scott & the Dynamite Three, rappers]
[Girls at Trinity Youth Centre, later Missi Roti]
[Ranvir Singh, TV presenter]
['Aunties' of Indian heritage girls]
[Agrawal's parents]
[Agrawal's work colleagues]
[Urja's neighbours]
[Members of Manchester Corporation Transport Committee]
[Delegation of Sikh Community Leaders]
[Mukhtiar Singh, first Sikh bus driver to wear a turban]
[Pratap Singh, mythological Punjabi warrior]
[Chetak, Pratap's horse]
[John Ayrton, founder of Manchester Central FC 1923]
[Chaprapati Shivaj Maharaj, Marathi warrior chieftain]
[Gyan-ji's sons]
[Gyan-ji's well-wishers and supporters]
[Lord Mayor of Manchester 1975]
[Crowds lining streets of Old Trafford for opening of Gurdwara]
[Gurdwara Committee Members]
[Twelve Elders' Guard of Honour]
[BBC News Reporter at opening of Gurdwara]
[Sergio Aguero, footballer]
[Freshers at MMU Sikh Society party]
[Claudia Jones, co-founder of Caribbean Carnival]
[Locita Brandy, co-founder of Caribbean Carnival]
[Steel bands, dance troupes at carnival]
[Revellers at carnival]
[Kanye West, rapper]
[Jimmy Cliff, reggae singer]
[Police officers at carnival]
[Hallé Orchestra]
[Northern Ballet Theatre]
[Luciano Pavarotti, tenor]
[Warren Beatty, actor and director]
[Courtney Pine, jazz musician]
[Nitin Sawhney, musician]
[Damien Hirst, artist]

[Lenny Henry, comedian]
[Johnny Vegas, comedian]
[Benji Reid, break-dancer]
[Mahendra's girlfriend]
[T.S. Eliot]
[Children bullying Khav at school]
[Jemadars, soldiers guarding the Great Hedge of India]
[Gandhi]
[Urja's Aunties]
[Emperor of Delhi]
[Pilgrims visiting Guru Nanak]
[Children in Platt Fields 1947]
[Manny Shinwell, Minister for Fuel & Power 1947]
[Clement Atlee, former UK prime minister]
[Staff at Buckingham Palace 1947]
[Circus Procession of Elephants, Manchester]
[Girls sitting on elephants dressed as Indian princesses]
[Easter Monday Bank Holiday crowds]
[Maharajah, an elephant]
[Lorenzo, Maharajah's keeper]
[Maharani, an elephant]
[Walter & Alice, Esther's parents]
[Esther's brothers]
[Courting couples inside Caterpillar]
[Spectators at Circus]
[Ringmaster]
[Trapeze artists]
[Cepheus, ancient King of Ethiopia]
[William Herschel, composer and astronomer]
[King George III]
[Paramedics from MRI]
[Ravi Das, a poet]
[Pooja Bedi, a Bollywood actress]
[Caitlin Mallone, glass artist]
[Group of people gathered round Homeless Woman]
[Harassed security official outside Contact Theatre]
[Young people from different countries taking part in Contact Biennale]
[Azrael, an angel]
[Onjali Q. Rauf, children's author]
[Jane Parry, Neighbourhood & Engagement Officer, Central Library]

[Punchkin, Indian Rapunzel]
[Ben Humberstone, Deputy Director of Health & Life Events Division, Office of National Statistics]
[Anonymous Sikh Community Leader]
[Paramedics taking Vikram to MRI]
[ICU Nurse, MRI]
[Tony Hart, presenter of Vision On]
[Sally, wife of Professor Brookes]
[Digger, a golden retriever]
[Thomas Mann, early trade unionist]
[W.B. Yeats]
[Victor Hugo]
[Marshall Foch, French General]
[Abbie Hoffman, US radical]
[George Bernard Shaw]
[Annie Horniman, founder of The Gaiety Theatre]
[Philip Larkin, poet]
[Plutarch, Roman historian]
[Contractors at Birley Hall of Residence, MMU]
[Ede & Ravenscroft, provider of academic gowns]
[Members of MMU Academic Board]
[Sarah Burton, fashion designer]
[Duchess of Cambridge]
[Michelle Obama]
[Lady Gaga]
[Gethin Jones, TV presenter]
[Scarlett Johansson, actor]
[Lizzy Maguire, character in the film 'Ghost Dance']
[Maggie Gyllenhall, actor]
[Kirsten Dunst, actor]
[Julia Styles, actor]
[Reese Witherspoon, actor]
[Buffy the Vampire Slayer]
[Principal from Buffy's High School]
[Kan Yasuda, sculptor]
[Mohini, female avatar of Vishnu]
[Gajasuras, elephant demons]
[Orpheus, Greek musician of legend]
[Eurydice, Orpheus' lost wife]
[Savitri, Hindu equivalent of Orpheus]
[Satyavan, Hindu equivalent of Eurydice]

[Charles Alexandre de Calonne, Comte D'Hannonville, pre-Revolutionary French politician]
[Nicholas Chamfort, Secretaire des Jacobins]
[The Buzzcocks]
[The Clash]
[Charles William Eric Fogg, composer]
[Graduands in Bridgewater Hall]
[Giovanni 'Sir John' Battista Barbirolli, conductor of the Hallé]
[Guang Li & Juan, proprietors of the Yang Sing]
[19th century workers at Great Northern Railway Warehouse]
[Waiters and waitresses at Platzki]
[Waiters at The Midland]
[Bao's father]
[Zhao Li's partners at accountants]
[Prince Albert, consort to Victoria]
[Jack de Manio, radio presenter]
[William Shakespeare]
[King James I]
[Sun Tzu, Chinese warrior and philosopher]
[Mrs Dale, fictional radio diarist]
[Chloe's teachers at school]
[Deng Xiao Ping, successor to Mao]
[Jhiang Zemin, successor to Deng]
[Hu Jintao, successor to Jhiang]
[Xi Jinping, successor to Hu]
[Martin Parr, photographer]
[Daniel Meadows, collaborator with Martin Parr]
[Amanda Window, photographer]
[Peter Walsh, photographer]
[Adam Burton, photographer]
[David Gleave, photographer]
[Adam Pester, photographer]
[Paul Wright, photographer]
[People in June Street photographs]
[People in Yates's Wine Lodge photographs]
[People in New Brighton photographs]
[The Charlatans]
[Victor Collins, boxer]
[Ivan Mauger, speedway rider]
[Denis Law, footballer]
[Clive Lloyd, cricketer]

[Crowds at dog tracks, football terraces]
[Oswald Mosley, fascist politician]
[Blackshirts, followers of Mosley]
[Participants in Mass Trespass]
[Gwynne Owen Evans, last man to be hanged in England]
[Wounded policeman at Moss Side]
[Giulia Lockhart, fashion designer]
[The Beatles]
[Yuri Gagarin, first man in space]
[Mourners for victims of Munich Air Disaster]
[Boys being soaked by elephant in Philips Park]
[Humphrey Jennings, documentary film maker]
[Old couple dancing beside Anderson Shelter]
[Children scavenging for shrapnel]
[Exhausted fire fighter drinking tea from enamel mug]
[Small child wearing outsized shoes pushing pram]
[The Black Arrows, forerunners of The Red Arrows, aerobatic flying team]
[Richard Perceval, linen weaver from Levenshulme]
[Thomas Tyldesley, Royalist soldier from Astley]
[Giovanni Cisinelli, sculptor]
[Ford Madox Brown, pre-Raphaelite painter of Manchester Murals]
[Khalil Gilbran, poet]
[Paul Heaton, landlord of The King's Arms, founder of The Beautiful South]
[Ian Brown, lead singer of The Stone Roses]
[John Squire, guitarist with The Stone Roses]
[Gary 'Mani' Mountfield, bassist with The Stone Roses]
[Alan 'Reni' Wren, drummer with The Stone Roses]
[Sir Thomas Egerton, 1st Earl of Wilton, designer of Heaton Hall and Park]
[Enrico Caruso, tenor]
[Billy Grimshaw, the 'Gramophone King']
[Beethoven]
[Prometheus]

Acknowledgements

(for *Ornaments of Grace* as a whole)

Writing is usually considered to be a solitary practice, but I have always found the act of creativity to be a collaborative one, and that has again been true for me in putting together the sequence of novels which comprise *Ornaments of Grace*. I have been fortunate to have been supported by so many people along the way, and I would like to take this opportunity of thanking them all, with apologies for any I may have unwittingly omitted.

First of all I would like to thank Ian Hopkinson, Larysa Bolton, Tony Lees and other staff members of Manchester's Central Reference Library, who could not have been more helpful and encouraging. That is where the original spark for the novels was lit and it has been such a treasure trove of fascinating information ever since. I would like to thank Jane Parry, the Neighbourhood Engagement & Delivery Officer for the Archives & Local History Dept of Manchester Library Services for her support in enabling me to use individual reproductions of the remarkable Manchester Murals by Ford Madox Brown, which can be viewed in the Great Hall of Manchester Town Hall. They are exceptional images and I recommend you going to see them if you are ever in the vicinity. I would also like to thank the staff of other libraries and museums in Manchester, namely the John Rylands Library, Manchester University Library, the Manchester Museum, the People's History Museum and also Salford's Working Class Movement Library, where Lynette Cawthra was especially helpful, as was Aude Nguyen Duc at The Manchester Literary & Philosophical Society, the much-loved Lit & Phil, the first and oldest such society anywhere in the world, 238 years young and still going strong.

In addition to these wonderful institutions, I have many individuals to thank also. Barbara Derbyshire from the Moravian Settlement in Fairfield has been particularly patient and generous with her time in telling me so much of the community's inspiring history. No less inspiring has been Lauren Murphy, founder of the Bradford Pit Project, which is a most moving collection of anecdotes, memories, reminiscences, artefacts and original art works dedicated to the lives of people connected with Bradford Colliery. You can find out more about their work at: www.bradfordpit.com. Martin Gittins freely shared some of his encyclopaedic knowledge of the part the River Irwell has played in Manchester's story, for which I have been especially grateful.

I should also like to thank John and Anne Horne for insights into historical medical practice; their daughter, Ella, for inducting me into the mysteries of chemical titration, which, if I have subsequently got it wrong, is my fault not hers; Tony Smith for his deep first-hand understanding of spinning and weaving; Sarah Lawrie for her in-depth and enthusiastic knowledge of the Manchester music scene of the 1980s, which happened just after I left the city so I missed it; Sylvia Tiffin for her previous research into Manchester's lost theatres, and Brian Hesketh for his specialist knowledge in a range of such diverse topics as hot air balloons, how to make a crystal radio set, old maps, the intricacies of a police constable's notebook and preparing reports for a coroner's inquest.

Throughout this intensive period of writing and research, I have been greatly buoyed up by the keen support and interest of many friends, most notably Theresa Beattie, Laïla Diallo, Viv Gordon, Phil King, Rowena Price, Gavin Stride, Chris Waters, and Irene Willis. Thank you to you all. In addition, Sue & Rob Yockney have been extraordinarily helpful in more ways than I can mention. Their advice on so many matters, both artistic and practical, has been beyond measure.

A number of individuals have very kindly – and bravely – offered to read early drafts of the novels: Rachel Burn, Lucy Cash, Chris & Julie Phillips. Their responses have been positive, constructive, illuminating and encouraging, particularly when highlighting those passages which needed closer attention from me, which I have tried my best to address. Thank you.

I would also like to pay a special tribute to my friend Andrew Pastor, who has endured months and months of fortnightly coffee sessions during which he has listened so keenly and with such forbearance to the various difficulties I may have been experiencing at the time. He invariably came up with the perfect comment or idea, which then enabled me to see more clearly a way out of whatever tangle I happened to have found myself in. He also suggested several avenues of further research I might undertake to navigate towards the next bend in one of the three rivers, all of which have been just what were needed. These books could not have finally seen the light of day without his irreplaceable input.

Finally I would like to thank my wife, Amanda, for her endless patience, encouragement and love. These books are dedicated to her and to our son, Tim.

Biography

Chris grew up in Manchester and currently lives in West Dorset, after brief periods in Nottinghamshire, Devon and Brighton. Over the years he has managed to reinvent himself several times – from florist's delivery van driver to Punch & Judy man, drama teacher, theatre director, community arts co-ordinator, creative producer, to his recent role as writer and dramaturg for choreographers and dance companies.

Between 2003 and 2009 Chris was Director of Dance and Theatre for *Take Art*, the arts development agency for Somerset, and between 2009 and 2013 he enjoyed two stints as Creative Producer with South East Dance leading on their Associate Artists programme, followed by a year similarly supporting South Asian dance artists for *Akademi* in London. From 2011 to 2017 he was Creative Producer for the Bonnie Bird Choreography Fund.

Chris has worked for many years as a writer and theatre director, most notably with New Perspectives in Nottinghamshire and Farnham Maltings in Surrey under the artistic direction of Gavin Stride, with whom Chris has been a frequent collaborator.

Directing credits include: three Community Plays for the Colway Theatre Trust – *The Western Women* (co-director with Ann Jellicoe), *Crackling Angels* (co-director with Jon Oram), and *The King's Shilling*; for New Perspectives – *It's A Wonderful Life* (co-director with Gavin Stride), *The Railway Children* (both adapted by Mary Elliott Nelson); for Farnham Maltings – *The Titfield Thunderbolt, Miracle on 34th Street* and *How To Build A Rocket* (all co-directed with Gavin Stride); for Oxfordshire Touring Theatre Company – *Bowled A Googly* by Kevin Dyer; for Flax 303 – *The Rain Has Voices* by Shiona Morton, and for Strike A Light *I Am Joan* and *Prescribed*, both written by Viv Gordon and co-directed with Tom Roden, and *The Book of Jo* as dramaturg.

Theatre writing credits include: *Firestarter, Trying To Get Back Home, Heroes* – a trilogy of plays for young people in partnership with Nottinghamshire & Northamptonshire Fire Services; *You Are Harry Kipper & I Claim My Five Pounds, It's Not Just The Jewels, Bogus* and *One of Us* (the last co-written with Gavin Stride) all for New Perspectives; *The Birdman* for Blunderbus; for Farnham Maltings *How To Build A Rocket* (as assistant to Gavin Stride), and *Time to Remember* (an outdoor commemoration of the centenary of the first ever Two Minutes Silence); *When King Gogo Met The Chameleon* and *Africarmen* for Tavaziva Dance, and most recently *All the Ghosts Walk with Us* (conceived and performed with Laïla Diallo and Phil King) for ICIA, Bath University and Bristol Old Vic Ferment Festival, (2016-17); *Posting to Iraq* (performed by Sarah Lawrie with music by Tom Johnson for the inaugural Women & War Festival in London 2016), and *Tree House* (with music by Sarah Moody, which toured southern England in autumn 2016). In 2018 Chris was commissioned to write the text for *In Our Time*, a film to celebrate the 40th Anniversary of the opening of The Brewhouse Theatre in Taunton, Somerset.

Between 2016 and 2019 Chris collaborated with fellow poet Chris Waters and Jazz saxophonist Rob Yockney to develop two touring programmes of poetry, music, photography and film: *Home Movies* and *Que Pasa?* In 2020 Chris was invited by Wassail Theatre Company to be part of a collaborative project with 6 other writers to create the play *The Time of Our Lives* in response to Covid 19 as part of the *Alternative Endings* project.

Chris regularly works with choreographers and dance

artists, offering dramaturgical support and business advice. These have included among others: Alex Whitley, All Play, Ankur Bahl, Antonia Grove, Anusha Subramanyam, Archana Ballal, Ballet Boyz, Ben Duke, Ben Wright, Charlie Morrissey, Crystal Zillwood, Darkin Ensemble, Divya Kasturi, Dog Kennel Hill, f.a.b. the detonators, Fionn Barr Factory, Heather Walrond, Hetain Patel, Influx, Jane Mason, Joan Clevillé, Kali Chandrasegaram, Kamala Devam, Karla Shacklock, Khavita Kaur, Laïla Diallo, Lîla Dance, Lisa May Thomas, Liz Lea, Lost Dog, Lucy Cash, Luke Brown, Marisa Zanotti, Mark Bruce, Mean Feet Dance, Nicola Conibère, Niki McCretton, Nilima Devi, Pretty Good Girl, Probe, Rachael Mossom, Richard Chappell, Rosemary Lee, Sadhana Dance, Seeta Patel, Shane Shambhu, Shobana Jeyasingh, Showmi Das, State of Emergency, Stop Gap, Subathra Subramaniam, Tavaziva Dance, Tom Sapsford, Theo Clinkard, Urja Desai Thakore, Vidya Thirunarayan, Viv Gordon, Yael Flexer, Yorke Dance Project (including the Cohan Collective) and Zoielogic.

Chris is married to Amanda Fogg, a former dance practitioner working principally with people with Parkinson's.

Printed in Great Britain
by Amazon